Andy McDermott is the bestselling author of the Nina Wilde & Eddie Chase adventure thrillers, which have been sold in over 30 countries and 20 languages. His debut novel, THE HUNT FOR ATLANTIS, was his first of several *New York Times* bestsellers. THE MIDAS LEGACY is the twelfth book in the series, and he has also written the explosive spy thriller THE PERSONA PROTOCOL.

A former journalist and movie critic, Andy is now a full-time novelist. Born in Halifax, he now lives in Bournemouth with his partner and son.

Praise for Andy McDermott:

'Adventure stories don't get much more epic than this' *Daily Mirror*

'If Wilbur Smith and Clive Cussler collaborated, they might have come up with a thundering big adventure blockbuster like this . . . a wide-screen, thrill-a-minute ride' *Peterborough Evening Telegraph*

'True Indiana Jones stuff with terrific pace' *Bookseller*

'A true blockbuster rollercoaster ride from start to finish . . . Popcorn escapism at its very best' *Crime and Publishing*

'If you're looking for thriller writing that will transport you into a realm very different from your own quotidian existence, Andy McDermott is your man' *Good Book Guide*

'A rip-roaring read and one which looks set to cement McDermott's place in the bestsellers list for years to come' *Bolton Evening News*

'Fast-moving, this is a pulse-racing adventure with action right down the line' *Northern Echo*

'A writer of rare, almost cinematic talent. Where others' action scenes limp along unconvincingly, his explode off the page in Technicolor' *Daily Express, Scotland*

'McDermott writes like Clive Cussler on speed. The action is non-stop' *Huddersfield Daily Examiner*

'An all-action read from one of Britain's most talented adventure writers' *Lan*

By Andy McDermott and available from Headline

Featuring Nina Wilde and Eddie Chase

The Hunt for Atlantis
The Tomb of Hercules
The Secret of Excalibur
The Covenant of Genesis
The Cult of Osiris
The Sacred Vault
Empire of Gold
Temple of the Gods
The Valhalla Prophecy
Kingdom of Darkness
The Last Survivor (A Digital Short Story)
The Revelation Code
The Midas Legacy

The Persona Protocol

ANDY McDERMOTT

THE MIDAS LEGACY

HEADLINE

First published in 2016 by
HEADLINE PUBLISHING GROUP

First published in paperback in 2017 by
HEADLINE PUBLISHING GROUP

2

Cataloguing in Publication Data is available from the British Library

ISBN 978 0 7553 8082 4 (B format)
ISBN 978 1 4722 4132 0 (A format)

Typeset in Aldine 401BT by Avon DataSet Ltd,
Bidford-on-Avon, Warwickshire

Printed and bound in Great Britain by Clays Ltd, St Ives plc

Headline's policy is to use papers that are natural, renewable and recyclable
products and made from wood grown in well-managed forests and other
controlled sources. The logging and manufacturing processes are expected to
conform to the environmental regulations of the country of origin.

HEADLINE PUBLISHING GROUP
An Hachette UK Company
Carmelite House
50 Victoria Embankment
London EC4Y 0DZ

www.headline.co.uk
www.hachette.co.uk

For Sebastian
My adventurer

Prologue

New York City, 1974

Henry Wilde took a deep breath as his name was called, summoning every scrap of self-assurance before standing. The twenty-plus people in the lecture hall regarded him expectantly as he headed for the lectern. A jury of his peers, he mused; the other undergraduates in his class. Some were friends – his roommate Jack Philby gave him a reassuring grin – but most were acquaintances at best, or even just faces in the crowd. The tall young New Yorker's obsession had put work ahead of socialising.

Obsession. That was perhaps hyperbolic, but he couldn't deny that his childhood fascination had intensified so much that it had determined his choice of degree. Now he was about to reveal that obsession to the jury.

And to the judge. Professor Orin Brighthouse stared at him over the thick black frames of his spectacles, the expression on his rumpled face one of bored disdain. *Another student with a chew toy for me to maul*, he didn't need to say out loud. Brighthouse was highly regarded in the field of archaeology, but he was also scathingly critical of ideas that challenged the status quo. It took a lot to impress him. So far, none of the other students had done that.

There was always a first time, Henry told himself as he

1

reached the front and took out his essay. He had rewritten it twice over the past two nights, trying to put forward his theory as clearly and convincingly as possible. Brighthouse's class made up only one part of his course, but it was an important one. A good result here would help him enormously in the future. A word from the professor could open many useful doors . . .

But first, he had to win that word.

'Peer review is an important part of the academic process,' intoned Brighthouse as if reciting the words from a cue card, before tipping his head back to look down his nose at the young man. 'But you already know that, because I've said the same damn thing to everyone else. So from here on, I'll skip the usual boilerplate. I'm sure you've all got anti-war demonstrations or love-ins or whatever kids do nowadays to get to.' A murmur of laughter from the audience. 'So, Mr Wilde: what are you going to tell us?'

This was it. 'I'm going to tell you,' Henry began, hoping he sounded more confident than he felt, 'the location of Atlantis.'

That certainly got the attention of the other undergraduates, whose own presentations to this point had been small in scale, subjects like the precise dating of various sites and relics discovered by others. Those who knew him weren't surprised by the announcement, Jack giving him a humorous shrug: *on your own head be it*. The reactions of the others were generally more negative. Incredulity, amusement, even head-shaking mockery. Yet a few seemed curious, so it wasn't an entirely hostile reception.

In fact, someone seemed outright intrigued. He had seen the pretty young woman sitting slightly isolated on the fourth row before – her ponytailed hair was such a vivid shade of red, it would have been almost impossible not to notice her – but their paths had never crossed socially; she had the same work-focused air as Henry himself. But she was now watching him intently, pencil poised as if eager to transcribe every word.

'So the word on the grapevine about your topic was true,' scoffed Brighthouse. 'Should I give you an F now and save everybody's time, or are you going to carry on and hope you can scrape a C for sheer imagination?'

'I'm still aiming for an A, Professor,' Henry replied, hoping his sudden feeling of nausea wasn't showing on his face. 'I think you'll be impressed. I've—'

'I wouldn't bet on it,' the academic rumbled.

'I've done my research,' Henry went on. 'Atlantis might be best known from Plato's texts, but there are plenty of corroborating sources describing a great seagoing empire that either pre-date them, or developed independently from the Greek dialogues. When you put them all together, you get a very interesting result.'

The red-haired woman had already started taking notes, her green eyes briefly meeting Henry's. The moment of contact gave him an odd feeling of reassurance, as if she were already convinced by his words. But it evaporated the moment he looked back at Brighthouse.

'Just because you find something interesting, Mr Wilde, does not guarantee that it is of worth,' said the professor, glowering. 'Some people find horoscopes, comic books or UFOs interesting. That doesn't mean the study of them has any value whatsoever.'

A twinge of anger fuelled Henry's reply. 'Well, maybe I'll change your mind.'

Brighthouse seemed to take that as a challenge. 'Then go ahead.' He leaned back in his chair, double chin pressed against his chest. 'Impress me.'

'I'll do my best.' Henry turned away from him to address the class. 'The legend of Atlantis has long been one of the world's most popular and enduring. A great civilisation swallowed up by the sea, taking all its wonders and treasures with it. People have spent their lives searching for it, but so far nothing has been found. The hunt for Atlantis is a great story, but that's all it is. Or . . . is it?'

His classmates were thankfully doing him the courtesy of appearing attentive. Jack, who already knew the basics of his theory, was waiting to hear the specifics – no doubt so he could pick holes in them and tell Henry he was wasting his time chasing a myth, as usual. But the redhead also seemed eager to hear more.

Well, two people were interested, at least. He pressed on. 'The Greek philosopher Plato gave us the first known references to Atlantis in Western culture, in his dialogues *Timaeus* and *Critias*. The general belief in academia is that Plato's Atlantis was fiction, a hypothetical; a way for him to expound his theories on a perfect society. But I believe there's more to it than that – I believe that his descriptions of Atlantis and its empire are based in fact. And here is why . . .'

The presentations of the other students over the past couple of days had generally weighed in at around fifteen minutes, followed by discussion: the peer review. Even as he spoke ever more quickly in his excitement, Henry's went on for almost twenty-five. Mouth dry, he finally reached his conclusion. 'So in summary, if a search for Atlantis is to be made, the kingdom itself is most likely to be found exactly where Plato stated it would be: beyond the mouth of the Mediterranean, in the Atlantic. But there must surely be other outposts still to be discovered. I've already mentioned potential sites in Morocco, Libya and Egypt, linked to the so-called Sea People. And there are possibilities even further afield, through central Asia all the way to the Himalayas. There is a whole world of opportunities to prove that Atlantis is more than just a myth, for those with the dedication and determination to find them. Thank you.'

A round of polite applause came from the audience. Jack gave him a grin. Henry looked up at the redhead to see that she was still taking notes with a look of intense concentration.

Before he had time to wonder what she was writing, a single loud handclap instantly silenced the students. 'A most interesting story, Mr Wilde,' Brighthouse said as he stood, voice oozing with sarcasm. 'If you were in a creative writing class, I'm sure it would have won you high marks. However, this is a *real* class. We deal in fact, not fiction. Evidence, not supposition. History, not myth.'

Despite his crushing dismay, Henry felt compelled to defend himself. 'I can back up everything I've just said, Professor. All my research has been cross-referenced with other sources.'

'Other sources that have no basis in fact! I know the usual suspects. Blavatsky leads to Donnelly leads to Cayce leads to none other than Heinrich Himmler and the Ahnenerbe, and back round again. It's circular logic, Mr Wilde, a conspiracy theory. Surely you wouldn't consider any of them credible?'

'Not the first three, no. But I do think there may be something to be learned from the German expeditions. I have a friend in Germany, Bernd Rust, who's been researching—'

Brighthouse's eyes widened. 'Are you actually saying that you give credence to the occult lunacy of the *Nazis*? Maybe you're going to propose that we start consulting crystals to find Atlantis.'

'Of course not!' Henry felt his cheeks flush as he heard mocking laughter from some of the undergraduates. 'But they sent out three expeditions, maybe more, searching for links to Atlantis, and the data they brought back still hasn't been fully analysed.'

'Because it's worthless!' proclaimed the elderly academic. 'They were more interested in phrenology and Aryan bloodlines than true archaeological research. And the idea that we might find outposts of Atlantis in the Himalayas, as you suggest – it's absolutely ludicrous.'

'But you can't deny that there are common aspects of the Western Atlantean mythology and legends from the Far East—'

'Exactly! Myths and legends. Many cultures have similar mythologies about a Great Flood, but it doesn't prove that all the world's animals went into Noah's Ark two by two.' Brighthouse took off his glasses, making a show of cleaning the lenses. 'I *will* give you credit for not backing down. You have the courage of your convictions. But Atlantis? Really? All the wonders of the ancient world that you could have put your obvious talents to researching, and you choose a pure fantasy?' He examined the spectacles, then donned them again, magnifying his intimidating stare still further. 'This is the real world, Mr Wilde. Chasing after legends will either get you nowhere, or into trouble.'

He faced the other students. 'Now I don't think we need open the floor to discussion on this occasion, because Mr Wilde has suffered enough humiliation already. We'll take a lunch break, and resume at two. With . . . Mr Jennings, I believe you are up next.' One of the students nodded. 'All right. I'll see you all then. Hopefully,' he added as he headed for the exit, giving the crestfallen Henry a snide look, 'with something more . . . well considered.'

Jack joined his friend as the other undergraduates filed out. 'Are you going to say it?' Henry asked him.

'Say what?'

'I told you so.'

'No, I'm not. I never like kicking a man when he's down.' The pair shared smiles. 'Brighthouse does have a point, though.'

'Ah, here it comes. The lecture.'

'I'm just saying he's right. You *are* talented, so why not put those talents to actual use instead of wasting time on myths? Especially one as fanciful as Atlantis.'

'Because I don't think Atlantis *is* a myth,' Henry replied. 'I always believed that, even as a kid – I don't know why, I just did.

But the deeper I look into it, the more certain I am. Whatever Brighthouse might say.'

'Well don't say I didn't warn you.'

'That's just a different way of saying I told you so, isn't it?' Henry grinned again as they left the lecture hall.

Their classmates had already dispersed – with one exception, he saw. The redhead was waiting near an exterior door, and judging from her earlier attentiveness, apparently for him.

'So, where shall we go for lunch?' asked Jack.

Henry only belatedly registered the words. 'Huh?'

'Lunch. You know, food and the consumption thereof?'

'Oh yeah, that.' But his attention was focused on the woman, who moved to meet him. 'Hi.'

Her eyes locked on to his. 'I believe you.'

He was a little startled. 'About . . . ?'

'Atlantis. Your theory about Atlantis – I believe it. You. Both.' She gave him a slightly embarrassed smile. 'I'm Laura, Laura Garde. We're in the same class. But I guess you already know that.' There was a distinct New England twang to her words, most likely Connecticut or Massachusetts, and Henry got the impression that she was from old money.

'Yeah, I do,' he replied, amused. 'You, ah, kinda stand out with your hair.' He indicated her vivid red ponytail.

'And you kinda stand out with your height. And *your* hair.' Henry's six-foot-four frame was topped by an ice-blond mop, which though he would never have admitted it to anyone he had modelled on Robert Redford's in the movie *Jeremiah Johnson*.

'Jack Philby,' said Jack hopefully from beside him.

'Hi,' said Laura, giving him a polite nod before turning back to Henry. 'I'd heard that Atlantis was your big thing, but I hadn't imagined you'd make such a convincing case for its location.'

'You thought it was convincing?' asked Henry, pleased.

'Absolutely. I don't think Professor Brighthouse was at all

7

justified in criticising your methodology. It seemed to me that you'd gone above and beyond to source your research. And you even had some things I'd never heard before.'

'You're interested in Atlantis too?'

Laura nodded. 'Although not nearly as much as you, it seems! I've loved reading about it ever since my mom told me the legend as a kid. Though maybe it's not a legend after all. Like I said, I believe you. And . . .' She looked down, coyly twisting the toe of one sandal against the tiled floor. 'I was wondering if you might be interested in talking some more about it.'

'Really?'

'Really. I'd love to see the rest of your work. You must have tons of notes.'

'A few pages,' Henry joked. 'Okay, I admit it: boxes.'

'I have to kick them out of the way every time I try to open my closet,' added Jack.

She laughed. 'Wow! I guess you really are an Atlantis expert.'

'So when would you like to talk about it?' asked Henry, not quite sure where this would lead. He'd had the occasional date since starting at Columbia University, but nothing serious; the fact that he inevitably ended up explaining his theories about Atlantis tended to lead to 'let's just be friends' very soon afterwards. Laura was attractive, and they definitely had common interests, but surely the universe couldn't be *that* generous?

'Whenever you like. I'm free after class today,' she told him. 'We could meet at your place, maybe?'

Henry took back his reservations about the generosity of the universe. 'Yeah. Yeah, we could,' he said, nodding a couple of times too many.

Jack huffed. 'I suppose you'll be wanting me to go see a movie, then?'

'That would be good!'

'No, no, you can stay,' said Laura at the same time. 'I don't want to put you out.'

Henry cursed silently, but not with any real annoyance. Just being able to talk about his obsession with someone who shared it would be enjoyable enough in itself. 'Cool. What time? Six?'

'Six is fine,' she replied. 'Where's your room?'

'McBain Hall, on 113th Street.'

'Okay, I'll see you there at six. It's a date. Well, not a *date* date.' She blushed a little. 'Not with both of you there. Free love is one thing, but that's going a bit too far.'

Henry laughed. 'Definitely for a first non-date date. So, see you later. Hopefully I won't bore you to death about Atlantis!'

'Don't worry,' said Laura as she turned to leave. 'I absolutely won't be bored.'

Once she had gone, Jack let out another huff, much louder. 'Goddamn, Henry! You got yourself a date without even asking. It's that hippie haircut of yours. Maybe I should try it myself.' He ran a hand through his own much shorter hair.

'It's not a date,' Henry reminded him, unable to hold in a broad smile. 'Well, not this time.'

'You think she'll want to see you again after you drone on about Atlantis for the whole evening?'

Henry moved to the exit to watch the redhead walk away. 'It's funny, but . . . yeah. Somehow I think she will.'

Laura headed through the spring sunshine across the quad, a smile still on her lips, towards a bench. An older woman, her hair a more auburn shade than Laura's, looked up at her approach. 'So?' she demanded. 'Is there anything to this Henry Wilde's theory?'

'I really think so, yes. It's actually very exciting!' Laura sat beside her, talking quickly in her enthusiasm. 'He didn't go into specifics, because he was mostly concerned with locating Atlantis itself, but he definitely believes that the Atlanteans established outposts as far afield as the Himalayas.'

'He actually said that?' Laura nodded. 'And he has evidence to back it up?'

'I just spoke to him. Apparently he's got boxes and boxes of research notes.'

'All well and good, but it's not finding Atlantis itself we're concerned about. We need to stay focused on Talonor's journey, and the cave.'

'Don't the others still want to investigate Santorini?'

The woman shook her head in annoyance. 'Yes. I think they're wasting their time, but we were outvoted, so . . .' Another shake, then: 'Anyway, if this boy has anything promising, it may render all that academic. You should try to get hold of his work and find out if he really has anything concrete about the Himalayas.'

Laura smiled. 'I'm meeting him tonight.'

'In his room?' The words were filled with disapproval.

'Oh, *Mother*!' protested the younger woman. 'It's not a date; his roommate'll be there.'

'Even worse! I know what these college boys are like.'

'I don't think I have anything to worry about. He seems very nice.'

'Does he now?' The woman regarded her daughter sternly. 'Just remember that this is business, for the Legacy. You're looking for anything that could lead us to the Midas Cave, not a boyfriend.'

'*Yes*, I know that,' Laura replied.

'Are you sure? Because I always know when you're not telling me everything . . .'

'Okay, yes, he's very tall and very handsome,' she admitted, exasperated. 'But he's also smart – and I genuinely want to find out more about his Atlantis theories.'

'So long as you keep your interest to the theoretical, that's fine.'

Laura sighed. 'I *do* at least have permission to enjoy myself while I'm doing it, don't I?'

'Ah, the joys of parenthood: sarcastic children.' Her mother stood. 'Well, since you clearly have everything worked out, I'll let you get on with it.' Her tone softened slightly. 'Do be careful, Laura.'

'I will, Mom,' she said, smiling again. 'But I think Henry's going to change things. I just have a feeling . . .'

1

Forty-four Years Later

Nina Wilde gazed in wonderment at the ruins of Atlantis rolling past beneath the submersible. Ten years had passed since she'd discovered the lost civilisation, using the lifelong work of her parents, Henry and Laura Wilde, as the foundations of her own research. The intervening decade had seen others join the task of excavating the wonders lost for eleven millennia, what had once been a rolling expanse of silt eight hundred feet beneath the Atlantic now dotted with buildings, many still surprisingly intact despite the earthquake and deluge that had dropped an entire island below the waves. It was an incredible sight.

But to her frustration, she wasn't seeing it in person.

The submersible was relaying the images picked out by its spotlights and laser scanners up an umbilical cable to a research vessel above, which in turn was transmitting them to an operations centre in the offices of the International Heritage Agency at the United Nations in New York. As much as Nina desperately wanted to revisit the site, she had – with deep reluctance – settled for watching the expedition unfold on a screen several thousand miles away. Adding to her annoyance, her husband *was* aboard the submersible . . . despite not especially wanting to go.

'Wish you'd kept up your dive certification,' said Eddie Chase over the comm system, his deep voice with its broad Yorkshire accent reverberating inside his spherical acrylic helmet. 'Then you could be freezing your bum off down here while I sit around drinking coffee in a nice comfy chair.'

'You remember what the IHA's office chairs are like, right?' Nina replied, a little tersely. 'And, y'know, having a baby kind of affected our priorities. You missed those new *Star Wars* movies; I didn't qualify to use a new version of a deep submergence suit. Not that I needed some certificate when I was running the IHA,' she added, with a glance at the man beside her. 'I just learned how to use the thing, then used it.'

Dr Lester Blumberg peered over his horn-rimmed glasses with a patronising smile. 'Yes, but we're a lot less – how shall I put it? – *improvisational* now than when you were in charge, Nina. Everyone needs proper training and certification for any IHA operation. Health and safety, you know.'

'Yeah, I know.' Nina's own smile was decidedly lacking in both humour and warmth. After her resignation almost four years previously, the post of director of the IHA had eventually been filled by the Minnesotan. Blumberg would not have even made it on to her shortlist, as she considered him merely competent at best – safe and unimaginative, a plodder – but she'd had no say in his appointment.

She turned her attention back to the screens. The main display showed a pilot's-eye view of the submersible's voyage, but one of the smaller monitors flanking it had an angle on one of its passengers, standing on a landing skid: Eddie. 'How much further?' he asked.

An Australian voice came over the comm. 'Be there in about three minutes,' said the couple's friend Matt Trulli from inside the sub. It could accommodate three, but today he was the only person in the cabin, making it far less cramped than normal.

The two men holding on to its hull had no such luxuries. On the other skid was a second diver, Nerio Cellini. The Italian was only young, in his mid-twenties, but already had years of experience of underwater exploration. His enthusiasm made Nina nostalgic for when she had been filled with the same youthful vigour, and also a little jealous of it.

'I see the site,' Cellini reported.

Nina looked back at the main monitor. The blue-green lasers used to pierce the water's murky cloak had the side effect of leaching away all colour except an eerie turquoise, but a small patch of white faded into sight at the screen's centre. 'That's it?' she asked Blumberg.

'That's it,' he replied. 'The Temple of Poseidon.'

The glow came from powerful spotlights standing on the roof of a massive structure rising from the sea floor. Even in ruins, the centrepiece of the lost city was still awe-inspiring. When Nina had first discovered it, the great temple had been largely buried by silt. Most of the surrounding sediment had since been cleared, but the building itself had suffered massive damage when her survey ship was deliberately scuttled and smashed down on top of it. Some of the RV *Evenor*'s remains were still in place, the wreck too big and costly to remove entirely. But parts had been cut away to give access to what remained of the temple.

The submersible approached the northern end of the huge vaulted ruin. The lights encircled an area where the damaged roof had been carefully opened up. Beneath it was the altar room, not merely a place of religious importance, but also an archive: the entire history of the Atlantean civilisation was recorded within, scribed into the sheets of gold alloy covering the walls. Some had been lost when the ceiling collapsed, but others were still intact, including an account of the doomed civilisation's last hours.

It was a different record that the expedition hoped to discover, however.

'Matt, move to drop-off position,' Blumberg ordered. 'Nerio, Eddie, you're up.'

The submersible stopped above the ring of lights, pulsing its thrusters at low power to hold position against the ocean's slow but relentless current. 'Okay, guys, we're here,' said Matt. The two divers each collected an equipment case, then Eddie leaned his shaved head closer to the camera and grinned at Nina, revealing the gap between his two front teeth, before stepping off the skid.

'Good luck,' she told him.

'Hope we don't need it,' Eddie replied. The deep suit – comprised of a hard casing around his body that let him breathe air at normal atmospheric pressure to eliminate any risk of the bends, heavy-duty seals at the shoulders and hips allowing his drysuited limbs to move freely – was neutrally buoyant, but the case was heavy enough to let him drift lazily downwards. A spool of hair-thin fibre-optic communications line played out behind him, keeping him in direct contact with the sub and the IHA. His feet made gentle contact with the ancient stone. 'Touchdown! It didn't collapse, so that's a good start.'

Cellini landed a few feet away. 'This part of the temple should be very stable,' he said. 'Only below the altar room is it . . .' He searched for the best English word, waggling his free hand from side to side. 'Wobbly.'

'And guess where we're going,' Eddie sighed. He became more serious as he surveyed his surroundings.

He had visited the altar room before, as well as near-identical copies the Atlanteans had built after abandoning their homeland; one in a vast cavern within a Himalayan mountain, the other deep in the jungles of Brazil. The archaeologists cataloguing the lost city on the Amazon had since discovered more chambers beneath its altar room – not hidden, exactly, but neither had they been immediately obvious. Meanwhile, the teams exploring Atlantis itself had uncovered references to a previously unknown treasure held somewhere within the Temple of Poseidon, and all the clues pointed to one of those secondary rooms.

There were two problems. The first was that nobody was sure if the Brazilian temple's chambers were exact duplicates of the original – sonar searches suggested open spaces beneath this altar room, but the results were far from conclusive. The second, and bigger, was that even if they existed, the *Evenor*'s destructive landing had dropped countless tons of debris into the temple's interior, making it impossible to know what was beneath.

Until someone remembered that Nina and Eddie had been inside the temple while it was still intact . . .

There was a camera mounted on the Yorkshireman's right shoulder. 'Nina, you seeing this?' he asked.

'Yes, all looking good,' his wife replied. 'I can see the stairs.'

An opening in one wall descended into darkness. The rubble blocking it had been removed, only for the IHA's explorers to find another, more solid obstruction further down. Small underwater drones had been able to squeeze past it to confirm that the stairway continued beyond, but in turn were stymied by further debris. To the fury of their controllers, the second blockage looked loose enough to be cleared by hand, but the little robots lacked the power to do so.

Which was why, the previous day, Cellini and another diver had used precision explosive charges to split apart the first obstacle. The blast had stirred up debris and sediment, turning the water in the tunnel completely opaque. It had now settled, so he and Eddie could check if the stairway was passable, and if so, explore its depths.

The Italian gestured to his dive partner. 'Are you ready?'

'Sure,' Eddie replied. 'I'll try not to wreck the entire place.'

He smiled to reassure the younger man, who clearly knew his reputation.

Blumberg's voice came through his earpiece. 'That would be appreciated this time.'

'Twat,' said Eddie under his breath, though deliberately just loud enough for his microphone to pick up. The IHA's director was making an implied criticism of his predecessor and her husband; despite their best efforts, the Temple of Poseidon was far from the only archaeological site to be seriously damaged after Nina had discovered it.

'What was that?'

'Must have been a fish farting. Okay, Nerio, let's go.'

Eddie used the controller stalk attached to the deep suit's chest to start its ducted propellers, gliding at low speed to the entrance. Cellini touched down beside him, directing his suit's lights down the steeply sloping passage. Stone steps receded into the murk for about twenty feet before the path came to an abrupt halt.

A huge stone slab had been dislodged from the ceiling, pulverising everything beneath it. It had originally come to rest at an angle, leaving a gap just big enough for the drones. Now, though, the space was much larger. The explosives had split the great block in two, the lower half dropping on to the steps and the upper wedging against it.

Rather than use the thrusters, Eddie carefully walked to the slab and took a powerful hand-held light from his case, shining it over the carved stone. It looked as if the divers could swim past – but first there was a question that had to be answered.

Cellini voiced it. 'Is it safe?'

'Who am I, Dustin Hoffman?' Eddie waited for a reply, but got only a bemused stare from the young man. 'You haven't seen *Marathon Man*?' Another blank look. 'You haven't even *heard* of . . . Oh, I give up. Kids today!'

'Just wait until *our* kid's older,' Nina joked. 'Macy'll be like, "Dad, all your cultural references are from the *twentieth century*! Mom's the archaeologist, not me."'

'I dunno, if ever a kid was destined to follow in her mother's footsteps . . .' He used his hands to test the blocks. They stayed firm.

Cellini added his torchlight to the Englishman's. 'So we will fit, yes? Help me through.' He swam to the gap. 'Is my suit clear?'

Eddie checked. There would only be a small space between the suit's fibreglass casing and the stone. 'Roll on your right so you don't bang your air tank cover on the ceiling.' Cellini did so. 'Okay, try to get through. Don't use your legs – I'll push you.'

Bracing himself, he carefully assisted the other man into the opening. Despite their best efforts, the suit scraped against the tight surrounds, with a tense moment when the control stalk caught the stone block, but a small roll brought Cellini clear. The hard carapace finally slipped through, and the Italian immediately angled downwards to get clear. 'I made it!' he cried.

'Wind out some of your fibre-optic so it won't catch when I come through,' Eddie told him. Cellini acknowledged. 'All right, here I come.'

He followed the other man into the opening. Cellini helped him through. Again, the inflexible fibreglass rasped against the stonework, but even though Eddie was considerably stockier than the lithe young man, the bodies of their deep suits were identical; if one could fit, so could its twin. A quick twist, and the Englishman was free.

'I'm through,' he told his listeners, bringing himself back upright. Without the spill of illumination from the altar room, the passage beyond the broken slab was much darker. He used his lamp to scan the floor, then the ceiling. 'Looks like some bits came loose from above,' he said, examining the broken stonework littering the steps.

'Is the ceiling intact?' Nina asked nervously.

'Yeah, but there are some cracks. Let's not stay in here too long, eh?'

'What about the second blockage?' said Blumberg. 'The robots couldn't get through it – will you be able to?'

'We'll soon find out.'

Eddie and Cellini carefully made their way down the sloping tunnel. Before long, another obstruction appeared. Eddie had seen a photo of the pile of rubble before diving, and saw at once that something had changed. Cellini realised the same thing. 'The explosion, it must have dislodged some of the stones,' he said. Although loose, the pile had previously reached to the roof, but now there were open areas at its top.

'We still won't fit through, though. Good job we brought these!' Eddie set down his case and opened it. Amongst other tools, it contained a steel crowbar and a folding shovel. He took out the former and made a few exploratory probes at the debris. The smashed stones shifted easily. 'You were right about it being loose.'

'How long do you think it'll take to get through?' asked Blumberg.

'Probably only a few minutes,' the Yorkshireman reported, knocking away a couple more pieces.

'Just make it a clean job,' said Blumberg. 'Smashing priceless sites apart isn't my style.'

Nina looked at the cardigan-clad man, whose retreating hairline had been feebly camouflaged by a swooping comb-over, but decided to keep her thoughts on his ideas of style to herself. Instead, she turned back to the monitors. Eddie and Cellini were indeed opening up the gap quite quickly. She was about to ask one of them to see if anything was visible beyond when someone entered the room. She sat up in surprise when she saw the new arrival. 'Oswald, hi!'

'And hello to you too, Nina,' replied Oswald Seretse. The urbane Gambian diplomat had acted as the IHA's interim director before Blumberg was appointed, but had since returned to the role of bureaucratic liaison between the semi-independent agency and the United Nations, with which she was sure he was far more comfortable. 'I heard you were in the building.'

'The UN grapevine's as quick as it ever was, I see,' she said, standing to shake his hand. 'It's been a while.'

'Three years, I believe. How is Macy?'

'Three years, I believe,' Nina echoed, grinning. 'No, she's great. Very precocious.'

He smiled. 'I am not surprised.'

'I understand you're responsible for getting me involved with this operation?'

'I am certain Lester would have remembered in due course that you and Eddie have personal knowledge of the temple's interior,' said Seretse, greeting Blumberg. 'After all, everyone at the IHA has surely read your book.'

'Of course,' Blumberg replied, hastily enough to give Nina the impression that he had skimmed it at best.

'My *first* book,' she told Seretse. 'The second's finished, and should be out by the end of the year.'

'I know,' he said. 'I have already read it.'

'You have?'

'Your publisher sent me proofs of the manuscript so it could be vetted for security purposes. I was sure you would not have included any classified information, and I was right, but I read it anyway.'

'And what did you think?'

'That it was every bit as detailed as your first.' She wasn't sure if that was a compliment. 'Oh, congratulations on your film deal, by the way! My son wants to know if I am in it.'

'Thanks,' said Nina. 'I honestly don't know what happens in the movie; after they bought the rights, they went off and did their own thing. I'll find out in a month or so, I guess!'

'I shall have to see it in a cinema like everyone else, then.' He regarded the screens. 'How are things progressing?'

'They're clearing the blocked stairway,' said Blumberg.

Seretse nodded. 'I will not distract you, then. I just wished to say hello.'

'It's good to see you again,' said Nina. 'And to be back at the IHA, actually. Even if it's only for the day.'

'A shame that you were not able to go on the expedition yourself. But I suppose one of you needed to be here for Macy.'

The redhead's smile became thinner. 'Yeah, a shame. I guess when only one of you's dive-certified, it makes choosing who stays home easier, right?' She forced a small laugh.

If he had registered her true feelings, the diplomat chose not to show it. 'Indeed. Well, I shall let you carry on. Do feel free to see me in my office later.'

'I will if I get the chance,' she told him, knowing that she almost certainly would not. Seretse said his goodbyes, then departed.

By now, the widening hole appeared almost large enough for the divers to traverse. 'Can you get through yet?' she asked.

'You in a rush?' Eddie asked. 'How long before you've got to pick up Macy from nursery?'

'Not for a while,' she replied.

'You *will* get her on time, won't you? Even if I'm about to discover an Atlantean UFO or something?'

'*Yes*, I will,' she snapped, mildly annoyed at being mocked.

He chuckled, then became more focused as a large piece of

stone fell away. 'Okay, I'd say that's big enough to fit through.'
He shone his light through the new opening. 'The tunnel looks
like it goes all the way down to the bottom.'

Nina and Blumberg exchanged looks. 'I'm *not* in a rush,'
the redhead said into her microphone, 'but: get your ass down
there!'

Eddie laughed, then cautiously swam through the hole. The
passage beyond was indeed clear to its end. 'All right,' said
Blumberg as Cellini emerged behind the Englishman. 'Nina,
Eddie, you've been here before. What can we expect?'

'The stairs came out behind the statue of Poseidon,' said
Nina. 'It was the biggest thing in the temple, about sixty feet
high. The place got flattened by the *Evenor*, though, so I'm not
expecting there to be much left of it. Some of the smaller statues
around it might have survived.'

'What about other entrances? Did you see anything that
matched what we found in Brazil?'

'Don't remember seeing any other doors,' said Eddie, as he
and Cellini approached the tunnel's end. More rubble came into
view below. 'We were a bit distracted, though.'

'There were alcoves along all the walls,' Nina recalled. 'Most
of them had statues in, so there could have been entrances
behind them. But as Eddie said, we didn't have a lot of time for
sightseeing. There were people trying to shoot us.' She had not
been the only one searching for Atlantis – and her rivals were
willing to kill to prevent her from reaching it first.

'Not today, though,' said Blumberg smugly. Then: 'Nerio,
what's that?'

The two explorers had reached the foot of the stairs, to
find that while the space beyond was choked with rubble from
the temple's collapsed roof, it was not completely blocked –
nor was all the debris mere stone. 'It looks like . . . gold,' said
the Italian in awe, his lamp picking out a twisted piece of

metal with an unmistakable hue. He knelt to pick it up. 'It is! It's gold!'

A warm reflection washed over Eddie as he shone his own lamp around. A low crawlspace remained open against the wall, a very large piece of sculpted metal forming a ceiling above it. Dents and tears revealed that its strength was provided by cast bronze – the Atlanteans had smelted together copper and tin thousands of years before the previously accepted beginning of the Bronze Age – but the surface was pure gold, almost a quarter of an inch thick.

Even without seeing the whole object, he knew what it was – and so did his wife.

'The statue!' Nina cried, staring in amazement at the main screen. 'It's part of the statue of Poseidon!'

'Must've got wedged against the wall when the roof caved in,' said Eddie. 'There's a gap under it.' He squatted to aim his light down the little tunnel.

Blumberg snapped his fingers, gesturing for an assistant to bring him a large folder. He quickly produced a floorplan. 'This is a diagram of what was left of the duplicate temple in Brazil,' he said, showing it to Nina. His finger tapped the representation of a set of stairs. 'That's the way up to the altar room, and *this*,' his finger slid across the page, 'is the entrance to one of the secondary chambers. If the other evidence we've found pans out, that's where we'll find the Secret Codex.'

She checked the scale. 'That's only . . . what, twenty-five feet away?'

'If that.' He regarded the screens. 'Question is, can anyone fit through?'

'I'm watching on the monitor,' Matt cut in from the submersible, 'and that looks like a job for an ROV if you ask me.'

'No, we can get through,' insisted Cellini. He dropped on to his front, head craned back to peer down the confined passage. 'It's low, but the suits will fit.'

'You sure about that?' asked Eddie sceptically.

Cellini pulsed his suit's thrusters to drive himself into the opening. With his chest plate scuffing the stone floor, the bulbous shell covering his air tanks slid beneath the golden ceiling with about an inch to spare. 'I told you,' he said once he was inside.

'The statue's not flat, though,' Eddie warned him. 'If it dips even by a couple of inches, you'll get stuck!'

The sight of the other man's flapping fins disappearing was the only reply. 'Really?' said Nina in exasperation. 'Eddie, you'd better make sure he's okay.'

'Would never've thought that having a three-year-old would be great practice for going on an archaeological dig,' said her husband as he followed his companion.

A low grumbling sound came over the speakers. 'Was that you?' Nina asked.

'What, you think I'd eat beans before getting sealed in this thing?' said Eddie, halting. He too had heard the noise, but couldn't pinpoint its source. 'Matt, there's nothing happening outside, is there?'

'The current's shifted,' the Australian told him. 'Started a couple of minutes ago. It's a tidal thing, don't worry about it.'

'I'm not worried about the tide. I'm worried about whatever made that noise.' He listened, but the deep rumble did not recur.

A higher-pitched grunt through the earpiece caught his attention. He looked ahead to see that Cellini had stopped, fins flailing uselessly. A swirl of sediment corkscrewed back towards Eddie as the younger man switched on his thrusters, to no avail. 'Eddie, I'm caught!'

25

'Hold on, I'm coming! Turn off your props.' The Englishman brought himself up behind Cellini, rolling for a better look at the ceiling. The bulbous back of the Italian's suit had jammed against some detail of the giant statue. 'Okay, I should be able to pull you out.'

'No, no!' Cellini protested. 'There is something on the other side, I can see it! We are so close! Push me forward.'

'You sure?'

Blumberg was about to speak, but Nina beat him to it. 'He's only about six feet from the entrance to the secondary chamber. You've got to keep going.'

'Just like old times, eh?' Eddie's tone was more sarcastic than nostalgic. 'I'm assuming everyone else is in favour?'

'We have to at least try,' agreed Blumberg. 'Don't take any risks, though.'

'Like crawling underneath a giant statue with fifty tons of rubble on top of it?' Eddie shook his head, then checked the golden surface. 'Okay, Nerio – it looks like you'll just about fit if I pull you back, then you slide to your left.'

'I can do that,' Cellini replied enthusiastically.

Eddie squirmed back, then braced himself and took hold of the other man's ankles. 'Ready?'

He pulled as Cellini levered himself backwards. The suit ground alarmingly against the protrusion, then came free. '*Sono libero!*' the Italian proclaimed.

'All right, go to your left,' said Eddie. 'Keep going . . . There, stop. Okay, go forward, slowly.'

The Yorkshireman carefully pushed the younger man. His air tanks again caught the sculpted fold, but this time the rasp was much fainter. 'You're almost through . . . All right, use your thrusters! Now!'

Cellini thumbed the throttle wheel on the control stalk. The suit's thrusters surged, and he popped free of the obstacle like a champagne cork. 'I did it!'

'*We* did it,' Eddie reminded him sardonically. 'Now, you going to help me through, or what?'

The Englishman's own journey through the gap was equally tight, but ultimately successful. Cellini helped him to his knees in a small space beneath what he realised was the statue's shoulder. 'Great, we're in Poseidon's armpit. And I bet he didn't use deodorant.'

'What can you see?' Nina demanded impatiently.

'You were right, Lester,' said Cellini. A curved alcove was set into the wall, an overturned golden statue partly buried beneath rubble – but behind it was a narrow passageway. 'There *is* an opening!'

Eddie brought up his light. The tunnel headed back beneath the altar room for around forty feet before turning to the right. There was debris on the floor, but it appeared traversable. 'Looks like we can get down it.'

'So what are we waiting for?' Cellini crawled forward until he had enough space to stand, then entered the passage. 'Eddie, come on!'

The older man shrugged as best he could in the suit, then followed. 'Rushing into ancient tunnels – it's like you're here with me, Nina. You sure you don't have any Italian relatives?'

'You and Macy are the only relatives I've got,' she replied. 'Which makes sending out Christmas cards a lot simpler. Okay, what can you see?'

Cellini reached the turning; Eddie caught up and put a hand on his shoulder. 'Careful,' he said. 'The Atlanteans really liked booby traps.'

The Italian was unconvinced. 'They would not still be working after all this time – and being under two hundred and fifty metres of water.'

'You'd think, wouldn't you?' Eddie took the lead, checking

the way ahead. The tunnel ran for thirty feet into a larger chamber. 'There's definitely a room down here,' he announced. 'If we swim in, we shouldn't set anything off.'

He kicked off the floor and tilted forward, using his flippers rather than the thrusters to move down the passage. They crossed the threshold, the walls opening out around them to reveal . . .

'*È incredibile!*' gasped Cellini.

Eddie was equally impressed. 'I think we've found what you were looking for.'

2

The room was not large, only a fraction of the altar room's size. But it was every bit as dazzling a find. Like its larger counterpart, the walls were covered with metal sheets: orichalcum, the red-tinted gold alloy favoured by the Atlanteans. At the sight, Nina unconsciously touched a pendant around her neck, made from a scrap of the same material by her father when she was a child.

Inscriptions filled the panels, recounting the history of the ancient civilisation. There was even a map, similar to one Nina had seen in the Brazilian temple. It showed the continents of the world, incomplete, distorted, but still recognisable. Lines weaved across both sea and land. The voyages of the Atlanteans?

She didn't have time to give it proper scrutiny, however, as something else had captured the divers' attention. They turned to point their cameras at a statue at one end of the room. A man, life-sized, and sculpted in gold – in its pure form this time, the metal an auric yellow. He was clad in robes, a sword sheathed at his side. His hands were raised before him.

Holding a large book.

Nina stared at the screen, more than ever wishing she was seeing it in person. 'Oh, wow. It's just like the Talonor Codex . . . which means,' she leaned closer to examine the statue's face, 'that actually might *be* Talonor!'

'I'd say it's a good bet,' said Blumberg, enraptured. 'So that's what he looked like?'

Talonor had been the greatest explorer of Atlantis, travelling as far as the Amazon basin to the west, and into the Himalayas to the east. The Talonor Codex, a record of his journeys, had been discovered in the underwater ruins several years earlier. It had given a whole new insight into the ancient civilisation, as well as leading Nina to another discovery: the Vault of Shiva, an astounding repository of Hindu artefacts high in the Indian mountains.

But it had not been his only record.

Further discoveries had led the IHA's archaeologists to believe that Talonor – a military leader as well as an adventurer – had compiled a *second* volume, the so-called Secret Codex. Rather than an account intended to impress the citizens of Atlantis with epic exploits in far-off lands, this was for the empire's rulers alone, written with a potential conqueror's eye: the strengths and weaknesses of the peoples Talonor had encountered, their riches and resources that could be plundered.

And it seemed that it had now been found.

Eddie moved closer. 'He's a bit smug.' The lean-faced man had a definite smirking curl to his lips.

'Well, when you're one of the greatest explorers in all recorded history, you're allowed to be pretty pleased with yourself,' Nina told him. 'The book – it looks like he's holding it, rather than it being a part of the statue?'

Eddie's gloved hand appeared on the monitor, brushing silt off the golden fingers. 'Yeah, it's a separate thing. You want me to pick it up?'

'No!' both Nina and Blumberg cried simultaneously, Cellini joining in the chorus from the ocean floor. 'We need to photograph and catalogue everything first,' she went on. 'I know it's been a while, but you remember the drill, surely?'

'I was hoping you'd forgotten the boring parts,' he replied.

'None of this is boring!'

'Different strokes, love.' Cellini's camera on another screen revealed that the Yorkshireman's smirk was as wide as Talonor's; he was trying to wind her up. 'I'll have a poke around while Nerio's taking pictures, then. Don't worry, I don't *literally* mean poke.'

Blumberg gave Nina a disapproving look. 'He does know what he's doing, trust me,' she said. 'After I beat it into him.' A faint mocking snort came from the seabed.

Cellini took a camera from his case and started to photograph the chamber. Blumberg switched the main screen to show the view from his shoulder cam as he worked. 'This is amazing,' said Nina, her knowledge of the ancient Atlantean language letting her pick out some of the words on the walls. They appeared to describe the lands the explorer had visited. The map was almost certainly a chart of his travels, then. 'Talonor's secret records chamber, still preserved after all this time.'

'It's incredible that anything survived at all,' said Blumberg. 'First Atlantis sinks, then a ship demolishes the temple . . .'

She ignored the hint of blame aimed at her for the latter. 'But there it is. Thank you for letting me be a part of this, Lester.'

'No problem,' he said, somewhat dismissively. 'Although there was only one route to follow down there, so we didn't actually need a guide at all.'

Now she made her annoyance plain on her face, but before she could come up with a spiky rejoinder, another low rumble echoed over the loudspeakers. 'What was that?'

Eddie felt it directly. 'The room just shook.' The floor had quivered beneath his feet, enough to unsteady him.

Cellini looked about in alarm. 'Earthquake?'

'No, mate,' said Matt. 'I've got readings from the seismic relays around the site. That was local, just in the temple.'

'If something was dislodged by the explosion, the change in the current might be affecting it,' suggested Blumberg.

'Oh, great, so it's going to fall down on us?' Eddie started for the tunnel. 'Come on, Nerio, time to go.'

'In a minute,' said the Italian. 'I have to photograph this first.' He approached the statue.

'What *is* it with archaeologists?' Eddie asked the universe in general. 'Look, if that big statue outside drops by even a couple of inches, we're not getting out of here! Forget taking pictures – just take the real thing.' He reached past Cellini and tugged the volume from Talonor's golden hands. It was heavy, its pages thin sheets of inscribed metal.

'Eddie!' Nina protested. 'What are you doing?'

'It's going to be taken out of here anyway, innit? I'm just saving some time—'

Another rumble, louder than before – and the whole chamber shuddered. Dust and silt dropped from between the ceiling's stone slabs, forming ghostly stalactites in the water.

'That was *not* me,' Eddie said firmly, glaring at the statue. 'That was a coincidence, not a booby trap!'

Cellini gave him a worried look. 'You are right. We should go!'

Both men launched themselves at the exit, using their suit thrusters to power down the passage before stopping at its end. Eddie squatted to check their escape route. It was still clear. 'Okay, you go first,' he told Cellini.

The Italian shook his head. 'No, you first! We have to get the Secret Codex out of here.'

'Your life's worth more than some book. And so's mine, for that matter!' But Eddie could tell the young man was not going to change his mind. He had seen the same attitude often enough in his wife. 'Oh, for— All right!' He threw the Codex as hard as he could into the low crawlspace. It spun through the water, skidding to a halt about ten feet in. 'I'll push it through ahead of me. As for you, you'd better be right behind!'

He dropped to his belly and pulsed the thrusters to move himself into the passage. Cellini took hold of his feet to push him onwards. When he reached the Codex, he shoved it along the narrow tunnel. A faint drumming reached him through the water. He put his fingertips to the ceiling. The statue was trembling.

Above him, he saw scrapes in the gold where the deep suits had ground against it. He rolled slightly to give himself as much clearance as possible. 'Nerio, I'm almost at the tight bit. Let me line up before you push me through.'

The Italian released his ankles. Eddie shuffled across to bring himself into what he hoped was the right alignment. 'Okay, now!'

Cellini pushed him again. The scrapes passed above his head . . . then the suit jarred against the ceiling, stopping him dead.

'Push harder!' he barked, trying to hold back his rising panic – not simply because he was caught, but also because now that he was in direct contact with the statue, the shudder was being transmitted into the hard body of his suit. It was an irregular pulsing thump, like a door banging in the wind, only something much bigger and heavier.

Whatever it was, it was getting worse.

He scrabbled at the floor with both hands as Cellini strained to force him through. His fingers brushed the Codex. He angrily pushed it away, wriggling and twisting as the ominous drumbeat grew louder—

A rasp – and suddenly he was free. Cellini released his legs. He kicked, the fins driving him forward. Another shove of the Codex, then he fired the thrusters to bring himself to the base of the stairs. 'I'm out!' he said, turning to look back into the cramped passage.

'What about the Codex?' asked Cellini.

'The stupid thing's here, don't worry. Hurry up, your turn!'

He aimed his light down the tunnel. Cellini was edging towards the lowest point beneath the statue. 'A bit to the right,' Eddie told him. 'That's it. Keep on coming, you can do it . . .'

The young man reached the clench point, his suit knocking against the ceiling. 'I can't fit!'

'Yeah, you can,' Eddie replied, trying to sound reassuring. 'Just roll a bit and you'll be able to get your air tanks through. Trust me,' he added with a smile.

Cellini nervously followed the instructions. 'That's it!' said Eddie. 'Come through, now!'

The Italian advanced. This time, the suit's carapace slipped beneath the obstruction, grinding against it as he squirmed forward—

Another deep rumble echoed through the water. The floor jolted – and displaced silt erupted through the passage as the great statue shifted.

Eddie felt as if he was inside Big Ben when the bell struck noon, a colossal metallic *boom* pounding him. Ears throbbing, he tried to hold himself in position. His vision was reduced almost to nothing by the swirling cloud. 'Nerio! Nerio, are you okay?'

No answer.

The reason wafted past him a moment later, a tiny point of blue light in the murk – the broken end of the Italian's fibre-optic cable.

'Eddie!' said Blumberg. 'We've lost contact with Nerio! What's happening?'

'His comm line's snapped,' Eddie replied. 'The statue moved.'

'Oh my God!' said Nina. 'Are you okay?'

'Yeah, but Nerio was right under it, and I can't see anything!' He groped until his fingers found the metal ceiling. There was still a gap underneath it, but how far had it dropped? An inch would trap Cellini – and anything more would crush his suit. At this depth, even the smallest breach would instantly kill its wearer.

Blumberg spoke again, but Eddie shouted him down. 'Quiet, quiet! Everyone shut up – I need to listen.' He waited for the radio chatter to cease, then called out Cellini's name.

All he could hear was the background hiss of his suit's air supply. 'Nerio!' he yelled again. 'Can you hear me?'

Still nothing, then . . .

'Eddie!' The voice was faint, reaching him through two thick acrylic bubbles and several feet of silt-choked water, but the Italian was alive. 'Help!'

'I can hear him!' Eddie reported. 'I'm going back into the tunnel.'

'You might get stuck too,' said Nina in alarm.

Blumberg joined in with a warning of his own. 'Eddie, if the statue shifts again, you could both be killed!'

'I can't leave him behind,' Eddie said firmly. He pulled himself back into the cramped tunnel. 'Nerio, I'm coming! Keep talking, let me know where you are!'

Cellini's voice grew louder. 'I'm here, I'm here! My radio is out!'

'I know, your line snapped. Stretch your hands out. I can't be far from you.'

Eddie looked ahead. The water was still an opaque soup . . . then it started to swirl. 'I'm almost there,' he said. 'Keep waving!'

Something flicked through the gloom, stirring up suspended silt. A moment later it moved back: Cellini's gloved hand. Eddie grabbed it. '*Mi hai trovato!*' gasped the Italian.

'Still got to get you out of there,' Eddie cautioned. 'I'm going to try to pull you. Are your thrusters working?'

'Yes, but they did not help.'

'We'll have to use brute force and ignorance, then. Usually works!' He gripped Cellini's wrist, using his other hand to take his own suit's control stalk. 'Okay, you ready? Start 'em up!'

Both sets of thrusters whined to full power. Eddie backed up, but halted again almost immediately as his arm reached full stretch, straining to pull the Italian. 'Are you moving?'

'I don't know!' Cellini replied. 'I . . . I hear the suit rubbing on the statue, but – no, no!' Excitement filled his voice. 'I can see the floor, I moved!'

'That's great!' Eddie growled, tugging at him. 'Keep it up—'

Another rumble shook the temple – and a sharp crack came from his suit's fibreglass back as the statue pressed down hard upon it.

He froze in fear, but no explosive inrush of water hit him. The section of casing covering the air tanks was cosmetic streamlining rather than structural. It had split under the weight, but the pressurised body had not been damaged.

Yet. If the statue dropped any lower, it would crush the shell like an egg—

An idea came to him. He twisted to test it, and found that even though the suit was still graunching against both floor and ceiling, he had slightly more freedom of movement. 'Nerio!' he yelled. 'Back up, as far as you can! You need to hit the ceiling harder!'

'What are you doing?' Blumberg demanded.

Cellini was equally bewildered. 'But the suit will break!'

'I know, I know – but if the *back* breaks, it doesn't matter! It's just a cover! If you flatten it, you'll be able to fit through.'

'Eddie, that's crazy,' said Blumberg, but the Englishman ignored him – and to his relief, so did Cellini. The Italian withdrew, Eddie letting himself be pulled deeper into the tunnel until he jammed against the statue.

'All right,' he called. 'Are you set?'

'Yes!' came the reply.

Eddie restarted his thrusters at full power. '*Now!*'

He lunged backwards, pulling Cellini with him – and the younger man slammed against his confines. There was a sharp snap of splintering fibreglass. 'Keep going, keep going!' Eddie shouted. He pulled Cellini's arm. 'You're moving!'

Another crack – and Cellini broke free, rushing forward with such force that he almost collided head-on with Eddie. The Englishman shoved himself backwards, swinging around as he reached the bottom of the stairs. The water was less murky here, letting him see the archaeologist's smile of relief as he emerged. His suit's back had been flattened, spears of broken casing jutting out like porcupine quills. But the tanks inside were still intact. 'You saved me! Thank you, thank you!' He moved as if to embrace the Englishman.

'We're not out of here yet,' Eddie reminded him. 'Get to the top, fast!'

'But the Codex—'

'I'll get it!'

'And I lost the camera—'

'Just *go*! God, bloody archaeologists!'

Cellini's thrusters surged and propelled him up the staircase. Eddie was about to follow, but decided – with aggrieved reluctance – that a promise was a promise. He flailed his fins until one touched something straight-edged on the floor. He grabbed the heavy book, then started after the Italian at full speed—

A rushing current swept past him as a stone slab fell into the space where he had just been.

His arm grazed a wall as he was thrown off course. He corrected, looking ahead to see Cellini passing over the rubble pile. The Englishman followed, manoeuvring the bulky Codex ahead of him.

The first barricade lay above, Cellini squeezing into the opening above the broken slab. The Italian's damaged suit bashed against the ceiling in his haste, clipping shards off the casing. He backed up to try again. More loud booms came from below. Eddie looked back.

A roiling wall of silt was surging up the tunnel. After ten years, the overturned statue had finally hit the floor, forcing the water beneath it out along its only escape route – straight at the two fleeing men. 'Go, *go!*' he yelled, shoving Cellini on before powering through the narrow space after him.

A dull *whump* as the shock wave hit the barrier, dislodging the broken block – followed by louder crunches as the ceiling gave way and fell into the tunnel.

Cellini was a human torpedo just ahead of Eddie, the turbulence from his thrusters buffeting the Yorkshireman. Lights rose ahead, the altar room coming into view—

They burst into open water as the churning wave hit and sent them both tumbling. The Codex slipped from Eddie's hands. Blinded by the silt, all he could do was let himself be carried along and hope he wasn't on a collision course with the surrounding masonry.

He gradually slowed and kicked upright, restarting the propellers to rise out of the swollen mass of sediment. The circle of lights returned to view, now broken where some had been knocked over.

'Eddie!' A voice in his ear: Matt. 'Can you hear me?'

'Yeah, I can,' he replied, recovering his breath. The submersible was some way above him, directing its lights downwards. 'Can you see Nerio?'

A tense pause, then: 'I got him! Lower than you, off to your left.'

Eddie caught sight of the other diver's lights. 'He looks okay.'

'Thank God!' exclaimed Nina. 'What about you?'

'My suit'll need some filler to patch up the dents, but I'm all right.'

She let out a relieved sigh. 'Okay. I feel kinda bad asking this, but . . . what about the Secret Codex?'

'I dropped it, but it's around here somewhere. When the water clears, we should be able to find it. Although,' he continued with a sudden weariness, 'to be honest, I'd rather get back up top. And Nerio probably would too.' He looked towards his companion – only to see him descending back to the altar room. 'Oh, you're kidding me! He's already gone to look for it. You archaeologists really are all as bad as each other!'

'We can't stop being who we are,' Nina said, amused. 'But you're right, you should get topside. And back home! Macy missed you this morning.'

'Let's not tell her about the whole "Daddy almost died" part of the day, shall we?'

'Yeah, probably best.'

Matt cut into the conversation. 'Hey, Eddie. Looks like Nerio found that book.'

Eddie saw the Italian ascending with the Codex. 'Great, we got the list of all the places where Talonor dug latrines. Now can we go? That's more than enough archaeology for me.'

Nina smiled at her husband's complaints. 'I'd be perfectly happy to keep going, but . . .' She checked her watch, eyes widening. 'Oh crap! It can't be that late already!'

'You haven't missed picking Macy up from nursery, have you?' Eddie asked.

'No, but I need to get moving soon. Like, now.'

'Okay, then I'll talk to you when I'm at the airport. Which'll be a while, seeing as I've got to get up to the ship and then take a chopper back to Portugal first.'

'I'll wait up. All right, I have to go. Love you.'

'Love you,' Eddie replied.

She smiled again, then took off her headset microphone.

'Well, thanks for coming in, Nina,' said Blumberg.

'No problem at all, Lester. If you need me for anything else, I'm more than happy to help. Although Eddie might be a bit reluctant! But if you want me to assist with the translation of the Secret Codex, I—'

He shook his head. 'That won't be necessary, thanks.'

'Are you sure? I know the Atlantean language as well as anyone, and—'

He cut her off again, more brusquely. 'The Secret Codex is now an IHA security matter. You'll be able to read the abstracts as they become available, of course, but we need to keep the actual translations classified for now. Talonor visited a lot of places; we can't afford to have treasure hunters ripping potential sites apart before we have a chance to investigate them. You know the rules.'

'Yes, I know the rules,' she snapped. 'I wrote most of them!'

Blumberg puffed out his chest. 'That's as may be, but you don't work for the IHA any more, so you don't have clearance to see the Secret Codex before we've determined what's safe for public release. I appreciate your help today, but you've done everything you can for us. So you should probably go pick up your daughter. You wouldn't want to be late.' He gave her a smug little smirk.

Nina stood, scowling. 'You know you're kind of a patronising jerk, Lester?' One of the IHA technicians stifled a giggle.

Her host was not amused, however. 'Thank you for stopping by, Nina.' He turned away, issuing commands to those aboard the research ship.

'Asshole,' Nina muttered as she headed for the operation centre's exit.

Despite her best efforts to rush through Manhattan, she still arrived fifteen minutes late at the Little Petals nursery. The elevator was old and slow and frequently out of order, the building undergoing renovation work, so rather than wait for it, she simply ran up the stairs to the second floor.

'Oh hi, Nina,' said Penny Lopez, as the redhead hurried into the cloakroom. Even though the teacher was smiling, there was still a critical undercurrent to her greeting. 'Look, Macy! Here's your mommy.'

'Hi, Mommy!' squealed Macy Wilde Chase, running to meet her mother. Nina hugged her, noticing to her dismay that her daughter's coat was the only one left on the hooks. 'We painted pictures today! I painted a ship, because Daddy's on one. Do you want to see?'

'I'd love to, honey,' Nina replied. Macy skipped away to get it. 'I'm *so* sorry I'm late,' she told Penny. 'I was helping with my old job at the United Nations, and Eddie . . .' She remembered the couple's discussion after he escaped the temple. 'I had to make sure he finished what he was doing.'

'That's fine,' said Penny. 'But it's not going to be a regular problem, is it? We're more than happy to have some flexibility around parents' schedules, but we need to know in advance.'

'No, no, this was a one-time thing. It seems.' She tried not to sound too despondent about being cut out of what had been her profession.

'Have you considered hiring a nanny? I can recommend some good people.'

'I don't think we're quite ready for that, thanks,' Nina said as her daughter returned bearing a large sheet of paper. 'Is this your painting?'

'Yes, it is!' Macy said, pointing out aspects of her finger-painted masterwork. 'That's the sea, and that's the boat Daddy's on, and that's a fish, and that's a sumb . . . sub . . . submarine!'

'Wow, that's really good,' Nina told her. For a three-year-old, it was quite advanced, everything Macy indicated a distinct object rather than a splodgy agglomeration, though rough circles and triangles were the limit of her artistic talents. 'Is Daddy there too?'

'He's on the sumbarine!' She jabbed at a pink thumbprint.

Nina smiled. 'It's a very good likeness. I'm sure he'll want to see it when he gets home. Let's put on your coat.'

'When is he coming home?' Macy asked.

'He'll be back tomorrow.'

'Tomorrow!' The little girl looked stricken. 'But he always reads me a story for bedtime!'

'I'll read you one tonight, hon. The one Daddy wrote for you, about the eggs?'

'But Daddy does the funny voices. You can't do funny voices.'

'Daddy has an advantage because he's *got* a funny voice,' said Nina. She put Macy's arms into her sleeves. 'Okay, are you ready? I'll take your painting, and you hold my other hand. Say bye-bye to Penny.'

They started for the exit. At the door, Nina paused, feeling a strange sense of incongruity. Less than an hour ago she had been involved in an archaeological expedition deep beneath the sea, and now she was collecting her daughter from school and discussing bedtime stories.

There was another feeling, too. It took her a moment to work out what it was, and when she did, guilt joined her emotions.

The abrupt return to everyday normality had left her *disappointed*.

3

'**I**'m back!' Eddie called as he entered the apartment.

'Daddy!' cried Macy, rushing to hug him. 'You're home!'

'Hi, love!' He kissed her. 'Where's Mummy?'

'Mommy,' his wife and daughter corrected as one as Nina joined them. 'I am *so* happy to see you. Safe and well.'

'And in one piece,' said Eddie. He scooped Macy up. 'Wow, look at you! I'm away for a couple of days and it looks like you've grown another inch.'

'Did you see fish in the sea, Daddy?' she asked.

'Quite a few. They went like this: *bloop-bloop-bloop*.' He mimed a big-lipped fish blowing kisses. Macy giggled.

'Did they bring the Secret Codex back to the IHA?' Nina asked as they went into the lounge.

'Yeah, Nerio took it. He was supposed to work at Atlantis for a few more days, but after what happened, they decided to give him a break.'

'It was a close call. I wish I'd been there with you.'

Eddie sat, Macy hopping off his knee and running from the room. 'Did you actually just say those two sentences one after the other? "You almost got killed. I should have been there so I could almost get killed too!"'

'Okay, maybe I needed more of a segue there.' Nina sat beside him. 'But I *did* want to see Atlantis again. For real, not on a screen.'

'I've seen that place way too—' Macy returned. 'Flipping much,' Eddie concluded.

Nina grinned. 'I'm still impressed by that. You said you weren't going to swear any more once Macy was born, and I thought you just meant in front of her. But you kept it up. Except when you called Lester something rude, and I'd consider that justified.'

'Yeah, it's funny that you swear loads more than me now.' Macy proudly displayed her painting to him. 'Hey, that's good! Is that the sea?'

She showed off the points of interest. Eddie made approving comments, then, as the little girl left to bring more drawings, looked back at Nina. 'So you didn't get to go there in person, but they still found something new thanks to us.'

'Thanks to *you*,' she said, with a hint of petulance. 'And as Lester took pleasure in pointing out, they didn't need us at all. Once they opened that tunnel, anyone could have explored it.'

'So what? It doesn't mean you weren't a part of it. Maybe you'll be able to add it to your new book.' He glanced at the desk, where a stack of pages sat next to Nina's laptop: the proofs for the second volume of her tales of discovery.

'It won't be much more than a footnote, though.' She leaned forward, feeling deflated. 'And I'd much rather be doing some-thing new instead of just writing about what I've already done. Although I started by finding Atlantis, and finished by finding the Ark of the Covenant! It'll be hard to top that.'

'Who says you're finished?' Eddie objected. 'And you don't have to do something massive and world-changing. You can still do something that's important to you.'

'I suppose. I've got no idea what, though.'

'You'll think of something,' he assured her. 'Besides, it's not like you haven't got other stuff to do. There's Macy, for a start.'

He could tell from the way Nina stiffened that she had not taken the remark as he'd intended. 'Yeah, I've got Macy,' she said tersely. 'You get to go and explore Atlantis, while I'm stuck here picking her up from playgroup!'

'I would *gladly* have stayed here if you'd had your dive certificate.'

'That's not the point! You've gone off to do other things before – you've got your consultancy work for your army buddy's company, and there was that business in the Canary Isles last year.'

'Someone needed my help,' he protested.

'And what if *I'd* needed your help? Or Macy?'

He held up his hands. 'Why're you getting mad at me? I've only been back five minutes.'

'I don't know. I'm sorry.' She shook her head. 'I think yesterday made me realise how long it's been since I actually went into the field and did some, y'know, *archaeology*. Being stuck at a computer writing books about it isn't the same.'

'It helps pay the bills, though. And there's the film coming up; you might be able to blag a trip off the back of that.'

'Oh, the film!' she said, keen to change the subject. 'I just remembered, I got an email from Marvin.' Marvin Bronze was the producer of the movie based on Nina's book, and the business partner of their friend Grant Thorn, Hollywood action star. 'They're having the premiere here in New York next month. He sent us an invitation.'

'Tchah!' Eddie exclaimed in mock outrage. 'I was hoping we'd get an all-expenses-paid trip to LA!'

'I haven't replied yet. We'd have to fix up a babysitter for Macy. It runs quite late.'

'I keep telling you, we should ask my niece while she's over here. She loves Macy, I'm sure she'd look after her.'

Nina smiled. 'Wait, you mean . . . we might actually be able to have a grown-ups' night out on our own? Although if we're going to see a Grant Thorn movie, I don't know if "grown-up" is the right term. I mean, they didn't even use the title of my book.' She gestured at a framed print of its cover above the desk, the words *In Search of History* and her name superimposed over an atmospheric photograph of a golden statue on the seabed. '*The Hunt for Atlantis*? It's not exactly subtle.'

'They'll have changed a load of other stuff too,' said her husband. 'It's Hollywood; they always do. They're not even using our names for the main characters.'

'Which makes me nervous from the get-go. They can have them do anything and we can't complain about it, because they're technically not us.'

Macy returned with more pictures. 'Oh, what are these?' her father asked. 'Are these fish too? They're really good!' He looked back at Nina as he perused the crayoned artworks. 'I wouldn't worry about it. Grant's a big star, and Marvin's a successful producer. They know what they're doing.'

'I know,' she said, trying to reassure herself. 'I just hope they didn't change *too* much . . .'

A month later, Nina had her answer.

'That was,' she hissed to Eddie as the credits began to roll to teen-friendly rock music, 'the biggest pile of . . . of *shit* I have ever seen!' As the other audience members applauded, she hurriedly stood and headed for the aisle, pulling her husband after her.

Eddie grinned. 'See, you *do* swear loads more than me now. I really enjoyed it, myself. Didn't like that they changed me into an American, but that's Hollywood for you.'

'You *liked* it? It was . . . it was *idiotic*! It was even more ridiculous than Grant's stupid car movies, and I didn't think that was possible. At the end, when they jump out of the jet without parachutes? There's no way they could have survived!'

'We actually did that,' Eddie pointed out as they exited

the auditorium and started down the stairs to the lobby.

She glared at him. 'Yes, but – but it didn't happen that way. Then there was that ludicrous action sequence where you – I mean *Jason Mach*' – a snort of contempt – 'steals a train and chases after me, or rather Eden Crest?'

'That happened too.'

'Shut up! And Eden Crest, what the hell kind of a name is that? Sounds like an environmentally friendly toothpaste. Also,' a deeper scowl, 'I *really* hated that they made you into the perfect hero and turned me into the damsel in distress who always needed rescuing.'

'Yeah, I wasn't keen on that either,' he admitted. 'Hopefully they'll fix it in the sequel. You should have a word with Grant at the after-party.'

'I don't want to *go* to the after-party,' she protested. 'I just want to get home and see my little girl.'

'After all that time you kept saying how great it'd be to finally have a night out without Macy, now you can't wait to get back to her?'

'This wasn't what I had in mind.'

Before he could ask what she did have in mind, they'd passed through the lobby doors – and Nina stopped in her tracks. Many of the members of the press attending the premiere had made a beeline for the foyer to catch the celebrity guests as they emerged. 'Oh God,' she moaned. '*Please* don't let anyone ask me what I thought of it.' She shook her head. 'I can't believe I accepted that clause in the contract about not publicly bad-mouthing the movie. Marvin might seem friendly, but I bet he'd slap me with a lawsuit in three seconds flat if I told a reporter what I *really* thought about it.'

'I can say whatever I want, though,' said Eddie. 'I didn't sign any contract.'

'Yeah, but you liked the damn thing!'

He squeezed her to him as more audience members thronged past them into the foyer. 'Come on, love. It wasn't that bad. And it's a Hollywood action movie! What did you expect?'

She sighed. 'I don't know. I guess I'd hoped it would be more like *Gorillas in the Mist* than some pulp mash-up of James Bond and Indiana Jones!'

Eddie laughed. 'You do remember all the stuff we've been through, don't you? Like how we first met? I pulled you out of a car at the bottom of a river!'

'I could hardly forget it. Although a lot of it, I'm still trying really hard to.' Her expression became serious, even downcast. 'To be honest, I almost walked out right at the beginning. That opening, where Eden Crest's parents were murdered just as they found a clue leading to Atlantis? It hit *way* too close to home.'

'That's what was bothering you?' he asked with sympathetic concern.

Nina nodded. 'It's not just that it was a dumb movie. It was a dumb movie that used my life for *plot points* – it took the worst thing that ever happened to me and reduced it to a way to get a character the audience's sympathy. It . . . it hurt, you know? My parents were all I had, and that scene brought back how it felt when I lost them.'

Eddie was silent for a moment, then took her hand. 'You're right, we should go home. Macy's probably still up waiting for us.'

'I told Holly to put her to bed at seven.'

'Macy never goes to sleep at seven for us; why would Holly do any better?'

They turned to leave – only for Grant Thorn to hurry across the lobby to intercept them. 'Hey, there you are!' drawled the Californian, looking sharp in a tuxedo. 'I was hoping to catch you. What did you think of the movie?'

Nina was about to let him know her true feelings, but the sight of Marvin Bronze and several journalists arriving in his wake – as well as the actor's puppy-like expectancy – persuaded her to be more diplomatic. 'It was . . . interesting,' she managed.

'Guys, this is Dr Nina Wilde,' Marvin said exuberantly to the reporters, 'the author of the book the movie's based on. You wanna find an ancient legend, you call her! She discovered Atlantis, King Arthur's tomb, even the Lost Ark of the Covenant. That was a few years back, though, so Nina: what've you done for us lately? Joke,' the tanned little man added on seeing her startled expression. 'So, how much did you love the movie?'

The redhead recovered her composure. 'Well, you changed a lot from my book, which was what *actually* happened, but it was all still very . . . exciting.'

Marvin chuckled. 'You didn't tell us everything, did you? All classified, very hush-hush,' he clarified for the journalists. 'We had to fill in some of the details ourselves. But we stayed with the spirit of the story, didn't we?'

'Insofar as Atlantis was being hunted for, yes . . .'

'You did a great job,' said Eddie, stepping in to save his wife. 'Some of the story was different from real life, but you can't have too many explosions, right?' A couple of chuckles from the group. 'But I just had a message from our babysitter saying our little girl's missing her mum and dad—'

'Mom,' Nina corrected automatically.

'—so we need to get moving. Family comes first, right?'

'Aw, man, that's a shame,' said Grant. 'You're not coming to the party? We got celebrities there, Masta Thugg's gonna do a set . . .'

'Afraid not.' Nina had rolled her eyes during the movie when she saw that Matt Trulli had been replaced by a wisecracking fictional character played by an American rapper. 'We have to get back to Macy.'

The name caught Grant off-guard. 'Macy. How . . . how is she?'

'She's great, thanks. She's three now.'

'Three! Man, has it been that long?' He seemed about to add something, but then eyed the recording devices nearby. 'I'm happy for you guys. And, y'know, calling her . . . It would have meant a lot to her.' Nina and Eddie's daughter had been named in memory of their friend, and Grant's girlfriend, Macy Sharif, who had died trying to prevent a group of Nazi war criminals from finding the secret of eternal youth.

The trio shared looks of mutual sympathy, then the actor straightened. 'Like you say, family comes first, right!' he said, in a performance as obvious as any he had ever given on screen. 'Glad you liked the movie, we're all very proud of it. And don't forget,' he added for the microphones, 'you want to find out what really happened, read Nina's book! It's called, uh . . .'

'*In Search of History*,' Marvin quickly said. 'Great story, we wouldn't have bought the rights otherwise!' He looked around. 'Hey, Claudia's over there with Leviticus Gold. Let's get all the stars together for the cameras, huh?'

'Catch you guys later!' Grant called over his shoulder as Marvin ushered his business partner and their entourage away.

'Bye,' said Nina, with distinct relief. She regarded her husband. 'Can we go now?'

He smiled. 'Yeah, I think we're done.'

They headed for the exit. Nobody tried to intercept them. Nina gave silent thanks that the journalists had more famous prey—

'Dr Wilde? Nina?'

'Goddamn it,' she muttered before turning.

To her surprise, the person who had called her name wasn't a member of the press but an elegantly dressed old lady. Nina guessed she was well into her eighties, white hair drawn into a carefully styled bun. Despite her age, the woman's green eyes were still bright and intelligent, regarding the redhead with a contemplative, almost approving air. 'Hello?' Nina said after an uncomfortable silence.

The woman blinked. 'I'm sorry,' she said, an upper-class New England accent clear even in just two words. 'It's just that . . . I've seen photographs of you, of course, but I hadn't been prepared for how much you look like Laura in person.'

Nina felt unsettled at her mother's name being used by a complete stranger. But as she looked back at the elderly woman, the feeling grew – because she was now also experiencing an odd sense of *recognition*. Something about her was familiar, almost disturbingly so. 'Do I know you?'

'No, I'm afraid you don't. But I did know your mother – and we should talk about her.'

'What about my mother?' Nina demanded. 'Who *are* you?'

The woman smiled. 'My name is Olivia Garde. I'm your grandmother.'

4

The lobby's hubbub seemed to fade as Nina stared at the old lady. 'That's . . . that's not possible,' she said. 'My grandmother died a long time ago.'

'Yes, I imagine that's what Laura told you,' said Olivia, with a small, sad shake of the head. 'But I can prove that I am who I say. If you'll let me.' A glance at the crowd. 'Perhaps somewhere more quiet?'

Nina was caught between the urge to find out more and telling the impostor – she *had* to be! – where to go. The former won out. 'We're just on our way home. You could meet us there.'

'Er, Nina?' said Eddie. 'We're putting our three-year-old daughter to bed, remember?'

'I wouldn't want to keep Macy awake,' Olivia told them. 'I can meet you at your convenience.'

'No, that's okay. It's okay,' Nina repeated to her disapproving husband. 'We'll make it quick. If that's all right?' she asked Olivia.

'That will be perfectly fine,' the older woman replied. 'I'll take a cab. What's your address?' Nina gave it. 'I'll see you there. Don't worry – and don't you worry either, Mr Chase. I'll explain everything.'

Nina and Eddie watched as she departed. She might have been old, but she still had a steady and determined pace. 'Wait, she knew who I am. And Macy,' Eddie said with a frown.

'That doesn't mean she really is my grandmother,' said Nina. 'She could have just googled me. Hell, I wrote about my parents in the book, so it's not as if it's a great secret.'

'If you don't believe her, then why'd you invite her to our house?'

'Because . . .' She wasn't entirely sure herself. 'Because there's something about her that . . . that makes me think she might be telling the truth. I don't know if she actually is,' she added, seeing his look of incredulity. 'But I want to find out for sure.'

'She'd better not be trying anything on. If this is some con trick . . .'

'Eddie, she looked about ninety. She'd have to be one hell of a grifter to try the long-lost-relative routine on us at that age.'

'Some people never change, however old they get.' He took her hand. 'Come on, let's find out what she's after.'

The journey home did not take long, but there was little conversation on the way. Despite Eddie's attempts to engage with her, Nina found herself gazing out of the window, replaying the meeting with Olivia in her mind.

The old woman couldn't *possibly* have been telling the truth. That would mean her own mother had lied to her through their entire life together. Nina couldn't accept that. And why on earth would Laura Wilde have told her daughter that her grandmother was dead if that were not the case . . .

'We're here,' Eddie said.

'Huh? Oh. Right.' Composing herself, she got out as Eddie paid the fare.

A yellow cab was waiting outside their building. 'Hello again,' Olivia said as she emerged. 'I'm glad you agreed to see me.'

'With a claim like yours, I could hardly say no,' replied Nina.

'Thank you.' The old lady surveyed the surrounding buildings. 'Quite a nice area. Your grandfather and I once lived not far from here. We had a wonderful view of the park.'

Nina recalled her mother once pointing out a Fifth Avenue

apartment building as a childhood home, but said nothing, not wanting to give the woman any hints about her past that she could weave into a fictional narrative. 'Come inside,' she said instead as Eddie joined her.

They entered the building. 'So what were you doing at the premiere?' Nina asked Olivia. 'A Grant Thorn action movie doesn't really seem like your kind of thing.'

Olivia laughed. 'Oh dear me, no. It was awful nonsense, all shouting and wobbly cameras.'

Nina smiled at Eddie as they boarded the elevator. 'Told you.'

'No, I'm quite well known in New York's social circles. There are few events to which I can't get an invitation if I choose. In this case, I came specifically to see you. I watched the first five minutes for politeness' sake, then had a meal at a little place around the corner before coming back. And,' she went on, with a faint sigh, 'when I realised who the characters at the beginning were meant to be, it ended any desire I had to see more.'

'What do you mean?' asked Nina, wanting to see if her guest shared her emotions about the opening scene – and why.

Olivia's emerald eyes turned upon her, sadness clear in them. 'The names were different, but they were meant to be your mother and father. My daughter, and her husband. I didn't want to watch what happened to them.'

'Nor did I,' Nina said, lips tightening.

The elevator arrived at the eighth floor. Eddie led the way into the apartment. 'Holly?' he called in a low voice. 'We're back.'

The thump of a pair of excited little feet jumping from a bed told both parents that any hopes their daughter might be asleep had come to nothing. 'Daddy!' cried Macy, running down the hall to greet them. 'Mommy, hi!'

Eddie embraced her. 'Ay up, someone's still awake when she shouldn't be. You been giving her coffee, Holly?'

'No, just a few lines of coke,' said the Englishman's niece as she followed Macy out of her bedroom. Holly Bennett was currently on the third year of her American Studies degree, spending it in the States as part of an exchange programme. Her eyes grew wide as she saw that her uncle and aunt were not alone. 'Ooh, sorry! Didn't realise you had company.'

'It wasn't planned,' Eddie told her pointedly.

'Holly, this is Olivia Garde, a . . . friend,' said Nina. 'We met her at the premiere.'

'How was the film?' Holly asked excitedly. 'Was Grant Thorn there?'

'Ludicrous, and yes. Olivia, our niece Holly, and our daughter. Macy.'

Olivia smiled at Macy, who hugged Nina before taking cover behind her, regarding the visitor uncertainly. 'She's very pretty. How old is she?'

'She's just had her third birthday.'

'She's three? They grow up so quickly, don't they?' Her expression turned wistful. 'I can see the family resemblance. She looks a lot like you – and like Laura. She certainly has the same hair.'

'Daddy said my hair means I'm a handful,' announced Macy proudly, showing off a strand of her deep red locks.

Nina gave her husband a stern look. 'Did he now?'

'Might have done,' Eddie replied with a grin. 'Come on, young 'un. It's way past your bedtime.'

'But I want to stay up with you!' Macy objected.

'And I want a Ferrari, but we can't always have what we want.' He kissed her. 'Mummy needs—'

'Mommy,' Nina said over him.

'—to talk to her friend.'

'What about?' asked the little girl.

'Grown-up stuff, you wouldn't be interested. Now, how

about me and Holly put you back to bed? We can tell you a story.'

Macy squeaked with excitement. 'The one about the eggs with legs!'

'I *told* you to send it to my publisher,' said Nina.

'I'll type it up tomorrow,' he replied. 'Say night-night to Mummy, Macy.'

'Night-night, Mommy!'

Nina smirked as Eddie groaned. 'Fighting a losing battle, aren't I?' he said as he and Holly headed for Macy's bedroom.

Nina waved to her daughter, then turned back to Olivia. 'So. I think we have some stuff to talk about.'

'We do,' the elderly woman replied. She was carrying a bulging leather satchel. 'As much as I dislike playing the little-old-lady card, may we sit down? This is quite heavy.'

'Sure. This way.'

Nina led her guest into the lounge, gesturing to an armchair. After peering at the numerous framed photographs decorating one wall, Olivia sat and placed the satchel on a coffee table, Nina sitting opposite. 'I wouldn't expect you simply to take my claim at face value,' she began as she opened it, 'so I brought proof.' She carefully drew out a plastic sleeve containing several photographs. 'I see you have a picture of your parents there.'

Nina glanced towards the wall. The image was of her teenage self with Henry and Laura Wilde, taken at an archaeological site in Turkey. 'Yeah.'

'I have some family photos of my own. Please, take a look.' She slid the sleeve across the table.

Nina took it. The first photograph was visible through the protective cover – and it gave her a momentary shock.

She recognised the smiling figure at the centre. It was her mother, a few years younger than Nina in the photo on the wall.

With her were two people she knew only from pictures: her grandparents, Thomas and Olivia Pearce.

She looked up sharply at the old lady. Even though several decades had passed, there was still a definite resemblance between the woman in the still and the one sitting before her.

'Yes, that's me,' said Olivia. She tapped the red-haired woman in the picture with a well-manicured nail. 'That was taken in, let me think . . . 1966. We were living near New Haven at the time. Tom, your grandfather, was an executive for General Electric in Fairfield.'

'And what were you doing?'

'Whatever I wanted. My family, the Gardes, were wealthy and influential. I went back to my maiden name after Tom died – not immediately, I hasten to add. That would have been very disrespectful. But there were . . . social advantages, one could say. More so for your mother than myself. I wanted the absolute best for her, to open the right doors, which is why she adopted it too.'

Nina nodded, keeping her face neutral. Again the story matched what she knew of her mother's background, but there was nothing so far that couldn't have been unearthed with diligent genealogical research.

She carefully slid the clutch of photos from the sleeve. More images of her mother and grandparents, the giant tail fins of a car in the background of one dating it to the late 1950s or early '60s. Time advanced jumpily as she flicked through them, her mother growing from a little girl into a young woman—

The last photo – and again she felt an emotional jolt. This featured only her mother and grandmother against a backdrop of trees and flowers. Laura had recently turned eighteen.

There was a reason Nina could date it so precisely. 'Excuse me,' she said, going into the main bedroom. She opened the wardrobe and took a cardboard box from the top shelf. Lifting the lid, she quickly found what she was looking for and returned to the living room with her prize.

It was another photograph, which she put down on the table next to the final one from Olivia's collection: its twin. 'Mom told me that was the last photo she had of her mother before she died,' she said, a tremor in her voice. 'Spring 1972. The Shakespeare Garden in Central Park. Now you'd better have a damn good explanation for why you have that photo, and how, if you really are my grandmother, you're alive and well despite what my mom told me. Because if you don't . . .' the tremor became barely contained anger, 'then age be damned, I'm going to kick your ass out on to the street.'

Olivia did not speak for several seconds, then the corners of her mouth slowly creased upwards. 'It's been a long time since I heard *that* tone of voice,' she said. 'You really are your mother's daughter.'

Nina was unmoved. 'I'm still waiting for an explanation.'

'And you certainly deserve one. I assume you think I'm pretending to be your grandmother to bilk you out of the money your fame has brought you – something like that?'

'The thought had occurred.'

'I don't blame you for being sceptical. But I assure you, I *am* your grandmother – and Laura's mother. The reason she told you I was dead was that we had . . . a falling-out. A very serious falling-out.'

'About what?'

'About your father.'

'What? Why?'

Olivia gave her a sorrowful look. 'Everyone makes mistakes in their life – mistakes where they are one hundred per cent convinced they are in the right until the sky falls on them. The greatest mistake I ever made was thinking I knew what was right for Laura better than she did. When she met your father, and fell in love with him practically overnight, and wanted to marry him and search for Atlantis with him . . . I thought she was throwing everything away, that she was turning her back on her family's legacy for a penniless archaeology student with a crackpot theory.' A deep breath. 'I was wrong. I've never been more wrong, and the greatest regret of my life is that I never got the chance to ask her forgiveness.'

It took Nina a moment to process what she had just heard. 'So you're telling me that Mom told me you were dead – that she lied to me – because you had an *argument*?'

'It was quite a serious argument,' the elderly woman clarified. 'I forbade her to marry him – in fact, I told her she couldn't keep seeing him. Now, knowing your mother, how do you think she took that?'

'Probably the same way I would have.'

'Exactly. And I'm sure you also remember what she was like once she had decided to do something. She was—'

'Stubborn.'

Another tiny smile. '*Determined* was the word I was going to use, but yes. It all happened very quickly; I don't think she had even talked about me with your father before they decided to get engaged. When she told me, the discussion became very heated, to say the least, and she . . .' Any trace of humour vanished, replaced by regret. 'She turned her back on me. She told your father that *both* her parents had died in the car crash, not just Tom, and once it had been said, she stuck with it.'

'So you *are* saying she lied to me my whole life.'

'I *was* dead – to her, at least,' said Olivia. 'The last time I spoke to her was shortly after she graduated, before her wedding. Our positions hadn't changed, I was still trying to talk her out of it, so . . . that was it. She wanted nothing more to do with me. She could have contacted me at any time, but chose not to. And I'm ashamed to say that I made no further effort to reach out to her either, even after you were born. Determinedness – stubbornness – is very much a family trait, especially in the women. Your husband may be right about it coming with the hair.'

'So why've you come to me now?' asked Nina, still not sure what to believe.

'For one, I'm eighty-nine years old. You're my closest living relative, and I realised that if I ever wanted a chance to get to know you, it would have to be now. But there is something else; something I thought you should have.' She reached back into the satchel, withdrawing several packed manila folders. She opened the topmost. 'These were your mother's. Her notes.'

Nina almost lunged to take out the first page when she saw what was written on it. 'This is her handwriting!'

'You recognise it?'

'I've still got all her research. My dad's, too. They were the basis of my entire theory on how to find Atlantis. They were nine tenths of the way there – they'd just got some of the details wrong. If they'd had more time . . .'

'Laura was always fascinated by the legend of Atlantis. It was why she studied archaeology in the first place. Well, I probably influenced her too. I was something of an amateur archaeologist in my youth,' Olivia added, on Nina's questioning look. 'I was never dedicated enough to match her achievements, though. Or yours.'

Nina turned back to her mother's notes. She had indeed recognised the handwriting, but at the same time she could tell that Laura had been younger when she wrote these notes than while seeking Atlantis with her husband. The calligraphy was more upright, less assured, but also with remnants of childish flourishes like circles above the lower-case letter 'i' instead of dots.

She switched her focus to the words. *Atlantis* leapt out at her. She read on from it.

Interesting. Even at this early stage, Laura had already developed the premise that the Atlantean empire had spread well beyond merely the Atlantic and Mediterranean. Nina knew from her own discoveries how far afield the ancient peoples had travelled, but in the 1970s such thoughts were considered the domain of cranks and New Age fabulists. But her mother apparently believed that the Atlanteans had sent an expedition along what would later become known as the Silk Road through Asia, travelling as far as the Himalayas—

Another word jumped out at her with almost physical force, making her flinch. 'This – this can't be real!'

'It hasn't been altered in any way – to be honest, I wouldn't know where to start.' Olivia pushed the other folders towards her. 'Everything here was written by Laura, before you were even born.'

'That's just it!' Nina protested. 'It *can't* have been written then. This,' she waved the sheet of paper, 'mentions Talonor, Atlantis's greatest explorer. But nobody even knew he'd existed until the Talonor Codex was found in Atlantis – which was only discovered ten years ago!'

'By you.'

'Yes, by me, but that's irrelevant. Mom *couldn't* have known about Talonor before she met Dad. Nobody could. It's not possible.'

'If you read her notes, I think you'll find some answers,' Olivia told her. 'Not to everything, because even Laura never found them. But you'll understand how she could know something that was still hidden from the world until you found it.'

Nina fixed her with an angry look. 'So why don't you just tell me now and save me the time?'

'Because it'll be better for you to see it for yourself.'

'No!' snapped the redhead, jumping up. 'I don't accept that Yoda "you cannot be told, you must learn for yourself" bullshit.

There are times when directness is the right approach, and this is one of them!'

Olivia raised an eyebrow. 'I see directness isn't a problem for you.'

A fuming Nina was about to add more when the door opened. 'All right, keep the noise down,' rumbled Eddie. 'We just got Macy to sleep. What's going on?'

'Nina was doubting the authenticity of what I've shown her,' Olivia told him.

'And what's that?'

'My mom's research,' said Nina. 'About Atlantis.'

Eddie peered at the thick folders. 'God, she made as many notes as you. Although are you saying this lot isn't real?'

'I don't know,' Nina admitted. 'This *is* her handwriting, I'm certain of it, and these photos,' she indicated the pictures, 'are definitely of her and . . . and Olivia. But she talks about Talonor, the Atlantean explorer—'

'Yeah, I remember who he is, love,' said Eddie, smiling.

'And she couldn't possibly have known about him,' Nina pressed on. 'The Codex wasn't found until over a decade after she died.'

Olivia stood. 'As I said, the best way for you to find answers is by reading her work. It *will* explain things, I promise. And I hope, when you see that, you'll want to speak to me again.' She produced a card from her purse. 'My number is on there.' When Nina didn't take it, she placed it beside the folders. 'It's getting rather late, so I think I should be leaving. I'll call a cab; there's no need to see me out.'

'It's no problem,' said Eddie, escorting her from the room – his glance at Nina telling her that he wanted to make sure she was out of their home.

He soon returned. 'Okay, obvious question: is she *really* your grandma?'

'I'm reserving judgement,' his wife replied. 'But I've got the feeling that . . . she might be.'

'But you told me your grandparents were dead.'

'That's what I thought! My mom always said they died in a car accident when she was eighteen, before she started at Columbia. But . . .' She swapped the page of notes for the Central Park photograph. 'I can't deny that she looks like an older version of the woman in this picture – hell, she looks like an older version of my mother.'

'Of you too,' Eddie pointed out.

'Great, so if nothing else, at least now I know what I'll look like when I turn ninety.' Nina picked up the page again. 'This was supposedly written before my parents first met in 1974. My mom was already looking for Atlantis, even back then. But . . . Well, you know who Talonor was,' she said. 'I don't see how she could even have heard of him, never mind tracked the route of one of his expeditions.'

'Olivia said to read all that lot to find out,' said Eddie, regarding the collection of notes. 'Are you going to?'

Nina let out an exasperated snort. 'I'll *have* to, won't I? I can hardly ignore it.'

They both turned as Holly entered. 'Everything okay?'

'Sure,' Nina answered. 'How's Macy?'

'She's soundo. I'll get going.'

Eddie handed her several bills. 'Thanks for looking after her.'

'Hey, no problem, Uncle Eddie! I loved doing it. Any time you need me again, just let me know. I'm only a subway ride away.'

'Get a cab home,' he told her, passing her another banknote. 'There's a lot of weirdos around after dark.' He cast a meaningful look at Olivia's card.

'Okay, thanks,' said Holly. 'See you again soon.' She hugged him, then waved to Nina. 'Tell Macy I said goodbye.'

'We will. Thanks,' Nina replied. Holly grinned, then departed.

'She's a good kid,' said Eddie.

'She is,' Nina agreed with a smile, which turned into something more pensive. 'Do you think I'm a good mom?'

The question surprised him. 'Course I do.'

'Because if Olivia really is my grandmother, that means my own mom lied to me – and my dad – about her my whole life. And they had such a huge fight that they never spoke to each other again. It was so bad that my mom told me she was dead rather than try to repair the relationship.' She looked towards her daughter's bedroom. 'I don't ever want that to happen with me and Macy.'

'Well, one day she's going to be a teenage girl,' said Eddie. 'Then she'll hate you no matter what.'

'Gee, thanks!' But the wisecrack had disarmed her. 'So when did you become an expert on the thought processes of teenage girls?'

'I've got an older sister, remember? Lizzie and my mum used to argue all the time.' He picked up one of the manila folders. 'So what're you going to do with this lot?'

'Read it.'

'You really think your mum wrote all this?'

'If it's a forgery, then somebody's gone to an insane amount of trouble. There must be two hundred pages here.' She pulled out a sheet at random. 'It's definitely her handwriting.'

'Two hundred pages? She really was as bad as you.' He tugged off the tie he had grudgingly worn for the premiere. 'I'm going to bed. You coming?'

'Sounds like a good idea.' She put the folders on her desk, pausing to peruse the loose page. 'I'll be right in.'

He paused at the door. 'No you won't.'

'Hmm?'

'You're going to start reading it right now, aren't you? I can tell.'

She hurriedly put the page down. 'No, I wasn't, I . . .'

He chuckled. 'It's okay. I know what you're like – but considering what that stuff is, I don't blame you. If someone gave me a bunch of letters from my mum, I'd want to read 'em straight away too.'

'Thanks, honey,' she said with a smile. 'Are you the most understanding husband in the world, or what?'

'I'm the sexiest, definitely.'

'Uh-huh.' They both laughed. 'I'll see you in a little while, then. Thanks.'

'Don't stay up *too* late. Night, love.'

'Goodnight.' They blew each other kisses, and Eddie left her with her mother's work.

Nina stared down at the folders. Where to begin?

At the beginning, she decided with a smile. She found what appeared to be the oldest pages, and started to read.

5

'*Please* don't tell me you were up all night,' Eddie said as he padded into the lounge.

Nina was at her desk, picking through her mother's notes. 'I wasn't, don't worry. You were asleep when I came to bed. I didn't get much sleep, though – I kept thinking about what I'd read, so I got up first thing and carried on working.'

'It's work now, is it?' He peered over her shoulder. 'So what've you found?'

'That there are other explorers in my family,' she said, unable to contain her enthusiasm. 'My great-great-something-grand-father, Tobias Barrington Garde, visited India and Nepal in the 1840s.' She rifled through the pages to find a particular passage. 'Some Buddhist monks showed him an artefact that described Talonor's expedition!'

'What, so your ancestor from a couple of centuries back found something from Atlantis?' Scepticism was clear in his voice. 'That's a bit of a coincidence. Are you *sure* this lot isn't fake?'

'More than ever,' she said, indicating a box of her parents' work she had brought in for comparison. 'It's definitely her writing. I don't believe in destiny, but it might explain why I've always been so obsessed with Atlantis, just like my mom and dad; it's woven into our family history.'

'If your mum knew about Talonor, why didn't she tell your dad?'

'I . . . don't know,' Nina had to admit. 'I can't think of any reason why she would have kept quiet about it. If my father had known about Talonor's expedition, it might have led him to the Himalayas much sooner.' She was quiet for a moment. 'And they might both still be alive.'

Eddie put a comforting arm across her shoulders. 'You okay?'

'Yeah. Thanks. But,' she continued, pushing the unhappy thought aside, 'whatever her reasons, the fact is that she *did* know about Talonor. And what he was doing. There was more to it than just exploration, or conquest – he was specifically looking for something. And Tobias found it. He called it the Midas Cave.'

'Midas?' said Eddie, surprised. 'As in turning stuff into gold?'

'It seems that way.'

'Thought that was a Greek myth, nothing to do with Atlantis?'

'It is. The story goes that King Midas was granted a wish by the god Dionysus for helping rescue his mentor Silenus, and he wished for everything he touched to turn to gold. Which backfired badly, as wishes usually do; whenever he tried to eat anything, it became twenty-four-carat inedibility, and as for when he hugged his daughter, well . . .'

Eddie looked towards Macy's room. 'Note to self: don't make stupid wishes.'

Nina smiled. 'But from what I've read so far, the Greek myth of King Midas might have originally *come* from Atlantis – they share a common pantheon of gods, so other legends could have been adapted by the ancient Greeks as well. In this case, though, Midas isn't a king. He's an Atlantean prince, and Talonor's friend and companion on the expedition. The cave was named after him.'

'Why? Is it full of gold?'

'I don't know. My mother didn't say anything about its contents. But whatever it was, it was important enough that the monks kept its location a secret.' She found a set of pages she had marked with a Post-it note. 'According to this, when the monks took Tobias and his companions to see the cave, the journey lasted three days, and they travelled most of the way in window-less sedan chairs to stop them from seeing the route. Once they arrived, Tobias was so amazed by whatever he saw that every time they stopped on the way back, he secretly took navigational readings, based on the bearings and inclination of the surrounding mountains, to try to re-create the path they took.'

Eddie nodded. 'Smart man.'

'Not smart enough. He never did find the cave again. But that didn't stop my mom from trying.' Nina unfolded a creased and yellowing map. The dense concentrations of contour lines immediately revealed it as a mountainous region. 'Western Nepal,' she said. 'See how she marked all the peaks?'

Her husband took a closer look. Starbursts of lines, most in pencil but some more decisively inked, were connected to numerous summits. 'I see what she's done,' he said. 'Trying to match the bearings Great-Great-Grandad Toby made to the real mountains.'

'Yeah,' Nina replied. She ran a fingertip along a zigzagging line of red ink. 'She thought this was the most likely route.'

There were other, less decisively marked, paths on the map. 'Doesn't look like the only option, though,' Eddie noted.

'No. I guess if he was taking the readings in a rush, they wouldn't be totally accurate. And the map itself dates from the 1940s, so probably isn't that precise either – certainly not compared to what we have now.'

'I take it your mum didn't find the cave.'

Nina shook her head. 'She thought that this,' she gestured at a particular region, 'was the right area, but couldn't pin it down any further.'

He checked the map's scale. 'Lot of ground to cover.'

'I know. Mom did think she'd narrowed it down at one point, but there's an old monastery near the end of her route. Tobias didn't mention any signs of civilisation, so it couldn't be the right place.'

'But you said he couldn't see where he was.'

'For most of the way, yes, but the final stages were too dangerous for the monks to carry the sedan chairs. He went up to the cave itself on foot.' She found another bookmarked page. 'Mom even wrote to the monastery to ask if they had any record of Western visitors in 1846, but they said no.'

'She was serious about finding this place, then,' said Eddie, impressed. 'How old was she when she did all this?'

Nina's face hardened slightly. 'She started working on it before going to university. But . . .' She tapped on a letter, typewritten text standing out amongst the freehand script. 'This is the reply from the monastery. It's dated March 1975. *After* she met Dad. She was still trying to find the Midas Cave even though she knew he was obsessed with finding Atlantis.'

A theatrical yawn from the hallway told them their daughter was out of bed. 'Hey, little love,' said Eddie as Macy entered.

'Hi, Daddy,' she replied. 'Hi, Mommy. What are you doing?'

'Work, honey,' Nina replied.

'But you finished writing your book,' said Macy, confused.

'This is different.'

'Is it because of that lady who was here last night?'

Nina smiled. 'Yes, it is. She brought me something that used to belong to *my* mommy.'

'Ooh! Can I see?' Macy tried to clamber on to her lap.

'It's just some letters, hon. Nothing much to look at.'

Eddie scooped up the little girl. 'Come on, let's let Mummy—'

'*Mommy*,' mother and daughter corrected simultaneously.

'—put all this stuff away while we make breakfast.'

'Thanks, I need a really strong coffee,' said Nina. She was about to gather the papers on the desk, but paused at the sight of Olivia's card.

'You're going to phone her, aren't you?' Eddie asked.

'What?' she said, feeling almost guilty.

'Your maybe-grandma. You want to find out more about your mum – and all of this.'

'I . . . hadn't decided.' The statement didn't sound convincing even to herself, and she could tell her husband didn't believe it either. After ten years together, he knew all too well when she was set on a particular course of action.

'We'll go out somewhere and leave you to it,' he said with exaggerated resignation.

'Thanks,' Nina replied, genuinely appreciative. 'You know how much I love you, right?'

'You can always show it by giving me a— Agh, I can't do my old rude jokes any more.' Eddie grimaced, looking at the child in his arms. 'Me and my promises.'

'You're a good dad, Eddie Chase,' said Nina, amused. Leaving her husband to take care of breakfast, she picked up the card and regarded it thoughtfully, then dug out her phone.

'I'm glad you called,' said Olivia an hour and a half later. 'There was always a worry that you would treat me like Laura did.'

'We'll see how things go,' Nina replied, wanting to maintain the upper hand. She showed the older woman into the lounge.

'Where are Macy and your husband?' Olivia asked as she sat.

'They went to the zoo. Eddie thought it'd be best if we had some time to ourselves.'

'I see.' She regarded the folders, which were laid out on the table between the two women. 'I assume you've read some of Laura's work.'

'Most of it. I'm a fast reader.'

'So was she. It runs in the family.'

'As do a lot of things, apparently. Like exploration. I'd never heard about Tobias Garde before.'

Olivia sighed. 'Yes. I suspected that in cutting herself off from me, Laura would also have kept our family's history from you.'

Nina glanced at the desk, where her laptop was open. 'I did a little genealogical research. He was my great-great-great . . . *great-*grandfather?'

Olivia nodded. 'That's right.'

'And a rich man. I also did some historical research.'

Another nod. 'The Gardes have never been short of money. Which, incidentally, your mother refused to take. She had a trust fund, but after our argument, she never claimed it. It's technically yours now. It's quite substantial.'

'I don't need money.'

'I know. You've made your own way in life, very successfully. I don't know if it will mean anything to you, but I'm proud of that.'

Nina was uncomfortable with the praise, but covered it. 'So. After forty-some years, my grandmother reappears.'

'You accept that I *am* your grandmother?'

'I'm prepared to accept the possibility. In which case, the question is: why now?'

'I told you last night,' said Olivia, with a gentle smile. 'I'm almost ninety, and I wanted to give my granddaughter her mother's work before it was too late.'

'And the page on top of the pile just happened to mention Talonor, right? Kind of funny how that happened.'

She had expected the elderly woman to respond with surprise or embarrassment at being caught, but instead her smile merely became more knowing. 'You noticed, then. I admit, I would have been a little disappointed if you hadn't.'

'So you set it up that way on purpose?'

'Of course! I would say I had an ulterior motive, but that sounds overdramatic. I just wanted to be sure I would catch your interest.'

'Consider it caught. Why?'

'Your family history is also my family history. And Laura's. Before she met your father and joined his crusade to find the lost civilisation of Atlantis, she was searching for a more specific part of it.'

'The Midas Cave.'

'The Midas Cave, yes. Tobias Garde saw it once, all those years ago, and spent the rest of his life trying to find it again. Whatever it contained, it was something wondrous, which nobody else has seen since.'

'Except the monks who hold the secret.'

'Perhaps not even them. You know that Tobias went back to Nepal?' Nina nodded. 'The monastery where the monks lived, the starting point of the journey to the Midas Cave, had been destroyed. It could have been by war, or a natural disaster – no one knew. There was nobody left who could tell him anything. He spent years exploring the mountains, but never found the cave.'

'And since then,' said Nina, taking out the annotated map, 'the family's been trying to follow in his footsteps?'

'On and off, yes. Laura was particularly intrigued. Enough to have put all this work into finding it.'

'But then she met my father and put her efforts into finding Atlantis instead.' She gave the words an accusatory edge, wanting to see how Olivia would respond.

But if she had hoped to draw out her grandmother's ulterior motive, she was disappointed. 'And they got so close,' Olivia said instead, with a mixture of approval and sadness. 'As you said, they almost found it.'

'Yeah,' Nina replied, her lips tightening. 'And then they were murdered.'

The older woman nodded, staring down at her daughter's research. 'Those responsible,' she said at last, 'you didn't say what happened to them. I understand why; your book is about the archaeological discoveries you've made, not what you went through to find them. But . . . was justice done?'

'They got what they deserved,' was Nina's quiet reply.

'Good.' A long pause, neither speaking, then Olivia looked up. 'It took you to see Laura's work through, Nina. She would have been so proud of you. The reason I wanted to give you her research is that I hoped you might see her *other* work through.'

'The Midas Cave?'

'Yes. It's not an understatement to say that this,' she indicated the folders, 'represents years of work on her part. She scoured every scrap of information we had about Tobias and his expedition, searched out other historical sources, even wrote to a Nepalese monastery—'

'I know. I saw their reply.'

'Before she met Henry, this was her obsession. She wanted to retrace Tobias's steps, rediscover whatever wonders he'd found in the cave. Now it seems like . . . unfinished business.'

'That I might be able to finish for her.'

Olivia smiled. 'You *are* the world's most famous archaeologist. If anyone can bring our family's history full circle, it's you. It *deserves* to be you.'

'And if I do, what's in it for you?'

That finally drew a startled response. 'That's rather cynical.'

'Born out of experience,' Nina replied. 'Painful experience, sometimes.'

'So I gather. But all I want is to know that Laura's work wasn't for nothing.'

'So if I find the Midas Cave, you don't want to know where it is?'

'Well of course I want to know where it is,' Olivia said, a little condescendingly. 'It's a family mystery we've been trying to solve for generations! But if you're concerned that my goals are solely financial, I can assure you that, like you, I don't need money. I have enough to see me through. Actually, considering my age, more than enough!' A chuckle, then she became more contemplative. 'You completed your parents' work when you found Atlantis. It would mean a great deal if you could complete your mother's work too.'

'It would,' Nina said quietly.

'I'll let you decide what to do, then.'

Olivia stood and they said their goodbyes, then the elderly woman left.

Now it was Nina's turn to stare at her mother's notes. She composed her thoughts, taking a moment to reach a decision, then picked up her phone and made a call.

6

'Nina,' said Oswald Seretse, greeting her with a smile. 'Always a pleasure.'

'Likewise,' Nina replied, shaking the diplomat's hand. 'You've got a new office. Nice.'

'Yes, the benefits of a promotion.' The windows looked out across Manhattan from the Secretariat Building's thirty-fifth floor. When Nina had been the director of the International Heritage Agency her view had been similar, but in a smaller office several storeys below. 'I now act as UN liaison for four other agencies in addition to the IHA.' After an exchange of pleasantries about each other's families, he asked: 'Now, what may I do for you?'

Nina took a breath. 'I'd like a favour, Oswald.'

She was not surprised when he didn't immediately offer his assistance. 'What is it?'

'I want access to the IHA's files on the Secret Codex.'

He gave her a curious look. 'I thought you already had it.'

'Only the abstracts. Lester decided I wasn't worthy of full access for security reasons.' She tried not to make her disdain for her successor too clear. 'I'd like to see everything.'

'For what purpose?'

'A personal project. I've come across something that might be linked to one of Talonor's expeditions, but I'd need to see the raw text to be sure.'

Seretse sat back. 'As you are aware,' he said carefully, 'I am not actually an archaeologist myself. A decision like that, especially considering the security implications, really needs to be made by the IHA's director.'

'Right.' Nina's disappointment was plain in the single word.

'While my personal instinct would be to say yes, I am sure you remember how you would have felt if I had made such a decision over your head when *you* were running the agency,' he said drily. 'But Lester is here today, so we can ask him in person if you wish.'

She nodded. 'That'd be great.'

After checking via Seretse's secretary that Blumberg was available, they took an elevator down to the IHA's offices. At the reception desk was a familiar face, who reacted to Nina's appearance first with surprise, then delight. 'Well, hell-o, stranger!' said Lola Adams. 'I haven't seen you for a while!'

'I know, Lola, I'm sorry,' Nina told her friend and former assistant. Their once-regular meetings for coffee had become less frequent of late. 'But you know what it's like when you have a kid. How is Gino, by the way?'

'He's great, thanks. He's at pre-K now – he's getting big! How about Macy?'

'The same. At the rate she's growing, she'll be taller than me by the time she's about eight!'

The big-haired blonde smiled. 'Dr Blumberg's in his office. You can go right in.'

'Thank you,' Seretse replied. 'Nina?'

She followed the diplomat into what had once been her own office. The decor had completely changed since her last visit; unsurprisingly, since she and Eddie had crashed an airship into the building's side while averting a poison gas attack on a meeting of world leaders, necessitating considerable refurbishment. But the layout was also different. She had positioned her desk facing the door, back to the windows to minimise the distraction of the view across Manhattan, while the new occupant had placed his workspace at one side of the room to give himself an uninterrupted outlook.

'Ah, Oswald,' said Blumberg, getting up to greet them. 'And Nina Wilde too! This is a surprise. Especially after our last meeting.'

'Hello, Lester,' Nina replied, staying polite; after all, she wanted something from him. 'How are things going?'

'Very good,' said the Minnesotan. 'We've made several impressive new finds along the route of the Exodus through Egypt and Israel.'

'Thanks to your discovery of the Ark of the Covenant,' Seretse added to Nina.

Blumberg nodded – a little testily, she thought. 'But we've made our own discoveries, too. We have a new dig in Armenia that seems very promising, and we've also got operations pending at Calakmul and Xi'an.'

'Sounds like everything's under control,' Nina said with a small smile.

'I like to think so. What brings you here?'

She glanced at Seretse to prompt him, figuring her request would have greater weight coming from Blumberg's superior. 'Nina was hoping to be granted access to the classified files relating to the Secret Codex,' he said.

'The Secret Codex?' Blumberg echoed, nudging his glasses higher on his nose. 'Like I said last time you were here, those files are classified for a reason. We don't want treasure hunters and tomb raiders tearing up Talonor's sites.'

'I'm well aware of that,' said Nina, annoyed at being patronised. 'But I'd hope you trust me not to drop the whole thing on to Wikileaks.'

'You are of course beyond reproach in that regard,' said Seretse, moving smoothly to calm the waters. 'Perhaps if you explain to Lester your interest, he may see no harm in granting your request.'

Blumberg gave her an expectant look. 'All right,' she said. 'I've received some research relating to a find made in the nineteenth century, in Nepal. It may be connected to Talonor, but without being able to read the Secret Codex, I can't confirm that.'

'Talonor certainly travelled through what is now Nepal, according to the Codex,' said Blumberg, nodding. 'Whose work are you basing this on?'

'Someone I hold in the highest regard – an unimpeachable source.'

'I'll need a *little* more than that.'

Nina narrowed her eyes. 'Let me put it this way. If it hadn't been for this person, I wouldn't have found Atlantis, and we wouldn't be standing here in this room, because the IHA wouldn't exist.'

'I see,' said Seretse, with an understanding tip of the head. Blumberg appeared confused, so he added: 'Surely you have read *In Search of History* by now, Lester?'

His reaction made it clear to Nina that he had lied to her the previous month about doing so. 'I . . . Well, of course!' he hastily replied. 'Congratulations on the movie, by the way, Nina. Have you seen it?'

'I was at the premiere last night. It's certainly . . . got a lot of action. But,' she went on, unwilling to let him change the subject, 'regarding the Secret Codex, I'd like to correlate what it says about Talonor's journey through Nepal with this new research to see if I can pinpoint the location of the nineteenth-century find.'

'It's been lost?'

'Unfortunately, yes. I have a general idea where it might be, but can't narrow it down without more data. If I identify it, then I'll obviously be more than happy to share that information with the IHA.'

Blumberg fiddled with his glasses again as he considered his options. 'You'd be willing to sign a confidentiality agreement in return for access?'

'Yes, I would,' she told him, irritation rising. 'You know you can trust me.'

'Of course,' said Seretse. Her last statement had not been directed at him, but she was glad of his support.

'Okay, then. All right,' Blumberg said. 'I'll get Lola to print out an agreement for you, and then I'll approve your access.'

'If that is all, then?' said Seretse. 'Thank you, Lester. I appreciate your time. And I am sure that Nina does too.'

'Yes, thank you,' she said. 'I'm very grateful.' A non-committal sound from Blumberg, then politenesses were exchanged and she and Seretse left the office. 'Thank you, too,' she told the diplomat.

'Considering how many lives you saved here at the UN, it was the least I could do,' he replied as they returned to the reception area. 'Now, you will just need to sign this agreement.'

'It won't involve giving up my firstborn, will it?'

Seretse looked amused. 'I believe that clause is hidden in the very small print.'

They both turned as someone called Seretse's name. 'Your secretary said I might find you here,' said a new arrival, waving a dismissive hand at the protesting Lola as he passed her desk to meet the Gambian.

'Fenrir,' said Seretse, surprised. 'What are you doing here?'

The tall, broad-shouldered blond man was around sixty, though with the almost ageless features of someone who had taken care to live cleanly. Nina pegged his accent as Scandinavian but couldn't pin it down precisely. He wore a well-tailored suit bearing a striped pattern that stood out as positively loud against the flat greys and blues favoured by those working at the United Nations. 'I need to talk to you about issues arising from the

Iranian nuclear deal,' he said. His pale eyes glanced briefly at Nina, then snapped back in a double-take. 'Are you Dr Nina Wilde?'

'I am, yes,' she said.

'Then I feel extremely privileged to meet you.' The man smiled. 'If not for you, I would be dead. I was at the United Nations during the attempted attack on the General Assembly. Thank you.'

'This is Dr Fenrir Mikkelsson,' said Seretse. 'He is one of the directors of the International Atomic Energy Agency, and also the senior UN negotiator for the recent nuclear weapons treaty.'

'Then I should be the one feeling privileged,' Nina told Mikkelsson, shaking his hand. 'Getting countries like North Korea to agree on limitations was a pretty impressive achievement.'

'It will not last for ever,' he said. 'Such things never do. But for now, the world feels a little safer, no?'

'I've got a three-year-old daughter, so I'll take a little over nothing at all.'

'I agree. I have a daughter myself, although she is much older.' He gave her an appraising look. 'If I may ask, are you returning to the IHA?'

She shook her head. 'No, I'm here on business.'

'An archaeological matter? Another remarkable discovery, perhaps?'

'Just a personal project. A lot less important than whatever you need to talk to Oswald about, I'm sure! Don't let me keep you.'

'Then I hope your project goes well.' He turned back to Seretse. 'Shall we discuss it in your office?'

'Of course,' Seretse replied. 'Although you did not need to come running down here to find me. I would have returned shortly.'

'It is not a problem. And exercise is always good. Good morning, Dr Wilde.' The two diplomats departed.

'Okay, weird,' said Lola. 'Wonder why he didn't just have Mr Seretse paged?'

'Must have been pretty urgent,' Nina said. 'Anyway, have you got a form for me?'

'Yeah, Dr Blumberg told me to print it off for you. What's it for? Are you getting involved in archaeology again?'

'I was never *un*involved,' she said as Lola took several sheets of paper from her printer. 'Oh, jeez. Don't tell me it's all of that?'

'Afraid so. Most of it's just boilerplate, though.'

Nina skimmed through the legalese. 'No "take my firstborn" clause, so . . . done,' she said, signing it.

Lola took back the pages. 'I'll email you a confirmation and login details as soon as I can. Oh!' She leaned closer eagerly. 'Tell me about your movie! Is it good?'

'If you like Grant Thorn movies, you'll probably love it,' was the best the redhead could come up with. 'Anyway, sorry, but I've got to go. I'll see you soon.'

'Don't leave it so long this time!' Lola called after her.

True to Lola's word, by the time Nina returned home and checked her phone, an email from the IHA was waiting. She resisted the temptation to log in at once, instead joining her husband and daughter. 'How was the zoo?' she asked Macy.

'It was awesome!' the little girl trilled. 'We saw some bears, and a red panda, and three different kinds of penguins!'

'Yeah, we had a nice time. Especially as we stayed longer than we'd planned,' said Eddie pointedly. 'What about you? You get what you wanted from the IHA?'

'Yes.'

His gaze twitched towards her laptop. 'I suppose you'll be starting work right away, then?'

'No,' she assured him. 'It can wait.'

'Good. 'Cause Macy wants to draw you all the animals she saw today. Don't you, love?'

Macy had already produced a box of crayons. 'You should have come, Mommy! We saw a snow leopard! It was very beautiful.'

Nina got some paper and sat with her family. 'I wish I'd seen it. But you can draw it for me, that's just as good.'

Macy started to scribble, her parents offering encouragement as her interpretation of the animal took on form. But before long, Nina couldn't help but glance towards the laptop – only to catch Eddie's silently accusing stare. With more than a twinge of shame, she looked back at her daughter's drawing.

'Night-night, Mommy,' said Macy, kissing Nina.

'Night, honey,' Nina replied. 'I'll see you in the morning, okay?'

'Okay, Mommy. But I wish you'd come to the zoo with us.'

'I had something else to do, hon. I'm sorry. I'll come next time.' She and her husband went to the door. Eddie blew Macy a kiss, then quietly shut the door behind them. 'Did she really miss me?'

'When I told her we were going without you, yeah,' he replied. 'Once she saw the animals, though, she was so excited she hardly even remembered *I* was there. But you should have come.'

'That sounded a bit accusatory,' she noted as they entered the lounge.

He shrugged. 'Just saying.'

'Because, you know, she's three years old now. She's already very independent, and it's a good time for her to start doing things without both of us there.'

Eddie dropped on to the couch. 'Or a good time for one of us to start doing things without *her*?'

She eyed him. 'That was *definitely* accusatory.'

'What can I say? Yeah, it was nice to get out last night and do summat different, but that's not the same as you going back to work for the IHA. That place never brought us anything but trouble.'

'I'm not *going* back to the IHA,' she said, sitting facing him across the coffee table. 'I want to follow up on my mom's research, that's all. Being able to check the IHA's database just makes it a hell of a lot easier. Besides, that,' she indicated her mother's notes, 'isn't work. It's personal, it's my family's history. How could I not look into it?'

'Yeah, I suppose,' he said, with reluctance. 'Well . . . go on then.'

'Go on then, what?'

He jerked a thumb at the desk. 'Go and do what you want to do. I can tell you're absolutely desperate to get started.'

'Are you sure?'

'If I don't let you, you'll probably explode, and then I'll have to clean up the mess.'

She scurried past him towards the desk, pausing to kiss the top of his shaved head. 'Have I mentioned lately that you're the best husband ever?'

'I'll remind you of that next time *I* want something,' Eddie told her, smirking.

She opened her laptop and went straight to her email. Lola's message contained the promised login instructions. Quickly clicking through, she soon had access to what she sought.

The Secret Codex.

The IHA had already done most of the translation work, amongst other things producing a list of the places where Talonor's forces had established outposts. This was the reason for the agency's secrecy; were the translations freely available, some locations – ports, peaks, passes – would be readily identifiable today, allowing anyone to set them as landmarks that could be used to find, and raid, potentially priceless archaeological sites.

Right now, though, Nina was only interested in identifying one of them: the Midas Cave. Atlantis, the greatest, richest, most powerful empire of pre-history, had not sent Talonor on his missions of discovery simply out of imperial greed, the endless need for *more*. He had been tasked with searching for something specific.

And now she was going to find out what it was – and where.

7

'That should be it,' Nina muttered, comparing the satellite image on her laptop's screen with her mother's annotated map. 'That *has* to be it. So . . . why isn't it?'

'Why isn't what?' said an irritable voice behind her.

She turned to see Eddie, carrying a yawning Macy, enter the lounge. 'Why isn't the Midas Cave where it ought to be?' she replied, frustrated. 'I located mountain peaks that match the bearings Tobias took, as well as my mom's work and the records of Talonor's journey from the Secret Codex. And I also factored in shifts in magnetic north over time, the Atlantean measurement and numerical system, even the video you got of that map in the temple, and everything I know about the region's history. It all points to the cave being *here*.' She jabbed at a point on the map. 'But it can't be!'

'What's Mommy talking about?' Macy asked, concerned.

'Before you were born, this is what she used to do,' Eddie told her. '*All the time*. She'd get so involved in some archaeological bol— thing that she'd forget to do other stuff. Like sleeping.'

'I know it's late, but I needed to—' Nina checked the laptop's on-screen clock and gasped. 'Wait, it's morning?'

'Yeah, it's morning!' said her husband sarcastically. 'You didn't come to bed!'

'No, that can't be right. I don't feel tired.'

Eddie regarded an empty mug beside the computer. 'How many coffees did you have?'

'I dunno, three, four? Oh. Yeah, that might explain it. Oh my

God, I can't believe I worked through the whole night!'

'Is Mommy okay?' Macy whispered to Eddie. 'She's talking weird.'

'She does that,' he said. 'Come on, let's get you some brekkie. Hopefully she'll have sorted herself out by then.' He headed for the kitchen with his daughter.

Nina followed. 'But I *should* have found it, that's the thing. In the Secret Codex, Talonor says the Midas Cave is on what the locals called Dragon Mountain. There's a place in Nepal that's sometimes called that even today, and it's exactly where the cave should be. But it can't be, because the only possible route up the mountain has a monastery on it – the same one my mother wrote to. Tobias couldn't have missed it . . . therefore he couldn't have gone that way. Which means I'm back at square one.'

'What's a monstery?' Macy asked as she took her seat.

'Where monsters live,' said Eddie.

'Ignore Daddy; it's where monks live,' Nina corrected.

He chuckled, then started gathering Macy's breakfast. 'So this Midas Cave is definitely a real thing?'

'Yes. Talonor named it to honour his friend Midas – the prince. Midas made some sort of sacrifice to find it, but the Codex doesn't say what. It wasn't his life, though; he travelled on with Talonor afterwards.' She glanced back at the map. 'It was the farthest point of that expedition, actually. They returned to Atlantis after finding the cave.'

'So they were specifically after whatever was inside it?'

'Looks that way. Talonor left a contingent to guard it and prepare for the arrival of something called "the Crucible", but he doesn't say what that is. The people he was writing the Codex for would already have known, so he didn't need to explain it. It was mentioned in Mom's notes too, but she didn't explain it either.'

Eddie sat with Macy and gave her a bowl of cereal. 'That's the end of that, then.'

Nina eyed him. 'You sound almost relieved.'

'It'll mean you'll come to bed at a non-ridiculous time. Or actually *come* to bed.'

'I don't see how I could have been wrong, though. Everything fits, until it all falls apart at the end.'

'Maybe your mum was wrong,' he suggested.

'I doubt that,' she snapped.

'Blimey, no need to get defensive. Everybody makes mistakes. Even me.'

'Yeah, I can think of one or seventeen.'

Macy was following the conversation with an ever-furrowing brow. 'Why do monkeys live on a mountain? I thought they lived in trees.'

Nina laughed. 'Not monkeys, honey – monks. They're men who believe in a god so much that they live in a special house called a monastery, where they can spend all their time thinking about it.'

'That's silly. Why would you build a house on a mountain? It might fall off.'

'Maybe they didn't want visitors,' suggested Eddie. He started on his own breakfast, pausing when he realised his wife had fallen unnaturally silent. 'Ay up. What?'

'I was just thinking,' Nina said.

'Yeah, that's never a good sign.'

'Oh Daddy's *so* funny, isn't he?' she snarked to Macy, who giggled. 'But why *would* they build a monastery on a mountain?'

Eddie shrugged. 'Monks do weird stuff. We went to a monastery way up a mountain in India.'

'Yeah, but when Tobias came back to look for the cave, the monastery he'd originally set out from had been destroyed. What if the monks hadn't been killed – but had *moved*?' She hurried back into the lounge, finding the letter her mother had received from Nepal.

'Why would they move?' Eddie called after her. 'Council tax went up?'

'Shush!' She quickly reread the letter. 'Every answer the monks gave Mom is a *non*-answer – like saying that parts of the monastery pre-date the 1840s. That could mean anything. They could have transferred statues or altars from the original site.'

'So you're telling me a bunch of Buddhist monks lied to your mum?'

'They're not technically lying, just being economical with the truth.' She came back into the kitchen with the letter and map. 'What if the monks who showed Tobias the cave and the monks who wrote to my mom are the same ones?'

'They'd be pretty old.'

'I don't mean *literally* the same ones. But they've been protecting the cave's secret all this time. To the point that when they realised Tobias might be able to find it again, they upped sticks and rebuilt their monastery on the only path up the mountain to make sure nobody could get past!'

'Bit of a long shot,' said Eddie dubiously.

'You said my mom might have been wrong. She was – but only in the sense that she'd been given bad data. The monastery was blocking her from seeing the right answer because, well, who's going to think that a Buddhist monk's lying to them?' She put the map on the table and tapped the spot she had indicated earlier. 'That's it. That's the cave. Talonor's journey meets Tobias's right there.'

'Okay, so you think you found it. Now what're you going to do?'

Nina stared at the map. After a long, thoughtful pause, she said: 'I'll need to make a couple of phone calls.'

* * *

'Hello? Can you hear me?'

Nina's first call had been to Lola at the IHA to obtain contact details for the remote monastery from the UN's databases, learning that it had a satellite phone for emergencies. After explaining herself to the surprised monk who answered her second call, she had been put through to the man she hoped could help her. The connection was poor, the speaker's voice echoing as if coming through a long metal pipe, but she could make him out well enough.

Would the answers she received be as clear?

'Yes, hello,' she replied, carefully enunciating each word. She could tell that his first language was not English. 'Is that Abbot Amaanat?'

'Yes, it is. Are you Dr Wilde?'

'I am. Thank you for talking to me.'

'We do not often get telephone calls, especially from famous archaeologists. It is my honour to speak to you.'

'Again, thank you. You've heard of me, then?'

'Oh yes.' Amaanat sounded quite elderly, giving her a mental picture of a hunched, bald old man in red and orange robes. 'We are not out of touch with the world, even here. What may we do for you?'

Nina composed herself before replying. 'It's a personal matter, actually,' she began. 'I recently received some old letters belonging to my mother, and found one that had been sent from your monastery. I believe you were the person who wrote it.' She glanced at the letter. The signature was incomprehensible to her, the curlicued Nepalese alphabet being related to Hindi, but beneath it had been written *AMAANAT* in tiny, careful capitals.

'I may have, yes. It can take some time, but we try to reply to every letter we receive. It is only polite. What do you wish to ask?'

'I want to finish her work. She had some questions about the monastery's history. Do you remember what you said?'

Even with the satellite link's time delay, it seemed that he hesitated before replying; not because he was searching his memory, but because her question had caught him off guard. 'I . . . do not remember anything like that recently.'

'Well, this letter was sent quite a long time ago. 1975 – March, to be exact.'

'That is a long time ago,' Amaanat agreed. 'Too long to remember one letter.'

'But you were at the monastery in 1975, yes?'

'Yes, I have been here for more than fifty years.'

Nina was caught between caution and her urge to push for the truth; there was nothing stopping Amaanat from hanging up if he resented being interrogated. 'I can remind you what she asked. The first question was simple: when was the monastery built?'

'Ah, that I can answer,' he said, with no hesitation this time. 'Parts of it date to the seventeenth century, the period of the Three Kingdoms.'

'And it's been in the same place the whole time?'

'It has been rebuilt several times. There have been avalanches, fires and earthquakes.'

'But you've never been at another location.'

'No. Since I became a monk, I have always been here.'

You should have been a lawyer, with answers that pedantic, Nina stopped herself from saying. 'I meant the monks, the order in general. Have they ever lived somewhere else?'

'In the past, we have sometimes moved when necessary, such as when the monastery was being rebuilt. But we are here now.'

Now she had to contain her exasperation at his becoming outright evasive – yet still without actually saying anything that could be proven as a lie. Maybe politics, not law, should have been his calling. 'My mother also asked about past visitors to the monastery. Do you know when the first Westerners reached you?'

'I am afraid I do not,' said Amaanat. 'Many have visited our monastery, but we do not keep records of all of them.'

'But would you know if some had come to you in, say, 1846?'

The very specific date prompted another pause. 'That was a year of great turmoil in Nepal,' the abbot said. 'It is very possible visitors came to us after the war with the British. But again, we do not have records.'

'I see,' said Nina, her patience finally running out. 'Tell me: have you ever heard of an Atlantean explorer called Talonor?'

A startled silence, though the constant hollow moan of the satellite link told her he was still on the line. 'I'll take that as a yes,' she went on. 'Now, I'm following up my mother's work from over forty years ago. She was trying to find an Atlantean outpost established by Talonor, which the monks – your monks, the same order – showed to an ancestor of ours, Tobias Garde.'

'Nepal is a very long way from Atlantis,' said Amaanat. The strain behind his voice implied that politeness was now the only thing keeping him from disconnecting.

'Yeah, but it's not far from Tibet, and I found an outpost of Atlantis there, so it's not really a stretch. You might know the one on Dragon Mountain – that *is* one of the local names for the mountain on which your monastery's built, isn't it?'

'It is,' he admitted.

'You could know it by another name. The Midas Cave.'

When Amaanat spoke again, courteous vagueness had been replaced by wary suspicion. 'What do you wish of us, Dr Wilde?'

'I told you, I want to complete my mother's work and find the Midas Cave.'

'Is that all?'

She wasn't sure what he meant. 'Yes. What else could there be?'

'If you believe that finding the Midas Cave will bring you riches, I am afraid you are mistaken.' It sounded almost like a threat.

'I don't care about riches,' Nina insisted. 'You said you know who I am, so you should know I'm not interested in money. I just want to see if my mother was right.'

'I cannot help you, Dr Wilde,' said the monk. 'I am sorry to have wasted your time. May you be well and happy.'

The conversation was clearly over. Unless . . .

'Wait,' Nina barked. 'If you don't want to help, that's fine. But it means I'll have to take everything I've learned about the Midas Cave to the International Heritage Agency and the Nepalese government, and mount an official archaeological expedition to find it.'

'You cannot do that!' said Amaanat, alarmed.

'Your monastery might be on the mountain, but you don't own it, do you? I can get permission to explore it easily enough.'

'There is only one route up the mountain, and you cannot reach it without going through our monastery. We will not let you do that.'

'Then we'll climb around you. Or even fly over you. I checked, and you're well below a helicopter's maximum altitude.' She let him think about the situation for a moment. 'You want to keep the Midas Cave a secret, don't you?' she asked, more conciliatory. 'I can give you my personal assurance of that.'

'You will not tell anything that you learn to others?'

'I told you, all I want to do is finish my mother's work. I give you my word.'

Another long silence from the other side of the world, then: 'We will not tell you more about the Midas Cave over the telephone. Only in person.'

'Wait, that's not what—'

Amaanat seemed to anticipate her objection, interrupting even with the time lag of the satellite transmission. 'If you come to the monastery – and keep your promise that you will not tell others of the Midas Cave – then your questions will be answered. And your mother's.'

'You want me to come to you? In *Nepal*?'

'If you decide to come, telephone and tell us when you will arrive. We will be waiting.' The line's hollow echo ceased abruptly.

Nina blinked in surprise. 'What the hell just happened?' she said.

But the more important question was unspoken: what was she going to do about it?

'You want to do *what*?' Eddie demanded.

'I want to go to Nepal,' repeated Nina. 'The monks at Detsen monastery know about the Midas Cave. The abbot said he'll tell me the secret – but only if I go in person.'

'Are you fu— frickin' kidding?' She had sent Macy to play in her room before starting a discussion that she knew would become heated. Even so, Eddie only barely managed to hold back an obscenity. 'You can't go to Nepal!'

'Why not?'

'Because it's fu— sod— *really* stupid! How do you know they're not having you on?'

'Eddie, they're Buddhist monks,' she said. 'I don't think they'd ask me to fly to the other side of the world for a joke.'

'I don't mean they're joking. I mean they might be lying.'

'Seriously?'

'They lied to your mum.'

'Yes, but to protect the cave's secret. Now that I know it's there, they're willing to tell me about it, in return for my keeping quiet.'

'And what if they decide to make sure you'll keep quiet by pushing you off the mountain?'

'Yeah, I'd thought of that. But I'll let the IHA know where I'm going, even if I don't say why, in case anything does happen to me. And you'll know too, of course,' she added.

'Of course,' he echoed sarcastically. 'So you're going to jet off to Nepal for a week on your own?'

'I won't be gone a week! Three, four days, tops. Fly out, travel to the monastery, see whatever's in the cave, leave.'

'Nepal isn't exactly known for its network of motorways and bullet trains.'

'I already checked,' she said. 'I can fly into Kathmandu and charter an internal flight to Bajura or Jumla. There's a road to within about ten miles of the monastery, and I can ride or hike from there.'

'Oh, just like that?'

'Eddie, I *have* done this before,' she protested.

He shook his head. 'It's still a stupid idea.'

Nina knew she wouldn't convince him with logistics alone. 'This is really important to me, hon,' she said, her voice softening. 'It's . . . it's a connection to my mom, one I didn't know I had until now.' She glanced across to the photograph on the wall of herself with her parents. The image brought back thoughts of the day it had been taken, the strands of which she tried to follow to other memories of her mother. But time had blurred and fragmented them, turning their life together into a dissociated collage . . .

'I'm *losing* her, Eddie,' she admitted. 'As I get older, and further away, she's fading in my mind. I don't want that to happen. I want to do something that'll bring us close again – something that'll honour her memory.' She gestured at the stacked notes. 'She worked on this for years, and was so close to finding the truth. If I go to Nepal, I can finish what she started.

There's something else, too,' she added, sensing that he was about to raise another objection. 'You remember at the movie premiere, when Marvin asked "What have you done for us lately?" That really hit home.'

He frowned, perplexed. 'It was just a joke.'

'Maybe, but it felt true. What *have* I done lately? I wrote my books, and I did the interview circuit and some lectures, but . . . that's all. I'm an archaeologist, and I've said it before: it's not just what I do, it's *who I am*. And for the past few years, I haven't done any new archaeological work. I haven't been able to be who I am.'

'That's 'cause you're something else an' all,' he reminded her. 'You're a mum. A good one, too – a bit weird, mind—'

'Thanks.'

'—but you've always been there for Macy. Isn't that more important?'

She gave him an icy look. 'Sounds like you're saying I should give up everything to stay home and look after my baby.'

Eddie was wrong-footed by the accusation. 'That's not what I'm saying, and you know it.'

'No? I never stopped you from doing what you felt you had to do after Macy was born. Well this is what *I* do, Eddie. It's a part of me, something I can't deny. And I can't fight it for ever. I've got the itch.'

He gave her a half-smile. 'There's a cream for that.'

Nina returned it. 'I knew the moment I said it that you'd come back with something like that.' But the joke had cut through the rising tension. 'Look, I know you probably think I'm crazy. But I need to do it. I need to *know*. You understand that, don't you?'

Eddie nodded reluctantly. 'Yeah, I understand. And I *do* think you're crazy . . . but I knew that when I married you.' He sighed. 'You're definitely, absolutely going to go, aren't you?'

'How can I not? But you and Macy'll be able to do whatever you want without me fussing around. I'm sure that'll be great fun—'

'If you're going, I'm going.'

Nina was startled. 'You want to come?'

'I don't *want* to come,' insisted Eddie. 'But I know what you're like. If I don't keep an eye on you, you'll get distracted by some ancient relic and start chasing around the world on a massive treasure hunt.'

'No I won't. I told you, as soon as I've seen the Midas Cave, I'll come straight back. But if you come, what about Macy?'

'We'll have to ask Holly to look after her.'

'What if she can't?'

'Then maybe, just maybe, it might be a good idea for you to wait a while before doing this,' he said pointedly. 'For that matter, maybe you should see what Macy thinks. She might not want her mum and dad to go away for three or four days.'

'Are you going away?' came a small voice. They both turned to see Macy peeking around the doorway.

'We might be, love,' said Eddie. 'We haven't decided yet.'

'Can I come with you?' Macy asked.

'I'm sorry, but no,' Nina told her. 'We'll have to go a long way, and it'll be very cold when we get there. And it might even be dangerous.'

Her expression became one of alarm. 'But what if you don't come back?'

'We'll come back,' Eddie assured her. 'That's why I'm going too, to keep Mummy safe.'

'But if you go away with Mommy to keep her safe, you won't be here to keep *me* safe!'

He gave her a loving smile. 'Glad you think that way about me, love. But nothing'll happen to you.'

Macy was not mollified. 'Hey, it's okay, honey,' said Nina,

picking her up. 'We're not going to go away for ever! We'd never do that, we love you too much. It's just something Mommy needs to do.'

'And Daddy needs to do to keep her out of trouble,' added her husband.

'Why do you need to go?' asked Macy.

Nina carried her to the desk, showing her the notes and map. 'Before I was born, my mommy looked for something special hidden in a country called Nepal. She never found it, but now *I've* got the chance to find it and finish off her work. Nepal's a long way away, though, so if I go, it'll be for a few days.' She gave Eddie a look. 'But if you don't want us to go, then . . . then we won't.'

Macy regarded the map for a moment. 'Did you love your mommy as much as I love you?'

'Yes, I did,' Nina replied, her voice catching unexpectedly. 'I still do, even though she's not here any more.'

'Will it make you happy if you find what your mommy was looking for?'

'I hope it will, yes.'

The little girl's face crinkled in deep thought. 'I don't want you to go, but . . . I want you to be happy. So you can go if you want to.' She managed an uncertain smile.

Nina kissed her. 'I love you,' she said. 'I love you so much.'

'Are you absolutely sure about that, Macy?' Eddie asked.

She hesitated before answering. 'Yes . . . ?'

'If we go, we'll ask Holly to look after you—'

The smile became wider. 'Oh yay! I love Holly! She's got nice hair, and she talks like you, Daddy! Only better.'

'Ha!' said Nina.

'She's a southerner, she can't even pronounce simple words like "bath" right,' he complained. 'But you'd be happy if she looked after you?' Macy nodded vigorously. 'That's that question answered, then. We still need to ask Holly if she's actually up for babysitting for a few days,' he reminded Nina. 'If she isn't, your whole plan's down the toilet, because there's no one else I'd trust to look after her.'

'I know,' Nina replied ruefully. 'We'll have to offer her more than fifty bucks this time, I guess! And as for you . . . are you sure you want to come with me?'

'You've got to do what you do,' he said. 'And I've got to do what *I* do. Which is watch out for you!'

'Hey, not for a while,' she pointed out. 'It's been more than three years since anything bad happened to us.'

He snorted. 'Great, you just jinxed it.'

'Oh come on. What could happen? The monastery's remote, but it's not like we haven't been to isolated places before – we went to frickin' *Antarctica* once! As long as we're prepped, we'll be fine. It's not as if there'll be any bad guys.'

'I'll remind you of that when half a dozen helicopter gunships start shooting at us,' he said, with a wry grin. 'But I actually know someone in Nepal, an old Gurkha mate. I'll see if I can get hold of him. He'll be able to sort things out for us. Although the first person I need to call is Holly.'

Nina saw Olivia's card still amongst the papers on the desk. 'I'd better make some calls of my own.'

'So you've found the Midas Cave?' said Olivia over the phone half an hour later. 'That's wonderful! Where is it?'

'I *think* I've found it,' Nina corrected. 'If I'm right, it's more or less where Mom thought it was all along. She just didn't consider that a key piece of data was flawed. If she'd known that, she might have found the cave forty years ago.'

'I'm so happy to know that. Oh, poor Laura. If only . . .' Olivia sighed, then her voice became more measured. 'So where exactly is it?'

'That's what I'll hopefully find out in Nepal. I'm going in a few days to see for myself.'

Her grandmother had clearly not expected that. 'What? You're going yourself?'

'Yes.'

'Surely that's not necessary. It's a lot of time and effort, and expense. And what about Macy?'

'Her cousin's agreed to look after her for a few days. And Macy actually seems quite excited at the prospect of our going away. I'm not sure if that's a relief or a worry!' She laughed a little, then went on: 'You know, I thought you of all people would want me to find out if the cave really exists.'

'I don't want you to take any risks on my account,' Olivia replied. 'I've only just met my granddaughter; I'd rather not lose her to an avalanche!'

'I know what I'm doing. I *have* done this before. And actually, the other reason I'm going – the reason I *want* to go – is something I should thank you for.'

'Me? What would that be?'

'Because you gave me a way to reconnect with Mom – a way to honour her memory. And it's also giving me a chance to get back to doing what I do best – being an archaeologist. So thank you.'

'My pleasure,' the elderly woman replied, though she sounded troubled. 'What are you going to do now?'

'Set everything up. We've got to book flights, arrange transport, deal with the Nepalese government – although I can call in some favours at the IHA to take care of that, so I'm not expecting any problems. There *are* some advantages to being famous.'

'Well, if you feel you must head off on a trek through the Himalayas, I doubt I'm going to talk you out of it. You certainly have your mother's . . . resolve.'

'I'm sure Eddie would use a different word.'

'Your grandfather felt just the same about me. It runs in the family.'

'Glad to find that out. Okay, I'll talk to you when I get back.'

'Good luck, Nina,' Olivia replied. 'And . . . take care.'

'Thanks.' Nina rang off. She briefly wondered why her grandmother had been so unsettled by the thought of her going to Nepal, but dismissed it; she imagined she herself would have much the same response if Macy declared she was heading off on a whim to some remote corner of the world. Something to look forward to once her daughter turned eighteen, she told herself, before directing her thoughts to her own impending journey.

8

Nepal

'Well, this is nice, innit?' said Eddie as he stepped down from the small turboprop aircraft. The runway of Jumla airport, over two hundred miles west of the capital Kathmandu, was a bumpy line of snow-scabbed asphalt along a narrow valley floor, meagre little fields abutting the boundary fence. The surrounding mountains were blanketed by clouds, a chill morning dampness permeating everything.

'Lovely,' Nina replied, huddling in her thick jacket. 'This friend of yours, will he be here yet?'

'Jayesh? Yeah. If he says he's going to do something, it gets done.' They collected their backpacks and headed for the small terminal building.

A short Nepalese man with a drooping grey-speckled moustache awaited them. 'Chase,' he grunted, the tip of the cigarette dangling from his mouth glowing red. 'Huh. You got fat.'

'I'm not fat! It's just the coat, you cheeky old git,' Eddie replied, grinning, as they shook hands. 'How've you been?'

The Nepali shrugged. 'All right, I suppose.'

Eddie made introductions. 'Nina, this is Jayesh Rai. I worked with him in Afghanistan when I was in the SAS – he's a Gurkha. Jayesh, this is my wife, Nina Wilde.'

'*Namaste*,' said Jayesh.

Nina almost extended her hand to him, before remembering from her research on the country that it was considered impolite for a man to shake a married woman's hand. '*Namaste*,' she echoed instead. He gave her a tiny nod that she took as approval. 'I've never met a Gurkha before. You're supposed to be the best soldiers in the world, aren't you?'

'They like to think so,' Eddie sniffed.

'Better than SAS. Got some stories about Chase,' Jayesh told her. 'Caught him once in training. Jumped out of a bush behind him and put my blade to his neck. Thought he was going to soil himself.'

She turned to Eddie, unable to hold in a smile. 'Really?'

'Nope,' he said, frowning at his former comrade. 'He's full of . . . poop.' Jayesh's stony face almost displayed something resembling amusement. 'So, you got transport?'

'Truck outside,' the Nepali said. 'Two hours to the end of the road. Got something else to go up the mountain. Come on, then.' He donned a brimless felt cap and a multicoloured scarf, then started for the exit.

'Right charmer, isn't he?' said Eddie as he and Nina followed him outside.

'He's . . . brusque, yeah,' she agreed. 'So are the Gurkhas really that good?'

He dropped his voice. 'Annoyingly, yeah. If you're ever in a fight, you don't want to be on the opposite side to the Gurkhas. Don't tell him I said that, though.'

They wedged their bags into the rear bed of a dented Toyota pickup truck. 'Cigarette, Chase?' asked the Gurkha, offering a crumpled golden packet.

'I gave up,' the Englishman told him.

That produced Jayesh's first visible display of emotion: surprise. 'Gave up? *You?*'

'Realised it wasn't doing me any good, so I quit. And I'm definitely not going to start smoking again – I've got a little girl now.'

Jayesh shook his head. 'Weird world,' he muttered, though it wasn't clear which of the two revelations he found more unexpected. 'Okay, get in.'

They boarded, Jayesh taking the wheel after reluctantly stubbing out his cigarette. Eddie regarded the gloomy mountains ahead. 'Glad I brought my warm socks,' he said. 'You ready for this, love?'

'Yeah, I am,' said Nina. 'Let's go in search of history.'

'I know it's the name of your book, but it's still a rubbish catchphrase,' Eddie replied. She glared at him. 'Think we'd better move before she chucks me out on the street,' he told Jayesh.

'She hasn't already? Must be love,' the Gurkha remarked before starting the engine.

Jayesh's estimate of the journey time proved optimistic, the road into the mountains in a dismal state of repair. But when the bumpy ride finally ended in a small village, Nina was even less impressed by the mode of transport the Nepali had arranged for the final ten miles. 'You're kidding, right?'

He shrugged. 'This, or walk.'

'I *might* walk!'

A trio of yaks, outfitted with colourful saddles and reins, had been brought to them by a round-faced local woman. 'You've ridden a camel,' Eddie reminded his wife. 'This won't be any harder.'

'I hated riding a camel,' she retorted.

'So hopefully this'll be an improvement!'

It wasn't. 'Next time I have the urge to travel to the butt-end of beyond,' Nina complained, desperately uncomfortable after straddling her shaggy-haired mount's broad back for an hour, 'remind me of this, will you?'

'Not much point, is there?' Eddie said with a smug smile. 'I do that every time, and you always still want to come.'

'You know, everyone hates a smart-ass . . .'

But the reason for the switch from four wheels to four hooves was clear. The terrain had soon become impassable for even the most capable off-roader, and only grew more extreme as they gained altitude. The narrow path they were following clung in places to steep cliffs, the yaks brushing the rock faces on one side while overhanging steep slopes the other. However, the animals, though ungainly-looking, were stable and sturdy, plodding tirelessly uphill.

The weather improved as they went higher. It was bitingly cold when the wind blew, but the clouds had parted enough for the midday sun to break through, lighting up the snowy wastes with an almost unnatural clarity. Nina's mood improved a little as she took in the stark beauty around them. 'Jayesh!' she called. 'How much further?'

Their guide was at the head of the little caravan, wreathed in cigarette smoke. 'About four kilometres to go,' he reported after consulting a map. He pointed at a mountain ahead. 'Go around that side and up, monastery should be there.'

Nina surveyed the peak. 'So that's Dragon Mountain? It's weird thinking that an ancestor of mine was here a hundred and seventy years ago – and that I knew nothing about it until now. Why wouldn't Mom have told me?'

'Maybe she didn't want you to rush off after him,' Eddie said. 'Would you want Macy to come up here?'

'Perhaps? When she was old enough? Okay, fair point,' she conceded, before a note of parental longing entered her voice. 'She must be missing us – I know I'm missing her.'

'Me too. But she sounded okay when we rang from

Kathmandu, and Holly said everything was fine. I'm more worried about what happens when we get to this monastery.'

'Why are you worried?'

'You tell 'em you've worked out their secret, and they invite you to come and see it in person, but only if you don't tell anyone? That's not suspicious or anything. But it's one of the reasons I asked Jayesh to give us a hand – in case things turn iffy.'

'Oh God. *Please* don't tell me that you asked one of your old army buddies to bring guns to a Buddhist monastery.' An alarming thought struck her. 'You haven't brought that stupid hand cannon of yours, have you?'

'No, I sold the Wildey before Macy was born,' replied Eddie, slightly offended. 'A gun in the same apartment as a kid? I'm not an idiot. Plus I got fed up of the faff of New York's gun rules.'

'Good.'

'But Jayesh still came prepared. Didn't you, mate?'

The Nepali held up a polished automatic pistol. 'Great,' said Nina, sighing in despair.

'He's more of a budda-budda Buddhist. But he's got something quieter too.'

Jayesh reached under his coat to draw something from behind his back. 'Yeah.'

'It's a kukri,' Eddie explained as Nina goggled at the eighteen-inch blade he had produced. It resembled a machete, though curved inwards past the dark wooden hilt rather than straight. 'Gurkha knife. They use 'em for all kinds of stuff, but in a fight . . . put it this way, you want to be *well* clear even if you've got a gun. I've seen a Gurkha chuck one of those and score a bullseye from over a hundred feet away – and it hit so hard, the blade went right through the wood.'

Jayesh put on a performance, flipping and spinning the kukri in his hand so quickly that Nina could barely follow before balancing it by the point of the blade on a fingertip – all while his yak continued its wallowing plod. 'Second World War, Gurkha unit killed a whole German squad without using a single bullet,' he said proudly. He tossed the blade into the air, then snatched it as it fell and smoothly returned it to an elaborate leather scabbard across his lower back.

'That's . . . cool,' said Nina, dismayed. The Yorkshireman grinned, while the Gurkha came his closest yet to cracking a smile.

They continued onwards. The path narrowed once more as they rounded the mountain, the wind whipping up little eddies of ice crystals, before eventually widening out into a natural amphitheatre, a large sloping bowl cut into the mountainside. A sheer drop at its lower end fell several hundred feet into a desolate valley. Above, at the rear of the great space, a towering wall of stone rose almost vertically towards the peak high above.

At its foot was the monastery.

Nina yanked the reins to halt her mount. 'Oh my God, Eddie! Look at that!'

He halted his own yak. 'All right, yeah – that's pretty impressive.'

Detsen monastery was a collection of wood and stone buildings strung out along the cliff's base, some dug into the sheer face itself. At the closest end of the ribbon of structures was a gate, the only apparent entrance, set into a high wall running the length of the remote retreat. At its far end, a tall tower seemed almost to be teetering at the top of the slope, hugging the rock face behind it. Long rope lines bearing dozens of brightly coloured pennants, Buddhist prayer flags, stretched from its snow-laden rooftop down to various points on the hillside. 'Impressive?' she hooted. 'It's stunning!'

'Get your camera out, quick. You could make a few quid selling pictures to the *National Geographic*.'

'Someone watching from the wall,' said Jayesh, as much in warning as observation.

Nina spotted a figure atop a small tower near the gate. The man gave scale to his surroundings, the wall over twenty feet high. It was clearly defensive, dotted with windows that were too small for anybody to get in, but large enough for those inside to aim weapons out. It would be almost impossible for anyone to gain access without the monks allowing it.

The monastery's residents also controlled access to higher parts of the mountain. Beyond the tower, she picked out some kind of pathway ascending across the cliff face. The only way to reach it seemed to be from the tower's top. Was it the route Tobias Garde and his companions had taken to the Midas Cave?

The trio set off again, their yaks shuffling through the snow towards the gate. As they got closer, Nina picked out details that deepened her suspicions about the monastery having been moved to protect the cave. Her archaeological training had familiarised her with architectural styles and techniques of the past, and it seemed that the higher, most ornate parts of the buildings dated from an earlier period than the lower levels on which they stood. It was possible that the monks had raised the top floors and built new ones underneath them . . . but more likely that they had reconstructed parts of the original monastery in their new home on the mountain.

They soon reached the gate. Jayesh called out to the man on the wall, who bowed his head before replying, then disappeared from view. A short wait, then the wooden blockade slowly swung open.

A reception committee waited in the narrow courtyard within. 'Hello?' said Nina as she dismounted with relief and approached a pair of orange-robed monks. 'I'm Nina Wilde – this is my husband Eddie Chase, and our guide Jayesh Rai.' She regarded the older of the two bald-headed men. 'Are you Amaanat?'

'I am he,' he replied, placing his palms together before bowing deeply. The younger man beside him did the same. 'I am the abbot of this monastery. This is Rudra.' Amaanat indicated his companion.

The abbot matched Nina's earlier mental picture, but with one major exception: he had a deep crooked scar running down the left side of his face from the crown of his forehead all the way to his jawline. He was also much more solidly built than she had imagined, still muscular despite his age. His eyes were gentle, but she couldn't help but feel that before becoming a monk, he had lived a hard and violent life.

'I'm honoured to meet you,' she said. '*Namaste.*'

'Hi,' said Eddie, offering his hand. Rudra regarded him with barely concealed disapproval, but Amaanat smiled and shook it.

'Welcome to Detsen,' he said. 'Was your journey pleasant?'

'I've had more comfortable ones,' said Nina, glancing back at the yaks as another monk gathered their reins.

'Yes. They are the only way to reach us. In summer, a yak train brings supplies every two weeks and takes back our goods to sell, but in winter the weather is too bad even for them. Had you wanted to visit a few weeks sooner, it would have been impossible.'

'So you're trapped here over the winter?' Eddie asked.

Amaanat shook his head – a motion that in Nepal meant *yes* rather than the Western opposite. 'We have everything we need. If there is an emergency, we have a satellite telephone. As you already know, Dr Wilde.'

'I'm glad you do,' she said. 'Communicating by letter would have been a lot more laborious!' The thought occurred that her mother hadn't necessarily written to the monastery *after* meeting her father; with the monks being cut off for part of the year, her questions may simply have taken a long time to reach them, and longer to be returned.

The abbot smiled politely. 'You have had a long trip. Please, let us offer you our hospitality.'

He led them into a large building nearby. 'Our debate house,' said Amaanat. The interior was dark, lit only by candles, but the square room was surprisingly warm considering the temperature outside. A statue of the Buddha dominated the wood-panelled space, the larger-than-life figure sitting cross-legged beyond the doorway. There was another door opposite the entrance, but the monk took them around the statue and through a side exit into a system of tunnel-like chambers carved from the rock. More candles lit the way, with an occasional electric light providing greater illumination. Other monks watched them curiously, moving respectfully aside to give them room to pass.

Amaanat and Rudra brought them to an egg-like space with a low table at its centre, plain plates already set upon it. 'Please, sit,' the abbot said, gesturing towards cushions on the floor. 'We will bring food, and tea.' His eyes met Nina's. 'Then I imagine you are impatient to see what has brought you here.'

Rudra spoke for the first time, his English more clumsy. 'You have already broken promise,' he said. He was calm on the surface, but obviously holding in anger. 'You promise not to tell anyone you come here. But you bring others with you!'

'Eddie's my husband,' Nina replied. 'What I know, he knows.'

'Plus there was no way I was letting her come here by herself,' Eddie added, giving the younger man a steely glare. 'Anything could've happened to her. Which is why I asked Jayesh to come along too.' He nodded at his stone-faced friend. 'He speaks the language, so if anything funny goes on, he'll let us know.'

Rudra frowned, about to say more, but Amaanat waved him to silence and smiled. 'There is no need to worry, Mr Chase. Or you, Dr Wilde. I believe you will honour your promise of secrecy. You will understand why the Midas Cave is best kept from the rest of the world. It was a mistake for our order to have shown it to outsiders at all, but at the time they believed it justified.'

'Why?' Nina asked.

Rather than reply, he rang a small bell. Two more monks entered, one bearing a tray of fruits and vegetables, the other an ornately decorated teapot and five cups. 'Please, eat and drink,' said Amaanat. 'Then I shall give you the answers you seek.'

9

Nina ate her meal as quickly as politeness allowed, waiting impatiently for the others to finish. Finally Amaanat sipped the last of his tea and rang the bell, and the monks returned to take away the empty trays and crockery. 'Thank you,' she said.

'It is our honour to provide for our guests,' the abbot replied. 'Now, if you are ready, I shall show you our monastery.'

'I'm definitely ready.' She stood, the men following suit.

Amaanat led them back through the rocky passages to the debate house, going through the door opposite the courtyard entrance. Beyond was a long hallway lit by hundreds of candles. The floor was old polished wood, a red carpet running down its centre between two ranks of prayer wheels: metal cylinders inscribed with Ranjana calligraphy. Tapestries depicting scenes and figures from Buddhist mythology hung from the walls behind them. 'Are you a spiritual person, Dr Wilde?' asked the abbot.

'Not particularly,' said Nina, slightly uncomfortable with the question. 'I'm concerned with finding tangible truths. The intangible, the spiritual . . . it's something I can't really connect to. I guess I'm a rationalist.'

'And there is nothing wrong with that,' Amaanat said. 'Without rationality, what are we but primal animals? But a mind that is not open to the possibility of there being more to the world than what we can see and touch seems . . . *imprisoned*, in a cell of its own making.' He carefully rotated one of the wheels, whispering under his breath, then another as he walked along. 'Perhaps you should try.'

She turned the same wheel as the abbot. It made a faint singing sound as the metal points of the hubs rubbed against their mounts, but the experience left her unchanged, and unmoved. 'Sorry, but it didn't do anything for me.'

Amaanat was not offended; rather, amused. 'Then you should start with something smaller.' He indicated a rack containing miniature prayer wheels on handles, each about the size of a tennis racquet.

'Or you could try that one,' Eddie suggested. At the passage's far end was a prayer wheel far larger than any of its companions, almost as tall as the Yorkshireman. 'Spinning that thing should put you in tune with the universe.'

'Either that or exhaust me,' she replied. They continued along the hallway, both monks turning more wheels as they went. Even Jayesh joined in, shooting Eddie a look as if daring him to comment. His friend merely grinned.

They passed a window. Eddie glanced through it, seeing that their yaks had been tethered to a ramshackle hitching post outside the monastery's wall. 'Will they be okay there?'

'If the weather turns, we will bring them inside,' said the abbot. 'Do not worry, they will be fed.'

The exit at the hall's far end led into a large building, a staircase ascending to a higher floor, but Amaanat instead indicated another flight going down. The level below was colder and darker. A stone passage used for storage ran back beneath the prayer wheel hall, countless boxes and sacks lining the walls. However, the abbot turned in the opposite direction, bringing them to a pair of doors. The one to the side was ajar. Nina glanced through, seeing metal cylinders in the shadows: gas canisters.

Amaanat stopped at the other, heavier door ahead and rapped

on it. A muffled voice came from inside. The old monk replied, and a hefty bolt was drawn back. 'In here, Dr Wilde,' he said, 'you will find your answers.' He opened the door.

A wave of heat hit Nina as she stepped through. The large stone-walled chamber contained a roaring furnace, seething blue flames being fed by propane tanks. Molten metal glowed in a ceramic crucible sitting above the fire. The sweating monk who had let them in bowed, then quickly returned to it. He used a set of iron tongs to lift the crucible and carefully pour its contents into a mould. Sparks spat as the glutinous liquid filled the rectangular space.

Eddie and Nina exchanged surprised looks. Neither needed to be a metallurgist to realise what he was making.

A gold bar.

Shelves on the rear wall bore more bricks of the precious metal. 'What's all this?' Eddie asked. 'I'm guessing you haven't taken a vow of poverty.'

'We pay for the upkeep of the monastery by crafting jewellery and sculptures,' Amaanat explained, crossing the room. He drew a key on a chain around his neck from his robes and unlocked another, smaller door. 'Until they are taken by yak train to be sold, they are kept in here. Along with . . . other valuable items. Please, enter.'

Nina went in. The room was dark, until the monk switched on a light and she saw what he meant. 'Oh, wow.'

More shelves lined the walls. The smaller items upon them were carefully wrapped in soft cloth, but the larger ones were on proud display.

Serene faces gazed back at her, figures of the Buddha ranging from six inches to almost three feet tall. All were made from exquisitely worked metal, some inset with precious stones. Even under the glare of the single overhead bulb, they gleamed warmly as if illuminated from within. 'These are beautiful,' she said.

'Thank you,' Amaanat replied. 'All are made by hand. I do not wish to boast, but our monks are very skilled.'

'You're not kidding.' She examined one more closely. 'Are they all made of gold?'

'They are. Our work is highly regarded. It is how we are able to keep the monastery alive.' He smiled. 'We do not receive many visitors in such a remote place, so donations are rare. But you have not come here to see what we make.' The humour disappeared from his face, replaced by earnest respect. 'You have come to see this.'

The abbot went to a squat metal chest in the furthest corner of the room. He used a second key to open a padlock, then Rudra helped him raise the heavy lid.

Inside was something tightly shrouded in red velvet, a shape resembling a book. Amaanat stood back as Rudra lifted it out and placed it on a table. Nina moved closer, watching as he gently peeled open the cloth.

She knew the item's origin immediately. The distinctive colour of the metal, tinged a deeper red than the golden Buddhas, was proof enough. 'It's from Atlantis,' she gasped. 'That's orichalcum.'

Amaanat fully removed the velvet. 'This is our oldest relic – older even than the Buddha himself. It was left many thousands of years ago by an explorer and general.'

'Talonor,' said Nina.

'Yes.'

'May I take a closer look?'

'Please do.'

Nina took out her phone, drawing a suspicious look from Rudra, and switched on its flashlight to get a clearer view. Like the Secret Codex, the book's pages were sheets of metal, Atlantean text inscribed upon them.

'Can you read it?' asked Eddie.

'Some of it,' she said. 'It's . . . a marker, I suppose, Talonor's equivalent of leaving a plaque on the moon. It says that he and—Midas!' she gasped on picking out a name. 'This says Midas! He really did travel with Talonor.' She read on. Some parts of the text were beyond even her ability to translate, while others were mere statistics: the number of men on the expedition, distances travelled, supplies consumed and other minutiae. That was not what interested her, though, and she reached to turn the page before hesitating. 'Can I touch it?'

'It is metal. You will not hurt it,' Amaanat replied.

All the same, she did so gingerly, trying to leave as few marks from her fingertips as possible. The next page turned out to be more of the same, a dry account of how Talonor's expedition had reached this place. But even here she picked out nuggets of interest. The Atlantean had definitely been searching for something specific; there were references to his dealing with local tribes, questioning them for knowledge of . . . 'A furnace?' she muttered.

Eddie glanced back into the hot room. 'What about it?'

'No, not here. Talonor was looking for what he calls a furnace, but it was obviously something very special.' She became aware that neither of the two monks had responded to her words; while Amaanat's expression was studiously neutral, there was a hint of what she thought might be worry behind Rudra's attempt to match it. 'You know what it is, don't you?' she asked the abbot. 'You know why Talonor came here – and what he found.'

'All the answers you require are to be found here,' Amaanat told her, indicating the metal book.

'All the ones I need, maybe, but what about the ones I *want*?' The old man's face remained an impenetrable blank. Annoyed, Nina read on. The text became less dry, more intriguing, as it returned to the subject of exploration, but still it did not give her any more insight, until—

'The cave!' she exclaimed. 'It's here! Talonor found a cave on the mountain, and it had something to do with this furnace he was looking for. He named it the Midas Cave in honour of Midas's . . . sacrifice, this says. His sacrifice in service of the empire. Something very important to him was lost in finding the cave.' She continued to scan the ancient text. 'It doesn't say what, though. They returned to Atlantis – it even says which route they planned to take! – intending to come back with "the Crucible".'

'Your mum talked about that,' he reminded her.

She nodded. 'And whatever it is, it was incredibly important to them – it was the entire reason Talonor was sent out to search the world in the first place. It seems their own furnace was dying, so they needed a replacement.'

'Well, if you've got a crucible, a furnace is a pretty good place to put it.'

'But what were they putting *in* it?' She faced Amaanat. 'You know. I can tell.'

It took all Rudra's self-restraint not to respond with anger at the accusation, but the old man merely bowed his head. 'You may believe what you wish. But there is nothing more for you to see here.'

'And what about the Midas Cave itself? You said you'd show it to me.'

'I said no such thing. All I said was that your questions would be answered. Now they are. You have finished the task your mother set herself, and learned that Talonor of Atlantis did indeed once travel to this place.' A small smile. 'Your quest is over.'

His calm denial infuriated Nina. 'My mother? You're going to bring up my mother? Okay, let me do the same: she died because of you!'

'You dare!' barked Rudra, stepping towards her. Eddie moved

to intercede, but Amaanat had already held up a hand. Scowling, the young monk retreated slightly.

The abbot fixed Nina with a level gaze. 'We cannot be held responsible for the actions of others. Your mother's loss was tragic, but we had no part in it.'

'Didn't you?' She retrieved an item from a pocket: the letter Laura had received from the monastery, inside a protective plastic envelope. 'She wrote to you asking about the Midas Cave – not directly, but you knew what she was after. You *knew*. And you lied to her!' She held it up in front of Amaanat's face, pointing out his signature. 'You, personally, lied to her. You didn't tell her anything about the cave, or Tobias Garde's visit, or that Talonor had ever been here.'

The monk's eyes flicked over the typewritten text. He was again expressionless, but now to cover his surprise at being presented with his own words over four decades on. 'She did not ask about them,' he said after a pause, 'so I could not have replied about them.'

'Semantic *bullshit!*' Even Eddie was startled by her explosion. 'Everything in this letter was deliberately intended to make her think Detsen monastery was the wrong place. And because of that, she died. If you had told her the truth, and she'd seen this,' she gestured at Talonor's record, 'it would have told her and my father how to find Atlantis. Talonor's route back would have led them right to it – and they would have found it forty years ago! But instead they spent the rest of their lives searching, until they got too close and were *murdered* for it. That happened because of *you*, Amaanat. You may not have pulled the trigger personally, but you put them in front of a firing squad!'

Rudra's voice was barely above a growl. 'You will leave. Now.' He clenched both fists.

Eddie squared up to him. 'Guess we'll see how far your whole non-violence thing goes, won't we?' Jayesh, who had remained near the door, moved to join him.

'There will be no violence,' said Amaanat firmly. He stared at Rudra. 'There will *not*.' The younger man shrank back, ashamed.

'I don't want violence,' Nina insisted. 'I just want answers. Where is the Midas Cave, and what's inside it? What did my ancestor see in there?'

Amaanat closed his eyes, drawing in a slow breath before answering. 'The monks of Detsen monastery have kept the Midas Cave a secret because to reveal it will bring only violence. What it holds will spark the greed of every unenlightened person in the world.'

'So pretty much everyone,' said Eddie.

'This is why we cannot show it to you,' the abbot went on. 'It is too dangerous. You cannot be trusted.'

'*I* can't be trusted?' Nina snapped. 'You do know what I've done for the past ten years, right?'

'Of course. You discovered archaeological sites – and showed them to the world.'

'That was only half my job. The other half was *keeping them secret*. The IHA's purpose isn't just to find lost wonders; it's also to protect them. Sometimes to keep them out of the hands of greedy, unenlightened people, but other times because what we found was too dangerous to be revealed. I'm not going to tell you what they are, for obvious reasons, but I've made discoveries that would make the Midas Cave look as big a threat as a wet bath sponge.'

'You do not know anything,' snarled Rudra.

'No? How about you let me decide that?' She took a breath of her own, trying to calm herself. 'Look, I may not work for the IHA any more, but I still share the same values. I want to find the hidden treasures of the past, and show them to the world . . . but only if it's safe to do so. There are some secrets that have to be kept. I know that for a fact, because I'm keeping them.'

Conflict was clear on the old man's features. 'Will you give your word of honour that you will keep *this* secret?'

'I will,' she promised.

'And your husband?'

The Englishman nodded. 'If Nina says she's going to keep quiet about it, then so will I.' Jayesh tipped his head in agreement.

A long silence followed, the elderly monk gazing intently at the two Westerners as if assessing their souls, then finally he placed his palms together and bowed to them. 'I believe that I may trust you,' he said.

'So you'll show us the cave?' Nina asked.

'I will. But you should be warned that it is not only the cave that is dangerous. The path to it has claimed many lives. You must be prepared, and careful.'

'We will,' said Eddie. 'We've both been up mountains before.'

Amaanat appeared almost amused. 'Not like this, Mr Chase. Dragon Mountain will certainly try to catch you off guard. Are you ready to face it?'

'We are,' said Nina firmly. She reached back and gathered her hair into a ponytail.

'Then,' he said, 'let us begin.'

10

The visitors prepared for the journey. Amaanat assured them they would not need the climbing gear Jayesh had brought, but Nina and Eddie still made sure they had survival and emergency equipment – and some extra for the monks, just in case.

They assembled in the courtyard with Amaanat, Rudra and five other monks. The Nepalis had donned outerwear that Nina considered worryingly light for the conditions. The new faces all bore cargo: one had a small haversack and two coils of rope slung from his shoulders, while the others wore larger backpacks. What was in them she couldn't tell, but it was clearly heavy.

Amaanat issued instructions, then spoke to Eddie and Nina. 'We are ready. Please follow – and once we are outside the monastery, be very careful.'

He set off, but not towards the main gates. Instead he led the group into the string of buildings, passing through the debate house and the hall of prayer wheels before continuing on past the stairs into other structures. Monks bowed as they passed. Finally they entered the base of the tall tower. A large golden statue of the laughing Buddha sat in the centre of the floor, one hand raised as if waving them off on their journey.

A staircase of well-worn dark wood spiralled upwards inside the framework of thick beams supporting the stone walls. Amaanat bowed to the statue and uttered a brief prayer, then led the ascent, pointing out features as they climbed. 'Many parts of this tower were brought here from the original monastery. These stairs are almost four hundred years old.'

'No wonder they creak,' said Eddie.

'It is the strongest part of the monastery. It was first built as a fort, for protection against bandits.'

'I assume the reason the monks demolished the original monastery and moved here was to make it harder for Tobias Garde to find his way back to the Midas Cave?' Nina asked.

'Yes,' replied the abbot. 'They showed your ancestor the cave in gratitude for his help. But later they realised the danger of outsiders taking control of it.'

'How did he help them?'

Amaanat did not reply, entering a room at the top of the tower. A door was set into the rear wall. 'This is the only way to reach the cave,' he announced as Rudra drew back a bolt and opened it.

A freezing wind rushed in. Even in her well-insulated clothing, Nina felt it slicing at her like tiny razor blades. 'Wow, that's cold.'

'It will get colder,' Rudra warned. Beyond was the near-vertical wall of the cliff behind the monastery. A sturdy plank was lashed to metal supports driven into the rock.

'How long'll the climb take?' Eddie asked.

'It depends on the weather . . . and if the path is still there.'

Nina and Eddie looked at each other. 'Yeah, that's totally reassuring,' she said.

Amaanat smiled. 'There are supplies to repair it along the way – ropes, wood.' He stepped on to the plank. 'This way.'

Rudra went next, followed by Eddie, Nina and Jayesh. The narrow gap between tower and cliff acted as a natural wind tunnel, intensifying the icy blast. More snow-caked planks were strung along the cliff to form a walkway – with two-foot gaps between them. Eddie let out a disbelieving huff, his breath forming a steaming cloud. 'You don't need to be a mountaineer to get up there. You need to be Super Mario!'

Amaanat sidestepped along the planks until he emerged from behind the tower, giving him enough room to face forwards. The others did the same. The force of the gale reduced once they were clear of the structure, but the biting temperature did not improve.

The abbot surveyed the vertiginous route ahead, then advanced, fingertips brushing the rock face to his left for support. Age had not affected his agility or balance, and he negotiated the tricky path with easy assurance. His guests found it more difficult, their inflexible boots actually a disadvantage when it came to finding grip.

The walkway slanted upwards, reaching a narrow ledge. The group continued along the curving wall overlooking the natural bowl until they reached a sharp fold in the mountain-side. A gap had been chiselled out of it, giving just enough room to duck beneath the overhanging rock to reach another path beyond.

Nina looked back at the monastery as the procession slowed to clamber through. The multicoloured prayer flags sweeping down from the tower fluttered in the wind, leading her eye to the precipice at the foot of the slope. More bleak mountains rose beyond it. Other than the tethered yaks, there was no sign of life, not even a distant tree. Although coldly beautiful, it was a desolate, dead landscape.

Yet it hid something extraordinary that her ancestor had seen over a century and a half ago – and that thousands of years earlier an explorer had come all the way from the mouth of the Mediterranean to find. Whatever was in the Midas Cave, they had considered it worth enduring the emptiness.

She followed Eddie through the gap, Jayesh standing ready to assist from behind. The drop to the boulder-strewn ground was a good sixty feet. If the monks wanted to silence the visitors, an 'accident' would be easy enough to stage . . .

But Amaanat and his people showed no signs of hostility; not even Rudra, whose present bad temperament was aimed at the elements. Reassured, she kept moving.

Before long, the new ledge levelled out and widened slightly. Bundles of planks and skeins of rope rested in a small hollow in the cliff. 'The path ends not far ahead,' Amaanat announced, stopping and moving aside so Rudra could pass him. 'From here there are more platforms. Talonor first built them so his people could reach the cave. We have maintained them, but the journey is not easy.'

Jayesh took advantage of the brief pause to light a cigarette, drawing disapproving looks from some of the monks. 'We'll cope.'

'I hope so. But be warned, parts of the path are very old.' He turned as Rudra returned and spoke briefly in Nepalese. 'The path does not need repair. We may go on.'

They resumed the journey, rounding another fold in the cliff. Nina halted when she saw what lay ahead. The path narrowed to nothingness, but the route continued onwards on a ragged line of more planks supported by logs jutting from the cliff face. The mountainside here was vertical, the drop at least two hundred feet and rising as the precarious walkway staggered upwards. Ropes threaded through eyelets hammered into the stone acted as a kind of handrail, though the slack in the lines did not inspire confidence. 'Are you *certain* it doesn't need repair?' she asked.

'This way has been used for thousands of years,' Amaanat pointed out. 'It is dangerous, yes, but it can be travelled safely if you take great care.'

'Nah, I was planning to wing it and run along 'em,' said Eddie sarcastically. He faced his wife. 'You sure about this?'

'We've come this far,' she replied.

'Yeah, and that's never got us into trouble before, has it?'

He let out a vaporous breath. 'Okay, just remember that we've got a little girl waiting for us to come home, right? Be really careful.'

'I wasn't planning to do anything else!' Nina told him. 'I guess we're ready.'

Amaanat bowed his head. 'Then let us go on.'

He retook the lead, stepping over the gap on to the first plank. It made a low warning groan as it took his weight. The sound did not deter him, and with his left hand lightly holding the guide rope he took measured paces along the wood to reach the next platform in line. 'Do not have more than one person on each step if you can,' he called back.

Eddie took a much firmer grip on the rope when his turn came to advance. 'One down, maybe five hundred more to go,' he said as he waited for Rudra to clear the next plank. 'Will we be able to climb all the way up and then back down before it gets dark?'

'If the path is clear, yes,' said Amaanat.

'And if it isn't?'

'There is a shelter,' Rudra told him. 'It is not big, but there is room for all of us.'

'Sounds cosy,' said Nina, not keen on the prospect – as much out of impatience to reach the Midas Cave as at the thought of being trapped for the night on a Himalayan mountain.

The little procession moved on. Once over her initial unease, Nina found the process almost straightforward: eight or nine careful footfalls along each length, then step up to the next platform. The blustery wind encouraged her to press close to the rock, but despite appearances, the guide ropes turned out to be firmly attached to the cliff.

Before long, she felt secure enough to divert a small amount of attention to her surroundings. Empty holes cut into the stone and the protruding stubs of worn logs or metal poles above and below the current pathway suggested that sections had been abandoned over time – or simply broken away and dropped into the void. Some were clearly much older than others. Talonor's original route to his prize, allowing him to get men and materiel to and from the cave? It seemed likely . . . but for what purpose?

Somewhere in the distance, she heard an odd noise, a rumbling hiss. It continued for several seconds, then stopped. 'Did you hear that?' she asked Eddie.

'Yeah,' he replied. 'Hey, Rudra. What was that?'

'The dragon,' the monk replied.

'No need to be sarcastic.'

'I was not.'

Eddie rolled his eyes at Nina, who shrugged, wondering what he meant. They resumed their trek.

The trudging climb continued around the mountain, revealing a new frozen vista beyond as empty as that behind them. It also revealed something new along their path – something worrying.

Eddie saw it too. 'You're f . . . lippin' kidding.'

'Amaanat! Are you sure that's safe?' Nina called to the abbot. He had reached a vertical cleft cutting deeply into the rock face, an ancient geological fault some fifteen feet across. The route upwards continued on its far side – but the only way to reach it was by traversing an extremely rickety-looking rope bridge.

'In my time at Detsen monastery, eighteen monks have fallen from this bridge,' he warned.

'That's kind of a huge no, then.'

'It is less than one every two years.'

'Still not filling me with confidence!'

The elderly man smiled. 'Watch me. Do what I do, follow my footsteps.'

A guide rope was stretched along the inside of the bridge. He gripped it with his left hand, then held his right arm out for balance as he took small, precise steps over the planks.

'You holding your breath?' Eddie whispered.

'Uh-huh,' Nina replied, not daring to exhale in case she blew the monk off his feet.

Amaanat reached the midpoint. He paused as a gust of wind set the bridge swinging, hunching down to dampen the motion, then continued. A few more steps and he reached the relative security of a short length of rocky ledge.

Nina finally allowed herself to breathe. 'That wasn't terrifying at *all*.'

'We've still got to get across it,' Eddie reminded her.

'Thanks for that, hon.'

Rudra crossed next, more quickly than the abbot, as if trying to prove a point, then it was Eddie's turn. The Englishman held the rope before gingerly putting one foot on the bridge. 'I should probably say something reassuring about now, shouldn't I?' he said, looking back at Nina with a strained grin.

'Yeah, that would help!'

'How about . . . at least we're not being shot at?' He winked.

'All right. Let's do this.'

He followed Amaanat's example, taking controlled, measured steps. The wood creaked underfoot. Nina cringed, but Eddie steadied himself, then carried on. Five feet to go, three, two . . . then he took a long step to take the waiting Rudra's hand on the far side. 'Thanks,' he said, before looking back at his wife. 'Take it steady, and you'll be fine.'

Nina clamped her hand around the guide rope. 'Look at the bridge, not the . . . total nothingness under it,' she muttered. From here, she could see that the cleft cut a good seventy feet into the mountainside, and stretched seemingly to infinity below. 'Okay. Take it steady. *Real* steady.'

She put one foot on the first plank. It shifted slightly beneath her. Steeling herself, she stepped forward.

Her heart began to pound. The whole bridge was swaying, and the wind was now picking up, snow being plucked from small outcrops below and spiralling skywards past her. 'It's all right,' called Eddie reassuringly. 'You're doing fine. Just keep going.'

'I'm sure as hell not going to stop,' she said as she continued her nervous advance. Halfway over, three quarters . . .

A sharp gust – and the entire bridge lurched.

Nina tried to drop as Amaanat had done, but the planks had swung out from beneath her centre of gravity, overbalancing her. The vertical cleft opened up below—

The guide rope snapped taut. Pain flared in her clenching fingers, but she maintained her grip. She crouched to steady herself, then took hold of the line with her other hand. 'Jesus!'

'Sh . . . oes!' yelled Eddie. 'Nina, are you okay?'

She somehow forced a smile. 'You still managed not to swear.'

'It was close! Are you all right?'

'Yeah, I'm fine, just feeling like my adrenal gland exploded.' She cautiously straightened. 'I'm coming over.'

She set off again, trying to balance the need for care against her desperate urge to reach comparative safety. Step, step, feeling the planks waver – and then Eddie grabbed her hand and pulled her on to the ledge. 'Got you.'

'Oh, thank God!' She hugged him.

Amaanat called back to her. 'Are you all right, Dr Wilde?'

'Yes thanks. That was close, though!'

'I warned you how dangerous this place can be.'

'It'd be less dangerous if you built a proper bridge!' said Eddie angrily.

Rudra scowled, but the abbot shrugged off the criticism. 'Our legends say that this' – he indicated the chasm – 'was cut by the sword of the bodhisattva Manjusri when he fought the dragon of the mountain. We cannot close the wound in case the dragon regains his strength.'

'I don't think dragons are what you should be worried about,' Nina complained.

The old monk smiled knowingly. 'You will soon see that is not so.' He went to the end of the ledge and resumed his precarious trek along the stepped platforms, Rudra following.

'Sure you're okay?' Eddie asked Nina.

She nodded. 'Yeah. But let's not do that again.'

'Still glad to be back out in the field?'

A narrow-eyed smile. 'Get moving, you.'

He laughed, then set off after the two monks. Nina waited until he had cleared the next platform before continuing, Jayesh and the other monks crossing the bridge behind her.

As the group made their way around the mountain, Nina's resurgent vertigo discouraged her from admiring the view, however spectacular. It also grew steadily colder as the sun moved behind the wall of rock.

The line of platforms eventually ended. She wondered if they had reached their destination, before seeing that they were instead changing direction – going straight up. Rungs had been driven into the sheer stone to create a ladder, ascending for about a hundred feet. Amaanat had already begun to climb. Rudra clambered up behind him.

Eddie reached the foot of the ladder. 'Think they need to spend a bit of the money they make from selling gold knick-knacks on Hammerite.' He tugged at one of the rust-scabbed metal bars. To Nina's relief, it didn't move.

He let Rudra open up a gap for safety, and was about to climb after him when he froze and looked across the valley with a quizzical expression. 'What is it?' asked Nina.

'Thought I heard a chopper.'

She followed his gaze. The distant echoing thrum of a helicopter's rotors reached her, but she could see no sign of any aircraft. 'You expecting company?' she called to Amaanat.

'Ever since the earthquake, there are many more helicopters,' he answered. Eddie still appeared dubious, but the sound soon died away. 'Be careful here. Some of the rungs need to be repaired.'

'Don't suppose you remember which ones, do you?' said the Yorkshireman, but he got no reply. With a sigh, he followed Rudra upwards, Nina behind him.

As Amaanat had warned, some of the rungs were in poor condition, a few so heavily corroded that they had sheared apart. 'Watch out on this one,' Eddie told Nina and Jayesh as he passed the halfway point, finding a particularly ragged example. 'Don't want to catch tetanus.'

'As if we don't have enough to worry about,' said Nina.

'Yeah. Don't think we packed anything in the first-aid—'

He had gripped a new rung – which lurched in its mounting holes. One of his feet slipped, the jagged end of the broken bar slicing an ugly gash into his boot. 'Ffff . . . ishing *hook*!' he yelled as he secured himself. Rudra stopped above him, looking down in alarm. 'You could've warned me!' The young monk appeared genuinely contrite.

'Are you okay, Eddie?' said Nina, worried.

'Just got a bit of a shock, that's all. Don't put any weight on this one.' He thumped the offending rung with a balled fist, taking a very careful look at the ones above before resuming his ascent.

The rest of the climb was made safely. To the visitors' enormous relief, the top of the ladder led to the solidity of a ledge. The group advanced along it, crossing another section of planks before reaching a further ledge. Ahead, a second ladder continued upwards, but something beyond it caught Nina's eye. 'Are we here? Is that it?'

A squat wooden structure was tucked against the cliff, half buried in snow. 'No,' said Amaanat. 'That is the shelter. I hope we will not need it.' He drew back the cuff of his coat, revealing a watch. 'Yes, you will be able to see what is inside the Midas Cave and return before sunset. The timing is perfect.'

'Timing for what?' she asked, but he began to scale the next ladder without answering.

Rudra went up behind him. Nina waited for Eddie to follow, but now he too was staring at something along the ledge – not the shelter, but a small crevice nearer to them. 'That's weird.'

'What?'

'The snow. I mean, the *no* snow.' A teardrop-shaped gap in the white covering directly in front of the little opening revealed bare rock, a rime of frost glistening on it. 'Looks like it's melted.'

'Why would it only melt there?' Nina wondered.

'Dunno.' He glanced back at Jayesh as the Gurkha joined them. 'Keep an eye out,' he whispered to his friend.

'You think they're going to try something?' said Nina.

'I dunno *what* they're going to do. Better safe than sorry, eh?'

The visitors made their way up the ladder. This one was fairly short, about thirty feet, and ended at a much larger and broader ledge strewn with boulders.

A cave entrance was set into the foot of the cliff, a small wooden hut to one side. As with the crevice below, the ground immediately before the opening was devoid of snow.

There was no indication that anyone else was already here, though: no footprints other than Amaanat's and Rudra's, no smouldering remains of fires. So what had caused the snow to melt?

'Is that the Midas Cave?' Nina asked, starting towards the entrance.

'It is,' replied Amaanat, holding up a hand to warn her back. 'But you must wait before we can go inside.'

'Why?' asked Eddie.

'You will see. In . . .' he checked his wrist, 'six minutes. Please, wait over there.'

The other monks assembled where the abbot had indicated, putting down their heavy packs. Now intrigued, Nina joined them, Eddie and Jayesh standing slightly apart from everyone else to maintain a discreet watch.

The minutes ticked by. 'So whatever's about to happen, it happens to a schedule?' Nina asked Amaanat.

'Always,' he said. 'You are lucky to be here at this time of the year. It begins at the end of winter and continues until summer. It has done so since Talonor first came to this place, and long before.'

'And it always happens on time?' said Eddie.

'Yes.'

'Whatever it is, we should get it to run the trains.'

Nina smiled, then looked at her own watch. Less than a minute, if Amaanat was right. Less than a minute before she had the answer that her mother had sought for so long . . .

She became aware of an odd, unsettling sensation, but couldn't identify it – until she realised that the ground itself was *shivering*. A low rumble gradually became audible, a hiss rising above it. 'What's that?'

'The dragon,' announced Amaanat. 'The dragon is breathing.'

No sooner had he spoken than the sound became a whooshing roar – and a great blast of steam burst from the cave mouth, sweeping across the bare stone before the dense cloud of rising vapour was caught by the wind, dispersing into tendrils. More rose from below as a smaller jet gushed out of the narrow crevice on the lower ledge. The thunderous expulsion continued for several seconds before fading. A few last puffs escaped the cave, then everything fell silent and still.

Eddie and Nina regarded the entrance in shock. 'What the hell was *that*?' she said, wide-eyed.

The abbot gave her a gentle, knowing smile. 'That,' he said, 'was the secret of the Midas Cave. And now I shall show it to you.'

11

The secret was not revealed immediately. To Nina's rising frustration, Amaanat insisted that they wait before entering; because of the heat, he said, but she couldn't help thinking there was more to it.

Her suspicion was confirmed several minutes later. Rudra went into the hut beside the steaming cave entrance, re-emerging clad in something that made her give Eddie a worried look. '*That's* reassuring.'

The monk wore a bright yellow hazmat suit, the thick plastic overall covering him from head to foot. More alarming still, he carried a boxy device that when turned on emitted an ominous crackling noise. 'Is that a Geiger counter?' said Eddie, taking an involuntary step backwards.

Nina was equally horrified. 'The cave's radioactive?'

Amaanat raised his hands to placate them. 'The steam is radioactive, not the cave. It will be safe, but we must wait for the readings to fall before we can go inside.'

'How long will that take?'

'Not long. Please, be patient.'

Rudra disappeared inside the tunnel. Minutes passed, then he returned, pulling back the hazmat suit's hood. 'It is clear,' he announced. The Geiger counter was still growling, but at a much lower level.

Amaanat spoke to the other monks, and all but one took metal containers the size of large paint tins from their backpacks. Their contents were much heavier than paint, though. One monk's fingers slipped, his canister dropping the few inches to the ground with a thud that sounded as if someone had pounded the earth with a sledgehammer.

Meanwhile, the man who had carried the ropes produced something about the size of a basketball, wrapped in thick layers of cloth. From the reverent way he handled it, it was clearly of great value. Nina was about to ask what it was, but the abbot spoke first. 'Please, follow me.'

Jayesh lit another cigarette. 'I'll stay here,' he told Eddie. 'Keep my eyes open.'

'See you soon,' Eddie replied. A nod was the only reply he needed for reassurance.

Rudra had by now removed the protective suit and returned it and the Geiger counter to the hut. He emerged carrying a pair of lanterns. They were clockwork; he gave a charged one to Amaanat, then began winding the handle to power up the other. 'He will follow us inside,' said Amaanat as he switched on his light and entered the cave. 'This way.'

'You absolutely *sure* it's safe?' Eddie asked. 'I don't want to end up with an extra head growing out of my stomach like Kuato.' Nina looked askance at him. 'From *Total Recall*,' he added.

'I know.'

'The original, not the crappy remake.'

'I *know*.'

He flapped his hands before his chest and put on a croaky voice. '"Start the reactor!"'

'Will you be *quiet*?'

'There is nothing to fear,' the monk told them as he made his way deeper. 'But we must leave before the next burst of steam. Which will be in . . .' he consulted his watch, 'forty-six minutes.'

Nina examined the walls, and the wooden beams supporting them. The condition of neither made her feel safer. But there was something odd about the rock, she realised. As they moved away from the entrance, she caught faint glints of reflected lamp-light from all around, as if tiny flecks of metal were embedded in the walls.

Not just the walls. The wood, too. Whatever it was, it covered everything.

The tunnel sloped downwards into the heart of the mountain, the air becoming hotter and more humid. As they rounded a bend, the light from behind was cut off. 'It is not much further,' said Amaanat.

Eddie spotted drips coming from a hairline crack in the ceiling. 'Water's getting in.'

'It is from the snow as it melts. But without it, what you are about to see could not happen.'

'So what *are* we about to see?' asked Nina.

The passage narrowed as they rounded another turn. 'This,' said Amaanat.

Nina and Eddie both stopped, stunned by the sight.

The cave was made of gold.

Every surface was covered in the precious metal, as if it had been slathered thickly over walls, floor and ceiling. Even the pit props had been absorbed into the shimmering coating. At the far side of the space, a six-foot-wide chasm dropped vertically downwards, the ragged rock also caked in gold. A tall, heavy-duty tripod spanned the gap, a pulley hanging from its top. The arrangement was the only thing in the chamber that had not been completely gilded, but even this had a distinct sheen to it.

'Whoa,' Nina said finally. 'Okay, now I understand why Midas's name is associated with gold.' She took in the whole of her incredible surroundings. 'But this isn't a natural seam. This has been . . . *deposited*. How?'

Eddie took a closer look at one wall, examining where a prop met the rock. The gleaming covering had softened any sharp edges as if it had oozed to fill every corner. 'It must be an inch thick! I don't even want to think how much this lot's worth.'

'And that is why we have kept this place a secret,' said Amaanat. 'The violence as greedy men sought to control it would be terrible.'

'Control it?' said Nina. 'Not just take it?'

'This is not simply a place that contains gold. It *makes* gold. Talonor found it, thousands of years ago, and it has been used to create riches ever since.'

Eddie shook his head sceptically. 'That's impossible.'

'Where do you think we get the gold to make our statues and jewellery? The monks of Detsen hold the secret, and we have used it. Carefully, a little at a time, to avoid attention. But we can create gold by the gram, by the kilo . . . or by the ton.'

'How?' Nina demanded. 'How is that possible?'

'I will show you.' The elderly monk moved towards the chasm – and Nina gasped as his light suddenly illuminated a figure hidden in the darkness.

'Who's that?' said Eddie, instinctively interposing himself between his wife and the lurker.

Amaanat replied quietly, almost reverently: 'That is the daughter of Midas.'

Her initial shock now past, Nina saw that the person was unmoving. A statue. No, not even that, more an abstract representation of the human form, all features smoothed to the nothingness of a sea-worn pebble. It was half crouched, twisted at the waist, both arms raised to shield its empty face.

She realised that Amaanat's words were literal, not merely naming a piece of sculpture. 'There's somebody *inside* it?'

'She died here,' he said, almost sadly. 'By radiation, by steam, being choked by gold – we do not know. But Talonor named the cave in honour of his friend's loss. She was Midas's only daughter. A woman of importance, a princess. She thought this

ANDY MCDERMOTT

place was exactly the same as another in Atlantis. She was wrong. The time between each breath of the dragon is shorter here, and she was caught inside when one took place.'

Nina nodded thoughtfully. 'And was turned into gold. Or coated in it, but it must have looked like the same thing. So that's where the myth of Midas came from. Atlantean history, passed down to become a Greek legend.'

'That'll be a good chapter for your next book,' said Eddie.

'Except we can't tell anyone about it, can we?' She looked at Amaanat. 'I gave my word.' The abbot smiled.

The tramp of feet signalled the arrival of Rudra and the other monks. The lantern-bearer was in the lead, a length of rope over one shoulder. The man carrying the shrouded object was behind him. The others bore the metal canisters. 'This is the true secret,' said Amaanat as the mysterious item was carefully unwrapped. 'Without it, there would be no gold; the cave would create nothing but radiation. This is the Crucible.'

The artefact mentioned in both her mother's notes and the Secret Codex. Nina watched as the last layer of cloth was removed, eager to see what was revealed . . .

It matched none of her expectations.

The name suggested a man-made vessel, but what Rudra lifted out resembled some sort of geode: a natural, roughly spherical reddish crystal. An opening at the top gave her a glimpse of the hollow interior. It was faceted, reflective, like an agglomeration of gemstones. Jagged rib-like ridges ran up the outer shell. From the great care the monk was taking, she guessed they were as sharp as they looked. The whole thing was contained inside a man-made cage of thick wire with a tall handle looping over its top.

Amaanat anticipated her next question. 'We do not know where it came from. That secret was kept by Talonor. But we know what it does.'

'Makes gold, at a guess,' said Eddie.

'*How* does it make gold, though?' Nina asked. 'It can't just magic the stuff up out of nothing.'

'We shall show you.' Amaanat stepped back as Rudra placed the Crucible on the floor near the tripod. 'But first you will need protection.'

The Englishman smirked. 'Too late for that, we've already got a kid.'

One of the other monks opened a bag and took out several breathing masks, which he distributed. His brethren donned them. 'The Crucible turns mercury into gold,' explained the abbot, voice muffled by the filter. 'But the mercury gives off vapour. In a confined space, it is poisonous.'

'You've got mercury in those cans?' said Eddie. 'Nasty stuff.'

'We take great care with it. We do not want to pollute the mountain – the water from this cave flows down into the rivers, and on into the sea.'

Nina remembered the drips from the ceiling. 'There isn't much of it, though.'

Amaanat stepped to the edge of the chasm. 'Not that water. *This* water.' He tilted his lantern to illuminate what lay below.

Nina joined him, looking down, and saw that the rift was flooded. The surface some thirty feet below shimmered gently, suggesting that it was being gradually filled by meltwater flowing through faults in the surrounding rock. The coating of gold stopped abruptly around five feet above the rippling pool.

'Okay,' she said, admitting defeat at any attempt to understand what she was seeing. 'What *is* this place? You say the Midas Cave turns mercury into gold, but how? How is that possible? You've got a pool of water, and some sort of weird crystal from Atlantis – how can that possibly have made all . . . all *this*?' She waved her hands to encompass the golden walls.

'The answer is simple, Dr Wilde,' said the old man. 'You are standing inside a nuclear reactor.'

At first Nina did not respond, unsure if she had heard him correctly. Eddie, on the other hand, jumped as if he had received an electric shock, clapping both hands protectively over his groin. 'A nuclear fucking *what*?' he yelped.

'Okay, that was definitely swearing,' said his wife.

'Yeah, and it was fucking justified!'

'It is a natural reactor,' Amaanat went on. 'There are uranium deposits in the rocks below.' He pointed. Veins of grey metal ran through the stone beneath the golden line. 'Now, they are safe. But as the water rises, it acts as a . . . neutron moderator.' His hesitation suggested he was familiar with the process, but had never explained it in English before. 'This brings the uranium to critical mass and starts a nuclear reaction. It becomes so hot, the water boils away – very quickly.'

'So you get that big blast of steam,' said Eddie.

'Yes. Once the water is gone, the reaction stops. Until the pool fills again, and another begins. The cycle takes fifty-eight minutes.'

Nina searched her memory. 'There was a natural reactor somewhere in Africa. I remember reading about it . . .'

'At Oklo, in Gabon,' the monk told her. 'It was discovered when the atomic authorities thought fissile uranium had been stolen from a mine, because there was less of it than there should have been. But the natural reactor had burned it up more quickly. That one died a long time ago when the fissile uranium decayed, millions of years. But this,' he gestured into the pit, 'is still alive. And it is used with the Crucible to make gold.'

'So there must have been another reactor in Atlantis!' The disparate fragments of information she had discovered suddenly came together. 'The furnace! That's what Talonor was searching for, the reason the Atlanteans sent him out to explore the world. They had their own literal gold factory, but it was running out of juice.' Excitement filled her voice at the realisation. 'Gold was at the heart of their civilisation – it was a symbol of their power, a way for them to show how rich they were compared to their rivals. But they didn't mine it, or plunder it. They *made* it. And when they realised they wouldn't be able to keep doing that, they needed to find a new reactor.'

'And they came all the way out here to find it?' Eddie said. 'They must have been pretty determined. Or desperate.'

'Everything Talonor learned came in useful when the empire's last survivors settled in the Himalayas, though.' The sound of a monk unscrewing the lid of a container in response to a command from the impatient Rudra caught her attention. 'Oh. Hint taken!'

She and Eddie donned masks as the monk removed the top. Lantern light glinted off a new kind of elemental metal: liquid mercury. Two other men held the Crucible firmly in place as he carried the heavy can to it.

Rudra placed a funnel inside the crystalline sphere. The quicksilver was carefully poured in, filling about a fifth of the Crucible. The empty canister was removed and the next brought. 'Does *all* of that turn to gold?' Nina asked, scepticism rising again. If it did, that meant the monks could produce *pounds* of the metal at a time, worth tens or even hundreds of thousands of dollars. Mercury was not cheap in such quantities, but even a few ounces of gold would more than cover the cost.

'No,' said Amaanat. 'There is a certain isotope of mercury found naturally in the whole. It is only a small part, but this is what is transformed.'

'How?' Eddie asked. 'This all sounds like magic – or, you know, legend. Midas touching stuff and it turns into gold.'

'A process called nuclear transmutation,' explained the abbot.

'One atom can be changed to another, and mercury is next to gold on the periodic table. Scientists discovered this could be done in a nuclear reactor in the 1940s, but the Atlanteans knew the secret of creating gold in a *natural* reactor many centuries before.'

'I bet when you became a monk you didn't think you'd end up studying nuclear physics, did you?' said the Englishman wryly.

Amaanat smiled. 'No. I became a monk to atone for a violent life.' He turned his head, the lamplight picking out the ragged scar down his face. 'I have learned much since then – but not everything. I am still a mere monk, not a scientist. My studies of the intangible are on a spiritual plane, not the subatomic.'

The strange geode was now over half full, the last canister of mercury being brought to it. 'How does it work?' said Nina. 'It looks like you're going to lower the thing into the water, then pull it out filled with gold. It can't be that simple.'

Rudra laughed. 'But it is!'

'We do lower it into the water,' said Amaanat. 'But that would not transform mercury into gold without the Crucible. It somehow traps and reflects the neutrons created by the chain reaction, and increases the chance that they will transform an atom of mercury.'

She shook her head. 'I still have trouble believing it.'

The last can was emptied. 'You soon will not have to believe,' Amaanat told her as he gazed into the chasm once more. 'You will *know*. Look.'

Something had changed below. The light in the cave was different, gradually brightening. It was not the stark white of the lanterns' LEDs, but a deep cyan. Nina peered over the edge – and was startled to see a glow coming from beneath the water's surface. The walls themselves seemed to be alight.

Eddie joined her, only to hurriedly retreat, shielding his crotch again. 'That's bloody radiation!'

'It cannot hurt you,' Amaanat said calmly, watching as the strange luminescence slowly intensified. 'Not yet. It is Cherenkov radiation, coming from the uranium as it reaches critical mass, but it is not strong enough to get through the water.'

'So when *will* it hurt us?' the Yorkshireman demanded.

'We still have time to leave the cave, do not worry.' The monks slung the rope through the pulley on the tripod, then tied one end to the Crucible's handle. With one man steadying the vessel, the others hauled on the line. The stand creaked as it took the weight of the mercury-filled sphere, but held. The Crucible was lowered slowly to just beneath the cut-off line of the gold on the walls, and the rope secured to hold it in place.

The water level was now not far below it, the eerie light strong enough to illuminate the whole cave. Nina saw for the first time that there was another passage to one side. 'Now we must leave,' said Amaanat.

'See you at the top,' Eddie told him, taking his wife's hand and leading her briskly towards the exit.

'Why the rush?' she asked. 'The monks aren't worried about it.'

'Maybe, but they're monks.'

'And?'

'They're not generally known for wanting kids!'

'You want another kid?' she asked, surprised.

'Not right now, but it'd be nice to have the option. If we don't get out of here, our bits'll end up glowing green!'

'I'm fairly sure our second kid won't be the Hulk,' she said, teasing, as they rounded the twist in the passage and saw daylight ahead.

A figure stood at the entrance: Jayesh. 'Where are the others?' he asked.

'On their way,' Nina told him. 'You might want to move back, though. That big steam blast? There'll be another one in a few minutes.' The taciturn Nepali's eyebrows twitched, and he followed them clear.

The monks emerged soon afterwards. 'Four minutes,' warned Amaanat as he joined the visitors. 'When it is safe to go back inside, you will see that I have spoken the truth.'

Time passed with infuriating slowness. Eventually the low rumbling began again. The hissing of subterranean steam grew steadily louder – until another vaporous eruption burst from the cave mouth, a second, smaller jet again gushing from the opening on the lower ledge. The rising plumes were quickly swept away by the wind.

Rudra retrieved the hazmat suit and Geiger counter from the hut. His safety check was soon completed, and he waved the onlookers back to the cave. 'Now you shall see what Talonor saw,' said Amaanat. The group put their masks on again as he led the way inside.

Far down the valley, a man watched through a powerful telescope as they disappeared into the darkness. He panned it on its tripod mount to find Jayesh, still standing watch. 'So, one bodyguard,' he whispered in Greek. Another look back at the now empty opening, then he withdrew and turned around.

Two helicopters stood before him, having landed on a higher plateau over four miles from the target zone. One was an elderly Polish-built Mil Mi-2 eight-seater in bright red civilian paint-work, the other a slightly larger but much newer AgustaWestland AW169 outfitted with an external winch. Swathes of black plastic had been taped over parts of their hulls to cover tail numbers and identifying logos. He went to the second aircraft, ignoring the bored Nepalese men inside, and collected a satellite phone before returning to the telescope. Resuming his observation, he made a call.

It was soon answered. 'Yes?'

'It's Axelos.'

'Ah, Petros!' said the deep-voiced man at the other end of the line. He spoke briefly to someone in English, then returned to his native language. 'Where are you, and what have you found?'

'I paid a customs officer at Kathmandu airport to hide a tracker in Wilde and her husband's baggage. We followed them into the mountains. They've gone into a cave with the monks.' He frowned, still watching the ledge. 'I don't know what's going on inside, but it's weird. A lot of smoke or steam blew out of it.'

'You don't need to worry about that. Just secure the Crucible. How long will it take you to get into position?'

'Thirty, forty minutes – we'll need to fly behind the other mountains so they don't hear us coming, and rope down higher up so we can attack from above.'

'And will the men be up to the job?'

Axelos glanced at his companions: a collection of local mercenaries, hurriedly hired through his boss's global network of contacts. All claimed to have military experience, but the black-haired Greek had many years of his own, and could tell that none were top-tier. But they were all he had. 'It would have been better if I'd been able to use people I already knew – people I can rely on.'

'I know. But when you need to act fast, you use what you have, not what you want, yes? Okay, do it.'

'Moving out now,' Axelos said.

He was about to end the call when the other man spoke again, sounding almost saddened. 'And Petros?'

'Yes?'

'I'd prefer there to be no violence. The Crucible is what matters. But . . .' His voice became harder, filled with meaning. 'I *must* have it. Understood?'

'Understood,' Axelos replied. 'I'll call you again when it's done.'

He disconnected and returned to the helicopters, calling out their passengers and getting one of the Nepalis to translate as he addressed them in perfect English. 'All right! We're moving out. You all know what to do, so follow my lead.' He waited for the non-English-speakers to respond to the translation, then continued: 'There's a guard outside the cave, so we deal with him first. He looks Nepalese, but he's not a monk, so you shouldn't have any trouble picking him out. Then we round up everyone else.'

A mercenary, one of twin brothers whom Axelos could only tell apart by their scarves, spoke in clumsy English. 'What we do if they do trouble?'

'Use the minimum force necessary,' he replied, 'but if anyone poses a threat . . . take them out.'

Nods of agreement, with some leering smiles. The Greek concealed his disdain, instead signalling to the helicopter pilots. The Mil's was a local Nepali, the AW169's an American named Collins, another employee of Axelos's paymaster. 'Let's do this.'

The eerie cyan glow had disappeared, only lamplight reflecting off the cavern's golden walls. Wisps of steam coiled from the chasm. Nina looked down into it as the monks prepared to raise the Crucible back to floor level. The strange sphere was now suspended some distance above the surface, where the meltwater had boiled away in a furious burst.

What she could see of the mercury within the Crucible looked no different, though. Was the whole thing just some bizarre lie?

The monks strained to lift the red crystal up the shaft, gingerly pulling it on to solid ground. Rudra brought one of the empty canisters and placed the funnel into it, inserting a fine wire mesh to act as a filter. A pair of men gently tipped the Crucible, pouring out its contents.

The mercury containers had remained in the cave, and Nina noticed that their dull metal had acquired a faintly lustrous sheen. 'Is that gold?' she asked, pointing it out to Amaanat.

'Yes.'

'How? They weren't in the Crucible.'

'The mercury vapour in the air touches everything. The neutrons inside the Crucible reach such an intensity that they escape in a burst – and some of the atoms of vapour are hit and transformed into gold. It is how the walls have become like this,' he said, touching one of the subsumed wooden beams. 'Layers of gold have built up over years, over centuries.'

The first container was now filled with mercury. Rudra carefully lifted the filter from the funnel. Another monk positioned a shallow bowl beneath it as he shook the little sieve, a few tiny flecks falling through the mesh, then tipped out the larger pieces that had been caught.

Amaanat brought his lantern closer. 'You see? Gold.'

Nina leaned in. The misshapen lumps were all small, resembling loose dental fillings, but they had the undeniable yellow gleam of the precious metal. Combined, she estimated they might weigh about half an ounce, so the entire contents of the Crucible could yield perhaps four times that in total. At current prices that was still worth a few thousand dollars, but it was not the overwhelming quantities she had expected. 'There isn't much there.'

'And it could've been in the mercury when you brought it up here, for all we know,' said Eddie.

Rudra gave him an irate look, but Amaanat simply shrugged. 'Why would we lie to you? We have asked you to tell no one about this, and you have agreed. We have nothing to gain.'

'He's got a good point,' Nina was forced to admit.

'There is more in the bottom,' the abbot went on. 'Steel will float on mercury, but gold will sink. From this Crucible, we will get perhaps ten troy ounces.'

'Ten ounces is quite a lot . . .' Belatedly she registered his phrasing. 'Wait, you said *this* Crucible. There are more?'

'There is one other,' he replied. 'Talonor had this one with him when he first found this place. The second was brought when he returned.'

'Two Crucibles, double the gold,' said Eddie. 'Not bad.'

The old monk smiled at some highly amusing secret. 'What is it?' Nina asked.

'Come, see for yourself,' Amaanat told her.

As the other monks continued to pour out the mercury, he led Nina and Eddie to the side passage. The walls were still caked in gold, but once they had rounded a corner, the coating vanished, leaving nothing but bare, damp rock.

'Here,' said the monk, holding up his lamp. 'Here is the second Crucible.'

The couple's eyes widened simultaneously. 'Okay,' said Eddie, 'double the gold was a bit of an understatement.'

'You're not kidding!' Nina replied, amazed. 'This thing could fill up Fort Knox!'

The second Crucible was much like the first in form, a rough spheroid of dark red crystal with an opening carved into its top. But it was very different in size. Where the first had been the size of a basketball, this one was almost as tall as Nina, a great bulbous cauldron inside a heavy metal cage. As for how much mercury it might hold, she guessed it would measure in the hundreds of gallons.

It would not produce ounces of gold. It would produce *pounds*.

'It has not been used for many years,' said Amaanat. 'To fill it would need so much mercury that people might become suspicious. It would also need many trips up the mountain to bring the mercury here, and you have seen how dangerous that can be. But we know it has been used in the past.'

'By Talonor and the people he left here,' said Nina, nodding. She peered inside the artefact, the monk lifting his lantern to illuminate the interior. The light reflected back in a dazzling display from countless gem-like facets.

'Where do you even get all the mercury?' Eddie asked. 'It's not like you can just order it from Amazon.'

Nina answered the question for him. 'Mercury's extracted from cinnabar, which isn't that hard to find. It's been mined since the Neolithic era. There are major deposits in China and other parts of Asia – Spain, too,' she added in realisation. 'Spain would have been under Atlantis's control when the empire was at its height. That's where they got the raw mercury, and they took it back to Atlantis to turn into gold. At least, until their natural reactor decayed and ran out of power.'

'You now see why we have kept this place a secret,' said Amaanat. 'To make gold in such great quantities – some men would start wars for that. We have saved lives, kept the peace.'

'While using it for yourselves,' she observed.

'We are in a remote place, and everything we need to survive must be brought to us. It is expensive. We use the small Crucible to create enough gold to support the monastery, no more. It has allowed us to protect the Midas Cave for hundreds of years.'

'But now we know about it,' said Eddie. Nina knew why he had made the pointed statement: if the monks were going to do anything extreme to keep their secret, it would be now, after their visitors had learned the truth . . .

But Amaanat merely bowed his head. 'You could tell the whole world, if you wished,' he said. 'But I do not believe you will. You have both seen the violence that can come from greed.' He looked up again, regarding them with a gaze that went deeper than their eyes alone. 'I trust you to keep our silence.'

'We will,' Nina assured him. Eddie nodded in agreement.

The abbot smiled, then led them back into the golden cavern. The other monks were still carefully draining the smaller Crucible, filtering out more nuggets of gold. 'We should wait outside,' he said, continuing towards the exit. 'It is cold, but the air is clean.'

The couple followed him up the tunnel. Jayesh was still standing watch. 'Finished, Chase?' he asked, drawing on another cigarette.

'Yeah,' Eddie replied as he took off his mask. 'We saw what we came to see.'

Jayesh shrugged. 'Not my business. Only here to keep you out of trouble.' He gave Nina the tiniest hint of a smile. 'Hard work with him, eh?'

'Tell me about it,' she replied.

'Me?' hooted the Yorkshireman. '*She's* the disaster magnet, mate. Anywhere you take her, something's bound to blow up.'

'Not for a long time now,' she reminded him. 'And hopefully never again.'

He made a sarcastic noise. 'You remember how jinxing works, right?'

'No problems here,' said Jayesh. 'Heard a chopper, but a long way off. Nothing else out there.'

'We get few visitors,' Amaanat said. 'None go further than the monastery. Nobody comes to this place.'

'If someone wanted to climb up here, they could,' Eddie pointed out.

'But they have not.' The abbot gestured towards the more distant peaks. 'There are far higher mountains for tourists to climb.'

'The steam vents could attract attention, though,' said Nina. 'And the whole place is called Dragon Mountain, which is kind of a draw.'

'The steam cannot be seen from the valley; it is hidden by the cliffs. If you are high enough on another mountain to see it, it looks only like a cloud or blowing snow, because you are so far away. Trust me, Dr Wilde,' he said, 'people do not come here by chance. Would you have come without good reason?'

'I guess not,' she admitted.

Eddie checked the sky. It was still daylight, but the mountains to the east were becoming shadowed by higher peaks as the sun lowered. 'We'll need to start back pretty soon.'

'We will be at the monastery before it is dark,' Amaanat assured him.

Eddie nodded, then looked back at Nina. 'So. You've seen the Midas Cave – now what?'

'Now?' she replied, pondering the question before giving a reluctant reply. 'Amaanat's right: it should stay hidden. Which is frustrating, because it's an incredible find! And seeing for myself that there's truth behind the Midas myth was also amazing – maybe not just Midas,' she added. 'There are other legends along the same lines. There was an Indian called . . . Nagarjuna, I think, an ancient alchemist who supposedly found a way to produce gold from mercury. And actually, isn't there a Buddhist myth about someone who turned other metals into gold?'

'Yes, there is,' replied Amaanat. 'He was also called Nagarjuna. They are not the same man, though. They lived many centuries apart.'

'So if you want your son to grow up to be an alchemist, that's a good name for him,' said Eddie.

Nina glanced back at the cave as the masked Rudra emerged, carrying the small Crucible. The other monks, bearing their own cargoes, filed out behind him. 'You know, a lot of the stories about alchemy involve mercury. And the Philosopher's Stone was used to create gold.'

'The one Harry Potter was after?'

'Not quite. But in mythology, it's often described as being reddish in colour, like the Crucibles. I suppose in a way they *are* the Philosopher's Stones – they literally do transform another element into gold. It's just that it's mercury, not lead. But you know something?' she proclaimed. 'It doesn't matter that I can't tell anyone what we found. Because that's not why I came here. I came to complete my mom's work, to see if she was right. And she was.'

'Yeah, she was,' said Eddie, putting his arms around her. 'But so were you. You were the one who actually put all the pieces together.' He kissed her, drawing disapproving looks from some of the monks, though their leader smiled. 'So how do you feel?'

'I feel . . . happy,' she told him. 'Sad in a way, because Mom couldn't be here. But . . . I finished what she started. I saw something incredible – I found that another ancient legend is actually true! I didn't just do what I came here to do, I did more than that. So, yeah. Happy.'

'If you're happy, I'm happy,' he said, with a broad grin. 'So we're done here?'

'We're done.'

'And we can go back home to our little girl?'

She grinned. 'Yeah, we can. God, I hope she hasn't missed us too much.'

'She'll probably have had such a good time with Holly that she'll have forgotten who we are.'

'That's what I'm worried about!' Nina addressed Amaanat. 'Thank you. Thank you so much for letting me see this.'

'It was my honour,' replied the elderly monk. 'And I know that our secret will be safe with you. We all do. Is that not true, Rudra?' The younger man, who was re-wrapping the Crucible, still appeared dubious but agreed reluctantly. 'Good. Then we shall . . .'

He trailed off, seeing the other monks looking around in confusion. A noise became audible, a thudding chop echoing from the surrounding mountains.

Growing louder.

Jayesh threw away his cigarette and snatched out his gun. 'Helicopter!' he warned—

Another sound, a flat clatter of boots on rock – and a man leapt down from above the cave mouth to slam the Gurkha to the cold ground.

An automatic weapon crackled, a three-round burst of bullets smacking into the snow at Eddie and Nina's feet. They looked up – to see that the gun was now locked on to them.

12

Ropes uncoiled and dropped snake-like to the ledge. Eleven more men abseiled down them, unslinging Kalashnikovs. A startled monk raised a hand as if to ward them off – only to earn himself a harsh blow from the butt of an attacker's rifle. He fell, clutching his bleeding temple. The mercury canister he had been holding rolled over the cliff to land heavily on the lower ledge.

The staccato pounding of the helicopter's rotors became a roar as the aircraft rounded the mountain, an Mi-2 sweeping past before banking away. A second, larger aircraft lumbered over a ridge on the mountainside above, then dropped into the valley to follow it.

'What the *hell*?' Nina gasped, raising her hands. The attackers appeared to be Nepalese, ranging from their early twenties to late thirties. Several wore equipment webbing bearing grenades.

Eddie was paying more attention to their firearms. All were Kalashnikov variants, but of several different types – ageing AK-47s, the marginally more modern AKM, a single AK-74, a Chinese-made clone, even one that he couldn't identify specifically but which was probably a knock-off from India or North Korea. That told him the intruders were mercenaries, but not an established group; they would otherwise have obtained their weapons from a single source, and made sure they could use the same ammunition. The AK-74's user would be stuck if he ran out of bullets, as his rifle used a smaller-calibre ammo than the others.

If they weren't used to working as a team, that could be to his advantage . . .

Not yet, though. They had their prisoners covered. 'Jayesh! You okay?' he called as he brought up his own hands in surrender.

The Gurkha groaned as two mercs dragged him to his feet. Another collected his pistol. 'Yeah. But lost my gun.'

Amaanat called out in Nepalese: a plea for there to be no more violence. Rudra appeared about to defy him, but a much sharper instruction from the abbot forced him to abandon any retaliation. The attackers rounded everyone up to stand near the cave mouth.

The man who had fired at Nina and Eddie quickly and expertly roped down from his perch. He was wearing new, expensive cold-weather gear and carrying a compact FN P90 sub-machine gun that looked as fresh from the box as his clothing. The newcomer pulled a scarf from his face to reveal olive-skinned Caucasian features. 'You are Nina Wilde,' he said to the American. It was not a question; he had known that he would find her here.

'Yeah,' she replied, cautious. 'And you are?'

He did not reply, instead giving Eddie an appraising look before issuing an order. 'Search him. And him,' he added, indicating Jayesh.

Both were rapidly patted down. 'No gun,' one man reported, stepping back. Eddie and his friend exchanged the briefest of knowing glances . . . but then the mercenary frowned, feeling a crease on the back of Jayesh's coat. He shoved the Gurkha on to his front and yanked the kukri from its concealed scabbard. Another man gave it an admiring look, then took the blade and slid it into his own belt.

'How did you know I was here?' Nina demanded, trying to conceal her rising fear.

'We watched you through a telescope,' the man replied. His accent was Greek.

'I meant here in Nepal.' Again he did not answer.

'What do you want of us?' asked Amaanat, head bowed in supplication.

'I want the Crucible,' the Greek told him.

Nina was shocked – how could he possibly know about it? – but Rudra's response was outrage, aimed not at the intruders but at her. 'You told them!' he yelled. 'You betray us!'

A gunman clubbed the monk with his rifle and sent him sprawling into the snow. 'You do not need to hurt anyone!' protested the abbot. 'We will not resist you.'

'Very wise,' said the Greek. He watched as Rudra rose painfully to his knees, then turned back to Nina. 'The Crucible. Where is it?'

'I don't know what you're talking about,' she said.

'No?' He brought up the P90 – and aimed it at Eddie's chest. 'Does this help you remember?'

'Please!' cried Amaanat. 'We do not want violence.'

'Then where is the Crucible?'

The old man sagged in defeat. 'There.' He pointed at the cloth-wrapped object. Rudra objected, but another rifle blow knocked him back to the ground.

One of the mercenaries collected the Crucible and brought it to his leader, who carefully peeled away the protective layers, reacting with a confirmatory nod when he saw what was inside. 'He knew what to expect,' Nina whispered to Eddie.

'Hmm?'

'The Crucible. He already knew what it looked like before he saw it. He had more information about it than I did.'

'Not enough to find it without you,' he replied.

The Crucible was covered once more. The Greek turned to Amaanat. 'And the *second* Crucible? The big one?'

It was the abbot's turn to be taken aback. 'How could you know about that?'

'Just tell me where it is.'

Rudra's only objection this time was a look of despair. Amaanat hesitated, then indicated the cave. 'Inside. There is a passage at the back.'

The Greek nodded. 'We will search it,' he said to two of his men, before ordering the rest to watch the captives. The crystal vessel was carefully placed on the ground, then the little group entered the tunnel. To Nina's shock, the Greek had a Geiger counter of his own. Not only did he know about the Crucible; he was also aware of the nature of the Midas Cave itself.

'What're we gonna do?' she hissed.

Eddie eyed the remaining gunmen. They didn't appear a particularly close-knit team, and he could tell from the way some held their fingers on their guns' triggers even when there was no immediate threat that their training was basic at best. Jayesh had reached the same conclusion, his eyes flicking towards the man nearest to him. The Yorkshireman at once saw why; the merc was so inattentive or amateurish that he had unwittingly pointed his AK-74 at one of his comrades as he turned to watch the Greek depart. 'We've got a chance, but we'll need a distraction,' he whispered.

'Anything in mind?'

Both helicopters were now flying a broad, lazy orbit above the valley. Eddie watched the larger one, confirming a detail he had glimpsed earlier, then brought his attention back to the guards. 'Yeah, but there's nothing we can do right now. If they come to get the big Crucible, though . . .' Nina had no idea what he meant, but a scowl and jab of the gun from a guard when he realised they were talking deterred her from asking any further questions.

After a few minutes, the Greek and his companions returned. Their wide eyes proved that they had found the cave's golden secret. The leader took out a walkie-talkie as the two Nepalis excitedly told the others what they had seen. 'Collins, we will definitely need the winch. Is this ledge wide enough for you to land?'

'Negative,' came the crackling reply, in an American accent. 'We'll have to hover to lift anything off there, and even then it'll be tight.'

The Greek pursed his lips in annoyance. 'Okay. I'll call you when we're ready.' He put away the radio, then took out another transmitter: a satellite phone. The call was answered almost immediately. A brief discussion, in Greek – the mercenary leader identified himself to the other party as 'Axelos' – then he addressed his men. 'There's a large crystal in the cave. We need to bring it out here so it can be winched up.' He waited for the translation, then continued: 'It will be heavy, and it needs to be moved very carefully. You, stand guard.' He pointed to four of the mercenaries, including the amateur near Jayesh. 'The rest come with me to move it. Anything else in there you can keep, but both Crucibles are mine.'

That last brought greedy excitement from the Nepalis, some casting unpleasant glances at the prisoners – already thinking about permanently ensuring their silence, Nina was sure. The foursome spread out to keep the monks and their companions covered as their comrades disappeared into the cave. 'You told them about the Crucibles,' Rudra growled at Nina as he got to his knees.

'How?' she protested. 'I didn't even know what they were until Amaanat showed me.' The guard glowered at her again, but did not try to silence her. 'And I definitely didn't know there were two of them! Someone else did, though.'

'That cannot be,' said Amaanat. 'The only outsiders who have ever seen the Midas Cave were Tobias Garde and his companions.'

'Then someone connected to his companions talked.' It occurred to her that in her desire to finish her mother's work, she had overlooked a question she should have asked her grandmother: who else had been with Tobias?

But that would have to wait until she got back to New York – if she ever did. The more pressing question was: what were they going to do now?

'If they try to airlift the big Crucible out of here,' Eddie said quietly, 'they'll have a job getting close enough to drop a winch line.' He glanced at the near-vertical rock face above the ledge. 'When they actually pick it up, that's when we'll get our chance.'

'To do what?'

Eddie didn't reply, instead looking at Jayesh. The Nepali slowly rubbed his coat as if scratching an itch in his lower back. Eddie nodded.

'Uh, okay,' said Nina, surprised. The two former soldiers had somehow shared a plan without needing to speak.

'There should be no violence,' said Amaanat, but with resignation. 'We do not need to—'

One of the guards barked at him in Nepalese. The abbot fell silent. Rudra gave the man a hostile glare, but did nothing.

Ten minutes passed before Axelos and the other mercenaries returned, straining to carry the larger Crucible by its metal cage. The Greek leading the way, they brought it almost to the edge of the flat ground before putting it down with relief.

'We have the Crucible,' Axelos said into the walkie-talkie. 'Move in to collect it.'

The larger helicopter approached. The other aircraft held a watching brief, though close enough to show that there was another man in the cabin as well as the pilot. The AW169 carefully slowed to a hover thirty metres out from the ledge, then edged closer.

The rotor downwash blasted a biting whirlwind of snow from

the ground. Some of the mercenaries shielded their eyes. Jayesh gave Eddie a meaningful look, but the Englishman shook his head almost imperceptibly: *not yet*. The guards were still watching their prisoners, weapons at the ready.

Nina realised that the chopper could not get close enough. The rotors were perilously near to the rock wall above, and she knew from experience that helicopters could become extremely unstable if they were hit by displaced air bouncing off a solid surface. The pilot quickly reached the same conclusion. The AW169 pulled back. A few seconds later, Axelos's radio crackled. 'I can't get any nearer. It's too dangerous.'

The Greek was not pleased. 'We *have* to take the Crucible. Can you lower the cable and swing it to us?'

The pilot sounded incredulous at the suggestion. 'If you want to risk being hit by it, sure.'

'Do it.'

'Okay, your decision . . .'

The helicopter's side door slid open and a man leaned out, operating the winch controls. A steel cable with a large hook on the end was slowly lowered towards the ledge. As it drew closer, the pilot began to rock his aircraft gently from side to side. The heavy hook swung like a pendulum, each sweep wider than the last.

'Get ready to catch it!' Axelos ordered. As his men moved hesitantly towards the hanging line, the guards watched the spectacle unfold, distracted from their charges.

Eddie tensed, preparing to act. Jayesh brought his hand towards the hem of his coat . . .

The Greek added, 'And watch them!' He pointed at the prisoners. The Gurkha's hand retreated as the four men returned their attention to their assignment. The Englishman muttered a curse.

Another swing, and the hook scuffed through the snow close

to the Crucible. The winch operator shouted to the pilot as Axelos's men hurried to grab it. The helicopter dropped a couple of metres, the line going slack, and the hook came to rest. The mercenaries surrounded it like hounds on a wounded animal. More cable played out, then the aircraft cautiously drew away from the mountainside.

Axelos slapped a hand on top of the Crucible's metal cage. 'Fix it here.'

The Nepalis attached the hook to the loop running over the top of the great crystalline sphere and locked a carabiner clip into place. Axelos tested that it was secure. 'It's ready,' he said into the radio. 'Take it up!'

'Get set,' Eddie whispered. Jayesh nodded; Nina took a deep, nervous breath, unsure what was about to happen but psyching herself up to react when it did.

Her gaze met Amaanat's. He too knew that the two ex-soldiers were about to take action, and was silently begging her to stop them. But she couldn't. While Axelos seemed interested only in the Crucibles, his men were now filled with a lust for the gold in the cave. There was no way they would let their prisoners live.

The old monk realised that violence was inevitable. For a moment Nina thought he was about to warn their captors . . . but then he gave her a look of almost infinite sadness, bowing his head and placing his palms together in silent prayer.

The pilot increased power. The helicopter slowly ascended, drawing the cable with it until it was almost taut. Axelos signalled to the winch operator, who worked the controls.

A shrill metallic *twang* came from the steel cable as it pulled tight. The Crucible lurched, slithering a few inches closer to the edge. The mercs hurriedly moved clear as the straining line vibrated like a plucked guitar string. If it snapped, the lashing end could easily decapitate someone.

Another look passed between Eddie and Jayesh. Their one chance was almost here . . .

Engines roaring, the helicopter tried to climb. The Crucible shifted again, rocking precariously on the cliff edge. The cable creaked, the ancient metal cage enclosing the strange artefact juddering under the stress, then the great sphere slithered off the ledge.

And swung outwards.

The helicopter was yanked down by the extra weight – but with the winch arm extending out from its port side, it also rolled unbalanced to the left.

Towards the mountain.

Those on the ledge reacted with sudden fear as the chopper veered at the cliff above them. The pilot frantically counteracted the movement, climbing and banking hard to starboard. But momentum was still carrying it closer to the looming rocks, closer—

The rotors came within inches of the cliff . . . then retreated. The Crucible swinging wildly beneath it, the AW169 lurched clear, its downwash blasting a hail of gritty debris over the ledge.

The mercenaries shielded their heads—

Eddie and Jayesh burst into action.

The Gurkha whipped both hands under the back of his coat. His kukri had been taken from him – but it was not the only blade in the scabbard. There were also two much smaller knives, a *karda* and a *chakmak*, used to hone the kukri itself to perfect sharpness. Yet they were still weapons in their own right – as Jayesh proved by stabbing them deep into each side of the neck of the inattentive guard.

The man let out a choked cry, spitting blood. Another mercenary whirled and fired, only for his comrade to take the bullet to his chest as Jayesh hauled his prey around as a human shield.

The dead man's Kalashnikov fell from his hands. 'Nina, *go!*' Eddie yelled as he dived for it. He caught the weapon, rolling on landing and firing back at the attacker.

The AK-74 spat out a stream of bullets. The rifle's fire selector was set to full auto, catching the Englishman by surprise; he hadn't considered that the merc might actually be as amateurish as he had appeared. But the rounds still hit home, ripping a bloody swathe across his target's torso.

Pandemonium erupted. The monks scattered, some running for cover amongst the boulders, others throwing themselves flat. A mercenary barged Amaanat aside, aiming at Eddie—

The abbot whirled – and drove the heel of his palm hard into the man's face, breaking his nose with a wet crack.

Another merc flinched in sympathetic shock and raised his AKM, only for a lightning-fast sweep of the old man's other arm to knock it out of his hands. But a third mercenary charged Amaanat like a bull, tackling him brutally into the snow.

Nina had followed Eddie's instruction and taken off at a run. But she did not head for the cover of the rocks – rather, towards the cloth-wrapped Crucible.

Rudra sprang up to follow her, the anger in his eyes directed as much at the redhead as the intruders.

Eddie jumped upright, searching for new targets amidst the chaos. He found them – but some of the fleeing monks were in his line of fire, freezing the Yorkshireman's finger on the trigger. 'Jayesh!' he yelled instead, racing for the rocks near the ladder.

The Gurkha started after him, bullets searing past—

One clipped his thigh. The wound was only shallow, but it was enough to make him fall. The shooter prepared to finish the job . . .

Eddie switched the selector to burst-fire mode as he scrambled behind a rock, sending a rapid three rounds at the gunman. None hit, but they served their purpose, drawing the mercenaries' attention away from his friend.

And towards him.

Ragged splinters of stone exploded from his cover as the gunmen opened fire. He pulled back behind it and glanced around the other side, trying to locate his wife.

Nina had been ignored in the mayhem, scurrying past the mercenaries as they regrouped. She grabbed the Crucible. The geode was heavier than it looked.

Now she searched for cover. The hut, or the cave? The latter would offer more protection, but the next burst of steam from the natural reactor couldn't be far off. If she went inside, she would be broiled – or irradiated.

The hut. She started for it—

Someone grabbed her from behind. She gasped and spun – to find Rudra trying to claw the Crucible from her grip. 'You cannot take it!' he roared.

'I'm trying to *save* it!' she cried. 'We can't let them steal it!'

He wrested the shrouded sphere free. 'You did this!' he screamed as he shoved her away. 'You brought them here!'

'I didn't—'

She stopped abruptly. Axelos had heard the altercation and realised they had the Crucible. 'There!' he yelled, pointing. 'Get them, stop them!' A mercenary took aim. 'No!' the Greek cried. 'You'll hit the—'

The man fired. Rudra took a burst of bullets to his upper chest and head. Nina screamed, feeling hot liquid splash her cheek as he fell. The Crucible thudded into the red-speckled snow.

The gunman watched with a satisfied leer as the monk crumpled, then switched targets to the American—

His own skull blew apart as three tightly spaced bullets from Eddie's rifle struck home.

Axelos ducked and scuttled behind a boulder. He shot a look at the Crucible, but dealing with the Englishman now took priority. 'Flank him!' he shouted. 'Spread out and go after him from both sides!'

'Eddie, they're coming for you!' Nina cried as she checked on Rudra. The young man was dead, a hamburger-sized hole in the side of his shaven head oozing disgustingly into the snow. Horrified, she retrieved the Crucible and hurried for the hut.

Eddie heard Nina's warning. He peeked around the rock to locate his enemies, but was forced to jerk back as a fusillade of bullets pockmarked the stone. The brief glimpse had revealed two of the mercenaries, but the flat chatter of Kalashnikovs warned him there were more closing on his position.

He switched the selector to single-shot – every bullet had to count now – and hurriedly checked his surroundings. More boulders poked from the snow behind him. He could dart between them for cover, but he would rapidly run out of man-oeuvring room. The ledge thinned to nothingness against the cliff face about sixty feet away. The mercenaries would quickly pin him down.

He had to move, though. Flinders burst inches from his head as one of the attackers came around to his left. A few more seconds and he would be exposed.

Only one way out. He fired a shot to force the man back – then sprinted for the ladder.

His rush caught the mercenaries by surprise. More bullets cracked past, but he was already weaving between the last few rocks. A glance back: Nina was almost at the hut. He didn't know how he was going to help her, but even a few seconds out of the line of fire would give him time to think up a plan.

The valley opened out before him as he reached the edge. He jumped, twisting in mid-air to grab the ladder's top rung as he dropped past it—

His right hand snagged the corroded metal – but the other slid off the icy surface. He swung around . . . and lost his grip.

The rungs whipped past him. He clawed desperately at them, fleetingly catching one, but the coating of ice splintered into nothingness in his grasp—

Impact.

Pain exploded through his legs as he hit the lower ledge. But the momentary pause in his descent had slowed him just enough to save him from a broken bone.

He was not safe, though. A shout came from above. One of the Nepali mercenaries peered over the top of the ladder, and saw him.

Eddie rolled to flatten himself against the cliff face as several bullets smacked against the ground behind him. His own gun had landed in the snow at the ladder's foot, but trying to recover it would get him shot. Instead he scrambled into the snowless crevice containing the steam vent. More rounds impacted on the bare stone, but there was just enough of an overhang to shield him from gunfire from above.

A low noise warned him of another danger, however. A deep grumbling sound came from the vent, slowly rising in intensity.

The cave was about to blow.

13

Eddie knew that if stayed where he was, he would either be scalded by radioactive steam or blasted off the ledge. He had to move.

The shelter—

It wasn't much, but it was his only option. He hopped over the fallen mercury canister and ran through the thick snow to the little wooden lean-to.

He pulled the door, but it didn't move. Frozen. He kicked at it, trying to crack the encrusted ice – then some sixth sense made him glance up. Another merc was leaning over the higher ledge, fixing him in his sights.

Eddie threw himself back against the cliff as a ragged bullet hole burst in the door. He looked up again, but a bulge in the cliff face now blocked the gunman from view. Safe, for the moment, but he couldn't go any further without becoming a target.

He edged sideways, back to the crevice, only to see steam drifting out from the vent. No way forward, no way back: he was trapped.

And a change in the engine note of one of the helicopters warned him of a new danger.

'He's on the ledge below us,' Axelos told the Mil's pilot over the radio. 'Move to a position where you can see him, then take him out.' He listened with growing annoyance to the reluctant reply, the chopper's pilot – and owner – not wanting to put himself or his aircraft in harm's way. 'Why do you think the man with you has a sniper rifle? Do it!'

The Mi-2 descended towards the mountain. Axelos switched his gaze to the AW169. The Crucible was still suspended beneath the larger helicopter, its pendulous swing finally slowing.

One prize was secured. But that still left the other. His boss had been very clear about wanting both.

He turned back to the cave. The smaller Crucible had gone.

The sight of the little hut's door closing told him where the redhead had taken it. 'You two!' he called to the nearest of his men. 'The woman's in there – get her!'

The cramped shack offered no place for Nina to hide. Shelves held the equipment the monks needed to make use of the Midas Cave, but nothing more. It wasn't even properly weatherproofed, with wide gaps between some of the planks.

And through one, she glimpsed two mercenaries hurrying towards her.

'Shit!' she gasped, searching for anything she could use as a weapon. There was nothing.

All she could do was run, but there was nowhere to go—

The stacked items started rattling against each other. Even over the noise of the helicopters, she heard the rising rumble from within the mountain.

Nowhere to go, but somewhere to go *past* . . .

Clutching the Crucible, Nina burst back outside. The tunnel was filling with vapour, the sound of the impending steam blast still growing. She looked back as she ran towards it.

The mercs were gaining.

Eddie saw the Mil's cabin door open as the helicopter swept down to hover a hundred feet from the ledge. A man leaned out.

The Englishman instantly recognised his weapon as a Russian

Dragunov sniper rifle, or a Chinese copy of one. His only chance of survival was to keep moving, and hope the chopper was unsteady enough in the shifting wind to affect the mercenary's aim—

Muzzle flash. Eddie had already darted sideways, the bullet smacking like a hammer against the rock right beside him. The rifle tracked him. This time the Yorkshireman dropped to the ground as the next round impacted where he had been standing. The mercury canister was only a few feet away; some instinct prompted him to grab it as he rolled to dodge a third shot. He wasn't even sure why – it wasn't as if he could throw it at the helicopter . . .

Not throw. *Shoot.*

He sprang up and dived into the crevice. Steam roiled from the vent, the angry hiss of pent-up pressure growing ever louder. A round shrilled off the rock face, but the crack in the cliff was just deep enough to block him from the helicopter's view. He jammed the container as far as he could into the opening, then turned and crouched, waiting.

The Mil returned, hovering directly in front of the crevice. It was close enough for Eddie to see the frustration on the sniper's face – which changed to sneering pleasure as he took aim again. He hadn't expected his prey to be so hard to hit, but now there was nowhere else for him to go . . .

Nina kept running, but the snow was like the ground in a nightmare, bogging down each step. Another look back. The two mercenaries were at the cave mouth, guns rising—

The rumble became a roar – and a searing blast of steam consumed them.

Eddie dropped flat as the thunderous noise reached a crescendo, tugging up his hood and burying his face in the snow to protect himself. 'Start the reactor!' he yelled.

With the vent plugged, the first jets of superheated steam gushed out around the mercury container with the shriek of a hellish kettle – but then the pressure became too much and the blockage was blasted clear.

It shot over the Englishman like a cannon shell – straight at the helicopter.

The pilot didn't even have time to scream before it punched through his window and hit him. The impact left little of his skull intact, the gory spray of blood and pulp mixed with shimmering quicksilver as the canister burst open. His body slumped, foot spasming on the rudder pedal – throwing the Mi-2 into a spin.

The sniper had unfastened his lap belt for greater freedom of movement, but now he was granted the ultimate freedom as he was thrown from the open door. His terrified shriek echoed off the uncaring wall of rock as he fell to the ground far below.

The helicopter kept whirling, reeling drunkenly towards the higher ledge . . .

The thunder of steam escaping the cave faded, the billowing cloud wafting upwards to reveal the two mercenaries writhing on the ground. Their faces had been scoured red-raw, horrifyingly blistered, with strips of skin hanging off as if they had been flayed alive. Airways seared shut, they couldn't even cry out in their agony. Nina felt a pang of appalled pity, even knowing that they had been about to kill her.

The venting steam had caught the other attackers by surprise. Most had dived to the ground in panic, one man on the fringe of the blast howling in pain at a burn to his cheek.

She looked around for Eddie – and instead saw the helicopter careering towards the ledge.

A moment of shocked paralysis – then, still clutching the Crucible, she ran for the ladder. Some of the stunned mercenaries reacted as she passed, only for any thoughts of shooting her to vanish in favour of self-preservation at the sight of the spiralling aircraft. Mercs and monks alike scattered.

The shrill of the Mi-2's engine grew louder. The chopper plunged towards Nina as if drawn by a magnet—

She screamed and dived as it swept over her, blowing up a blinding swirl of snow in its downdraught before its rotor blades hit the unyielding cliff face. The impact flung the helicopter around, slamming it hard against the cave entrance. The fuselage was smashed flat, fuel tanks rupturing—

The aircraft exploded, scattering burning debris across the ledge. One mercenary was impaled through the torso by a javelin-sized shard of rotor blade. The ageing wooden beams inside the tunnel were blasted apart, the ceiling collapsing with a pounding *boom* of falling rock.

Burning shrapnel struck Nina's shoulder. She cried out, rolling over to extinguish the flames. Her coat was torn and singed, but the pain was more from the blow than the fire.

She recovered the Crucible and sat up to see the Gurkha nearby, his guards sprawled around him. 'Jayesh!' she called. She was about to tell him to head for the ladder, but he was already moving, launching himself at the nearest dazed mercenary and cracking an elbow down on the back of his head with brutal force. The man slumped into the snow. Jayesh pulled his kukri from the merc's belt and turned towards Nina – then suddenly hurled the blade.

It whooshed just inches above her head. Before she could even be shocked, she heard a solid *chut* and a truncated scream from behind. Whirling, she saw the gunman at the top of the ladder facing her, his AK dropping from numbed hands as blood pulsed from the machete embedded in his throat. He collapsed, twitching.

'Go! Go down!' Jayesh ordered, before yelling more

commands in Nepalese. Amaanat hurried to the cliff edge and called for his fellows to follow him.

Nina held the crystal in the crook of one arm and rapidly descended the ladder, to her immense relief finding a familiar face waiting below. 'Eddie! Oh, thank God!'

He saw the rip in her coat. 'Are you all right?'

'It's nothing. What happened to the helicopter?'

'Things got a bit steamy. Come on, we need to move before they come after us.' He picked up the Kalashnikov from the snow as the monks came down the ladder.

'No bullets?' said Nina at his grimace when he checked the magazine.

'Not enough. Is Jayesh okay?' Single-shot cracks from an AK at the top of the ladder gave him an answer. 'Yep, he is. Jayesh! We're going!'

'So don't wait – shift your arse!' the Nepali called back.

'I guess he picked up some English slang in training,' said Nina as Eddie led her to the first of the wooden platforms.

'Not the only thing he picked up, the dirty sod,' the Yorkshireman said with a half-grin, before becoming completely serious. 'We'll have to go a lot faster than we did coming up.' He looked back. Amaanat was now descending, Jayesh crouching above ready to come after him. Eddie aimed his rifle at the upper ledge. 'Get going, I'll cover you. If anyone pokes their head over the top, they'll regret it.' Nina nodded and started along the walkway.

Jayesh fired a last couple of rounds, then shouldered his gun and yanked his kukri from the corpse's throat to slot it effortlessly into its scabbard. He scuttled down the ladder after the abbot. A mercenary appeared at its top, only to hurriedly retreat as Eddie shot at him. As soon as Amaanat cleared the foot of the rungs, the Gurkha let go and dropped to the ledge.

Nina moved as fast as she dared along the platforms. They

had been precarious enough on the way up; now they felt little wider than a shoelace. Holding the Crucible under her left arm, she clutched at the rock with her free hand, desperately seeking out any holds.

A look back. Axelos peered from the higher ledge, but the Greek was careful not to expose himself to fire from Eddie or Jayesh.

He could see her, though. A rush of fear went through Nina as he took aim, then thought better of it. 'Eddie!' she called. 'They aren't shooting at me – they don't want to risk losing the Crucible!'

'Doesn't help the rest of us,' he countered. The monks lined up behind him at the end of the ledge, Jayesh at the rear. 'Okay, I'll go first so I can cover you when I reach the next ladder,' he told them. 'Jayesh, watch my back.'

'They have what they came for,' said Amaanat as the procession started along the platforms. 'There is no need for more violence!'

'They still want the other Crucible,' Eddie replied. He checked behind him, to see a mercenary aiming at the pathway. He fired a single shot, driving him back – but too late. The man had already pulled the trigger. A ragged bullet wound tore open in the shoulder of the monk following the Englishman. He wailed, staggering . . . and one foot slipped over the plank's edge. He tumbled down the mountainside, his petrified cry fading to nothingness.

Eddie watched him fall, helpless, then snapped his attention back to the clifftop. He still had five monks to protect as well as Nina. All too aware of the alarming creaks of complaint from the weather-worn wood beneath his boots, he increased his pace.

Nina reached the next ledge and found cover behind a small outcrop. Relieved, she leaned out to check on the others. Eddie was moving across the platforms at a pace that made her heart freeze, the monks filing along in his wake.

Axelos reappeared, a mercenary beside him—

'Eddie, look out!' she warned. Her husband twisted to fire his AK, Jayesh unleashing another couple of shots. None of the bullets found their targets, but they drove the attackers back out of sight.

He hopped from the last platform on to solid rock. 'Keep going past me,' he shouted to the others.

Nina headed for the ladder. 'Why couldn't the Atlanteans have invented cable cars?' she muttered.

Eddie alternated his gaze between the advancing monks and the upper ledge. It seemed that none of the mercenaries were willing to put their heads above the parapet.

For now. Axelos was surely planning something . . .

The first monk reached him. 'Come on, keep going and you'll be safe,' Eddie said, trying to give the fearful young man some reassurance as he squeezed past. The next monk arrived a few seconds later. 'That's it! Keep coming!'

A head popped into view. Axelos. Eddie locked his rifle on to him, but the Greek had already dropped out of sight. Recon; he was checking on the progress of his targets.

Preparing for an attack—

'Everyone down! Jayesh!' yelled Eddie, keeping his AK-74 aimed at the ledge. The Gurkha echoed his warning in Nepalese, crouching and bringing up his own gun as figures sprang up over the lip of the little plateau.

Eddie and Jayesh fired first. The Englishman's instincts had been correct: Axelos had ordered his men to make a simultaneous assault on the fleeing group, gambling that sheer firepower would catch them. One merc reeled as a bullet clipped his arm, others hurriedly diving back into cover as rounds whipcracked past.

But the Greek's gamble was not a complete failure. A burst of bullets chewed a line across the cliff, hitting a hunching monk in the back. He keeled over, one hand clawing feebly at the rock before he toppled from the platform.

Eddie sent a furious shot at his killer, but the merc had already ducked. The nearest monk stared at him, eyes wide in terror. 'Come on!' yelled the Yorkshireman, hoping the man wasn't paralysed by fear. If he were, it would be almost impossible for the others to get around him. 'You can do it! Now!'

The monk gritted his teeth, then to Eddie's relief started moving. The Englishman kept his gun fixed on the ledge as the man passed. The others followed, Amaanat, then finally Jayesh. 'You okay?' Eddie asked the Gurkha, seeing blood on his leg.

Jayesh shrugged. 'Yeah. Why aren't they following?' He glared suspiciously back at the little plateau.

Eddie looked beyond it, at the second helicopter. The AW169 had retreated into the distance, the larger Crucible still hanging beneath it . . . but it was now making a slow, wide turn to reverse course. 'Shit. They're going to pick us off from the chopper! How many rounds've you got left?'

'Two. You?'

'One. So we're fine if we're attacked by the Fun Boy Three, otherwise we're pretty much screwed!' He looked for Nina. She was waiting at the top of the long ladder. He quickly caught up with Amaanat and explained the situation.

The elderly monk's face was filled with sadness. 'This is as I feared. Revealing the secret of the Midas Cave has brought nothing but violence and death.'

'There'll still be more coming unless we get out of here. Follow us.' There was just enough room on the ledge for Eddie and Jayesh to squeeze past the monks; they moved ahead and hurried to the ladder.

A simple headcount had given Nina the bad news. 'Oh God, I'm so sorry,' she said to Amaanat as the group arrived.

'It is all right,' he said, through tightly drawn lips. 'We shall all become again, in time.'

'We'll try to make it a long time,' Eddie assured him. The helicopter had passed out of sight as it turned, but the thud of its rotors was growing louder. 'Okay, I'll go down. Once I'm in position at the bottom, everyone follow me. Jayesh'll cover you from up here. Fight to the end, mate,' he told his friend as he started his descent.

'Fight to the end,' the Gurkha echoed.

'Eddie,' Nina called after him. 'Stay safe. Macy's waiting for her daddy.'

A strained grin. 'No pressure, then.'

He quickly clambered down. Thirty feet into the descent, a damaged rung reminded him that he was nearing the one that had almost caught him out on the ascent. Which was it?

The split rung beneath it helped him identify the danger, about twenty feet below. A glance along the valley: the helicopter was still blocked from sight, but it couldn't be far away. He continued downwards, carefully negotiating the risky rungs. A relieved breath, then he picked up the pace again. Two thirds of the way down, three quarters. He checked for the helicopter once more—

A rung snapped under his foot.

He only had one hand on a higher bar, caught mid-movement. His other foot slipped on icy metal. He dropped sharply before jerking to a halt—

His handhold tore out of the cliff.

14

'Eddie!' Nina screamed as he plunged. No ledge to catch him this time, just the valley floor far below—

The rung was still in his hand. A desperate swing and it hooked the ladder's very bottom step with a piercing *clank*, jarring him to a brutal stop against the unyielding rock.

He fought through the pain to keep his death grip on the rusted metal bar. 'Chase! I'm coming!' Jayesh shouted.

The bottom rung shifted, rasping out of the rock in stuttering half-inch steps. Toes scraping against the cliff, Eddie reached for the nearest wooden platform. It was just beyond his grasp. He strained to raise himself higher—

The rung jolted another inch out of the stone, spitting flecks of corroded iron into his face. The scabrous bar started to bend . . .

Jayesh neared him. 'Hold on!'

'Thanks for the tip!' Eddie yelled back. 'What do you bloody think I'm doing?'

'Being an idiot who falls off cliffs!' The Gurkha swung down on to the platform. He crouched and grabbed a secure rung. 'Here!'

The Englishman stretched out his free arm. Jayesh's hand clamped around it, then he pulled hard to lift him. 'Okay, I'm going for it,' Eddie warned, giving his friend a moment to brace himself – then lunging for the platform—

The bottom rung finally tore free, spinning into the void below with the makeshift hook. But Eddie's hand had found solid wood.

Jayesh shouted for the others to climb down, then pulled Eddie up. 'You okay?'

'Yeah,' said Eddie between gasps.

'Good. Wouldn't want to lose you. Bad for my rep.'

Eddie managed a strained smile. 'Glad you're not getting sentimental on me.' But he knew the Gurkha well enough to recognise the glimmer of amusement in his eye. 'You'd better go first. Where's that chopper?'

The answer came as the AW169 lumbered into view. The Crucible was still suspended beneath it, swaying in the down-draught. 'Shit!' Eddie looked up, seeing Nina coming down the ladder with her own crystalline container held awkwardly in one arm, the monks above her.

The winch operator peered out of the chopper's side hatch as it approached. Eddie still had the Kalashnikov, but with only one bullet remaining couldn't risk wasting it, and the man was currently too far away to be a viable target.

Jayesh set off along the platforms. Eddie helped Nina on to the plank, then started after the Gurkha. 'All right, follow me. Quick!'

'Jesus, Eddie!' she called after him. 'I thought you were going to die! Are you okay?'

'I'm not going to disappoint Macy yet,' he said, hopping across a gap. 'Plenty of time for that when she's older.' He looked back, seeing the first monk reach the platforms – and the AW169 looming ever closer. 'Jayesh!'

'Seen it,' Jayesh replied. He stopped, bringing up his rifle and firing a single shot. From the aircraft's abrupt bank away from the mountain, Eddie guessed it had scored a hit. 'Only one round left.'

'Snap,' the Yorkshireman replied grimly. They carried on along the platforms. The helicopter overtook them, staying well clear. The thought occurred to Eddie that he didn't know what

Axelos and the remaining mercenaries were doing. He looked back, spotting someone cautiously making his way along the higher ledge. 'They're coming after us,' he warned.

'Oh, like we don't have enough to worry about!' said Nina.

'They're sending the chopper ahead to block us,' he realised. 'If it can pin us down from the front, the others can pick us off from behind.'

'Mr Chase, Dr Wilde!' called Amaanat. 'If we give them the Crucible, they may leave us in peace.'

'They won't.'

'You have such little faith in others?'

Nina gave the abbot a world-weary look. 'If they catch us, we'll all be reincarnated pretty damn soon!'

The helicopter pulled into a hover two hundred metres from the mountainside. The larger Crucible swung beneath it. The winch operator supported himself against the door frame and leaned out—

'*Gun!*' yelled Jayesh.

Eddie had seen it too. The mercenary was armed only with a handgun rather than a rifle, but was still within range. 'Everyone down!'

The winch operator fired, twice, three times. He was concentrating his fire on the greatest threats, the two armed men – but hit nothing except stone. One round cracked off the cliff wall between the crouching Eddie and Jayesh, but the other bullets impacted below the ledge.

'He missed!' Nina cried.

Eddie was less jubilant. The shooter hadn't been *that* far off target, even firing one-handed through the turbulent downwash of an unsteadily hovering helicopter. The merc reached the same conclusion, shouting an order to the pilot. The aircraft tipped sideways, lazily moving closer.

Jayesh lifted his gun. 'Wait!' said Eddie. The Nepali arrested the movement. 'Let him get nearer.'

'Are you crazy?' Nina said.

'We've only got one shot each. We need to be sure of hitting him.'

'He'll hit *us* soon,' snapped the Gurkha. But his rifle remained still.

Eddie watched the helicopter intently. The AW169 was well within his Kalashnikov's range; the question was, could he be absolutely certain of hitting his target? Given even one more round he would already have fired, using the first as a sighter for the second, but right now he couldn't afford to miss . . .

The mercenary shifted, muscles tensing. About to fire . . .

Jayesh snapped up his own rifle. His last bullet cracked across the gap—

And missed. Only by a couple of centimetres, shock flashing across the merc's face as it struck the cabin roof above him, but it may as well have been by a mile. Jayesh hurled the useless gun into the void in frustrated defiance.

The helicopter kept closing. The mercenary recovered, lining up his pistol—

Now Eddie fired.

His shot was on target.

The final Kalashnikov round hit the mercenary squarely in the centre of his face, splintering as it tore through bone and brain before bursting from the back of his skull. The dead man flopped grotesquely out of the open door and plunged into the valley below.

Jayesh gave Eddie an approving nod as the helicopter made a hurried retreat. 'Good shot.'

'Not that good. I was aiming for the pilot!' The Yorkshireman grinned to make it clear he was joking, then threw away the empty rifle. 'Okay, we're clear! Come on!'

Jayesh led the group along the line of planks. He soon reached the bridge, making short work of the treacherous crossing. Eddie took hold of one of its support posts and leaned out from the ledge so the others could pass. 'Everyone across, quick!'

Nina gave him a worried look, but started across the gap, still cradling the small Crucible in one arm as she held the guide rope with the other. The monks lined up ready to follow. Eddie glanced across the valley. The helicopter was returning, the pilot realising that the fugitives were now unarmed. His wife reached the far side. 'Okay, your turn!' he told the first monk in the queue. The man tentatively made his way on to the crossing.

Axelos, leading the remaining mercenaries towards the ladder, signalled them to stop as his radio crackled. 'They're going over a bridge,' the pilot told him. 'They can only cross one at a time, though.'

'Can you stop them from getting across?'

'How?' came the incredulous reply. 'I'm in a helicopter!'

The Greek scowled. 'Yes, you're in a helicopter. So use it!'

One by one, the monks reached the far side, continuing along the platforms past the waiting Jayesh and Nina. Amaanat clearly wanted to be the last across, but a younger man insisted that the abbot go before him. Reluctantly, he did so.

The last monk started to cross the moment Amaanat was clear. He had only taken a few steps when a harsh gust rocked the unstable crossing, forcing him to stop and crouch to regain his balance.

But the wind only grew stronger – and the helicopter's roar became louder. 'Christ, he's trying to blow us off the bloody ledge!' Eddie cried as the AW169 dropped towards them, hot downwash forcing him to squint into the blowing ice and grit.

The monk froze again as the bridge lurched violently. The aircraft kept descending. Eddie grabbed the rock face for support, knowing from painful experience how hard it was to hold on against the force of a helicopter's rotor blast. 'Keep hold of the rope!' he yelled. The monk clawed at the line, but the wind was now pummelling him so hard that his feet slipped off the icy wood. 'No!' Eddie cried, seeing his hold on the rope weakening. 'Keep hold, keep—'

Terror filled the man's eyes – then the rope was left flapping in the gale as he plummeted into the chasm below.

But the Englishman had no time to feel rage over his death. The helicopter drew closer, angling as if to slice him up with the tips of its rotor blades—

Jayesh snatched out his kukri and hurled it at the aircraft.

It slammed against the cockpit window beside the pilot, the long blade punching straight through the thin Perspex before the broader wooden hilt jolted it to a halt. The man yelped in fear, any thoughts of attack instantly vanishing as he stared at the machete's needle-sharp tip less than three inches from his face. He twisted the throttle to full power and yanked up the collective control lever, hauling the chopper back towards the safety of the sky.

Eddie straightened. 'Okay, now *that* was a good shot,' he called across the gap.

Jayesh blew out an aggrieved breath. 'That was my favourite kukri. Doubt I'll get it back!'

'I'll buy you a bloody gold-plated one.'

'Might hold you to that.'

'Just don't tell Nina.'

'Standin' right here,' said his wife. 'Come on, quick, get across before—'

She broke off in alarm. The helicopter was still retreating, but its sudden change of direction had again set the large Crucible swinging pendulously beneath it, the hanging crystal rushing towards the mountainside like a wrecking ball. 'Oh *shit!*'

Jayesh pushed her ahead of him along the platforms after the monks. Cautious steps were no longer an option – they both vaulted on to the next plank as the Crucible whooshed at them.

It reached the end of its arc, slowing almost to a stop and glancing off the rock wall with a sound like the ringing of a glass gong before falling away again. Nina watched it go. 'Damn, that was close!'

'Chase, hurry up!' Jayesh shouted.

'And here I was about to have a picnic and enjoy the view!' was Eddie's sarcastic reply. He started across the bridge, moving as quickly as he dared – then looked up in cold shock as the giant geode swung back towards him. The pilot had overcome his panic, realising he had a new weapon.

And using it.

The Crucible rushed at the bridge—

Eddie threw himself back on to the ledge as the massive crystal hit the crossing. Planks smashed and ropes broke like thread as it swept into the deep cleft in the rock, then arced back the way it had come.

Eddie stood to find himself facing a fifteen-foot gap over a very long fall. The only part of the bridge that had survived intact was the guide rope, still attached to the posts at each side of the chasm. 'Oh, that's just bloody brilliant!'

The helicopter pulled back out into the valley, its pilot satisfied with the destruction he had caused. Jayesh came back and yanked at the hanging rope. 'This should hold! Climb across!'

'There isn't time!' Eddie had already made his own assessment. Even though it had survived the assault, the supporting post on his side had been partially uprooted. He would have to make a slow and careful traversal, and with Axelos and the remaining mercenaries probably already descending the ladder, it wouldn't be long before they could shoot at him.

He backed up along the ledge. 'What are you doing?' cried Nina.

'I'll have to jump it! Jayesh, get ready to catch me.'

'Are you *crazy*?'

'Probably!'

Nina and Jayesh retreated to make room for Eddie's landing as he psyched himself up for the leap. The gap was only about half the length of the world long-jump record, so in theory he could make it, but he didn't have much of a run-up – and athletes who fell short had soft sand to land in rather than empty air. 'You ready?' he called. The Gurkha nodded. 'Okay, here I come!'

He burst into a run. It took only a moment to reach the end of the ledge. He leapt—

Wind shrilled in his ears as he flew across the gap – and realised he wasn't going to make it.

He flung out his arms—

The wind was knocked from him as he hit the end of the planks at waist height. Jayesh grabbed his wrists as he fell backwards. The Nepali strained to hold him, feet slithering on the frozen wood. 'Chase!' he gasped. 'I'm slipping!'

Eddie swung his legs, toecaps barking against the cliff. One caught a jagged protrusion – it was barely half an inch deep, but just enough to give him purchase. Jayesh shifted position, securing his own footing, and pulled the Englishman up; slowly at first, then faster as Nina grabbed him from behind to add her own strength.

The plank bent under their weight, the poles and ropes securing it to the cliff face creaking in protest. Eddie managed to bring one knee on to the platform, then levered himself all the way up. 'I'm okay,' he wheezed. 'Get back before this fucking thing breaks!'

Nina hopped to the next platform, where she had put down

the wrapped Crucible. 'You sure you're all right?'

Jayesh helped him stand. He grimaced as he straightened. 'Feels like someone whacked me across the stomach with a fucking golf club, but yeah.'

'I guess the dam's broken on your not swearing, then.'

'Well, after three fucking years I've saved up a whole bastard load of shit-cock bollocking arse-wank shitehawk buggeration and fuckery fuckington *fuckety-FUCK*! Twatnoodles.'

'Feel better now?'

'Yep. Come on, get moving. They'll be here soon.' He looked up at the helicopter, which had pulled away to keep watch from a distance.

'They can't get across the bridge, though.'

Eddie turned back to the cleft. The post supporting the guide rope on this side was still solidly mounted in the rock. 'They can still use this. Jayesh, don't suppose you've got anything we can cut it with?'

The Gurkha glanced towards the chopper, where his kukri was still jammed in the window. 'Used to.'

'Arse chives. We'll just have to hope it slows 'em down long enough for us to get back to the monastery.' He recovered his breath, then followed Nina and Jayesh down the line of platforms after the monks.

Axelos's radio squawked. 'Come in, come in,' said Collins.

The Greek and his men had just descended the ladder. He halted, the mercenaries following suit. 'Did you stop them?'

'No – and they, ah, took out the bridge.'

The American's hesitancy made Axelos suspect that he was not telling the whole truth, but there were more important concerns. 'Will we still be able to follow them?'

'There's a rope across the gap, so maybe. I wouldn't want to risk it myself, though.'

'That's very helpful,' said Axelos, annoyed. 'Do they still have the other Crucible?'

'Yeah. The woman's carrying it.'

'Then keep tracking them. We'll try to catch up.'

He waved the other men on. Before long, they arrived at a rocky ledge before a deep cleft in the mountainside and he saw what the pilot had meant. The two halves of what had been a rope bridge hung limply down into the gap. All that remained intact was a single line spanning the void, and the post holding it at this end was damaged. He peered at its counterpart on the far side. It looked intact. 'Keep hold of this,' he told the Nepalis, indicating the crooked support. 'I'm going to climb across. If I make it, follow me.'

'What if you fall?' asked one of the twins. He did not seem concerned by the prospect.

'Then you can go back and keep all the gold in the cave for yourself. If you can dig it out. And if you can get down from this mountain once you have it. And if the monks don't warn the government what happened here.' He gave the Nepali a stern look. 'So it's best for everyone that we stay together and get the other Crucible before they do.'

The brothers exchanged glances, then moved to secure the pole. Axelos started his crossing.

15

The end of the long run of platforms was in sight, to Eddie's great relief. The first monks had almost reached the ledge with the little hollow containing wood and ropes. After that, there was only the last stretch of the plank walkway before the monastery.

He looked back. No sign of their pursuers, but he doubted the bridge's destruction would slow them much. The helicopter was still a constant presence, flying languid circles over the valley. If the mercenaries had been unable to cross the chasm, he was sure it would have been summoned to collect Axelos—

'Speak of the devil,' he growled as a figure came into view around the mountain's edge. 'We need to go faster!'

Amaanat reached the ledge. 'They are still a long way behind us.'

'Yeah, but a bullet'll catch up pretty quick,' Nina pointed out as she stepped gratefully on to solid ground behind him.

Jayesh and finally Eddie arrived on the ledge. 'Get around this corner,' the Englishman said, ushering everyone onwards into cover. 'They'll have a clear shot at us while we're on that last lot of planks to the tower, though.'

'You're right,' said Nina, remembering how the route followed the great curving wall of the natural amphitheatre. 'What do we do?'

Eddie spotted the repair supplies. 'We'll move a lot faster on the ground. Get the ropes – we'll climb down the cliff and run up the hill to the monastery.'

Amaanat called back the other monks as he reached the little nook. 'I do not know if the ropes will be long enough.'

'There isn't anything to fasten them to either,' said Nina.

'We'll tie them together, then wedge those planks inside the cave and fix the rope to 'em,' Eddie told them. 'And if it doesn't reach the ground, we'll jump the last bit. Snow looks pretty thick down there.'

Nina peered over the edge. 'You do know that falling off a real cliff into real snow won't be like in *Frozen*, right?'

'Aw, let it go.' He grinned, then started to haul out the hollow's contents.

With everyone working together, it took only a short time to knot the ropes and secure them to the planks. Eddie examined the piecemeal line. 'How long is it?'

'About twenty metres,' Jayesh replied.

The Yorkshireman made a concerned sound. 'That's never a good noise,' said Nina as he went back to the drop. 'How high's this cliff?'

'More than that.' Twenty metres was about sixty-five feet; he estimated the ground to be over eighty feet below. 'I'll check it's survivable.'

'How?'

'By seeing if I survive!'

'Not funny.'

'I wouldn't go down there if I didn't think it was doable. Here, give me that.' He took the Crucible from her and unwrapped its top, fastening the end of the rope in a loose knot around its wire handle. Then he held the line over the edge and quickly lowered it. Once the rope had reached its full length, he took a firmer hold of it. 'We'll make it,' he assured Nina. 'We've got to.'

'I hope you're right,' she said nervously.

'See you at the bottom.'

Without a harness or the time to wrap the rope around his body to abseil, he was forced to descend in the crudest possible way, relying on raw muscle to take his weight as he walked himself downwards. Ten feet, twenty, without difficulty, the knots acting as handholds. Thirty feet, half the rope's length. He looked down, and got his first clear view of the gap between the end of the line and the snow beneath it. It was more than twenty feet – and the drift itself was probably a few feet deep. Even if he hung from the very end of the rope, he would still have to fall about sixteen feet. The snow would cushion the landing to some degree, but if there were any rocks buried beneath it, the impact could be fatal.

No choice now. He kept descending, muscles starting to ache. Fifty feet, sixty, and he was at the end of the rope. The Crucible hung below him. He awkwardly reached down and tugged at the knot. It popped loose with only a little effort. Snagging the handle with his fingers, he swung the sphere outwards before releasing it. It landed in a snowdrift with a soft *whumph*.

It had survived; would he? Eddie looked up, seeing faces peering over the ledge. He managed a brief wave to Nina, then lowered himself to grip the rope's frayed end. The snow along the cliff's base undulated ominously, suggesting fallen rocks beneath the pristine surface. He would have to jump clear to land farther out, and hope no boulders had rolled down the slope.

He leaned back, bending his legs . . . and threw himself outwards.

A moment of freefalling fear, not knowing what was hidden below—

Eddie hit the snow with a thump, pain jarring his back as the drift compressed beneath him. He lay still for a moment. The sensation faded. Nothing was broken. He sat up, pushing a hand down through the flattened snow to find hard rock only a few inches beneath him. It had been deep enough to absorb his landing – just.

He stood. 'I'm okay!' he yelled. 'Come down!'

Nina was first to follow. He watched anxiously as she started her descent. She had been a regular – well, semi-regular – visitor to the gym since Macy's birth, so he was sure she had the strength to make the climb, though her clumsy movements showed how long it had been since she had done anything like this in the real world.

But she passed the halfway mark with little difficulty. Relieved, he moved to get a view back down the valley. The mercenaries were halfway along the line of platforms, moving briskly despite the danger of falling. 'Come on, faster,' he muttered, returning to watch his wife continue down the rope.

She reached its foot. 'What do I do?'

Eddie pointed at fresh snow next to where he had landed. 'Aim for there.'

'Okay.' She hesitantly sidestepped, the rope trembling as her arms strained – then closed her eyes and jumped with a shriek.

A cloud of powder burst from the drift as she vanished into it. No cries of pain came from the hole, however. Eddie yomped across to her. 'You okay?'

She sat up, blowing snow from her face. 'Yeah. Macy'd probably love that. If it was a lot lower and there wasn't a risk of death, I mean.'

He smiled and helped her stand. The rope was already twitching as Amaanat started to descend. Despite his age, the abbot was moving considerably faster than Nina, having clearly had plenty of climbing experience during his years living on the mountain.

'You should get to the monastery,' Eddie told her.

'I'm staying with you,' she insisted.

He sighed. 'I'd argue, but we've been together ten years now, and I know how well *that* works out!'

By the time she recovered the Crucible, the abbot had reached the bottom of the line. Without a word, he leapt backwards to land heavily in a drift. 'Bloody hell!' cried Eddie, running to him. 'You all right?'

Amaanat stood painfully. 'I am fine. How far away are those men?'

'Not far enough!' The next monk was already beginning his descent, leaving only one more and Jayesh still on the ledge. 'You need to warn the monastery that there's trouble coming. '

'Use the satellite phone to call for help,' Nina added.

'I . . . Yes, I will go ahead,' Amaanat said, with deep reluctance. 'But you must follow quickly.'

'Don't worry, we'll be running after you as fast as we can!' she promised. The abbot placed his palms together and bowed, then started a trudging jog through the snow.

The descending monk soon reached the end of the rope. Eddie pointed to a patch of virgin snow. 'Over here.' The man positioned himself, then launched off the cliff – only to wail on landing. The Englishman hurried to him. 'What is it?'

'Hurt . . . arm,' the monk gasped, clutching his left shoulder. A dark grey rock was exposed in the impression where he had fallen.

Nina joined her husband. 'Can you move your hand?' The monk grimaced, but managed to flex his fingers. 'I don't think it's broken, but you need to get to the monastery to check it. Do you want me to come with you?'

'No, I am okay. I go with Abbot Amaanat.' A pained bow, then he followed the old man's path through the snow.

Eddie glared at the rock. 'That's what I was worried about. These things could be all over the place like a bloody minefield.'

'At least they won't explode.' Nina watched the last monk's progress. Above him, Jayesh shouted in Nepalese, getting an alarmed response from the descending man. 'Oh, he didn't like that.'

'Getting the feeling I won't either,' said Eddie, before raising his voice. 'Jayesh! What're you doing?'

'Coming down now!' the Gurkha replied.

'What, two on one rope?'

'Can't wait! Bad guys almost here.' The Nepali dropped over the edge and scrambled down the knotted line. The monk below him let out a fearful yelp as the rope jerked in his grip.

'Jayesh!' Eddie yelled. 'For Christ's sake slow down, or you'll knock him off!' The Gurkha reduced his pace, but only slightly.

The Englishman could do nothing but clench his teeth and watch the two men clamber towards him. The monk was clearly struggling, but eventually he reached the bottom of the rope. 'Here,' said Eddie, indicating a clear patch of snow.

The monk dived from the rock face with a panicked cry. To Eddie's relief, there were no screams as he landed, just frantic gabbling in Nepalese.

'I don't speak the language,' said Nina, seeing the monk shoot an angry look at Jayesh, 'but I'm fairly sure that wasn't complimentary.'

'What's the Buddhist line on calling someone a bell-end, anyway?' Eddie asked the monk, whose only reply was a bemused stare. 'You don't speak English? Probably for the best. Amaanat, that way.' He pointed at the retreating monks. The man hurried after them.

Nina looked up. The Gurkha was moving faster now that the line was free. 'Aim for a clear patch!' Eddie called up to him.

Jayesh found a landing spot – and jumped.

He disappeared into a snowdrift. Neither the Yorkshireman nor his wife needed to see him to know that he had been hurt. The dull snap of breaking bone as he hit a buried boulder was more than enough. 'Shit! Jayesh!' Eddie cried, finding his friend's face screwed up in agony. 'What's broken?'

'Leg,' Jayesh rasped. 'Left ankle . . .'

Eddie scooped away the snow around his foot. 'I'm going to check it. Hold on.'

Jayesh braced himself. The Englishman carefully ran his fingertips over the other man's ankle. The Gurkha flinched, but made no sound. 'I can feel the break, but I don't think it's come through the skin,' Eddie told him.

'Leave me,' said the Nepali, voice strained. 'You get out of here.'

'Don't be a bloody idiot. Nina, help me lift him.' Jayesh continued to protest, but the couple hoisted him upright and supported him on their shoulders. 'Okay, try and hold up your foot so it doesn't drag in the snow.'

The other man made a choked snort that could almost have been a laugh. 'Yeah. Easy to do that!' But he lifted his knee as high as he could as the trio set off, following the monks' trail.

Axelos raised his gun as he reached the ledge and hurried along it. Collins had already reported that the fugitives had descended to the ground below, but he quickly checked in case they had left a rearguard in ambush. Nobody was there.

Their means of escape was obvious. He went to the rope. No one directly below, but tracks had been cut through the snow. His eyes followed them – to see three people about to round the base of a cliff.

One of the twins raised his rifle. 'Wait!' Axelos barked. 'I don't want to risk damaging the Crucible.' He faced his men. 'We'll go down after them.'

Nina looked back as she and Eddie, carrying Jayesh, made it to cover. Figures watched them from above. 'Oh crap. They're on the ledge! Can we get to the monastery ahead of them?'

Eddie didn't reply, that exact thought already dominating his mind. The great natural bowl opened out before them as they rounded the cliff's foot. The religious redoubt awaited at the top of the slope, prayer flags fluttering. Ahead, the other monks had caught up with Amaanat. The abbot paused to check on the progress of his visitors; on seeing Nina and Eddie supporting the wounded Jayesh, he gave an urgent command and one of the monks ran back to meet them, Amaanat and the other continuing on to alert their brothers at the monastery.

'Careful!' Eddie warned. 'He's got a broken ankle.' The monk didn't appear to understand English, so he directed him to hold the Gurkha under his knees. Nina shifted to put her free arm beneath his lower back as Eddie took up position to carry his friend from behind, arms supporting his shoulders. With the load spread between them, their pace up the hill quickened.

A monk appeared on the wall, bewildered by Amaanat's arrival from an unexpected direction. The abbot called out to him. After a moment, the gates began to open.

'The mercs'll have a hard time getting through those,' said Nina, panting as the slope became steeper.

'Won't keep 'em out for ever,' Eddie countered.

'Maybe not, but the monks are going to call for help on the satphone.'

'And how long'll it take to get here?'

'You know, sometimes I hate being married to a realist . . .'

A noise rose behind them. Apparently responding to an order from Axelos, the helicopter descended towards the foot of the slope, aiming for a patch of relatively flat ground. The large Crucible still hung beneath it, the pilot slowing to lay it in the snow as gently as possible before sliding his aircraft sideways to land beside it.

As it touched down, the mercenaries emerged from behind the cliff – but by now, Amaanat and his companion had reached the safety of the monastery. The others passed the tethered yaks, which raised their heads in bemusement to watch them. 'We're going to make it!' Nina cried.

Eddie was less exuberant. 'Split up! They're going to shoot!'

Nina let go of the Gurkha and darted clear, ducking. The monk was confused, but the flat thud of a bullet smacking into the snow a few feet away was more effective than any translation. The Yorkshireman pulled Jayesh from him to take the other man's whole weight himself. His friend held in a gasp as his injured foot brushed the snow.

Another round kicked up a little fountain of powder beside them. 'Nina, run!' Eddie yelled. '*Run!*'

Nina rushed for the gate. Splinters spat at her face as one of the wooden doors took a bullet impact. She gasped, but then was inside, the monk following. 'Eddie, come on!'

A Kalashnikov opened up on full auto as her husband struggled towards the entrance. Only the first couple of rounds landed anywhere close to the two men, the others going high and hitting stonework as the rifle's recoil pushed the muzzle upwards.

But a single shot from Axelos's P90 passed much closer, searing an inch above Eddie's head to hit the door. And the mercenary leader would be refining his aim—

Jayesh realised the same thing, both men diving flat as one. The Gurkha let out a screech as his broken ankle hit the ground. A split second later, another round cracked over them. Had Eddie still been standing, it would have struck him squarely in the back of the head.

There was no time to celebrate. The Englishman scrabbled through the snow, staying flat. 'Come on, crawl!' he hissed, grabbing Jayesh's arm. His friend cried out again, but managed to push forward with his uninjured leg.

More bullets struck the ground and walls, the mercs realising they were about to lose their prey – but the two ex-soldiers were now at the gate, hands helping them through. Other robed men pushed the doors shut. They met with a heavy boom, a thick wooden beam being dropped into place to bar them against a fusillade of thudding impacts on the other side.

Nina rushed to Eddie and hugged him as the gunfire stopped. 'You made it! You're okay!'

'Yeah, except for my underpants!' He spotted Amaanat. 'Jayesh's broken his ankle. Get him indoors, somewhere secure – everyone else too. Those tunnels where we ate, can you seal them off?'

'Yes,' the abbot replied. 'The door can be locked. But we will not be able to use the satellite phone underground.'

'We'll do it,' Nina told him. Both men regarded her questioningly. 'I'll call Seretse at the UN – he'll be able to talk to the Nepalese government directly and get them to act a lot faster than by going through regular channels.'

'But you will be trapped outside!'

She held up the Crucible. 'This is what they want. If they come after us, they'll leave you alone.' There was a large pile of straw near the gate; she shoved the crystal into it.

Eddie gave her a dubious look. 'Yeah, that'll keep it safe.'

'They'll never think to look for it there, and I'll be able to move a lot faster if I don't have to carry the damn thing!' A monk ran up and presented Amaanat with a chunky and outdated telephone handset with a long, fat antenna. Nina turned back to the abbot. 'Look, if I call the United Nations, they might get help here before those guys can even break through the gate. Please, let me try.'

Amaanat handed her the phone. 'Very well. Do you know how to use this?'

'Yeah, no prob—'

A monk on the tower by the gate shouted in alarm. Ripples of panic spread through his brothers. 'What was that?' Eddie asked.

'They are outside the doors,' the abbot said. 'He says they have . . . bombs?'

Nina blinked in surprise. 'Bombs?'

'Not bombs,' Eddie said sharply. '*Grenades!* Everyone take cover, *now!*'

Amaanat shouted in Nepalese. The monks scattered, some heading for small outbuildings around the courtyard while the majority hurried for the debate house. Nina and Eddie followed the latter group. The Englishman looked back, expecting to see grenades arcing over the gate – but instead he heard several metallic clunks as objects hit its outer side. 'They're gonna blast their way in—'

The gate blew apart.

16

Eddie dived on top of Nina to shield her from the explosion. He looked up as the echoes faded to see that a car-sized chunk of the wooden barrier had disintegrated. A monk was screaming, a deep bloody gash in his side where flying debris had speared into him. 'Get up, *go!*' the Yorkshireman yelled, shoving him into the arms of one of his fellows. 'They're coming!'

Nina helped another dazed man to his feet. 'I've got to call Seretse!'

'Do it on the move,' Eddie told her as they ran to the debate house. Most of the monks had now made it inside, Amaanat and those bearing Jayesh among them. 'Hope you remember his number.'

Gunfire crackled behind them as they reached the door. Eddie whirled to see a man crouching at the hole in the gate, firing up at the watchtower. Its occupant toppled from the wall. Another mercenary appeared alongside the first, aiming at the stragglers fleeing into the debate house—

The couple flung themselves through the doorway, landing hard on the wooden floor as the injured monk and his helper were cut down on the steps. A shriek came from outside as bullets ripped into a third monk.

More rounds tore through the entrance and smacked off the statue of the Buddha. 'Get behind it!' yelled Eddie. He and Nina rolled and jumped up, skirting around the sitting figure as the last monks piled into the tunnels. One waved urgently for them to follow, but Nina signalled for him to retreat. The man slammed the thick door shut as she and Eddie ran across the room.

The Yorkshireman kicked open the other exit. The hall of prayer wheels stretched out before them, countless candles glowing along each wall. Nina ran down the red carpet as Eddie closed the doors, looking for anything he could use to wedge them. Nothing presented itself. He cursed, then followed his wife towards the exit—

The doors behind them burst open.

Nina leapt for cover between the ornate cylinders. Eddie did the same a few paces behind her, thudding against the wall beside one of the racks of miniature prayer wheels. Metal clanged off metal in a discordant cacophony as the attacker hosed a wild spray of gunfire down the hall, sending the damaged wheels spinning furiously.

The onslaught stopped. Another man shouted in Nepalese – and hurled a grenade.

The olive-green sphere thumped to a stop on the carpet just past Eddie. 'Oh, *fuck!*' he gasped. It was out of his reach, and scrambling from cover to throw it would leave him exposed—

Instead he snatched one of the small prayer wheels from the rack – and swung it by its handle like a golf club, hitting the grenade and sending it flying towards the hall's far end.

It exploded at the doors. Candles flew in all directions, shrapnel striking the prayer wheels like hailstones on a tin roof. The largest of them was torn from its mounts, toppling sideways and slamming down on the carpet with a deep ringing boom.

Eddie looked back. Their attacker reappeared at the doorway with his gun raised, only to glare at it in frustration as he pulled the trigger to no effect. The Englishman burst from cover and ran, Nina doing the same. 'Count your shots, dickhead!' Eddie yelled as the man hurriedly ejected the empty magazine and fumbled for a replacement.

Flames from the scattered candles were already consuming the wall hangings. Nina squeezed past the giant prayer wheel. She was almost at the shrapnel-scarred doors when a burning ceiling beam crashed down in front of her. Smoke and sparks sprayed her face as she jumped back. 'They're blocked!'

Eddie braved the rising flames to tug at the handles. The doors opened, but not nearly enough to fit through. He kicked at the obstruction. It barely moved.

He hurriedly retreated – and saw that not only had the mercenary at the other end of the hallway reloaded his AK, but the other man had joined him. *'Down!'*

They dropped behind the prayer wheel as more gunfire spat down the hall. The great drum juddered and rang as bullets from two rifles pounded it. They were powerful enough to pierce the metal, but not to go all the way through to the other side. Even so, Eddie flinched as a smashed round impacted by his head with a clang. 'Jesus!'

Another length of flaming wood hit the floor. 'We've got to get out of here!' Nina cried.

The gunfire paused as one of the mercenaries ran down the hallway towards them. 'How?' Eddie demanded. 'If we come out from behind this thing, they'll shoot—' An idea came to him. 'Okay, we *don't* come out from behind this thing!'

'What do you mean?' she asked, but he had already risen to a crouch. He put both hands against the prayer wheel and pushed.

Metal creaked, and the cylinder started to roll. 'Help me!'

Nina shoved the phone into a coat pocket, then slapped her palms against the metal beside Eddie's and dug her soles into the carpet. The prayer wheel picked up speed. They pushed harder—

The advancing mercenary opened fire again. More bullets pounded the cylinder, stitching lines around its circumference as it rolled towards him. 'Come on, *come on*!' Eddie yelled as his pace increased to a hunched jog. 'Faster!'

'I'm fastering!' she snapped. The gunfire ceased. Eddie risked raising his head. The mercenary had burned through another magazine, clumsily changing it before looking back at his targets – and realising they were closing on him. He pulled back into a gap between two prayer wheels.

'Stop!' Eddie told Nina. She immediately halted and ducked. He kept going, sidestepping to one end of the rolling drum and pushing harder on that side. It changed course, angling towards the wall.

The mercenary poked his head out to see the great cylinder growling towards him. He fired again. Eddie dived flat to the carpet, letting the juggernaut's momentum carry it onwards—

It struck the mount of one of the standing prayer wheels, knocking it over to pound down on the mercenary's head like a sledgehammer. He fell to the floor – and the bullet-riddled cylinder rolled over him. The man's scream was abruptly cut off by a horrible *crack* as his ribcage collapsed under the weight.

The big wheel kept on turning. It deflected off another stand to continue down the hall. The second man hastily retreated through the doorway as it thundered towards him—

Another crack, much louder – and the floor gave way, carpet tearing and planks splintering apart as the prayer wheel plunged through to the stone corridor below with an almighty clang. More candles went flying, tapestries now alight at both ends of the hallway.

'Bloody hell, it's Flat Stanley,' Eddie said, glancing at the corpse as he stood. 'Nina, come on! Down the hole!' They ran to the ragged gap in the floor.

The second mercenary reappeared at the doorway—

Nina and Eddie leapt into the hole as bullets cracked above them.

They landed on crushed boxes eight feet below. The now-buckled prayer wheel had flattened more supplies before blocking a door at the passageway's end.

Nina helped her husband up. 'We can get out down there,' she said, pointing back at the stairs they had descended earlier in the day.

'If we can reach them!' he replied, hearing footsteps above. He pushed Nina ahead of him into the narrow aisle between the stacked provisions as the merc fired down into the hole. Flour exploded from ruptured sacks behind them.

A thump told Eddie that the man had jumped down into the stone hallway. He toppled the stacks in his wake to block their attacker's line of fire. 'Down!' he yelled as the Kalashnikov's flat hammering started again.

Wood splintered, bullets tearing into boxes of canned food and sacks of dried rice. But none of the rounds made it through the makeshift blockade. The shooting stopped, the mercenary snarling in frustration as he clambered after them.

Loud cracks echoed from the blazing hall above as more wooden supports surrendered to the flames. Nina weaved down the claustrophobic aisle, finally reaching the stairwell – only to stop in alarm as she looked up it. 'Oh, great!' The fire had already spread beyond the prayer wheel hall, the stairs ablaze.

Eddie tried the door to the room containing the gold furnace. Locked – but there was no keyhole, so it had to be bolted from inside. He pounded on it. 'Hey! Let us in!'

No reply, and the door remained firmly closed. Crashes came from the corridor as the mercenary kicked aside obstructions. 'In here!' said Nina, opening the neighbouring storeroom door. 'There might be something we can—'

She gasped as she was driven back by a wave of heat. A fallen beam from the floor above had punched through the ceiling, setting the room ablaze. The mere act of opening the door had fanned the flames, streams of fire swirling through the air like miniature dragons. 'Or maybe not!'

Eddie shielded his face as he looked into the smoky storeroom. Its contents were all related to the furnace: crucibles of various sizes, moulds, bags of sand . . . and numerous cylinders of propane. As he watched, the valve on one of them started to squeal in protest at the rising temperature, jetting out a thin stream of gas.

But he saw something else: a large waist-high metal chest, faded olive-drab paint covered with stencilled symbols. Chinese, a container for some sort of military supplies that had passed through various hands to end up here. He hurried to it and opened the lid. Cardboard cartons of what he guessed were metalworking consumables were inside, taking up about a quarter of the space . . .

'Nina, get in!' he shouted. 'Quick!'

'Are you crazy?' she cried. 'We'll get cooked!'

'It's the only way!' He strained to tip the chest on its side, spilling its contents across the floor. He was surprised to see that some rusted old rifle parts had been at the bottom, but had no time to wonder what they were doing in a monastery, instead shoving the case into a corner near the door.

Nina was about to voice another objection when the crash of falling boxes warned her that the mercenary had forced his way through the obstacle course. She darted into the storeroom. Eddie slammed the door as a bullet splintered the frame behind her. 'Get in!'

She clambered into the overturned chest and curled up as tightly as she could. Eddie squeezed in with her and swung down the lid. 'If the fire doesn't kill us, he will!' she gasped, the heat already rising. 'It's not as if there are many places we could have hidden!'

He gripped the lid's inner lip, holding it shut. 'He won't even get in here.'

'Why not?'

'You ever seen *Backdraft*?'

'What, the movie?' She suddenly realised his plan. 'Oh my God! We've been together for ten years – how did I not notice that you were *completely fricking insane*?'

The mercenary kicked open the door—

Fresh air rushed in – and the fire became an inferno.

The man's skin was seared from his face as a wave of flame gushed over him, but he didn't even have time to scream before the leaking propane tank exploded, taking its neighbours with it. The blast tore through the doorway and blew a hole in the monastery's outer wall, hurling the mercenary's charred remains into the open as debris rained down on the snowy slope outside.

The chest was slammed against the corner, its lid buckling – but it held, the pressure actually forcing it even more tightly closed. Eddie nevertheless maintained his hold until the noise from outside died down, then cautiously opened it a fraction of an inch. He took their not being instantly incinerated by an inrush of flame as a good sign and pushed it wider.

The little in the storeroom not already ablaze had joined the rest of its contents. But the smoke was swirling upwards through the now-larger hole in the ceiling as clean air was drawn through the ragged gap in the outer wall. The explosion had also blasted open the furnace room's entrance, the thick wooden door hanging off its hinges. Eddie stood up, then helped Nina out of the chest. 'We can get outside. You've still got the phone?'

'Oh yeah,' Nina said, pained. The bulky device had jammed hard into her side inside the crate.

They hurried into the passageway. Eddie peered through the hole. The first thing he saw was the dead mercenary transfixed upon the horns of an aggrieved yak, which was doing its best to shake off the corpse. 'Guess he was feeling horny.'

'Oh God,' Nina groaned. 'I haven't missed *those* for the past three years.'

'What?'

'*Quips.*'

'Black humour's a perfectly valid coping mechanism for dealing with death and horror,' said Eddie, straight-faced. Nina gave him a suspicious look. 'What? I did some reading. Come on.'

The ground was about ten feet below. He started to climb out, but stopped when he saw the helicopter down the slope. The large Crucible was being manoeuvred into its cabin by two men. One he guessed was the pilot; the other was one of the mercenaries, a Kalashnikov slung across his back. 'Arse! Can't go that way – there's no cover. And I don't think we'd outrun them on a yak.'

Noises from the corridor made Nina look around. 'Someone's coming!'

Eddie forced open the damaged door. 'In here.'

'But it's a dead end!'

His expression told her that he was well aware of the fact. The furnace was still alight, propane burners roaring and the glow of molten metal coming from the Crucible atop it, but there was no sign of the monk who had been in the room earlier. 'Where is he?' Eddie said.

Nina glanced towards the anteroom containing the golden treasures. 'He must be in there.'

Her husband went to it. 'It's padlocked.' He frowned. 'But the main door was bolted from *inside* . . .'

Neither had time to consider that any further as said door burst open and one of the mercenaries rushed in, AK at the ready.

Eddie threw himself behind a bench bearing the recently cast gold bar. Nina was still in the open, the furnace the only nearby cover. She ran for it—

The man fired as she dived, a bullet striking the ceramic Crucible. Blobs of luminous metal sprayed from its open neck. Nina screamed as one burned through her coat sleeve, managing to shake off the searing droplet before it ate into her flesh.

The Nepali ran around the furnace to find his target on the floor behind it, clutching her scorched arm. He took aim—

'Oi!'

He turned at the shout – and was hit in the face by twelve kilograms of gold. Teeth cracked, his upper lip bursting open. He fell, the thrown gold bar thunking down beside him.

Nina rolled clear as Eddie vaulted the bench and charged at the downed man. If he could get the rifle . . .

It swung towards him – but he booted it from the mercenary's hand. He moved to stamp on his opponent's head, only for the man to kick his knee. Eddie staggered, toppling towards the blazing gas jets—

He twisted as he fell, barely missing the burners and landing heavily beside the furnace. A still-molten glob of gold sizzled on the stone, close enough for him to feel the intense heat on his cheek. He rolled away, but the Nepali had already jumped to his feet. He slammed a boot into Eddie's chest, then aimed a second kick at his groin. Eddie thrust himself backwards to take the impact on his thigh instead. He kept retreating, fending off more strikes, but came to an abrupt stop against one of the banks of shelves.

The Nepali snatched up a set of long iron tongs and swung them at the downed Yorkshireman. Eddie whipped up both arms to protect his head. Metal struck his forearm, painfully paralysing his left hand.

The man drew back to hit him again – then realised that his gun had landed not far away. He threw the tongs at Eddie and darted for the Kalashnikov.

Nina scrambled back upright, seeing him snatch up his gun—

She kicked the furnace, hard. It fell over, the Crucible hitting the floor with a ringing note and splashing its glowing contents across the stone slabs.

The molten gold gushed around the mercenary's feet. At over a thousand degrees Centigrade, the liquid metal instantly melted the soles of his boots and set his clothing aflame. He fell backwards with an anguished screech, landing in the searing pool. There was a sizzling crackle of burning cloth and flesh as the man was suddenly wreathed in fire, limbs flailing for a couple of seconds before every nerve in his spinal cord was burned to blackened ash.

Nina jumped back, rounding the overturned furnace to drag Eddie clear. 'Jesus! Are you hurt?'

'Won't be juggling for a while,' he growled, cradling his aching left arm. 'Where's the gun?'

The Kalashnikov had landed in a tongue of superheated gold. 'Getting blinged up.'

'Great.' A shout came from outside. 'Shit, more of them!'

'What're we gonna do? There's no way out of here.'

Eddie surveyed the walls. 'The room was locked from inside, so there must be . . .' His eyes fixed upon a cabinet in one corner. Behind it, about five feet up, a wooden beam was set into the stone wall. A lintel? 'A secret door!'

He ran to it, Nina behind him. 'This isn't a haunted house,' she said, unconvinced.

'You've never heard of a priest hole?' He strained to pull the cabinet away from the wall.

'Monks aren't priests.'

'All right, a bloody monk hole!'

'*You're* a monk hole!' She helped him swing the old cupboard aside, revealing a squat opening behind it. 'Oh. Okay. You were right.'

'Apology accepted,' he said with a pained grin. Beyond the

little doorway was a narrow passageway. Eddie peered down it, seeing the foot of a ladder at the end. 'It's clear!'

They ducked through the opening. The ladder ascended to a trapdoor. Eddie cautiously raised it, recognising the interior of a building they had passed through to reach the cliff path. The way back towards the main gate was blocked by fire, the conflagration spreading.

He climbed out, left hand still numb. 'We'll have to get out through the tower.'

'There's no way down to the ground from there!' Nina protested.

'Maybe not, but you'll be able to use the satphone once we're outside.' They ran from the flames.

The second of the brothers rushed into the furnace room. 'Hermanga!' he called – then saw the burning figure lying in the spilled gold. A moment of shock . . . followed by a scream of anguish as he realised the body was that of his twin. He stood shaking for a moment, before spotting the hidden door. Roaring obscenities, he ran after his brother's killers.

Axelos retreated into the courtyard, looking back at the string of buildings as smoke and flames advanced along them like a lit fuse. He had reached as far as the prayer wheel hall before deciding that heading any deeper into the monastery would be suicide. The twins, however, had gone in pursuit of Wilde and her husband, leaving only one man with him. 'We're pulling out,' he said into his walkie-talkie. 'Everyone back to the helicopter, now.'

He waited several seconds, but there was no response. A faint shake of his head: *amateurs*. That was what happened when you rushed into a mission without the right people. 'Let's go,' he told the remaining Nepali.

The man gestured towards the outbuildings. 'Monks in there.

Kill them?'

'No. Enough people have died already.' He regarded the bodies sprawled outside the debate house with regret. What should have been a straightforward operation had turned, to use an American expression he particularly liked, into a cluster-fuck. He headed for the gate, bringing up the radio again. 'Collins! Is the Crucible loaded?'

'Just secured it,' the helicopter pilot replied. 'Did you get the other one?'

'No,' he said – unknowingly passing just a few feet from his prize. He turned at a loud crash to see the roof of the prayer wheel hall collapse, sending a great spray of sparks into the air. 'One will have to be good enough.'

'I'll let you be the one to tell him that.'

'Just get ready to take off. I'll be with you soon.' He and the Nepali set off at a jog down the hill.

Eddie threw open the tower's entrance. 'At least this isn't on fire.'

'Yet,' said Nina. The blaze seemed to be actively pursuing them through the monastery. She looked back as they rushed through, seeing fire licking along the corridor's ceiling beams – then flinched. 'Oh my God! But he's dead!' The man she had killed in the furnace room charged around a corner, rifle in hand.

Eddie stared in disbelief, then slammed the door. 'And you said this wasn't a haunted house!'

They ran past the laughing Buddha and pounded up the wooden staircase. Explosions came from somewhere nearby, more gas cylinders or stocks of fuel going up with enough force to rattle the tower's ancient timbers. But any hope that their pursuer had been caught by the blasts vanished as the Nepali barged through the door.

He saw them and yelled in rage, opening fire. Nina and Eddie ducked as bullets ripped through the wood around them. The banister splintered, holes exploding through the steps at their feet.

Then the shooting stopped – but only while he changed magazines—

More explosions, these much closer – and larger. The entire tower jolted as if hit by an earthquake, knocking the gunman off his feet. His Kalashnikov skidded across the age-worn stone slabs and vanished into a great crack that tore open in the floor.

Eddie and Nina fared little better. The Englishman almost fell through the broken banister before his wife grabbed him. The whole tower swayed sickeningly, like a ship pitching in a heavy sea. 'What the hell was that?' she cried.

Another detonation below, a smoky shock wave belching up from the widening chasm. The tower tipped further over, stones grinding and wood creaking to the point of fracture before it slowly reeled back upright. A smaller but more violent movement rose beneath it – a frantic shuddering, unyielding blocks crunching over each other . . .

Slowly, but inexorably, the entire tower tore away from its base and began to slide down the hillside.

With Nina and Eddie inside.

17

Axelos was two thirds of the way to the helicopter when he heard multiple explosions from the monastery. He looked uphill – and his eyes popped wide in surprise as the tallest tower leaned forward as if bowing, before shakily tipping back up-right . . . and then the stone wall at its foot crumbled and collapsed. The gridwork of thick wooden beams making up its foundations burst through the debris, acting like the runners of a sledge as the whole structure began to slither downhill.

His initial disbelief became astonishment; he expected the tower to shake itself into rubble, but somehow the ancient build-ing held together. It gradually picked up speed, tilting forward again as the gradient became steeper—

Another shock ran through the Greek, this one of fear as he realised it was coming straight at him.

And the helicopter.

'*Run!*' he shouted at his Nepali companion, before charging through the snow towards the AW169, waving furiously at Collins. 'Take off, *take off*!'

Cracking plasterwork showered Nina with dust. The building was lurching like a truck traversing rough ground – which, she saw to her horror as the burning monastery slid past one of the narrow windows, it actually was. 'Oh my *God*!' She tried to haul Eddie to safety—

A huge jolt sent her reeling. Her head hit the wall with a painful smack – and she lost her hold on her husband.

Eddie grabbed at one of the banister's supports as he went over the edge. He caught it with his left hand, but his prickling fingers lost their grip.

He fell to the quaking floor below. Even rolling to absorb the impact, the landing still hurt.

'Eddie!' Nina cried.

'I'm okay!' he shouted back, feeling anything but. The mercenary, whom he now realised must be the twin of the dead man, staggered to his feet. 'Get up to the door to the ledge!'

'But we're *moving*, the whole tower's—'

Nina's words were lost beneath the twin's enraged roar as he charged at the Englishman.

Eddie scrambled aside, darting beneath the golden statue's outstretched arm – then abruptly reversed direction as the mercenary followed, grabbing the Buddha's forearm and using it to pull himself up and deliver a two-footed kick into the Nepali's chest. The man flew backwards, catching himself at the edge of the crack.

The Yorkshireman dropped back to the floor, looking up to see Nina ascending the shaking stairs. He was about to run after her when sudden disorientation struck him. It felt as if he was leaning backwards . . .

He *was* leaning backwards. Nina's words finally registered. The entire structure was on its way down the mountainside, pitching forward as the slope steepened—

Floor and wall switched places as the tower toppled past the point of no return and smashed down on its front.

Debris showered the interior as chunks of the walls broke apart, debris showering the interior – but somehow the building as a whole remained intact, its fortified framework withstanding one final assault. Great sprays of snow came in through the holes in the stonework as it careered roof-first down the slope like a massive toboggan.

Eddie skidded down the new floor and hit the underside of the staircase. Momentarily dazed, he opened his eyes to see the great statue of the Buddha looming over him. It was still fixed to the tower's stone base, clinging like a rotund spider to a surface that had now tipped past the vertical, but the spreading cracks in the surrounding slabs warned him that it would not hold on for much longer.

But the metal figure was not the most immediate danger. The mercenary had grabbed the Buddha as the tower went over, and now he let go, jumping down to land in front of Eddie. A kick caught the Englishman in the side as he tried to stand. The Nepali screamed at him, oblivious to the perils around him in his vengeance-fuelled rage.

Eddie scrambled out from under the staircase, only to take another blow to his stomach that sent him slithering downhill. The mercenary snatched a knife from his belt and bore down on his winded target—

Stone exploded, the statue finally breaking loose and dropping with a metallic boom.

It rolled like a boulder, rapidly picking up speed and smashing straight through the wooden staircase. The mercenary whirled – and was mown down by the laughing holy man.

Eddie dived aside as the golden figure tumbled at him, the protruding hand delivering an agonising karate chop to his shin as it passed. Then it was gone, demolishing another leg of the stairs as it continued towards the tower's roof.

'Nina!' he roared. '*Incoming Buddha!*'

Nina had been thrown across the tower when it fell, hitting the wall hard. Debris bombarded her. The satphone flew from her pocket and skittered away.

Eddie's shout gave warning that something else was coming towards her. Half blinded by swirling snow, she looked up – to see the Buddha burst through the staircase like the Kool-Aid Man, his smile now anything but reassuring.

She shrieked, flinging herself out of its path. The statue thundered by, obliterating another section of stairs before slamming to a halt against the thick beams supporting the topmost floor.

Nina gawped at the golden figure, then heard her husband call her name. She turned and saw him half climbing, half sliding down the wall. 'You didn't get Buddha'd, did you?' he asked.

'No,' she replied, relieved. 'But I dropped the phone! I've got to get it!' She started through the whirling blizzard towards the roof before he had time to object.

Object he still did, though. 'You remember what's at the bottom of this hill, don't you? *A fucking great cliff!*'

Axelos and his companion jumped aboard the helicopter, but despite Collins jamming the throttle to full power, the aircraft's rotors still had not reached takeoff speed. The Greek stared in horror at the overturned building rumbling towards them like a torpedo. 'Go!' he screamed. 'Go, go! Get us up!'

The pilot's gaze flicked between his instruments and the rapidly approaching tower. 'What do you think I'm *trying* to do?' he yelled back, regarding one dial intently as its needle crept towards a particular mark. 'Come on, baby, come on . . . *Yeah!*'

He brought up the collective control lever. The AW169 rocked, slithering backwards down the hill for a few feet before finally leaving the ground. The loss of weight from its much-reduced passenger complement was more than counteracted by the added bulk of the Crucible, the aircraft struggling to gain height.

The tower rushed towards it, trailing lines of flapping prayer flags. Axelos grabbed the door handle, about to dive out. 'It's going to hit—'

The pilot jammed the cyclic stick hard over to the left. The helicopter rolled sideways – and the tower hurtled past, one corner of its pagoda-like roof whipping between the aircraft's wheels. Flags lashed the fuselage, ripping the plastic sheeting.

Breathless, Axelos spun in his seat to watch the building plough towards the precipice.

Nina squinted into the rush of snow as she reached the Buddha. The phone was wedged against the statue. 'Got it!' she cried.

Eddie pushed past to enter the topmost room. The doorway that had led to the path to the Midas Cave was now above them, and the door had broken loose. He stood under the opening. 'Here! I'll help you up.' He braced himself and boosted Nina upwards. She grabbed the door frame and struggled through.

The whirlwind of snow lessened as she clambered on to the tower's upper face. The helicopter was pulling away to one side, but she gave it barely an instant's notice. The terrifying view ahead completely dominated her attention. The cliff sliced across the snowfield before them, the drop into oblivion beyond only seconds away.

Eddie dragged himself up behind her. 'Buddharation and fuckery!' he gasped. At the speed they were going, if they jumped from the tower's side they would keep tumbling downhill and go over the edge before they could stop themselves.

They had to counter some of that speed. He grabbed Nina's hand. 'Run!' he yelled, pulling her with him back up the tower's length.

She tried to protest, but the only sound she could manage was a panicked scream as they leapt into the maelstrom of churning snow in the building's wake—

The whiteout consumed them. Pain overpowered their remaining senses as they hit the ground and somersaulted through the snow, coming to a stop on the very lip of the precipice.

Silence suddenly fell as the tower shot over the edge. The only noise they registered for a couple of seconds was their own panicked breathing . . . then came an almighty bang from below. The sound echoed off the surrounding mountains, reverberating for several seconds before fading.

The haze of snow drifted away in the wind. The couple looked at each other. 'Are you okay?' they both asked simultaneously. Eddie let out an exhausted laugh. 'Yeah, I'm all right,' he said. 'You?'

'I don't think I'm any worse than before I jumped off the tower,' Nina replied, panting. 'Compared to how I felt this morning, though . . .'

He chuckled, then peered over the edge. The tower's remains were strewn across the valley floor, a small mushroom cloud of pulverised stonework rising from the impact site. 'That was too bloody close,' he said, helping her to her feet—

The helicopter's roar made them both turn in alarm.

The AW169 had levelled out, wheeling about to head up the valley. It passed a hundred feet away, close enough to make out Axelos in the co-pilot's seat. The Greek stared down at them. Eddie glared back, adding a pair of middle fingers to his disapproval.

For a moment, Nina thought the mercenary leader might return to finish the job, but then Axelos looked away. The helicopter retreated into the distance, a yellow logo revealed through torn plastic sheeting flapping on its flank. 'They got the Crucible,' she said, dismayed.

'Only one of 'em,' Eddie reminded her. 'But to be honest, I'd be fine if they'd got both. Or the other one'd gone over the cliff with that tower.'

'So those monks would have died for nothing?'

He frowned at the implied criticism. 'We almost died too. So did Jayesh. And for what?'

Nina looked past the burning monastery, picking out the pathway along the cliff. 'Those guys knew what the Crucible is, and what it does. Which means they knew what the Midas Cave is – that it's a natural nuclear reactor.' She turned to watch the disappearing helicopter. 'The fact that they took the Crucible and didn't care about the cave means they've got some other way to make it do what it does. Something nuclear.' She faced her husband again. 'Eddie, this is a security issue. An ancient artefact – an *Atlantean* artefact – that uses nuclear power to turn other elements into gold? That whoever stole it is willing to kill for? We've got to tell the IHA.'

His expression remained stony. 'We don't work for them any more.'

'But they're already involved. *I* involved them; I called in favours to get here. And this kind of thing is their department. It's what the IHA was set up to do.' She held up the satellite phone. To her relief, it seemed undamaged.

'Before you start making calls to the UN,' said Eddie firmly, 'we need to get back to the monastery and help them. People are hurt. And,' he added, seeing her unwillingness to wait, 'you promised Amaanat you'd keep all this a secret. If you're going to go back on that, you should at least talk to him first. You got *him* involved too, and all the rest of the monks.'

It was her turn to prickle at the criticism, but she knew he was right. 'Okay,' she said with a sigh.

She started to trudge up the slope, Eddie ruefully regarding the smoking buildings before joining her.

Most of the fires had burned themselves out by the time they reached the monastery, the wood and flammable materials consumed to leave only cold, hard stone. Only shells of structures remained, walls still standing while the timber-framed roofs were gone.

There were survivors, though. Nina and Eddie arrived in the courtyard to find some two dozen robed figures bustling about. Some were tending to the injured, other men exploring the ruins to see what could be salvaged.

The Yorkshireman recognised one wounded figure. 'Jayesh!' he said, hurrying to his friend. The Gurkha lay under a blanket, his broken ankle being splinted by a young monk. 'You okay?'

'Chase?' Jayesh replied, sounding surprised and relieved before adopting his usual stoic air. 'You made it. And Nina too. Good.'

Eddie squatted to examine his injury. 'How's the ankle?'

'Hurts,' was the reply. 'What did you expect? It's broken.'

'Just checking,' said the Englishman. 'You grumpy old bastard.' Jayesh's mouth twitched into an infinitesimal smile.

Nina retrieved the Crucible from beneath the straw, then spotted Amaanat and hastened to him. 'Thank God you're all right,' she said. 'What about the rest of your people?'

The abbot's downcast expression added about a decade to his age. 'Eight of us are dead. Many more are hurt.' He cast his gaze over the smouldering ruins. 'And we have lost almost everything. Food, clothing, medicines . . .'

'I've still got the satellite phone, so you can call for help. But I have to ask you something.' She held up the Crucible. 'About this.'

His face fell further at the sight of the crystal. 'They did not take it, then.'

'No.'

'It would perhaps have been best if it had been lost . . .' A glum sigh. 'What do you wish to ask?'

'I want – with your permission – to take the Crucible back with me to America, to keep it safe. Your secret's out,' she added, indicating the fire-blackened buildings. 'But the IHA can help arrange security for the Midas Cave.'

'No, I do not know . . .' But his response was more uncertainty than outright refusal.

Eddie joined them. 'Some of the mercs got away,' he said. 'They saw the gold. Sooner or later, you'll have visitors.'

'We shall get them anyway,' the monk replied. 'Officials, politicians, soldiers – none can resist gold.'

'The IHA will do everything it can to protect the site,' Nina insisted. 'And other agencies will probably get involved as well. It's a natural nuclear reactor, after all – which means it's a matter of global security. Your monastery's protected it for long enough.'

'It would have remained protected if I had not agreed to let you come here.' For the first time, Amaanat's words had anger behind them, but it was aimed at himself rather than the archaeologist. 'All this has happened because of my weakness.'

'That's not true,' said Nina. 'Those guys may have followed me here, but they knew more about the Midas Cave and the Crucible than I did. A lot more. They would have found it themselves sooner or later.'

'There is no way to know that,' the old monk said quietly. A moment of thought, then he placed his hands together and bowed to her. 'But I still believe you are a woman of your word, Dr Wilde. If you say the IHA will protect the cave, then I shall accept that. Take the Crucible. But . . . be very careful,' he added, giving her an intense look. 'Perhaps not even the IHA should be told of it just yet.'

Nina was about to tell him that she would have to brief her former organisation, but something in his urging gaze changed her mind. For all she knew, the leak that had allowed the mercenaries to find her had been at the IHA itself. It didn't seem likely, but after the carnage that had just taken place, she couldn't risk anything similar happening again. 'You're right,' she told him, nodding. 'I won't tell them about it until I'm absolutely sure it's safe.'

'Thank you.' The abbot bowed again.

'Okay. Now I think you need to call for help.' She handed him the phone.

Eddie was already sceptical. 'So you're going to bring that thing back to New York? I think someone might notice at customs if it's just stuffed in your carry-on bag.'

'Yeah, I was kinda wondering how to do that myself.' She thought for a moment. 'As soon as Amaanat's finished, I'll make another call.'

'To the IHA?'

'Yeah, but not Seretse or Blumberg.' She gave him a sly smile. 'I was thinking more of somebody who can actually get things done.'

'You want me to do *what*?' said Lola Adams in a strained whisper.

Nina's call had been to her friend and former assistant. 'Arrange a United Nations diplomatic courier for a package that I need bringing from Nepal to New York,' she repeated. 'I don't want anybody, not even customs officials, seeing it.'

'I heard what you said,' Lola protested. 'I just can't believe you said it! I could lose my job, or worse.'

'You've done it for me and Eddie before.'

'Yeah, but you were my *boss* then! I can't—' She fell silent at the sound of conversation nearby, resuming even more quietly when whoever was talking had gone past. 'If Dr Blumberg finds out—'

'Why would he?' Nina cut in. 'I never demanded to sign off on every single diplomatic packet when *I* was director, and I can't imagine Lester does either.' A moment of doubt: Blumberg was, after all, as much by-the-book bureaucrat as archaeologist. 'Does he?'

'No,' Lola admitted after a moment. 'But it's still too big a—'

'Lola, please – it's really important. I've found something out here, something major. I will tell the IHA about it, but not yet. I don't want to risk any more lives.'

'*More* lives?' she echoed. 'Wait, has someone been hurt? Are you and Eddie okay?'

'We're okay, yes, but there are people here who aren't,' Nina told her grimly. 'Which is why I need to keep this thing a secret.' When there was no immediate reply, she went on: 'I know I'm asking a lot. But trust me, I wouldn't ask if it wasn't necessary. You're the only person who can help me.'

'I'll . . . see what I can do,' the blonde said reluctantly. 'But if I lose my job, *you* can pay for Gino to go through school, okay?'

'It's a deal,' said Nina. 'I'll give you all the info you'll need as soon as I get to Kathmandu, okay?'

'Okay. Ugh. You know, Nina? You can be a real pain in the ass sometimes.'

The redhead smiled faintly. 'It's been said.' She ended the call.

Eddie, holding the Crucible, had been listening. 'Let's hope Gino goes to community college and not Harvard.'

Another small smile. 'Yeah. But at least we can get that thing out of danger.' She regarded the crystal.

'That's if it doesn't bring danger back home with it.'

She could tell he wasn't entirely joking.

18

New York City

Oswald Seretse was waiting for Nina and Eddie at JFK – not in the arrivals area, but actually at the exit from the jet bridge where their airliner had pulled up. 'Okay, that's not a good sign,' said Eddie as he spotted the tall Gambian diplomat beside an airport official. 'Since when does he come to meet us?'

'Oswald, what are you doing here?' Nina asked as they reached him.

'I wanted to speak to you as soon as possible,' he replied. 'I have a car waiting to take us to the United Nations.'

'I don't want to *go* to the United Nations,' she objected. 'I want to go home. Our daughter's waiting for us.'

'I am sorry, but this takes priority.'

'You don't get to tell us what's a priority any more, Ozzy,' Eddie said, frowning. 'Maybe we'll just get a taxi instead.'

Seretse sighed. 'Very well. If we are able to finish discussing this matter by the time we reach Manhattan, I will tell the driver to take you to your apartment instead. Is that acceptable?'

Nina looked at Eddie, who reluctantly nodded. 'Yeah,' she said. 'You'd better start talking then.'

'Considering the nature of the matter, it would perhaps be best to wait until we can discuss it in private.' An electric cart stood nearby. The official took the wheel, and once the others had boarded, they set off through the terminal.

Nina made a phone call, putting it on speaker when she got a reply. 'Holly, hi. We're back – we're at JFK.'

'That's such a relief,' said her niece. 'Are you both okay?'

'We're fine,' Eddie told her. 'More or less.'

The young woman's voice filled with concern. 'Meaning that . . . you're not fine, but you don't want to talk about it because you don't want to worry me or Macy? What happened out there?'

'We're okay, we're back home, and you and Macy really *don't* need to worry,' Nina said firmly. 'Is she there?'

'Yeah, she's in her room . . . Macy! It's your mum and dad on the phone!'

The sound of running footsteps getting closer was audible even over the phone's little speaker. 'Mommy!' cried Macy. 'Daddy, hi! Where are you?'

'We're at the airport, honey,' said Nina. 'We're on our way home – we'll be with you soon.' She gave Seretse a pointed look.

Her daughter cheered. 'I missed you, Mommy.'

'And what about me?' Eddie asked, after a worryingly long silence from the other end of the line.

'I missed you too, Daddy! I wanted you to read me a story!'

Mother and father shared a smile. 'I'll read you one tonight, love,' said Eddie.

'The one about the eggs with legs!'

'Yeah, eggs with legs. Again.'

'We both love you,' said Nina. 'Can I talk to Holly again?'

The phone was handed over, Holly confirming that everything was in order at home. 'Oh, and your friend rang a couple of times,' she added.

'Which friend?'

'The old lady, the one who came here after the film premiere.'

'What did she want?' Nina asked warily.

'She just wanted to know when you'd be back. She left a number – shall I tell her you're home?'

'No, that's okay, I'll phone her later.' She tried to keep her expression neutral, not wanting Seretse to ask any questions. There were others she wanted Olivia to answer first.

'All right. We'll see you soon, then.'

Nina said goodbye and rang off. By now they had reached passport control, Seretse using his diplomatic credentials to see them waved through. Before long, the cart arrived at one of the airport's exits. A black limousine was waiting outside. Seretse ushered them into its rear, then sat facing them. The car set off.

'Now we can talk freely,' said the diplomat. The screen between the rear compartment and the driver was shut. 'What happened in Nepal is a most troubling situation.'

Eddie snorted sarcastically. 'That's a bloody understatement.'

'By requesting the help of the IHA, you involved the United Nations. As a result, the Nepalis are now demanding answers from us.'

'We told them everything we could before we left Kathmandu,' said Nina.

'Not everything they want to know – and need to know.' Seretse's tone, already serious, became positively grim. 'Another UN department is now involved: the International Atomic Energy Agency. The discovery of a natural nuclear reactor in the Himalayas has created a stir, even though everything possible is being done to keep it classified.'

She nodded. 'Yeah, I can see that it might.'

'What's happening with finding out who attacked us?' Eddie asked.

'Interpol is working with the Greek government to identify this man Axelos,' the diplomat replied. 'As yet, they have not found anything. It is not an uncommon name. Nor have the Nepalese authorities tracked him down. He has not left Nepal by any commercial flight, but that does not mean he is still in the country.'

'How would he sneak out with something as big as . . . the artefact?' said Nina, almost letting the Crucible's name slip.

'If they could afford to charter a couple of helicopters and pay a team of mercs, they'd be able to book a private flight to get it out of there,' replied her husband.

'This . . . artefact,' said Seretse carefully. 'You were unusually vague in your description of both its appearance and its purpose.'

'I have my reasons for that,' Nina replied. 'I hope you'll accept for now that they're good ones.'

He frowned slightly, but nodded. 'On the basis of your past record, I shall. For now. The artefact that Axelos stole, though: it was the only one, was it not?'

The redhead tried to hide her apprehension. 'It's what he came for, yeah.'

'That is not what I asked.'

'Something to say, Ozzy?' said Eddie, fixing him with a stony stare.

Seretse was not intimidated. 'I merely ask. I was curious about your arranging a United Nations diplomatic courier transfer of an unspecified item from Nepal.' His own gaze became more penetrating. 'To your home address.'

'Ah.' Nina took a deep breath. 'So you found out about that.'

'Did you really expect that I would not? I know you quite well, Nina. And you too, Eddie. It is not the first time you have . . . I hesitate to say "abused" the service to send items around the world without customs checks.'

'Please don't blame Lola for this,' said Nina. 'I asked her to keep it secret for a very good reason. The same reason I haven't told anyone about the nature of the artefact. Artefacts.'

'And would you care to share that reason with me?'

'I will, yes. But not right now.' He frowned again. 'Look,

Oswald, as you said, you know me. And you know I wouldn't do this on a whim. What we found, we couldn't leave in Nepal.'

'Is it dangerous?'

'Not in itself. But someone's willing to kill to get hold of it. I didn't tell anyone in the Nepalese government about it before we left – my priority was to get it as far away from the Midas Cave as possible. Enough people died or got hurt there already.' The wounded, including Jayesh, had been airlifted from Detsen.

Seretse leaned back, face stern. 'So why not turn it over to the IHA immediately?'

'There was a leak somewhere,' said Nina. 'Not many people were in the loop, but Axelos knew I was going to Nepal, and why. I don't want to risk anyone finding out that I've got this item, not yet. Not until I've had a chance to investigate it further.'

'I suppose I should be flattered that you consider me trustworthy enough to admit that you brought this object back to the United States, even if you will not tell me what it is.'

Eddie gave him a mirthless grin. 'Well, if anyone comes looking for it, at least now I'll know who to have words with.'

The diplomat responded to the implied threat with an equally humourless smile. 'Then let us hope it will not come to that.' He turned back to Nina. 'I could simply make a telephone call and have the package diverted to the United Nations. But I am going to place my trust in *you*, Nina. I will allow you to maintain secrecy about this artefact until you have done what you need to do. The condition I place on my assistance is that you inform me of everything you learn in due course – and that you turn it over to the IHA if I request.'

'Agreed,' Nina said grudgingly. 'Does anyone else know about this?'

'The diplomatic package? Other than Lola, no. I decided not to inform Dr Blumberg until I had discussed it with you. For now, I will maintain my discretion.'

'Thanks.'

'That is not to say that I shall continue to do so should the circumstances change. But we do trust each other to keep our respective words, yes?'

She nodded. 'Yes, we do.'

Seretse glanced at Eddie. 'All of us?'

The Yorkshireman folded his arms and glowered, but also managed a small nod. 'Yeah.'

'Good. Then for now, our discussion is over.' He pushed an intercom button and ordered the driver to divert from the United Nations to East 78th Street. 'I believe your daughter is waiting for you.'

Macy was delighted to see her parents, and vice versa. To Nina's surprise, she found herself becoming tearful as it hit home that she had been away from her daughter for three days. 'Oh, I'm *so* happy to see you again!' she told the little girl, hugging her tightly. 'I thought I wasn't—' She stopped herself from finishing the sentence, not wanting to worry either Macy or Holly.

Her niece was no fool, though. It was obvious from their bruises and cuts that the trip had been eventful. 'Sooo,' Holly said, lips pursed, 'are you going to tell me what happened? Or do I just need to go on to Google and look for anything that exploded in Nepal recently?'

'Yeah, things weren't as simple as I'd hoped,' Nina admitted as Eddie picked up Macy and kissed her. 'But we're back home now, so everything's good. Really!' she added, seeing the younger woman's sceptical expression.

'Was everything all right here?' Eddie asked.

Holly nodded. 'Macy was brilliant. I took her out to do things every day, and we had a great time.'

'You managed okay with only having a three-year-old for company?' said Nina.

She smiled. 'I didn't throw any wild parties after I put her to bed, if that's what you were wondering.'

The doorbell rang. Nina went to the intercom to be told that there was a courier downstairs. 'They're certainly efficient,' she said after buzzing him in. 'Holly, I don't want to seem as if I'm throwing you out, but Eddie and I would like some time with Macy, if that's okay?'

'I can take a hint,' the younger woman said with a grin. 'No problem.'

The courier arrived, bearing a box inside a sealed plastic anti-tamper envelope emblazoned with United Nations diplomatic logos. Nina signed for it, then she, Eddie and Macy said their goodbyes to Holly. She departed, leaving the family alone. 'What's that?' Macy asked as Nina put the package on her desk. 'Is it a present?'

'It's just something for Mommy's work,' Nina told her, to the child's disappointment. 'Listen, shall we have some food, then you and Daddy can go somewhere cool together?'

Macy looked stricken. 'What about you? You only just got home . . .'

'I've got to talk to someone about Nepal.'

'Can't it wait?' said Eddie.

Nina detected his undertone of aggravation, but did not let it change her mind. 'The sooner I get some answers about that,' she indicated the package, 'the sooner we can get back to normal. There's only one person who can give me those answers.' Her face hardened. 'And she'd better have them.'

'Nina, hello,' said Olivia. 'I'm so glad to see you again.' Nina showed her into the living room, the old woman's eyes immediately going to the now-unwrapped box on the coffee table. 'Where are Eddie and Macy?'

'Out,' Nina replied. 'I wanted to have a private conversation.'

Olivia picked up on her frosty air. 'Am I to assume that it might get rather . . . intense?'

'That's one way of putting it. Take a seat.'

The old woman made a show of carefully lowering herself into the armchair. 'You know, you really are so much like Laura. She used to have exactly the same tone when she was angry with me.'

'I'm not angry,' said Nina. 'Not yet.' She sat facing Olivia across the table. 'We'll just see how things develop, shall we?'

Olivia gazed at the box. 'That's something you brought back from Nepal, I assume.' Nina nodded. 'Then . . . you went to Detsen monastery? You found the Midas Cave?'

'We found it, yeah.'

'And you went inside?' Even though Nina was sure she was well practised at displaying only the emotions she wished to present to the world, Olivia couldn't contain her rising excitement.

'We did. And we found this.' She lifted the lid and took out the heavy crystalline sphere, placing it on the table between them.

Her guest stared at it, rapt. 'The Crucible . . .'

'So it's more than just a name to you,' said Nina accusingly. 'You know what it is.'

'Of course. Tobias Garde described it.'

Her eyes narrowed. 'And you know what it *does*.'

There was no attempt to prevaricate. 'Yes, I do,' Olivia replied. 'It turns mercury into gold.'

'You knew that the whole time – and you didn't tell me?'

'Would it have affected your decision to search for the cave?'

'It might!'

'Then you know why I kept it from you.'

Nina stared at her, aghast. 'So you *used* me? This whole thing was all about *gold*?'

228

'It was about much more than that,' Olivia insisted. 'You might think that I used you, but I did it for the best of intentions. I did it for my family. For *you*. And for Macy.'

'What are you talking about?'

'The Midas Cave gave us our family's legacy. Tobias discovered it; his fortune was the gold he was given from it. That fortune has been passed down through the generations, but nothing lasts for ever. Now that you've found the cave *and* the Crucible, though, it can be restored.'

Nina fixed her with a sardonic look. 'That might be harder than you think.'

'Why?'

'The cave's been destroyed.'

Olivia sat bolt upright, shocked. '*What?*'

'Someone knew I was going to Nepal to look for it – they knew I was going to Dragon Mountain. We were attacked.'

'By whom?'

'A team of mercenaries. They killed some of the monks, and nearly me and Eddie too. They also took the other Crucible, the big one.' Nina watched her grandmother's response closely; there was no surprise at the revelation of a second artefact. 'One of their helicopters crashed and collapsed the cave entrance.'

'My God.' Olivia regarded the crystal, then looked up at Nina. 'I'm glad you're both all right.'

'We nearly weren't. And *I'm* glad you remembered to be sympathetic, however belatedly.'

'This is not my fault!' she protested.

'Then whose is it? Whoever sent those men not only knew about the Midas Cave, they knew about the Crucibles, plural. Which is more than I did, or Mom.' An unpleasant thought came to her. '*Did* Mom know? What the Crucibles were, I mean. The name was in her notes, but there was never any explanation of what it meant. I'd thought that was because she didn't know, but now I'm wondering if it's because she *did*.'

Olivia was silent for a moment before answering. 'She knew the Crucible was part of the process of how the cave created gold. Beyond that . . . no, no she didn't. I hadn't told her, because there was no need for her to know at the time. But,' she went on, more urgently, 'that's not important right now. Who were these mercenaries? Who hired them?'

'I don't know,' said Nina. 'They were Nepali, but the leader was a man called Axelos.'

'That isn't a name I recognise, I'm afraid.'

'Did you think you might?'

'It was possible. You see, our family isn't the only one that made its fortune from the Midas Cave. Tobias Garde's companions shared the gold with him, and passed it down to *their* descendants too.'

'You think one of them sent the mercenaries?'

'I can't imagine that they would, but . . .' She lightly chewed her bottom lip, deep in thought. 'Nina, it's time you learned the full truth about your mother's past – your *family's* past.'

Nina leaned towards her. 'I'm listening.'

'Not here, not from me alone.' Olivia hesitated, apparently making a big decision. 'You need to meet the other members of the Midas Legacy.'

19

Iceland

Eddie peered out of the descending airliner's window at the raw, rugged landscape below. At this time of year the Icelandic lowlands were thawing, but the higher ground in the distance was still an unbroken vista of white. 'Can't believe I agreed to this,' he grumbled. 'We get back from Nepal, and the next day we're off to bloody Iceland!'

Macy, in the seat between her parents, let out a little gasp. 'Daddy! You said a bad word!'

'It's not a bad word in America, love,' he assured her. 'And when Americans say it, it sounds wrong anyway.'

'It's still a bad word in England, though,' Nina reminded him.

'No it's not. It's more like punctuation.'

'All the same, Daddy's going to stop saying it. Isn't he?'

'Bloomin' right,' said Eddie, but with a smile at his daughter.

A few minutes later, the Icelandair flight touched down at Keflavik international airport. Macy squealed first in alarm, then excitement. 'There you go, honey,' said Nina. 'You just finished your first airplane ride!'

The little girl craned her neck to see out of the porthole. 'Can we do it again?'

'Yeah, we'll be going back to New York soon,' said Eddie. He gave Nina a meaningful sidelong look. 'I hope.'

'I'm sure we will,' she replied.

She couldn't help feeling trepidation, however. Olivia had been annoyingly opaque, insisting only that the meeting she had set up would answer all Nina's questions about the Midas Cave – and her mother. She had not even expanded any further on the nature of the mysterious Legacy until Nina put her foot down and told her that without at least some clue about what to expect, she wasn't going to leave New York, never mind the country. 'I have a seat on what we call the Midas Legacy,' Olivia had finally said. 'It's not nearly as mysterious as it sounds – it's simply a rather self-aggrandising name Tobias and the others came up with, and that the three families have kept ever since because . . . well, we rather like it. It's essentially a council that meets every so often to make decisions concerning the fortune.'

Beyond that, however, she had not been forthcoming, which had made convincing Eddie that they should travel to Iceland a drawn-out process. But eventually he'd acquiesced, the condition being that Macy go with them; their daughter had had a passport for some time in anticipation of eventual travel. Nina had been more than happy to agree.

By international standards, Keflavik was a relatively small airport, so it did not take long to clear passport control. The only minor delay was when they had to wait for one of their items of luggage. Nina had checked the Crucible in as oversized baggage, the crystal well-protected in the same box used to transport it from Nepal. 'Well, it made it this far,' said Eddie as he collected it from the claim counter, with a wary look around.

'The only people who knew it was in New York were Lola, Oswald and Olivia,' said Nina. 'And Olivia was the only one who knew it was coming here. I don't think she'd send goons to steal it herself.' She put Macy into a puffy winter coat, then took her hand and started for the exit.

'Considering that she lied to you to find the thing in the first place . . .'

'Eddie,' Nina warned him quietly. Despite his misgivings – and her own, for that matter – about the sudden reappearance of her long-lost relative they had agreed not to air them in front of their daughter. He made a disapproving noise, but said nothing more.

A man approached them as they emerged from the arrivals gate. 'Dr Wilde?'

'Yes?' Nina said cautiously, aware that Eddie was subtly taking up a defensive stance, ready to react to any threat. The man – around thirty, with bristling light brown hair and a wide, tight-lipped mouth that gave an unsmiling edge to his otherwise handsome face – eyed him, clearly realising what he was doing.

'I am Rutger De Klerx. Mrs Garde is waiting for you in my car.' At first Nina thought his accent was German, but on hearing his name, she quickly revised her guess to Dutch. 'If you and your daughter will come with me?'

'And her husband too,' rumbled Eddie.

'Yes, and you, Mr Chase,' said De Klerx, though not without a dismissive exhalation. Eddie started to mutter something rude, but held it back after a glance at Macy.

They followed De Klerx to his waiting car, which was more imposing than expected. 'So we're getting a lift from the Fall Guy?' said Eddie, looking up at their ride. It was a bright red Ford Expedition EL, already a large vehicle capable of seating seven people, but made even taller by the fitting of massive off-road tyres and a jacked-up heavy-duty suspension. Banks of spotlights ran across its radiator grille and roof, a rack on the tailgate holding ropes, chains and jerrycans of fuel.

'It's a monster truck!' cried the amazed Macy.

Even smiling, De Klerx did not appear to be amused. 'They call them "super jeeps" here in Iceland. They are the only way to reach some parts of the island when there is snow.' He folded down a step and opened the rear door to let them in.

'I guess we're going somewhere snowy?' said Nina as she clambered aboard. Eddie lifted Macy up after her.

'The Electra hotel,' said Olivia from the front passenger seat. She greeted them, then continued: 'One of the Legacy's other members owns it. We sometimes use it for meetings because we can be sure of privacy. It's a little out of the way.' She smiled at Macy. 'Hello, dear. Did you enjoy your trip on an airplane?'

Macy began an enthusiastic recounting of the journey as Eddie climbed into the cabin. 'See you planned ahead,' he said, gesturing at the child seat into which Nina was buckling their daughter.

'I always do,' Olivia replied.

De Klerx got into the driver's seat and started the engine. The Expedition's big V8 sounded as if it had been considerably beefed up, exhaust pipes roaring. He pulled away, the studded tyres crunching noisily over the road surface.

Keflavik was some distance from the Icelandic capital Reykjavik, a long and lonely highway running parallel to the coastline before reaching the city's outskirts. Rather than heading into the centre, the Expedition skirted around it, taking a road that climbed into the hills to the east. The patches of snow on the ground grew larger as they went higher, soon joining to cover the entire landscape. The road itself was relatively free of ice – the Icelanders were well practised at ploughing and clearing their thoroughfares even in the wilderness – but the only vehicles they saw as they crossed the high plains were other super jeeps, in the form of pumped-up SUVs, pickups and even buses.

Eddie kept Macy occupied with an animated conversation about animals that might live in snow. 'Not many people out here,' Nina observed. The scenery was beautiful, but no less devoid of life than the mountains of Nepal.

'You should see this road when the Northern Lights are active,' said Olivia disapprovingly. 'It's almost as congested as Manhattan on a Friday evening. Endless busloads of tourists on their way to Thingvellir in the hope of getting a good view.'

'What's a Thingvellir?' Macy asked.

'It's a national park. There's a very big lake there, and it's also the place where the Icelanders used to have their parliament. Do you know what a parliament is?'

'I've got some words to describe the British one, but I can't use them in front of the little 'un,' said Eddie with a grin.

'It's where people meet to vote on what they're going to do,' Nina told the confused girl. 'Like Congress in Washington DC.'

Realisation lit Macy's face. 'Oh, where all the idiots are!'

'I see you've been offering commentary on the news,' Olivia said to the couple, amused, before addressing Macy again. 'The Icelanders called it the Althing, and it was their government. I suppose we're going to our own little Althing, except only three families vote in this one. Mine is one of them.'

'Who else is there?' Macy asked.

'That's a very good question,' Nina said pointedly.

'You'll meet them soon,' Olivia assured her.

The super jeep continued on, the large lake eventually coming into view to their right. Against the stark white backdrop, it appeared so deep a blue as to be almost black. Further along the road, Olivia pointed out a rocky chasm stretching back towards the ice-speckled waters. 'At the moment, we're technically in North America,' she said as the Expedition reached a curve in the road that crossed over it. 'And now . . . we're in Europe.'

'Wish it was that quick to get between 'em all the time,' said Eddie. 'It'd save a lot of waiting around in airports.'

'Was that the continental rift?' Nina asked, watching the cleft retreat behind them.

'Yes, between the North American and European plates.'

Olivia gestured at the distant hills to the east. 'This valley's gradually getting wider as new rock is formed beneath it. The place we're going is also on the rift, actually. One of its unique selling points, to use the jargon.'

The Ford soon reached a crossroads. De Klerx headed north, heading into some higher peaks. After a few miles he turned on to another road, a signpost bearing an exclamation mark and the bilingual warning *Ófært; Impassable*. Its accuracy soon became clear, the asphalt disappearing beneath deepening snow. Yellow marker posts snaked into the distance, tyre tracks showing that the buried route had been recently taken by other vehicles. 'There's a hotel all the way up here?' Nina asked dubiously.

'Good for skiing, I suppose,' said Eddie.

'You would think, but it's actually closed to the public at this time of year,' Olivia told him. 'The conditions are a little too extreme for the average tourist. The Icelanders prefer that their visitors not die of exposure.'

The Dutchman guided the Expedition onwards, kicking up compacted snow from its oversized wheels. A few miles on, they reached a small frozen lake, the icy surface glittering in the sunlight. Low cliffs rose beyond it, the markers curving around the shore to meet them. He slowed to ascend an incline, then applied a burst of power to propel them over its crest. Macy giggled at the engine's roar.

'There it is,' announced Olivia.

They had reached a broad plain, deep snowdrifts rippling across it like albino sand dunes. Beyond them, a building stood at the base of a low hill, its assertively angular architecture of pale wood and concrete and glass in sharp contrast to the natural surroundings. It seemed almost to be floating above the ground, a pair of long wings each two storeys high jutting out of the hillside. Where they joined, two stainless-steel chimneys rose skyward, plumes of pure white steam drifting from them.

'That's . . . pretty spectacular,' said Nina, impressed.

More super jeeps were parked in front of the structure. As they approached it, a young man in dark clothing hurried to meet the new arrivals. De Klerx lowered his window. A brief exchange, then the Dutchman guided the SUV towards one end of the hotel. 'He wants to meet us at the east entrance,' he told Olivia.

She was not impressed. 'Does he now?'

De Klerx said nothing, instead bringing the super jeep to a stop in an area free of snow beneath the building. From here, Nina saw that the hotel was actually Y-shaped in plan, the broad leg from which the two elevated arms extended partially buried in the hillside. Close up, the structure's gravity-defying nature was revealed as extremely clever design, steeply raked pillars bearing the load.

De Klerx opened the doors for his passengers. Another man in dark clothes took their baggage, though Eddie kept a firm hold on the Crucible. The group followed their driver up a flight of steps. Seeing that she was having difficulty, Nina moved to assist her grandmother. 'Are you okay?'

'Yes, thank you,' Olivia replied testily. 'If we'd used the main entrance we could have taken the elevator, but no, Fenrir has his own plans.'

The name was familiar, but for the moment Nina couldn't place it. 'Do you need a hand?'

'No, I'm fine,' the old lady insisted. She gripped the banister more tightly and continued defiantly upwards.

They entered a lobby. The man carrying their bags continued down a hallway, but rather than go with him, De Klerx brought the visitors into a large room occupying the entire end of the wing. Two whole walls were glazed, giving a breathtaking view of the snowy wilderness. But Nina's eyes went to its sole occupant. The room was a gym containing ranks of top-of-the-range exercise machines, but the man they had apparently come to meet was lying on his back on a bench, lifting a set of weights.

Now she knew where she had heard his name before. 'Dr Mikkelsson?' she exclaimed.

Fenrir Mikkelsson looked around at the new arrivals, the mechanical rhythm of his exercise not missing a beat. 'Ah, Dr Wilde! A pleasure to meet you again.'

'Who's this?' Eddie asked her. 'Haven't been seeing someone behind my back, have you?'

She gave her husband a sarcastic smile. 'I met him at the United Nations. Dr Mikkelsson's a director of the International Atomic Energy Agency . . . so I'm kinda surprised to see him here.'

'I am not only a member of the IAEA,' said Mikkelsson, raising his weights one last time before levering them back on to their rack with a clang. 'I am also a member of the Midas Legacy. I assume that Olivia has told you about us.' He sat up, wiping his face with a flannel. Despite his exertion, he was barely sweating.

'Yes, she has,' Nina replied, frowning at her grandmother. 'Although she's been very cagey about the details – like who else is involved in it!'

Eddie eyed the weights. 'A hundred-kilo bench press? Bit risky without a spotter.'

'One hundred and ten,' Mikkelsson corrected, 'and there is no risk, Mr Chase. I often lift far more.' He stood and donned a white robe over his black tracksuit. 'Welcome to the Electra hotel, Dr Wilde, Mr Chase.' He crouched before Macy. 'And who are you?'

'Macy,' the little girl replied, a little hesitantly.

'How do you do, Macy? My name is Fenrir.' Mikkelsson extended his hand. 'Do you like Iceland?'

She smiled and shook it, then pointed out of the panoramic window. 'There's a lot of snow.'

'There is! It can be very cold. But not in here; we keep it warm.'

'I assume you had us come in by the side door so you could give us a tour of your pride and joy,' said Olivia.

Mikkelsson rose to his full imposing height and faced her. 'Of course. What other reason would there be?'

'So that you get to meet Nina before the others and try to make a good first impression, perhaps? Just like when you *happened* to bump into her at the UN.'

The Icelander gave a mocking smile. 'You are becoming cynical in your old age, Olivia. Not everyone is as devious as you.' Her own smile in return was distinctly icy. 'Dr Wilde – may I call you Nina?'

'Sure,' Nina replied.

'Thank you. Nina, I really do wish to show off my hotel to you. I am quite proud of it.'

'I wouldn't have expected the boss of the UN's nuke-counters to be Basil Fawlty as a sideline,' said Eddie.

Mikkelsson was evidently not familiar with classic British sitcoms, but he got the gist of the comment. 'It is owned by my family's company, of which I am also the chairman.'

'You must be busy,' Nina said.

'Those who say there are not enough hours in the day are simply spending too much time asleep. Now, if you will allow me to get dressed, I shall give you a tour.'

A few minutes later, he emerged from a side room wearing a tailored suit, its chequered pattern more forceful than the one he had worn in New York. 'Shall we?' He gestured towards the doors. De Klerx opened them, and the group followed Mikkelsson through the lobby.

The hotel's interior was as neatly minimalist in design as outside, simple and elegant without seeming stark. 'One of my other business interests is renewable energy,' Mikkelsson continued. 'Iceland is the world leader in geothermal power. This site was originally used to test a new design of steam turbine – our island is formed by volcanoes, so it is very easy to drill down to a depth where the rock is hot enough to boil water. But we also have a beautiful landscape, so I thought: why not build more than a power station, so others may also enjoy it? Neither the government nor the elves objected, so I went ahead.'

'Elves?' Eddie said, surprised.

'Icelandic folklore. Many believe it is unwise to alter their land without appeasing the "hidden people"; it brings bad luck.' A small smile. 'So far, in life, I have stayed on their good side.'

'Kind of ironic that a nuclear expert would be so into renewable energy,' Nina observed.

'Few countries are as fortunate as we are to be able to take advantage of geothermal power. Nuclear energy is also vital if the world is to meet the needs of an ever-growing population. Ideally, we would use thorium rather than uranium in new reactors, as it is a more common element and produces less waste. Unfortunately, it cannot be used to make nuclear weapons.'

'*Un*fortunately?' exclaimed Eddie.

'From the point of view of governments. Because there is no weapons potential, nations are less keen to invest in developing it.' They reached the end of the hall, entering another, larger lobby at the hotel's main entrance. Banks of elevators flanked the reception desk, at which stood a man in dark clothing. Mikkelsson brought them behind it to a door that he unlocked with a contactless keycard. 'This is the turbine hall.'

Beyond was a large, high-ceilinged room, every surface painted a pristine white. A complex network of gleaming stainless-steel pipes ran through the space to a pair of great metal tanks attached to humming electrical generators. The constant low whooshing thrum of pumps echoed through the hall. 'A mixture of superheated water and steam is brought up from below the ground,' explained Mikkelsson, indicating the large conduits before them. Signs in Icelandic and English beside some of the valves warned that the contents were extremely hot. 'The water is redirected and cooled so it can be reused, and the steam sent to the turbines. This was only built as a test facility, so the turbines produce just two megawatts. That is more than enough to power the entire hotel, though.'

'So it's self-sufficient?' Nina asked.

The Icelander nodded. 'We have backup diesel generators, but they have never been needed. The only waste product,' he indicated another set of pipes, these bearing warning stickers with the symbols for both flammable and explosive substances, 'is hydrogen sulphide.'

'Isn't that poisonous?'

'And kind of smelly,' Eddie added.

'It is not a pleasant smell, no,' Mikkelsson told him. 'But the gas is condensed in the next room and stored in tanks so it can be treated with a catalyst and broken down. We actually sell the sulphur that is produced as fertiliser.'

Nina grinned. 'Recycling in action.'

'It turns it into something much more valuable. Which,' he continued as he directed his visitors back to the door, 'is in a way why you are here.' He had until now seemed almost to have deliberately avoided looking at the box Eddie was carrying, but now he gave it his full attention. 'The Crucible, I assume?'

The Englishman nodded. 'So is this where we finally get to find out what you know about it?'

'It is,' replied Mikkelsson. 'I shall introduce you to the others.'

He took them back through the lobby into the hotel's other wing, a mirror image of the first. At the far end was another large room with a stunning view, this a luxurious lounge. A well-stocked bar ran along the rear wall. Before the windows stood a circular table, several chairs arranged around it.

Some were occupied, but rather than go to meet those already in the room, Mikkelsson instead crouched to speak to Macy again. 'Would you like to see something very cool?' he asked.

She looked up at Nina before answering; her mother nodded. 'Okay.'

He led her to a raised round pool to one side. Rising from its centre was a stylised sculpture of a volcano. Faint wisps of steam rose off the water surrounding it. 'Do you know what a volcano is, Macy?'

'Of course I do!' she told him proudly. 'It's a mountain, but it's full of lava! It's very hot because the rock is all melted.'

'You are a most knowledgeable young lady,' said Mikkelsson. 'But this volcano is a little different. Would you like to see why?' She nodded. 'Watch this.'

He straightened and moved to one of several metal pedals set around the pool's base. As Macy watched with anticipation, he slowly moved his foot over it, then pressed. With a loud hiss, a geyser of steaming water burst from the volcano's mouth and splashed down around it. She flinched back before laughing in delight.

'That is water from the power plant,' Mikkelsson explained. 'We also use it for all the hotel's hot water and heating. No, no,' he added gently as Macy stamped on another pedal. 'It takes a little while to recharge. A deliberate feature,' he told the adults, 'otherwise nobody in here would ever hear anything except the volcano erupting.'

'I guess you have kids,' said Eddie.

'I have. In fact, you are about to meet her.' Mikkelsson crossed to the table, where a tall blonde woman in her early twenties stood to greet him. He kissed her cheek, the woman returning it before embracing him. 'This is my daughter, Anastasia Fenrirsdottir.'

'We Icelanders don't have surnames like you do in Europe and America,' said Anastasia, seeing Eddie's quizzical expression. Her English was as good as her father's, but much more easy and informal. 'Mine means Fenrir's daughter; his means Mikkel's son.' She glanced past Nina at De Klerx, the redhead noticing that she couldn't quite contain a smile at the sight of him.

Mikkelsson beckoned to an older woman, also blonde but smaller and more willowy than Anastasia. 'And this is my wife, Sarah.'

'Hi,' said Sarah. 'Nice to meet you.' Her quiet accent seemed to Nina to be French Canadian, but it sounded as though she had lived in Iceland for a long time. She smiled at Macy. 'Oh, what a beautiful little girl! I remember when Ana was that age. You've got so much to look forward to.'

'Thank you,' said Nina, pleased and proud.

There were two other people in the room, who bustled over as if afraid of being left out. They were a slender, well-groomed man in his mid fifties, and a curvaceous woman at least twenty years younger, with long dark hair and a low-cut dress. 'Dr Wilde!' said the man; he was American, more specifically a New Englander. 'A great pleasure to meet you. We were looking for the same thing, but you were, ha ha, rather more successful.' The laugh was slightly awkward, his discomfort growing when all he got in return was a look of confusion. He faced Olivia. 'I take it you haven't told her about our search for Atlantis.'

Olivia treated him to a wry smile. 'I hadn't gotten around to it.'

'Ah. So much for my opening conversational gambit.' Another hesitant laugh, then he thrust his hand at Nina. 'Spencer Lonmore. It genuinely is a pleasure to meet you. And your husband.'

'Thank you,' she replied, shaking his hand. Eddie followed suit.

'My wife,' Lonmore went on, introducing the brunette. 'Petra.'

'Great to see you, hi,' said Petra, her voice more valley girl than Pioneer Valley. Nina couldn't help but sense an air of disdain towards her from both Mikkelsson's family and Olivia.

'So,' said her grandmother, 'now you've met the Midas Legacy. I told you it sounds far more mysterious and conspiratorial than it actually is. It's just three families with a shared history.'

'There is more to it than that,' said Mikkelsson. 'But now that you are here, Nina, it is time that we told you about it.' He went to the table, Sarah and Anastasia following. The Lonmores quickly took their seats, Olivia finding hers in a more leisurely manner.

Nina regarded the chairs. 'Are we missing someone?' The Icelanders, the Lonmores and Olivia made six; there was an extra place.

'Not at all,' said her grandmother, gesturing at the empty chair beside her. 'This one? It's yours.'

20

Nina regarded the six seated people in bewilderment. 'What do you mean, it's mine?'

'I mean,' said Olivia, 'I want to give you a seat in the Legacy.'

Lonmore broke off from sipping a glass of whisky to raise a finger. 'Ah, now strictly speaking you want to *offer* her a seat in the Legacy, Olivia,' he said. 'Her acceptance is still subject to approval by at least one of the other families. As you well know.'

The elderly lady fixed him with an unblinking stare. 'Well, of *course* I know, Spencer. After all, you needed *my* approval when you wanted to give your new wife a seat after your son . . . departed.' A disapproving look from Anastasia suggested that said approval had not been unanimous. 'And far be it from me to take any unilateral actions without consulting the other members.'

'Such as giving Laura's notes to her daughter so that she might find the Midas Cave for you?' said Mikkelsson, his own gaze on Olivia equally steely.

'Okay, Laura's daughter is standing right here,' Nina said loudly. 'I haven't accepted any offers, and I sure as hell didn't go looking for the Midas Cave for anyone except my mother. The only reason I'm here is because I want to find out what's going on!'

Eddie quickly passed the Crucible to Nina, then took Macy's hand and ushered her towards the pool. 'Hey, love, shall we go and play with the water volcano? Mummy's getting a bit red-haired again.'

'I heard that,' Nina snapped after him, before turning back to the table. 'What *is* this thing?' she demanded, holding up the box. 'People have died because of it, and I was nearly one of them. So was my husband. I'm here because I want answers. If I don't get them, I'm leaving – and I'm taking this with me and giving it to the IHA.'

Lonmore's face flashed with alarm, but Mikkelsson's response was more measured. 'We will tell you everything you want to know. But first, may I beg your indulgence?'

'For what?'

'May we see the Crucible?'

Nina surveyed the faces at the table, her gaze sweeping clockwise from the empty chair: Anastasia, Mikkelsson, Sarah, Lonmore, Petra and finally Olivia. Having already seen the crystal, her grandmother was the only one not filled with visible anticipation, instead watching her intently.

Beneath their expectancy, the others betrayed other feelings. Lonmore was still nervous, as if afraid that she might walk out, taking the Crucible with her. Petra was also concerned, but on a less personal level, more that she was taking a cue from her husband. Both Sarah and Anastasia appeared impatient to see the artefact, the daughter far more overtly. Only Mikkelsson was unreadable, calmly awaiting her answer.

'Okay,' Nina finally said, deciding she had let them hang for long enough. 'Here's your damn Crucible.' She opened the box.

All eyes fixed upon the crystal as she held it up. 'Exactly as they described it,' said Mikkelsson. 'It really exists. And you found it, Nina.'

'Yeah, I found it,' she replied testily. 'So you got your answer. Now I'd like mine.'

'Then please, take a seat.' He gestured at the chair beside Olivia.

'That's *a* seat,' Lonmore hastily clarified. 'Not *your* seat. Just wanted to make that clear.'

'Whatever,' said Nina dismissively. She returned the Crucible to the box, then sat. 'Okay. Start at the beginning. My ancestor was in Nepal in the nineteenth century, I'm guessing with your ancestors. What happened?'

Olivia started the tale. 'Tobias and the others, Valmar Patreksson and Aldus Lonmore,' she nodded towards Mikkelsson, then Lonmore, 'were explorers, but they were also traders. The aftermath of the war with Britain had opened up Nepal, and they wanted to take advantage of it.'

'They were in the north-west of the country when they realised there was a lot of gold doing the rounds,' Lonmore continued. 'They went looking for the source, and ended up at a monastery. In return for goods and supplies they needed, the monks agreed to pay them in gold – and to show them the Midas Cave.'

'Which they tried to keep secret by hiding the route from them,' said Nina. 'I read that in my mother's notes.'

Olivia nodded. 'What wasn't in Laura's notes was that the amount of gold they were paid was substantial. Enough to set them all up for life.'

Mikkelsson took up the tale. 'It made all three of our families very wealthy, and influential. They could have simply divided it equally, but they realised the returns would be higher if it were pooled. So they established the Midas Legacy.' He spread his hands to encompass those at the circular table. 'Which still exists today.'

'Decisions about the Legacy were made democratically,' explained Lonmore. 'Each family had two seats, and a chairman was chosen on a rotating basis, with a proxy taking their place while they held the position.'

'I am the present chairperson,' said Mikkelsson. 'Sarah is currently acting as my replacement. She slots in very efficiently.' He gave his wife a small smile, receiving a still fainter one in return. 'Decisions are reached by simple majority rules, with the chair voting only as a tiebreaker.'

Nina looked around the table. 'I'm seeing kind of a numerical disparity here.'

'Indeed,' Olivia said tartly. 'Our family used to be represented by myself and Laura, when she was old enough.'

'Mom was a part of this?' Nina tried to hide her shock.

'She was. However, she didn't keep her seat for very long, because once she met your father, she not only wanted nothing more to do with me, she also left the Legacy.'

'What happened to Laura was a terrible tragedy,' Mikkelsson said to Nina. 'She is greatly missed. Not only as a member of the Legacy, but personally. She was a very good friend.'

'Thank you,' Nina replied, recognising his sincerity. The others around the table offered more muted regrets. She turned back to Olivia. 'Is that why you wanted me here? So you wouldn't be outvoted?'

'You really are extraordinarily cynical, Nina,' said her grandmother.

'Shoot at me once, shame on you. Shoot at me, I dunno, the three hundred and seventy-six times in my life someone's tried to kill me . . .'

'Nobody's trying to kill you here. I'm offering you something that by right should already be yours: a seat in and a share of the Legacy. And before you tell me you're not interested in money,' Olivia added, 'remember that it isn't only about you. It's also about your family.' She smiled at Macy, who was playing at the fountain with her father. 'Yes, you've made some money from your book, and I'm sure this new movie will earn you some more, Hollywood accounting notwithstanding, but will that be enough to last you for the rest of your life? To provide Macy with everything she needs – including a good education?'

'I'm sure we'll manage,' said Nina, though she was forced to admit she had already had those exact concerns about the future.

'But there's no need for you to *manage*. You can be secure.'

'It is not a full-time job, Nina,' said Mikkelsson. 'We usually meet only two or three times a year, whether here or in America.'

'Kind of a stockholders' meeting,' Lonmore added. 'We get an update on how the Legacy is performing, and vote on any proposals. Which we still need to do, by the way.'

Olivia waved a hand to shoo away the suggestion. 'It can wait. This is more important than some fool idea to invest the Legacy in a hedge fund.' Her frown at Lonmore told Nina who had put forward that idea.

Mikkelsson gave her a wry look. 'I think we know which way you will be voting, Olivia.'

'I've been very clear about this for years. Putting the Legacy in the hands of the piranha pool that calls itself Wall Street is a sure-fire way to see it vanish before our eyes.'

'It's already vanishing!' Anastasia said. 'Especially after so much was *wasted*.' She glared at Lonmore.

'What my family does with its share of the Legacy isn't your concern,' he replied, more flustered than angry.

'It is when it goes *beyond* your share—'

Mikkelsson tapped on the table. The noise was not loud, but it still silenced the argument. 'That is enough,' he said. 'Perhaps Olivia is right that this can wait. After all, Nina still wants answers. For a start, I imagine she is curious to know how the Crucible can possibly turn mercury into gold.'

'The monks didn't go into specifics, beyond it being some kind of nuclear transmutation,' said Nina, glancing at the strange crystal sphere. 'They didn't *need* to, I suppose; they already knew the process worked, so the "how" part didn't matter to them.'

'It matters to us, though,' Anastasia said. 'Fortunately, we have a nuclear physicist who's worked it all out.' She gave her father an admiring look.

'I am not merely a diplomat,' Mikkelsson told Nina, seeing her surprise. 'To be an effective negotiator in a matter as complicated as nuclear proliferation, it is necessary to understand all aspects. Governments are by their nature devious and secretive, especially about their nuclear capabilities. But by knowing as much about the technical aspects as their scientists – and certainly more than their politicians – I can determine if they are trying to deceive us.'

'So you know how the Crucible works?' Nina asked.

He nodded. 'Much of it is theoretical, as I have not seen the process for myself. I based it upon the accounts of our ancestors when they visited the Midas Cave. But the physics are sound. Did the monks know anything about the process by which the natural reactor functioned?'

'Yes, they told me that much. Rising water starts a chain reaction in the uranium deposits. The neutrons it produces hit mercury atoms in the Crucible and cause them to transmute into gold. When the uranium gets too hot, the water boils off and the reaction stops.'

'Was the reaction as violent as Valmar described?'

Eddie had been half listening from the pool. 'Enough to shoot down a helicopter, so yeah.'

Mikkelsson appeared impressed. 'A very rapid process, then. Much faster than Oklo . . .' He mentally filed away the new information, then continued: 'The water acts as a neutron moderator, initiating a chain reaction. Under normal circumstances, it would also absorb the neutrons that are released.' He stood and rounded the table to Nina's position, peering into the Crucible's gem-like interior. 'However, I believe that this acts as a neutron *reflector*. Neutrons can penetrate its outer shell, but once inside, the majority are trapped.' He reached for the crystal. 'May I?'

Nina hesitated before replying, overcoming an unsettling

feeling that allowing anyone else to touch the Crucible would somehow end her control over it. 'Sure.'

He carefully lifted the artefact. Holding it up to the daylight, he turned it to examine the reflections within. 'Intriguing,' he remarked at last, returning it to its container. Nina felt surprisingly relieved to have it back.

'So does it match your theory?' Olivia asked Mikkelsson as he sat again.

'It does,' he replied. 'The internal facets somehow reflect the neutrons back inwards. When the Crucible is filled with mercury, this greatly increases the odds that a neutron will collide with an atom of mercury-196. This isotope occurs naturally in liquid mercury,' he explained to Nina, though she noticed that Petra was also listening intently, as if taking notes. 'Since it is only present in very small quantities, an attempt to transmute mercury in a nuclear reactor would not produce much gold, because most of the neutrons would not strike any mercury-196.'

'But because they're reflected back into the Crucible and pinging around in a small space . . .' said Nina.

'Precisely. As the chain reaction continues, more and more neutrons enter the Crucible, but then find it hard to escape. At a certain point, they reach a critical state of their own – causing a neutron burst of such intensity that it cannot be contained. Any remaining atoms of mercury-196 that have not already been transmuted now do so, even if they are not inside the Crucible itself.'

'So that's why the cave walls were covered in gold?' said Lonmore.

'The mercury vapour inside the cave is also partially composed of mercury-196,' Mikkelsson confirmed. 'It too is transmuted by the neutron burst. Those atoms in contact with a surface become bonded to it.'

'That's what happened to Midas's daughter,' said Nina, remembering the faceless figure in the cave. 'She was in there when the reaction happened. Fried by radiation, boiled like a lobster or coated in gold and suffocated: however she died, it wasn't in any good way.'

'Are there any good ways?' asked Sarah quietly.

'If you have lived a good life, you can die a good death,' said Mikkelsson. 'But I hope none of us will have to worry about this for some time.' He glanced at Olivia, who as the oldest in the room by some margin was not enthused by the thought. 'The question now is what to do about the Crucible.'

An animated discussion broke out around the table, the members of the Legacy clearly having strong – and differing – ideas. Mikkelsson tapped on the table again. 'One at a time, please. Spencer?'

'The answer's obvious,' said Lonmore. 'We go ahead with my hedge fund proposal, and let Wall Street work its magic with the full remaining value of the Legacy. Only now, we have security. If we need more gold, we can have it. We can *make* it.'

'Using what?' demanded Olivia. 'This place is a geothermal plant, remember, not a nuclear reactor.'

'And the Midas Cave is on the other side of the world,' Anastasia reminded him. 'We can't just drop by whenever we need more gold.' She leaned towards the crystal. 'There is another option. We *sell* the Crucible.'

Both Olivia and Lonmore regarded her in disbelief. 'What?' he gasped.

'You can't be serious,' said Olivia.

'I'm entirely serious. How much would a nation state, or even some ultra-wealthy individual, pay for the ability to produce unlimited gold? We could name our price. The Legacy would be secured for ever.'

Olivia shook her head. 'That is unbelievably naive, Ana.'

'It'd also be a one-time deal,' Lonmore pointed out. 'With my proposal, we keep hold of the Crucible—'

Nina couldn't hold in her own opinion any longer. 'Excuse me!' she said loudly, waiting for all eyes to turn to her. 'Hello, hi. Can I point out a few things? Firstly, the Crucible is a priceless archaeological relic, not your personal ATM. Secondly – and I could have gone with this first, as it's the biggie – it's not yours to use!'

'It isn't yours either,' said Anastasia frostily. De Klerx edged up behind her, facing Nina, and folded his arms. The intimidating gesture did not go unnoticed by Eddie, who broke off from playing with Macy to move closer to the table.

'If it belongs to anyone, it's the monks of Detsen monastery,' Nina insisted. 'But their abbot entrusted it to me, so for now, I'm the person who decides what to do with it. That might mean handing it back to the monks, or turning it over to the IHA. But it definitely isn't going to be put up on eBay! And as for using it to make more gold, you'll find that kinda hard, since the Midas Cave was destroyed.'

That caused shock around the table. 'What!' cried Lonmore. 'Why didn't you tell us?'

Nina treated the question with richly deserved sarcasm. 'Oh, I'm sorry, I didn't realise I was your employee and was supposed to brief you the moment I arrived.' Eddie laughed.

Lonmore was flustered, but Olivia responded with amusement. 'She told me.'

'And you decided not to tell *us*?' he snapped. 'It's the same old story with you, isn't it, Olivia? Control information, let it out in little trickles when it's to your best advantage!'

'Please, Spencer, be calm,' said Mikkelsson in a placating tone. 'Nina is right. Though it would have been better, Olivia, if you had shared what you knew before the meeting.'

'I thought it best if Nina gave her account of events in her own time and as it suited her,' Olivia replied, nothing but genteel innocence in her voice.

'I can give you a very quick precis right now,' Nina said. 'Eddie and I went to Nepal, we convinced the monks to let us see the Midas Cave, then after we did, we were attacked.'

'Attacked?' said Lonmore, eyebrows rising. 'Who attacked you?'

'We don't know,' Nina admitted. 'Most of them were Nepalese mercenaries, but the leader was a Greek called Axelos. We don't know who he was working for, though.'

'Greek?' A look of perturbation crossed his face. 'Wait – you weren't joking about shooting down a helicopter?' he asked Eddie.

'Nope,' said the Englishman. 'There were two choppers, full of . . .' He remembered that Macy was in earshot. 'Bad guys. I took one out, but the other got away.'

'With the big Crucible,' added Nina.

'How could anyone have known where you were?' asked Anastasia.

'That's a question I've been asking myself. Very few people knew we were even going to Nepal. Now, I trust the people I dealt with at the United Nations, so the leak must have come from either inside the Nepalese government, or . . .'

'Or?' Anastasia demanded.

'Or this end, I think she's saying,' Eddie finished on his wife's behalf.

'That's absurd!' Lonmore protested. 'Why on earth would anyone here do that?'

'I dunno, maybe to cut out the middleman – or the middle-woman, rather – and take the Crucibles for yourself.'

Lonmore reddened, about to object more forcefully to the accusation, but Mikkelsson interceded calmly. 'I understand why you might think that, but there is a flaw in your reasoning. If we already had the large Crucible, we would not be interested in the small one. We would also have known that the Midas Cave had been destroyed. So there would be no need for you to come here.'

'Yeah, that's . . . actually quite a good point,' Nina admitted.

'There's another reason why the leak couldn't have been from the Legacy,' said Olivia. 'It's a very simple one: I didn't tell any of the other members enough to act upon it.'

'You hardly told us anything at all,' complained Petra.

'I did as much as I needed to, according to our own rules.'

'After you ignored those same rules when you brought Nina into this,' said Mikkelsson acerbically.

'Do you tell the rest of us every time you discuss something related to the Legacy with a member of your family? I've held the chair too, Fenrir; I know all the procedural games.'

'The point still stands, though,' the impatient Anastasia said to Nina. 'None of us would have anything to gain from attacking you in Nepal. So who did?'

'We all know a Greek,' said Olivia. Though addressing the whole table, her eyes were fixed upon Lonmore. 'Some of us better than others.'

'What? Yes, I know a Greek,' he spluttered, 'but I've never told him anything about the Midas Cave, the Legacy – anything like that!'

'He *is* your friend, though,' Mikkelsson said.

'And I haven't spoken to him for . . . for almost a year. Olivia only got Dr Wilde involved in this less than two weeks ago.' The others seemed unconvinced. 'Oh come on! As you said, you all know Augustine. Just because one of these mercenaries was Greek doesn't mean he hired him.'

'Nina, do you know anything else that might identify the person who sent these men?' asked Mikkelsson. 'Or you, Mr Chase?'

Nina shook her head. 'Axelos spoke to him – assuming it *was* a him – on a satellite phone, but we never heard his voice.'

'In what language?' said Anastasia.

'Greek.'

All eyes darted back to the increasingly uncomfortable Lonmore. 'That still doesn't prove that Augustine had anything to do with this,' he said, though with noticeably less conviction than before.

Mikkelsson addressed Nina and Eddie again. 'What about the helicopters? Was there anything that might help trace them?'

Nina gave a helpless shrug. 'I'm not really the expert. There was a big one and a smaller one, but that's about as much as I know. Eddie?'

Her husband stood beside her. 'The little one that got blown up was a Mi-2, and there are thousands of 'em. The big one was a Westland 169 . . . but the registration was covered up,' he recalled.

'They must have been worried that it could be traced,' said Olivia.

'They'd covered something else too!' Nina said, suddenly remembering her last view of the helicopter as it swept past them. 'But the plastic got torn when the monastery tower slid down the mountain . . . Long story,' she added, seeing the confusion of the others.

'Happens to us a lot,' said Eddie. 'She just didn't put any of this kind of stuff in her book. The film's actually closer to reality.'

'It is *not*,' Nina insisted firmly.

'Do you remember the tail number?' Mikkelsson asked.

'No, but . . . there was a logo on its side.' She closed her eyes, trying to visualise the aircraft. 'It was yellow.'

'A yellow circle,' her husband added. 'With—'

'With five triangles radiating outwards from the centre,' said Mikkelsson.

Nina was startled. 'Yes. How did you . . .'

Lonmore finished his drink in a single gulp, then slumped in his seat, ashen. 'It's the logo of Augustine Trakas's company. The Greek – my friend,' he clarified. 'He's in shipping. Well, transport in general. He owns a cargo airline as well as ships. And I'm sure he has helicopters in his fleet.'

Anastasia fixed him with an accusatory glare. 'How the hell did he find out about the Midas Cave?'

'I don't know!'

'He obviously knows more than you think he does,' said Nina. 'How do you know him? How *well* do you know him?'

'We've known each other since the 1970s,' said Lonmore. 'The members of the Legacy at the time thought we might be able to locate the Midas Cave by finding Atlantis itself, based on what our ancestors had learned about Talonor's journey. Our theory was that Atlantis was in the sea off the island of Santorini, in Greece.'

'Yeah, I know where that is. I'm kind of an expert on Atlantis.'

He looked embarrassed. 'Yes, of course. But at the time, it seemed a good bet. So we arranged an expedition. Augustine was a nobody at the time, starting out in business with just one ship. We hired it to use for our dives.'

'Laura would have come with us,' Mikkelsson told Nina, 'but then she met your father, and after reading his work she dismissed Santorini as a possible location. So she did not join us. A great shame.'

'I became friends with Augustine,' Lonmore went on. 'In a way, I'm responsible for his success, as I gave him tips on how to run a business, and put him in touch with people who could help him—'

'And look how he repaid you,' Olivia interrupted, her tone caustic. 'He tried to kill Nina, and he stole the Crucible!'

'What's he going to do with it, though?' Eddie asked. 'The

Midas Cave's now the Midas Rockpile. It'd take months to dig back into it, if you even could. Unless he's got a nuclear reactor in his back garden, the most he can use the big Crucible for is a hot tub.'

'Actually,' said Mikkelsson, 'that is not true. The Crucible would not need a nuclear reactor to create gold from mercury. A particle accelerator would also work. The source of the neutrons needed to produce nuclear transmutation does not matter; the effect will be the same.'

'Well, he's not going to have a particle accelerator in his back garden either, is he?' Eddie scoffed. 'Unless he lives next to the Large Hardon Collider.' Nina held in a laugh.

'That is "Hadron",' Mikkelsson corrected.

'I know, but my version's funnier.'

The diplomat did not appreciate his joke. 'Do you know how many particle accelerators there are in the world, Mr Chase?'

'Twenty, thirty? I dunno.'

'I know they're not all as big as the Large *Hadron* Collider,' said Nina, enunciating the word carefully. 'Two hundred, maybe?'

Mikkelsson allowed himself a little smile. 'Over thirty thousand.' At the couple's surprise, he went on: 'And that is only counting the high-powered ones. There are many more that are smaller. They are used for physics research, but also by industry and the medical profession, for all kinds of purposes. The technology is simple; even an old cathode-ray tube television is technically a particle accelerator. Scaling it up to the size of the LHC is when it becomes difficult and expensive.'

'So does Trakas have a particle accelerator?' Olivia demanded of Lonmore.

'How would I know?' he shot back. 'He has all kinds of business interests. I don't have a list.'

'Perhaps you should ask him,' said Mikkelsson.

'What, you're suggesting I go to Greece and accuse my friend of stealing something that doesn't actually belong to us, but that he ought to hand over anyway? That would mean revealing the Legacy's existence!'

'I think that bird has already flown, Spencer,' said Olivia. 'Although I have another proposal.' She turned to her granddaughter. 'Nina should see him.'

'What?' Nina said, taken aback.

Eddie was also far from enthusiastic. 'Are you kidding? He tried to kill us!'

'I still can't believe that he would do that,' said Lonmore, shaking his head.

'I can,' Nina told him scathingly, before responding to Olivia. 'Why me? Eddie's right: the last person I want to go see is someone who sent a gang of mercenaries after me!'

'Because you can offer him both a carrot *and* a stick,' said the elderly lady. 'The carrot is simple enough: a share of the gold created by the Crucibles. As for the stick, the threat of the IHA and international law enforcement coming down upon him ought to convince him to see sense.'

Anastasia's expression was one of sour disapproval. 'So you're saying we should cut him in on the Legacy? Give him a quarter of everything we have as a *reward* for what he's done?'

'Not the Legacy, no,' Olivia replied. 'The promise of an equal share of any *new* gold, though? Augustine is a businessman, after all. A quarter of something is better than all of nothing – or a spell in jail.'

'Or,' said Eddie, 'he might just try to make sure we never tell anyone.'

'I don't think he will,' said Lonmore. 'Not if . . . if I go with you. He *is* my friend, after all. If I'm there, I'm sure I can convince him. An extra carrot, so to speak.'

'Some kind of vegetable, certainly,' Anastasia said under her breath. Lonmore, across the table, did not hear her, but Nina did – as did Mikkelsson, his mouth twitching into a small smile.

'This isn't our problem,' Eddie objected. 'We went to Nepal to find this thing – which I was against doing from the start,' he reminded his wife, 'and almost died doing it. But we got it, so I think we should hand it over to the IHA.'

The proposal aroused varying degrees of outrage from around the table. Anastasia was the most vocal. 'You can't do that!' she cried, half rising from her chair.

'Yeah, we can,' said Eddie, noticing De Klerx's fingers flexing as if about to draw six-guns from imaginary holsters. He gave the Dutchman a warning look. 'Unless someone's going to try to stop us?'

'Of course not,' said Mikkelsson. De Klerx retreated, hands stiffening. 'That decision is Nina's. But I would hope you will hear us out,' he continued, addressing the redhead.

'Remember what I said, Nina.' Olivia turned to her. 'This isn't just about the six of us here. It's about you too – your family, your legacy. And your *mother's* legacy. That was once her seat; it's yours now, if you're willing to take it. You said that the monks entrusted the Crucible to you? We're also entrusting something to you: our future.'

Before Nina could answer, a small voice caught her attention. 'Mommy, what's going on?' Macy joined her parents, regarding their hosts with concern. 'Why is everybody angry with you?'

'Nobody's angry, honey,' said Nina. 'These people just have . . . some differences of opinion, that's all. They want me to do one thing, and your daddy wants me to do something else.'

'What thing?'

'It doesn't matter. Because I already decided what I'm going to do.'

The others almost unconsciously leaned forward, anxious to hear her decision. Nina faced them again. 'I'm going to go back to New York and turn the Crucible over to the IHA. Like I should have done in the first place.' She raised her voice over the protestations. 'They can work with Interpol to investigate Trakas and find out if he really has got the other Crucible, and if he has, then the international courts can deal with him. But Eddie's right: this isn't my problem. And I don't want to discuss it any more. After everything I've been through, I just want to go home and be with my family.'

'By turning your back on another part of your family?' said Anastasia, indicating Olivia.

'It's not the decision I was hoping she would make,' said the old lady, downcast. 'But it *is* her decision. We can't force her to do something she doesn't want to do.'

'Thank you,' Nina said.

'Are we going home?' Macy asked. 'But we only just got here!'

Mikkelsson spoke in Icelandic to the clearly angry Anastasia, who drew in a frustrated breath, then he turned to Nina. 'It would be a shame if you were to leave so soon. You are welcome to enjoy the hospitality of the hotel.'

'Thanks for the offer, but it'd be better if we left,' Nina replied. She knew that if they stayed, she would be subjected to non-stop pressure to change her mind.

Macy tugged at her sleeve. 'Mommy, I don't want to go yet. I want to play in the snow.'

'I'm sorry, honey, but we have to leave.'

'It was very nice to meet you, Macy,' said Mikkelsson. 'I hope I will see you again sometime. I am afraid you have quite a wait for the next flight to New York, though,' he added to her parents. 'It does not leave until this evening. Are you sure you do not want to stay here until then?'

'I think they've made their decision,' Olivia said, standing. 'We should respect it.'

Mikkelsson nodded. 'Of course. Then may I suggest you visit

Reykjavik before your flight? It may not be Manhattan, but it has its attractions. And some very good restaurants.'

Nina hesitated, wanting to leave with no further fuss, but Eddie spoke first. 'What do you reckon? Got to be better than airport food.'

'There is that, yeah,' she admitted. 'We'll take your advice, then,' she said to Mikkelsson. 'Thank you.'

'My pleasure,' said the Icelander. 'Rutger can drive you there.'

'I'll come with you,' said Olivia. She caught Nina's attempt to hide her suspicion. 'Don't worry, I won't try to change your mind. I have to fly back to the States anyway, and since I've no more business here . . .'

'Okay,' said Nina, with reluctance.

'Thank you. I'll just wrap things up, then we can leave. Fenrir?' Olivia ushered Mikkelsson away, beginning a quiet discussion. Lonmore looked put out at not being included.

'Bit of a shame to come all the way out here only to go straight back home,' Eddie said to his wife. 'Still, at least we're not paying for it.' Olivia had covered the cost of the air fares.

'Yeah,' Nina agreed, though she couldn't help wondering if some other price for her decision would follow down the line. Feeling oddly defensive, and unsure why, she collected the Crucible, holding it tightly as she waited to leave.

21

The atmosphere inside the super jeep was as frosty as outside.

'Anyone fancy a game of I Spy?' Eddie joked to break the tension as they rounded the frozen lake. 'I spy, with my little—'

'Snow?' said Macy.

'Tchah! How'd you guess? Your turn.'

Olivia, in the front seat, sighed. 'We're not going to have this all the way back to Reykjavik, are we?'

'We can talk about anything you want,' said Nina, 'as long as it's not what I said I absolutely wouldn't discuss.'

'You've clearly made up your mind, and I respect that. And I'm sure I don't need to restate my own position.'

'No. You don't.'

The old woman turned to give Nina a look that was somewhere between disappointed and irked. 'There's no need to be so curt. All I wanted was what was best for my family.'

'What was best for your family, as long as it involved finding the Midas Cave,' Nina shot back. Eddie quickly diverted Macy's attention with another round of I Spy. 'You know, you could have come to me at any time in my entire life. Like, I don't know, maybe *twenty years ago*, after Mom and Dad died?' She was hit by a sudden surge of anger, which she struggled to contain so as not to upset Macy. 'I was completely alone, Olivia. You could have seen me then, told me what happened between you and Mom for her to shut you out of her life. Out of *my* life. But you didn't! You waited until I could *do* something for you. That might have been what was best for you, but it sure as hell wasn't for me.'

'I know, and I'm sorry. But it wasn't out of some monstrous sense of self-interest, I assure you. You lost your mother . . . and I lost my *daughter*.' She glanced at Macy. 'My only child. I hope to God you never have to go through that experience. Not even losing Tom, the man I loved the most in all the world, compared to how I felt after Laura died.'

Nina's anger was quickly replaced by guilt. She had attended Macy Sharif's funeral, and witnessing the grief of the young woman's parents had been one of the most emotionally painful experiences of her life. 'I'm sorry.'

'It's all right. Time may not heal all wounds, but it does at least dull the pain. As for why I didn't come to you until now, Laura had made it very clear that she didn't want me in her – or your – life. As painful as that was, I respected her wishes before she died. And afterwards, how could I simply turn up and tell you who I was? It would mean revealing that she'd lied to you, *and* to your father. I didn't want to dishonour her memory. But you're my family, Nina. You're so much like Laura that . . . that's it's almost as if she's still here.' A deep sadness filled her eyes. 'Whatever else may have happened, I'm still glad that I got to meet you. And I hope I can get to know you better in the future.'

Nina had no comeback to that. 'Thank you. I hope so too,' was all she could say. Olivia smiled, then looked back at the icy vista ahead.

They eventually returned to the paved road, De Klerx turning at the crossroads to take them back to civilisation. Once they reached Reykjavik, rather than retrace their route to the airport, he instead followed a road that took them towards the city's centre along its northern waterfront. 'I suggested we go this way,' said Olivia. 'It's slightly longer, but it gives the best views. It's actually a very pretty town.'

'Yeah, I see,' said Nina, gazing across a wide bay to the mountains beyond. Most of the snow had gone near sea level, but the distant peaks were still capped in white. Looking the other way, she saw that Reykjavik itself was very spread out, plenty of open green space between the relatively low-rise buildings. 'How often have you been here?'

'Enough to know the best restaurants. Fenrir and his father always preferred to hold meetings in their own country rather than in the States whenever they had the chair. But it's not a hardship coming here, as long as there isn't a blizzard blowing. It's a beautiful country.'

Eddie regarded something at the water's edge. 'That's pretty cool.'

'The *Sun Voyager*,' explained Olivia as they passed the sculpture – a skeletal representation of a longboat in stainless steel. 'The Icelanders are very much into art and culture. I suppose it comes from being stuck indoors due to darkness and bad weather for half the year. If you had more time before the flight, I'd be more than happy to show you around the galleries and museums.'

'Thanks, but that's fine,' said Nina. 'Dinner will be enough.'

Olivia nodded. 'Rutger, take us to Vonarstraeti, then.'

De Klerx guided the super jeep past the impressive modernist block of the city's concert hall before turning down a broad street into the heart of the capital. Even here, everything was spaced out with lots of greenery. Traffic was only light, a huge contrast to Nina's native Manhattan. 'So, where are we going?' she asked.

'There's a very good restaurant overlooking the lake,' said Olivia. 'It does excellent fish. Although that can be said of most places in Iceland, really.'

'Sounds good to me,' said Eddie. 'Macy, do you want to try some—'

He broke off at a noise from behind: a car suddenly accelerating with a screech of tyres. De Klerx also heard it, eyes snapping to the rear-view mirror.

'Daddy?' Macy asked, alarmed.

Both Eddie and Nina whirled in their seats as a dark blue SUV roared past. Brake lights flared, and the truck skidded to block the super jeep's path. De Klerx swore and stamped on the brake, trying to swing up on to the pavement to get around it, but there was not enough room for the oversized vehicle. The Expedition bounded to a halt outside a glass-fronted bookstore-cum-coffee-house.

Three men jumped from the SUV, faces covered by dark balaclava masks – and guns in their hands. Pedestrians fled at the sight. Macy screamed, Nina lunging to shield her as Eddie stabbed at his seat-belt release.

One man ran to the driver's door and yanked it open, slamming his pistol against De Klerx's head. The other two went to the other side of the super jeep, the man at the rear aiming at Eddie while his companion flung the front door wide. 'Don't move!' he bellowed, locking his own weapon on to Olivia. He had a thick accent, English not his first language. 'The Crucible! Where?'

'In the back!' Nina shouted, holding Macy tightly. 'Don't shoot, *don't shoot*! We've got a child!'

De Klerx's attacker rushed to open the Expedition's tailgate. Rather than carry the Crucible around with him for the rest of the day, Eddie had put it in the trunk with the survival gear. The man snatched up the box, then called out to his companions – in Greek, Nina realised.

The man threatening Olivia gestured for her to unfasten her seat belt. 'Out!'

'I'm not going anywhere with you,' she replied in fearful defiance. His response was to sweep a balled fist at her stomach. She folded, gasping.

'Olivia!' cried Nina, shocked.

The attacker released the old woman's seat belt, then dragged her from the super jeep. The man carrying the Crucible hurried past and scrambled into the SUV. The third man jabbed his gun in warning at Eddie, then followed.

The Englishman immediately reached over the back seat to snatch up the first heavy object he saw, a kettle-sized propane cylinder. 'Eddie, no!' Nina shouted as he opened his door. 'They'll kill you!'

He ignored her, jumping out. The gunman hauling Olivia was almost at the SUV, the other rounding the vehicle to get in. 'Hey!' he roared. Her captor looked back—

Eddie hurled the cylinder. It crossed the few metres between him and his target in an eye blink and struck the gunman squarely on the forehead, sending him crashing to the ground. Olivia fell beside him, her head hitting the pavement.

The Yorkshireman rushed at them. If he could grab the masked man's gun before he recovered or his companions escaped . . .

Too late. The SUV's engine snarled, the truck jolting over the kerb before turning hard to swing back on to the road. It powered away, one of its doors still open.

The downed man was already recovering. Eddie changed direction and threw himself into the shop doorway, expecting a gunshot—

None came. The man was fleeing.

Eddie raced after him. A fence ran along the street's central divider. The gunman vaulted over it, heading for a small park. The former soldier angled to follow, about to make the jump himself when his daughter's terrified wail stopped him. He aborted his leap and slammed into the barrier, glaring furiously after the retreating gunman. A shrill of tormented rubber came from along the street as the SUV screamed around a corner to make its own escape.

'Shit!' he yelled, banging a fist on the fence before looking back at the super jeep. Nina ran to help Olivia, De Klerx staggering from the vehicle with a hand pressed against his head. Macy peered from the rear door, crying in fear and confusion. A last glare at the running man before he disappeared behind a building, then Eddie hurried back.

Nina was helping Olivia to sit up, revealing a cut on her temple and a vivid graze down one cheek. 'Are you okay?' she asked her grandmother.

Olivia gingerly felt the bruise. 'I . . . I think so,' she said in a shocked, tremulous voice. 'Oh my God! Are you all right? Is Macy—'

'I'll get her,' said Eddie, satisfied that Olivia's injuries were not life-threatening. 'Hey, hey, it's okay,' he told the little girl as he picked her up. 'It's all right. We're all safe.'

'Daddy . . .' she whimpered, nuzzling against his cheek. He held her more tightly, giving Nina an anguished look as she and De Klerx raised Olivia to her feet. His wife made sure she could stand, then went to her family.

'What the *hell* was that?' Eddie demanded, jaw tight with a seething, barely contained rage.

Nina wrapped her arms around her husband and daughter. 'I don't know,' she said. The super jeep's rear door was still open, giving her a view of the interior – and the empty space where the Crucible had been. 'But they got what they were after.'

Police and an ambulance quickly arrived, summoned by emergency calls from onlookers. Paramedics assessed Olivia's injuries before putting her on a stretcher. De Klerx shrugged off all attempts to do the same for him, instead phoning Mikkelsson to inform him what had happened.

The police were equally keen to find out, to Nina's frustration. 'That's my grandmother!' she told them as Olivia was loaded into the ambulance. 'I should go with her.'

'Look, let her take our little girl and go to the hospital,' Eddie said to the senior cop, who to his relief spoke excellent English, as seemed to be the case with most Icelanders. 'I'll tell you everything I can. Not that it'll be much, 'cause I don't have a bloody clue what just happened.'

The policeman held a brief discussion with the other officers, then turned to Nina. 'Okay, you can go with her. But we will need to talk to you all at the hospital.'

'Thank you,' Nina replied. She took Macy from Eddie and kissed her husband. 'See you soon. I love you.'

'Love you too,' he replied. 'Okay, so what do you want to know?' he said to the cops as Nina and Macy climbed into the ambulance.

The journey to Reykjavik's Landspitali hospital, less than a mile away, did not take long. Nina waited nervously as Olivia was taken into a private room to be examined. 'Will she be okay?' Macy asked. She had stopped crying, though her cheeks were still stained with tears.

'Yeah, I'm pretty sure,' said Nina, trying not to let her concern show. 'We'll find out soon.'

It was about thirty minutes before Olivia reappeared, in a wheelchair. 'It's just precautionary,' she said when she saw Nina and Macy waiting. 'I'd be back on my feet right now if they'd let me.' The blonde nurse pushing the chair smiled, then left them to talk.

'So you're okay?' asked Nina.

Olivia touched the Band-Aid covering the cut on her temple.

'I've survived much worse. Are you two all right?'

'Yeah, we're fine. Macy was scared, though. She's still shaken up.'

'I feel better now,' Macy assured her, though her voice was muted.

'I'm just glad you're okay. What about Eddie?'

'That's good timing – you can ask him yourself,' Nina said, seeing a familiar figure jogging towards them. 'Hey!'

'Hey,' Eddie replied as he arrived, kissing Macy before regarding Olivia's wheelchair with alarm. 'That doesn't look good.'

'Just a precaution,' Nina assured him. 'What happened with the police?'

'I told 'em what happened in the street,' he said, not reiterating any details for Macy's sake. 'As for *why* it happened, I was a bit cagey. They knew who you were, so I said they took an archaeological relic, without saying exactly what it was. I figured that the fewer people who know about a nuclear gold-making crystal, the better.'

'Did you tell them who attacked us?' asked Olivia.

'No, 'cause I didn't know myself.'

'I've got a good idea, though,' said Nina. 'I heard one of them shouting in Greek.'

The elderly woman raised her eyebrows. 'They were sent by Augustine Trakas?'

'It seems likely. He didn't get everything he wanted in Nepal, so he sent people after us here too.'

'They were taking a huge risk. An armed assault in the middle of Reykjavik? They must be desperate.'

'Or greedy.'

'Trakas always was,' said Olivia, shaking her head. 'He was determined to make a fortune in business, but he also made a couple of attempts to run for the Greek parliament. Not that he ever won.'

Eddie gave a mocking snort. 'What's worse than a politician? A *wannabe* politician.'

'A failed one, at that,' said Nina. 'But he succeeded at something: he got both the Crucibles.' Her expression hardened. 'And he threatened my family to do it. He *hurt* my family. I'm not going to let him get away with that.'

22

Greece

The mountains of Greece rolled past beneath the chartered business jet as it cut across the country on its way to Athens International Airport. Nina was not admiring the view, however, instead reading a digest of a scientific paper about nuclear transmutation on an iPad.

Eddie was not looking through the window either, but nor was he engrossed by a screen. He was watching his wife with a pensive expression that became deeper – and more aggrieved – as the minutes passed.

Finally he could contain his feelings no longer. 'We shouldn't have done this.'

Nina looked up from her tablet. 'What?'

'Come to Greece. Or left Macy with Holly again.'

'We could hardly bring her,' she said. 'I'm not prepared to put her at risk, not after what happened in Iceland. Especially when we're going to see someone who's attacked us twice already.'

'Which is why we shouldn't even have come in the first place. You should have handed the whole thing over to Interpol and let them sort this twat out.'

'I would have – if Trakas hadn't made it personal. I want to confront him face to face about what he's done.'

'And he's letting us do that,' Eddie said suspiciously. 'How do we know we're not walking straight into a trap?'

'For one thing,' said Lonmore from a nearby seat, where he was enjoying a glass of whisky, 'he's got nothing to gain. He's got both Crucibles, so it's not as if there's anything else he wants from us – and he must know that we've told other people we're meeting him. If anything happens to us, he's the number one suspect. For another . . . I *know* him. He's been my friend for over forty years – he's my son's godfather!' He shook his head. 'To be honest, it's hard to believe that he's behind all this.'

'Well, maybe he's changed. Money does that to people. Especially when it's in the form of a shitload of gold.'

'We'll see.' The businessman sighed. 'I hope you're wrong. I really do.'

'How old is your son?' Nina asked.

'Oh, he's not mine,' Petra quickly clarified from beside her husband. 'We've thought about having kids, but haven't gotten around to it yet. We've only been married for two years.'

'Spencer was my son with my first wife,' said Lonmore. 'She passed away twelve years ago. Cancer.'

'I'm sorry,' said Nina. Lonmore nodded in appreciation.

'Sorry,' Eddie echoed, before continuing: 'Hang on, you named your son after yourself? That's such an American thing. If you did it in England, nobody would ever stop taking the piss out of you.'

'Fortunately, we don't live in England,' said Lonmore. 'But Spencer's now twenty-five, and he's gone his own way.'

'I'm surprised he isn't on the Legacy with you,' said Nina.

Lonmore and Petra exchanged looks. 'That's, ah . . . kind of a contentious issue,' he said, shifting awkwardly. 'He actually *did* have the Lonmore family's second seat. But he had some personal problems, so he . . . stepped down. But,' he quickly continued, escaping the uncomfortable topic, 'it's not the first time

273

someone's left the Legacy. Laura did the same when she married your father.'

'You knew her?'

'Yes, although not too well, I'm afraid. She was several years older than me. Fenrir knew her much better. I do remember that she was very sharp, though, very smart. She could easily have had a career in politics or law. But she was also very focused on what she wanted to do, which was archaeology, so . . . Well, no one knows better than you. I guess you've got a lot in common with her.'

Nina smiled a little. 'Thanks.'

'How does it work if someone leaves the Legacy, then?' Eddie asked. 'Seems like it'd mess up the balance.'

Lonmore put his hand on Petra's; she grinned in response. 'I was lucky because I had Petra to take Spencer's place.'

'Yeah, over some objections,' she said, her good humour dissipating at the memory.

Nina cocked her head, intrigued. 'Sounds like they don't like new blood coming in.'

'The others like to keep it in the family, yes,' said Lonmore. 'Especially Fenrir.' His voice dropped, becoming almost conspiratorial. 'Sarah only has a seat because she's his proxy while he holds the chair. He may be married to her, but it's Anastasia he fully trusts with the Legacy. She's utterly devoted to him.' A snigger. 'It's a little creepy, actually.'

'And what about Olivia?' asked the redhead.

The businessman slowly leaned back and drained the remainder of his glass. 'I'm not sure it's my place to tell you this kind of thing, but . . .' He popped back upright. 'Okay, she was absolutely livid when Laura left. They had a huge bust-up over her wanting to marry your dad, yes, but some of it . . .' He hesitated, only continuing at Nina's urging look. 'It meant that Olivia lost a huge amount of her say in the Legacy, because she didn't have another family member to back her up.'

'Two against two against one, right?' said Eddie.

Lonmore nodded. 'Sometimes worse than that. But she's been in that position since the 1970s, and it's stuck in her craw.'

The pilot announced that they were on their final approach. 'So, this bloke Trakas is expecting us,' said Eddie after everyone had fastened their seat belts. 'Which is a bit Bond villain-ish. What can we expect from *him*?'

'There's a helicopter waiting to take us to his yacht,' said Lonmore.

'Also Bond villain-ish!'

'He's out somewhere in the Cyclades islands. Once we meet him, I guess we'll have to play it by ear. He's a direct man, so you won't need to beat about the bush about telling him why you're here, Nina.'

'Good,' she said. 'Because I wasn't planning to.'

'On the other hand, flat-out accusing him to his face of robbery and murder might not go down too well, so . . . maybe I should handle things to begin with?'

Nina folded her arms. 'Fine by me. Just so long as you know I'm going to do what I came here to do.'

After landing and clearing customs, the two couples were escorted to the waiting helicopter – which bore a familiar sun-like yellow logo. It took off, turning south-east and soon clearing the coastline to head out over the Aegean.

Islands were strewn across the sea like gravel scattered over blue baize. Most were volcanic in origin; Nina knew that farther out was Santorini, once thought to be a possible location for Atlantis. The helicopter's destination was closer and more northerly, however: the little island of Poria, nestled amongst dozens of still smaller rocky offspring.

They landed on a beach. A man with the salt-etched features

of someone who spent a lot of time at sea waited on a nearby jetty with a motor launch. He helped the new arrivals aboard, then set off. 'So where's Augustine?' asked Lonmore.

'On his yacht,' said the driver, pointing out to sea. There were several vessels cruising between the islands, but the one he indicated was considerably larger than the others.

'Big boat,' Eddie commented. It was a twin-masted sailing vessel, long and sleek.

Petra nudged her husband. 'Why don't we have a yacht, babe?'

Lonmore chuckled. 'There's a saying: what's the quickest way to become a millionaire? Be a billionaire and buy a boat.'

The launch headed towards the yacht. The water was choppy, a stiff breeze kicking up whitecaps. While it made the ride uncomfortable for the visitors, it was clearly to the taste of the local sailors, some of the smaller craft gleefully racing each other. Someone was even parasailing, gliding high above the sea behind a speedboat.

As they approached the yacht, the name on its hull became clear: *Pactolus*. The streamlined gantry of a double boat hoist extended out over the vessel's stern. One place was occupied by a speedboat, hanging chains beside it waiting for a companion, but rather than take the space, the launch manoeuvred to a small retractable dock below. A pair of crewmen secured it, and the occupants disembarked.

A short flight of steps led up to the aft deck. The mainsail blotted out the sun as it swung across from one side of the ship to the other. Nina instinctively ducked, remembering a painful encounter with a moving sail on the far smaller yacht of a friend of her parents as a child, but from here this one was well above head height. The mainmast was rooted amidships, behind the wheelhouse, so anyone on the uppermost deck would need to watch out for the moving boom. Stairs to one side descended into the hull, while a set of sliding glass doors at the super-structure's rear led inside the ship.

A bearded Greek man in a pristine white epauletted shirt greeted them. 'Mr Lonmore! It has been a while.'

'Captain Rouphos, isn't it?' Lonmore replied, shaking his hand. 'You're right – the last time I saw you was on Augustine's old yacht. It was a lot smaller than this one.'

'Mr Trakas has traded up,' said Rouphos with a smile. 'Welcome aboard. He will be back soon.'

'Back?' said Lonmore. 'Where is he?'

Rouphos pointed at the parasailer, who was about half a mile behind them and closing. 'There.'

The speedboat approached the yacht. Rather than slow so the flyer could make a gentle descent into the sea, however, it swept past. Trakas pulled the release to free his harness from the tow rope, working the steering lines to zigzag down towards the aft deck. The observers held their breath as it seemed that he would collide with the boat hoist, but he brought his legs up to glide over it and make a near-perfect touchdown on the teak planks. A couple of crewmen raced to him and collapsed his parachute before the wind could yank him backwards off the stern.

Eddie chuckled. 'Talk about making an entrance.'

'He always did like to show off,' Lonmore said with an affectionate smile.

Trakas removed his life vest and crash helmet, then strode to meet his guests. 'Spencer!' he boomed in a voice as big as he was. The Greek tycoon was both tall and broad, with a bronzed and hairy barrel-like torso on display through an unbuttoned yellow short-sleeved shirt. He sported a chunky gold necklace and an outsized and over-engineered gold watch, as well as several nautically themed tattoos. 'My friend! So good to see you again!' He embraced Lonmore in a bear hug, the slender American looking decidedly overwhelmed.

'Augustine, hi!' Lonmore managed to say in return. 'Yes, it's been a while.'

'Too long. We should see each other more often.' Trakas released him and went to Petra, taking her hand and bowing to kiss it. 'And the beautiful Petra. I haven't seen you since the wedding!' He straightened, then turned towards Nina. 'And you must be Dr Wilde, the famous archaeologist.'

'Yeah, I must,' she replied, finding herself struggling not to like him. Their host's larger-than-life bonhomie was instantly infectious – but she reminded herself that he was responsible for her almost being killed. 'My husband, Eddie Chase.'

Trakas reached for her hand. She turned it on its side, making it clear that she would go no further than a shake. He did so with a shrug and a small smile before facing Eddie. The Englishman gave him a perfunctory but firm handshake before pulling away, stone-faced.

'You are not so pleased to see me, I can tell,' said the Greek, unconcerned. 'But I always welcome guests, so please! Come inside.'

He led the visitors through the glass doors, the temperature immediately dropping as they entered an air-conditioned combination of gym and lounge. Trakas headed through it and along a lengthy passageway with more rooms to each side. The scent of cooking food wafted up from the deck below as they passed a flight of stairs. 'My chef will have something good for you,' he announced. 'Swordfish, freshly caught. I landed it myself,' he added proudly.

'With help, I bet,' said Lonmore.

Trakas laughed. 'Spencer is still bitter about the time I took him fishing and he hurt his hands trying to bring in a swordfish *this* long.' He held his palms about eight inches apart. 'Including the sword!' Another booming laugh, then he opened a door and stepped through. 'Please, in here.'

The new room was another luxurious lounge, wraparound windows giving a panoramic view of the ocean. Glass doors were open to the bow deck, a couple of crew members beyond the foremast. A table had been laid for a meal. Trakas took the seat at its head. Nina noticed that six places had been set, rather than five.

'So,' said the Greek as his guests sat, 'you want to talk to me.'

Lonmore spoke first. 'Yes, we do. It's about the—'

'It's about the Crucibles,' Nina cut in. 'The Atlantean artefact your mercenaries stole from the Detsen monastery in Nepal.'

Trakas showed no surprise. 'Yes, the Crucible. What of it?'

'What of it?' Eddie echoed scathingly. 'We want you to give the bloody things back!'

'And why should I do that?'

'Because if you don't,' said Nina, 'we'll bring down Interpol on you. There'll be plenty of charges, but the biggest ones will be the theft of Atlantean artefacts – which the UN consider protected items under the jurisdiction of the International Heritage Agency – and multiple counts of murder.'

'Murder?' barked Trakas. 'I have killed nobody.'

'But you hired mercenaries who did. It amounts to the same thing. If you don't cooperate, you'll be arrested and extradited to Nepal to stand trial.'

'But if you turn the Crucibles over,' said Lonmore, in a more conciliatory tone, 'I'm sure we can come to some mutually beneficial arrangement.'

Trakas shook his head dismissively. 'You say I am responsible for these deaths. But that is not the version of events I have been told.'

'We were there,' said Eddie. 'We saw it for ourselves.'

'And so did the man who told me.' He called out in Greek. Someone came down the passageway – and Eddie and Nina reacted in shock as Axelos entered the lounge.

The Yorkshireman jumped up. 'What the *fuck* is he doing here?'

'This son of a bitch tried to kill us!' Nina cried.

'Please, please, be calm,' said Trakas, gesturing for Eddie to retake his seat. 'Petros works for me – he is my chief of security. I sent him to Nepal to obtain the Crucibles, but because of the short timescale, he was forced to hire local men instead of more reliable ones he had worked with before. This was,' he brought his hands together as if in prayer, seeming genuinely contrite, 'a mistake.'

'No shit,' Eddie growled.

'It was you and your friend who made the first kill,' said Axelos with disdain. 'If you had let us leave with the Crucibles, no one would have died.'

'Oh, please,' snapped Nina. 'The moment those assholes you hired realised the cave was full of gold, they decided they were going to kill us and take it. You were damn lucky they didn't decide to kill you too.'

'But you *did* cause the first death, did you not?' Trakas asked.

'In self-defence,' Eddie insisted.

'All wars start with a first shot, and the man who pulls the trigger is to blame. Yes, I used extreme means to get the Crucible. But they are needed in extreme times – and I have very good reasons. As soon as I learned you were going to Nepal to find the Midas Cave, I had to act quickly.'

'You knew that?' said Nina, surprised. 'How?'

Lonmore was just as curious. 'Yes – how could you possibly have known anything about the Midas Cave, or the Crucibles?'

Trakas chuckled. 'Why, *you* told me, of course!'

'Me?' Lonmore gasped. 'What? No, I didn't!' He glanced towards his companions as if trying to convince them. 'Of course I didn't!'

The grinning tycoon picked up one of the glasses before him

and peered through it at his friend. 'Ah, Spencer, you don't even remember? Well, we were young, and you never could take your alcohol. But surely you remember the bar, down the little back street near the top of the mule track from the harbour in Santorini? It served a very good ouzo.'

Lonmore was about to say something else – then his face froze as a long-lost memory resurfaced. 'The bar, yes. We went in there almost every night after the dives. But I didn't . . .' He trailed off, his expression now riven with uncertainty.

'You did,' said Trakas smugly. 'You were drunk, my friend; very, very drunk! You told me about the Midas Legacy, your great cache of gold – and why you were in Greece. It was not to search for Atlantis, no? You were looking for a way to find the Midas Cave.'

'Oh my God,' whispered Lonmore, going pale. 'I can't have told you. I *can't*! I couldn't have been that stupid . . .'

Trakas snorted in amusement. 'I am not a mind-reader, Spencer. How else would I know? Ever since then, I have been very interested in you, and the others in the Legacy. As I became rich, I was able to use . . . certain means to observe what you were doing, even from Greece.'

The American was appalled. 'You were *spying* on us?'

'I am afraid so, yes. I used to use private detectives, but now there are people who can find out everything with just a computer. What you buy, where you travel, who you phone . . .'

'Jesus.' Lonmore slumped, both hands to his head. 'All this time, and you were just *using* me to find the Midas Cave?'

'I really have been your friend,' Trakas insisted, almost hurt. 'For years I did not believe it was even real. Yes, your families got their fortunes from somewhere, but a cave of gold in the Himalayas, left by people from Atlantis? It seemed like a fairy tale! But then,' he gestured at Nina, 'Dr Wilde *found* Atlantis. The legends were true. And if Atlantis was real, then so too was the Midas Cave – as was the story of Midas himself. The ruler with the golden touch – I can appreciate that. So then I took a whole new interest in the Legacy . . . especially when I learned that she was Olivia's granddaughter.'

'But if you knew that, you must have known I had no connection with her, or the Legacy,' said Nina. 'I didn't even know she was still alive until last week!'

'I knew *her*, though. I was sure she would some day use you to find the cave. And I was right. When I was told you were going to Nepal, I sent Axelos to follow you and obtain the Crucibles.' He leaned towards her. 'I am sorry that people were hurt, I really am. It was not what I wanted to happen.'

'But it *did* happen,' she shot back. 'And you can split hairs all you want about who shot first, but if you hadn't sent those mercenaries, nobody would have died. You *are* responsible.'

'For all I knew, going into the cave would have killed you,' said Trakas, his geniality fraying. 'It is a natural nuclear reactor! Perhaps the monks themselves wanted to silence you by letting you go inside, hmm?'

Lonmore broke out of his self-tortured gloom, looking at the Greek in surprise. 'Wait – how did you know about the reactor? I couldn't have told you that in Santorini, because I didn't know myself! It was Fenrir who figured it out, and that wasn't until he had his doctorate . . . which was *after* the dive in Greece.'

Trakas smiled. 'No, you did not tell me, Spencer. But you could say that without you, I would not have been able to find out.' His amusement growing as he saw Lonmore's confusion at his riddle, he spoke to Axelos. 'Petros, please fetch my other guest.'

Axelos went back down the passage and knocked on a door. It opened, and someone else accompanied the Greek back to the lounge.

Neither Nina nor Eddie recognised the trendily and

expensively dressed young man who entered. But the Lonmores reacted with open-mouthed shock. 'What . . . what are you doing here?' Lonmore spluttered.

The new arrival treated him to a contemptuous sneer, folding his arms defiantly across his chest. 'What do you think? I want my share of the Midas Legacy . . . *Dad*.'

23

On the *Pactolus*'s foredeck, a crewman named Velis squinted into the sun with growing suspicion at an approaching motor yacht. Augustine Trakas was both a rich man and someone who had accrued enemies, and kidnappings of either were far from unknown in Greece.

One of his shipmates had also spotted the craft, ahead off the port side. 'Is it coming at us?'

'It'll be close.' While the *Pactolus* had engines, at the moment it was using its sails alone to make around nine knots. The motor yacht was slightly faster, pounding through the waves on a course that would cut in front of the sailing vessel – or even intercept it. 'I'll warn the captain.'

He jogged aft, glancing through the lounge windows as he passed. His boss was engaged in what looked like a heated discussion with the visitors. Not wanting to interrupt, he continued on along one of the narrow side decks and entered a door to climb a ladder to the bridge at the front of the level above. Rouphos was at the wheel. 'Captain! There's a ship coming towards us.'

Rouphos nodded. 'I've seen it. We're to her starboard, so we should have the right of way, but . . .' He regarded the cruiser warily, then made a decision. 'Take the wheel – if she gets to one hundred metres without changing course, turn hard to port and start the engines to get us clear.' The crewman nodded and stood at the controls. 'I'll go and warn Mr Trakas that we might—'

He stopped. The incoming cruiser was now less than two hundred metres away, but its pilot had apparently realised at last that the vessels were converging. It swung lazily to port, angling away from the yacht as it crossed its path.

Rouphos retook the wheel. 'Bloody tourists,' he complained.

'I don't like that it came so close,' said Velis. 'Especially when we've got these people aboard with Mr Trakas. Should we issue weapons?'

'Not yet.' Rouphos watched the ship as it pulled away. 'It can't do anything to us from there.'

The cruiser was indeed retreating from the *Pactolus* . . . but just before it crossed the yacht's course, some of its passengers had dropped unseen into the sea from the far side of its superstructure.

Beneath the choppy surface, several scuba divers approached the sailing vessel. Each was being pulled along by a diver propulsion vehicle, essentially a powerful electric motor with a propeller. Even the fastest DPV couldn't keep up with a ship moving at almost ten knots, though, which was why the group had entered the water ahead of the yacht. Now, they had only one chance to intercept it.

The sailing ship closed on them in eerie silence, the only sound reaching the divers over the hissing whine of their own DPVs was the slap of the waves above. The leader and two of his companions curved across its course to run parallel to its starboard side, the others staying on its port. The keel sliced through the water between the two teams of divers, rapidly overtaking them even with the DPVs at full power—

The leader clamped a disc-shaped object hard against the yacht's hull as it swept past. The others did the same, their limpet-like suction devices all sticking firmly in place. One by one they let their DPVs fall away, then used second limpets to climb upwards.

The yacht continued onwards, its occupants unaware of the new stowaways beneath the waterline.

'So, we going to get any introductions?' said Eddie loudly over the angry babble that had erupted in the lounge. 'I'm assuming from the whole "Dad" thing that this is Junior Lonmore.'

'Don't call me that!' snapped Spencer Lonmore Jr. 'I'm not some *adjunct* of my father. I'm my own man, and I live my own life. At least,' a poisonous glance towards the elder Lonmore, 'until *he* cut me off!'

'I did everything I could to support you!' Lonmore protested. 'And I still am – I'm paying your allowance!'

'My *allowance*? You say it like I'm ten years old and I'm using it for candy and Pokémon cards!'

'You're still paying for everything he wants?' Petra said to Lonmore, surprised and also annoyed.

'He's my son, what else am I going to do?'

'You could maybe tell him to grow up and earn his own money instead of mooching off of you!'

'Mooching?' cried Spencer, with a bitter laugh. 'That's rich, coming from the gold-digger!' Petra drew in an affronted breath.

'Hey, *hey*!' said Nina, blowing a shrill whistle. 'Time out, okay? Everyone shut up and calm down.'

'You can tell she's got a three-year-old, can't you?' Eddie said, amused.

'If people act like three-year-olds, what do they expect? All right, what's going on?' She looked to Trakas for an explanation.

The Greek nodded towards the new arrival. 'I have known Spencer ever since he was a boy. When he found himself in, ah, financial difficulties,' a faint smile, 'he came to his godfather for help.'

'He wasn't in financial difficulties,' Petra responded sarcastically. 'He was kicked out of the Legacy for going on a spending spree with everyone else's money!'

'And you were all set to replace me, weren't you?' snarled Spencer. 'Poisoning the others against me so you could have my seat!'

'It wasn't like that,' said Lonmore. 'I gave you every chance I could to turn things around.'

Petra sneered at the young man. 'But you liked being a playboy too much, didn't you? You just couldn't give up the cars and the casinos and the hookers.'

'At least hookers are honest about what they do,' he fired back.

'Do *not* make me whistle again!' Nina cut in before the furious Petra could reply. She turned back to Trakas. 'You were saying?'

'I wanted to help Spencer, of course,' Trakas continued. 'And I knew from my investigators that he had been a member of the Legacy: the same people, meeting in the same place at the same time so often? So I offered him a deal that would help us both. He accepted.'

Lonmore stared at his son, shocked. 'You told him about the Midas Cave? You told him *everything*?'

'No more than you did when you were drunk off your ass,' Spencer replied. 'And you had the nerve to criticise *me* for having a good time?'

'I used my own resources to try to find the cave,' said Trakas. 'With no success. But then I learned that Olivia had contacted you, Dr Wilde.'

Spencer's expression slid into smugness as he swaggered to the last place at the table and sat facing his father. 'You and the others met Olivia in New York right afterwards. That must have pissed you all off, that she went ahead and did it without discussing it first. Not that I'd expect her to change after all this time.'

'And then,' Trakas went on, 'my sources learned that you were going to Nepal, Dr Wilde. To find the Midas Cave.'

'Which brings us back to why we came here,' said Nina, anger simmering. 'Are you going to turn over the Crucibles, or do I have to get international law enforcement involved?'

'International law!' barked Trakas, almost spitting out the words, as if they tasted foul. 'International law is a sick joke, Dr Wilde. Do you have any idea *why* I want the Crucible?'

'To make enough gold to turn leprechauns even greener, I'm guessing,' Eddie offered.

Nina nodded. 'I've met a lot of very rich people over the years. The one thing they had in common is that they all wanted to be even richer.'

Trakas drew back in his chair, almost offended. 'You think the gold is for *me*?'

'It isn't?' asked Lonmore, confused.

The tycoon banged a fist on the table. 'I am a patriot! Greece is my motherland, and I will fight for the honour of my country, whatever it takes. We have been betrayed and humiliated by the banks, by politicians, by our so-called friends and allies.' He rose to his feet, glaring down at his visitors as if they were personally responsible for his nation's grievances. 'I will avenge that humiliation! And I will use the Crucible to make our betrayers *beg* our forgiveness!'

The remaining crewman near the bow, a man called Galatas, watched the cruiser as it headed away from the *Pactolus*. It hadn't been a threat, then, just bad seamanship. Nothing to worry about . . .

An odd noise, somewhere behind him. He looked around. There was nothing loose on the foredeck, and it hadn't come from the headsail or its mast; he was experienced enough to know the sounds made by a ship at sail.

It came again, a dull thud. He crossed the foredeck to investigate. Nobody on the starboard walkway. Another muffled bump. He headed past the lounge and down the side deck to a hatch. It was open, but there was nobody inside. So what had made the—

Something stabbed into his calf from behind – and every muscle in his body locked solid in paralysed agony as fifty thousand volts coursed through him.

Galatas fell to the deck. Unable even to scream, he could only watch helplessly through pain-clenched eyes as two wetsuited figures clambered over the railing. One drew a silenced handgun from a large waterproof pouch and aimed it at the crewman's face. He didn't need to speak to communicate his intent: *make a sound and you die.*

The current cut out, Galatas slumping. 'How many crew?' demanded the gunman, in English.

Even in his dizzied, nauseous state Galatas still thought to feign ignorance of the language, but the man's cold expression warned that he would be considered either cooperative or useless – and the latter would not be good for his chances of survival. 'Eight,' he gasped.

The second intruder – a woman – produced a gun of her own. 'If you're lying, you'll be the first to die.'

'We have eight regular crew, and the captain,' Galatas insisted. That seemed to satisfy the gunman, though the woman was reserving judgement.

Another man, the one who had shot the taser into his leg, climbed over the railing. How they had scaled the yacht's smooth side without lines the Greek didn't know, but he had no chance to investigate as the latest arrival secured his hands behind his back with a plastic zip-tie.

The leader donned a headset, speaking quietly into the mic. 'Everyone's aboard,' he told the woman after others responded, then he issued a command. 'Secure the crew before we move in on Trakas. Use tasers to subdue them, but shoot anyone who's a threat. Okay,' he continued, addressing his companions, 'let's move.'

The second man forced Galatas through the hatch, the leader and the woman heading aft. Even if he hadn't still been suffering the after-effects of the electric shock, the zip-tie prevented the Greek from taking any action against his captor. A feeling of shame flooded through him at the realisation of how completely he had failed his boss.

But all was not lost. While he had technically told the invaders the truth – that the *Pactolus* had eight full-time crew including himself, plus the captain – he had not mentioned the chef, whom Trakas had brought on board for the day specifically to cook for his guests.

And she, like the yacht's regular crew, was also a trained bodyguard.

'What humiliation?' said Lonmore, bewildered. 'Augustine, what are you talking about?'

Trakas snorted. 'How typical. When you are safe and secure in your own rich little world, you think you can ignore everything outside it. But when everything is suddenly taken away' – a glance at Spencer, who nodded knowingly – 'then you will understand.'

Eddie regarded their luxurious seagoing surroundings. 'Kept this from the bailiffs, did you?'

'I still have my wealth,' the Greek replied. 'But my country does not! Before the financial crash, the banks and the European Union encouraged Greece to borrow, borrow, borrow – as much money as we wanted. So she borrowed, because we were told that nothing could go wrong.'

'And then it did,' said Nina.

'It did,' he echoed. 'The crash came, and suddenly the banks wanted all their money back – with interest. Billions of euros of interest. And the European Central Bank, and the International Monetary Fund, which had encouraged my country to borrow in the first place? Now their plan became clear! They would lend us the money we needed to survive, but only if we obeyed their orders. Sell off our assets, destroy our welfare system, let foreign companies take over our infrastructure – turn us into a third-world nation, a puppet of banks and bureaucrats!'

'But you could have said no,' Lonmore pointed out. 'If you'd left the euro, you would have been able to control your own exchange rate, set interest rates—'

'Do you think I do not know that?' Trakas barked, slamming his hand on the table again. 'I pushed for Greece to leave the euro! But the people voted to stay, and our fate was sealed. As long as we are in the eurozone, we cannot control our own economy. We will be in debt for ever, and everything we built will be sold to foreign vultures to pick apart!'

'Yeah, that's a bit crap,' said Eddie. 'But what's it got to do with the Crucibles?'

'It has *everything* to do with the Crucible, Mr Chase. Do you know how much gold is held by the European Central Bank and the IMF?'

'Not off the top of my head, no.'

'But I'm sure you're going to tell us,' Nina said.

A sarcastic chuckle. 'Yes, I am. The ECB has reserves of over five hundred metric tonnes of gold, worth more than twenty billion dollars at today's rate. The IMF holds almost three *thousand* tonnes, worth over one hundred and twenty billion dollars!'

'That's Dr Evil money,' said Eddie, impressed.

'All that gold is used to stabilise the world's economies. And the Crucible,' said Trakas, his anger metamorphosing into something close to expectant glee, 'can make it all worthless. If I choose, I can *wipe them out*. Not just the global banks, but the other countries that tried to crush Greece under their boots. Germany, France, Italy, all the others. With the Crucible, I can turn their gold into *nothing*.'

'But the Crucible *makes* gold,' said Eddie, puzzled. 'Was there a reverse button on it I didn't notice?'

Nina suddenly realised what Trakas intended. 'You're not just going to make gold,' she exclaimed. 'You're going to make a *lot* of gold. Enough to flood the market and drive down the value of their reserves.'

Lonmore gaped at the Greek. 'But . . . but that would destroy the entire global economy!' he stammered. 'It'd make the 2008 crash look like a blip. You're talking about causing a worldwide depression!'

'I am,' said Trakas, satisfied. 'But . . . there is a simple way that I can be persuaded not to do it.'

'And that way is?' demanded Nina.

'I will use the Crucible and a particle accelerator to create gold. The process will be recorded and witnessed to prove it is not fake. Once that is done, the *threat* of my making more will be enough to force the banks to do what I wish: to wipe out all of Greece's debts, every last cent. If that does not happen, then I shall release the proof of what I have done to the media, which will terrify and destabilise the markets . . . and then I shall sell tonne upon tonne upon tonne of gold. Its price will crash.' He smiled. 'If they know what is good for them – and they do, they are very clever people –' the words sounded more insult than compliment, 'I will not need to do that.'

'It'll never work,' said Lonmore. 'The US government has the world's largest gold reserves – they'll never let anyone hold them to ransom. They'll stop you, whatever it takes.'

'The American economy is backed by more than gold,' Trakas replied. 'They will survive a crash and recover quickly, just as they did after 2008. And they can even profit from it; they will be able to set their own terms to help those who were wiped out. Germany and the others will know how Greece felt!' Another smile, more gloating. 'But I hope it will not come to that. It will be much easier for everyone to give me what I want, and help one small country. Then after I have rescued Greece, who knows? Perhaps she will reward me with something more valuable than money.'

Nina almost laughed at his sheer gall. 'What, this is your presidential bid?'

'Why not? With no debt, the banks will have no power over us. The country can be run for its people, not for vultures and parasites. If I am chosen to lead, I shall be honoured. But even if I am not, I have still done my duty as a patriot. I will reclaim the legend of Midas for Greece, Dr Wilde. But this time, my golden touch will not be a curse.'

Lonmore stared at him in disbelief, then turned to his son. 'Spencer, why on earth would you want to go along with this? It would wipe out the value of the Legacy's gold as well. We'd be ruined!'

'It won't just wipe out the Legacy's gold,' Spencer sneered. 'It'll wipe out the *Legacy*. Everything you've built, everything you've done over a hundred and fifty years? Gone.'

'There'll be nothing left for you either,' said Eddie.

The young man shrugged. 'Augustine's taking care of my money issues whatever happens. I won't be broke any time soon, trust me. Unlike the rest of the Legacy.' He smirked at his father and stepmother. 'I just hope I get to see Fenrir and Olivia's faces if it happens. It'll be worth it just to see that arrogant sociopath and that old bag squirm.'

'Hey!' snapped Nina. 'That's my grandmother you're talking about.'

'The grandmother who only told you she was still alive because she realised she could get you to find the Midas Cave?

Yeah, she's worth standing up for. Just like the rest of them.' Spencer gave his father a look of disdain. 'All that crap you fed me about using the Legacy's money to do good for society? What a bunch of hypocritical bullshit. We all know it's just to cover up how our families got rich in the first place.'

'That's not true,' said Lonmore, but with an uncomfortable defensiveness.

'No? And what about you, Dr Wilde? You want to join the Midas Legacy even after finding out the truth about it? You're as bad as the others.'

'I *don't* want to join the Legacy,' Nina shot back. Spencer's surprise at learning that was plain. 'And what truth? What are you talking about?'

Spencer gave his father a mocking laugh. 'You haven't *told* her? Oh my God! Olivia never even . . . Damn.' He shook his head, laughing again. 'I never thought even she'd be that stone cold.'

'About what?' Nina demanded.

Trakas smiled. 'Perhaps you should tell her the family secret, Spencer.'

'Spencer, no,' said Lonmore in a warning tone.

His son ignored him, turning to Nina with a smug expression. 'You know why Aldus Lonmore and the others were actually in Nepal? They sure as hell weren't explorers.'

'So enlighten me,' she said, frowning – but also wanting to find out more.

'I thought you'd know, but I guess you're an archaeologist rather than a historian.' A smirk at his little joke. 'Nepal was falling apart in the 1840s, with power struggles between the royal family and other nobles. It got so bad that when someone murdered the queen's favourite general, she had everyone she thought might have been even slightly involved rounded up, brought to her palace and executed on the spot. So it wasn't exactly the most stable country. But you know what kind of people you'll always find looking to make a fast buck in that kind of situation?'

'Mop salesmen?' Eddie suggested.

'I'll tell you,' Spencer said, ignoring the interruption. '*Arms dealers!*'

The intruders spread out silently through the yacht, hunting down the crew.

One man was caught as he cleaned Trakas's stateroom, turning at a noise over the whine of his vacuum and taking a taser dart to his chest. Another man emerged from the head to find a wetsuited stranger just feet away, not even having time to shout in alarm before one shock was overpowered by another.

The other crewmen were also quickly taken down. Out on the open sea, they had thought they were safe, and paid the price for their complacency. One by one they fell, whether to the paralysing power of a stun gun or more physical blows.

The last to be taken was Captain Rouphos in the wheelhouse; focused on guiding the *Pactolus* through the choppy waters, he didn't register someone entering behind him until thousands of volts sent him sprawling over the controls. His attacker, the woman, secured the sailor's hands behind his back, then brought him at gunpoint down to the lower deck.

A burning smell made her nose twitch, her concern rising as she realised a thin haze of smoke was coming from the galley. She peered in to discover that the cause was a large fish on a grill. One side was black, the flesh turned to charcoal.

She almost walked on, but then it occurred to her that the smoke could trip a fire alarm, warning Trakas that something was wrong. Keeping her gun fixed on her prisoner, she turned off the grill's twin propane burners. 'Okay, keep going.'

Rouphos trudged aft down the central passage. The other

bound crew were crammed together in a storage hold under armed guard. The leader of the attackers shoved the captain down with his men, then spoke into his headset. 'Is Trakas still in the same room?' The reply was in the affirmative. 'Okay. Let's go. Honnick, stay here and watch them.' A man with a cut and bruise on his forehead took up position at the door. Everyone else headed for the main deck.

The woman glanced into the galley again. The burnt fish was still smouldering, but the smoke was being drawn out through an extractor fan. Since the alarm hadn't already gone off, it was unlikely anything would trigger it now. Reassured, she trailed the leader to the stairs, the other men behind her.

The only movement in the galley was the gentle swirl of smoke rising from the half-incinerated swordfish . . . then a cabinet door slid open.

The chef, a Greek woman called Sperou, leaned out, listening. All she heard was the clump of retreating feet. She carefully slid out of the cabinet.

It was sheer fluke that she had escaped capture. She had been about to turn the fish when she glanced to check a simmering pan and caught a reflection in its gleaming stainless-steel side. Even distorted by the curved surface, she instantly recognised that the figure in the passageway was not one of the crew . . . and was holding a gun.

By the time he entered the galley, Sperou had already found a hiding place. Assuming that one of his companions had already captured the cook, the intruder gave the room a cursory search, then departed.

Now Sperou blew a relieved kiss at the pan before going to a wall cabinet. Assorted packaged ingredients were within, but she pushed them aside and retrieved a box, opening it to reveal a compact Glock 26 handgun and magazine.

It took only a moment for the woman to load and check the pistol, her six years in the Greek army and specialist bodyguard training beyond that familiarising her with a multitude of weapons. What had happened to the yacht's crew she didn't know, but she assumed from the number of people passing the galley that they were being held prisoner in one of the holds.

She had to free them.

'That's right,' Spencer went on, seeing Nina's dismay. 'Our ancestors, the founders of the Midas Legacy, weren't in Nepal to make any amazing discoveries. They were gun-runners! They were selling rifles – to both sides.'

'And that's how they got their gold?' she asked.

Spencer nodded. 'The monks at Dragon Mountain were allied with . . . I don't even know who, but it doesn't matter. All that Buddhist peace and love crap didn't get a look-in when they had a chance to arm up their side. And they were so happy to get the guns that as well as paying their suppliers a fortune in gold, they also showed them their biggest secret – the Midas Cave. And our three families have been living off the back of that ever since. Just with the embarrassing part about how they actually got rich in the first place pushed aside.'

Nina looked at Lonmore for a denial, but could tell that one would not be coming. 'And I don't suppose you or Olivia or anyone else would have mentioned this if I *had* decided to join the Legacy?' she asked him.

'It's not something we're proud of,' said Lonmore. 'But it happened, and since then the three families have tried to do what they can to make up for it.'

'Yeah, I'm sure you've been making regular donations to charities in Nepal,' Eddie said scathingly.

'But now you know,' Lonmore continued. 'So what are you going to do, Nina?'

Nina drew in a breath, trying to control her anger. 'I'll tell you what I'm *not* going to do,' she said. 'And that's have anything more to do with your pathetic little secret society. And believe me, the next time I see my grandmother – if she's ever brave enough to show her face to me again – I'm going to tell her exactly what I think of her for using me to do her dirty work! Right now, though? I came here for a reason. Which was,' she turned back to Trakas, 'to ask you to turn over the Crucibles to the IHA.'

'I think you know my answer, Dr Wilde,' Trakas replied, his earlier good humour evaporating.

'Yeah, I think I do,' she said, the unpleasantly familiar feeling that the situation was about to change for the worse rising in her stomach.

Eddie sized up Axelos, whom he realised was doing the same to him. 'So do I.'

'Augustine, there's no need to do this,' said Lonmore, pleading. 'We can come to a deal. The Legacy is willing to cut you in on an equal share of the gold we make if you let us have both Crucibles. Everyone can benefit. Even you, Spencer,' he added. His son's only response was another scornful sneer.

'Do you have your own particle accelerator?' scoffed Trakas. 'I think not. And why do you keep saying I have both Crucibles? I only have the big one.'

'No, you took the small one too,' said Nina.

He looked puzzled. 'I did not.'

'Yes you did! You sent your men to take it from us in Iceland.'

Trakas asked Axelos a question in Greek. The younger man shook his head, just as surprised as his boss. 'I only have one,' the tycoon reiterated. 'I wanted both, but I do not *need* the small one. I do not know where it is; Petros thought you lost it on the mountain.'

'No, we brought it back . . .' Nina trailed off, suspicion rising.

She glared at Lonmore, but he was equally bewildered. 'If you don't have it, then who—'

A sudden scuffle of running footsteps from behind Axelos made the Greek whirl – to find a silenced handgun aimed at his chest. 'Nobody move!' yelled the wetsuited man holding it.

This time, Nina and Eddie knew the face. 'Rutger?' cried the surprised Lonmore as De Klerx barged into the room, shoving Axelos backwards. The bodyguard recovered, about to lunge at his attacker – only to topple and crash to the floor as a taser barb fired by a second diver behind the Dutchman stabbed into his torso. At the same moment, two more figures ran along the side deck outside the lounge's windows and rushed in through the foredeck entrance.

One of them was Anastasia Fenrirsdottir.

'Hello, Augustine,' she said, pointing a gun at Trakas. 'I believe you have something that belongs to us.'

24

Sperou moved cautiously to the galley door and checked the passageway outside. Empty. The group who had just passed had come from aft. She leaned out to look in that direction. One of the doors was open, a shadow warning her that someone was standing just inside it.

The Glock raised, she padded quietly down the passage. The shadow's source gradually came into view as she neared the hold. A man, wearing a wetsuit; and beyond him she glimpsed the ship's crew sitting on the floor, heads down.

She could simply sneak up to the guard and shoot him, but the gunshot would alert the other hijackers. Instead, she carefully judged his height. She would only get one chance . . .

Sperou crept up to the doorway, readied herself – then whipped around it and smashed the base of the Glock's grip against the guard's temple. Caught completely unawares, Honnick reeled in blinding pain, crashing against a bank of shelves. She drove home a second brutal blow. This time the guard went down and stayed there.

The prisoners looked up at her, surprised and relieved. 'Is everyone all right?' she whispered.

Rouphos tried to stand; she helped him up. 'Yes. They had guns, but they used tasers on us first.' He turned to show her the plastic band trapping his wrists. 'Get this off me!'

'Hold on,' Sperou replied. There was nothing in the room that could cut the zip-tie, so she hurried back to the galley, quickly returning with a pair of meat shears. A single snip, and the restraint fell off.

Rouphos took Honnick's gun, then helped the other crewmen up, the chef cutting each free in turn. 'There are guns hidden in the other hold,' said the captain. He nodded at the two nearest men. 'Come with me to get them. Everyone else go with Sperou to the weapons locker. Once we're all armed, I'll go up to the bridge and retake the controls. The rest of you find Mr Trakas and either get him off the ship – or kill those pirate bastards!'

'What about the people who came to see Mr Trakas?' a man asked as the group began to exit.

'If they're working with the hijackers,' replied Rouphos grimly, 'kill them too.'

'Ana!' shouted Lonmore, jumping to his feet. 'What the hell is this?'

'Has he given up the Crucible?' Anastasia replied, indicating Trakas.

'No, but—'

'Then we're doing what should have been done from the start.' The blonde turned her gaze to the younger Lonmore. 'And you – you're working with Trakas? I should have known you'd sell out the Legacy to get revenge. You bitter, greedy little boy.'

'Hey, fuck you, Ana!' Spencer snapped back, only to flinch away as the scowling De Klerx pointed his gun at him.

Trakas regained his composure. 'You think the Crucible is here? I will have to disappoint you, Anastasia.'

'Then where is it?' she demanded.

'At one of my facilities.'

'Which one?'

The Greek shrugged. 'If you kill me, you will never find it.'

'But you'll be dead,' said De Klerx. 'Gold is no use to you then.'

'Oi!' Eddie said loudly, drawing everyone's attention. 'You're all pretty wound up about this, but you know what? It's not our problem. We'll just be on our way and leave you lot to it, if you don't mind. Come on, love.'

He stood, about to lead Nina to an exit – but Anastasia flicked her gun in their direction. The weapon did not remain aimed directly at the couple, but the threat was clear. 'Stay here,' she said. 'Nina, I'm not going to let Trakas keep the Crucible, but giving it to the IHA is not acceptable either.'

'Point that fucking thing somewhere else,' Eddie warned her. 'Or you'll regret it.'

De Klerx turned away from Spencer and Axelos to jab his own weapon at the Yorkshireman. 'If you threaten her again, I will kill you!'

'It's okay, Rutger,' said Anastasia. 'Nina, I don't want to do anything drastic. But we are not leaving Greece without the Cru—'

A gunshot – and De Klerx's man at the lounge's aft doorway fell, blood spouting from a ragged bullet hole in his back. Anastasia flinched away in shock, while Petra screamed.

Two of the yacht's crew rushed down the passageway and darted into the cover of rooms to each side, the cook covering them with her smoking gun from the stairs to the lower deck. 'Let Mr Trakas go!' she shouted.

The Dutchman flattened himself against the bulkhead beside the entrance. The other man who had followed Anastasia into the lounge brought up his gun to shoot down the passage—

The tycoon's hand whipped under the table and snatched out a revolver that had been taped beneath it. He fired without hesitation at the hijacker, the round ripping into the side of his chest. The man flopped to the carpet like a rubber bag full of water. Lonmore yelped in horror.

De Klerx spun to face the unexpected danger – and Axelos

burst into action, hurling himself bodily at the Dutchman. His gun arm was knocked away from its new target as he fired, the bullet blowing out one of the large windows. A great waterfall of shattered safety glass fell to the floor behind Nina and Eddie.

Axelos slammed De Klerx against the bulkhead. But even with the wind knocked from him, the brown-haired man kept fighting, grappling with the bodyguard. Trakas aimed his revolver at a new target: Anastasia. She stiffened as the gun swung at her. 'Ana! Tell your man to stand down.'

'Rutger, stop,' Anastasia said with angry reluctance. De Klerx gave Trakas a rage-filled glare, then ceased fighting. Axelos shoved him face-first against the wall before stripping him of his other weapons and equipment.

'This is not the first time I have been threatened on my own ship,' said Trakas. 'Now, Ana. Drop your gun.' Her pistol clunked to the carpeted deck. 'Good.' He moved to her and kicked the fallen weapon clear, then shifted position to cover his guests. 'Greece is a seafaring nation. We do not like pirates.'

'Augustine, I swear I had nothing to do with this,' said Lonmore, hands spread in entreaty as he stepped closer to his friend. 'This wasn't—'

He moved between Trakas and Eddie – and the Englishman responded instantly. 'Nina!' he yelled, grabbing the table and flipping it over. It hit Lonmore, sending him reeling into Trakas and Anastasia. Before either Greek could react, the couple had leapt through the broken window and run aft down the port-side walkway.

'Where are we going?' Nina shouted.

'Off this fucking boat!' Eddie looked towards the stern. The launch that had brought them aboard was still moored at the dock—

An armed crewman rounded the rear of the superstructure. The Englishman swerved, pulling his wife with him through a hatch. A narrow passageway lay before them, but he suspected it would lead back to the central corridor, and Trakas's people. 'Up here,' he said instead, scaling a steep ladder to the deck above.

Nina followed him up into what turned out to be the bridge. It was unmanned, an autopilot apparently steering the yacht. 'Ghost ship,' she said.

'Sounds like there'll be more ghosts aboard soon,' replied Eddie as gunfire erupted from the decks below. The crew were retaking the vessel. He looked around. The only other exit was a sliding door at the wheelhouse's rear that led on to a long sun deck running the length of the superstructure, the mainmast rising from it like a gleaming redwood. 'There's a ladder at the far end – or worst comes to the worst, we can jump down.' He threw open the door.

More crewmen rushed into the lounge, aiming at anyone unfamiliar. 'Mr Trakas!' one shouted. 'Are you okay?'

'Yes, I'm fine,' Trakas replied. 'Watch her.' Even in the midst of a tense situation, he still gave Anastasia's athletic wetsuited body a look of leering appreciation, which she did not fail to notice. Nor did De Klerx, whose lips curled into a snarl. 'What's happening? How many others are there?'

'We saw seven as well as these two, but there might be more.'

'Two less now.' Trakas gave the dead men a dismissive glance. 'Where's Rouphos?'

'On his way to the bridge.'

'Good. We need to—' He broke off as another exchange of gunfire from the deck below was accompanied by a detonation that rattled the floor. The shrill clamour of a fire alarm echoed through the ship.

'What was that?' gasped Lonmore.

'The gas tanks!' Trakas replied, concerned. 'One of your idiots must have shot them.'

'They're not *my* idiots!' the American insisted. 'I'm telling you, I came here to negotiate as a friend, not—'

The Greek waved him to silence. 'Later. Much later!'

'We've got to get you off the ship,' Axelos told his boss.

Trakas's reluctance at abandoning his yacht was clear, but he nodded. 'Okay. Bring them with us.' He gestured at the four prisoners. 'There are two more, a bald man and a woman,' he told his crew. 'Find them!'

Nina and Eddie raced along the upper deck. The mainsail's long boom extended out over the water off the starboard side, the great canvas triangle pushed firm by the wind. 'Christ, now what?' said Eddie as a strident alarm sounded.

'Great, the ship's on fire!' replied Nina. 'Just what we need.'

'At least there's plenty of water to put it out— Shit!' A crewman was scaling the ladder in the deck's aft corner.

A rack holding several life vests was mounted on the side railings. Eddie snatched one up and hurled it at the crewman. The man instinctively raised an arm to protect his head. The impact of the flotation device knocked his gun from his hand, sending it clanging to the deck below. He cursed, glancing after it before realising that the approaching intruders were unarmed.

'Get to the boat!' Eddie called to Nina as the crewman reached the deck and rushed at them. She swerved clear as the two men collided. The Greek had hoped his charge alone would be enough to knock the other man down, but Eddie was prepared for it, dropping and twisting to take the impact on his shoulder while simultaneously driving a punch into his attacker's stomach. 'Go on, go!'

She hesitated, but while the man was much younger than her husband, he was also obviously a far less experienced fighter. Winded, he swung a couple of flailing blows at Eddie's head, neither of which landed more than a glancing impact as the

Yorkshireman drove him backwards. Now confident that the brawl would end quickly, she ran to the end of the deck.

The launch had been joined at the floating dock by the speedboat that had towed the parasailing Trakas. A choice of two – and no one else in sight. She hurriedly descended the ladder. 'Eddie, come on!'

Above, Eddie whipped up his arm to deflect another blow before snapping a punch at the crewman's face. The younger man reeled back, but didn't fall.

He had to put the Greek down before he and Nina could escape. Fists raised, he advanced—

The crewman glanced past him – then shouted. Eddie was sure nobody could yet have caught up from behind, but the flash of hope in the other man's eyes hadn't been faked. He risked a split-second look back at the wheelhouse. A figure was visible inside. Rouphos. If he had a gun, the situation was about to get a lot worse.

Eddie made another lunge at the crewman, who hurriedly retreated. He followed, aiming to trap the sailor in a corner to bring the fight to a rapid end—

The deck rocked under his feet as the yacht made a sharp turn. Rouphos bellowed something in Greek.

Eddie hurriedly stabilised himself, expecting the crewman to make a counterattack, but he too had braced against the change of direction, dropping low. What had the captain warned about?

The answer came a second later as the mainsail's swinging boom smacked against the back of Eddie's head.

A moment of insensate blackness . . . then pain filled his skull to overflowing as he regained full consciousness. He forced open his eyes to find himself looking up at the sky, the crewman standing over him with a mocking smile. Rouphos arrived, handing his subordinate a gun and issuing a command before helping him drag the woozy Englishman upright. 'If you were a sailor, you would have kept your head down around the mast!' the captain said. Eddie tried to think of a comeback, but all he managed through the pulsing throb assaulting his brain was an irate groan.

Shouts caught Rouphos's attention. Eddie endured a moment of nausea as he turned to watch him hurry to the aft railing – and beyond him saw Nina reach the yacht's stern.

But the captain wasn't looking at her, instead calling down to someone on the deck below.

Nina glanced back, hoping to see Eddie following her, but instead saw Trakas, Axelos and a number of the ship's crew emerge from the superstructure. Spencer was with the burly Greek, his father and Petra being pushed along behind them with Anastasia and De Klerx. Rouphos stood at the end of the deck above, framed by a plume of dark smoke rising from the ship's side.

Now she spotted Eddie behind him, but to her horror he was being held by the sailor. The fight had gone badly. And things were about to go the same way for her too, as Trakas's bodyguards caught sight of her.

Nowhere to hide on the dock—

Instead she leapt down the nearby stairwell, landing hard at the bottom as a gunshot cracked from above. She threw open a door and rushed inside.

'No, don't shoot her!' Trakas barked at the trigger-happy sailor. 'Get after her, catch her!' The man ran to the stairwell.

'You want her alive?' Axelos asked as the group reached the dock.

'She might be useful,' said the tycoon thoughtfully, before his attention returned fully to the situation at hand. 'Put them in the launch. Keep them well guarded,' he ordered, before having a partial change of mind. 'No, the girl comes in the speedboat with me.'

'Ana!' yelled De Klerx as he and Anastasia were separated. He lunged at the man holding her, but another crewman dragged him back.

'What about me?' asked Spencer.

'You come with me too,' Trakas told him. He looked back at Rouphos on the upper deck. 'That one as well!' he shouted, pointing at Eddie. 'Bring him—'

A loud, deep *whump* from somewhere within the *Pactolus* shook the deck – and a moment later a second explosion erupted into the open as a section of the starboard side amidships blew apart. Everyone staggered—

De Klerx smashed an elbow into the gut of the man holding him, folding him double. Before anyone could react, he vaulted off the launch's bow into the sea, bringing up both arms to enter the water in a dive.

Two crewmen fired after him, bullets smacking into the waves as the dark figure dropped beneath the surface. 'Rutger! No, stop!' Anastasia cried from the speedboat.

Axelos ran to the end of the dock. The yacht was rapidly pulling away from the expanding splash marking the Dutchman's landing, still making almost ten knots. 'I don't think we got him,' he reported. 'He went deep enough for the water to stop the bullets.' He looked back at Trakas. 'We can go after him in the boats when he surfaces.'

Another blast from the ship's innards made everybody turn. A noxious black cloud was now boiling from the ruptured hull. 'What the hell?' gasped Lonmore as fire whipped past. The sea itself was alight, the *Pactolus* leaving a ragged trail of flame in its wake.

'The fuel tanks!' Rouphos cried. 'We're leaking fuel!'

By now the sailor had brought Eddie to the aft deck. 'Abandon ship!' Trakas ordered. 'Everyone get off while we can!'

'The fire control systems should be able to handle it,' Rouphos insisted.

'If they could stop *that*, they already would have!' Trakas pointed at the mainmast. The fire swirling from the hole in the yacht's side had swept up to reach the sails. 'We leave, now!'

'What about him?' asked Axelos, pointing after De Klerx.

'Forget him! We need to get to shore.'

Eddie didn't understand the exchange going on between the Greeks, but the combination of the renewed rush to board the boats and the flames licking along the yacht's starboard side meant that he got the gist of it very quickly. 'Where's Nina?' he demanded as he was ushered at gunpoint to the dock. 'Where is she?'

'She went back inside!' Petra cried from the launch.

'What? Then bloody get her out of there!' he yelled at Trakas.

The magnate waited for the Englishman to be put into one of the speedboat's rear seats beside Anastasia before boarding himself. 'I have sent one of my men after her. If he finds her, they will follow in the last boat.' He glanced up at the remaining craft, still on the hoist. 'If he does not, then she will either swim – or burn!'

The fire swirling around the mainmast deterred Rouphos from returning to the wheelhouse to sound the evacuation alarm. Instead he jumped down to the aft deck and went to open a wall panel in the gym, revealing a control board inside.

He flicked a switch to sound the general alarm, then activated the PA system. 'Abandon ship!' he snapped in Greek. 'All hands to the boats!' It was not standard procedure, but given the circumstances – gunfire was still being exchanged further forward – it was the best he could manage. Job done, he ran back to the stern to assist with the untying of the two boats, hoping the rest of his crew would reach them in very short order.

Had the captain gone to the bridge, though, he would have immediately spotted a new danger.

He had deactivated the autopilot to make the sharp turn that had taken Eddie out with the boom, then re-engaged the system as he hurried back to help secure the prisoner. The yacht had still been turning as he did so, but now it had settled on to its new course.

Straight towards a small uninhabited island, a ragged line of cliffs rising out of the sea like a rotten tooth.

25

Nina ran through the lower deck, hearing chasing feet behind her. Unlike the single central corridor bisecting the main deck, this was a minor maze of much narrower passages, winding past the engine room, holds and crew cabins.

And while her pursuer knew his way around, she had no idea where she was going.

She rounded a corner – only for flames and smoke roiling from an open hatch ahead to bring her to an abrupt stop. No way past. But a steep companionway to one side led back to the deck above. She hesitated, knowing that Trakas and his men might still be up there, but then her pursuer appeared behind her.

He shouted in Greek, but she was already haring up the ladder. Throwing open the hatch at its top, she emerged to find herself on the starboard-side deck. Thick smoke swirled past her, making her cough. Going forward would take her deeper into the choking miasma; her only options were to head aft or jump overboard.

A glance at the oily rainbow sheen on the water put her off the latter choice. The yacht was leaking fuel, lots of it, and fires were spreading over the surface. She wouldn't be swimming from the *Pactolus*, at least not from this side.

A recess housed a cabinet of emergency equipment. She pulled it open, hoping to find something she could use to jam the hatch shut behind her, but found only first aid kits, survival blankets, rope . . . and distress flares. She grabbed one – not to summon help, but to ward off the crewman – and hurried back towards the stern.

The two boats had gone.

The launch and the speedboat were pulling away from the stricken yacht, swinging hard to its port side to avoid the floating fires in its wake. Both vessels were full to the point of overloaded, Trakas's remaining crew having crammed aboard. She saw Eddie in the speedboat with the Greek. Other men were in the water, their wetsuits revealing them as members of De Klerx's team. Some had grabbed life vests before leaping over the side, others simply taking their chances and hoping their comrades would come to their aid.

But no one was coming to hers.

She looked at the last boat, still swinging from the hoist over the stern. How long it would take her to get it into the water she had no idea. And a bang from behind warned that even if it only took seconds, it would not be fast enough. She spun to see the sailor emerging from the hatch.

Nina backed on to the aft deck and raised the flare, pointing it at him. His reaction was almost amusement. 'I'll do it!' she warned, hooking her index finger around the pull-tab in its base. 'I've done it before. Back off!'

His mouth curled into a grin, and he lifted his gun—

She yanked the tab.

The flare shot from its tube with a muffled bang and crossed the gap between them in an instant, hitting the sailor in the chest. He shrieked, stumbling backwards as his clothing was set alight, and fell over the railing into the ocean below. The sizzling flare went with him . . .

Landing in the spilled fuel.

Burning wreckage had already ignited the marine diesel, but the fires had not been hot enough to spread far, the dense oil being naturally hard to light. But the flare's magnesium heart was blazing at over two thousand degrees Fahrenheit, and not even water could extinguish it.

The result was instantaneous.

A swirling wall of flame burst upwards. Nina staggered back in shock as the heat hit her. The deck's edge was already alight, paint and varnish blistering. She ran to the port side, knowing she would now have to take her chances in the water – only to stop at the railing in fear as she saw a new danger.

The blaze was spreading out *behind* the yacht, its wake stirring up the burning fuel. One of De Klerx's men had leapt from the ship, only for the fire to consume him as the *Pactolus* swept on. He screamed, vanishing into the blaze.

The same would happen to her if she jumped overboard.

Flames rose behind the stern, hot tongues lashing up at the remaining speedboat. If she released it, it would fall straight into the firestorm. No way off . . .

A shadow crossed over her: the mainsail shifting as the wind changed direction. The boom! At the limit of its swing, it extended far out from the yacht's side. She looked around to see if she could climb along it to get clear of the fire—

The sail was alight, flames eating away at the great canvas sheet, but that wasn't what froze her in fright. It was what was visible beyond the bow.

A wall of rock.

The *Pactolus* was charging straight at a cliff.

Even with the mainsail holed, the other sails were still catching enough wind to maintain the vessel's brisk speed. 'Crap,' she gasped. 'Crap, crap!' The ship's fiery wake was if anything wider and fiercer than before. Traversing the boom was now her only hope of escape.

She ran to the ladder and climbed to the upper deck, only to freeze in dismay as the burning mainsail split apart, a great swathe of smoking canvas slapping down before her. The boom swung back until the weight of material dragged it to a standstill. Even if she climbed all the way to its end, she would barely clear the ship's side, never mind the waterborne conflagration behind it.

The cliffs loomed ever closer beyond the wheelhouse. She stared in desperation after the retreating boats as they carried Eddie and the others away to safety—

Something caught her eye near the boat hoist. Trakas's parachute.

After landing from his parasailing jaunt, he had needed help to stop him from being dragged off the stern by the wind . . .

There was no one left to tell her how crazy her instantly improvised plan was, so she did it herself as she jumped back to the aft deck and ran to the hoist. 'This is absolutely *insane*!' she gasped, collecting the chute. The sailors had repacked it after their boss's return – at least she hoped they had. 'Seriously, what is *wrong* with you?' she added as she fumbled her limbs through the various straps. Trakas's torso was considerably larger than hers, the harness hanging loose. She struggled to pull it tighter. The cliffs kept growing, swallowing the horizon ahead. 'Eddie's the one who has the mad ideas, not me!'

The straps finally drew snug around her chest. She clambered up the hoist, the Hadean sea of fire churning frighteningly below, and leapt across to land on the speedboat's bow. It rocked beneath her, almost pitching her into the flames before she caught the top of the windscreen.

The shallowing ocean became more choppy. Coughing as vile smoke streamed past, Nina clambered into the hull, making her way to its rear. The *Pactolus* was almost at the cliffs. She stood and faced forwards – then yanked the ripcord.

The pilot chute popped from its pouch, catching the headwind and snapping backwards . . . too slowly. It dropped as it dragged the main chute out with it, falling towards the fire. Her wild gamble had failed—

The main chute suddenly inflated as it too caught the slipstream. A sharp tug on Nina's harness sent her lurching backwards off the boat's stern. She screamed – as the parachute opened fully and lunged upwards, dragging her with it.

The *Pactolus* speared away as she was carried higher. Trailing smoke, it raced on through the breaking whitecaps – and ploughed into the cliff. The bow shattered in an explosion of fibreglass and wood, followed by an escalating series of detonations that ripped the ship apart from within. The forward mast snapped as if it were a matchstick, the taller mainmast lashing crazily before tearing out of the deck and toppling into the water like a felled tree.

Nina grabbed the parachute's steering lines and swung herself away from the boiling black cloud rising to engulf her. The cliffs rolled past, still growing larger as her momentum carried her towards them, larger—

Bare rock whipped past her dangling feet – then she was clear, turning back out to sea. She straightened out, letting the parachute take her away from the disintegrating wreckage.

A sharp smell hit her nostrils. It wasn't the burning yacht or its flaming trail of fuel. This was more like melting plastic . . .

Fear returned in full force. It *was* plastic: nylon.

The parachute was on fire.

A flame-ringed hole was opening up in the brightly coloured canopy, glowing globs of molten material dropping away as the fire ate through it. 'Oh, *shit*!'

Nina pulled on both lines, trying to bring herself down to the water more quickly. But her descent was already accelerating as the burning parachute started to collapse. Another scream as she dropped towards the ocean—

She still had enough presence of mind to take a deep breath just before she hit. A wave smacked hard against her face as she went under amidst a rush of churning bubbles. Disoriented, she tried to right herself and return to the surface, only to find herself entangled as the remains of the parachute came down on top of her.

The harness and pack were dead weight on her back. She pushed at the buckle on her chest to release them. A muted clunk, and the straps popped free. She shrugged clear and kicked out from beneath the overbearing jellyfish, but some of the lines had wrapped around her legs.

Her panic returned. She forced herself to stop swimming, bringing up both legs in front of her as she tried to unravel the cords. Currents shoved at her like impatient subway crowds. One leg freed, but the other was still snagged, the lines pulling tighter around her ankle as the floating chute was yanked back and forth by the waves.

Calm, stay calm, she told herself as she unlooped them. The pack sank past her, other lines pulling at her leg. She resisted the gentle but unyielding pressure, using her arms to propel herself back up before continuing her task. Only a few more to go. A distant thudding rumble reached her through the water, the sound of an engine, but she couldn't spare it any thought as she finally tugged away the last cord and swam clear of the parachute.

She burst into open air, gasping. More waves slapped at her. Spluttering, she blew away water as she tipped backwards to keep her face clear of the surface, then tried to get her bearings.

The column of black smoke rising from the cliffs made it impossible to miss the wreckage of the *Pactolus*. The luxury yacht's remains were barely identifiable as a ship, the mangled mass wreathed in fire. There was no beach, the weather-worn rocks rising straight out of the sea. Nowhere to get safely ashore.

She looked the other way. This low in the water, she couldn't see the small boats carrying Eddie and the others, but she did spy another vessel, a motor yacht, heading towards where she had seen De Klerx's men. It was going to rescue them . . . and, she desperately hoped, her.

'That's the ship that cut across our course!' Velis said, seeing the other vessel moving towards the bobbing mercenaries.

Trakas turned to Anastasia, who along with Eddie was being watched at gunpoint by Axelos. 'Your ship, I assume?' he asked her in English. Her only reply was a dismissive narrowing of her eyes. 'Your friends will be saved, then. Those who are still alive.'

'Never mind them,' Eddie said angrily. 'What about Nina? We've got to see if she got off the ship!' The smoke from the *Pactolus* had blocked his view of the yacht's last moments.

'We're not going back,' Axelos said coldly. 'It's too dangerous.'

'A pity,' said Trakas. 'Dr Wilde would have been useful.'

'For what?' the Yorkshireman growled, but no answer came.

'Where are you taking us?' Anastasia demanded.

Trakas chuckled humourlessly. 'You came here for the Crucible, no? Now you will see it.'

'Hey!' Nina cried, waving her arms. 'Over here, hey!'

She had been in the water for twenty minutes, reluctant to move too far from the smouldering wreck of the *Pactolus* for fear that anyone coming to investigate might miss her. But now the motor yacht was finally approaching, having picked up the men in the sea.

A figure on its deck signalled to her: De Klerx. Both relieved and aggrieved to see him, she swam exhaustedly to the ship. He and another man reached down and pulled her from the sea. 'Are you all right?' the Dutchman asked as she slumped to the deck, water streaming from her soaked clothing.

'Yeah, no thanks to you,' she replied, wringing out her hair. 'What the hell were you and Anastasia doing? We came out here to talk to Trakas, not start World War Three.'

'You were never going to succeed,' he replied with a dismissive sneer. 'A man who would go to such lengths to get the Crucible would never voluntarily give it up.'

'So you decided to take it anyway, huh?' Another man offered her some towels. She gratefully wrapped one around herself. 'What about Eddie, and the others? Where are they?'

'Trakas took them.'

'Where?'

De Klerx went to the cabin door, gesturing for her to follow. 'We think a place called Riklos. He owns a shipyard there.'

'You think? You don't know?'

'The two men I left on this ship had to choose between following him and rescuing us.' They entered the cabin. The other survivors of the failed raid were inside, now down to four. 'But I have spoken to Mr Mikkelsson. Even while we were travelling to Greece, he had used his diplomatic connections to obtain information about Trakas's businesses. Riklos is the only place he owns that could operate an industrial particle accelerator.'

'You think that's where he's keeping the Crucibles?' The Greek's denial of any knowledge about the smaller of the two Atlantean artefacts came back to her, but she put it aside; there were more urgent concerns.

'It must be.'

A hatch at the cabin's rear was open. The room beyond was dark, but Nina glimpsed distinctly military-looking cases stacked within. Weapons. 'You're planning to raid the place?'

'Yes. It will be night by the time we arrive, but we can still find the Crucible – and rescue Anastasia and the others.'

'I hope that's not the order of priorities,' said Nina, dropping on to an empty chair.

'No. Getting Anastasia back is my top priority.'

'Yeah, I bet it is.' That there was something going on between the Dutchman and the young Icelander had been hard to miss. 'Just remember that getting Eddie back is *my* top priority – and the Lonmores, too.'

'I am sure you will not let me forget.'

'Don't worry, I won't,' she said, responding to his sarcasm in kind. 'And I hope this operation goes better than your last one.'

26

Eddie surveyed the shoreline ahead as the helicopter began its descent. 'Guess that's where we're going.'

The two boats had taken their passengers to the island where he, Nina and the Lonmores had landed before travelling to the *Pactolus*, the chopper returning at Trakas's summons. With Axelos and one of the surviving yacht crew acting as armed guards, the prisoners were put aboard. Trakas took the front passenger seat, leaving Spencer to sit uncomfortably in the rear under the glares of his father, his stepmother and Anastasia.

The flight west to the Greek mainland took over an hour. A cove at the edge of a range of rocky hills was home to a sprawling boatyard. Numerous craft of varying sizes were under construction or being maintained, but a large factory-like building some way back from the waterline suggested that more went on at the facility than simple repair work. An electrical substation was located beside it, fed by high-tension lines running down from the hillside.

The helicopter landed near a perimeter gate. Eddie saw that it was guarded – and that the two men who hurried to meet the aircraft were armed, Italian Spectre sub-machine guns slung at their waists.

The new arrivals were quickly escorted to the factory, the chopper lifting off behind them. Trakas was greeted by a man in thick-framed glasses, whose report was well received by the shipping magnate. 'This way!' he told his unwilling guests with a smile.

'Where are we going?' demanded Anastasia.

'To see the Crucible! Is that not what you wanted?' He led the way through the facility, accompanied by the man in glasses. A number of assembly lines snaked around it, the mechanical guts of several boats in the process of being pieced together, but the Greek's destination was off to one side of the long building.

Eddie felt concern when he spotted radiation warning signs on the walls. 'Oh, great. First the Midas Cave, now this – I'll be lucky if I don't sprout a third bloody arm.'

'There is no need to worry,' said Trakas. 'It is perfectly safe.'

'What's safe?' asked Lonmore.

The Greek brought them into an area separated from the rest of the interior by a long partition. 'This!' he announced with pride.

A boxy piece of equipment emblazoned with more warning trefoils was raised on a stand. It formed one end of a machine, a hefty yellow-painted metal pipe that ran the factory's length. The tube was encircled at regular intervals by large coils of copper wire, thick skeins of electrical cabling running to each. 'A linear accelerator,' said Anastasia.

Trakas nodded. 'It was used to strengthen metal parts for boats and stop them from rusting. Ion implantation, it is called. But I have had it modified for a greater purpose.' He started along the device, Axelos ushering the others after him. 'Behind us is the particle source. They are accelerated by the magnets in these rings.' He gestured at one of the copper coils as he passed. 'By the time they reach the other end, they are going very fast – enough for the neutrons to get through the outer shell of the Crucible.'

'But not fast enough to get back out,' said Eddie, remembering Mikkelsson's description of the process.

Trakas glanced back at him. 'Indeed not, Mr Chase. They are trapped, to bounce backwards and forwards until they hit atoms of mercury-196. They join together . . . and turn to gold. Just like the legend of Midas.'

Anastasia's already angry expression deepened as she glowered at Spencer. 'You told him about this. All of this is my father's theory!'

'His theory, but Augustine's the one who's going to put it into practice,' the young man replied.

'Very soon,' Trakas added. He pointed ahead to where people were clustered around the linear accelerator's far end. 'Everything is ready for the first test. If it works, and I believe it will, then the bankers will be forced to give up their hold on my country.'

'You really think you'll be able to hold the world's financial system to ransom?' Lonmore said.

'I do, my friend,' the Greek replied. 'I do.'

The group approached the pipe's far end. The assembly that had been used to support boat parts for ion implantation had been shifted into a corner, replaced by a much larger and heavier box made of thick metal plates. The messiness of the welding suggested it had been put together at short notice. The container was open at the top, a hinged lid three inches thick raised by a heavy chain running to an electric hoist overhead.

More chains were slowly moving an object from the back of a flatbed truck into the imposing container.

The Crucible.

'There it is,' said Trakas proudly as Lonmore and his wife stared in amazement. Even Anastasia could not contain her wonder. 'It will be filled with over a thousand litres of mercury. According to Fenrir's theory, that much mercury should produce over twenty kilograms of gold. If it falls short, it does not matter; what matters is that any gold is produced at all.'

Eddie looked up at a man on a walkway who was filming the operation with a video camera. Other cameras were fixed upon stands around the accelerator, silently recording every moment.

'And all this is to prove you're not faking it, at a guess.'

'Yeah,' said Spencer. 'Everything's time-coded, so they'll know we haven't made any edits. My idea,' he added smugly.

'Bet you're full of parental pride right now, aren't you?' Eddie said to Lonmore. The businessman's disheartened expression served as his answer.

'You will also be witnesses,' added Trakas. 'I hoped Dr Wilde could be here too – the testimony of the world's most famous archaeologist would be hard to ignore.'

'Then maybe you should've bloody gone back to get her,' said the Yorkshireman angrily.

'There were survivors, Mr Chase. With luck she was one. But she is not the only one who will be believed.'

They reached the end of the steel tube. By now, the Crucible had disappeared inside the container. The chains were detached from its cage and pulled clear by the hoist. The truck moved off to stop at a roller door nearby.

'This containment chamber is my father's design,' Anastasia said of the box, with deep disapproval. She rounded on Spencer. 'You stole that too?'

'Why should it go to waste?' he shot back. 'The Legacy was never going to use the Crucible anyway. All you would have done was argue about it and block each other's plans.'

Lonmore turned to his son. 'I can't believe you've betrayed the Legacy like this, Spencer,' he said. 'You've given away our secrets – and why? Out of spite?'

'You know what *I* can't believe, Dad?' Spencer replied with an angry sneer. 'That you'd kick me out – your own son! – so you could give my seat to some bimbo who worked as your secretary! Can you *get* any more clichéd?'

'Don't you *dare* call me that,' hissed Petra. 'And maybe if you hadn't been an out-of-control spoiled brat, he wouldn't have needed to kick you out!'

'Now, now,' Lonmore said, feebly trying to interpose himself between the pair. 'That's not really fair, Petra.'

'Oh, so now you're standing up for your ungrateful waster of a son rather than your own wife?' she snapped. 'He *is* spoiled, Spencer! That's the only word for him! No, actually, I can think of quite a lot more, but I'll keep them to myself. But if you hadn't indulged him in absolutely everything he ever wanted, he might have taken more responsibility for his life instead of relying on you to bail him out!'

Spencer turned his back on the couple. 'I'm not going to be lectured to by some gold-digger from the typing pool. But this is what happens when blood doesn't stand by blood, isn't it? Everything falls apart.'

'That goes both ways,' Lonmore said, clearly distressed by the argument.

The man with glasses, who was apparently in charge of technical matters, called out to Trakas. 'We are ready to fill the Crucible,' the mogul announced expectantly.

The procedure took some time, but the last of several drums of liquid mercury was finally emptied, its contents pumped into the Crucible. Trakas eagerly issued a command, and the container's lid closed with a deep, reverberating clang. A rumbling sound came from machinery beside it as vacuum pumps drew out the air. The barrel-chested Greek ushered everyone back behind a free-standing concrete wall that on closer examination had a core of dense, dark metal. 'Lead,' he explained. 'The case is a radiation shield, lined with more lead. It should hold in the radiation, but it is best to be safe, yes?'

The technician made final checks, then returned to the particle source and signalled to those at the far end of the accelerator. 'We are ready to start!' Trakas announced, now almost childishly excited. A shout to the cameraman, who gave him a thumbs-up from the walkway. 'The cameras are rolling. We can begin!' He turned to Eddie. 'Thanks to your wife, Midas is about to save Greece. A pity she could not be here with us to witness this.'

The Yorkshireman eyed the armed guards. 'Yeah, I bet she'd be loving it.'

Trakas waved to the technician. The factory's overhead lights flickered as a basso hum came from the accelerator. It rose in pitch and volume. 'When the power has built up, neutrons will be fired into the Crucible,' he explained. 'If your father's theory is correct, Anastasia, when the neutrons trapped inside the Crucible reach a certain intensity, there will be a burst of radiation.'

'That's what happened in the Midas Cave,' Eddie told the Icelander. Despite her angry mood, she nodded, intrigued by what was happening.

The electrical sound from the machine kept climbing. The technician called out again, closing a circuit with a clack loud enough to be heard even down the accelerator's length. The lights flickered again, and a harsh droning buzz joined the noise. 'The neutrons are being fired!' said Trakas.

Even Petra was now engrossed. 'How long will it take?'

'I do not know.' He looked at Eddie. 'In the Midas Cave, how long?'

'A few minutes,' replied the Englishman. 'But there was a pool that had to fill up with water before anything happened, so . . .' He shrugged.

Trakas nodded. 'We will know when the neutron burst comes. There is a radiation meter inside the box.' He turned back to the accelerator, peering at it through a slot-like window of thick dark glass.

Eddie surreptitiously glanced at the others to see if they were equally transfixed. The guard's attention seemed divided between the humming device and his charges . . . but as Eddie slowly turned his head towards Axelos, he realised the security chief was watching him closely from just beyond easy reach, his gun held ready. Having faced the former SAS man before, he was unwilling to give him a second chance at escape. The Yorkshireman gave him a sardonic look, then looked back at the machine.

A minute passed, more – then the sudden clamour of a bell made the onlookers jump. 'Is that it?' asked Lonmore.

'Not yet, not yet,' Trakas replied, eyes wide with anticipation. 'But soon, very—'

Before he could finish speaking, a shrill siren sounded over the bell. The Greek whirled to look back along the accelerator, expression worried, but a shouted report from the technician quickly calmed him. 'There is no radiation leak,' he said.

'Great,' said Eddie, trying to cover his own relief. 'I can take off my lead codpiece, then.'

'Did it work?' asked Spencer.

'We will find out soon,' Trakas told him. The buzz and hum of the linear accelerator ceased as the technician shut it down, then he hurried past the observers to its other end, summoning the other workers to help him begin a series of checks.

It took several minutes before they were completed, but eventually the man smiled and gave Trakas a thumbs-up. His boss congratulated him, then faced his guests. 'There *was* a neutron burst,' he announced. 'We will soon see if any mercury has turned to gold.'

A loud hiss came from the box as it was refilled with air. The technician made more checks, then collected a Geiger counter and signalled for the hoist to be operated. The chain rattled, and the lid began to open.

The counter crackled alarmingly as vapour swirled out, but the man with glasses seemed unperturbed. He took a reading, then called out to Trakas. 'It is safe,' said the Greek. 'There is not enough radiation to be dangerous.' He led the group out from behind the wall.

'So what about the gold?' Spencer asked.

'We will soon know.' With the radiation danger gone, the other workers went into action. They pushed a wheeled stepladder into position alongside the box, a man wearing a hazmat suit and breath mask climbing to its top. The others passed a long tubular probe attached to a hose up to him. He leaned over and carefully lowered the tube into the Crucible, edging it down until it reached the bottom of the crystalline cauldron. 'Gold is more dense than mercury,' Trakas explained, seeing that some of his audience were puzzled. 'It will sink to the bottom. That machine,' he indicated a portable pump nearby, another hose running into a large empty barrel on a pallet, 'will suck it out and filter it from the mercury. Then we shall see how much gold I have!'

Another worker started the pump. It rattled and strained, then the hose running from the Crucible pulsed in the arms of the men supporting it. Quicksilver spat from the end of the second tube into the waiting canister.

The pump operator intently watched a glass jar attached to its side as the machine shuddered with the effort of drawing the heavy liquid metal out of the Crucible, then thrust his head nearer as if unable to believe his eyes. He sprang upright, calling out to Trakas in excited Greek.

It took all the tycoon's effort not to rush over to see for himself. Instead he issued a command. The worker shut down the pump, the other men waiting expectantly as he carefully detached the jar, then hurried with it to his boss.

The cameraman quickly descended from the walkway and joined the group to capture the moment. Trakas took the jar and held it up to the light, making sure the camera had a clear view of its contents. Eddie and the others leaned closer to see for themselves.

Just as in the Midas Cave, another metal had been extracted from the mercury. The system here was more effective than the simple mesh filter used by the monks, the bottom of the jar covered by a layer of what looked like fine sand. Dotted amongst it were larger grains, the biggest a lumpen nugget over a quarter of an inch long.

Their colour revealed that they were more than mere grit.

Trakas gasped in delight, turning the jar to examine the gleaming residuum from every angle. 'It works,' he said. 'It works!' He reluctantly handed the jar back to the worker, who quickly returned to the pump to reattach it and resume the task of extracting more. 'The legend is true,' the Greek tycoon continued to his guests. 'Midas could create gold. And now, so can I.'

27

De Klerx's ship squatted in the darkness offshore, all its lights off. From its foredeck, Nina surveyed the boatyard. She saw movement on the distant waterfront. 'Looks like they've got guards patrolling.'

De Klerx stared through binoculars. 'I see . . . three men along the water. Two by the slipways, and another at the docks.'

'Let me look.' The Dutchman passed her the field glasses with what she couldn't help feeling was annoyed reluctance. 'It's all right, I won't break your precious toy.'

She slowly panned her magnified view from left to right. Part of it was blocked by the rusting hulk of a half-submerged ship about a hundred yards out into the water, behind which was a jetty with a couple of small yachts moored. At its end, concrete took over from rock where a pair of dry docks cut into the land's edge. One had its gates open to let in the sea. The hull of a ship rose above the other's closed lock, a temporary cover of scaffolding and plastic sheets over a hole in its deck left where a large part of the superstructure had been lifted away by a crane. Along from the dry docks was a slipway leading up to several large open-sided structures, beached boats on stands inside them. Tall fences ran right to the water at both sides of the boatyard's perimeter.

'It'll be hard to get ashore without being seen,' Nina said. 'We definitely won't be able to take the boat all the way in.'

'I know that,' said De Klerx testily. 'We will have to swim.'

'I'd kind of expected that from the wetsuits.' The men aboard the darkened cruiser had, its pilot aside, donned dark neoprene. 'But I still say taking all that other stuff is a bad idea.' The stockpile of weapons in the rear cabin had been brought out; as well as several compact UMP sub-machine guns, it included a Steyr AUG machine gun and a Milkor MGL grenade launcher, six rounds loaded in its fat revolver-like cylinder. She was glad they hadn't been used in the first failed attempt to obtain the Crucible, but now De Klerx could not be dissuaded from employing them in a second. 'I'm not an expert, but I'm pretty sure that when you're doing a hostage rescue, it helps if you find out where the hostages are *before* you start shooting.'

There was acid in De Klerx's reply. 'I do know what I am doing, Dr Wilde.'

'So you shouldn't have any problems with proving it, should you?' She focused her view beyond the shoreline. More boats were lined up on stands behind the shelters, while past the crane was a jumbled maze of ship parts, machinery and junk. 'There are more men farther back, but have you noticed where most of them are?' She returned the binoculars. 'The big building, with all the lights in the windows – it's under guard. There are guys walking around it, and I'm guessing they aren't trying to prevent deep-vein thrombosis.'

'Yes, I saw them. And that is the only building here that could contain a particle accelerator powerful enough to use the Crucible.'

'So the guards probably mean that Trakas is in there.'

'And Anastasia and the others.'

Nina nodded. 'Let's hope he's the kind of villain who likes to gloat and show off to his prisoners rather than lock them up somewhere. Or just kill them.' She took in the whole of the boatyard again. 'Okay, so what are we doing?'

'We?'

'Yeah, we. I'm coming with you.'

He didn't even deign to look at her as he dismissed the suggestion. 'I do not think so. This is a task that should be left to professionals.'

'Yeah, you were *so* professional on the yacht when you brought your girlfriend with you and let her get captured.' That drew De Klerx's eyes, which gave her an irate glare. 'Or when your prisoners escaped and the whole damn boat blew up around you. Real pro work.'

'I served in the Korps Commandotroepen!' he snapped.

'For all I know, that's the catering corps. What I *do* know is that charging in there with guns blazing won't go any better than on the *Pactolus*. So whatever plan you've got, revise it so that "kill people and blow shit up" isn't the first line. Or preferably *any* line.'

His gaze hardened, revealing actual anger. 'Dr Wilde, you do not tell me what to do.'

'Yeah, I get told that all the time. Only as "Mommy" rather than "Dr Wilde". And I don't take it from a three-year-old either. So just remember that the point of being here is rescue, not revenge, and let's see if we can get everyone back safely without having to, y'know, murder anyone. Okay? If you start shooting, Trakas might kill his hostages. That includes Eddie – *and* Anastasia.'

De Klerx's mood did not improve when he saw that some of his men were smirking at his telling-off. 'Of course this is a rescue operation. And I have a plan.' He pointed at the wreck. 'We will take the boat in behind the sunken ship so we are not seen, then swim in. There is a ladder at the end of the open dock. We will climb up it and conceal our scuba gear in the hut there,' his finger shifted towards a small brick ruin close to the dry dock, 'then use the shadows to make our way to the big building.'

Nina gave the rest of his team a dubious look. 'You won't

have much chance of sneaking through the place unseen with a squad of huge guys with machine guns.'

'You are going to suggest again that you come with me, aren't you?' said the disapproving Dutchman.

'It's not my first time doing this kind of thing, sad to say. Trakas has got someone you love, yes? Well, he's got someone I love too. If you go, I go. You'll have to tie me up to stop me.'

De Klerk's displeased expression suggested that he was considering it, but instead he nodded. 'Very well. But remember that I advised against it.' There was a faintly menacing edge to the words. He turned to his men. 'Beel, wait with the boat behind the wreck until I radio that we have found Miss Mikkelsson and the other hostages, then move in to the dock. The rest of you, once we are safely ashore, swim in and stay in hiding until I signal. If we are discovered,' he went on, with a look at Nina daring her to challenge his orders, 'move in immediately and use any force necessary to rescue Miss Mikkelsson. Her safe return is the highest priority.'

'And everyone else's safe return,' Nina reminded him pointedly. She went into the cabin to collect a wetsuit and scuba cylinder. Her deep suit certification had lapsed, but she hadn't forgotten how to dive. 'Let's get them back.'

The man in the hazmat suit ran the nozzle of the hose around the bottom of the now-empty Crucible, then shouted down to the pump operator. The noisy machine wheezed into silence.

The mercury it had extracted had been drained into a line of metal drums, a man in a mask closing the lid on the last. Leaving Axelos and the other guard watching Eddie and the rest of the prisoners, Trakas strode to the pump as its operator again removed the glass jar.

It was considerably fuller than before.

The man grunted with the effort of lifting it. Under his boss's watchful gaze and the unblinking stare of multiple cameras, he brought it to a weighing scale nearby and carefully lowered it on to the plate. Trakas waited eagerly for the digital readout to settle, then laughed in pure glee at the final result. 'Seventeen kilograms!' he cried, hurrying back to his guests. 'Over seventeen kilograms of gold!'

'That's . . . that's worth quite a lot,' said Lonmore.

'It is!' The Greek produced a phone and brought up an app to enter a figure, getting an answer that widened his smile still further. 'At today's price, that much gold is worth over seven hundred thousand dollars! And,' he went on, becoming more thoughtful, 'it means that most of the mercury-196 in the Crucible was converted to gold.'

As much as Anastasia was unwilling to help him, she still nodded. 'Liquid mercury contains 0.15 per cent mercury-196. A thousand litres of mercury would weigh over thirteen metric tonnes, so the numbers add up.'

'I see you also paid attention to your father's theory. Yes, it is an efficient reaction.'

'Except now you're stuck with a load of leftover mercury,' said Eddie. 'And you'll need a load more every time you use the Crucible. It can't be cheap.'

Trakas shrugged. 'It is much cheaper than gold. And I have many factories, many businesses that have legitimate uses for it. I can buy it by the tanker if I want! But hopefully, I will not need to.' He spoke to the cameraman, who switched off his device. 'I now have everything I need. I have the Crucible, I have the gold it made, and I have proof that I can create as much of it as I wish.' He smiled again, this time in triumph. 'The bankers will *have* to give me and my country everything I ask for, or I will ruin them!'

★ ★ ★

After the boat had taken up a position of concealment behind the wreck, Nina and De Klerx rolled overboard to begin their swim to shore. It did not take long, the boatyard's lights making their destination clear even from underwater. They entered the flooded dock together. The ladder was in one corner; she angled towards it—

A silhouette obscured the lights above: a guard moving unhurriedly along the dockside, a slung sub-machine gun clear at his side even through the distortion of the waves.

Nina froze, hanging beneath the water's surface. She had cut in front of the Dutchman, who bumped against her. To her relief he also held still the moment he realised the danger, but both of them were close enough to be spotted if any movement drew the patrolling guard's attention.

Movement like bubbles from beneath the surface.

Nina held her breath. The scuba regulator would only release spent air into the water when she exhaled, but how long could she hold out?

The figure ambled along the dock . . . and stopped.

The redhead felt a surge of fear. Had they been seen already? She couldn't tell which way the man was looking, his head obscured by the glare of a light. Seconds passed. The waves slapping against the dock's concrete confines washed her gently back and forth, but she also felt herself slowly rising; there hadn't been time to prepare her diving weights for exact neutral buoyancy. The tank on her back was blue, not black – it would be visible even before it breached the surface.

One of the guard's arms moved towards his gun . . .

And withdrew. A moment later, a spot of orange appeared – the flame of a cigarette lighter.

Nina almost let out a breath of relief before catching herself. The man above lit up, taking in a long drag, then turned and walked away.

She let out a surge of stale bubbles, then she and the Dutchman continued towards the ladder.

It did not take long to reach it. She looked up. The only movement above came from rippling water. She rose cautiously to the surface, sound returning as she lifted her head. All she could hear was the endless wet flap of waves against concrete.

De Klerx breached beside her and took hold of the ladder with one hand, reaching down to unfasten his flippers with the other. He wedged them behind a rung at water level, then carefully started to ascend, leaning back to give himself a wider view of whatever was above. 'It is clear. Move.'

Nina took off her flippers and followed. The crane at the foot of the quay between the two docks came into sight, its elevated control cabin illuminated, but empty. De Klerx reached the top and moved aside. She shook off as much water as she could from her badly fitting wetsuit before climbing from the ladder; a big puddle and a trail of drips would be a dead giveaway that someone had just come out of the sea. The brick hut was not far to their left. Another check for movement, then she dropped low and scurried towards it.

There was a ragged hole in the brickwork. De Klerx paused to check for broken glass or rusty metal on the floor beyond, then squeezed through. 'Leave your diving gear in here,' he said, removing his cylinder and harness as Nina entered.

She shrugged off her own equipment. 'Where do we go now?'

He checked the dock again. Another man had come into view near the covered workshops at the top of the slipway, but he was far enough distant that he would not see them if they stuck to the shadows. 'Behind those boxes,' he said, indicating a pile of broken crates before moving his pointing finger to an overturned rust-scabbed hull, 'then across to that old boat.' He took his sub-machine gun from a waterproof bag. 'Let's move.'

He scurried out into the night, Nina advancing nervously behind him.

'Augustine, please,' said Lonmore. 'Don't do this. I know you think it's the only way to get Greece out of debt, but trust me, it won't work. You really believe the IMF and the other world banks will just cave in to your demands? They'll do whatever it takes to find you – and crush you.'

Trakas gave him a small smile. 'I am not going to walk into the headquarters of the European Central Bank with an ultimatum, Spencer. I will not even let anyone know that I am behind this until Greece is free! They will receive the video proof and perhaps a hundred thousand dollars of gold, to show I am serious, as well as my instructions and the deadline for carrying them out. In the meantime, I will use the Crucible to make more gold – two or three million dollars' worth should be enough to begin with. If they have not agreed to my terms – and I do not imagine they will, at first – I will sell it all on the open market.'

'Three million dollars of gold isn't that much in the global scheme of things. It's a blip at most.'

'No, but it will catch their attention. The next instalment will be bigger. The one after that . . . well, you know my business. My planes, my ships, my trucks – imagine them all filled with gold, on its way to be sold.'

'Nice little rhyme,' said Eddie. 'I'll have to remember it to tell my daughter at bedtime. It'll make a change from the story about the eggs with legs.'

Spencer frowned at him. 'Do you ever shut up?'

'Nope. You need a smart-arse comment or a crap pun, I'm your man.'

Petra was amused, but she was alone in her feelings. Anastasia merely tutted in disdain, while the faintly baffled Lonmore turned back to Trakas. 'So you're going to stay anonymous until you get what you want? You'll just let your demands speak for you?'

'No, someone else will speak for me.' Trakas's eyes fixed upon Anastasia. 'You!'

Nina and De Klerx crept along the line of boats behind the workshops. They had managed to slip past a couple of patrolling guards, but now the Dutchman raised his hand as he saw movement ahead. Nina crouched, leaning to look past him. Another armed man had just come into sight, patrolling the boatyard's outer fence. 'He will not see us,' whispered the Dutchman.

'Let's not take the chance, huh?' Nina retreated slightly, then sidestepped into the darkened gap between two of the boats. She stretched out one hand, cautiously sweeping her path. 'Careful here,' she warned as her fingers met cold, grimy metal. 'There's an anchor or something leaning against it.' She worked her way around the unseen obstruction, her back rubbing against one of the hulls. Despite the boat's size – it must have weighed several tons – an unsettling creak still came from the stand supporting it. 'God, are they balancing these things on toothpicks?'

'It does not feel safe,' De Klerx quietly agreed as he followed her past the blockage. To their relief, no further sounds came from the boat.

Nina reached the other end of the cramped passage, hunching behind a propeller. Movement caught her eye off to the left, a guard walking past a cage-like rack of gas cylinders, but he was heading away from the intruders. The large factory was ahead, beyond a couple of smaller structures. It was one of the latter that she fixed upon. 'If we climb up on that hut, we should be able to jump over to the annexe on the big building without anyone seeing us.'

De Klerx looked for himself. 'And then we can climb that to

the roof.' He indicated a ladder running up the factory's side.

'Good. I always like it when the bad guys have an easy way into their secret base.'

The Dutchman did not smile. 'If we go between those containers, they should keep us out of sight.' He made sure nobody was visible in either direction along the line of boats, then pushed past Nina and scurried across a rutted roadway to vanish into the shadows between a pair of shipping containers. She quickly followed.

'What do you mean?' Anastasia demanded.

'I mean, you will tell the banks what you have seen here, and confirm that it is true,' said Trakas. 'Dr Wilde would have been the best person to do so, as she is both famous and has a connection to the United Nations, but then so do you. The daughter of Fenrir Mikkelsson, the UN's top nuclear arms negotiator – she will be believed when she says what the Crucible can do.'

'I won't help you,' she said.

'You will.'

Her frown deepened. 'Fuck you.'

Spencer snorted. 'Classy, Ana. Classy.'

Trakas drew in a breath of irritation. 'You never liked me, did you, Anastasia? I must say, I have always felt the same about you. And your father. You are both . . . arrogant. *Cold*. I suppose it comes from living on a grey rock at the edge of the Arctic. Even Sarah; she had a warm heart when she was younger, but it has been frozen over the years.'

'Do not insult my father!' snapped Anastasia. 'I won't do what you tell me.'

'You do not have a choice.' He stepped right up to her, her tight-fitting wetsuit making her look even slighter against his broad torso, and took hold of her wrists. Disgust flashed across her features as she tried to pull away, but she couldn't break his grip. 'You are in my world now. Here, Midas is not king – *I* am. When I ask for something, it—'

She whipped a knee up at his groin – but Trakas had been prepared for such an attack, twisting back to take the impact against his leg. His response was immediate: a hard slap across her cheek. She flinched away, drawing in a sharp, shocked breath.

'Augustine!' cried Lonmore as his wife gasped. Even Spencer seemed taken aback. 'What the hell?'

Eddie made an abrupt move towards Trakas, fists clenched, only for Axelos to snap his gun up. The Englishman stopped, giving the bodyguard a glare of deep menace.

Trakas released Anastasia. She retreated, one hand to her stinging cheek. 'You okay?' Eddie asked her.

'Yes,' she said, regarding the Greek with loathing.

He looked back at Trakas. 'You're a tough guy, hitting a woman half your size. You fancy trying that on me? Without your little gofer holding a gun on me, I mean.'

'If I am hit first, I hit back,' said the tycoon, unimpressed by the threat. 'No matter who hits me. You are welcome to find out for yourself, Mr Chase. But not now. It is my country's honour I am protecting, not my own. The IMF, the banks, they need to know that I am serious.' He addressed Anastasia again. 'You will do that for me of your own free will, or I will make you do it.'

'How about you make *me* do it?' countered Eddie.

'You? Why would anyone care what *you* tell them?'

'They usually don't – until I tell 'em they're fucked and they realise I'm right. But you wanted Nina to do your little hostage video? Well, I'm the next best thing. Nearly as good-looking, and they know me at the UN too. I've saved their arses often enough. So if I tell 'em what you've done, and what you want to do, they'll believe me.'

Trakas considered his offer, then nodded. 'Okay. You do it. But I will tell you what to say, yes? No tricks, no hidden codes.'

'Okay,' said Eddie. The Greek nodded again, then turned away to speak to the cameraman. Axelos lowered his gun, but kept it pointed in Eddie's general direction. Spencer went for a closer look at the gold.

Anastasia sidled up to the Yorkshireman. 'Why did you do that?' she whispered. 'You shouldn't have given in to him!'

'Because the guy's just conjured up over half a million dollars of gold and could make as much as he wanted, but all he cares about is putting the boot in to the banks,' Eddie replied. Lonmore and Petra took an interest, leaning closer to listen. 'He's not going to stop, not now he thinks he might actually win. And when someone gets to that point, especially when they're a rich bastard who's used to always getting their way, they stop caring if other people get hurt.'

'And you're here to protect us?' Anastasia asked snidely.

'Someone's got to. I don't see your boyfriend here to do it.' That prompted a startled reaction. 'Oh, come on, you couldn't have made it any more bloody obvious if you'd started shagging each other on the yacht's dining table.' Lonmore raised his eyebrows, while Petra suppressed a giggle.

'It's not a secret,' the Icelander huffed.

'*I* didn't know,' said Lonmore, with a mixture of amusement and prurient interest.

'You didn't know your own son'd sold you out to your best mate either,' Eddie pointed out, to the older man's embarrassment. 'And another thing: we've been *kidnapped*. I know that should be obvious, but I thought I'd better point it out, since you still think Trakas is your friend. He can't let us go now, not until he's got what he wants. We'd give him away.'

'So what do we do?' asked Petra.

'Play along, try to drag things out for as long as we can. Some of your guys got away,' he told Anastasia, 'so they might be able to figure out where we are. Trakas can't have *that* many places where he can put a particle accelerator—'

He fell silent as the tycoon returned. 'Mr Chase. We are ready to begin. Are you?'

'Yeah, I am,' Eddie replied. 'What do you want me to say?'

28

De Klerx and Nina reached the shadows behind a small brick hut close to the much larger industrial structure dominating the boatyard. The concrete sidewalk around the factory was brightly lit, with no cover or hiding places. A guard made his leisurely way down the building's long side. His gun was slung at his hip, one hand resting upon it. Trakas's men were prepared for trouble, but not actually expecting it.

They waited for the man to pass on the other side of the hut and move on, then climbed up on to it and made running jumps across to the top of a long single-storey extension abutting the large building. The ladder was near the far end of its roof. Staying low, De Klerx reached it and started to climb. Nina followed, quickly finding that she couldn't match his pace. By the time she reached the top, he had already climbed across the sloping roof to investigate a skylight. 'Wait for me, dammit,' she muttered, cautiously crawling over the tiles after him.

She caught up at the window and looked down through it. The interior appeared to be a factory, conveyors and overhead tracks snaking through the space. Everything was stationary, but the low rumble of machinery suggested that something was active . . .

Nina shifted position, and saw what was making the noise.

Running the length of the far wall was a hefty tube mounted on stands. Trakas's particle accelerator? It seemed likely; each end was contained inside a large box bearing radiation warning symbols—

Her heart jumped as she saw Eddie at the furthest.

He was with the Lonmores and Anastasia, Axelos and another armed man keeping watch on them. Nina brought her head lower and spotted Trakas addressing his unwilling guests. Spencer stood with him, smirking. 'They're all down there,' she whispered.

De Klerx brought up his radio and told his men that they had found the hostages, and to move in on the factory. He saw Nina's disapproving look. 'We have to be prepared to get them out under fire.'

'It'd be preferable if we got them out *without* any shooting.' She moved to get a better view of the interior. 'There's a catwalk a couple of windows over,' she said, gesturing towards it. 'We should be able to climb down if we can get the skylight open.'

'The guards will see us,' the Dutchman warned.

'Not if we stay behind that pillar. Besides, they're watching the prisoners – and their boss.'

'Okay. But if we are seen . . .' He brought a hand closer to his gun.

'Just don't do anything stupid, please,' Nina told him wearily. She started across the roof, De Klerx behind her.

'Hold on, hold on,' said Eddie as the man with the camera prepared to start filming. 'Is my eye light set up properly? And I might need some powder, I'm a bit sweaty.'

Trakas frowned. 'What are you talking about?'

'You want this to look good, don't you? I've been on a film set. This is what Grant Thorn was like for every single shot.'

'You are a very funny man,' said Trakas, with a noticeable lack of amusement. 'Just say what I told you to say.'

'Okay, all right. But if you shoot from this angle, you'll cross the action line and have to spend a fortune to fix it in post.' Reluctantly accepting that he had delayed for as long as he could,

Eddie faced the lens. The shielded box at the end of the linear accelerator, out of which the Crucible had been hoisted to be visible to the camera, was framed behind him. 'Okay. You rolling?' He cleared his throat. 'Right. Hi. My name's Eddie Chase, and I'm married to Dr Nina Wilde, the world-famous archaeologist. I'm making this video to tell you—'

'Stop, stop,' Trakas cut in irritably.

'What?'

'You are doing a stupid voice.'

'No I'm not!' Eddie protested, offended. 'I'm from Yorkshire – this is how I talk!'

'You do kind of sound like that guy from *The Simpsons*,' said Petra. 'You know, the bad actor?'

'Troy McClure? Tchah! Everyone's a critic.'

'Just do it properly!' snapped the Greek. 'Start again.'

'All right, bloody hell.' Eddie shook his head, then composed himself for a retake. 'I'm Eddie Chase, and I'm married to Dr Nina Wilde, the world-famous archaeologist. I'm doing this to let you know that what you've been told about the thing behind me, the Crucible of Midas, is all true – I've seen it with my own eyes. It can be used with a particle accelerator to turn mercury-196 into gold, and do it on an industrial scale . . .'

He paused. With everyone else's eyes on him, he was the only person facing away from the accelerator and across the rest of the factory – and he had just glimpsed movement past the long partition, somebody dressed in black briefly coming into view as they climbed over part of the production line. Since Trakas had dismissed all the workers, that meant someone else was now in the building . . .

'The other video you got with this one hasn't been faked,' he hurriedly continued. 'The Crucible made about seventeen kilos of gold – you've been sent some of it as proof.' Both Trakas and

Axelos gave him odd looks as they registered that his speech was becoming more urgent; he tried to moderate it, but was all too aware that his acting skills didn't even match up to those of Grant Thorn. 'The bloke who's got it says he's going to keep making more and more gold to make the price crash, unless you give him what he wants. I reckon he's willing to do it, so—'

A noise from beyond the partition caught Axelos's attention. He snapped his head around to find the cause – as De Klerx vaulted the barrier and landed behind the group, his UMP at the ready. 'Drop your guns!' he snarled. The guard hesitated, then did so.

Another figure scrambled over the partition with rather less grace. 'Nina!' cried Eddie.

'Hi, honey,' she replied. 'Did you miss me?'

Anastasia's response to the Dutchman's arrival was more restrained, though no less heartfelt. 'Rutger! You found us!'

'Your father figured out where Trakas had taken you,' he said, gun quickly flicking towards the tycoon before locking back on to Axelos. 'I said drop the gun.'

Axelos regarded the unsuppressed weapon warily. 'If you shoot me, the guards will hear.'

'But you will be dead. And I am not alone; the rest of my men are on the way.' His face hardened, trigger finger slowly tightening. With angry reluctance, Axelos placed his gun on the floor, then stepped back.

Eddie collected it, moving to cover the four Greeks. 'All right, that's a wrap,' he told the frightened cameraman. 'Nothing'll happen to you as long as you don't do anything stupid.'

Nina went to him. 'Is everyone okay?'

'We're all fine, thanks,' said Lonmore, relieved. 'Thanks for your hospitality, Augustine, but I think it's time we left.'

'What about him?' Petra asked, glowering at Spencer. The younger man had the expression of a child caught with his hand in the cookie jar, only with a fear of something considerably worse than a chiding.

'I think we're due a serious family talk,' Lonmore said sternly. 'Come on, let's get out of here.'

'We need to take the Crucible with us,' Anastasia announced imperiously.

'What?' said Nina. 'The hell with that – let the cops handle it. Once they secure it, the IHA can take over.'

'Do you really think a man like him' – a disdainful jab of the finger at Trakas – 'won't have friends in the police? We came to Greece to get the Crucible back. I'm not leaving without it.'

'What do you mean, back? You never had it in the first place!'

Anastasia ignored her. 'How did you get here, Rutger?'

'Our ship is just offshore,' he replied. 'It is on its way to the docks.'

She pointed at the flatbed truck. 'If we load the Crucible on to that, can you get it aboard the ship?'

'Yes, if we can reach it. There are guards around the shipyard.'

'How many men do you have left?'

'Five, and one on the ship.'

'Is that enough to fight our way out?'

'If we have to.'

'How about we make bloody sure that we *don't* have to?' said Eddie, concerned by the direction the discussion was taking. 'Forget the Crucible. Getting everyone out of here safely is what matters.'

'He is right,' said Trakas. 'If you sneak out by yourselves, you might get away. But you will never get the Crucible to your boat without being seen.'

Anastasia shook her head. 'You see?' she said to Nina. 'If we leave the Crucible, he'll have it removed and hidden before the police or the IHA can get involved. We're taking it with us.'

'Really bad idea,' Eddie told her. 'Look, let's just tie these arseholes up so they can't raise the alarm, then get to this boat of yours. We don't need—'

A message over De Klerx's radio caught everyone's attention. 'My men are on the roof,' the Dutchman reported. He looked up as black-clad figures began to drop down through the skylights.

Trakas and Axelos exchanged worried looks. 'Spencer, my friend,' the industrialist began, addressing Lonmore, 'we can still all get what we want. You want gold? I can make gold – *we* can make gold, as much as we need, and more. You have the Crucible, I have the particle accelerator. We can work together! I can save my country, and the whole Legacy' – he swept out a hand to encompass the Lonmores, Anastasia, even Nina – 'will be rich again. We can make a deal.'

'There won't be a deal,' said Anastasia coldly.

'Now wait a minute, Ana,' Lonmore said. 'If there's a chance to resolve the situation in a way that benefits everyone, don't you think we should investigate it?'

She fixed him with a stare every bit as dismissive as any she had directed at Trakas. 'This isn't a board meeting. We're not going to vote on this, Spencer.'

'But that's exactly what we should be doing! This affects the Legacy, so all the members should be involved. Augustine, you've got a phone there – we should call Fenrir and Sarah, and Olivia. We can decide what to do about your offer together.'

'Oh, for God's sake,' said Nina, exasperated.

'I'm glad you don't run a bloody fire brigade,' added Eddie. 'By the time you'd held a vote on whether or not to kick open a door, everyone'd have burned to a crisp!'

Lonmore looked offended, but before he had a chance to say more, De Klerx's men arrived. One had a handgun in addition to his UMP; at a nod from De Klerx he gave the smaller weapon to Anastasia. She immediately pointed it at Trakas, to the Greek's consternation. 'The Crucible,' the Dutchman ordered. 'Load it on to that truck.'

'No, wait, wait,' said Lonmore, shaking his head firmly. 'Nobody does anything until we've had a chance to discuss this.'

'Do it,' Anastasia snapped. The men bustled into action.

Lonmore spluttered in disbelief. 'Now wait! You're not in charge here, Anastasia!'

'Nor are you,' she replied. 'This is not a time for democracy and debate. We need action.'

Spencer gave his father a humourless mocking grin. 'Now you know how I felt when I lost *my* say in the Legacy, Dad.'

'Okay, enough with the power plays,' said Nina as one of the men started the truck and reversed it towards the radiation shield. 'We need to get out of here before some guard decides to check on his boss.'

Eddie indicated Trakas. 'We should take him with us. If nothing else, it'll stop his goons from shooting at us.'

'You won't get away,' rumbled the Greek. 'My men are very loyal. If you take me, they will stop at nothing to rescue me.' He turned back to Lonmore. 'You have always been the sensible one, Spencer – the team player, as you say in English. But now you need to be the leader! Olivia and Fenrir always do whatever they want without asking for a vote. You should do the same. Take the deal. We will both be rich – we will *all* be rich. What do you say?'

Lonmore rubbed his chin, thinking. 'I'd say it's a good deal, yeah. What about you, Petra?'

'It sounds good to me,' said his wife, with a little uncertainty.

The hoist whined as it moved along its overhead tracks, sliding the Crucible towards the idling truck. De Klerx's men climbed up on to the flatbed to secure it. Anastasia watched, then rounded on the Legacy's other members. 'I told you there won't be any deals. We are leaving, and taking the Crucible with us.'

Trakas let out a growl. 'Spencer. Tell this *girl* she is not in charge here – you are!' Behind him, the Crucible touched down on the truck, the men rapidly snaking chains through its surrounding cage to hold it in place. 'I am offering you everything you want! Take the deal, and we will all leave here rich!' He stepped towards his friend, arms wide—

Anastasia shot him.

29

The burly Greek clutched at his chest, a breathless groan escaping from his mouth, then he dropped heavily to his knees and fell face-down on the concrete floor. Petra screamed and ducked behind her husband. Lonmore himself gasped, staring at the downed man in sheer disbelief.

Axelos was also stunned – but only for an instant, as a rage-fuelled urge for vengeance took hold. He hurled himself at Anastasia—

De Klerx bodily intercepted him, slamming him to the ground. Both men rolled, Axelos clawing for the gun – but De Klerx pulled the trigger. The first shot hit the Greek's hand at point-blank range and blew off two of his fingers. Before he could even cry out, the Dutchman fired twice more into his chest and throat. Axelos slumped on to his back, convulsing as blood gushed from his neck wound before falling still. The guard turned to flee, but another shot downed him.

A brief silence, broken by Nina's yell of 'Jesus *Christ*! What the hell did you just do?'

Anastasia's eyes remained fixed upon Trakas for a moment before she responded, facing the redhead with an expression that betrayed little other than surprise at her own actions. 'He . . . he was going to attack me,' she said.

'No he wasn't!' cried Lonmore. 'He was making a deal – he was going to *hug me*!'

'He was going to attack me,' Anastasia repeated, her brief uncertainty now gone. 'Again! I was not going to let that happen.'

'You did the right thing,' said De Klerx, standing.

'No she bloody didn't!' Eddie yelled. 'Now every fucking goon in the place knows we're here – and'll be trying to kill us!'

The cameraman finally overcame his paralysis, dropping to his knees and gabbling in clear fear for his life. De Klerx turned towards him, but before he could do anything threatening, Nina hurriedly interposed herself. 'Don't! This has already gone *way* past far enough. We've got to get out of here.'

'Where's this boat?' Eddie demanded.

Nina pointed. 'The docks are that way.'

He signalled for the Lonmores and Anastasia to follow him. 'Okay, come on. You an' all,' he added to Spencer.

The young man was ashen, unable to take his wide eyes off the dead men. 'I . . . I should stay here, explain what happened . . .' he stammered.

'All they'll care about is that someone killed their boss,' Nina warned, 'and you're a someone! They'll shoot you just as quickly as the rest of us.'

'She's right,' said Lonmore. 'Spencer, we've got to get some-where safe. Come with me. Please!' He was almost pleading. Spencer looked up at his father in surprise before frantically nodding.

'I'm staying with Rutger,' Anastasia announced. She followed the Dutchman as he joined his men at the truck.

'Take the Crucible to the boat,' he ordered. 'Get there quickly!' He opened the cab door for her, then followed as one of his team raised the large roller door. The truck started towards it, the men on the flatbed hunching down around the Crucible with their weapons at the ready.

'Why do I get the feeling we just became decoys?' said Nina.

'Better get to this bloody boat before they do,' Eddie growled. 'Come on!' He took the lead as the group headed across the factory floor towards an exit, Spencer following at his father's urging. 'How many guards did you see on the way in?'

'At least eight,' Nina told him. 'And they were all armed.'

'Well obviously— Shit, down!' One of said guards burst through the exit ahead of them, spotting the approaching fugitives. He fired at them – only to fly backwards with a pained scream as he was hit in the shoulder by a round from Eddie's weapon. 'Fuck's sake!' growled the Yorkshireman. 'I was really hoping I wouldn't have to shoot anyone else. It's a bad example for Macy.'

'Yeah, let's not tell her about all this,' said Nina.

They reached the door. Eddie swept out with his gun raised. There was nobody in immediate sight, though he was certain that situation would not last long. 'Okay, where are we going?'

They had emerged from the factory some way along from where Nina and De Klerx had arrived. The crane gave her a landmark. 'Over there,' she said, gesturing.

Eddie turned to the Lonmores, who were still in shock. 'Okay, we're gonna get you out of here. Just stay with us and keep your heads down.' Lonmore and Petra nodded, wide-eyed. Spencer looked to be eyeing alternative escape routes for himself, so the Englishman grabbed him by the arm. 'You, stick with me.' The order was half advice, half warning.

Nina went first, the other married couple close behind as they headed for a low brick building. Eddie pushed Spencer ahead of him, gun at the ready. Still no guards. Nina and the Lonmores reached the hut—

Two guards raced around the far end of the factory, one shouting into a radio. 'Get into cover!' the Yorkshireman yelled as he shoved Spencer onwards. A moment later, gunfire cut through the night air. A round smacked into the brickwork just behind Eddie as he reached the hut.

Petra squealed. 'They're shooting at us. They're really shooting at us!'

'What did you expect, that they were going to politely but

firmly escort us off the premises?' Nina said scathingly. Across a rutted pathway beyond the hut was a half-built section of hull. She waved the Lonmores past her. 'Get behind that!'

They ran into the shelter of the skeletal ship. Nina followed. Crackles of gunfire echoed through the boatyard. De Klerx and the others in the truck were encountering resistance.

She reached the hull, pausing in its shadow to let her husband catch up. Lonmore and Petra continued past another ship under construction and one of the racks of gas cylinders—

More shouts – from ahead.

'Look out!' Nina cried. The Lonmores darted behind an upturned superstructure as the guards opened fire with their Spectres set on full auto.

Bullets clanged against the rack, the wire mesh gates doing nothing to shield its contents from the gunfire—

A spear of bright flame erupted from a maroon gas cylinder. Nina immediately realised the danger and dived backwards – as the acetylene tank exploded.

The blast ripped through its neighbours in a fiery chain reaction, some of the oxygen and acetylene cylinders blowing apart while others rocketed out of the inferno on trails of high-pressure flame, spiralling hundreds of feet into the air or pounding the grounded ships like cannonballs.

Eddie saw Nina throw herself down just in time to follow his wife's lead, hauling Spencer with him. 'What the fuck was *that*?' the Englishman yelled as another errant cylinder went up like a bomb.

Nina hurriedly scrambled further behind the unfinished ship as burning chunks of metal smacked down around the crater where the rack had once stood. 'That's why our apartment's all-electric!'

Spencer stared at the inferno in horror. 'Dad! *Dad!* Are you okay?'

No reply for a few seconds . . . then Lonmore's voice reached them. 'Spencer!' The older man sounded dazed. 'We're okay! Are you all right?'

'Yeah, yeah!'

Eddie stood and quickly reached Nina. 'You're not too crispy?'

'I'm fine,' she replied. 'Don't think we'll be going that way, though.' A ragged wall of flame stretched across their path, cutting them off from Lonmore and Petra – while leaving the guards' line of fire all too clear. 'Spencer, Petra! Keep going – head for the crane and you'll see the dock! Stay in cover!'

'So how do *we* get there?' asked Eddie.

Nina gestured to their left. 'There's a line of boats. They go most of the way, and they should give us protection.'

He nodded, then gestured to the young man behind him. 'Come on.'

They picked their way through the dockyard until they reached the muddy roadway running along the row of standing boats. Eddie peered out from behind a dumpster of rusty scrap, spotting the crane beyond the beached vessels. 'Get across, I'll cover you. Spencer, you too.'

Nina started over the road towards the boats, Spencer behind her. Eddie briefly held back to cover them, then followed—

An engine roared – and a pickup truck skidded around the end of the road to his left, racing towards them.

Spencer froze. But Nina had already seen a man in the rear bed standing up. She shoved the young man forward as the guard fired at them, flames sputtering from his Spectre's muzzle. 'Move!'

They ducked between two of the boats. Bullet impacts kicked up mud and gravel, then splinters flew as the gunman tracked them behind the hull. Spencer shrieked. 'Keep going!' Nina yelled.

Eddie jumped out from cover and fired at the bounding pickup. The man in the rear unleashed another burst, but the vehicle's wild ride over the uneven ground made accurate aiming all but impossible. The Yorkshireman was stable – and more skilled. He let off three rounds, the first striking the truck's radiator grille. He instantly refined his aim. The second bullet shattered the windscreen – and the third hit the driver squarely in the head.

The pickup veered sharply as the dead man slumped over the wheel, flinging the gunman from the rear bed to hit a boat's mast and fold around it with a horrific crunch of bone. Out of control, the truck skidded on before hitting a bump and being thrown into the air . . .

It smashed into the line of boats, ripping one in half before burying itself nose-first in a second. The force of the impact collapsed the stands supporting the hull. It toppled over – hitting the boat beside it.

Which hit the next in line.

One by one, the grounded ships fell like dominoes, masts snapping and lines flailing. The line of destruction marched towards Nina and Spencer. 'Shit!' Eddie cried. 'Get out of there, *run!*'

Spencer hurried for the boats' sterns, but stumbled over debris hidden in the darkness. Nina ran into him from behind. They both fell. The ship to their left lurched as another vessel collided with it, then toppled sideways.

Even in the shadows, there was still enough spill from the boatyard's lights for Nina to see the ship's bronze propeller slicing towards her—

It jolted to a stop barely a foot above her as the rolling boat smashed against its neighbour. 'Go, *go!*' she shrieked, scrambling forward. Spencer gasped in fear and followed, both flinging themselves clear as the other ship rolled from its stand to continue the chain reaction. The first boat's abbreviated fall concluded, the propeller's edge burying itself a foot deep in the wet ground where they had been lying.

'Holy crap!' Nina gasped, pulling herself clear as smashed wood rained around her. She checked the almost hyperventilating Spencer. 'Are you okay?'

'Yeah, I – I think so.' He tried to stand, but his shaking legs gave way. 'Oh my God!'

She heard her husband shout her name. 'Eddie, we're here!' she answered.

'Thank fuck!' Eddie said, staring at the wreckage. There was no longer any space between the overturned boats, and he didn't fancy climbing over them either. Snapped spars jutted from the crushed hulls like the teeth of a Venus flytrap, lines from fallen masts entangling everything in a crazed spiderweb.

He looked to the right, seeing the nautical cascade finally end as the last boat in the line smashed against the ground at the edge of the nearest dry dock. 'I can't get to you! Head for the dock, I'll catch up with you there.' He waited for an acknowledgement, then ran along the roadway.

Nina stood. She and Spencer had emerged by one of the workshops at the top of the slipway, the dark shapes of boats lurking inside the open-sided shelters. Beyond them she saw the dry docks – and approaching the further of the two, the vessel on which she and De Klerx's team had arrived.

Bursts of gunfire sounded from elsewhere in the boatyard as the truck made its way to the waterfront. 'We've got to get to the ship,' she said, pulling Spencer to his feet. 'I don't trust Anastasia not to leave without us as soon as she's got the Crucible aboard.'

'I never trusted her anyway,' he replied. 'She always was a

sanctimonious bitch, doing whatever Daddy Dearest told her to do.'

'Unlike you, blowing the family fortune.'

'Hey, at least I wasn't a hypocrite about it. But Jesus Christ, she killed Augustine!' he went on, before she could ask him what he meant. 'Right in front of everyone! It must run in the family; I knew Fenrir was stone cold, but fuck me!'

'No thanks.' She set off again. 'Right now, though, we're relying on her and her boyfriend to get out us of here.'

Spencer quickly caught up. 'Rutger?' he snorted. 'Now he's a cold-blooded asshole.'

'No arguments here.' They reached the first dry dock. 'Shit,' Nina muttered. There was no easy way to get around it to reach De Klerx's ship in the second; the wreckage of the last grounded boat, its hull crushed like a dropped eggshell, had fallen right at its edge, the mast and superstructure jutting out over the concrete basin and blocking their way.

'We could climb over it,' suggested Spencer.

'Only if you want to get shot.' She hurriedly crouched behind some barrels, pulling him with her. A man with a rifle was climbing the ladder to the crane's control cabin.

She looked towards the sea. The lock gates of the nearest dock were both closed, keeping out the water. There were no railings along their tops, but they still looked wide enough to traverse. 'Across there.'

Spencer grimaced. 'Are you crazy? We'll either fall in the sea or thirty feet on to concrete – and we might still get shot!'

'We can make it. And I don't think the guy in the crane'll be looking in our direction.' A furious exchange of gunfire came from somewhere across the boatyard. Had the guards managed to regroup and intercept the truck?

A glance back at the crane. The man had reached its cabin. 'Quick, before he gets his gun ready,' she said, scurrying towards the lock. Spencer gave the guard a nervous look, then hurried after her.

The roadway turned sharply away from the waterfront. Eddie kept going in a straight line, picking his way between a clutch of containers and stacks of metal plates. He had also heard the barrage of gunfire, coming to a similar conclusion as Nina: Trakas's men had probably set up a roadblock.

He reached the side of the first dry dock, pausing in the shelter of the containers. A ship was in the drained tank, the rear half of its superstructure suspended overhead from the crane. Where was De Klerx's boat?

There – creeping into the second dock. It was running dark, a ghostly shape fading into view as it entered the wash of the boatyard's floodlights. To reach it, he would have to either skirt around the inshore end of the dry dock past the crane, or cut across the gangways leading to the disassembled boat; the smashed remains of a yacht blocked the way to the lock gates bridging the seaward end.

The first route, he decided. It was longer, but seemed safer. The dry-docked craft was missing large sections of its deck, shadows making it hard to tell what was merely darkness and what was an open hole. He broke cover and ran—

The echoing boom of a rifle from above and the piercing crack of a bullet splintering concrete just behind him came as one.

Someone was in the crane, high up enough to have been obscured from Eddie's hiding place. He cursed and changed direction. He was too far from the containers to retreat without giving the sniper a clear shot at his back. Instead he charged up one of the gangways. Another shot snapped past him, impacting against the ship's hull. He reached the deck. There was a hatch not far away, but it was closed, and taking even a second to open it would leave him a sitting duck.

But closer was a missing panel in the bulkhead. He leapt through it into the black void beyond—

Discovering to his horror that it really *was* a void. There was no floor!

He dropped—

Something hit him like a baseball bat to the chest.

A girder, one of the missing deck's supports. He caught it with one arm, pain punching at his heart through bruised ribs. His gun fell and banged off unseen objects a worrying distance below.

Eddie hung helplessly for a moment before finding the beam's edge with his now-empty hand. He swung his legs, but no footholds presented themselves, forcing him to draw himself upwards by sheer muscle until he could hook a heel over the girder—

A shrill hammerblow reverberated through the metal as another round hit a few feet away. The sniper had fired through the gap in the bulkhead. Even though he was clear of the point of impact, the clatter of ricocheting bullet fragments was stark warning that the Yorkshireman was not out of danger.

He hauled himself on to the beam, finding just enough remaining deck on its far side to allow him to stand. Sufficient light was coming from outside to let him pick out his surroundings. Sidestepping to a doorway, he slipped through into a passage. Its aft end was open to the night. He cautiously made his way down it, realising that the superstructure had been removed to give access to the engines below. Heavy machinery was visible through the gaping hole.

A gangway led from the deck to the quay between the dry docks. De Klerx's ship was still approaching the open lock – and Eddie felt a flash of alarm as he saw two figures traversing the closed one ahead of him. Nina and Spencer were picking their way across the top of the huge gates. Too quickly. They must have thought the sniper had been firing at them, and were now rushing for solid ground. If either slipped and fell into the dock, they would be killed when they hit the concrete below.

But they would also be killed if the sniper saw them. If Eddie made a run for the quay, he could draw the guard's fire—

He belatedly registered a new sound, a low mechanical moan. It was close by, but he couldn't work out what it was – until he saw the shadows on the deck shift as something passed in front of the floodlights.

Something large.

Realisation struck – as the section of suspended superstructure hit the ship.

30

The lock gates were eighteen inches wide, thick wood reinforced with steel to withstand the sea's immense pressure. They should have been straightforward to negotiate, but their tops were slimy with algae and splatterings of bird excrement, forcing Nina to take each step with great care.

But now she was three quarters of the way across the dry dock's entrance. Ahead, De Klerx's ship was almost at the mouth of the second dock. She risked a brief look inland, for the first time seeing something of the ongoing gunfight. Some of the boatyard's guards had blocked the road to the docks by dragging a section of mast across it. She couldn't see the truck bearing the Crucible, but it sounded as if the Dutchman's men had spread out to exchange fire. One of the defenders lay unmoving at the roadside, but she couldn't tell if the intruders had taken casualties of their own.

Movement to her side. She glanced at the crane, fearful that the man in it had spotted her – but instead saw the towering machine turning, swinging its suspended cargo at the berthed ship—

The hanging block of decks and bulkheads smashed into the rest of the superstructure with a colossal cacophony of rending metal.

The impact threw Eddie against a wall. Steel screamed around him, the ship warping and tearing as its two sections were crushed back together. Rivets burst loose and clanged off the bulkheads like bullets. He had to get outside—

A spar six inches thick punched through the side of the passage and lanced at his stomach.

He jerked sideways – not quite quickly enough. Its edge tore through his clothes and slashed his waist before burying itself in the wall behind him. The whole corridor twisted, turning into a demented funhouse as it closed in. He tried to duck under the beam, but more jagged spears ripped through the ruptured wall at him—

A deep, monstrous boom like the tolling of a satanic bell . . . and everything stopped.

The ship tipped sideways beneath him before slowly rolling back upright. Groans of tortured metal echoed through the vessel. Eddie gasped in relief and fear at the sight of a crooked knifepoint just inches from his chest. The swinging section was entangled in the rest of the superstructure. He had to make a break for it before the crane moved again.

He turned – and stopped in sudden pain as something dug into his ankle.

A deck plate had crumpled like paper, bending upwards over his foot. He tried to pull free, but another girder was wedged behind his heel.

The vessel jolted again, a shrill whine rising over the ear-splitting scrape of steel against steel. He redoubled his efforts to twist his foot from its cage, but the gap was too small.

Trapped – and suddenly he felt himself rise sickeningly as the crane ripped the whole of the mangled superstructure from the hull.

The man in the crane looked down at the ship with both anger and an almost boyish glee at the destruction he was causing. All he knew was that someone had killed Mr Trakas, and armed intruders were on the loose in the boatyard. He had seen one go into the dry-docked ship, and was doing everything he could to ensure he never came out.

The crane's motors wailed as it hauled the wreckage upwards. Shredded debris rained back into the gaping hole in the deck. No sign of his target, though. The opening the bald man had gone through was now buried in a crumpled mass of metal. He had to make sure he didn't find another exit . . .

A derelict building on the far side of the other dock caught his eye – as did a ship slipping in through the open lock. His boss's killers were trying to get away by sea! His anger returned, and he snatched up his rifle, before remembering his original target. He shoved a control lever forward to slide the hoist and the wreckage it was lifting to the far end of the jib, then worked another to set the crane into a turn.

One that would smash its cargo into the old brick structure like a wrecking ball.

Floodlights along the waterfront came into sight as the crane rotated, giving Eddie a clear look at the metal pinning his foot. He would never get free unless he could bend back the floor plate. But even he wasn't strong enough to do so with his bare hands . . .

A steel bar jutting through the wall rattled as the superstructure shook.

He strained to reach across and grab it. The bar moved, but only a little, a rivet attaching it to a hefty metal plate.

The approaching ship came into view through the passage's twisted end. The crane would carry him across the second dry dock ahead of it. A sudden fear struck him – was the sniper going to drop the decks into the water, drowning him? He tugged harder at the length of metal. The rivet groaned in protest. He could feel it working loose, but now he was over the dock, running out of time—

A crack – and the rivet sheared apart.

He hurriedly jammed the bar into his foot's prison. Not much space: it was pressed hard against his ankle. This was going to hurt . . .

He gritted his teeth, then shoved with all his strength. The bar ground against bone, pain drilling through his lower leg. But he had no choice except to endure it and keep pushing.

The dock's far side came fully into sight. The crane wasn't stopping, instead taking him back towards land . . .

A memory of the view across the dry docks flashed into his mind. There was a building near the empty dock's corner – and the wrecked superstructure was being swung right at it.

A new fear gave him extra strength. He let out a roar as he drove the bar forward, the protruding bone of his ankle feeling as if it were about to be crushed—

The deck plate cracked, and the crowbar suddenly jerked free. He threw it down and pulled out his aching foot, then ran as best he could for the open end of the corridor.

The dark waters spread out before him. He jumped—

A moment of freefall, giving him a glimpse of a man bearing a bulky weapon leaping ashore from the incoming ship – then he hit the sea.

The shock of the temperature change blew all thoughts of the pain from his mind. Bubbles swirling around him, he fought through his disorientation and struggled to the surface—

The superstructure smashed into the derelict building.

Bricks disintegrated, rotten beams exploding into matchwood as several tons of twisted metal ploughed through the ruin. The wreckage slewed around, the section that had been ripped loose from the ship tearing free and dropping on its side with a cacophonous bang that shattered concrete and sent boulder-sized chunks of the dockside tumbling into the water. Waves pounded

Eddie, washing over his head. Choking, he turned to swim clear—

The fallen deck section teetered, then toppled into the dock.

A wall of water hit the fleeing Yorkshireman like a tsunami, pounding him against the wall. He scraped painfully along it until the wavefront passed and he was able to right himself and resurface. Secondary ripples smacked his face. He grabbed one of the rusty metal pillars along the dock's side, pulling himself above the waterline.

The first thing he heard over the waves was the continuing crack of gunfire as the guards faced off against De Klerx's team. But then he picked out something else, close by – a staccato *chak-chak-chak*—

The realisation that it was a rotary grenade launcher came a split second before the first explosion.

Five forty-millimetre high explosive rounds detonated in rapid succession, the blasts rippling across the makeshift road-block and sending the guards and pieces thereof flying. The shooting stopped.

The ship's erstwhile pilot, Beel, regarded the devastation with satisfaction, keeping the Milkor and its last grenade at the ready in case any resistance remained.

It did – but not where he was looking.

A bullet from the crane tore through his shoulder.

The sniper felt a surge of vengeance-fuelled exultation as he saw the man on the dockside fall. He stopped the crane's turn. The hanging deck was buried inside the collapsed building, the other section sinking into the water beside it. From his elevated vantage point, he now had a view across the inshore part of the boatyard – and saw for the first time the attacking force.

Several armed men in wetsuits were hurrying along the road to the docks. Behind them, a flatbed truck pulled out from behind the cover of a half-built boat. There was something large on its back; he couldn't identify it, but he had seen it taken into the factory earlier. The invaders hadn't just killed his boss, they were stealing from him too!

The wetsuited men jogged to the mast blocking the road and dragged it clear. The truck headed for the dock.

'You're not getting away,' growled the sniper, taking aim again.

De Klerx leaned from the passenger-side window to shout instructions to his men. 'Get to the ship and load the Crucible aboard! But watch out for whoever fired that shot. There's still someone—'

The windscreen shattered – and the driver's lower jaw blew apart in a hideous shower of bone and shredded tissue as a rifle bullet ripped through it into his throat.

Blood sprayed across Anastasia's face. She sat frozen and stunned for a moment, then screamed. De Klerx threw open his door and hauled the blonde out as a second round smacked into the middle seat behind them. Now driverless, the truck veered off the road to crash into a stack of barrels. The Dutchman pulled Anastasia down behind the front wheel as the engine stalled. 'Sniper!' he yelled. 'In the crane!'

His men scattered as more shots came from on high.

Eddie dragged himself up on to the dockside just in time to avoid being mown down by the now-unmanned ship as it ground along the concrete. He dropped behind the side of its hull, but the gunfire from the crane wasn't aimed at him. The sniper had found new targets. He spotted the truck, and De Klerx and Anastasia hiding behind the stationary vehicle.

Another shot. One of De Klerx's men fell, the leg of his wetsuit flapping open as the round sliced through his thigh.

Retaliatory fire lanced up at the crane, only to clang ineffectually off the heavy pivot plates beneath its cabin. The sniper had superior positioning, Eddie saw, protected by the metalwork around him, and a clear view of every foot of ground between the truck and the slowing ship. Even if he'd still had his gun, shooting the guard would be difficult . . .

At least, if he shot a *bullet*.

He turned, seeing the wounded pilot – and the distinctive six-barrelled shape of a Milkor MGL grenade launcher beside him. There had only been five explosions . . .

Staying low, Eddie hurried to the downed man. 'I'm with De Klerx!' he said as Beel groped for a holstered pistol. 'Just need to borrow this.'

He scooped up the MGL, pulling a release hook beneath its stubby barrel to swing it open at the breech. As he'd thought, there was one unused round remaining. He snapped the weapon shut. He had fired similar launchers before, both during his military career and afterwards. They were reasonably accurate as such weapons went, but relied less on pinpoint targeting than blast and shrapnel to do damage.

Now he would have to be dead-on first time.

The launcher was fitted with a simple reflex sight, a red crosshair glowing in the eyepiece. He fixed the reticle on the cabin's open window, adjusted for elevation and windage – and fired.

The shot made surprisingly little noise. A reflected flash as the grenade arced past a floodlight, then it was lost to sight—

The cabin exploded. The burning torso and one remaining leg of the sniper somersaulted from the crane and smashed down inside a small boat, toppling it from its stands. 'B3, hit,' Eddie said, before calling out across the suddenly silent dockyard. 'It's clear! Come on!'

'Eddie!' Nina's voice. He looked across the ship's bow to see her and Spencer running down the quay between the two dry docks. They reached its end, passing the crane as Lonmore and Petra emerged hesitantly from behind a container.

De Klerx's men regrouped and headed for the ship, two of them carrying the wounded man. The Dutchman and Anastasia climbed back into the truck, restarting it. Nina hugged her husband as she reached him. 'Thank God you're okay! And, uh, wet.'

'Good job you're wearing a wetsuit,' he replied. 'Is everyone else all right? Apart from the obvious,' he added, assessing the injured man's leg wound; he would live.

'We're fine,' said Lonmore, breathless from the short run. 'Spencer, what about you? That explosion behind us – we thought you'd been caught in it!'

'I'm fine, Dad.' An awkward pause, then the two men embraced. 'I'm glad you are too.'

'We're not out of here yet,' cautioned Eddie. Over the truck, he heard a new sound: sirens. Distant, coming from the nearest town, but approaching quickly. 'Everyone get on the boat.' He tossed the MGL on to the bow, then ushered Nina and the Lonmores aboard.

De Klerx's men stayed on the dockside, waiting for their boss to arrive. The Dutchman pulled the truck up alongside them and jumped out. 'Load the Crucible!' he ordered. They climbed up to release the chains holding the great sphere in place.

'What about him?' Eddie protested, pointing at Beel. The pilot had passed out, the pool of blood from his shoulder wound spreading across the concrete.

'The Crucible is our top priority,' said Anastasia, coming around from the other side of the cab. 'But I'll help you with him.'

Nina recoiled at the sight of her blood-splattered face. 'Jesus! Are you okay?'

'Just shaken up,' the blonde replied.

Eddie joined them, and together they brought the unconscious pilot on to the ship. Behind them, De Klerx's remaining men strained like pallbearers to carry the Crucible. 'You should drop that fucking thing in the sea,' muttered the Englishman, glaring over his shoulder at the glinting artefact.

Anastasia didn't reply, instead returning to De Klerx the moment the injured man had been laid on a bench inside the cabin. Annoyed, Eddie searched for a first-aid kit, then started to treat the bullet wound.

By now, the Crucible had reached the ship, the raiding party lifting it on to the foredeck. The sirens drew nearer. 'Come on, quickly,' snapped De Klerx. The sphere was finally lowered into place. 'Tie it down! You two, get Doyle's body.' A pair of men went back to the truck and lifted the driver's corpse from its cab, returning to the ship with their grisly cargo. De Klerx went to the wheelhouse and put the engines into reverse, backing the vessel out of the dock. Once it was in open water, he swung about, then powered into the blackness of the Aegean.

Anastasia stood beside him, looking through the front windows – not at the sea, but the Crucible on the deck before them. 'We got it,' she said, tiredness driven aside by triumph. 'We got it!'

'Was it worth it?' Nina demanded from behind them. 'All those people dead, including some of your own – and Trakas. Was it worth becoming a murderer?'

Again, she did not reply.

31

It took most of the night before the ship finally made port, the vessel forced to travel below its top speed out of caution at navigating the island-strewn Aegean in darkness. The eastern sky was starting to brighten by the time it heaved to at a pier. An ambulance awaited, taking away the two injured men as well as the dead driver. Nina was certain they were not going to a public hospital, or anywhere else that might ask questions about how they had received their gunshot wounds.

Another two of De Klerx's men went to get the panel van and minibus in which the team had travelled to reach the dock, backing the former up to their vessel. The sun had breached the horizon by the time the Crucible was loaded, and was well clear of it when the vehicles finally brought the exhausted group to Athens airport.

A business jet awaited them. The fact that the Crucible and the group's weapons were put aboard without being checked by customs officials told Nina that she was not the only person willing to abuse United Nations diplomatic procedures to move items from country to country. Fenrir Mikkelsson had undoubtedly had a hand in it.

By now, though, she was too tired to care. 'Next stop, New York,' she said as she slumped into one of the cabin's comfortable chairs.

'Well, Boston,' said Lonmore from across the aisle. 'Although I'm sure we could make a diversion,' he went on at her stony glare. He ducked into the cockpit, returning after a discussion with the pilots. 'Okay, New York it is.'

'What's the flight time?' Eddie asked.

'Just over eleven hours, they think. Apparently there's a strong headwind over the Atlantic that'll slow us down.'

Nina yawned; her sleep on the ship had only been fitful. 'Great. Wake me when we get there.'

The aircraft was larger than the one that had brought her to Greece, with enough seats to accommodate all of De Klerx's men as well as the Dutchman and Anastasia. After the Crucible had been put into the hold, they trooped past Nina, Eddie and the Lonmores to fill the rest of the places. Anastasia gave Spencer a cold look as she went by, which he returned. The pre-flight checks were completed, then the aircraft departed, leaving Greece – and the chaos that had erupted – behind.

Despite her fatigue, Nina slept little better than she had on the ship. The main culprits for her frequent returns to bleary consciousness were the Lonmores, father and son, who were engaged in a long discussion. But Anastasia also woke her with a phone call to her own father, brushing past to visit the cockpit. Eventually, though, sheer weariness wore the redhead down, and she slumped against Eddie's shoulder.

She had no idea how long she had been asleep when her husband nudged her back to wakefulness. They were over the ocean, thickening clouds casting shadows over a slate-grey sea far below. 'What time is it?' she mumbled.

'Too early,' Eddie replied. His wary tone instantly put her on guard, residual sleepiness evaporating. Something was wrong.

'What do you mean?'

'We just started descending, but we've only been in the air for six and a half hours. There's no way we're close enough to the States to be coming in for a landing.'

Nina sat up. He was right: the jet's engines had throttled back, and its nose had tipped slightly downwards. She looked around. Petra and Lonmore were both asleep, an empty glass on his lap, while Spencer stared blankly out of a porthole. He caught her movement and peered at her. 'What's wrong?'

'Do you know why we're descending ahead of schedule?' she asked.

'We are?'

'We are,' said Anastasia from behind them.

Lonmore jerked awake, stirring Petra, and blinked at her. 'Huh? What was that?'

Nina turned in her seat, Eddie standing and facing the Icelander. De Klerx rose too, staring back at him almost challengingly. 'What's going on?' rumbled the Yorkshireman.

'We're making our descent,' Anastasia announced. 'We'll be landing at Reykjavik airport in thirty minutes.'

Commotion erupted in the cabin. 'What the hell?' Nina cried. 'We're supposed to be going to New York!'

'I told the pilots to change course.'

'Then tell 'em to change back,' said Eddie angrily, advancing on her.

De Klerx immediately blocked his path. 'Sit down.'

'Shove a tulip up your arse. We need to get back home to our daughter, not go to fucking Iceland!'

Lonmore stood as well, putting a hesitant hand on Eddie's arm. 'It's okay, I'm sure this is just a . . . miscommunication.'

'I doubt that,' Nina growled.

'We need to secure the Crucible as quickly as possible,' said Anastasia. 'The safest place is the hotel, so that is where we are taking it.'

'The safest place is the IHA!'

Eddie turned and marched to the cockpit door. He tried the handle, but it didn't turn. 'It's locked,' he said, giving Anastasia an accusing glare before banging on it with his fist. 'Oi! Open up!'

'They won't open it,' said the blonde.

The Englishman started back towards her, but De Klerx gestured with a raised hand. His men stood in unison behind him. 'I told you to sit down.'

'Going to be like that, is it?' Eddie growled, but he knew there was little he could do about the situation. Instead, he pointedly leaned against a seat rather than sitting.

'The plane will take you back to New York when we're done,' Anastasia said. 'But first, we *are* going to Iceland.'

Nina gave her a scathing look. 'You know, I'm more glad than ever that I've got nothing to do with your precious Midas Legacy.'

Neither Nina's nor Eddie's mood had improved by the time the plane landed.

It touched down at Reykjavik airport on the outskirts of the Icelandic capital, rather than at Keflavik. Again, there was a marked absence of customs officials. Confirmation that this was Fenrir Mikkelsson's doing came when Nina and Eddie disembarked to see the tall Icelander and his wife standing beside a line of super jeeps waiting to collect the aircraft's passengers and cargo, the largest 4x4 a jacked-up Ford F150 king cab pickup ready to accept the Crucible.

'Pabbi!' cried Anastasia as she ran to her father and hugged him.

Mikkelsson patted her shoulder, looking over her to watch the jet as its cargo door opened. Sarah greeted her daughter with relief. A forklift rolled up to extract the Crucible, which had been lashed to a pallet prior to its loading in Greece. 'Dr Wilde,' he called to Nina. 'Mr Chase, welcome back.'

'We're not here by choice,' Nina snapped. She was not dressed for cold weather, and the wind blowing across the concrete was biting.

'I apologise. But I am sure you understand why I wished the Crucible to be brought here without delay.' Flanked by De Klerx's men, the forklift made its careful way to the pickup truck and deposited its crystalline cargo upon it.

'I understand. But it doesn't mean I approve. Or forgive.'

'You've got the bloody thing now,' said Eddie. 'So if you get 'em to stick some more fuel in the plane, we'll be on our way.'

'It will be at your service soon. But first, I would like you to come with us.'

'No thanks,' Nina told him firmly. 'We just want to leave.'

'Olivia is at the hotel. She wants to see you.'

'Well, I don't particularly want to see her. Not after I found out that she'd been lying to me this whole time.'

Anastasia whispered something to him. 'Spencer told you what the founders were really doing in Nepal?' he said, shooting the younger Lonmore a disapproving look as he descended the steps after his father.

'Yeah. The Midas Legacy came from arms dealing. That's something to be proud of, huh? No wonder Olivia didn't mention it to me.'

'It is the future of the Legacy that we must discuss, not the past,' said Mikkelsson, unconcerned.

'You should come with us,' Lonmore said to Nina. 'I wasn't expecting to be here either, and believe me, I'm no happier about it than you are. But it means you'll be able to say your piece to Olivia – and to the rest of us, as I think you've probably got a lot to get off your chest. Plus it'll be a lot warmer.' He chuckled, the laughter quickly fading to silence at Nina's unsmiling expression.

'You will be back in New York by tonight,' said Mikkelsson. 'Please?' He opened the lead jeep's rear door.

De Klerx had by now supervised the Crucible's loading, directing his men to transfer the various cases of weapons from the hold before joining Anastasia. Eddie eyed him suspiciously, then turned to Nina. 'I'm not sure about this, but you do have some things to sort out with Olivia. If nothing else, you might feel better after giving her a good kick up the arse. Verbally, I mean.'

'I might not limit myself to that,' his wife replied. 'But . . . yeah. Okay. On two conditions.'

'Which are?' Mikkelsson asked.

'That as soon as we're done, this plane takes us back to New York. And that I can call home to check Macy's okay.'

'Of course. This jeep has a satellite phone, I believe.' He glanced at De Klerx, who gave him a confirmatory nod. 'Shall we go?'

Nina exchanged a look with Eddie, then reluctantly nodded. 'Okay. Let's get this over with.'

Even though Reykjavik's small airport was closer to their destination than Keflavik, it actually took longer to reach than on their first visit. Iceland's notoriously changeable weather was showing off for the visitors, flurries of snow swooping in to blind the convoy of super jeeps and reduce their pace to a crawl before vanishing as quickly as they had come. Eventually, though, the vehicles reached the buried road and followed the marker poles around the frozen lake on to the rippling plateau before the hotel.

The 4x4s stopped in the shelter of the overhanging wings to be met by black-clad security personnel. The passengers quickly headed inside, De Klerx's team receiving orders from their leader before continuing to the upper floor, where presumably luxuries like showers and fresh clothing awaited them. 'Lucky bastards,' muttered Eddie, whose own clothes still stank of seawater.

'After everything that's happened, you're just leaving the Crucible outside?' Nina asked Mikkelsson. The now snow-caked artefact was still on the back of the pickup truck.

'It will be safe,' he replied as he led everyone towards the lounge at the western end of the floor. 'Once we have reached a decision about what to do with it, we will bring it inside.'

'Or take it away again,' she said. He did not respond.

They entered the lounge. Olivia was the only occupant, the elderly lady gazing out across the wilderness from a chair near the panoramic windows. 'Thank God you're all safe,' she said, standing as the new arrivals trooped past the fountain to the circular table. The graze on her cheek had faded, but was still visible. She was about to speak to Nina when she saw Spencer. 'Well. I didn't expect *you* to show your face here again.'

Spencer smiled mockingly. 'I know how much you love surprises, Olivia.'

She glowered at him, then turned back to her granddaughter. 'Nina, I'm so glad you're all right. I understand things didn't go smoothly.'

'You could say that,' Nina answered, with a nasty look at Anastasia and De Klerx. 'Seeing as *someone* decided to mount a unilateral commando raid on Trakas's yacht!'

'Unilateral?' scoffed Spencer. 'I told you in Greece, she never does anything without Daddy Dearest's approval.'

The redhead regarded Mikkelsson coldly. 'Is that right?'

'We have much to discuss,' said the Icelander. 'Please, sit.' He gestured at the table. A box about a foot on each side sat before his place, its dimensions triggering a sense of unease in Nina.

Mikkelsson and his family members took their seats, Lonmore and Petra doing the same. Olivia went to her chair and gestured for Nina to take the empty one beside her. 'Huh. Only seven,' said Spencer sarcastically. 'Guess I'm meant to stand here like a naughty boy.'

'So you should,' Olivia told him. 'You've caused a lot of trouble – and you aren't a member of the Legacy any more.'

'Yeah, well, nor's she,' he replied, indicating Nina.

'And glad of it,' Nina said pointedly as she took her place, making her reluctance clear.

Eddie dropped into an armchair near the fountain. 'I'll just wait here then,' he announced, as sarcastically as Spencer. 'Don't suppose the bar's open, is it? Get me a pint, Tulip.'

De Klerx shot him a contemptuous look before Mikkelsson spoke quietly to him. The Dutchman nodded, then left the room. 'You need to fire your HR department,' said Eddie. 'Speaking as someone who's worked in private security? The kid's shit. Too big a temper and his trigger finger's got fucking Tourette's – plus the only person he's bothered about rescuing is his girlfriend! I wouldn't hire him to secure a bloody ice cream van.'

Anastasia half stood, anger on her face. 'Don't you dare say that about him. Rutger saved us!'

'Rutger kicked off the whole fucking mess in the first place when he let Trakas's crew take back his boat. And let's not forget how you made things worse when you shot the bugger!'

Olivia reacted in surprise. 'Who got shot?'

'She killed Trakas,' Nina told her.

Surprise became shock. 'What – he's *dead*?'

'He hit me,' said Anastasia, sitting at a subtle gesture from her father. 'I wasn't going to let him do it again.'

'He wasn't going to!' Lonmore protested. 'He was going to hug me! You know what he's like.'

Olivia shook her head. 'So, the whole affair was—'

'A disaster?' Nina finished for her. 'Pretty much. Lots of people dead, and for what?'

'For the Crucible,' said Mikkelsson. 'While the loss of life is regrettable, and possibly avoidable—'

'No "possibly" about it,' scoffed Spencer, who had pulled up another armchair behind his father's seat and sat with his legs splayed wide.

'—it does mean that we at last have the Crucibles. Both of them.'

The unease that Nina had felt earlier returned with greater force. 'What?'

Mikkelsson carefully lifted the lid of the box and placed the object inside on the table.

The small Crucible.

Even though the lowering sun was hidden by scudding clouds, the crystal still glinted in the light from the broad windows. She stared at it, then snapped her gaze to those around the table. Lonmore and Petra appeared genuinely surprised to see it. The same was not true of Sarah and Anastasia . . . or Olivia.

Nina faced her grandmother, appalled as she realised what that meant. 'You . . . you knew it hadn't been stolen. You *faked* it being stolen!' The masked men hadn't been working for Trakas, but De Klerx – and therefore Mikkelsson.

'This wasn't faked,' said Olivia, putting a hand to the mark on her cheek. 'I really did get hurt.'

'That's – that's not the point! You *lied* to me, you set me up!'

'I am afraid so,' said Mikkelsson. 'But it was necessary.'

'The hell it was!' Nina looked back at Olivia. 'So you staged the attack – and terrified my little girl – to trick me into going to Greece? As what, a *distraction*, so Anastasia and her asshole boyfriend could raid Trakas's yacht and force him to give up the Crucible?'

'We didn't know about any of this, believe me!' said Lonmore, equally shocked by the revelations. 'Not the raid, not that the other Crucible was still here, none of it. I went to see Augustine in good faith, in the hope of coming to a deal. And he would have agreed – if Ana hadn't shot him!'

'She wouldn't have done that if she hadn't felt threatened,' said Sarah defensively.

'It wasn't self-defence,' Spencer said, voice scathing. 'It was straight-up murder! Bam, dead! Yes, he'd hit her, but—'

'Then it was self-defence,' Mikkelsson cut in. 'There should be no argument about that.'

'Not sure the Greek police'd agree with you,' said Eddie.

'And you're being incredibly blasé about all this,' Nina told the diplomat. 'You're a senior United Nations official, and you're just brushing off the fact that you and your daughter are directly involved in murder, piracy and God knows what else! Diplomatic immunity only goes so far. This won't just end your career if it gets out; you could go to jail.' She gave Anastasia a pointed look, before turning her gaze upon her grandmother. 'And you wouldn't be the only one.'

'Nobody is going to jail,' said Mikkelsson, sounding fully confident in that belief. 'And I am not concerned about my career at the UN.'

'You seem to be forgetting that Trakas almost killed you when he stole a protected Atlantean artefact in the first place,' Olivia told Nina haughtily. 'I haven't done anything illegal.'

'That doesn't mean you haven't done anything *immoral*, though,' Nina replied. 'You manipulated me into finding the Midas Cave, you faked the attack in Reykjavik, you lied about that Crucible being stolen – and you kept quiet about your guilty little secret!'

The last accusation brought the strongest reaction, Olivia actually looking concerned. 'What secret is that?' she said cautiously.

'About what Tobias Garde and the others were really doing in Nepal in the 1840s. They were gun-runners! They weren't exploring, they were trying to profit from a civil war. And they did, more than they could ever have imagined!'

Olivia exchanged looks with Mikkelsson and Lonmore; the latter couldn't quite meet her gaze, abashed, while the Icelander's expression was unreadable. 'You told her?' she said to Lonmore, before rounding upon his son. 'No – *you* told her!'

Spencer leaned forward in his chair. 'Yeah. I did.'

'You . . . you absolute *cretin*! Why would you do something so stupid and irresponsible?'

'Like kicking me out of the Legacy? You're damn right I told her! She's got every right to know what kind of people the founders were. And what kind of people are in it now. I mean, Jesus!' He stood and swept a hand around the table at each member in turn, going clockwise from Anastasia. 'Daddy's little sociopath; sociopath Daddy; don't know what the hell *you* do, you're just there filling a seat,' he said to the affronted Sarah, before continuing on to his own father. 'Dad, you're basically a nice guy, but I'm afraid you're a wuss who always plays it safe and folds like a cheap lawn chair whenever anyone puts pressure on you. Then we've got the gold-digger,' he continued to Petra, before coming around to Olivia, 'and finally Mrs Machiavelli, who'd stab herself in the back for fun if she could reach around far enough.'

The old woman gave him a piercing glare. 'You are hardly in a position to criticise anyone else here, Spencer. You're nothing but a wastrel – no, worse than that, a parasite! As if leeching off your father to support your debauched lifestyle wasn't bad enough, then you started stealing from the rest of us by dipping into the Legacy itself! And when you were caught, rather than taking responsibility like a grown man, you went crying to someone outside and betrayed us. Pathetic. Absolutely pathetic.'

'Now hold on, Olivia,' said Lonmore. 'I think we should all calm down and take a—'

'You want to know what's *really* pathetic?' snapped Spencer, stabbing a finger at Olivia. 'Ordering your own daughter to date someone because you want to steal his research on Atlantis!'

Olivia didn't reply, frozen with fury – and something else, a deeper emotion. Nina stared at her, recognising . . . fear? Shame? She looked back at Spencer. 'What are you talking about?'

'I'm talking about *her* guilty secret,' he replied. 'It's bad enough that the Midas Legacy was founded by arms dealers, but she's hiding something a lot more personal. Aren't you, Olivia?'

For the first time since meeting her, Nina realised her grandmother had been completely wrong-footed, with no idea what to do next. 'Is what he just said true?'

'It's . . . no, it's not true,' Olivia replied, flustered. 'That's not what happened at all.'

'But something *did* happen, right?'

'Of course it did!' said Spencer. 'It's what she does. She sets people up! She set you up to go to Greece and distract Augustine, she set you up to find the Midas Cave for her – and she set up your mom with your dad! All she cared about was whether his work could lead her to the cave, but when Laura fell in love with him for real, Olivia kicked her out of the Legacy and cut her off!'

'It didn't happen like that!' insisted Olivia. 'Laura cut herself off from *me*, not the other way around. I never wanted her to go!'

'You're not denying the rest of it, though,' said Nina, horrified. 'Oh my God!' She drew back from her. 'You really *did* tell Mom to go out with Dad, didn't you? The only reason they met is because you wanted a short cut to the Midas Cave!'

'And they fell in love!' Olivia protested. 'That had nothing to do with me – it was practically in spite of me! Yes, I asked Laura to find out more about Henry's research, in case it was useful to the Legacy. But everything that happened after that was entirely their own doing, not mine.'

'It doesn't change the fact that you set them up in the first place!' Nina stood, sickened. 'Mom lied to me, and to Dad – and you lied to me too! My whole life, it's . . .' She shoved the chair away and hurried for the exit. 'It's all based on lies!'

'Nina, wait!' Olivia cried after her.

'Go to hell.' She shoved open the door and rushed out, with no idea where she was going other than away from the old woman.

32

Eddie ran after her, catching up in the long hallway. 'Whoa, Nina! Hold on. It's okay.'

'It's anything *but* goddamn okay, Eddie!' she said. 'I just found out that – Jesus, I can hardly even think about it without wanting to throw up!' They entered the lobby, Nina going to a set of couches facing the hotel's front windows and dropping despairingly on to one. 'The only reason I even *exist* is because my grandmother was so greedy for gold that she forced my mother to go on a date with my dad!'

He sat close beside her. 'Did she really force her?'

'Does it matter? The end result's the same. What would you think if when Macy was older I told her to date a particular guy because there was money in it for me?'

'I wouldn't be happy, no. But you wouldn't do that.'

'So what does that say about Olivia? My own grandmother – my own family? She lied and manipulated, my mom did the same . . . and if you go further back, Tobias Garde was a goddamn arms dealer! That's right up there with "slave trader" and "Grand Wizard of the Ku Klux Klan" as things not to be proud of in your family tree.' She leaned back, looking despairingly up at the ceiling. 'Everything I thought I knew about my family is a lie.'

'Your mum did love your dad, though,' said Eddie, trying to comfort her. 'And she loved you too.'

'I don't know. I don't know any more . . .' She put a hand over her eyes, wanting to shut out the world. 'Money. That's what everything comes down to, isn't it? Fucking money. And the people who deserve it the least are not only the ones who have the most, but will do whatever it takes to get more.'

'Way things are, I'm afraid. I mean, how many evil billionaires have we met?'

'Have we ever met a *nice* billionaire? Is there even such a thing?' She wearily shook her head, then sat up again. 'But those people back there,' she jerked a thumb at the lounge, 'they aren't even billionaires. Sure, they've got money, but it's not a massive amount. And yet they're still fighting and lying and plotting against each other even for that. This is . . .' She let out a deep, gloomy breath. 'This is humanity, isn't it? People just fucking each other over for that little scrap more than anyone around them. And Macy's growing up into their world. She might even end up *as* one of them.'

'She won't,' Eddie said firmly. 'Not with us as parents.'

'You think?'

'Yeah. She might end up as an obsessive, passive-aggressive gobshite who makes crap puns and has a weird accent that's halfway between New York and actual York, but she won't be the sort to screw people over for a few extra quid.'

'*Who's* passive-aggressive?' Nina demanded, but with a very small smile. Eddie grinned. 'Oh God,' she said, the upward curl fading from her lips. 'I don't know what to do. I don't know what to *think*.'

'About what? Olivia, or . . .'

'Olivia, my mom – anything. It feels like a big part of my past has suddenly been taken away. I always thought my parents got together because they both believed in the legend of Atlantis. That's what they told me: that the first thing my mom ever said to Dad was "I believe you." But did she really? I don't know any more. Maybe it was another lie, all part of Olivia's scheme . . .' She wiped away a tear, slumping back in despondency once more. 'It wasn't about Atlantis. It was about gold. Just money.'

'If that was true, though,' Eddie said quietly, 'she would never have married your dad, would she? He didn't have any money, and she gave it up to be with him. You were never exactly rolling in cash as a kid. But your mum and dad still went looking for Atlantis anyway. She wouldn't have done any of that if she hadn't genuinely believed in it.'

Nina knew he had a very good point, but in her current frame of mind she didn't want to accept it. 'I don't know,' was all she said. Eddie recognised her need for silent contemplation and added nothing more, simply sitting with her as she stared unhappily out at the stark landscape.

They stayed like that for some time, watching the sun fall towards the horizon. Squalls of snow occasionally obscured the view, but the darkening sky slowly cleared of clouds. 'Be a good night for seeing the Northern Lights,' Eddie said at last.

'Great,' Nina replied. 'That means there'll be a traffic jam of tourist buses blocking the road back.' She straightened. 'I want to go home.'

'Same here.' He looked towards the lounge. Nobody had yet emerged from it. 'We should tell 'em we're done here so we can go. If they're still not finished arguing, I'll take one of those bloody jeeps myself. I always wanted to drive a monster truck.'

'We should, but I really don't want to have to deal with any of those people again. Especially not Olivia.' The mere thought of her grandmother produced a groan of disgust. 'Ugh, God. You know, if you'd just left the Secret Codex in that chamber when the ceiling collapsed, none of this would have happened.'

'Oh, this is all my fault, is it?' But the words were said with humour.

'Of course it is!' She managed a smile. 'That's what I always tell Macy. When something goes wrong, it's Daddy's fault. Every time. Page one of the Secret Codex for moms.'

'Mums.'

'*Moms.*' They both laughed a little.

'Thank you.'

'For what?'

'For being you. For always being there when I need you the most.'

'Keep the missus happy and life's about a million times easier,' he said, grinning. 'Page one of the Secret Codex for dads.'

A sound from behind made them both turn. The door of one of the elevators flanking the entrance to the power station opened and De Klerx stepped out. He had changed his clothes and was now wearing a dark suit. Some of his men had travelled from the upper floor with him, remaining in the lift. The Dutchman issued a quiet command, then the doors closed. He headed for the lounge as the elevator continued downwards.

Eddie watched until he passed out of sight. Nina felt him tense. 'What is it?'

'He had a gun under his jacket.'

'You sure?'

'Yeah. I know how to spot a shoulder holster. And where are all his goons off to?'

Nina glanced out of the windows. The snowy landscape was turning a deep and beautiful shade of blue as dusk fell, but there was no sign of vehicle lights or any movement that might have prompted the hotel's security detail to investigate. 'Y'know, I'm thinking it's really time that we left.'

'Yeah.' Eddie stood and crossed the lobby to a position where he could see down both the long corridors. De Klerx was entering the lounge, while at the opposite end of the building a guard emerged from a side door and started down the stairs of the eastern entrance. Light briefly gleamed on metal as he descended.

The man had a gun slung over his shoulder. 'Definitely.'

They made their way briskly down the hall after De Klerx. The sounds of an ongoing argument reached them as they opened the door. 'I don't really see that we have a choice,' said Lonmore plaintively.

'Well, you would say that, wouldn't you?' snapped Olivia. 'You were willing to hand over a quarter of everything to Augustine, so I can't say I'm surprised that you'd try to make a deal with someone else.'

'So what would you do?' demanded Petra. 'Build our own particle accelerator? That would probably cost more than the gold we could make from it.'

'We're not cutting in someone else just because they have the facilities we need. That leaves us open to blackmail – or a *renegotiation*.' The word dripped sarcasm. 'Why would someone settle for a quarter of the gold when they could have a third? Or half? And as for your idea of simply selling the Crucibles outright, Ana, that's every bit as bad, if not worse. A one-off payment in exchange for something of potentially limitless value? That isn't any kind of legacy; it's the same short-term thinking that's ruining the world.'

Anastasia leaned forward in forceful refutation. 'We'd be in exactly the same position as before. No, we'd be better off, because we wouldn't just have the Legacy, we'd also have tens of millions more dollars!'

'Thank you for proving my point. You're talking about millions, when the Crucibles used properly could make *billions*! Yes, it would require a capital investment, but—' Olivia looked around as she realised that someone had entered the room, seeing first De Klerx lurking near the bar, the Dutchman having entered silently, then Nina and Eddie passing the fountain. 'Nina!' she said, standing and going to meet them. 'You came back. I'm so glad. I wanted to apologise for—'

'We're not staying,' Nina interrupted coldly. She deliberately bypassed her grandmother to address Mikkelsson. 'You said the plane would take us back to New York when we wanted. Now we want.'

Mikkelsson nodded. 'Of course. If you will allow us to conclude our discussion, I will make the arrangements.'

'It doesn't sound as if you're going to reach an agreement any time soon, so just get someone to drive us.'

'Give me the keys if you like,' added Eddie.

'It would be preferable if you stayed until we are finished.' The Icelander was as calm as ever, but something in his tone served notice that he was not open to negotiation. 'This also concerns you, after all.'

'I don't see how,' Nina replied, growing annoyed. 'I kept telling you that I don't want to be a part of the Midas Legacy, and after everything I've seen, I'm more certain of it than ever. Keep your gold, spend it on particle accelerators or Lamborghinis or even do some good with it; I don't care. What I *do* care about is getting home to my daughter, and also making sure that the Crucibles end up with the right people.'

Anastasia gave her an unfriendly look. 'And you don't think we *are* the right people.'

'That's kind of an understatement, yeah.'

Spencer chuckled. 'See?' he said. 'This is what happens when you treat your own family like shit.' He was addressing Olivia, but the statement was obviously meant for the Legacy as a whole. 'You shouldn't be surprised when they get pissed off at you.'

'I never treated you badly,' protested Lonmore. 'I supported you even after the others voted to kick you out! You're my son, what else could I do?'

'Not let them. And not let someone else take my place.'

'Spencer. Nobody ever could.'

The younger man seemed about to make some retort, but his

father's unexpectedly heartfelt words had clearly affected him. 'I . . . appreciate that, Dad.'

'This is all very lovely,' said Anastasia impatiently, 'but we need to make a decision.'

'We do,' said Mikkelsson. 'As chair, I am going to call a vote. That is entirely my prerogative,' he went on as both Olivia and Lonmore objected. 'There are three proposals. Olivia, you wish to keep the Crucibles and use the Legacy's remaining funds to construct a particle accelerator in order to produce our own gold. Spencer,' he turned towards Lonmore, 'you suggest a similar deal to the one you offered Augustine Trakas, whereby we come to an arrangement with an as yet undetermined third party for use of their particle accelerator. And Ana, you propose selling the Crucibles to an entity or nation state for a large sum of money. Is that correct?'

Nods of assent. 'Very well,' said Mikkelsson. 'First we will vote on Olivia's suggestion. All in favour?' Olivia raised her hand, glowering when no one joined her. 'All against?' Four other hands went up. Since it was not a tie, Mikkelsson, as chairperson, did not get to vote. 'The motion is rejected. Next, Spencer's suggestion. All in favour?' Predictably, the result was two for and three against. 'The motion is rejected,' the Icelander went on. 'And now, Anastasia's plan?'

This time, it was again three against two, Olivia and the Lonmores versus Anastasia and Sarah. 'And no decision is reached,' said Olivia. 'As usual.'

'Democracy in action,' Eddie joked.

'Since you can't decide what to do with the Crucibles,' said Nina, 'I'd say that puts the matter in my hands. They're going to the IHA. Where I should have taken them to start with.'

'Nina, please,' said Olivia. 'There must be something that can persuade you to do what's best for your family. For Macy, and her future.'

Nina bristled. 'The best thing I can do for Macy is to set a good example – and that means not lying to her, and not trying to manipulate her!' She looked past her grandmother at Mikkelsson. 'Okay, you had your vote. I'm done here. We're going.'

'Actually,' said Mikkelsson, 'there is one more matter. I have a proposal of my own.'

Lonmore frowned. 'Anastasia made your family's proposal. You can't just pitch another one.'

'I am making this proposal in my role as chair of the Legacy, not as a representative of my family. It is within the rules.'

'At a stretch,' complained Olivia.

'But still permissible. My proposal is actually very similar to Anastasia's, but I chose to hold it back in the hope it would not be necessary.'

'You want to sell the Crucibles?' asked Lonmore dubiously. 'We just said no to that.'

'There is one vital difference. I have already found a buyer.'

The response was vocal disbelief and outrage. 'You can't do that!' cried Lonmore.

'You took a decision like that without consulting the rest of us?' Olivia added.

Anastasia huffed sarcastically. 'You're in no position to complain about anyone taking unilateral action, Olivia.'

Petra had a different question. 'For how much?'

'The agreement is for thirty million dollars in hard currency, and sixty million dollars in gold,' Mikkelsson told the room, as casually as if he were reciting prices on a menu.

She gasped. 'Ninety million dollars?'

'Oh, you can add up at least,' scoffed Spencer, but he was as taken aback as the others.

'Thirty million dollars for each family,' continued Mikkelsson. 'If you agree to the deal.'

Lonmore appeared shell-shocked. 'That, ah . . . that would more than rebuild the Legacy's funds. But you really shouldn't have made a deal without the approval of the rest of us.'

'You were going to make a deal with Trakas,' said Anastasia.

'I *proposed* one – but I would still have brought it to a vote before it was finalised.'

'And so shall I,' Mikkelsson said. 'This arrangement has been agreed in principle, but it will not go ahead until the other members of the Legacy have cast their votes.'

'Agreed with *whom*?' demanded Nina.

He gave the tiniest shrug of amusement. 'That does not concern you. As you have made clear, you are not a member of the Midas Legacy.'

'It concerns me in every sense of the word,' she shot back. 'The Crucibles aren't yours to sell – and who's willing to pay ninety million dollars for them in the first place? Especially when they're giving you sixty million of it in gold. Who would need to make gold if they've already got that much going spare?'

'That's a very good point,' said Olivia. 'I think we need to know all the details before we make any decisions.'

Lonmore exchanged whispered words with his wife, then nodded. 'Agreed.'

Anastasia was angered, Sarah worried, but Mikkelsson merely gave another little shrug. 'As you wish. The client is a nation state with which I have dealt on a diplomatic level for some time. In the process of doing so, I made personal connections with senior officials. As soon as the prospect of finding the Midas Cave became a reality – even before you left for Nepal, Nina – I approached them in secret. Given what the Crucibles could provide them with, they were eager to accept my proposal in principle.'

'*Who* was eager to accept?' said Nina.

Mikkelsson fixed her with an unblinking stare. 'North Korea.'

There was an uncomfortable silence, finally broken by Eddie's disbelieving '*What?*'

'You made a deal with *North Korea?*' said Olivia, equally shocked. 'Are you mad?'

'Quite the contrary,' Mikkelsson replied. 'As I discovered during my negotiation of the nuclear treaty, they have the technical capabilities to make use of the Crucibles, as well as the urgent desire to obtain what they can produce.'

'But they obviously already have gold if they're willing to pay us in it,' said Lonmore, confused.

'They are not interested in gold. Well, that is not strictly accurate – like any nation, they maintain reserves, though in their case it is to make purchases on the black market rather than to support their currency. But the Crucibles can be used to produce something far more valuable. Gold is not the only element they can create by nuclear transmutation. They can also make plutonium.'

Again, the Icelander's statement was so matter-of-fact that it took a moment to sink in. '*Plutonium?*' Nina said, horrified. 'You mean they can use it to make *nukes?*'

Mikkelsson nodded. 'I realised long ago that the same process that creates gold from mercury can also create plutonium – in this case, from uranium. North Korea has plentiful reserves of uranium-238. This is non-fissile, so useless for military purposes, but it can be transmuted into plutonium-239. Doing so in a nuclear breeder reactor would produce large amounts of the unwanted contaminant plutonium-240. The Crucibles, however, would create almost entirely pure plutonium-239: "supergrade" plutonium.'

'You mean weapons-grade,' said Eddie.

'Exactly. The more pure the plutonium, the smaller the amount needed to create a nuclear weapon. And the smaller the weapon, the easier it is to mount upon a ballistic missile.'

Nina shook her head, struggling to accept what she was hearing. 'Did I step into a mirror universe this morning? You're the UN's senior nuclear negotiator – your whole job's supposed to be about *stopping* countries from building nukes!'

'I have my reasons,' Mikkelsson replied, still as calm as ever. 'But I do not wish to get into a political debate.' His gaze flicked between the members of the other families. 'First we must put it to a vote.'

'I'd think you were joking, but I know you too well,' said Lonmore. 'You're actually serious about this, aren't you?'

'I am, yes.'

'This is lunacy,' said Olivia. 'Sheer lunacy! Do you know what would happen if you broke a nuclear arms embargo? Ninety million dollars is no use if you spend the rest of your life in jail!'

'I know very well what would happen,' said Mikkelsson. 'I helped draft the treaty that set the penalties. But the risks are minimal, and I have contingency plans should the sale be exposed.' He straightened, setting both hands firmly upon the table to either side of the small Crucible. 'Now. The vote. My proposal is to sell both Crucibles to North Korea, for a total sum of ninety million US dollars. All in favour?'

Anastasia and Sarah raised their hands. There was a marked lack of movement from the others. 'I see,' he said. 'All against?'

Lonmore hesitantly lifted his hand, followed by Petra. Still standing with Nina, Olivia raised hers more firmly. 'The motion is defeated,' she said. 'Thankfully.'

Mikkelsson shook his head slowly. 'That is most disappointing,' he said. 'Of all people, Olivia, I thought your greed would lead you to make the right choice.'

'She *did* make the right choice,' said Lonmore. 'Making a deal with an insane dictatorship? You must be mad yourself, Fenrir! How could you possibly think we'd go along with it?'

'I had sincerely hoped you might,' he replied, 'but I suspected you would not. Which is why I prepared for this outcome.'

He gestured to De Klerx – and the Dutchman advanced, drawing a gun from inside his jacket.

'Shit!' Eddie gasped, hurriedly moving to shield Nina. 'I fucking *knew* it!'

'What the hell are you doing?' gasped Lonmore, jumping up from his chair. Petra squealed in fear, grabbing his hand. Behind them, Spencer half rose from his own seat before freezing as the muzzle flicked towards him.

'The Legacy has lost its ability to function,' said Mikkelsson, standing. Sarah looked on with apprehension; Anastasia with anticipation. 'It has lost its *purpose*. If it cannot fulfil its purpose, then it must be replaced.'

'Fenrir, please!' cried Lonmore, wide-eyed. 'We – we can talk about this, we can reconsider! We'll take another vote!'

'You have already cast your ballots,' the Icelander said. 'Now we will cast our bullets.'

'No, wait—'

Another gesture – and De Klerx opened fire.

The first rounds tore bloodily into Lonmore's chest. Petra screamed and tried to run, but only made a single step before another rapid-fire fusillade cut her down. Behind them, Spencer leapt from his chair and sprinted in panic across the room—

De Klerx tracked him. A couple of bullets narrowly missed the running man, one of the panoramic windows exploding – but another hit him in the shoulder, shattering bone. Overcome by blind agony, Spencer collided with a chair and fell to the floor. De Klerx rounded the table and closed on him. Before the young man could recover, a last bullet hit him in the side of his head, an exit wound bursting open on the other side of his skull and spraying its contents across the pale wood floor.

Eddie saw that the gun's slide had locked back: the magazine was empty. 'Nina, run!' he yelled, but the Dutchman was already replacing it with a new mag from the strap of his shoulder holster and bringing his weapon to bear.

Nina, Eddie and Olivia froze by the fountain. An ice-spiked wind blew in through the broken window as De Klerx looked to Mikkelsson for instructions. 'What are you waiting for?' the Icelander snapped. 'Shoot them!'

33

The Dutchman glanced at Anastasia, who smiled, then back at his targets—

Nina stamped on a metal pedal.

The fountain gushed into life, boiling water erupting from the model volcano – and instantly producing a blinding, choking cloud of steam as it hit the freezing air from outside. The gusting wind swept it across the lounge, swallowing De Klerx.

'Run!' Nina yelled. She raced for the exit, hauling her grandmother behind her.

Eddie had nearly been caught by the scalding steam. 'Jesus!' he gasped as he darted clear and followed the two women. 'You almost lobstered me!'

'Better red than dead!' she replied. Eddie overtook and barged open the doors. Behind them, the cloud was already dispersing. 'We've gotta get to the jeeps!' Nina headed for the nearby stairs to the west entrance, but the exterior doors below crashed open. 'Whoa, not that way!'

Eddie snatched a fire extinguisher from its wall clips and hurled it down the stairwell. Honnick, charging up the steps, tried to dodge, but not quickly enough. The heavy metal cylinder struck his skull, bowling the hapless mercenary back to ground level with another deep cut to his head to add to those he had received in Reykjavik and aboard the *Pactolus*.

The Englishman was about to vault down to grab his gun when he saw the shadows of more guards running towards the glass doors below. 'Keep going!' he yelled instead, reversing course.

He quickly caught up with Nina and Olivia. 'Come on, come on!' the redhead cried, tugging at the old woman's wrist.

'I can't!' Olivia protested. 'I'm eighty-nine years old!'

'You want to reach ninety? Then move your bony ass!'

Olivia looked offended, but before she could say anything, Eddie scooped her up and threw her over his shoulder in a fireman's lift. She shrieked. 'Sorry,' he said as he ran down the corridor alongside Nina. 'But she's right, it *is* on the bony side.'

'You—' the elderly lady began, only to gasp in fear as two men reached the top of the stairs behind them. 'Look out!'

Nina darted around a corner as they entered the main lobby. Eddie swerved after her. Plasterboard exploded behind him as bullets hit the wall, but the rounds didn't penetrate, impacting against concrete beneath the surface.

They were still far from safe. The gunmen were already haring after them, and a gust of cold air warned that more guards were coming up the stairs from the main entrance below. 'In there,' said Eddie, running for the geothermal power plant's entrance.

'You think there's another way out?' asked Nina.

'I bloody well hope so!'

'There is,' Olivia told them. 'At the back. I've got a keycard.'

'Great.' He put her down. She produced the card and swiped it across the lock.

They entered the cavernous white chamber. There was nobody else inside. Nina slammed the door, seeing a bolt and shoving it closed, even though she knew it wouldn't stop their pursuers for long. 'Which way?' she asked Olivia.

'There.' Her grandmother pointed. The hydrogen sulphide pipes ran into the rear wall, a doorway nearby. 'There's a door to the outside past the storage tanks.'

Eddie spotted something mounted on the wall beside a fire hose and veered away as they ran across the room. 'Keep going! I'll catch up!'

Nina looked back. 'What are you doing?'

'Slowing 'em down!' He grabbed a fire axe and rushed back to the pipes leading into the twin turbines. The door banged as someone tried to open it. Another thump, louder: a kick. The bolt buckled.

Eddie reached a set of valves. Red-painted wheels allowed the flow of superheated water to be controlled manually. A deep breath, then he raised the axe.

A crack as the bolt snapped and the door flew open. A man burst in. He saw the Englishman directly ahead and took aim—

Eddie swung. The axe sheared off one of the valve wheels – and the jutting stub of pipe to which it was attached.

He dived clear as a high-pressure water jet blasted at the doorway. It hit the gunman and hurled him back into the lobby, his skin instantly blistering and liquefying. He skidded across the floor, other guards scrambling clear as boiling droplets sprayed off him.

The stench of rotten eggs filled the room as suspended hydrogen sulphide escaped into the air. Eddie coughed, rolling back to his feet. Some of the super-hot spray had caught him, the exposed skin of his hands red and stinging. He looked at the doorway. It was shrouded in steam, the fist-thick jet still rushing through it. Nobody else would be coming in that way.

There was another entrance higher up the wall, though, an elevated walkway leading around the turbine hall to a ladder. It wouldn't take De Klerx's men long to reach it.

He caught up with the women at the rear door. Olivia was panting, her gait unsteady. 'I'll carry you!' he shouted.

'Please, no!' she insisted. 'At least leave me *some* dignity!'

'You want to die with dignity,' Nina said, 'go to Switzerland—'

The whine of the machines suddenly fluctuated and dropped in pitch. Alarms shrilled as the bright overhead fluorescents flickered, then went out. A moment of darkness – then illumination returned, but at a much lower level as emergency lights came on. Both turbines spun down to silence.

'What happened?' asked Nina, blinking into the gloom.

'I think the emergency generators just kicked in,' replied Olivia. 'But that would mean something had happened to the geothermal pumps.' She saw the dripping axe in Eddie's hand. 'Ah. Mystery solved.'

He smirked. 'Just be glad this isn't a nuclear plant.'

They opened the door. The room beyond was as tall as the turbine hall, but less deep, complex pipework connecting a row of large stainless-steel tanks. Eddie hefted the axe, but the chamber was empty. At the room's far end was another door. 'There are some offices through there,' said Olivia. 'There's an emergency exit past them.'

A bang from behind as one of De Klerx's men barged through the upper door. 'Time to go!' Eddie said, bundling the women into the room. The guard fired. A bullet whipped past the Yorkshireman's back and clanked off a piece of machinery.

Nina grimaced as she saw a warning sign; she couldn't read the Icelandic text, but the international explosive hazard symbol was clear even in the half-light. 'Jesus! It's lucky he didn't blow the whole place up.'

Eddie glanced at the sign, then – to her alarm – grinned. 'Yeah, 'cause it means I can give him another chance.'

'What does he mean?' Olivia asked her granddaughter with growing concern.

Nina took her hand again. 'When he gets that face? You want to be moving away from him, fast.' She hurried down the line of gleaming gas tanks, drawing Olivia with her. Eddie didn't follow. 'What're you doing?'

'Just get outside.' He flipped the axe around to favour the sharp point at the other end of its head. 'I need to pass some gas.'

'No, don't!' the horrified Olivia cried as he swung. 'It'll expl—'

The point stabbed into the first tank's steel skin with a clang – then was blown clear as hydrogen sulphide jetted out.

Eddie reeled as the escaping gas tore at his clothing. If the smell in the turbine room had been bad, this was more like a chemical attack. He closed his eyes and held his breath, burying his face into the crook of his arm for protection – he was now literally standing in a cloud of poison. Another alarm wailed as detectors registered the deadly substance.

He waved the axe in what he thought was the direction of the exit, trying to find a pipe to use as a guide, then abruptly drew it back. Stainless steel, at least the kind used to contain explosive chemicals, wouldn't spark, but that might not be true of the blade. He turned it over to grip it by the head, using the wooden handle like a blind man's stick to feel his way forward. He had to get clear before the guard reached the entrance.

The handle barked against something in front of him. The route to the exit had been clear of obstructions. He was off-course, and realised with growing fear that he had lost his bearings. The roar of gas echoed off the walls, seeming to come from all around him. The howling alarms increased the confusion. A couple more sweeps of the axe revealed an open path . . . but was he facing the exit, or back towards the turbine room?

Even closed, his eyes were stinging. If he opened them, however briefly, they could be permanently damaged. He had to get clear of the ruptured tank, but if he went the wrong way, the gunman would kill him before the gas could.

He knew what he had to do. It was a huge risk, but there was no choice. He moved his arm just enough to expose his mouth, using the last of the air in his lungs to shout, '*Nina!*'

Even exhaling, that was enough to burn his lips and sear his tongue. He clamped his mouth shut again. If Nina was replying, he couldn't hear her over the noise. But he couldn't call out again without taking a fatal breath.

He had to move. A fifty-fifty chance: either he was going towards her, or he would die. Sweeping the axe again, he started forward. Another roar, but this was inside his own head – blood rushing in his ears as his body ran out of oxygen—

'*Eddie!*'

Faint, seeming miles distant – but ahead. He found some reserve of strength and increased his pace. The wooden shaft thunked against pipework, again and again – then nothing. He remembered that the pipes turned inwards at the base of each tank. The way the steel vessels were spaced, that put him about twenty-five feet from the leak. Far enough to risk a breath? Not yet.

Nina shouted again, but now his reserves were gone. He shuffled on, feet turning to lead. *Thunk, thunk, thunk* of wood against steel—

Another gap. Fifty feet. The hole was only small, and the room big. Was he far enough away? The alarms kept wailing, but with a gas this toxic they would warn of even a small release. Wouldn't they?

It didn't matter. If he didn't breathe right now, he would pass out—

He drew in a desperate gasp of air.

The disgusting taste filled his mouth . . . but he stayed conscious, and upright. He might suffer some after-effects, but he was clear of the most deadly concentration of the gas. Tears stung his eyes as he opened them, but he saw Nina at the doorway, frantically urging him on. 'Eddie, over here!'

He headed towards her, pace quickening as he took another breath. 'Get out,' he rasped. 'Get outside! Quick!'

She was about to protest, but then realised from long experience that something catastrophic could happen at any moment. She darted through the door. Eddie ran after her, glancing back at the punctured tank as he reached the exit. A plume of gas was still gushing from the hole, swirling around the pipework before dispersing invisibly into the air.

The turbine room door crashed open.

The gunman charged through, staggering to a halt and clapping a hand over his nose and mouth as the stench hit him. He was about to retreat when he saw Eddie. The Englishman deliberately held his ground as the guard's weapon came up—

Now Eddie moved, slamming the door – as the man fired.

The gunshot was drowned out by a massively larger detonation as the muzzle flash ignited the flammable gas. The hydrogen sulphide instantly became a fireball, incinerating the man a fraction of a second before his charred corpse was disintegrated by the exploding gas tank.

The blast tore apart the pipework, releasing still more fuel into the conflagration – and the other tanks went up like a chain of truck-sized firecrackers.

The switchover to the emergency diesel generators had warned Mikkelsson that something was badly wrong in the generator room, prompting him to speed up his departure plans. 'Ana, take this,' he told his daughter, handing her the small Crucible. 'We're going to the airport.'

'Already?' she asked, surprised. 'There's no way Olivia and the others can be a threat to us now. They'll never get out of here.'

'It's not Olivia I'm worried about. De Klerx!' The Dutchman, who had stayed to protect the family rather than join the hunt for the fugitives, snapped to attention. 'Sarah and I will take the jeep with the large Crucible. You drive. Follow us,' he added to Anastasia, who had been about to object to being separated from her lover. 'Take one of the men as a bodyguard.'

'You're that worried about Nina and her husband?' asked Sarah as De Klerx used his radio.

'I've read their IHA file,' Mikkelsson replied, leading the way past the bodies of the Lonmores towards the exit. 'Chase is especially dangerous – he's a trained killer – but even Nina has a talent for survival. I would never underest—'

A percussive thump shook the floor – then the entire hotel seemed to jump a foot off the ground as a series of pounding explosions ripped through the building. Mikkelsson staggered, De Klerx rushing to shield Anastasia as more windows shattered. 'Oh my God!' Sarah cried. 'What the hell was that?'

Mikkelsson opened the doors to the hallway. The main reception area was shrouded in steaming mist, but now swirling black smoke broke through it and spread malignantly along the ceiling towards them. 'The hydrogen sulphide tanks,' he growled. 'They must have blown them up!'

'Then they're dead,' snapped De Klerx. 'Nobody could have survived that.'

'I'm not going to bet our lives on it.' He jabbed a finger at the Dutchman's walkie-talkie. 'Call in your men, find out how many are still alive. We're leaving, *now*. Make sure Olivia and the others don't follow.'

Nina had just reached the exterior door and pushed Olivia through when the gas tanks exploded. She was thrown against the wall, a hot shock wave of reeking air rushing past. New alarms clamoured in meaningless warning. 'Oh God,' she gasped. 'Eddie!'

'Nina, wait!' called Olivia from outside, but she ignored her, hurrying back down a flight of stairs into a thickening haze. The stench of both smoke and residual hydrogen sulphide grew worse. She covered her face as she turned a corner to find the corridor strewn with wreckage. The suspended ceiling had been torn down, wire skeins and battered sections of aluminium ducts littering the floor. The door was ahead, all but wrenched from its hinges. Fires burned beyond it.

Big fires. If Eddie was still in there . . .

Coughing, she picked her way through the rubble. No sign of her husband. 'Eddie!' she cried. 'Can you hear me? Where are you?'

No answer. The heat was rising, the flames in the processing facility raging harder. There was no way anyone in the chamber could still be alive.

A rattle of shifting debris – and a section of collapsed ceiling shifted aside to reveal a singed, bruised, but still very much alive bald Yorkshireman beneath. 'Ay up,' Eddie managed to gasp, before erupting into a coughing fit.

Nina pulled him from the wreckage. 'You *maniac*! What happened?'

'Muzzle flash plus flammable gas equals, well, that,' he said between coughs, jerking a thumb at the ruins of the adjoining room. 'I'm okay, just a bit scorched.' He recovered the axe, then they made their way down the corridor. 'Where's Olivia?'

'Outside.' She glanced nervously back. 'I don't think Fenrir's hotel will be taking many guests this season.'

'The elves'll be pissed off too.'

Olivia was waiting just outside the building, shivering in the icy wind. 'Eddie, my God! After that explosion, I was sure you'd been killed.'

'We've still got to get out of here,' said Nina. They were on the hillside behind the hotel, the section housing the geothermal plant partly dug into the ground. The east wing was ahead down the slope, many windows broken and smoke rising from within. Only emergency lights remained lit, but they were enough to pick out hulking metal shapes sheltering beneath the elevated structure.

'The jeeps!' Olivia said through chattering teeth. 'We can drive back to Reykjavik!'

Eddie was less confident. 'If we can get to 'em. Still plenty of arseholes with guns around.' He started downhill, snow crunching under his feet.

Nina and Olivia followed. 'You're freezing!' the redhead said in alarm, feeling her grandmother tremble.

'I'll be all right,' Olivia insisted. 'I just need to get somewhere warm.'

'It's nice and warm inside, but that's not really an option,' said Eddie. He reached the end of the power station's wall and cautiously peered around the corner. Some super jeeps were parked near the stairs to the main entrance, but his attention snapped to the pair heading away from the hotel. 'Shit! They're already leaving!'

Nina recognised the lead pickup. 'They're taking the Crucible!' She looked back at the parked trucks. 'We've got to stop them.'

They hurried to the nearest super jeep. 'Hope they left the keys inside,' said Eddie. 'Be just our luck if they're in someone's coat—'

A shout cut through the wind's shrill. A man scurried down the main stairs, bringing up his gun—

Eddie flung the axe. The blade slammed into the man's skull with a bone-splitting crack, neatly bisecting his face as he toppled backwards. The gun fired as he fell, bullets spraying the concrete above.

More shots from further away. Another armed man ran at them from the far end of the east wing, firing as he came. 'Shit! Down!' Eddie barked, throwing himself behind the super jeep.

Nina pulled Olivia into the cover of its oversized front wheel. Bullets struck the truck, the driver's window shattering. Olivia screamed. 'It's okay, it's okay!' Nina said. 'We're behind the engine – he can't shoot through it.'

'No, but he can run around it!' she countered.

Eddie searched for better cover, but found nothing they could reach. He looked up at the truck itself, one of those that had collected everyone from Reykjavik airport . . .

Before he could act on the thought that was forming, another burst of bullets hit the jeep. One of the huge tyres blew out. The unbalanced truck crunched down on to its front-left wheel hub, the rear corner opposite kicking up into the air. Muffled thumps came from inside as the cargo shifted. 'Stay put!' he shouted.

'I wasn't planning on going for a stroll,' snapped Olivia as he scuttled to the rear passenger door.

'What're you doing?' Nina demanded.

He opened it, staying low as more rounds punched through the bodywork. With the vehicle now tipped towards the oncoming man, he was hidden from sight, though not shielded from bullets. 'The guns and stuff they brought back from Greece?' he said as he clambered inside. 'They're in here!'

The back of the truck was filled with bags and boxes. He fumbled open a case, his hand falling on an angular object inside. *First time lucky*, he thought as he pulled out a Steyr AUG – only to discover there was no magazine loaded, the receiver empty. His groping fingers failed to find any ammunition.

He dropped the useless weapon and scrambled deeper into the rear bed – as a bullet tore through the roof above him and blew out one of the side windows. A cascade of fragmented safety glass scoured the back of his head. The gunman was still coming.

Another case contained magazines, but he knew from their shape that they were for UMPs, not the full-sized machine gun he had found first. No sign of the weapons they were intended to fit.

He threw open another container. The low light from outside

picked out the grenade launcher he had used at the shipyard – and beside it a squat ammo box. He grabbed the MGL, tearing at the box's latch. Dull metal hemispheres stared at him from inside like dead eyes: the warheads of half a dozen forty-millimetre grenades. He snatched one out and crawled to the rear door, pulling the launcher's release hook. It swung open to expose the cylinder.

The running man kept firing. Another window burst apart. Eddie slammed a grenade into the topmost chamber and snapped the launcher shut, then pulled the rear door handle to throw open the tailgate. The movement immediately drew fire, more bullets clanging against the back of the truck as the Englishman dived out.

He hit the ground, rolling to face the gunman – and pulled the trigger.

The grenade sailed over its target – but the man's surprise and relief was very short-lived as it hit the hotel's underside behind him and exploded.

A storm of shrapnel lacerated his back. Blood spouting from countless wounds, he crumpled to the ground and lay twitching. Stray shards of metal struck the truck, but Eddie was beyond the grenade's lethal radius.

The Yorkshireman scrambled upright, returning to the super jeep in the hope of finding a matching gun and magazine, but shouts from inside the hotel prompted him to abandon the search. Instead he grabbed the MGL's ammo box and ran for another jeep, waving for Nina and Olivia to follow. 'Get in, quick!'

This vehicle was a Toyota Land Cruiser – and the key was in the ignition. He tossed the launcher and ammunition on to the passenger seat and started the engine. The truck's headlights and roof-mounted spots flared. Nina pushed her grandmother through the rear door before jumping up after her. 'Okay, go!'

Eddie put the super jeep into gear and floored the accelerator. It sprang forward, the massive tyres getting full traction on the snow-free paving beneath the hotel before ploughing into the packed drifts beyond. It slewed almost sideways, the Englishman hurriedly feathering the power to regain control. 'There, over there!' said Nina, pointing. The rear lights of the Mikkelssons' jeeps were tiny red sparks in the distance. 'Catch up with them!'

'We've got to get away from that lot first!' Eddie shot back, seeing three more men rush out of the hotel and pile into another super jeep. 'Grab the grenade launcher and load it.'

She picked up the weapon. 'How?'

'There's a hook in front of the cylinder – pull it and it'll swing open. Get rid of the dead one inside and load the others. Turn the cylinder after you put each one in; it's got a kind of clockwork spring that brings round the next grenade when you fire.' He turned the heater controls to full. 'Are there any coats or blankets back there?'

'I think so,' the shivering Olivia replied. 'These jeeps usually have survival equipment in the trunk.'

'I'll look,' said Nina, breaking off from her task to rummage through the super jeep's cargo. There was indeed a blanket, which she passed to Olivia. The elderly woman accepted it gratefully and drew it tightly around herself. The redhead resumed loading the launcher, pausing as she glanced ahead. 'Eddie, you're going the wrong way!' The other jeeps were off to their right, and heading away.

'We'll never catch up with them if we just follow that track,' he said, guiding the 4x4 across the rippling snowfield. 'They're going around the lake; if we cut straight across it, we can get in front of them.'

'You do remember we're not in a boat, right?'

'The lake's frozen – it should hold us.' He looked back at Olivia. 'Shouldn't it?'

'I'm hardly the expert,' she objected.

'Maybe not, but you've been here before. Is it usually still frozen this time of year?'

'I think so, but I'm not entirely—' Her eyes widened in fear. 'Look out!'

Eddie snapped his gaze back ahead – to see the snowy ground dropping out from under the jeep's lights.

He stamped on the brake pedal, but it was too late to stop. The Toyota shot over a rise, bursting through a snow-bank and going airborne for a couple of seconds before pounding back down in another explosion of snow. The heavy-duty shock absorbers bottomed out with a tooth-jarring bang, then the truck bounced back up and slewed across a wallowing dip.

None of its occupants were wearing seat belts. Eddie managed to keep hold of the steering wheel, but Nina ended up sprawled over her grandmother. 'What are you *doing*?' Olivia shrilled. 'Didn't the army teach you to keep your eyes on the road?'

'What road?' Eddie replied. The super jeep was now angling up another steep rise, almost rolling over before he managed to point its nose straight up the incline. He glimpsed headlights in the rear-view mirror, closing fast. 'Shit! Get down!'

Nina dropped flat, pulling the startled Olivia with her. Cracks of gunfire reached them over the engine's roar. A round punched through the rear door with a flat *thunk* and hit the gear in the cargo area. Olivia gasped.

Another bullet glanced off the truck's flank as Eddie made an evasive swerve. 'The launcher!' he yelled. 'Is it loaded?'

The MGL had fallen into the rear footwell. Nina groped for it. 'Yeah, but it's not closed.'

'Just swing it shut – it should lock.'

She did so. The cylinder snicked into place. 'Okay, what do you want me to do with it?'

'What do you think? *Shoot those wankers!*'

The super jeep crested another rise, scattering snow. The Mikkelssons' jeeps briefly came back into view in the distance before the Land Cruiser dropped sharply down the other side. Nina yelped, then squirmed around and lowered her window. A freezing gale blasted in, clods of snow kicked off the front wheel's chunky treads spattering her as she leaned out and tried to bring the bulky grenade launcher to bear.

The glare of the pursuing super jeep's spotlights preceded its appearance over the crest, giving her a target. She took aim, waiting for it to appear . . .

It burst through the snow. She pulled the trigger – just as her own vehicle reached the foot of the slope and levelled out. The abrupt change of gradient threw off her aim. The grenade hit the ground twenty feet ahead of the jeep and blasted a crater out of the snow and frozen soil.

Anastasia looked around in surprise at the sound of an explosion – not from the burning hotel, but somewhere off to her left. For a moment she saw nothing, then a flare of lights marked the appearance of a super jeep over one of the moraine crests. Another surged into view behind it, clearly in pursuit. A flash of orange light was followed by the delayed boom of a second grenade blast.

She grabbed her jeep's radio handset. 'It's them! They're coming after us!'

Her father's normally controlled voice was edged with anger. 'I said we should not underestimate them!'

'We can't let them catch us.' Her driver had put his UMP on the dash; she took it. 'I'll stop them.'

De Klerx came on the line. 'Ana, no! It's too dangerous. I can handle it.'

'You've got to get my parents and the Crucible out of here,

Rutger,' she countered. 'I'll be right behind you.'

Sarah took the mic. 'No, we should stay together. It's safer.'

'I can *do* it,' she insisted. 'Go after them!' The driver obeyed, skidding the truck off the track into the deeper drifts beyond.

'Anastasia!' barked Mikkelsson. 'Come back! You've got the other Crucible – we need both of them!'

The basketball-sized crystal was nestled in her lap. She glanced at it, then spoke into the radio again. 'I won't let you down, Pabbi,' she said, before replacing the handset and taking the gun in both hands.

'Be careful, Ana,' said Sarah, but her daughter barely heard her, focused only on the lights ahead.

34

Nina was blinded by flying snow as the super jeep vaulted over another rise. 'Damn it, Eddie, I missed again! Hold this thing steady!'

'If I do, we'll get shot!' he shouted back. The other jeep crested in their wake, two men leaning out. Eddie swerved as one opened fire. The rear window exploded.

Nina flinched, then aimed the MGL again. The enemy driver swept his truck across to the other side of her super jeep, trying to block her line of fire. She pulled the trigger anyway, but the grenade went wide and exploded behind its target. 'Son of a bitch!'

'You've only got two shots left,' Olivia cautioned.

'Mom taught me to count, thank you!'

Eddie applied more power as the 4x4 started uphill once more. The snow was getting deeper, giving him an idea. 'Nina, get back in!' he called. 'I'm going to try something.'

'What?' Nina asked as she retreated.

'Depends what's at the top of this hill! Just hold on really tight, both of you – and get ready to shoot when I say.'

'Why am I not filled with confidence?' muttered Olivia as Nina ducked down beside her.

More bullets struck the super jeep's rear and blew out one of the tail light clusters. Eddie hunched as low as he could, still charging up the slope. Deepening snow swamped the jeep's headlights, spray coming up over the bonnet and hitting the windscreen. He turned on the wipers. Black sky rose above the spotlit white glare. Almost at the top—

He switched off all the Toyota's lights as they reached the crest.

The view ahead became nothing but darkness as they bounded over the summit. Eddie spun the wheel hard to the left as they landed, bringing the truck around in a barely controlled power slide back up the hill. 'Get ready!' he yelled to Nina.

She still had no idea what he was doing – until the second jeep exploded through the snow to their left, crashing back down into the drifts below. Eddie kept turning, coming about to complete a full circle and swing in behind it. The men inside were confused by their prey's apparent disappearance . . . until the Yorkshireman switched the spotlights back on, pinning them in the merciless beams. '*Now!*'

Nina had already leaned back out of the window. This time, she didn't miss.

The grenade punched a neat hole through the super jeep's rear window – and exploded, the blast ripping the three men in the cabin to shreds and blowing out all the windows. A moment later, the shrapnel-ravaged fuel tank detonated, flinging the hulking vehicle into a blazing somersault. It smashed back down on its roof, two of the oversized wheels flying off as what remained of the body tumbled to a stop.

Eddie hurriedly changed course to avoid the burning wreck. 'Nice shooting.'

Nina dropped the MGL on the front passenger seat. 'We've still got to catch up with Fenrir's jeeps.' She closed the window as the truck climbed again. 'For that matter, we've still got to find them—'

Her eyes widened in shock as Anastasia's GMC Yukon erupted through a snowdrift and charged straight at them.

Eddie jammed down the accelerator and tried to swerve out of its path – but too late. The onrushing super jeep hit theirs at an angle, caving in the rear wing. The impact threw everyone sideways, Nina's head banging against the window.

The truck slewed around, for a moment travelling sidelong as the other off-roader barged against it before Eddie broke away. The Toyota lurched, flinging its passengers back across the rear seat.

Anastasia's jeep rammed them from behind. Eddie scrabbled for the grenade launcher, but it had fallen into the footwell, out of his reach. 'Nina! I can't get the—'

He broke off as the lights in the mirror shifted. The Yukon pulled to the left, trying to overtake on his side, and he saw Anastasia's arm emerge from the front window. '*Gun!*'

Flames spat from the sub-machine gun as she opened fire. Eddie dropped low, making another hard turn away from his attacker. The side window behind him burst apart, a bullet shredding his headrest. Another clanked against the hefty roll cage – but a third hit flesh.

Nina screamed as the searing round tore through her left bicep. Hot blood caught Olivia's face, the elderly woman shrieking.

Despite the pain, Nina threw herself over her grandmother as another round whipped through the broken window. 'I'm okay,' she gasped, clapping a hand over the wound.

Eddie sliced back in front of the other super jeep to cut off Anastasia's line of fire. 'Where are you hit?'

'My arm,' Nina told him. 'I think the bullet went through.'

'As soon as we get away from these fuck-knobs, I'll look at it— Shit!' The Yukon veered left again to give Anastasia another shot. He turned to block it, curving across the snowfield as more rounds narrowly missed the Toyota. 'We'll end up going in bloody circles at this rate!'

Olivia raised her head in sudden alarm. 'How far are we from the road to the hotel?'

'I dunno, I can't see it. Why?'

'Because we might be heading for the lake!'

He gave her an aggrieved glance. 'That's where I *want* to go!'

'But the cliff gets higher the farther you are from the road – and we're heading away from it!'

He hurriedly looked ahead, but the truck was descending into a dip, only snow visible. Not that he had time to scan the landscape. The pursuing 4x4 jinked left again, this time accelerating enough to pull its nose past the rear of the Englishman's vehicle, preventing him from cutting back across its path.

Instead he braked hard and made a skidding turn to the right, speeding up to pull away from his adversary. The Yukon arced around to follow him.

Anastasia leaned out to shoot, but before she could pull the trigger the Toyota cleared the next rise, dropping out of sight. Eddie wondered whether he would be able to pull off the same trick that had taken out the first super jeep – but then saw a sharp edge to the snowfield directly ahead, coming up fast.

The lake. And Olivia had been right about the rising cliff, the drop at least twenty feet.

He was about to brake and turn away when spotlights reappeared behind him, followed by flashes of gunfire. Only one place to go. 'Hang on!' he shouted. 'We're going over!'

He accelerated, the engine snarling as the super jeep surged towards the cliff edge—

The Icelander's bullets struck home.

One of the rear tyres blew out, ruptured rubber flaying the wheel arch before ripping from the hub. The super jeep swerved. Eddie jerked the wheel back, but the 4x4 had already reached the cliff.

It flew over the precipice, the weight of the engine tipping its nose down towards the ice—

Impact.

Even with the beefed-up tyres and suspension taking the shock of the landing, the Land Cruiser still wiped out as it hit the ice, a front wheel tearing from the axle. The frozen surface cracked, stress lines shooting outwards like lightning bolts as a huge splash of icy water burst from under the truck. But there was still enough play in the surviving wheels to catapult the super jeep back upwards, sending it careering across the lake and bouncing once, twice, before slithering to a stop.

Despite being braced, Eddie had still slammed painfully against the steering wheel. He slumped back, the sudden silence left by the stalled engine almost shocking. 'Nina,' he said, turning his head painfully. 'Are you—'

A new noise, the roar of another big V8 behind them – which abruptly changed in pitch as the driver tried to stop before reaching the cliff . . .

He failed.

The second super jeep hurtled over the edge in a spray of snow, landing short of the hole where Eddie's truck had hit the lake. The front suspension collapsed, one of the shock absorbers stabbing up through the hood – and the ice smashed beneath it, dropping its nose into the frigid water.

More fractures shot through the surrounding surface, frozen chunks breaking loose and rolling in the waves. The jagged lines lanced across the ice towards the Toyota—

A dizzied Nina had just raised her head to check on Olivia when the super jeep pitched backwards, its rear wheels dropping through the breaking ice. Everything in the cargo bed hit the tailgate, then was swallowed by a freezing deluge as the bottom of the smashed rear window dipped beneath the surface. 'Jesus!' she gasped. 'We're sinking! Olivia, get out!'

Olivia grabbed the nearest door handle. The latch clicked, but with the 4x4 now tipping ever more steeply, the door's own weight was holding it shut. She strained, forcing it open a few inches. Nina crawled closer to help, only to be tugged to a stop. Her foot was caught in something. She kicked, trying to free herself, but to no avail. A seat belt had entangled her leg. She groped in the darkness for the strap—

With a scrape of ice, the super jeep slid deeper into the lake.

Eddie was about to bail out when he remembered the grenade launcher. He leaned over the centre console and clawed in the footwell. The truck jolted again, grinding backwards into the water. He grabbed the MGL, then threw open the front door and rolled out.

Even dry, he was still freezing. The temperature was sub-zero. 'Nina!' If they didn't reach shelter or summon help, without outdoor clothing they would rapidly suffer the effects of exposure—

Another kind of death was closer.

A bullet hit the jeep's flank just inches from him. Eddie whirled and saw Anastasia staggering towards him, silhouetted by the spotlights of her own wrecked vehicle. The small Crucible was clutched in one hand, her UMP in the other. The Yukon was slowly sinking nose-first, the splashed blood on its cracked windscreen telling Eddie that her driver had not survived the touchdown.

He started to lift the grenade launcher – but her gun locked on to him, any residual dizziness from the crash now past. He froze, knowing that he would never be able to aim the awkward weapon fast enough to take a direct shot.

And Anastasia knew it too. 'You thought you could beat us?' she crowed. 'Nobody can beat my father!'

'Give me time,' Eddie replied. ''Cause I already beat *you*.'

She hesitated, surprise in her voice. 'What—'

He pulled the MGL's trigger.

The launcher's barrel was pointing at the ice between them. The grenade hit – and punched through, continuing onwards like a torpedo until the water slowed it . . .

Underneath Anastasia.

It armed – and exploded. The screaming blonde was flung into the air amidst a churning fountain of spray. Bones broken by the shock wave, she plunged back down into the freezing water, chunks of ice pounding her as she vanished into the black depths. The gun followed her, the Crucible landing at the edge of the jagged hole.

Eddie dropped the empty launcher and turned back to his stricken super jeep, Anastasia already forgotten. The Toyota had tipped backwards almost to the vertical. It had also slewed sideways, the water up to the edge of the rear door.

And his wife and her grandmother were still inside.

He tried to open the door, but its lower corner was blocked by ice. He leaned through the broken window. 'Get out of there, it's sinking!'

'What do you think I'm *trying* to do?' Nina yelled back. 'My foot's caught!'

Eddie cursed and ran around the truck. The other rear door was ajar, and still above the lake, its corner pressing into the ice like a piton. He yanked at it, feeling the surface under his feet flex and groan as his weight shifted. Metal scraped against frozen water – then crunched free. He hauled the door open. 'Olivia!'

She stretched out a hand and he pulled her clear. 'Get away from the edge,' he ordered before dropping to all fours, holding the door open with his back as he looked into the truck. The only illumination came from the other 4x4 behind them, but it was enough to pick out the belt snagging Nina's ankle. He crawled partway inside and tried to untangle her—

The super jeep jolted, ice snapping malevolently beneath it.

Opening the door had let him reach Nina, but the truck was now held up only by whatever parts of its underbody were caught on the lake's edge. Its sheer weight was dragging it relentlessly downwards, inch by inch, as the frozen surface crumbled. He pulled at the seat belt. The tension lock clunked. 'Bend your leg,' he told Nina. 'I need to loosen it.'

'Easier said than done when your car's turning upside down!' she protested. Squirming around, she twisted her leg. Eddie made another attempt to free the strap, pulling more gently.

This time, the lock released. He carefully drew out a few more inches. 'Okay, I've got it—'

Water surged around her seat from the flooded rear bed as the vehicle sank deeper. Nina shrieked as it soaked through her clothing. 'Oh my God, Eddie!'

He grabbed her foot and forcefully unravelled the belt, then backed up. 'Come on!' The door pressed down hard on his back as he cleared the cabin – and the pressure kept rising. 'Quick, this thing's fucking crushing me!'

She slithered out feet-first, gasping as the freezing wind caught her wet legs. Spicules of ice spat at her face from creaking cracks. Eddie strained to hold fast against more than two tons of metal. 'I can't . . . keep it . . .'

Nina rolled clear. He tried to follow her, but the edge of the door caught his left leg as it dropped. The metal ground against his shin, crushing it into the ice. 'Agh, *fuck*! It's got me, it—' His words became a yell of pain.

She grabbed the door and pulled at it, a wail of her own joining her husband's as her wounded bicep burned. But her efforts were just enough to ease the pressure, if only for a moment – and he jerked his leg free. Nina let go and fell backwards. The door thudded down flat on to the ice. Its hinge creaked as the Toyota continued to slither into the lake, bending it to its limit . . . then with a protesting moan of metal the vehicle jolted to a stop, held in place by the buckled panel.

Eddie tried to stand, only to stumble back to the ice as a bolt of agony speared through his leg. It was not broken, but he wouldn't be managing anything more than a hobble for several hours.

If they lived that long. Panting, he crawled to Nina. Her face was screwed up in pain, palm again pressed to the bullet wound. 'Get back from the water,' he said, still hearing alarming sounds from the overstressed surface. 'How's your arm?'

'I actually wish it was colder,' she replied, grimacing. 'That way, I wouldn't be able to feel it!'

He managed a faint smile as she helped him stand. 'Let me see it.' She reluctantly lifted her hand, stifling a cry as the ragged wound was exposed. Eddie examined it. 'It doesn't look too deep,' he told her with relief, 'but it'll need stitches. I'll see if there's a first aid kit.'

'Everything in the back of our jeep is underwater,' she said, before looking across the lake. The Yukon's hood was completely submerged, but its rear was still above the ice. 'That should have something inside— What the *hell* is she doing?'

A figure was skirting the broken hole in the ice between the two trucks: Olivia. She had lost the blanket, her clothing fluttering in the wind. 'Olivia!' Nina cried. 'Get back here!'

The older woman shouted back to her. 'I'll get their survival gear before it sinks!'

'No, come back – I'll get it!' Eddie started after her – but staggered as his bruised leg almost gave way.

'I'll go,' Nina told him. Before he could object, she hurried past him to follow her grandmother.

Ahead, Olivia continued her trek towards the stricken 4x4 – then spotted something at the edge of the ragged star of nothingness blasted by the grenade.

The Crucible.

She hesitated, looking between the truck and the crystalline sphere . . . then changed direction. 'No, don't!' cried Nina. 'Leave it! It's too dangerous!'

'I can reach it!' the old woman insisted, picking her way closer. 'It's right here, I can . . .' She bent down, reaching out to lift the Crucible away from the water. 'Got it!'

She turned – and the ice under her feet shattered.

Olivia plunged into the water, going chest-deep before catching the edge with her arms – by fluke rather than intent, the shock of the cold overpowering all rational thought. The Crucible jolted from her grasp and rolled across the surface.

Nina broke into a run. '*Olivia!* I'm coming!'

Ominous snaps came from underfoot as she got closer, forcing her to slow. Pieces of ice calved away into the inky water around the flailing woman. 'I'm almost there!'

'Nina!' A glance back to see Eddie limping after her. But she couldn't wait for him to arrive. Olivia's splashing was already becoming more feeble, her whooping breaths ever shallower.

Ice crackled as Nina dropped to her knees. Water swelled up through fractures, soaking her shins. She gasped, but knew it was only a fraction of what her grandmother was experiencing. 'I'm here, I'm here!' she said. 'Grab on to me!'

Olivia clutched at her, but her hands were already numbed, unable to grip. Nina strained to raise her higher. More snaps and hisses came from the ice as it sagged under their combined weight.

The older woman's waist cleared the surface. Nina kept pulling, squirming back from the edge—

The ice beneath her gave way.

35

Nina dropped into the water, the cold like a punch to her heart. She was going under—

A thud from behind – as Eddie dived and skidded on his belly across the ice to grab her beneath her arms. 'Keep hold of Olivia!' he yelled, dragging her out of the new hole. She managed to maintain her grip on her grandmother even through the biting chill assaulting her body. Both women collapsed on to the frozen surface.

Eddie crawled backwards, pulling them with him. 'Come on, get up,' he said. 'We've got to find some shelter before she gets hypothermia.'

'Where?' Nina asked, shivering as she surveyed the surrounding emptiness.

'The . . . the other truck,' Olivia said, her voice a quavering whisper. 'In the back, there should . . . be a tent.'

Anger filled Nina, its heat almost driving away the cold. 'But you went for the goddamn Crucible first?' The crystal sphere was only a few feet away in the snow. 'That thing's almost gotten me and Eddie killed half a dozen times already – and now you're joining in as well!'

'Nina, hey,' said her husband, trying to calm her. 'We need to get her warmed up, *then* you can have a go at her. See if you can get anything out of the other jeep before it sinks. I'll get her back to ours, it's the only shelter we've got.' He picked up Olivia, holding her tightly as he limped back towards the Toyota.

Nina shook off freezing water, then, shivering, made her way to the other truck. It was still slowly sinking, trapped air bubbling up as its nose tilted downwards. The rising water had reached the rear bed. She pulled as much as she could out on to the ice and hurriedly examined it. There was no tent, but a waterproof bag contained a bivouac. There was also a small portable gas heater and a first aid kit; she collected them along with a few other items, then hurried after Eddie.

She passed the Crucible. A pause – then, almost disgusted at herself, she picked it up and continued towards the super jeep, the cold wind tearing at her wet clothes like the fangs of a wolf.

Sarah looked back across the snowscape with concern. 'It's been too long. Where is she?'

Mikkelsson followed her gaze. Beyond the light from the 4x4's roof-mounted spots, there was nothing but darkness. 'She must be out there somewhere.'

'I can't see her truck.'

'I can't see Olivia's either. Perhaps Ana has dealt with them and gone back to follow us around the lake.' The words were spoken with his usual matter-of-fact conviction, but couldn't disguise an edge of concern.

De Klerx gave his boss a worried glance. 'Something might have happened to her.'

Mikkelsson took the radio handset. 'Anastasia, come in. Where are you?' He waited for several seconds, but there was no answer.

'Maybe the aurora's blocking the transmission?' Sarah suggested hopefully, eyes flicking towards the dim green fog in the sky.

He shook his head. 'It would have to be much stronger than that.'

'Something's wrong,' said De Klerx. He released the accelerator. The super jeep quickly slowed in the dense snow.

'What are you doing?' demanded Mikkelsson.

'We've got to go back and look for her!'

'Yes, we do,' Sarah said, nodding. 'She might be hurt.'

The tall diplomat's face hardened. 'No.'

'What do you mean, "no"?' his wife asked, confused. 'You don't think she's hurt, or—'

'We have to keep going. De Klerx, go.'

The security chief stared at him. 'She's your daughter!'

'Yes, and she is as committed to our plan as I am.' He gestured at the large Crucible in the pickup bed. 'It is more vital than ever that we get the Crucible out of the country quickly. If Nina warns the authorities before we leave, we will be arrested at the airport.' Seeing his companions' disbelief, he went on: 'If Anastasia is still alive, then Olivia, Nina and her husband are dead and we have nothing to worry about. Even if her jeep has been damaged, she knows how to survive out here.'

'And if she . . .' Sarah couldn't bring herself to voice the alternative. 'And if Olivia and the others aren't dead?' she managed instead.

'Then it is imperative that we leave right now.' He stared at De Klerx. The younger man hesitated, then wilted under Mikkelsson's unblinking gaze and pushed down the pedal.

'Fenrir!' cried Sarah, appalled. 'You . . . you're just going to *leave* her?'

He faced her. 'She is okay, I am sure of it. She will catch up with us. But if our positions were reversed, she would do the same thing. You *know* she would,' he insisted, reaching out to put a hand against her cheek. 'Don't you?'

She almost flinched at the touch, uncertainty clear on her face. 'I . . . yes, I do.' Another look back, but there was still nothing behind her but darkness. 'She's okay. She'll be okay, right?'

'She will,' Mikkelsson said, stonily regarding the way ahead.

* * *

Eddie watched the super jeep's lights drop behind a distant rise. 'Least they didn't come back to finish us off,' he said through chattering teeth as he duck into the cramped bivouac. Olivia lay on a groundsheet inside, covered by a blanket with the heater beside her. With no way to swap her wet clothing for dry, all they could do was try to keep her warm.

Nina sat with her, legs curled under a corner of the blanket in an attempt to mitigate her own exposure. 'Yeah, but that means they're getting away with the big Crucible – and taking it to North Korea.'

'North Korea.' Olivia managed to project disbelieving disdain even through a strained whisper. 'It's like something from that terrible movie they made of your book, Nina! Fenrir must be out of his mind.'

'I don't know, I can see a kind of demented logic to it,' she replied. 'He has the diplomatic connections, he has access to classified intel about their nuclear programme, and he knows how to use the Crucible to make plutonium for them. I mean, the man's a nuclear physicist!'

'The man's *insane*. I can't . . .' Olivia coughed hard, struggling to recover her voice. 'I can't believe I never realised before.'

'He's a sociopath. He's very good at hiding his true intentions, and getting people to do what he wants.'

'Like Anastasia,' said Eddie. 'His own bloody daughter. That's what I can't believe. No way would I ever push Macy into doing something that could get her hurt.'

'I doubt that he pushed her,' Olivia said. 'Children naturally want to please their parents . . .' She trailed off, shuddering.

'Are you okay?' Nina asked, worried.

Olivia gave her a pained look. 'I just fell in a frozen lake and have never been s-so cold in my entire life. So on balance, I would have to say no.'

'I see being a smart-arse runs in the family,' said Eddie. He held his hands over the heater. 'I'll try to get the truck's radio working and send out a Mayday. The battery should still be dry, so hopefully I'll be able to get power to it.'

'If Fenrir hears it, they might come back,' said Nina.

'We don't have much choice. That heater won't last for ever. And we can't stay out here all night.'

Olivia tipped her head towards him. 'You mean . . . *I* can't.'

'No,' he said, with a heavy sigh. 'Not wanting to sound like a cock, but . . . not at your age. If you were forty or fifty, you could probably make it even after a soaking like that. But at ninety . . .'

'Eighty-nine, thank you.' She managed a small laugh, which turned into another cough. 'There's a certain irony. I smoked, drank, ate red meat and sugar, all the things that are supposed to kill you, but I never imagined a mountainside in Iceland would finish me off.'

'You're not finished yet,' Nina said firmly. She took her grandmother's hand – and tried to hide her reaction.

Olivia still caught her flickering change of expression. 'Th- that cold, am I?'

'You're *not* finished,' repeated Nina, squeezing her frozen fingers between her palms. 'I'm not finished with you.'

Taking a flashlight with him, Eddie backed out of the shelter. 'I'll get started on the radio,' he announced, carefully opening the upended truck's front door.

Olivia let her head loll back to its original position. 'So you've got something to say to me?'

'You're goddamn right I have,' said Nina, her earlier anger resurging. 'How could you have been so *stupid*? You went after the Crucible rather than get to safety – and you almost *died*!'

'The night's not over yet,' Olivia replied. 'But I had to get the Crucible. I *had* to. It's . . . it's our family's legacy. It's *your* legacy.'

'I don't give a damn about our family's legacy!'

'Then why did you save it too?' Her gaze went to the corner, where the red sphere sat glinting in the low glow of the gas heater. 'If you don't care about it, then why make the effort?'

'Because . . . because it's a priceless Atlantean artefact,' Nina said after a moment. 'After everything I've been through to get it, I wasn't going to let it end up at the bottom of some lake.'

'I see. And the real reason?'

'That *is* the real reason.'

A small smile. 'You really are so much like your mother. In so many ways. Including facial expressions. I always knew when Laura wasn't telling me the whole truth.'

'I'm not Laura.'

'Oh, I know. You're very much your own person.' Olivia closed her eyes. 'She would have been so proud of you. Not just for what you've accomplished as an archaeologist. For who you are. I'm . . . I'm proud of you, too. I just wish that . . .' She coughed again, her whole body straining before she brought it under control. 'That I'd told you that many, many years ago.'

Nina felt tears. 'Hey, hey, stay with me,' she said, finding her grandmother's other hand. 'I'm not done with you yet.'

The old woman forced her eyes half open. 'And again, you sound just like Laura. Just like her.' She blinked, a tear of her own slowly running down her cheek. 'My poor girl . . . oh, my poor baby girl . . .'

Her granddaughter squeezed her hands more tightly. 'What happened with you and Mom – and Dad? What really happened? Was Spencer telling the truth?'

'I'm afraid so,' Olivia replied, with a small, sorrowful nod. 'I was the one who first told Laura to . . . to make contact with your father.' A cough threatened to erupt, but she managed to fight it down. 'But everything after that was entirely her choice. I opposed it, every step of the way, but . . . but I was wrong. She found true love and happiness with her husband – and her daughter.' A faint smile up at the younger woman, but it quickly faded. 'While all I had was . . . was a big empty house and greedy dreams of gold. I had the choice between family or money, and I made the wrong one. And – and I'm still making the wrong choice, even now! My own granddaughter thinks I'm an idiot for chasing after some damn stone rather than saving myself. And . . . she's right.'

'We're all idiots,' Nina assured her, with a sad laugh. 'You, Mom, me – we *all* spent our lives chasing after the past. I guess that kind of idiocy runs in the family.'

'But at least you and Laura had purer motives.' A bang from outside made her start; Eddie had opened the truck's hood to access the electrics. 'I did try, you know.'

'Try what?'

'I tried to . . . do *something* that wasn't solely for my own benefit. I got you involved in this, not just for gold, or the Legacy, but because I wanted to pass on a legacy of my own. To you, and to your daughter. Even if I wasn't . . . freezing to death on a glacier, I won't be around for much longer—'

'Don't talk like that,' Nina cut in firmly. 'We'll get out of here.'

A glimmer of humour crossed Olivia's face. 'Interrupting your elders is very rude,' she said. 'Didn't your mother teach you anything? But I didn't want my life to end with a house of mourners, and all of them just . . . acquaintances. Not one of them family. I didn't want that. I don't want that.' A fearful realisation, even revelation, lit her eyes. 'Oh God, Nina, I don't want that! I don't want to have no one to remember me! No one to . . . to *care* about me!'

'You don't have no one,' the redhead insisted. 'You've got me.'

'After everything I've done? All the half-truths, all the . . . lies?' That seemed the biggest confession of all.

'Yeah.' Nina smiled at her. 'And you know why? Because now that I've got a family, I'm not about to let it go. Any of it.'

Olivia's eyes closed again, her voice a mere sigh barely audible over the wind. 'You may not . . . have a choice. I'm so cold.'

'Oh no. No no *no*,' Nina said in defiance. 'You don't get to die on me. Okay? I've never had a relative come back from the dead before, and I'm sure as hell not letting you renege on that!' She pulled off the top layer of her own clothing and put it over Olivia, against her grandmother's feeble protestations. 'We *are* going to get out of here, and—'

She broke off at an electronic squawk from the super jeep. 'Yes!' whooped Eddie. 'You fucking beauty.'

'You got the radio working?' Nina asked.

'Yeah. Did a bit of rewiring to run it straight off the battery rather than having to start the engine. Dunno how long it'll last, so I'd better get cracking.' He reached into the cabin to take the handset. 'Mayday, Mayday, Mayday,' he said. 'Our jeep has crashed on the way to the Electra hotel in the . . . What's the name of this place again?'

'Thingvellir,' Olivia said quietly. Nina relayed it to him.

'In the Thingvellir national park. I repeat, our jeep has crashed on an ice lake on the road to the Electra hotel. There are three of us; two are injured. Mayday, Mayday, Mayday, please respond.' He waited for a reply, hearing only static on the open channel, then repeated the message.

'And for a moment I . . . had hope,' said Olivia.

'Someone'll hear him,' Nina told her. 'You said yourself that the main road's a tourist route, and there's an aurora tonight. People will have come out here to see it.'

The old lady replied, but too quietly for Nina to make out. She took her grandmother's hands again, huddling beside her in the meagre warmth of the heater. Outside, Eddie kept repeating his SOS. The hiss of dead air was the only response. Nina turned her head to listen, as if she might somehow catch a message that her husband had missed, then looked back at Olivia – only to find that she had gone still. 'Olivia? Olivia!' She gripped her cold hands more tightly. 'Olivia, wake up! Wake up!'

She shook her – and Olivia's lips clenched. 'I'm . . . I'm here,' she whispered. 'Did Eddie . . . get through?'

'Not yet, but I know he will. He will.'

'It's . . . too late.' Another tear swelled in the corner of Olivia's eye, but even it was too weak to roll free. 'I'm so tired . . .' She fell silent again.

'Olivia!' Nina cried. 'Stay with me! You've got to stay, I'm not letting you go now! I'm—'

A new voice cut through the cold. 'Hello, hello,' said a man over the radio, his Icelandic accent strong. 'Can you hear me?'

'I hear you!' Eddie replied. 'Did you get my Mayday?'

'Yes, I did. We have told the rescue service, but we are coming to you now. We are on highway thirty-six. Can you hold on?'

'Yeah, but we've got someone in hypothermic shock. How fast can you get to us?'

'Twenty minutes, thirty minutes? Where are you exactly?'

The Yorkshireman gave their position as best he could. He had just enough time to get an assurance that the rescuers were on the way before the jury-rigged radio went dead. After swearing loudly, he returned to the shelter. 'Oh God, you're freezing!' said Nina as he squeezed in beside her.

'I feel warmer knowing we're not going to be stuck out here all night.' He examined Olivia. 'How is she?'

'Not good. She's asleep . . . or unconscious.'

'She'll be okay.'

'You sure?'

'I'm sure. I heard what you were saying to her. She's family – yours *and* mine. I'm not going to let her go either. Even if,' a wry half-smile, 'she did get us into this bloody situation in the first place!'

'She can't take all the blame,' said Nina. 'I'm just as responsible. And I'll make sure she knows that when she wakes up.' She looked down at her grandmother once more. 'You hear me? You *are* going to wake up.'

Eddie put an arm around her. Together they sat in silent vigil until the distant rumble of an engine told them rescue was finally drawing near.

36

New York City

'This is a most grave situation,' said Oswald Seretse, shaking his head. 'I cannot believe that Fenrir Mikkelsson would do this. I *cannot*!' The outburst, though little more than his raising his voice, was nevertheless the strongest display of emotion Nina had ever seen from the normally unflappable diplomat. 'But,' he continued, 'whatever I believe, the evidence is undeniable.' He went to the windows, staring disconsolately across Manhattan.

'I'm afraid so.' The speaker was a man named Howard MacNeer, a senior official of the US State Department. 'We lost track of his jet once it entered the commercial air corridor over Russia, but picked it up again in Chinese airspace heading for North Korea.'

'You couldn't intercept it?' Eddie asked. 'America's got loads of planes in South Korea.'

'Intercepting it would have risked starting a war,' replied MacNeer. There was a world map on one wall of Seretse's office; he indicated the Korean peninsula, a tiny stub hanging off the eastern edge of China. 'They never entered international airspace, so we couldn't touch them.'

'You could've still got a missile lock from hundreds of miles away. Shoot 'em down, and if the North Koreans complain, say you had a weapons malfunction or something.'

MacNeer clucked patronisingly. 'This isn't a Tom Clancy novel, Mr Chase. But the jet landed at Tonyong, a military base about forty miles north of the DMZ. It took off again a half-hour later and flew to Shenyang in China, where it's stayed. We're trying to track down Mikkelsson and the others there, but haven't located them yet.'

'You think he's in China?' asked Nina.

'Would *you* want to stay in North Korea any longer than you absolutely had to?'

'Point taken.'

Seretse joined the other official at the map. 'What is the significance of Tonyong? Why would Fenrir go there?'

'It's a North Korean weapons development facility,' MacNeer answered. 'It's underground, built into a mountain – they even dug one end of a runway into it so planes can be loaded without our surveillance satellites seeing what's going on. There's been a lot of activity over the past couple of years; more tunnels being excavated, judging from the amount of rubble that's been dumped nearby.'

'Big enough to build a particle accelerator?' said Nina.

'Maybe. We don't know for sure – it's one of the hardest countries in the world to get reliable intel out of. The North Koreans have a nasty habit of imprisoning or straight-up executing anyone they even *think* might be spying. Most of their big-money facilities have been involved with their nuke programme, and we know where they are, but particle accelerators have multiple uses – including separating enriched uranium-235 from useless uranium-238. We invented the technique as part of the Manhattan Project in the 1940s, so it's not as if it's a big secret. Considering how desperate they are to build up their nuclear arsenal, it wouldn't surprise us if the North Koreans have been using every possible method to get fissile material out of their uranium deposits.'

'And if Mikkelsson's right about how the Crucible works, they can use it to turn their useless uranium into plutonium,' she said gloomily. The small Crucible had been recovered along with the three survivors on the frozen lake, and was currently being kept under guard at a secure location pending a decision on what to do with it. 'They can make the jump from A-bomb to H-bomb.'

MacNeer gave her a bleak nod. 'The thermonuclear test they did in 2016 was a fizzle, whatever Kim tried to tell the world. But if they start to manufacture plutonium on a large scale, it's only a matter of time before they have the real deal.'

'So what's being done about it?' Eddie asked.

The two officials exchanged looks. 'What?' said Nina, realising the subject had already been discussed before she and Eddie arrived.

'There has been a proposal by the State Department,' Seretse said carefully. 'Or more accurately, US intelligence. However, I suspect you will not like it.'

Eddie made a face. 'That's a really good start.'

'What is it?' Nina demanded. 'What proposal?'

Seretse retreated to grant his guest the dubious honour of presenting the bad news. 'As I said, it's hard to get reliable intel out of North Korea,' MacNeer began. 'It looks likely that Mikkelsson delivered the Crucible to the North Koreans, and they've taken it to Tonyong – but we don't know for sure. We hardly know *anything* about what's down there. But what we do know – and this isn't just the United States talking, but an agreement between the other nuclear powers in the IAEA – is that North Korea cannot under any circumstances be allowed to mass-produce nuclear weapons. Not only would that be a hugely destabilising threat to the world, it would violate the treaty that North Korea itself just agreed to.'

'A treaty that Mikkelsson convinced them to sign,' added

Seretse. Another shake of his head. 'What game are you playing, Fenrir?' he added, almost to himself.

'Under the terms of the treaty,' MacNeer went on, 'there's a provision that allows direct action to be taken against any nation that wilfully violates the agreement. If North Korea arms itself with thermonuclear weapons, that would definitely qualify as a violation. The US, or any other involved nation for that matter, would be justified under international law in using any means necessary to prevent it.'

'That sounds more like it,' said Eddie. 'So you're going to send over a few stealth bombers loaded with bunker-busters?'

'No action can be taken without proof,' Seretse told him solemnly. '*Solid* proof. After what happened in Iraq with the weapons of mass destruction that turned out not to exist, the United Nations requires a higher standard of confirmation before it will approve such risky measures.' He gave the State Department official a hard look.

MacNeer let the implied criticism slide. 'The thing is, getting that proof is going to be hard, and take a long time. We just don't have the assets in place. Unless . . . we recruit some.'

Nina felt decidedly uneasy about the way he was looking at her and Eddie. 'I'm going to guess that you're not talking about bribing some North Korean guard to sneak in a camera.'

'I'm afraid not. We need someone who can get in there by offering the North Koreans something they need – and then get back out to tell us what they've seen.'

Eddie's eyebrows rose as he realised where the American was leading. 'You mean us? You want *us* to go on a spying mission into North fucking Korea?'

'You're the only people who can do it,' MacNeer explained. 'You found the Crucibles in the first place, you retrieved them from the Greek, and you know how they work – both in turning mercury into gold *and* uranium into plutonium. There isn't anybody else who could conceivably offer the Crucible you recovered to the Koreans. It would be too suspicious.'

'It'll be suspicious anyway!' Nina protested. 'What, are we supposed to rock up to the North Korean embassy and tell them, "Hey, we know that Fenrir Mikkelsson sold you the big Crucible, but we'll let you complete the set if you show us your secret underground base"?'

MacNeer almost smiled before catching himself. 'That's kind of a sarcastic way of putting it, but . . . yes, in essence.'

'And why the bloody hell would they believe us?' said Eddie.

'Because they do not know you,' said Seretse. 'If you make them an offer that seems mercenary, even positively rapacious in its demands, they will think you are simply after money – because the North Koreans believe all foreigners, especially Americans, are greedy, imperialist monsters.'

'Except for Dennis Rodman, I guess,' Nina said.

'If there's one thing they love to do,' added MacNeer, 'it's show off all the incredible technology that they're going to use to destroy America and conquer the world. Granted, most of it's twenty to thirty years behind us, but that doesn't mean they won't give you a guided tour if you tell them you want to hand over the Crucible in person.'

Eddie was still dubious, to say the least. 'Okay, so even if they decide to let us in, then what?'

'All you need to do is confirm that they're manufacturing plutonium, or intending to. Once you're safely out of the country and report in, Special Forces will take care of the rest.'

'How? They can't just take a cab across the DMZ.'

MacNeer gave him a knowing look. 'North Korea's air defence radars can't pick up our stealth aircraft, and we're sure of that because we've been doing covert overflights for years. And the B-2 can deliver more than bombs.'

'What, they can carry *paratroopers*?' Eddie said in disbelief. 'Since when?'

'Since we built pressurised drop pods that fit in the bomb bays.'

Eddie laughed. 'Thought you said this wasn't a Tom Clancy novel!'

The official held in his amusement, then became serious once more. 'Once you confirm that the facility's being used to develop nuclear weapons, a team will HALO-jump on to the mountain above it, inside the perimeter, so the North Koreans won't even know they're there. They'll descend to a position above the runway tunnel, which based on our thermographic analysis is the only way in or out, and plant explosives. When they're clear, they'll blow the charges and collapse the tunnel. Problem solved.'

'But how will the soldiers get out of the country?' Nina asked.

'By doing what they're trained to do. I'm sure Mr Chase knows what I mean.'

Eddie was still unconvinced. 'Not saying I couldn't do it, but getting out of *North Korea* without support? Not easy.'

'They can do it,' said MacNeer. 'But it's up to you whether or not they get the chance. If you don't go, it might take months to confirm what's going on by other means.'

'And by then it may be too late,' Seretse added sonorously.

'You're asking a hell of a lot,' said Nina, worried. 'We're not spies, but you want us to go on an espionage mission into one of the most paranoid regimes on the planet! If they suspect *anything*, we won't get out again even if a former president flies in to Pyongyang to ask for our release, like Bill Clinton did for those journalists.'

'I know one former president who'd fly in just to tell 'em to keep us,' muttered Eddie.

'We'd be putting ourselves in danger again,' Nina continued, 'and we only just got *out* of it!' She gingerly touched her arm, where a bandage under her sleeve covered the now-sutured bullet wound. 'I got shot, and my grandmother almost died. And we've got a daughter now – if anything happened to us . . .' She let the statement hang in the air.

Seretse nodded. 'I completely understand your reluctance. But at the same time, I am sure you are aware of the seriousness of the threat. Perhaps if you take some time to think the proposal over?'

'Not too much, though,' said MacNeer.

'I'm already fairly sure what my answer will be, but . . . yeah. We'll think about it,' she said. Eddie nodded in agreement. 'I'll let you know our decision as soon as we've made it.'

The State Department official was clearly disappointed, but kept his expression neutral as he shook their hands. 'Do please give the matter full consideration,' implored Seretse. 'There is a great deal at stake.'

'We will, don't worry,' Eddie told him. 'All right, let's go and get Macy.'

They made their way through the Secretariat Building to the IHA's offices, where Macy had been left with Lola. When the couple arrived, they found that their daughter had drawn a small crowd of other colleagues. 'Hey, Macy, here are your mommy and daddy!' Lola trilled.

'Told you it was "mommy".' Nina nudged her husband, smirking.

'*Mummy*,' he sighed, before picking up the little girl. 'Ay up, love! Did you miss us?'

Macy shook her head. 'Lola let me talk to all her friends!' She waved at the smiling group around her.

'Good to feel wanted,' Eddie said with another sigh.

'Is everything okay?' Lola asked Nina as the others laughed. 'You look a bit . . . you know, that look you get when something's about to catch fire or explode.'

'We're fine,' Nina assured her. 'We've just got something big to think about, that's all. Was Macy okay with you?'

The blonde grinned. 'Are you kidding? She's gorgeous. You two have made one heck of a little girl. She's been drawing, singing – even showing off how much she knows about archaeology.'

Eddie groaned. 'And so it begins.'

'Quiet, you,' said Nina. She took Macy from him. 'We've got to go now, honey.'

'Where are we going?' the little girl asked.

Nina paused before answering, then smiled. 'To see your great-grandma.'

When Nina cautiously entered the hospital room, she thought at first that Olivia was asleep. She was about to withdraw when a weak voice reached her. 'Nina?'

'Hi,' she replied softly, going to the bed. Her grandmother looked older and far more frail than when she had first met her. Her skin was still pale from her ordeal. A colourless fluid ran down an intravenous line into her arm. 'How are you feeling?'

Olivia opened her eyes. They at least still had the same spark as before, even through her exhaustion. 'I'm as good as could be expected, thank you. A little lighter, though. They had to amputate two of my toes. Frostbite.'

Nina was horrified. 'Oh my God!'

'One from each foot, so fortunately they balance out.' A faint weary smile. 'Apart from the need to buy a completely new collection of shoes, I should make a full recovery, they tell me. Again, as well as could be expected for an eighty-nine-year-old. But,' another smile, this time a little wider, 'at least I should make ninety. Thanks to you and Eddie.' She tilted her head, trying to see past Nina to the door. 'Is he here?'

'He's just outside. With Macy.'

'You brought Macy?'

'Yeah. I wanted her to meet her great-grandmother. Properly, I mean.'

'Looking like this? I'm more likely to send the poor girl running screaming. What about you two? Are you both okay?'

Nina indicated her bandaged arm. 'I've had worse gunshot wounds. Which is kinda terrifying when you think about it, but yeah, we're fine. I'll go get them.' She went to the door and called her family in.

'Ay up,' said Eddie. He was carrying a large bouquet of flowers. 'You're looking . . . all right.'

Olivia sighed. 'Damned with faint praise. But thank you anyway. Both of you. If not for you, I'd be . . .' She glanced at Macy, who was taking more of an interest in the monitoring equipment beside the bed than its occupant. 'I wouldn't be here,' she finished. 'You have my eternal gratitude.'

Eddie nodded, then presented her with the flowers. 'These'll brighten up the place,' he said, regarding the starkly decorated room.

'Thank you. But there's someone here who does that much better than any number of carnations.' She strained to sit up to see Macy.

'Hey, no need to do that,' said Nina, seeing that the bed had a remote control. She pushed the button to raise Olivia higher. 'Macy, come here. I want you to meet someone.' She perched her daughter on the edge of the bed.

Macy peered at the elderly woman. 'You're the lady who came to our house.' A quizzical look. 'Your hair's different.'

The tight bun Olivia had worn before was now hanging in loose strands, hairstyling a low priority for the medics. 'Yes, I am. And yes, it is.'

'Macy, this is Olivia,' said Nina. 'She's your great-grandma! That means that she's my grandma. Say hello to her.'

'Hello,' said Macy politely, holding out a hand.

Olivia gently squeezed it in her palm. 'Hello, Macy. I'm very, very happy to meet you.' She gave the young girl the broadest smile she had managed in a while.

Her great-granddaughter returned it. 'Are you very old?'

'Yes, I am,' she said, laughing. 'Ah, children. I'd forgotten how direct they can be.'

'They're fun, aren't they?' said Nina with a grin.

'They are. Oh, I wish I'd met you at this age . . .' Olivia's eyes became wistful for a moment, then she looked back at her visitors. 'But at least I know you now. I shouldn't regret what I didn't have, but be thankful for what I *do* have.'

Nina nodded. 'Good words to live by.'

'Can I smell your flowers?' Macy cut in. 'They're very pretty.'

'Of course you can,' replied Olivia, passing the bouquet to her.

'What do you say, Macy?' Nina prompted.

'Thank you, Great-Gamma!' Macy cried, hopping from the bed and scurrying to a chair to examine her gift.

The old lady smiled after her, then became serious as she addressed the couple again. 'Is there any word on Fenrir or the Crucible?'

'Yeah, and none of it's good,' Eddie told her.

'We just came from the UN,' Nina elaborated. 'It looks like he delivered the Crucible to North Korea.'

Olivia's face fell. 'Where is he now?'

'China, apparently. Where he's going to go from there, I have no idea, but I imagine he's got something planned.'

'I have absolutely no doubt about that. Fenrir always thinks three steps ahead.' She paused, regarding Nina with curiosity. 'Laura used to get exactly the same look when there was a problem preying on her mind. There's something else, isn't there?'

'You could say that,' Eddie rumbled.

Nina nodded. 'Yeah. They – by which I mean the UN and the State Department – want us to go to North Korea to find out if they really are using the Crucible to make plutonium for H-bombs.'

'They want *you* to go?' Olivia exclaimed. 'Why you?'

'Because we're the only people the Koreans might accept as willing to sell the small Crucible. If we offer to deliver it in person, we might be able to confirm what they're doing, so action can be taken to stop it.'

'Action of the *wheee, boom* kind,' added Eddie, miming a bomb being dropped and exploding.

Olivia nodded. 'Fenrir told you how to profit from the Crucible, so it's not beyond the bounds of plausibility that you might want to cash in.' She caught her granddaughter's disapproval. 'Since they don't know you personally and know that you never would, of course.'

'Of course,' Nina echoed. 'It's all academic, though. Because there's no way we're going.'

Eddie reacted with mild surprise. 'Thought we were going to think about it first.'

'What? Oh come on, Eddie. You can't possibly *want* to go.'

'God, no. But it's not just about what *we* want, is it? Some fat dictator with hair like Dilbert's boss'll be able to crank out nukes like Volkswagens if the Crucible does what Fenrir said. That's not a good thing.'

'No,' she protested, 'but as you're so fond of saying, we don't work for the UN any more. It's not our problem. And you stopped being a soldier a long time ago. You're a *dad* now. You want to risk leaving Macy on her own?' Their daughter looked up from the flowers in alarm.

'It's okay, love, don't worry,' Eddie said to her, before glowering at his wife. 'See, that's why we need to talk about this properly, *in private*.'

'I don't think there's anything to discuss,' Nina replied, bristling.

'Before you get any deeper into an argument, may I offer some advice?' said Olivia quietly. 'From a historical perspective.'

'What do you mean?'

'I mean that while you're both old enough to remember the Cold War, neither of you can really appreciate what it was like at its height.'

'What's the Cold War got to do with anything?' asked Eddie.

'Everything. I'm talking about what it was like to live under the constant threat of nuclear armageddon. It was a frightening time, especially in the 1960s and '70s. When Laura was growing up,' she added, giving Nina a look laden with meaning. 'An anxious, fearful time, because there was nothing you could do about it. Unless you were willing to live in a concrete bunker in some godforsaken desert wilderness, money couldn't offer you any protection. And if there's one thing parents should always do for their children, it's try to protect them.'

Nina lowered her voice so as not to scare her daughter. 'Our ending up in some North Korean hellhole, or worse, is hardly going to protect Macy.'

'There's a bigger picture to consider, Nina. It's not just your child, it's everyone else's children too. We're living in dangerous times, just as dangerous as the Cold War – and more unstable. Fenrir giving a megalomaniacal madman a way to mass-produce nuclear weapons is not going to help matters. North Korea already has rockets; they'll be able to target hydrogen bombs on Seoul, Tokyo, Honolulu, San Francisco . . . maybe even further afield. And who's to say he won't start selling them to other countries, or terrorists? That threat, that *fear*, isn't something I want to live through again – and I certainly wouldn't wish it upon anybody's children.' She gazed at Macy, who was counting the petals on a flower.

Eddie looked thoughtful. 'Me neither. I remember when I was a kid, twelve or thirteen, I was on my way to school when an air-raid siren started up. I thought it was the four-minute warning! Never did find out what it was, but it scared the' – a glance at his daughter – 'poop out of me. Thought everyone I knew was about to get nuked! It was probably one of the reasons I ended up joining the army. At least that way I'd actually be fighting against it in some way.'

'I didn't know that,' said Nina.

'Hadn't thought about it until now. But I don't want Macy to *have* to fight against it. The world's got enough bad stuff going on already without adding this.' His face became as grim as she had ever seen it. 'Especially when we've got a chance to stop it.'

'You really *do* think we should go, don't you?' she said, dismayed.

'It's not that I want to, believe me. But that guy from the State Department was right that we're the only people who could offer them the second Crucible and be believed.'

'*Might* be believed. It's a big difference.'

'It's that or nothing. And we know the Crucible works with a particle accelerator, 'cause we saw it in Greece. If they've built one already . . .'

'Oh God.' Nina turned away from him, heavy-hearted.

Macy immediately picked up on her expression and crossed the room to her. 'What's wrong, Mommy?'

'We . . . might have to go away again, Macy.' It took an almost physical effort to force out the words.

The little girl was distraught. 'But you only just came home!'

'I know, honey. I know. We're still thinking about it; we haven't decided for sure yet.' Even as she spoke, though, she knew with an increasingly leaden sense of inevitability that the choice had already been made. 'But we'll be as quick as we can. I'm sure Holly will look after you. You like Holly, don't you?'

Tears were forming in Macy's eyes. 'Yes, but she isn't you! You keep going away! I don't *want* you to go away!'

Nina felt a tear run down her own cheek. She smiled sadly and hugged her daughter. 'I love you, Macy.'

Eddie joined her. 'I love you too. We both do. And we'll be back before you know it, okay?'

'Why do you have to go?' Macy cried.

'Because nobody else can,' said Nina, kissing her.

'But that's not fair!'

'I know. I know.' She and Eddie continued to embrace the little girl, then unwillingly withdrew. 'Better get it over with,' Nina told her husband. She took out her phone. 'Oswald,' she said, once she had been put through to Seretse. 'It's Nina.' A long, deep breath. 'We'll do it.'

37

North Korea

The view from the jet's windows as it crossed the border from China into the so-called Hermit Kingdom revealed a striking contrast. Along the northern bank of the winding Yalu River sprawled numerous Chinese towns and cities, lights blazing in the night. To its south, though, was almost a wilderness, what settlements there were far smaller and more dimly lit than their counterparts across the water. The blackness was so empty that it could be mistaken for open ocean, only the occasional smudges of illumination breaking the illusion.

Eddie peered down at the isolated country below. 'They must've forgotten to pay their electricity bill.'

'Eddie,' Nina cautioned quietly. The mission briefing by MacNeer and a coterie of State Department and CIA advisers before they left the United States had warned that not only would the trio of stony-faced North Korean 'guides' ostensibly accompanying them to translate and assist really be spying on everything they said and did, but also that the plane – and any other vehicle they travelled in – would be bugged.

The Yorkshireman was unconcerned, however. 'What? There's so few light bulbs, it looks like Norfolk down there.'

'I assume if I were British I'd find that hilarious.'

'If you were British, you'd say words like "mum" and "herb" properly.'

She gave a mocking snort, covering her nervousness as she noticed one of their minders seemingly taking a mental note of their conversation. To distract him, she asked a question. 'How long before we land?'

Another of the guides glanced at his watch. 'In twenty-five minutes, approximately.' The Koreans spoke reasonably good English, but strongly accented.

'Good. It's been a long trip,' said Eddie. They had flown from New York to China by commercial airline, being picked up by the North Korean plane for the last leg of the journey. 'And the service hasn't exactly been first class,' he added in a fake whisper to his wife. 'They didn't even offer us a bag of peanuts.' The nearest guide frowned slightly.

North Korea was a small country: at its narrowest point, less than two hundred miles separated the Chinese border from the heavily fortified demilitarised zone that lay between the Democratic People's Republic and the vastly wealthier South Korea. Before long, the aircraft entered its final approach. Below was a large military airbase, the first brightly lit place they had seen since crossing the Yalu. A long, wide runway slashed across the landscape. The plane touched down on it, soon coming to a stop.

One of the guides opened the hatch and lowered the stairs. Nina and Eddie stood; another translator moved as if to take their single item of baggage, but the redhead quickly collected it. 'Thanks, but I'll carry that,' she told him, lifting the padded plastic case containing the small Crucible.

Cold air hit them as they stepped on to the concrete. North Korea was nowhere near as frigid as Iceland, but there was still a bitter chill to the wind. To the new arrivals' relief, a car was waiting for them, a large Chinese-built SUV. Eddie was not looking at the vehicle, however, but at something beyond it. 'Bloody hell. That's a *big*-arse plane.'

'You're not kidding,' Nina agreed. Looming over its surroundings, so huge that its tail rose higher than the roof of even the largest hangar, was a Russian Antonov An-124 cargo aircraft. Built for the Soviet military, this one had been transferred to private hands, an air freight company's name emblazoned on its side in Cyrillic lettering. It was slightly shorter than a Boeing 747, but much more bulky; practically the entire length of its swollen fuselage was a cavernous cargo hold, built to swallow trucks, helicopters, even tanks. 'Wonder what that's doing here?'

'Maybe it's carrying all the gold we asked for.' They shared wry grins as their minders ushered them into the car.

The SUV set off, heading away from the runway towards a checkpoint in a high fence. Several guards were on duty, one shining a flashlight suspiciously over the vehicle's occupants before waving to a comrade to let it through. They started up a winding road into the darkened hills beyond. Nina gave her husband a concerned look when she realised there were no safety barriers, only white-painted stone markers warning of the steep drop into the densely forested valley below. The surface had been asphalted, but it was broken and potholed, giving them a very bumpy ride.

They passed under a double line of electricity pylons, doing so again several minutes later as the twisting road doubled back upon itself. 'Something up here needs a lot of juice,' she whispered.

'Maybe they really do have a . . .' Eddie began, before noticing one of the guides surreptitiously tipping his head towards them. 'Massive hairdryer,' he finished. 'Those things use a load of power.'

'How would you know?' his wife said, rubbing his shaved head. The remark proved that their travelling companions were indeed listening in, as one tried to hide a smirk.

The SUV continued its zigzagging ascent. A half-moon lit the landscape, revealing the brooding silhouette of a rocky peak rising above the forest. Eventually the road flattened out, leading them to another checkpoint. The driver's credentials were checked, the passengers scrutinised by armed men, then finally a radio call was made to confirm that all was in order before they were allowed to pass through.

What awaited Nina and Eddie came as a surprise.

They knew there was a runway built on a plateau halfway up the small mountain, and that one end had been dug into its side – but they hadn't been prepared for just how deeply it went into the heart of the peak. Lines of bright overhead lights receded into the distance, the runway continuing into the rock for almost as far as it extended in the open.

And the excavations were continuing, even at night. Trucks were bringing rocky debris out of the mountain and dumping it over the side of the plateau, going back underground for more as soon as they had delivered their loads. 'Must be a *really* massive hairdryer,' Eddie remarked.

Nina noticed a group of armed soldiers at the dump site; between them she glimpsed men and women in dirty grey clothing picking up rocks that had not gone over the edge. Prisoners? A forced labour detail? What she knew about the brutal North Korean regime, its appalling human rights abuses condemned by the UN in language as strong as diplomacy permitted, suggested that either guess was likely to be correct.

But the SUV swept onwards before she could get a clear look. The driver brought them down the runway, which was considerably narrower than the one at the base below, towards the gaping tunnel mouth. On each side of it were gun emplacements, turrets surrounded by sandbags. 'Miniguns,' said Eddie, seeing that the weapons were six-barrelled Gatling guns. 'One way to put off the Jehovah's Witnesses.'

'I guess they really don't want uninvited visitors,' Nina replied.

They drove down the long tunnel. What she had thought was a concrete wall at its far end turned out to be a blockhouse, presumably to keep any planes with faulty brakes from careering into the still larger space that widened out beyond it. The SUV pulled up at the broad structure, where a rank of soldiers stood to attention. Two officers waited before them, watching their guests' arrival.

One of the guides opened the door for Nina and Eddie. 'Dr Wilde, Mr Chase,' he said, 'welcome to People's Special Engineering Facility Number 17.' He saluted the officers. 'This is the base commander, Colonel Kang Sun-il.'

The older of the two men regarded Nina and Eddie disparagingly. Although he was short, not even Nina's height, he exuded menace, his eyes narrow and almost snake-like in their coldness. 'Welcome to Democratic People's Republic of Korea,' Kang said, sounding anything but cordial.

'And the facility's chief of security,' the translator continued, indicating the younger man beside the commander, 'Major Bok Jeong-hun.'

'Delighted to make your acquaintance,' said Bok with a predatory smile. His English was fluent and confident, even more so than the translators'. He was several inches taller than his commander, the absence of the other soldiers' tight-faced haggardness suggesting that his upbringing had been relatively privileged.

Unsure of protocol, Nina settled for a modest bow. Eddie gave the two officers a brief bob of his head. 'We're both glad to meet you,' she said. 'So, shall we get down to business?'

The colonel took a moment to decipher what she had said, prompting the guide to repeat her words in Korean, which in turn drew a snapped rebuke. The translator shrank back, head bowed in craven apology for his presumption. 'Yes, business,' Kang said, eyeing her case. 'You have Crucible?'

'You have our money?' Eddie countered, remembering the part they were playing.

'Ten million dollars American, ten million dollars gold. Yes.'

Nina opened the lid of the case, letting the two men glimpse the crystalline sphere inside. 'It's here. The money?' She was all too aware of the weakness of her position; there was nothing stopping the Koreans from taking the Crucible by force, or shooting the visitors where they stood.

But Kang simply nodded. 'Come,' he said, starting around the blockhouse.

Nina surveyed her surroundings as everyone followed. The hulking concrete building was apparently a control tower, a high line of windows looking out along the runway. Below them was a trio of giant portraits: Kim Il-sung, Kim Jong-il and Kim Jong-un, the three generations of family who had ruled North Korea as absolute dictators since the 1940s. 'Oh, herro,' Eddie said quietly, barely hiding a grin.

'Don't you frickin' *dare* start quoting *Team America!*' Nina hissed. 'They'll probably shoot us just for having watched it.' But she had to admit that the late Kim Jong-il did indeed closely resemble his puppet counterpart from the satirical comedy.

Noise ahead caught her attention. A large elevator platform bearing several tons of rubble rose from a wide shaft to stop at floor level. More workers in filthy clothes began to unload the lift's cargo for transfer into a waiting truck. An emaciated man staggered under the weight of a rock, falling to the concrete floor. A soldier rushed up to him and repeatedly slammed his rifle butt against the man's back, screaming abuse with each strike. None of the other workers dared even look, struggling with their own burdens.

Bok saw Nina's shock. 'Criminal elements,' he said

dismissively. 'They work for the glory of our nation to pay for their crimes.'

'And what crimes were those?' Eddie asked, disgusted. The prisoners were a mix of male and female, young and old.

'Does it matter? They are guilty.'

'Guilty of not being able to carry a big lump of stone?' The beaten man collapsed, other soldiers surrounding him to deliver brutal kicks. 'You've got some real tough guys there, going four against one.'

If he had registered Eddie's sarcasm, Bok chose to ignore it. 'All the troops protecting this facility are our country's very best,' he said proudly. 'They will fight without fear against any threat, and bring defeat to our enemies. They each proved their unflinching dedication to their duty by executing a criminal with only a bayonet, or their bare hands.'

'That's . . . dedicated, yeah,' said Nina, trying to conceal her horror.

They passed beyond the edge of the runway tunnel into a broad passage along the blockhouse's wall. Lined up before them were numerous vehicles; mostly jeeps and trucks, though some were more exotic. 'Hang on, I saw those in a film,' said Eddie. '*Die Another Day*, right?' He gestured at a group of small four-seater hovercraft – which had undergone extensive modifications. Sloping wedges of armour covered their noses, narrow slits providing the only visibility for their pilots. Large-calibre guns were mounted on pintles at the top of the shields. 'You're nicking ideas from crappy James Bond movies? Don't tell me you've got an invisible car an' all.'

Kang glared at him, but Bok was amused. 'Yes, there,' he said, pointing at an empty space.

'Good one,' Eddie replied with a humourless smile. His gaze turned to another collection of oddball machinery. 'And you've got some Little Nellies, too.' These were ultralight aircraft, barely more than powered hang-gliders with oddly shaped bodywork enclosing the tandem seats. The fabric wings and faceted bodies were all a dull charcoal grey. 'They're hardly stealth bombers, though.'

Kang clearly understood, but chose to respond in Korean, the translator relaying his words. 'That is exactly what they are, Mr Chase. They can fly over the demilitarised zone invisible to radar, and drop bombs.'

'You can't exactly carry a blockbuster on one of those little things, though.'

'They can also land commandos behind enemy lines. We do not need to spend billions on one plane for it to be a good weapon.' The colonel puffed out his chest in smug pride as the group rounded the blockhouse and the depths of the underground space came into full view.

It was an irregularly shaped artificial cavern the size of several football pitches. Hefty pillars were dotted throughout to support the fifty-foot-high ceiling, upon which was an endless grid of harsh lights. It was not the scale of the facility that made Eddie and Nina stop in surprise, though. It was what it was being used to build.

A production line occupied most of the vast space. But it was not making vehicles.

The seemingly random collection of metal pieces at one end gradually took on deadly form as they progressed through the factory. Curved plates became fuel tanks, mating with pumps and pipework and enclosed in cylindrical bodies, all to the percussive accompaniment of rivet guns and the crackle of welding torches. The bell-like nozzles of rocket motors were fitted at one end, conical nosecones at the other. The final results were revealed in all their sinister glory at the end of the line.

Missiles.

A fully completed example hung in a cradle, several white-overalled men inspecting it carefully. Sixty feet long and five in diameter, its two stages were painted a mottled camouflage green. There were no fins or anything else to break up its shape, a harsh, uncompromising digit of death.

This one was not yet ready to leave its birthplace. But it had siblings that were.

Parked at the line's end were three enormous trucks, Chinese lumber transporters adapted for military purposes to avoid the arms embargo. Each vehicle had sixteen wheels, spreading the weight of a hefty hydraulic lifting system designed to raise its cargo from its horizontal bed to the vertical. They were TELs – transporter erector launchers, built to ferry ballistic missiles by road and fire them without the need for expensive and easily targeted silos.

And these were loaded. Each TEL bore a missile. 'Shit,' said Eddie as he stared at the weapons. 'Those are ICBMs!'

Kang stopped, his subordinates all following suit. 'You know our weapons?' he asked with evident suspicion.

'Call it a hobby,' the Englishman replied with what he hoped was a disarming smile. He decided not to mention that his knowledge of missiles came largely from SAS briefings, where he had been taught to identify the weapons of hostile powers for the purposes of sabotage. 'That looks like a modified Scud first stage with a copy of a Russian sub-launched missile on top of it. Just a guess, mind.' He smiled again.

Kang's scowl confirmed he was probably right, but the North Korean was not about to admit that his country was reliant upon second-hand designs. 'You guess wrong. That is *our* latest missile, the Hwasong-15.'

Eddie shrugged. 'I'll update Wikipedia.'

Nina had noticed something about the missiles – not just the ones still under construction, but the completed articles on the TELs. Or rather, the *incomplete* articles. The tapered nosecones were abruptly truncated at the tip, looking like empty bullet casings. 'They're missing something.'

Eddie had spotted it too. 'Yeah, looks like you haven't put the warheads on 'em yet.'

Kang's small smile was both unexpected and alarming. 'They will soon be ready. Now come.' He set off again, his men falling in behind him. Nina and Eddie exchanged concerned glances, then followed.

They continued around to the far side of the blockhouse, seeing more of the colossal space. Across the cavern were ranks of huge cylindrical tanks marked with red warning symbols; the missiles could be fuelled for launch before being loaded on to the TELs. The group's destination was closer by, however. A large opening in the floor housed a trio of elevator tracks that descended deeper into the bowels of the mountain. A chain-link fence was the only barrier around the gaping chasm, the two waiting elevator cars open-topped cages with folding metal gates. 'I guess North Korea isn't big on workplace safety,' Nina muttered.

A soldier hurried ahead of the two officers to open the gates of one car. Kang and Bok entered, the translator gesturing for Eddie and Nina to join them. A couple of the other troops followed them in, the remaining soldiers entering the second car.

The elevator was manually operated, the first soldier closing the gates and going to a control board to take hold of a large brass lever. He pulled it, and the car began its lumbering descent, the cables shrilling alarmingly. The second car followed on the parallel track. A stifling breeze gusted up from below, the shaft providing ventilation as well as access.

Rough rock walls slid past, opening out some eighty feet below to reveal another subterranean floor. This was not as large as the first, though still cavernous in its own right. More production lines were at work, some producing the microlight aircraft they had seen above, others an assortment of heavy weapons. Facility 17 was operating at full tilt to build up the North Korean war machine.

Bok saw Nina's trepidation. 'Impressive, yes?'

'Seen bigger,' Eddie replied, dismissively and truthfully.

The major smiled with all the charm of a rattlesnake. 'But we have a lot more to show you.'

Nina's worry grew stronger still. North Korea was revealing its military secrets to two foreigners – one of whom was a citizen of its most hated enemy. Even if they believed she was purely motivated by financial greed, it seemed unlikely that such a show would be given without consequences.

A new floor rolled by, markedly smaller, with several tunnels leading out of the main space. It was home to another assembly line, but this was not currently in operation, the machinery covered by dust sheets. There was still plenty of activity going on out of sight, however: an endless clinking and hammering of tools on stone. Down one of the tunnels she glimpsed a conveyor belt carrying stones towards the cargo elevator she had seen earlier. The rubble dumped in the forest was excavated from here – by hand, there being no noise from drills or jackhammers. Nina didn't even want to imagine how many unfortunates were being forced to expand the underground base.

But her own concerns quickly returned as the lowest level came into view below. The air was now unpleasantly hot, banks of whirling fans at the shaft's foot forcing it upwards. Whatever was going on was producing a lot of waste heat.

The car stopped. The other elevator arrived alongside it and everyone filed out. The three Kims, larger than life, watched them beatifically from a wall.

Kang waited for the group to assemble before leading the way through a set of double doors. Beyond was a short corridor. He exchanged words with a man in a captain's uniform, then nodded and dismissed him. The young officer disappeared into a side room occupied by several other soldiers. The colonel continued on to the end of the passage, where a pair of metal sliding doors emblazoned with strident warnings in Korean blocked the way. He swiped a keycard through a reader and the barrier rumbled open. 'In here,' he said.

Nina and Eddie followed him into a large, softly lit control room. It resembled that of a power station, banks of monitoring equipment lining the walls and large boards covered with indicator lights showing the status of numerous systems. The hardware's styling was dated, the moulded plastic panelling straight out of the 1970s, but a cluster of flat-screen monitors and a brace of laptops showed that at least some of the systems were up to date. Several technicians in white coats stood and bowed respectfully to the facility's commander. Behind them, a bank of windows overlooked a large subterranean chamber, though from where she stood, Nina couldn't see what lay below.

Kang spoke to a senior technician, then faced the Westerners. Bok stood beside him with an air of malevolent anticipation. The soldiers spread out behind Nina and Eddie, blocking the exit. 'All right,' said Eddie, 'what's all this?'

'We've brought you the Crucible, just as we promised,' Nina said, trying to sound confident. 'So you can keep to your side of the bargain and give us our money.'

'There will not be any money, Nina,' said a new voice. 'Not for you.'

Eddie and Nina whirled – to see Fenrir Mikkelsson entering the control room. The soldiers' guns snapped up, all aimed at the couple.

'I think,' said Eddie as he took in the line of weapons, 'this definitely qualifies for a "buggeration and fuckery".'

'*I* think,' Nina replied, 'that's a fucking understatement.'

38

Mikkelsson strode triumphantly to Nina and Eddie. Sarah and De Klerx appeared behind him. 'You were not expecting me to be here,' said the Icelander. 'You thought I had flown on to China, yes?'

'Something like that,' Nina replied. 'I can't imagine there are many places to spend ninety million dollars in North Korea.'

'The gold will become far more valuable soon. I stayed here because I suspected you had survived to inform the United Nations and the IAEA what I had done. Since that meant they would be looking for me, remaining in the one place they cannot search was very much to my benefit. Did Olivia also survive, by the way?'

'She did.'

'What a shame.'

Sarah whispered something to him. She was pale and drawn, eyes red-rimmed with dark shadows beneath. 'Yes, soon,' her husband said with dismissive impatience, before addressing Eddie and Nina again. 'Another reason I chose to remain here was because there was a high probability you would approach my hosts with some foolhardy proposal to sell them the second Crucible as a ruse to recover the first.'

'You think we came here as a *ruse*?'

He smirked. 'Come now. I imagine Howard MacNeer played upon your patriotism and your desire to save the world yet again. He is as predictable as he is dull-minded. No doubt he had Oswald to support him. Poor Oswald, I shall miss him. A good friend, but he was always a diligent follower of policy, never a man with the determination to make it.'

'We came here of our own accord,' Nina insisted.

Mikkelsson turned his gaze to what she held in her hand. 'The Crucible. I assume there is a tracking device artfully hidden in the case? But I doubt it will be able to transmit through a hundred metres of solid rock.' He took it from her and placed it carefully upon a desk.

Nina decided to play out her deception for as long as possible. 'There's nothing in it but the Crucible. We came here to sell it to someone who could actually make use of it.'

'Thanks for letting us know they were interested, by the way,' Eddie added.

'If you can profit from it,' Nina went on, 'I don't see why we shouldn't too.'

Mikkelsson's response was a mocking shake of the head. 'Oh, Nina. You are not a good actress – I imagine that is why the producers of your movie did not ask you to play yourself. After all those times you insisted that you would not take your seat in the Legacy because you did not want money, you did not *need* money . . . now you expect me to believe that you have turned mercenary overnight?' He tutted. 'Even your husband, whom I know used to *be* a mercenary, could not have convinced me. He is too much of a white knight. And giving North Korea the power to build an unlimited number of hydrogen bombs would not be the act of such a man.'

'So what kind of man does that make you?' Nina demanded.

'A man who sees through the hypocrisy of the United States, and its puppets at the United Nations,' he replied. 'The longer I worked for the IAEA, the more I realised that I was being used. The assertion that nuclear weapons are a destabilising force is a myth, a lie. The US works tirelessly to prevent others from developing what it already has, in numbers sufficient to wipe out the population of the world several times over. It is not interested in peace, only in preserving its own hegemony.'

'So letting a bunch of nuts like North Korea have nukes is *good* for world peace?' asked Eddie sarcastically. 'No offence,' he added to Kang and Bok. 'But you're pointing guns at me, so I reckon that entitles me to gob off.'

'They provide security,' said Mikkelsson. 'The threat of mutually assured destruction kept the peace for fifty years.'

'Except for, y'know, little things like the Korean War,' Nina pointed out. 'The Vietnam War, the Gulf War . . .'

'Precisely! Small wars, proxy wars, held in check by the Soviet Union and its own arsenal. The global balance of terror was maintained. Once the Soviet Union collapsed, America believed it had the power to act unchecked. And look at the result! An arrogant giant could stamp freely all over the world – until it stepped on a wasps' nest and was stung. Then, in its blind pain and rage, it caused more damage and chaos than its enemies could ever have wished. New tyrants rose, freedoms were destroyed, countless innocents died, because there was no deterrent. But this' – he gestured at whatever was beyond the windows – 'will bring back that deterrent.'

'And what *is* this?' said Eddie. 'It's pretty retro. Looks like we're on the set of *Space: 1999.*'

Bewilderment from the Koreans, but Mikkelsson gestured for Nina and Eddie to join him at the windows. Warily, they did so, the soldiers' guns tracking them. 'This is North Korea's newest and largest particle accelerator,' he proclaimed.

Circular tunnels led out of each side of the large chamber below. Running through them was a thick tube of polished metal, its slight curvature hinting that it formed a loop several hundred metres in diameter. The accelerator was supported by a series of heavy-duty braces almost buried amongst a dense tangle of pipework and wiring: housings for the powerful electromagnets used to guide the particle beams.

Protruding from the accelerator directly before the control room was a set of heavy hinged panels, opened and closed by hydraulic pistons. They were currently in the former position, revealing that the accelerator passed through the shielded box. A large metal framework was mounted on tracks so it could be rolled towards the metal tube – which split into two, one branch continuing uninterrupted while the other had a gap in it. That surprised Nina, whose research had told her the particle beams needed to be contained in a vacuum to be brought almost to the speed of light.

A partial explanation came when she saw what was inside the framework.

The Crucible.

The larger of the two crystal spheres squatted within a high-tech copy of the cage that had formerly held it. The whole arrangement, particle accelerator and all, was nothing less than a man-made version of the natural nuclear reactor high in the Himalayas; once the accelerator was running at full power, the Crucible – containing uranium rather than mercury – would be slid into the beam's path to trigger the transmutation process. Nature was being duplicated in steel and concrete.

Mikkelsson could tell that she had understood its purpose. 'Yes, they have replicated the Midas Cave.'

'How'd they do it so fast?' Eddie asked. 'You only just gave them the bloody thing!'

The Icelander chuckled. 'Did you think I make everything up as I go, like you? I have planned this for some time. The accelerator had already been built; the Koreans intended to use it to transmute uranium to plutonium, ironically enough. But the Crucible will let them do so far more quickly and efficiently. I told them the principles after the discovery of the Secret Codex provided a way to find the Midas Cave. I intended to use my security clearance and friendship with Oswald to read the IHA's files with the intent of locating the cave myself, but you, Nina, saved me the trouble. Once you described the Crucible in detail, I quickly designed an articulation frame to hold it. They have done a very good job of modifying the accelerator to accept it. It works perfectly.'

It took a moment for the full import of his words to sink in. 'It's already *working*?' said Nina, shocked.

'You are just in time for a demonstration,' Mikkelsson replied.

Kang straightened proudly. 'We have plutonium for two warheads. Now we make three.'

'Uh-oh,' muttered Eddie. 'I just remembered how many warheadless missiles they've got parked upstairs.'

Kang issued an order. The technicians went to their stations, two scurrying down a flight of steps to a lower level. A series of confirmations as instruments and readouts were checked, then the lead technician, with a degree of ceremony, pressed a switch. The lights flickered and a low thrumming sound echoed up from the chamber below, rising gradually in pitch and volume.

'The accelerator is building up power,' said Mikkelsson, peering at the monitors. 'When it reaches four teraelectronvolts, the particle beam will be redirected from the main loop down the branch' – he pointed at the tube with the gap – 'and into the Crucible. Once the intensity is high enough to trigger a neutron burst, the uranium will be transmuted into plutonium.'

Eddie eyed the system. 'Should I have brought my lead-lined underpants?'

'The panels form a radiation shield. After the uranium sphere is in position, the shield will be closed. We are quite safe.' As he spoke, the two technicians came into view below. They were pushing a trolley, on which sat an orange-sized sphere of a dull grey metal. Despite its small dimensions, it was obvious from the men's movements that it was extremely heavy. 'Uranium-238,'

Mikkelsson went on. 'In itself, useless as nuclear fuel or for nuclear weapons. But it can be converted into plutonium-239. By normal means it would contain a large number of undesirable contaminants, such as plutonium-240.'

'Which can't be used to make a bomb, I'm assuming,' said Nina.

'Correct. At least not at the Koreans' current level of development. Plutonium-240 emits a great deal of harmful neutron radiation, with a high risk of a fizzled detonation, or even a premature one.'

'Premature detonation's a big problem for some men,' Eddie quipped.

The Icelander ignored him. 'But the Crucible achieves an almost total conversion of uranium-238 to supergrade plutonium-239, with practically no impurities. The ancient Atlanteans had the key to literally limitless power, but not the knowledge to use it. Now we have both.'

The technicians used a small crane arm to lift the sphere off the trolley and carefully lower it into the Crucible. Once it was in place, they quickly retreated. The sound of the particle accelerator had now risen to a shrill whine. A large digital readout in the control room was climbing with increasing speed; Nina didn't know what it was displaying, but some of the staff were paying it close attention.

The lead technician gave a command. One of the operators pulled a lever, and the panels of the radiation shield edged shut, sealing in the Crucible with a flat bang. Another noise could be heard over the accelerator: a deep rumble of vacuum pumps.

The readout was rapidly approaching five thousand. A technician adjusted a dial, the rate of increase slowing slightly. The man in charge raised a hand, saying something in Korean that the visitors could only interpret as 'Get ready . . .'

Five thousand – and the lights went out, plunging the room

into a darkness broken only by the dim glow of the instruments. The technician barked an order. Another man worked a control. There was the clack of a heavy-duty circuit closing, and the room returned to full illumination. 'Think you need to fix your fuse box,' said Eddie.

'They have switched in the second-stage power,' Mikkelsson explained. 'The accelerator is now at its maximum output. The liquid nitrogen cooling system has been brought to full capacity to stop the electromagnets from melting.'

The readings kept rising, the accelerator's pulsing whine becoming a shriek. Tension was clear on the technicians' faces as the seconds passed, then minutes. Nina imagined that if something went wrong with the process, the glowering Kang would hold them personally responsible for the failure.

The head technician bent over one of the displays, watching it unblinkingly. He began what sounded like a countdown. The Koreans all held their breath—

A strident buzzer made Nina jump. There was a rush of activity around the room as the techs rapidly worked the controls. The digital readout, which had just topped a figure of twelve thousand, plunged back towards zero as the electrical wail died down.

'That's it?' Eddie asked, moving his cupped hands from his crotch.

'It is,' Mikkelsson confirmed. 'That was the neutron burst.' He looked over the shoulder of one of the white-coated Koreans at a screen, nodding in approval. 'I believe the process has been successful. But we shall soon see for ourselves.'

A loud hiss of air came from below as the vacuum inside the radiation shield was breached. The panels opened, a vaporous cloud wafting out. The lead technician's gaze snapped to a red-painted box on one wall, a radiation warning trefoil stencilled on frosted glass, but it remained unlit. He gave more instructions, his men completing the accelerator's shutdown procedures while the two who had loaded the Crucible returned to extract its contents. The crane arm descended again, slowly lifting out the sphere.

'It's changed,' said Nina. It was still dark grey, but subtly different in lustre.

'Pure plutonium-239,' said Mikkelsson, watching as one of the men ran a Geiger counter over it. The readings were to his satisfaction, and relief. 'The uranium-238 was cast so it could be fitted straight into an already manufactured warhead after conversion. The North Koreans have a stockpile of such warheads based on proven Soviet designs, simply waiting for their nuclear cores.'

'And I thought it was *South* Korea that was supposed to be super-efficient,' Eddie said. 'So that's the plan, is it? Crank out a load of nukes, then tell the world, "Better not fuck with us"?'

'These warheads are not for North Korea,' Mikkelsson replied. 'Not the first ones, at least.'

'Then who?' asked Nina, surprised.

Kang answered her question. 'Saudi Arabia.'

That brought a splutter of disbelief from Eddie. 'What?' said Nina. '*Saudi Arabia?* What the hell does Saudi Arabia want with nukes?'

'The balance of terror,' said Mikkelsson. 'The Saudis want to strengthen their hand against Iran, and Israel. Nuclear weapons will give them that strength. The United States has refused to grant the Saudis access to nuclear technology because of the threat to Israel, but North Korea is willing to supply it in exchange for hard currency – and more importantly, oil.'

'The Israelis'll go fucking apeshit!' Eddie protested. 'They've got nukes of their own, and there are plenty of Israeli politicians who've been itching for an excuse to use 'em.'

'This'll destabilise the entire Gulf,' added Nina. 'Iran only just stopped its nuclear weapons programme – how do you think they'll react to having one of their biggest enemies getting hold of them?'

'They will buy them from us also,' said Kang smugly. 'An agreement has been made.'

'Violating a treaty that took years to work out?'

'The Iranian treaty will not be violated,' Mikkelsson said. 'I know, I helped negotiate it. It prevents Iran from developing its own nuclear fission weapons using uranium from its existing facilities. It does not stop them from buying plutonium-based *fusion* weapons from other nations. The importation of weapons systems was specifically excluded from the terms.'

Eddie let out a disgusted breath. 'Fucking diplomats. Always leaving loopholes!'

'And I guess there were other loopholes in the treaty you negotiated with North Korea, right?' said Nina.

The Icelander nodded. 'Restrictions were placed on the production of fissile material in its nuclear reactors. This,' he nodded towards the particle accelerator, 'is not a reactor. Therefore it is outside the terms of the treaty.'

'I doubt the US will see it that way.'

'What the United States thinks is irrelevant. By the time they learn the truth, North Korea will already have an arsenal of thermonuclear ballistic missiles capable of striking South Korea, Japan, even mainland America. The balance of terror will be restored, North Korea will feel safer from American aggression – and a country that feels secure is less inclined to take overtly aggressive acts. You only have to look at your own country before and after 9/11 for proof of that, Nina.'

'Peace through fear, huh?' she said scathingly.

'As the writer Heinlein – an American, I might add – once said, "An armed society is a polite society." Soon, many more nations will be armed. When everyone has a finger on the trigger, they become very careful about pulling it.'

'And what happens when someone sneezes when their finger's on the trigger?' Eddie demanded.

Before Mikkelsson could provide a smug answer, Sarah again whispered to him, more forcefully than before. 'Yes, soon,' he snapped.

'No, *now*, Fenrir,' she said. 'I've got to know. *We've* got to know!'

'We do, sir,' added De Klerx, glaring at Nina and Eddie.

'Very well,' said Mikkelsson – but before he could say anything more, the group was distracted by the return of the two technicians from the lower chamber. They were carrying between them a small but heavy metal case.

'Hold on,' said Eddie in alarm, retreating until a jab from a soldier's rifle brought him to a halt. 'You're bringing fucking *plutonium* in here?'

Mikkelsson smiled. 'It is perfectly safe. Colonel, if I may?' Kang nodded. The diplomat had a brief exchange in Korean with the senior technician, who then gave an order. The two men set down the case and opened it. Eddie tried to edge away, but the Icelander indicated the red box on the wall. 'If the radiation readings were at even half a dangerous level, that alarm would have sounded.'

'My sister thought that about her smoke alarm, until she burned some toast and it turned out the battery was flat,' Eddie retorted.

'I assure you, we are safe. If we were not, I would not do this.' He reached into the case and – with effort – lifted out the sphere.

'You can *touch* it?' said Nina, both amazed and aghast.

'I told you, it is pure plutonium-239. It produces almost no radiation; it is plutonium-240 that is dangerous. This emits only alpha particles, and they are so weak they cannot even penetrate the skin.' He held it out to her. 'Here. Touch it.'

She hesitated, but Kang and Bok's expressions made her fear

that refusal might not be a choice. Instead, she gingerly brushed the sphere with a fingertip – and involuntarily flinched back.

'What is it?' Eddie said, alarmed. 'Is it electrified?'

'No, it's just . . . warm.' She put her finger on it again. The metal felt hotter than body temperature, but not uncomfortably so. Nevertheless, she withdrew after only a few seconds.

'You have had a rare privilege,' Mikkelsson told her. 'Few people have touched pure plutonium with their bare hands.' He looked at Eddie. 'And you?'

'I'll give it a miss, thanks,' said Eddie firmly.

Mikkelsson shrugged, carefully returning the sphere to its case and closing the lid. The head technician spoke with the officers, then Bok used a walkie-talkie to issue a command to someone elsewhere in the base. 'So now what?' Nina asked as the other technicians began another series of checks and the two men who had brought the plutonium sphere up from the lower level headed back down the stairs.

'Now, the particle accelerator is being readied to convert another sphere of uranium to plutonium,' Mikkelsson said. 'While this one,' he gestured at the canister, 'will be transported with the others, along with their warheads and missiles, to a launch facility at al-Sulayyil in Saudi Arabia.' He crossed the room to the case Nina had brought. 'As for the second Crucible, Colonel Kang agreed that we should let you bring it to North Korea, but I am wondering if I should buy it back. It does belong to the Legacy, after all. And soon it will be a great advantage to have our own gold factory. The markets always panic in times of instability and buy gold, raising the price.'

Kang frowned. 'The Crucibles are ours.'

'I am sure we can negotiate something to our mutual benefit. My gold will be too heavy to take it all in our jet. Perhaps some could be left with you for . . . safe keeping?'

Bok understood his meaning at once and grinned slyly; Kang

took long enough to translate the suggestion that the guide began to do so for him before being curtly shouted down. 'Yes. We can negotiate. For the good of North Korea,' the colonel added, giving the translator a stern look of warning that he should never tell anyone else what he had heard. The man quailed.

Several more soldiers entered, led by the broad-jawed captain Kang had spoken to outside. He snapped to attention before his commanding officer, his team following suit. Kang acknowledged with a salute of his own, then reeled off commands. The captain responded smartly, his men loading the canister holding the plutonium on to a small cart, though with the same wary trepidation as Eddie.

'How come they're not juggling the thing about if it's so safe?' said the Englishman.

'The dangers of a small amount of knowledge,' the Icelander replied. 'North Korea operates on the principle of need-to-know, and its soldiers do not need to know *anything*. They probably believe, like the uneducated in the West, that all nuclear materials are equally dangerous and instantly deadly. Captain Sek is responsible for delivering the plutonium and the warheads; all *he* needs to know is that if anything should go wrong, he is accountable.'

'I guess they don't need to know English either,' said Nina. 'Otherwise they'd wise up with us talking about it.'

'It is not encouraged,' said Bok with a smirk. 'Not for the ordinary people.'

Kang gave more orders. The team wheeled the cart out of the control room. The particle accelerator started to build up power again, its noise rising. 'Fenrir,' said Sarah in a tone of pent-up frustration.

'In a moment,' Mikkelsson answered, turning to Kang.

'No. *Now*.' She rounded him to stand before Nina and Eddie. 'Where's Anastasia? What happened to her, where is she? Where's my daughter?' Frustration was replaced by desperation, her voice quavering.

Nina couldn't help but feel a pang of empathy. 'She's . . . I'm sorry. She's dead.'

Sarah's expression froze as she struggled to take in the words. 'What?' barked De Klerx, his own shock holding back anger. 'What do you mean?'

'I mean, she's dead.'

'She . . .' Sarah's face crumpled into anguish. 'No, no, she . . . she can't be. Not my girl, she . . .' Behind her, Mikkelsson was unreadable, staring silently at the couple.

'I'm sorry,' Nina repeated.

De Klerx clenched his fists into tight, furious balls. 'How did she die?'

'She fell into the frozen lake.'

He shook his head. 'No. No! She knew Iceland, she knew the lake. She would never have been that careless! What really happened?' His eyes narrowed, fixing upon Eddie. 'What did you do?'

'Does it matter?' Eddie asked, assessing the Dutchman's mental state. He was close to snapping in sheer rage, meaning he might be provoked into doing something unwise . . .

'Yes, it matters!' De Klerx snarled. 'Tell me! Tell me now!'

'Remember that grenade launcher you had in Greece? I fired it into the ice underneath her. Boom.' He mimed pulling a trigger, then raised his hand to blow smoke from an imaginary gun. 'She went swimming with the elves.' Sarah was shocked, Mikkelsson's face still an emotionless mask – but De Klerx was now at the point of explosion.

'Eddie . . .' said Nina in surprised warning.

He pressed on, forcing a mocking smile. 'Yeah, I killed her. What're you gonna do about it, clog boy?'

Detonation. 'I will kill *you*!' De Klerx's voice rose to a shriek as he launched himself at the Yorkshireman.

39

The attack caught the North Koreans by surprise, the soldiers hurriedly pulling back as De Klerx ploughed into Eddie. One brought up his gun, but Kang waved him down. A soldier hauled Nina away as Eddie fought back. The two brawling men lurched across the control room.

'Rutger, stop!' Sarah cried, but De Klerx ignored her as he drove a series of furious punches at the Englishman. Eddie blocked most of them, but a couple got through, making him stagger backwards. The soldiers moved to encircle the fight, turning the room's centre into a ring. Some of the technicians left their stations to get clear, others watching in fascination.

'*Ik zal je vermoorden!*' De Klerx shrieked, sending another frenzied blow at his opponent. Eddie swept his forearm up to intercept it, then snapped a punch under the Dutchman's guard to hit his mouth. De Klerx's head jerked back. The taste of blood from his split lip enraged him even more – and he charged at the other man with an incoherent scream.

Eddie raised both arms to block him, but De Klerx had momentum on his side. Both men thumped into the human wall surrounding them. The soldiers retreated, one stumbling over a technician's chair. Eddie slammed a fist into De Klerx's stomach, making him gasp, but before he could follow up the attack a North Korean clubbed him with a rifle butt. He yelled in pain, stumbling forward, only to take a blow to his jaw.

Kang laughed. Now having approval from their superior officer, the soldiers broke their silence to jeer and holler at the battle as if it were a boxing match. Or, Nina realised from the sadistic glee on their faces, a *cage* match, a cockfight. They had enjoyed similar spectacles before, and were looking forward to seeing one of the contestants being beaten half to death.

Or fully.

'Stop them!' she cried. Even the head technician was entranced, letting out thrilled little gasps each time a punch landed. 'This is insane!' She turned to the Mikkelssons. Sarah was weeping, her face buried in her husband's shoulder, while the tall Icelander watched the brawl with cold intensity.

'They are fighters,' said Kang, mouth curling with relish as blood began to speckle the white-painted floor. 'Let them fight.'

Nina turned away in disgust as the two technicians in charge of loading the Crucible ran up the stairs to see what was going on. One of the other operators suddenly remembered that he had a task to perform and whirled back to his control panel. He pulled the lever to close the radiation shield, the grumble of the vacuum pumps becoming audible over the accelerator's whine. That done, he turned back to watch the fight.

The large digital wall display climbed again, two thousand and rising . . .

Eddie jerked sideways to avoid a kick. He jabbed at De Klerx's head again, but only caught the Dutchman a glancing blow. A snarl, and another strike came – aimed at his groin. He twisted away from it—

A rifle butt thudded against his shoulder. He gasped, reeling as hands shoved him back into the centre of the amorphous battleground. De Klerx was waiting, his boot heel hitting Eddie's knee. The Yorkshireman yelled as his leg gave way, only just catching himself as he dropped to the floor. Another swing of his enemy's foot struck him in the side. The impact bowled him into the soldiers' shins. They jumped back, a technician looking over their shoulders almost falling as they collided with him.

Kang cackled, the others echoing the sound sycophantically.

More kicks, this time from the Koreans. Eddie scrambled clear. De Klerx was right on him, his foot thumping painfully against his hip. He rolled again, this time using the movement to jump upright. De Klerx advanced, balled fists raised. Eddie made a circling retreat, trying to stay out of reach of the soldiers behind him—

'Eddie! The power's building again!'

Nina – but why would she tell him *that*? He glanced towards her. She was beyond the wall of leering soldiers, another man holding her arm with one hand. The Type 58 rifle in his other was pointed at the ground, not his prisoner. And just behind her were the control panels, the operators gawping at the fight rather than watching their instruments . . .

He realised what she was trying to tell him. Another glance, this at the stairwell to the lower floor. Nobody was watching it. An escape route – if they could reach it.

Which was a *big* if.

De Klerx closed in. Eddie hurriedly sidestepped so the Dutchman was between him and Nina – then dropped his head and made a screaming charge at the other man.

They collided with a *whump*. De Klerx lurched backwards. He hit two of the soldiers, one in turn reeling into Nina and her guard. The redhead arrested her fall on a control panel, slapping a hand down on to it – and twisting the dial controlling the power flow.

It was only a tweak, as she didn't want to risk drawing attention. She didn't even know if it would be enough to make a difference. But as her guard recovered and pulled her away, she checked the large display. The numbers were still climbing, now well past four thousand . . . and rising faster than before.

Nobody else was watching the indicator, though. All eyes returned to the brawl as the soldiers forced the Yorkshireman back into the makeshift ring. De Klerx leapt after him, smashing another blow against his head. 'You dyke-poking *fuck*!' Eddie snarled, anger powering a new volley of punches against the Dutchman. De Klerx bobbed and jinked, blocking most – but then crying out as one cracked his nose. Blood squirted from his nostrils.

He drew away, huffing to clear his airways before wiping his face on his sleeve. Eddie circled to position his adversary between himself and Kang. The soldiers shifted, blocking any retreat. He glanced at the digital display – approaching the five thousand mark – but then locked his eyes back on De Klerx as the Dutchman rushed at him.

Eddie swept up one arm to knock away a punch – only for a second jab to catch him squarely in the face. It was not a fight-ender, but it jarred his senses enough that he was too late to block the next. He fell against the hooting soldiers behind him. They shoved him back into the arena—

De Klerx wound up for a brutal haymaker, Eddie stumbling right into its path. He tried to dodge, but had nowhere to go.

The punch hit his skull like a sledgehammer. He went down hard to the floor, the metallic tang of blood filling his mouth. His vision blurred, sounds suddenly echoing. He looked up, seeing howling faces whirl nightmarishly around him. Kang's took on form, the little colonel pumping a fist in glee.

De Klerx stepped in front of him, anger joined by victorious exultation. He drew back a foot to smash his steel toecap into Eddie's defenceless face—

Nina's voice cut through the hubbub. '*Fix the fusebox!*'

The senior technician suddenly realised that nobody was monitoring the particle accelerator. He whirled to check the readings – as the display reached five thousand, sooner than he had expected—

The control room was plunged into darkness.

De Klerx hesitated before delivering his kick – but Eddie had already moved in instant response to Nina's coded warning, twisting to dodge the attack and grabbing the Dutchman's foot with both hands.

The technician scrambled for the control to activate the second-stage power supply as the accelerator drew greedily upon every erg of electricity from the rest of the base. The circuit closed with a bang, the lights coming back on.

Eddie forced himself up, still gripping De Klerx's foot and driving the flailing Dutchman backwards. He hit Kang, sending the short man spinning into Mikkelsson and Sarah. Husband and wife both fell as the Yorkshireman threw De Klerx to the floor.

The soldiers recovered from their momentary blindness, guns snapping up – but their commander and chief of security were too close to their target. The only man with a clear line of fire was Nina's guard. He fumbled to bring his rifle to bear—

Nina threw herself against him. The man stumbled – and tripped over Mikkelsson. His gun skidded across the floor . . .

To be snatched up by Eddie.

The Englishman whipped around and pulled the trigger. The Type 58, an AK-47 copy, was set on full auto, its thudding bark almost deafening as bullets ripped through the soldiers and technicians. They fell screaming, blood spouting from their wounds. Bok dived behind the desk, the bullets meant for him instead sending the senior technician flying against the control panels with gushing rosettes of blood across his white coat.

The rifle's bolt clacked. It had only taken three seconds to empty the magazine, but that was all Eddie needed. The last rank-and-file soldier still alive was Nina's guard, who lifted his head – only for it to slam back against the floor with a crimson spurt as the Yorkshireman used the empty gun as a club. 'Nina, go!' he shouted, dropping the Type 58 and looking for a replacement. None of the dead soldiers' weapons were in immediate reach – and now Kang was fumbling for his holstered pistol, Bok doing the same.

Eddie ran for the stairs, stamping on De Klerx on the way. Nina was already heading for the exit, pulling a particular lever as she passed. He held back for a second to let her by, then clattered down the steps after her – as a bullet from Kang's pistol blew a chunk out of the wall just behind his head. 'What did you do?' he asked as they reached the floor below.

'Opened those!' She gestured towards the radiation shields, which were slowly parting, exposing the Crucible within.

'But we'll get fucking *zapped*!'

'Not if we get clear! We saw it in the Midas Cave. Radiation travels in straight lines, but the tunnels curve!' She ran for the nearest circular entrance. 'We've got about a minute before the neutron burst!'

'A minute? But you sped up the fucking countdown!'

'Oh. Yeah, I did, didn't I? Oops.' They reached the tunnel. It followed a sweeping arc into the distance, the gleaming steel tube of the accelerator and its pipework-entangled electromagnets disappearing around the bend a hundred metres distant. 'Better run if you don't want a glowing butt!'

They raced down the tunnel as the accelerator's shrill grew ever louder.

Bok ran to the window. 'They're in the tunnel!'

Kang took in the strewn corpses of his men with shock. The translator was among them. 'Get another squad down here! Go after them!' Bok barked urgent commands into his radio.

Mikkelsson stood, helping Sarah up. 'I think we should leave,' he said in English as the few surviving technicians hastened to their workstations. 'And I suggest you do too, Colonel. This area is not safe with Wilde and Chase on the loose.'

'We will catch them,' said the security chief.

'*I'll* catch them,' snarled De Klerx. He grabbed a gun from the floor, looking back at Sarah. 'I'll make them pay for Anastasia.' He hurried down the stairs.

Mikkelsson took his wife's hand and started for the elevators, collecting the case holding the small Crucible. 'Colonel,' he said in Korean. 'Are you coming?'

Kang stared at the container, caught between his desire for revenge and the prospect of riches. 'Yes,' he decided. 'Bok, come with us. Until more men are down here, you're our bodyguard.'

'Yes, sir,' Bok replied, also eyeing the case. Kang ordered the technicians to regain control of the huge machine below and complete the transmutation process, then the group quickly departed.

Fixated on their own readouts, conditioned by the secrecy and paranoia of North Korea to focus only on their own task and not question what was happening beyond it, none of the operators thought to look out of the window at the open radiation shields below . . .

'How much further?' asked Eddie as he followed Nina painfully along the curving tunnel.

'Not far,' she replied. 'I think.' She looked back to see if the shields were still visible beyond the tunnel's mouth.

They were – but now so was De Klerx. He stopped to take aim—

'Gun!' she cried. Eddie ducked as the Dutchman opened fire. Bullets clanged off the accelerator's casing. Its curvature meant that from De Klerx's position they were partially protected by it, but he was already running again, unleashing single shots to force his targets to stay in cover.

Eddie tried to squeeze underneath the accelerator, but pipework and cabling beneath it blocked him. He swore, then scrambled to join Nina behind a support brace – the ring of powerful electromagnets immediately making their presence felt. 'Bloody hell!' he gasped, jerking his left arm away. 'Feels like it's trying to pull the pins out!' The titanium rods that had been used to splint the bones of his forearm after a break several years earlier were weakly magnetic, and the effect was like invisible hands pawing at him.

'Too bad they don't work on bullets,' Nina said grimly. 'What do we do?'

'If we stand up and run, he'll have a clear shot at us.' The accelerator was only chest-high at its tallest. 'You stay low and keep going. I'll try and jump him.'

'Eddie, he'll kill you!' The brace and its pipework extended merely a foot outwards from the metal tube. 'You can't hide behind that!'

'It's all we've got! Go!'

De Klerx had already closed the gap as Nina reluctantly hurried away. He glimpsed the movement and fired. She shrieked as bullets cracked off the concrete beside her – and the impacts got closer as he came around the tunnel, bringing her into clear view—

He spotted Eddie's shadow behind the brace.

The Dutchman switched targets to the greater threat – and his lover's killer. He ran to the support, about to rush around it and spray Eddie with bullets—

The rifle was snatched from his hands.

It smacked against the electromagnets. Startled, De Klerx lunged to retrieve it – only to be tackled by Eddie, who drove a brutal punch into the mercenary's stomach and threw him back against the tunnel wall. 'Fuckin' magnets, how do they work?' Eddie growled, hitting him again.

But De Klerx was far from finished. He hurled himself at the Englishman, sending them both crashing against the shrilling accelerator. Eddie caught him under his chin with a flailing uppercut. The Dutchman spat out blood, only to retaliate by slamming a knee into his opponent's side. Eddie fell. De Klerx whirled for his gun—

Nina leapt at him from behind. De Klerx hit the brace chest-first. Winded, he dropped to his knees.

She tried to pull the rifle free, but the magnets were too strong – all she managed was to turn it in place. But she couldn't bring it to bear on De Klerx as he hauled himself back up, the muzzle wedged against the cables—

Not cables. *Pipes*.

She pulled the trigger.

The bullet blasted through the tubing – unleashing a steaming jet of liquid nitrogen.

It gushed over De Klerx's legs, the supercooled liquid instantly freezing them solid. Nina flung herself clear with a shriek of pain as stray droplets hissed on her clothing.

But it was nothing compared to the Dutchman's agony. He screamed, his howl echoing through the tunnel even over the noise of the particle accelerator.

Eddie dragged Nina clear as ice clogged the end of the ruptured pipe, cutting the flood to a spray – then sent a sweeping kick at De Klerx's frozen knees. 'Chill out!'

Both the wailing Dutchman's legs exploded into blood-red shards. The rest of him dropped to the floor, his head falling straight through the still-escaping liquid nitrogen. His scream was instantly cut off, his skull flash-freezing before bursting apart into a million glittering fragments as it hit the concrete.

'Did it get you?' Eddie asked as he lifted Nina to her feet. 'Are you hurt?'

'I dunno, I dunno!' She checked the backs of her legs. The splashes were tiny patches of pure white on her trousers, but they felt as if she had been burned by cigarettes. 'I can still move.'

'Great, 'cause we need to!' He looked back through the swirling steam. The control room was still partially visible beyond the tunnel entrance. He saw a face appear at the window, staring down at the open radiation shields with first disbelief, then fear. 'Come on!'

They both ran, leaving the smashed corpsicle behind. 'Did you *really* just say "Chill out"?' Nina panted.

'Pretty sure I already used "Ice to see you" somewhere,' he replied. Another glance over his shoulder as they continued around the tunnel. The chamber finally passed out of sight, blocked by concrete and solid rock, but he had absolutely no intention of stopping.

The technician looking down at the accelerator screamed a warning. Another operator scrambled to reach the unattended console with the radiation shield control, but too late—

A flash of indescribable colour from the Crucible – and the radiation alarm screeched, warning lights flashing.

Nobody in the control room was alive to pay heed. The neutron burst had penetrated the thin walls, and everything within. Neutrons were even more damaging to organic matter than gamma radiation, the technicians' flesh almost liquefied as they collapsed dead over their instruments.

With no one to shut down the particle accelerator, it kept running at full power, temperature gauges rising as the liquid nitrogen systems struggled to cool the electromagnets. One readout in particular rocketed upwards as the vital fluid dribbled out over the remains of Rutger De Klerx . . .

The elevator was halfway back to the runway level when an alarm sounded. Kang and Bok both blanched, the security chief shouting into his walkie-talkie and getting no reply. 'What's happened?' asked Sarah, seeing her husband's concern.

'Radiation!' gasped Kang. 'A radiation leak!'

'What? But how—'

'They must have sabotaged the shields,' said Mikkelsson. 'If there was an unprotected neutron burst down there, it will have killed everyone in the control room.'

'What about Rutger?' His silence gave Sarah her answer. 'Oh my God! What about us, are we safe?'

'We're shielded by the rock. Even high-energy neutrons can only penetrate a short distance.' He looked over the car's side. 'But there is a chance that contamination might be drawn upwards by the ventilation system. Colonel, you should evacuate the facility until a hazmat team can secure the accelerator.' Kang nodded, then gestured for Bok to hand him the radio.

'And . . . *them*?' Sarah said, hesitating before saying the names. 'Nina and her husband?'

'I don't know. If they got far enough around the tunnel, they might have survived.'

'But they can't get out, surely? The tunnel's a loop – they can only go back to the control room, and that'll kill them!'

Bok frowned in realisation. 'There are ladders to the level above.'

Kang broke off from issuing the evacuation order to bark a new command: 'All security forces! Find the Westerners – and *kill them*!'

40

Eddie looked back in the direction of the flash as he and Nina hurried around the tunnel. 'What the fuck was that?' he shouted over the accelerator's wavering screech.

'The neutron burst,' she gasped in reply. 'If we'd been any closer, we might have ended up like Lot's wife!' He gave her a blank look. 'From the Bible? Turned into a pillar of salt?'

'You remember that I skived out of Sunday school, right? But are we safe even if we weren't in line of sight of it?'

'We shouldn't have been directly exposed. But I don't think it'd be a good idea to go back.'

'Hopefully we won't need to.' Eddie pointed ahead. There was an alcove set into the inner wall, a ladder leading upwards. Some of the accelerator's cabling branched off and ran up the narrow shaft alongside it. 'Must go to the next level.'

'Anywhere's better than here.' They climbed over the gleaming tube—

A thudding jolt shook it. 'What was that?' Eddie said, jumping down on the other side.

'I don't know,' said Nina, 'but I doubt it was anything good . . .'

Confirmation came a moment later as the boom of an explosion echoed down the tunnel.

Without coolant, the electromagnets had overheated – and blown apart, the blast ripping through the pipework and cables around them. More liquid nitrogen erupted from the main feeder pipe. Without the magnetic field to guide the beam around the loop, the racing subatomic particles now wanted to travel in a straight line. They smashed into the wall of the metal tube, within seconds turning it red hot. The neighbouring electromagnets also overloaded as their coolant supply was cut off, a chain reaction tearing the enormous machine apart—

Eddie and Nina ran for the alcove as the blasts ripped towards them. A dense wall of swirling mist raced through the tunnel ahead of the explosions – not steam, but the air freezing as liquid nitrogen gushed along the floor. He practically flung her up to grab a higher rung before scrambling into the narrow shaft behind her. The icy wavefront gushed past below, detonations rattling the ladder as more magnets blew to pieces.

'Keep climbing!' Eddie yelled.

'You think?' Nina shot back sarcastically.

The top of the dimly lit shaft was a small dot a long way above. They continued their hurried ascent – as another, more violent explosion shook the walls.

The overload reached the accelerator's particle source, on the opposite side of the huge loop from the control room. It exploded, sending one final surge of energy through the failing system. The electromagnets guiding the beam into the Crucible fluctuated, the stream of superfast particles burning into the crystalline sphere's support frame. It melted like wax under a blowtorch, pitching its contents to the floor as more liquid nitrogen swilled from ruptured pipes—

Extreme heat met extreme cold as the Crucible hit the ground. There could only be one result. Not even the strange material of the Atlantean artefact could withstand such stresses. It burst apart, shimmering splinters scattering across the chamber.

Before they had even come to rest, a wall of fire tore through the room, obliterating everything.

★ ★ ★

A sudden rush of wind from the tunnel below warned Nina and Eddie that danger was coming their way. '*Hang on!*' cried the Englishman.

A thunderous shock wave pounded the shaft, tearing away the ladder's lowest section and jolting those above so hard that they both almost lost their grip. Smoke and embers surged upwards, blinding them in a hot, stinking haze. Then the noise faded, residual echoes of disintegrating machinery still rolling through the underground passage.

Nina coughed, squinting downwards. Her husband was still gripping the ladder below her. 'Keep going,' he gasped, 'or we'll choke on this crap.' They resumed their climb, the bullet wound in Nina's arm burning with renewed pain. 'So, you think everything that just blew up was expensive?'

'I'm going to guess that any *sane* poverty-stricken country wouldn't even have considered it,' she replied.

'You haven't met many dictators, have you?'

'Have you?'

'More than I'd like.'

'Why am I not surprised?' Nina reached the top of the ladder. 'Okay, big-ass manhole cover blocking the way.'

'Let me see.' She leaned aside so Eddie could peer at the obstruction. 'No locking bar on this side. Either we can just push it open, or . . .'

'Or?'

'Or it's locked from the top.'

She sighed. 'I will be really, *really* pissed if the thing that keeps us from getting out of here is a buck-fifty padlock.'

'Pretty sure there'll be more than that trying to stop us. Shift over.' She squeezed against the cables, Eddie squirming up beside her. 'This is cosy.'

'Mind on the job, mister.' They both managed their first smiles in some time. 'Are you ready?'

'Yeah.' He wedged his shoulder against the cover, bracing his feet. 'On three.'

He counted down, then both pushed upwards. For a moment the heavy metal disc remained firmly in place, before shifting with a graunch of rusted metal. Eddie shoved harder, Nina seeing faint lights through the gap as it widened. 'Looks like a tunnel,' she said.

He raised a foot to a higher rung and strained again. The cover rose, Nina forcing it sideways. A few more seconds of effort, then Eddie lowered to bring it down flat on the floor before shoving it clear. 'That's given me a chip on my shoulder – out of the fucking bone.'

He retreated to give Nina space to climb out. 'Are you all right?' she asked, helping him up.

'I'll be fine, so long as I don't have to carry any sacks of coal.' He surveyed their surroundings. 'Okay, now where the hell are we?'

They had emerged in a tunnel, rectangular in cross-section rather than circular. Other passages branched off it. 'This was the level they were digging out, wasn't it? Maybe they haven't finished it yet.'

Eddie's gaze followed the path of the cables from the shaft to the ceiling, where they joined other thick skeins running overhead. 'They all go that way,' he said, pointing down one leg of the gloomy tunnel. 'Those power lines we saw on the way up the mountain came in through the runway tunnel, so if we follow 'em, they should take us to the way out. Eventually.'

'We've still got to get up there, though,' Nina reminded him as they started down the passage. 'I don't think calling the elevator will be a good idea.'

'Hopefully there's more ladders— Oh balls.' A sound from somewhere ahead: the echoing clatter of running feet, growing louder. 'They're probably not here to give us a guided tour.'

They hurried into a dimly lit side passage.

'Where do you think this goes?' Nina asked.

'Somewhere that hasn't got a shitload of soldiers running towards us, I hope.' They rounded a corner, seeing a crossroads ahead. 'Great, it's a fucking maze.'

'Look, more cables.' Another set of heavy-duty power lines ran across the intersection. 'Do we follow them?'

'Yeah,' he decided. 'They probably join up with the ones behind us.' They ran to the crossing and turned right.

The tunnel complex turned out to be extensive. Following the power cables, they went through chambers that had been completed but stood empty, awaiting new production lines. The chatter of the soldiers' boots was still behind them, but dispersing as they spread out to search. The open manhole had been found.

Other noises became audible ahead. Underlying everything was the wail of an alarm, but through it they heard a constant chittering: the clash of metal tools against rock. 'This must be where they're digging,' said Nina nervously, remembering that the slave workers were being overseen by numerous armed guards.

Eddie saw brighter lights where the tunnel opened out. 'Shit, we might have to go through that to get to the way out.'

The cables ran into the new chamber. They had not recently passed any side routes that might safely skirt the excavations – and Nina's glance back caught the distant flare of a flashlight. 'They're coming!'

'Fuckeration,' muttered Eddie. 'Okay, we don't have much choice . . .'

They slowed as they approached the end of the passage. A ragged cavern had been blasted out of the mountain's heart, now being shaped by hand. Eddie crouched and led Nina behind a pile of rubble just inside to survey the scene. About two dozen prisoners were working in the irregular space, some hacking at the stone walls with picks while others cleared the debris and loaded it on to a conveyor belt heading down the tunnel into which the cables ran. They were overseen by three soldiers: two with Type 58 rifles, the third with a shotgun. The trio seemed unsure how to respond to the alarm. Even in the troops' confused state, though, there was no way Nina and Eddie could reach the exit without being seen.

'Okay, what do we do?' Nina whispered.

Eddie's gaze followed the conveyor, seeing a stack of red-painted wooden crates near the tunnel mouth. Explosives, he guessed; dynamite or something similar. A potential weapon, but he would be shot long before reaching them. He looked back at the piles of broken stone around the cavern's perimeter. 'Maybe we can sneak round these if we—'

A voice blared over a loudspeaker. Even without knowing the language, both recognised it as Bok's. 'What's he saying?' Nina wondered.

'Probably warning about us,' Eddie replied, but the sudden change in the guards' expressions revealed that something else was going on. Confusion gave way to shock as Bok continued to bark commands – then the emotion spread to the workers, a wave of fear running through the chamber. A few broke from their places, pleading in horror.

That small show of resistance was enough to snap the soldiers out of their bewilderment. Faces turning as hard as the surrounding stone, they spread out, shouting at their prisoners and gesturing for them to gather together in the centre of the space. Most went meekly even in their obvious terror, but a few fled, scrambling behind the rubble.

'Shit,' Nina gasped. 'They're going to kill them!' The alarm was probably a radiation warning, prompting an evacuation – and the slave workers were considered disposable, too much trouble to corral and bring to the surface.

A woman burst from the main group and sprinted around the edge of the cavern, towards the passage behind Eddie and Nina. Two soldiers hurried to intercept her, bellowing orders. She ignored them, crossing an open space between the mounds of rubble—

One running guard fired his shotgun. The frightened woman's grimy clothing shredded in a spray of red as the pellets ripped into her chest. She tumbled limply to the floor, trailing blood. The prisoners screamed, more of them scattering.

The other soldiers turned, about to unleash automatic fire upon the helpless crowd—

There was a pickaxe on the pile of stones by Eddie. He snatched it up as he charged from cover at the man with the shotgun, swinging it – and impaling him through the back, its long spike bursting out of the soldier's chest with a torn chunk of his heart transfixed upon the end. The Korean let out a gargling shriek, the Englishman grabbing his gun as he fell.

The nearest soldier spun in surprise—

Eddie lunged at him, pumping the shotgun to load a new shell and firing it into his stomach. The point-blank blast tore a hole right through the soldier's body, a gruesome fountain of blood and intestines exploding out of his back.

The third soldier, forty feet away, whirled to face the new threat—

Eddie rapidly pumped the shotgun again before body-slamming the dead man at chest height and ramming the weapon straight through the gory hole in his torso. Bullets smacked into the corpse's upper body and punched messily out just above the Englishman's head.

Hand inside the dead soldier's guts, he pulled the trigger again.

The shotgun boomed. Forty feet was still well within its lethal range, the tightly packed spray of red-hot pellets reducing the

North Korean's face and upper chest to bloody mince. He staggered backwards, firing a last few rounds before collapsing.

Nina scrambled over the debris. 'Eddie! They're coming, behind us!' The tramp of approaching feet had grown faster at the sound of gunfire.

'Get that gun!' he shouted, pointing at the last soldier's fallen rifle. She ran past her husband as he snatched up the second man's weapon and hurried back to the rubble near the tunnel entrance. He dived on to the pile of stones, taking aim at the opening.

More soldiers rushed from the passage—

Eddie's rifle blazed, bloodily cutting down the half-dozen North Koreans. He jumped up and ran to the fallen troops. One was still moving, clawing for his gun. A single shot to the back of his skull ended the threat. The Yorkshireman peered around the corner. No movement in the gloom. 'Nina, we're clear. Come on!' He swapped his empty weapon for one of the fully loaded ones on the floor, then headed for the exit.

'What about the workers?' Nina said. She had picked up the Type 58, the prisoners regarding her fearfully. 'The soldiers will kill them!'

'Don't suppose any of you speak English?' Eddie called to them.

To his surprise, he got an answer. A skinny man with a swollen purple bruise on one cheek tentatively raised his hand. 'I . . . speak English,' he said quietly, hardly daring to meet their gaze.

'Okay,' Eddie replied. 'I'm Eddie, she's Nina, and we're leaving. All of us. The guns over there – get them. We'll have to shoot our way out.'

That only intensified the man's fear. 'We're trapped down here too,' said Nina. 'They're trying to kill us, just like you – we don't have a choice.'

'If you get the guns, at least you can fight back,' Eddie added. Nobody was yet in sight down the main tunnel, but the wailing alarm and the conveyor's rattle prevented him from hearing if anyone was approaching from its side passages. 'Even if you don't want to come, tell the others so they can decide for themselves.'

The man hesitated, then spoke in his native language to the prisoners. It quickly became clear that there were two groups: those who had been so traumatised and crushed by their jailers that they were afraid even to consider the possibility of escape, and a smaller number who while just as physically ground down still harboured a spark of resistance. These latter moved warily away from the others as if expecting some cruel trick; when it became clear they were not about to be punished, they went to the dead soldiers and shared out their weapons. When all the guns were taken, the remainder gathered pickaxes, determined not to be left defenceless.

'What about you?' Nina asked their translator, who had not armed himself. 'What's your name?'

'Ock,' he replied, finally finding the courage to look her in the eye. Some of the other prisoners were regarding her with expressions that went beyond simple curiosity. It took a moment to realise why: they were staring at her hair. North Korean propaganda posters, she knew, sometimes demonised Americans as red-headed, freckled thugs.

'Will you help us?' When he hesitated again, she continued: 'You're the only one who can speak English – we need you to talk to the others.'

'I . . . I do not know,' he stammered. 'My wife, she is here also, on another floor.' His eyes flicked upwards. 'If I help you, they will kill me – and they will kill her!'

'They were going to kill you anyway,' Eddie pointed out as he examined the red crates.

'Yes, but . . .' The strain of trying to resolve the dilemma made him tremble.

'Ock,' Nina said softly. 'We'll do everything we can to help you, and to find your wife. I'm not a soldier, but Eddie is. A very good one. If anyone can get all of us out of here, he can.'

'So long as we don't stand around here all day with our thumbs up our arses,' the Yorkshireman added.

'He's also a very *rude* one,' she said, glaring at him. But he had a point. 'We've got to get out of here. Are you coming with us?'

Ock finally whispered an answer. 'Yes. I will help you.'

'Thank you.' She looked at the reluctant prisoners. 'Try to get as many of them to come with us as you can, then tell the ones with guns to do what Eddie tells them.'

'Did any of the guards in here smoke?' Eddie asked, opening one of the wooden boxes.

'Did they smoke?' echoed Nina uncertainly. 'Why?'

He lifted out something that could have come straight from a cartoon: a stick of dynamite wrapped in red paper with a fuse hanging limply from one end. 'So I can light these!'

Ock gawped at him, then pointed at the guard impaled by the pickaxe. 'Him.'

'Get his lighter, or matches, whatever.' Eddie stuffed several sticks into his pockets, along with a couple of longer coils of fuse, then returned to the tunnel. From somewhere in the distance he heard a thudding drumroll: the sound of rifles firing in unison. 'Those *fuckers*,' he said, realising what it meant. 'There must be other workers on this floor – they're killing them! We've got to move *now*, before they trap us down here.'

Nina scurried to the dead soldier, digging gingerly through his pockets and pulling out a crumpled book of matches. 'Got them.'

'Great – let's go.' He started down the tunnel at a rapid jog, moving alongside the conveyor so he could use it as cover if anyone appeared ahead. Nina ran to catch up, followed by the armed prisoners. Ock had a hurried discussion with the other workers, then the group – with varying degrees of reluctance – came after them.

The tunnel met with another a couple of hundred yards ahead, a larger passage slicing across its end at an angle. The conveyor stopped at another belt, dropping the last few pieces of broken rock that had been loaded before Bok's announcement on to its still-laden counterpart.

That was not the route concerning Eddie, though; rather a smaller side passage that appeared to link the two main shafts. 'Hold on,' he said as he approached it, signalling those behind to slow. He stared intently at the darkened opening, and saw flickers of light washing along its walls from within. 'Shit! Someone's coming. Nina, give me those matches!'

She handed him the matchbook. 'You're going to use *dynamite*?'

'If we run out of bullets, we're fucked.' He pulled out one of the sticks, then struck a match. 'None of those soldiers back there had spare mags. The Norks probably can't afford 'em.'

'That's great, Wile E., but it won't matter if you bring the roof down on us!'

But he had already lit the fuse. 'Everyone down!' he snapped. Nina hurriedly ducked behind the conveyor, Ock yelping a translation to the prisoners before joining her in cover.

Eddie ran to the passage, holding the sputtering explosive in one hand. He peeked around the corner – and saw the silhouettes of several soldiers advancing on him, one holding a torch.

The beam snapped up and locked on to his face—

Eddie jerked back as bullets smacked against the wall, stone chips stinging his head. He flung the dynamite around the corner, then dived to the floor and covered his ears. Shouts of panic came from the passage, followed by a scuffle of footsteps as some of the soldiers turned and fled, while another made a desperate scramble to tear out the fuse.

He failed.

A piercing *bang* came from the tunnel, followed by a surge of flying dust and grit and body parts. Deeper booms shook the floor as part of the ceiling collapsed, crushing what remained of the soldiers into oblivion.

Even covered, Eddie's ears were still ringing from the detonation. 'That's another bloody step closer to needing a hearing aid,' he complained, returning to the others. 'We need to keep moving.' They set off again, the Koreans glancing down the wrecked tunnel with expressions that suggested hope was rising within them for the first time in years.

They reached the main intersection. Eddie waved for caution as he went to the corner and checked the new tunnel, but the only movement was the ceaseless trundling of the second conveyor belt. The power cables ran along the roof. 'Does this go to the way out?' he asked.

Ock peered nervously past him. 'To the lift that takes rocks to the surface, yes.'

'If it takes rocks up, it can bring soldiers down,' Eddie warned, signalling for everyone to follow him along the tunnel.

41

It took the fugitives a few minutes to reach the tunnel's end. Two other conveyors ran into the chamber beyond from adjoining passages, their termini choked with mounds of rubble. The reason it had not been cleared was instantly apparent: all the slave workers had been shot, bloodied corpses littering the floor.

'Bastards,' Eddie growled. He surveyed the area, but the soldiers who had committed the murders were gone. 'The guards must've evacuated.'

'Yeah, but they're coming back!' Nina said in alarm. A large elevator shaft was cut into the room's side – and the cables within were moving.

'Everyone with a gun, with me!' Eddie shouted, running towards it. The armed prisoners followed as Ock relayed the command.

'What are we doing?' asked Nina.

'If anyone gets out of that lift, we're screwed, so we make sure *no one* gets out of that lift!' He looked up the shaft, seeing the descending car less than a hundred feet above.

'How?'

'You ever heard of anyone wearing bulletproof *shoes*?' He opened the elevator's wide gate as the large rectangular platform came towards them. It would only be seconds before it dropped below ceiling level and the soldiers aboard would be able to see out—

Eddie pointed his gun straight up and pulled the trigger, stitching a weaving line of bullet holes into the elevator's underside. Nina followed suit, the Korean prisoners joining in. Splinters rained down on them as the wooden platform was perforated by a storm of metal. The cacophony was deafening, but even over the thunder of the guns they heard screams from above – which were cut off as the onslaught continued.

Magazines ran dry. The shooters pulled back as the elevator reached floor level – and continued past it, the soldier operating it slumped dead over the controls. 'Oh bollocks!' Eddie gasped, jumping down on to the platform and navigating the two dozen or so bullet-torn bodies to drag the man off and shove the large brass lever to the neutral position. The elevator stopped with a squealing jolt. He pushed it the other way to bring it back up, stopping with another clash from the cables. A couple of corpses flopped out grotesquely. 'Basement!' the Yorkshireman announced. 'Perfume, stationery and garden tools. Going up!'

'That's great,' said Nina, stepping with trepidation over the lacerated soldiers, 'but now we're out of ammo.'

Eddie tossed away his empty rifle and replaced it with a slightly bloodied one from the lift's deceased passengers. 'North Korea really is an arms supplier!' The floor was riddled with holes, but the wood still seemed intact enough to take everyone's weight. He kicked out more bodies to make sure, then waved everyone on to the platform. 'All aboard!'

The prisoners stepped on to the elevator, some reacting with fear or revulsion at the dead men before the hope of freedom took over. Eddie operated the lever. A whine of motors some-where high above, the cables singing, then it began its ascent.

'They're probably waiting for us at the top,' said Nina, peering up the shaft. Patches of light marked the levels above.

'I dunno,' her husband replied. 'How long is it since they gave the evac order? Ten minutes, twenty? If it was a radiation alarm, that'll have encouraged everyone to get their arses outside pretty damn quick.'

'It was radiation,' Ock confirmed. 'First they gave the order for soldiers and technicians to get out. Then Bok said to kill the prisoners. The elevators could not take everyone fast enough.'

'This place is like an underground *Titanic*,' Nina muttered.

To her surprise, Ock almost smiled. '*Titanic*. It is a good movie.'

'You've seen it?'

'On a DVD, smuggled from China. I watched it with my wife.' The smile disappeared. 'I hope she . . .'

'We'll try and find her,' Eddie assured him. 'But you're right, Nina – this place is like the *Titanic*. 'Cause it's gonna go down.'

'How?' she asked. 'I forgot to pack my iceberg.'

'Remember where they were building the missiles, on the top level? They were making fuel for 'em too. And I just happen to know,' a sly smile, 'that North Korea uses kerosene and some stuff called red fuming nitric acid for fuel in its Scud knock-offs. If they come into contact with each other . . .' He spread his hands apart to mime an explosion.

The elevator rose through the next level, which had also been evacuated. 'You want to *blow up* the base?'

'Saves someone else doing it, doesn't it? Seeing as they really were using it to make nukes.'

'The nukes,' Nina echoed. 'Damn it, they're probably on their way out of here already!'

'Yeah, along with Mikkelsson. And his money, and his gold, *and* probably the bloody Crucible too – the small one, anyway. Hopefully the big one got buried when the particle accelerator blew up.'

'Great. They can just start the whole process all over again. We've got to stop him.'

'Let's worry about getting out of here alive first, eh?' He looked towards the approaching top of the shaft. 'Okay, this is it. Anybody wearing a stupid big hat with a red star on it, shoot 'em!' He waited for Ock to pass on his instructions, then asked him: 'You sure you don't want a gun? Doesn't look like these twats have exactly been treating you well.' He indicated the lurid bruise on the Korean's face.

Ock bowed his head. 'No, I . . . I am not a soldier like you.'

'I haven't been a soldier for a long time now. Doesn't stop me from protecting myself. Or people who need it.'

'No, no. I cannot. I just . . . I just want to find my wife and go home.'

Eddie and Nina traded downbeat looks: the chances of Ock's wife still being alive were vanishingly small. But they said nothing, instead watching the upper gate draw closer. 'Everyone get ready,' said the Yorkshireman, readying his gun. The action told the others what to do without the need for a translation. He took hold of the control lever. 'And . . . now!'

He slammed it to the stop position, one of the unarmed workers throwing open the gate. Everyone rushed out.

Half a dozen soldiers stood by a truck at the end of the runway. Only a couple had time to react to the unexpected new arrivals before the prisoners opened fire, bullets tearing them apart. More rounds ripped into the truck's cab, blood from the driver's head splashing the splintering windscreen.

Another couple of soldiers were standing near the blockhouse. Both fell to sharp bursts from Eddie's rifle. He checked the area. Nobody else in sight.

Nobody *alive*. There were large piles of rubble that had been brought up from below but not loaded for disposal. As before, the reason was appallingly clear. More workers lay still and bloodied amongst the debris, twisted in the frozen agonies of death.

Ock let out a keening cry, staring in horror at one of the bodies. He ran to the motionless woman and fell to his knees. Nina felt a deep dread. 'Is she . . . your wife?'

The quivering man's eyes filled with tears. He had to choke back sobs before being able to speak. 'Yes . . .'

She regarded the dead woman with an almost overpowering sadness, knowing she would feel just as lost in the same situation. 'I'm sorry. I'm so sorry.'

He tried to reply, but couldn't form the words. All he managed was a moan as he bent lower until his face almost touched the floor, gripping his wife's still hand. The other prisoners looked on with sympathy, some offering whispered condolences. Finally a word in Korean escaped his lips – spoken not with grief, but with anger. He jerked back upright and repeated it in an enraged scream as tears rolled down his face.

Eddie looked on sorrowfully, then noticed something in the huge hangar beyond. Or rather, the *absence* of something. 'Shit!' The three missile transporters were gone – along with their cargo. But he could still hear the echoing roar of powerful diesel engines. With some of the prisoners following, he ran to the runway. The sound grew louder. He peered cautiously around the corner to look down the main tunnel.

The TELs were approaching its mouth, travelling in a convoy with several jeeps, another two-ton truck like the bullet-ravaged one nearby, and the 4x4 in which he and Nina had been brought to Facility 17. As he watched, one of the jeeps veered off sharply and skidded to a halt, its occupants jumping out. Even at this distance, Eddie could tell from his clothing that one was an officer rather than a regular soldier.

Bok.

The echoes of massed gunfire from the runway's far end had alerted Bok that something was wrong. He ordered his driver to swing out of the convoy and stop.

The other vehicles all slowed in response. 'Bok!' barked Kang over the walkie-talkie. 'What's happening?'

The security chief got out and stared back down the tunnel. In the distance, he saw figures spilling from one side of the blockhouse – and dead soldiers on the ground. 'Some of the prisoners have escaped! They've—' One person stood out clearly, even from this distance. Red hair. 'The American woman, she's still alive!' he cried in disbelief.

Kang's voice turned even colder than usual. 'None of them get out. Do you understand?'

Bok stiffened at the understated but clear threat. That Wilde and her husband had survived in the first place was already a black mark for him; his rank and privileged background would not help him if he failed to prevent them from escaping the facility. 'They'll be dead when you reach the airbase, sir,' he replied.

'It had better not take that long, Bok.'

'Yes, sir.' The major shouted hurried orders into the radio. Three more jeeps pulled over to form a barricade across the runway, the soldiers jumping out and aiming their rifles down the tunnel. The rest of the convoy accelerated again, clearing the mountainside and rumbling away into the night.

Bok clipped the radio back to his belt, trying to conceal his worry, then looked around. At this range, without telescopic sights, his men's Type 58 rifles would be all but useless, but there were other weapons nearby that could do the job. Flanking the runway just outside the tunnel entrance were the two minigun turrets, intended to repel invaders trying to enter Facility 17 . . . but also able to turn through a hundred and eighty degrees to prevent anyone from *leaving* it.

'The guns!' he shouted. 'Man the guns – point them into the facility.' Two men ran for one, while he and a soldier from his jeep started for the other. 'No one gets out of there alive!'

Eddie saw the North Korean troops head for the turrets. 'Shit! Everyone get back, get into cover!' He pushed Nina around the

499

corner as he withdrew, but several prisoners had already raced past him on to the runway. Without Ock to translate, they didn't understand his warning – and by the time they realised for themselves, it was too late.

The miniguns opened fire with chainsaw snarls, sending twin streams of bullets down the runway, tracers giving them the appearance of laser beams. The gunners swept them across the end of the hangar, fifty rounds impacting every second. Concrete splintered under the onslaught, lines of death homing in on the running figures—

The miniguns only used standard 7.62-millimetre ammunition, allowing them to draw upon North Korea's vast reserves of Kalashnikov-compatible rounds, but fired at such a fearsome rate that the result was like being struck by cannon shells. The first man to be hit literally *disintegrated*, his body blasted into a bloody spray. The woman beside him screamed as her arm was ripped off at the elbow, but her agony lasted only a moment before the gunfire cut her in half.

The other escapees tried to retreat, but there was nowhere to hide. More fell, exploding into bloodied shreds. A few managed to get behind the truck, but it did not save them. The minigun streams tore its bodywork into shrapnel, tearing apart the men and women cowering behind it before its fuel tank exploded, scattering blazing wreckage all around.

The gunners focused their attention on the spot where the fugitives had emerged. Eddie and Nina fled as the corner of the cavern wall shattered behind them, blasted apart by the six-barrelled weapons—

Sudden silence as the miniguns ceased firing. 'What happened?' Nina gasped. 'Why've they stopped?'

Eddie signalled for everyone to stay put, then moved back through the haze of dust to risk a brief peek around the bullet-gnawed corner. Both turrets still pointed down the runway. 'Run out of targets. Probably worried about wasting ammo, too – if those miniguns are like American ones, they can fire over three thousand rounds per minute.'

'So what can we do?'

'There's no way we'll get past 'em,' he replied, grim-faced. 'We—'

Ock pushed past him, now holding a rifle. 'We kill them,' he growled. 'We kill them!'

Eddie dragged him back. 'No, don't!' cried Nina. 'They'll kill *you*!'

'I do not care! She is dead, she is *dead*!' A despairing wave at his wife's body. 'I have nothing left!'

'You'd be dead before you got twenty feet,' Eddie told him. 'You'll die for nothing! Would your wife want that?'

The question shook Ock. 'No, she . . .' He slumped. 'No. But what can we do? We are trapped!'

Eddie looked back into the cavernous underground factory. His gaze fell upon the ranks of vehicles near the cargo elevator. 'Come on,' he said, hurrying to one.

'You want to *float* out of here?' Nina asked incredulously. 'In that?' Even with its military modifications, the four-seater hovercraft seemed almost toy-like.

'I want to see how thick this armour is.' He examined the wedge of plating covering the craft's nose. 'Everyone get back!' He waved for the others to retreat, then raised his gun and fired a single shot. The round banged off the armour and screamed away into the depths of the hangar. The drab camouflage paint spalled away around the impact point to reveal dull grey metal beneath, but the surface itself had only a slight dent.

'What was that for?' Nina asked.

'Miniguns use regular rifle ammo,' he replied. 'And a rifle round hardly scratched this.' He knocked on the armour. 'Looks like Chobham, or summat similar. They'll have built these to charge through the demilitarised zone – the South Koreans won't be able to hurt 'em with regular weapons until they're already over the border.'

'At which point they can just shoot them in the back as they go past,' Nina pointed out, indicating the hovercraft's open, unprotected body behind the plating. 'And they'll do the same to us if we try to get out in these!'

'I wasn't thinking of getting out in 'em.' A glance at another vehicle, one of the microlight aircraft. 'We've got to take out those turrets first, and I think I know how . . .' He turned to look across the runway. Some of the giant fuel tanks were visible beyond the blockhouse. 'Ock!' he called. 'Tell everyone I need help with some hover bovver!'

Bok stared intently down the runway. The dust from the miniguns' assault had settled, nothing moving at the tunnel's far end except the flames licking in the wrecked truck. He had glimpsed someone looking out around the corner, but they retreated before the guns could be brought to bear.

He was about to raise his radio to order some of the men along the barricade to move into the tunnel when a low growl reached him from the depths of the mountain. 'They've started an engine,' he announced instead. 'They must be making a run for it. Whatever they're driving, I don't want it to reach the exit.'

Acknowledgements crackled through the ether. The man operating the turret pointed the minigun at the bullet-riddled corner. Bok watched as the distant engine roared, eagerly awaiting its appearance.

But nothing came into view. It sounded as though the vehicle was being driven across the facility behind the blockhouse. 'They're up to something! Everyone be ready!'

★ ★ ★

Ock stood in the hovercraft's front passenger seat, looking over the armour as Eddie piloted the little vehicle across the factory floor. 'Right, right!' the Korean shouted as it drifted towards a stand of machinery on the missile production line. 'Go right!'

The Englishman flicked the rudder, bringing the hovercraft around in a wide, slithering turn. The narrow viewing slits were practically useless, too low to give him a clear view even when hunched down in the uncomfortable fibreglass seat. 'Are we clear?' he asked as the obstacle slid past.

'Yes, yes! Go forward!'

Eddie straightened out. He had driven similar vehicles before and knew how much of a handful they could be, but the nose-heavy North Korean example was even harder to control. He glanced back, seeing several prisoners following at a run. 'How much further?'

'Not far . . . Stop! Stop, now!'

Eddie closed the throttle. The hovercraft wallowed, skidding along on a residual cushion of air before its Kevlar-toughened rubber skirt deflated. The Korean grabbed the mounted gun to steady himself as the vehicle lurched to a stop. 'You okay?' Eddie asked.

Ock's eyes still betrayed his grief-stricken rage. 'Yes,' was his curt reply. 'What are we doing?'

The Yorkshireman climbed out. Before him were the fuel tanks, ranks of great metal cylinders rising above a rat's nest of pipework. 'There should be two different kinds of fuel. One'll probably be kerosene – or paraffin, it's called in Britain. The other'll be a kind of nitric acid.'

Ock surveyed the tanks, spotting warning signs. He pointed at one of the larger vessels. 'Yes, that is kerosene. And that' – he turned to indicate a group of smaller, but still capacious, tanks about a hundred feet from the first set – 'is acid.' He gave Eddie an odd look. 'You said you were a soldier, but you know this. Are you a scientist?'

The Englishman laughed. 'Not even close! I don't know if Nina'd find that funny or be offended.'

The other prisoners arrived. 'Okay, we need a barrel of the stuff from those tanks,' Eddie pointed at the kerosene store, 'and another barrel from those.' He turned to indicate the containers of augmented nitric acid as Ock translated his instructions. 'Fill 'em about two thirds full. But whatever you do, *do not fucking spill any*. If they mix, if they even *touch*, they'll explode – and the more there is, the bigger the explosion.' Widening eyes told him that the danger had been successfully communicated. 'It looks like you can drain stuff using those valves, so get a barrel of each and bring 'em back to the hovercraft. *Really* carefully,' he added as the group split up.

'What are you going to do?' Ock asked.

'If we load up the hovercraft with the barrels, we can send it down the runway to crash into those jeeps they've set up as a barricade. The barrels go flying, the stuff inside mixes – and *boom*. We've got our way out.'

The Korean was sceptical. 'It is a very big runway.'

'It'll be a very big boom. Trust me.' The metal drums he had seen stacked near the tanks were of a standard fifty-five-gallon size, over two hundred litres. If they were filled as he had asked, the combination of more than seventy gallons of hypergolic fuel and oxidiser would produce an extremely satisfying explosion.

The remaining prisoners, Nina with them, approached pushing one of the microlights. 'Okay,' she demanded, 'why exactly did you want us to bring this?'

'Because we need a way out of here.'

'And the half-dozen jeeps back there aren't suitable because . . . ?'

'Because A, they'll never catch up with the missile convoy on that twisty road, and B, there'll probably be a shitload of troops coming back *up* the road once they realise what we've done.'

'Which is?'

'Blow this place to fuck.' He took out a stick of dynamite, then smiled and nodded towards the fuel tanks. 'About fifty thousand gallons of rocket fuel ought to do it.'

'Yeah, it might,' she said with alarm.

'And speaking of . . .' Eddie watched as three straining men carefully carried a barrel of kerosene towards the hovercraft. A lid had been placed loosely over its top, but he could still hear its contents sloshing about. 'Put it here,' he said, pointing at one of the rear seats. Ock relayed the command, the trio carefully lowering it into position.

By the time they were done, the other group had returned from the more distant tanks. The noise from their drum was far more worrying: a frothing hiss as the nitric acid tried to eat through the metal. The lid had been pushed down more firmly to hold in the choking fumes, though one of the prisoners carrying it had a very sickly appearance from accidental exposure while filling the barrel. Eddie directed them to the other rear seat. 'Careful, *really* careful,' he warned as they lowered it. 'Okay, that's good.' There was a rolled-up camouflage tarp in the rear; he used it to wedge the second container in place. 'Let's get this thing moving.'

'Wait, so now what?' Nina asked. 'You're just going to push it out and hope it goes in the right direction? These things steer like cows on ice skates!'

Eddie was about to make a sarcastic reply, but Ock spoke first. 'I will drive it.'

'You what?' said the Englishman. 'You can't – you'll be killed!'

The Korean fixed him with an unwavering look. 'I do not care. I have lost everything.' He gestured in the direction of his late wife. 'I want to kill them. I want to kill *Bok*! If I do, you can all get out of here.'

'There has to be another way,' Nina said, pleading.

'No. I must do it. Now, before . . . before I become afraid.' He pushed past Eddie to climb into the pilot's seat.

'They'll be shooting at you, so let's at least give you a chance to shoot back,' Eddie told him. As well as the tarp, the hovercraft held various other supplies, including an ammunition box. He opened it and pulled out a belt of bullets. The weapon on the pintle was a North Korean copy of a Soviet-era PK machine gun; while Ock was familiarising himself with the vehicle's controls, he quickly loaded the belt. 'Okay, that's about a hundred rounds,' he said. 'There's a lever there to aim it, and,' he pointed out the mechanical linkage running down from the gun's trigger to between the front seats, 'if you pull that? Ock's gon' give it to ya.'

Ock nodded, then restarted the engine, the skirt inflating. 'I am ready,' he said, testing the rudder pedals. Even with the main propeller only idling, there was enough airflow to nudge the craft's tail around.

Nina hurriedly retreated from the blades. 'You don't have to do this.'

He looked back at her, fearful but also determined. 'Yes, I do.'

'My Korean's a bit rusty, so you'd better tell the others that if this works, they need to run for the outside as soon as the way's clear,' said Eddie. Ock did so, then the Yorkshireman held out his hand. 'Good luck.'

'Thank you.' The Korean shook it before turning back to the controls. 'Goodbye. I hope you see your home again.'

'So do I,' said Nina morosely.

Eddie pulled off both barrel lids, then Ock edged the main fan to full power. The hovercraft moved off, making a sweeping turn towards the tunnel.

★ ★ ★

The return of the distant engine noise had drawn the attention of the soldiers at the tunnel entrance. 'They're coming!' Bok shouted into his radio. 'Ready all weapons!' The men along the vehicular barricade raised their rifles, the two miniguns spinning up their barrels ready to fire.

The hovercraft came into view. 'There it is – quick, quick!' the major snapped, waving for his gunner to lock on. By the time he found his target, it had already turned on to the runway and started towards them, rapidly gaining speed. '*Fire!*'

The buzzing rasp of the miniguns and the stuttering bark of the soldiers' rifles was drowned out by the thunderous clanging of bullets off the hovercraft's frontal armour. Ock cried out in terror, before realising that he was still alive . . . and still moving, the tunnel walls rolling past at an increasing pace.

He squinted into one of the narrow slits in the plating. Paint flecks whipping through it stung his face, but he still made out the line of jeeps, and the gun emplacements on each side.

Bok was in one of them. He knew that an explosion at the runway's centre had the best chance of clearing the way for the prisoners to escape – but the thought of the man who had ordered his wife's murder made him veer angrily to the right instead, aiming straight for the turret.

More bullets pounded the armour like a hail of hammers. Fibreglass cracked behind him, the propeller's hooped cowling splintering. His turn had exposed the rear of his craft to the other minigun, and it would only get worse the closer he got to the tunnel mouth.

The gun—

He turned the handle to swing the PK towards the left side of the entrance – then pulled its trigger control.

The noise was almost deafening, broken links from the ammo belt showering down on his head as the machine gun roared.

The pounding of bullets against the hovercraft's prow abruptly halved as the minigunner dropped behind sandbags. Another look ahead. Bok's turret was right in front of him. The flame from its Gatling gun grew brighter, the storm of lead hitting with greater force as he closed in.

The hovercraft shuddered with each impact. Ock glanced back at the two barrels. Fumes trailed from the drum of nitric acid, the kerosene beside it slopping and splashing almost to the open top. He swung the machine gun back across and pulled the trigger again, sending a snarling burst of bullets at his target. The strobing flame briefly cut out as the gunner ducked, then returned with even more fearsome intensity.

The other minigun locked back on – and this time caused more than superficial damage. One of the rudders shredded, its supports shearing away. The hovercraft slewed around. Ock tried to counter it, but the vehicle was now even harder to control, swinging away from the turret.

He cursed, struggling to straighten out. More rounds hammered the armour – which started to warp and buckle under the relentless assault. One of the jeeps came into view through the slits. He was running out of both room to manoeuvre and time. Finally regaining control, he aimed the hovercraft at the vehicle with a defiant roar—

Bok clenched a fist in triumph as a chunk of armour blew off the hovercraft, only for the gesture to freeze in surprise as he saw something in the rear of its passenger compartment.

Barrels, one of them leaving a wispy trail of what looked like smoke . . .

Not smoke. *Vapour*.

The fugitive had come from the rocket fuel stores. His mind made the connection—

'*Run!*' he screamed in horrified realisation, scrambling over the circle of sandbags surrounding the turret even though he knew he was doomed. The gunner looked around at him in surprise. 'Get out of here, run!'

The hovercraft's main propeller was torn apart by the withering gunfire, shedding blades – but it was too late to stop it.

Ock howled as the hovercraft ploughed into the jeep. The barrels flew forward, their contents sluicing out . . .

And mixing.

The spontaneous ignition of the two chemicals was instant – and devastating.

Both vehicles disintegrated in a colossal ball of fire.

42

The explosion vaporised everything within fifty feet and tore a crater in the concrete. The soldiers further away were no better off, the shock wave flipping the other jeeps in flames across the runway and pulverising bones and organs.

Even at the end of the tunnel, the noise of the detonation was overpowering. 'Christ on a bike!' said Eddie, wincing. He looked down the runway. The vehicles that had made up the barricade were scattered like unwanted toys, crumpled and burning. Both gun emplacements had been flattened. 'I knew that stuff was dangerous, but I didn't realise *how* dangerous.'

Nina regarded the smoking crater sadly. 'Oh God. Ock . . .'

'He didn't die for nothing,' Eddie assured her. He turned to the prisoners, who were staring in shock at the destruction. 'This is your chance – go, go!' When nobody responded immediately, he switched to communicating by gesture, shooing them away. '*Vamos*, go on, get out! Leg it!' They finally got the message and hurried towards freedom.

'What about us?' Nina asked.

He looked back at the microlight. 'We need to get that thing ready to fly, then I'll rig the rocket fuel tanks to blow.'

They ran to the little plane, Nina eyeing it dubiously. 'How long will that take?'

Eddie took out the dynamite and fuses. 'Hopefully not as long as it takes for the Norks to send more men back to get us!'

★ ★ ★

Colonel Kang turned sharply in his seat at the sound of a powerful explosion higher up the mountain. A fiery glow was visible through the trees. 'Bok!' he snapped into the radio. 'Bok, report! What was that?'

No answer came. 'Rocket fuel,' said Mikkelsson from the rear seat. 'That is the only thing that could cause such a blast. It must be Wilde and Chase.'

The numbed Sarah looked around at him. 'They . . . they're still alive?'

'They will not be for long,' Kang growled, switching channels. 'This is Kang! Send squads from the evacuation muster point back to the base. The spies have escaped, with the aid of criminals – find them and destroy them!'

Eddie and Nina moved the microlight on to the runway. 'Okay,' said the Englishman, taking hold of the trailing edge of one of the pusher propeller's blades, 'hope I can do this without chopping any fingers off!' He checked that Nina was holding down the starter button, then sharply shoved the blade down, jerking his hands clear as the engine clattered into life. The prop buzzed up to speed, a snap of displaced air stinging his fingertips – and the plane immediately began to roll along the concrete. 'Whoa, whoa! Pull back the throttle!'

'It *is* pulled back!' Nina protested as she jogged alongside it. Even at minimum revs, the propeller was still spinning fast enough to push the lightweight aircraft along.

'Hit the kill switch!' She pushed another button. The engine spluttered and cut out. The propeller abruptly stopped, the microlight trundling to a halt. 'Okay, that's not ideal,' he said, catching up. There was nothing to hand that might serve as chocks for the wheels. 'I'll have to start it right before take-off.'

'*After* you light the fuses?' Nina said unhappily. He had

already rigged the tanks with explosives, using the full lengths of both coils.

'Yeah, I know. Help me move it back over there so I won't have to run as far.'

They wheeled the little plane to the runway's end. The microlight was basic in the extreme, the tandem seats bolted to a simple tubular frame coated in something resembling Teflon, presumably a radar-absorbing substance; Kang had claimed that the tiny craft had stealth capabilities. From outside, the faceted front bodywork shielding the pilot appeared quite high-tech, but beneath it was revealed as nothing more than wooden panels painted with the same material. 'Yeah, this fills me with confidence,' Nina said, holding up a safety belt – a simple lap strap of the kind found on airliners.

'Could be worse,' Eddie joked. 'At least it's *got* seat belts. Beats holding on with your bare hands!' They brought the plane into position. 'Okay, I'll light the fuses.'

'How long will we have before they blow?' Nina asked as he ran off, rifle slung over a shoulder.

'A minute. Maybe.'

She got into the rear seat. 'Confidence? Still not filled with it!'

Eddie grinned, then continued to the fuel tanks. The gap between them was too wide for the fuses to meet, ruling out a simultaneous detonation; he figured instead that blowing the nitric acid tanks first, then spilling kerosene on to the flood, would give him the best chance of escape. 'Let's see how the big bang theory works in practice,' he said, lighting a match and touching it to the first fuse.

A spark sizzled along the length of line. He checked his watch, then raced to the second fuse and ignited it before running at full pelt back to the microlight.

Another glance at his watch as he reached the plane. Only thirty seconds remaining. 'Okay, let's get this thing started!'

Nina leaned over the front seat to push the starter as he spun the propeller. It made a half-turn . . .

And stopped.

The microlight shuddered, the engine coughing briefly before falling silent. Eddie tried again, with the same result. 'You pushing that button?'

'Yes, I'm pushing the damn button!' Nina snapped.

'Okay, okay! Let's give it another shot.' A third attempt. The engine wheezed mockingly at him as the blades juddered once more.

He looked at the fuel tanks. The spark was almost at the dynamite he had planted on the nitric acid containers. 'Oh *arse.*'

'Still pressing the button!' his wife said with rising alarm.

Eddie swung the propeller again, and again, glaring at the portraits of the North Korean dictators smirking down at him from the blockhouse. 'You can . . . fuck right off, Kim . . . Nobhead!' he growled between pushes.

The engine stuttered and caught. The prop whirled—

The fizzing spark reached the dynamite.

Sharp blasts ripped open two of the tanks, a sizzling hiss echoing through the cavern as a tsunami of acid burst out and swept across the floor. To Nina's dismay, part of the wavefront was heading for them. 'Time to go!'

The aircraft was already moving. Eddie caught up and jumped into the front seat. Too late, he realised he was sitting on his seat-belt buckle, but there was no time to pull it out and secure himself. 'Great, I *am* gonna have to hold on with my bare hands!' he complained as he pushed the throttle lever fully forward. The engine noise rose to a screech, the microlight shimmying on its little tricycle wheels before straightening out.

He looked along the runway. In the distance, debris from the explosion littered the concrete, along with the burning wrecks of the vehicles that had formed the barricade.

More explosions behind them – and the huge cavern filled with flame as the spraying kerosene met its oxidiser.

A massive chain reaction tore through the facility, the ranks of fuel tanks detonating like hundred-ton bombs and smashing support pillars. The ceiling collapsed on to the missile production line with earthquake force, forcing the fireball through the tunnel.

A gunpowder explosion down a rifle barrel – and the microlight was the bullet.

A fragile, flammable bullet.

'Eddie!' shrieked Nina, feeling rising heat as a wall of fire rushed after them.

'Yeah, I know!' Eddie yelled back. The wing's fabric snapped taut as the airflow started to generate lift. He pulled back the joystick to raise the nose. The front wheel left the ground . . . then dropped back again. 'Shit! Come on, take off, you piece of crap!'

They were rapidly approaching the tunnel mouth – but the fireball was gaining, pushing a wave of searing air before it. Eddie angled to avoid the largest pieces of debris from Ock's suicide attack, but there were so many that a collision seemed inevitable.

He pulled back the stick again. The nose strained upwards, but they still hadn't reached take-off speed. The rear wheels skipped and hopped over the concrete.

The rubble field rushed at them—

Eddie swerved to avoid a football-sized lump of stone. The front wheel cleared it by inches, only to hit one of the rears, snapping off the outrigger supporting it. The plane tipped sideways. He pushed the stick to level out, but in doing so the front wheel thumped back on to the runway.

A blazing jeep loomed. Flames ahead and behind as the inferno swept towards open air—

Eddie yanked the joystick again. This time the little plane left the ground – and remained airborne.

Heading straight for the jeep.

He yelled and veered away, the fuselage barely missing the wreck – only for the other outrigger to be clipped off. He fought to keep control as the plane burst out into the night—

The tunnel mouth erupted like a volcano.

An enormous gush of flame blasted from the entrance, lighting up the surrounding landscape with a hellfire glow. Debris arced across the plateau, the blast hurling metal and stone for hundreds of metres as Facility 17 was consumed by an explosion powerful enough to shake the entire mountain.

The dazzling flare faded . . . revealing the microlight straining skywards.

'Oh my God!' shrieked Nina. The heat of the explosion had singed her hair, exposed skin feeling as if she had leaned into an oven, but she was still alive. She looked up to check that the wing had not caught fire, and was thankful to see that the fabric was intact.

Her relief was short-lived as she realised their situation. They were far from safe. The plateau spread out below as they gained height. Lights stood out on the winding road descending the mountainside: the missile convoy making its way down . . . and trucks coming back up. Soldiers sent to reclaim the base – or what was left of it – and hunt down the escaped prisoners. Beyond was nothing but dark forest all the way to the airbase far below. Even from this distance, the enormous Antonov freighter stood out clearly at one end of the long runway.

Eddie brought the microlight around in pursuit of the TELs. The plane had reached its top speed, which he estimated to be only around fifty miles per hour; there was no speed indicator, or for that matter any instruments beyond a crude artificial horizon and a couple of gauges. 'We should be able to catch up.'

Nina had to raise her voice over the wind and the buzzing engine. 'We're really going after them?'

'It's all we can do. Well, apart from letting a bunch of pissed-off North Koreans torture and kill us. I know this thing's supposed to be stealthy, but I don't fancy our chances of crossing the border without getting flak shot up our arses. And that's if we can even reach it.'

'So our choices are get killed, or try to stop them escaping with a set of nuclear missiles – and *then* get killed?'

He looked back at her, downcast. 'Afraid so, love. We're stuck in North Korea with no backup, and we've just made 'em really, *really* mad at us. And it's not like we can blend in with the locals – the red hair's a bit of a giveaway.'

'Just a little. But what can we do to stop them?'

'I've still got one stick of dynamite. We can fly over the first transporter and bomb it. If we get lucky, it'll block the road – the other trucks might even crash into it.'

'And after that?'

'No idea. But I don't think . . . I don't think we're going to get home to Macy.' The name was abruptly choked off by emotion.

Nina felt the same overwhelming sense of loss and grief. 'We shouldn't have come here,' she said, tears blurring her vision. 'We shouldn't have done this! Oh God, Eddie, why the *fuck* did we do this? We're going to die and we're . . . we're going to leave Macy all alone!'

'She won't be alone. She—'

'She won't have *us*! Eddie, she's going to have her parents taken from her – she's going to go through the same thing as I did! Why did we . . . *Why?*'

Her husband was silent for a long moment as she sobbed. Finally he spoke. 'If we hadn't come here, they'd still be shipping out the missiles and they'd be knocking out even more plutonium from the Crucible. At least we stopped them making any more nukes, and we've still got a chance of keeping those down there from leaving the country.'

'I'm sure that'll make Macy feel so much better,' she said bitterly.

'Yeah, I know. But even if Mikkelsson thinks that if everyone has nukes nobody'll dare use 'em, he's full of shit. It only takes one psycho megalomaniac and it'll all kick off, and it's not like there's any shortage of them in the world.' He made a course adjustment, then looked at Nina again. 'I don't want Macy to have to face that. So if we're going to die either way, then at least we can do like Ock and make it count for something.'

'Fight to the end, as you like to say?'

'I say it because I believe it. We can still make a difference. I'd prefer to do that without fucking *dying*, but, well . . .'

She wiped her eyes, then squeezed his shoulder lovingly. 'You know something, Edward J. Chase? Probably nobody else but me would think so, but you are actually kind of noble. In your own special, sweary way.'

'I try my best. All I can do, really.' He leaned over to regard the vehicles below. 'Okay. Let's do this.'

The convoy had just emerged from a zigzagging series of hairpins on to a relatively straight section of road. The SUV carrying Kang and the Mikkelssons was in the lead, the truck bearing Captain Sek and his team – and the warheads – following. Behind that was a jeep, then the three TELs and their deadly loads, the missiles lying flat in their hydraulic cradles. Bringing up the rear was a second jeep.

Eddie fumbled the dynamite and matchbook from his pocket and passed them to Nina. 'Get ready to light it when I say.' The convoy was picking up speed, going faster than seemed safe considering the state of the road and the sheer size of the trucks. Kang was presumably in a rush to reach the airbase. The Yorkshireman looked ahead. 'Bollocks.'

'What?' asked Nina.

'Power lines in the way.' He peered into the moonlit darkness. 'I'll have to come in from the valley to avoid the wires.' He changed course, swinging out over the steep-sided gorge below. 'You ready with the dynamite?'

'Yeah – if I can light a match in this wind.'

He looked over at the road, now to their right. The leading vehicles were still picking up speed, though the driver of the first TEL was apparently having second thoughts, allowing a gap to open up. That was good – a slower target would be easier to hit. Eddie judged the speeds and distances again. 'Okay – light it!'

The rearguard jeep had three soldiers aboard. They were in the dark about what was happening: all they knew was that Facility 17 had been attacked, and their job was to protect the missile transporters at all costs. The brutal discipline of North Korea's military had been drummed into them, hard; taking actions or even asking questions about anything beyond the scope of their orders was an invitation for punishment.

So when the man in the rear seat heard a buzzing noise in the dark sky, he did not immediately open fire upon it. Since their instructions had been to stop anyone pursuing them by *road*, he merely tapped the shoulder of the driver, his immediate superior. 'Sir! There's something up there – I think it's one of our little planes!'

The driver, his rank the Korean equivalent of a lowly private, first class, was no more ready to take risks than his subordinate – especially when said risk would involve shooting at a secret aircraft of the People's Army. 'Get on the radio to Colonel Kang,' he ordered the other passenger. 'Tell him about the plane, and ask what we should do.'

The soldier made the call, twitching in fear when Kang's voice roared back at him. 'What do you *think* you should do, you idiot? Shoot it down – *kill them*!'

The two privates hurriedly raised their rifles. A small flickering light appeared on the aircraft, giving them a target . . .

It took Nina three attempts to light a match, and another two before the fuse caught. 'Okay, it's fizzling!'

The microlight was now level with the second TEL, passing over the line of pylons. Eddie got ready to turn for his bombing run. 'Give it to me!'

She reached out to put it into his upraised hand—

Gunfire sounded from behind. Bullets whipped past, a couple punching holes through the fabric wing and another striking the engine block just behind Nina. She shrieked, flinching just as Eddie threw the aircraft into a hard bank away from the road, snapping his hand back to grab the dashboard. The dynamite tumbled into the forest.

'Shit!' he yelled as a loud detonation came from below. 'So much for stealth!'

The firing stopped. Nina looked back through the propeller at the retreating lights. 'Great, now what do we do? That was the last stick!'

Her husband curved the plane around, gaining altitude. 'We either give up and see how far this thing can take us before we run out of fuel . . . or we do something crazy.'

'Crazy, or stupid?'

'Usually the same thing with us, isn't it?' The convoy came back into view. 'If I can get *on to* one of the transporters, I can take out the crew, then go full Mad Max and use it to ram the others off the road.'

'You're right,' Nina exclaimed. 'That's crazy *and* stupid. And what would I be doing while all this was going on?'

'You'd be flying the plane, obviously.'

'Well obviously!' she hooted.

'It's pretty easy. Like playing a video game.'

'I hate video games!'

'Except for when you were obsessed with Candy Crush! You'll get the hang of it long before you hit the ground.'

'I'm not reassured. And how am I supposed to take the controls when you're in the front seat?'

'You'll have to wait till I've jumped out!' He twisted to give her a small smile. 'You can do it, trust me.'

'It's *you* I'm worried about,' she replied unhappily. 'Once you jump . . . that's it. We'll never see each other again.'

The smile disappeared. 'Yeah, when you put it like that, it really does seem like a shit idea.' He sighed. 'But I'm not just going to give up and run until they shoot me.' He altered course to cross behind the convoy and take the plane over the trees above the road. 'And I've got this,' he added, nodding at the rifle on his shoulder. 'So at least I've got a fighting chance.'

'But I don't. Eddie, what am I supposed to do without you?' It was a question that went beyond the immediate future.

A long pause. 'What you always do,' he said. 'You survive. Somehow.'

'Not this time.' Her voice quavered. 'Not without you.'

'Hey, you never know – maybe we'll both survive. I dunno *how*, but . . .' His smile returned, warm even through sadness. 'But I'll only get one shot at this, so I've got to take it. I love you.'

'I love you,' she replied, wrapping both arms around his chest. 'I love you so much.'

'Enough not to think I'm insane for doing what I'm about to do?'

'I wouldn't go *that* far.' She wiped away tears. 'Go on then, you damn fool. Go and save the world. Again.'

'We really need to start charging for it, don't we?' The convoy was now out of sight behind the trees, though occasional flickers of light through the foliage gave away its position. He turned the plane towards it, pulling back the throttle lever. The engine slowed, the propeller noise dropping considerably. 'Huh. Okay, maybe it's stealthier than I thought. I did think that trying to cross the border in a squad of lawnmowers probably wouldn't work.'

'So what's the plan?'

'They won't be able to see us until we come over the trees. I'll bring it as low and slow as I can, then jump out. The second I go, you climb over the seat and grab the controls. You'll be heading out over the valley, so that should give you enough time to sort yourself out before you hit anything.'

'And then what?'

'I'd tell you to fly this thing as far away as you can, but . . .' Both knew full well that she had no intention of leaving him. 'Just make sure you get clear.' One last loving look back at her, then: 'All right, here we go.'

He brought the microlight lower over the moonlit treetops, angling to cut across the road. The leading vehicles came into sight, Kang's SUV and the troop truck now some distance ahead of the rest of the convoy. 'Okay, get ready, get ready . . .' He tensed, swinging both legs over the side. 'Get ready . . .'

The transporters swept into view below, the aircraft crossing above the rearmost—

'*Now!*'

Eddie jumped.

The drop on to the missile was not great, only around eight feet – but there was no purchase on the smooth, curved surface. He slithered off, hitting the rocket's hydraulic crane arm, hard, and rolling off it towards the ground below—

One hand caught the transporter's side as he fell. He swung from it, dangling with the huge wheels churning just inches away. 'Arsing cockery!' he gasped as his gun bounced off the road and disappeared over the edge of the gorge.

He flailed his free arm, managing to get a secure hold. Relieved, he pulled himself higher, glancing forward to check the road ahead.

Startled eyes stared back at him in the truck's wing mirror.

The transporter's driver barked a hurried command to the other men in the cab – as the chatter of gunfire resumed from behind.

43

The men in the trailing jeep could hear the microlight still shadowing them, but couldn't see it – until it overflew the transporter ahead. They opened fire as it continued across the valley.

Eddie's leap threw the little aircraft wildly off balance, sending it into a steep climb as it banked drunkenly to the right. Nina, clambering into the front seat, screamed as she was almost pitched after her husband. Bracing herself, she pushed the stick to the left, levelling out with a lurch – only for more bullets to lance up at her.

The wing took several hits, fabric tearing. She looked up to see a yard-long rent in the dark material, its edges flapping furiously. The microlight rolled again. 'Oh shit, *shit!*' she panted as it veered back towards the road.

The convoy reappeared below, growing larger as the plane lost height. She was past the third transporter, heading for the second as another burst of fire came from the jeep. The wing puckered again, the engine taking more hammerblow impacts – and stuttering.

She tried to swing away from the looming TEL, but the controls felt as if they were submerged in molasses. The nose pitched upwards, too slowly. Glaring red tail lights swelled before her like devilish eyes—

The little plane finally banked, but too late.

The wingtip clipped the missile, swinging the microlight sharply back around. It crashed against the rocket's left side, its wing snagging on the great hydraulic clamp securing the weapon for transport.

The fuselage tore loose. Nina was almost flung on to the road, just catching one of the ladder rungs running along the length of the missile's erector arm. The broken bodywork hit the road below her, breaking apart.

Eddie hauled himself up on to the third transporter, crouching on a narrow footplate beside the missile. The gunfire from the trailing jeep had stopped – he guessed they were afraid of hitting the rocket – but he could no longer hear the microlight's engine. Hopefully Nina had got clear—

The reason for the aircraft's silence was frighteningly revealed as its mangled remains bowled past. The propeller clanged off the TEL's side just beneath him, slashing a foot-long tear in the sheet metal. The jeep swerved to avoid the debris, falling back.

Nina hadn't been in the wreckage. He looked ahead, desperate for any clue to his wife's fate. The road curved, bringing the rest of the convoy back into view – and revealing her hanging from the second transporter's side.

The TEL's wheels whirled beneath Nina. Above the long blank slab of the transporter's side the ripped wing flapped like a flag, the lines that had secured it to its frame now whipping in the wind.

Shock giving way to fear, she pulled herself up. Arms straining, she swung and tried to hook a foot over the edge of the bodywork—

Lights flashed behind her. The third transporter had pulled out, the driver waving furiously from his side window.

Warning the soldiers in her own vehicle that she was there.

★ ★ ★

Another message crackled over the SUV's radio. Kang listened with growing disbelief, then shouted an order into the mic. 'They are still alive!' he snarled to his passengers. 'They are on the transporters!'

'Perhaps we should stop so your men can get a clear shot,' said Mikkelsson icily. 'They seem to have trouble with moving targets.'

The colonel glared at him. 'We will not stop! Two people cannot have destroyed the entire facility – they *must* have had help from the American special forces you warned us about. If they take the warheads or the plutonium, it will be a disaster for my country!'

'And for you,' Sarah said quietly, her face expressionless.

Kang regarded his companions with fury. 'We will *not* stop.' He bellowed more commands into the radio. 'I want those spies dead before we reach the airbase! Do not stop for any reason! If they damage the missiles, I'll have you all shot as collaborators!' His voice rose to a spittle-flecked screech. '*Kill them, right now!*'

The jeep pulled out to overtake Eddie's TEL, the huge vehicle obligingly shifting to the right of the road to make room. As it drew alongside, the soldier in the front passenger seat stood and grabbed the ladder rungs, pulling himself aboard the transporter. The man behind him followed suit, the jeep dropping back once both were clear.

Eddie scrambled forward. The Koreans still couldn't risk shooting at him, but the first man had drawn a knife or bayonet, and his companion was doubtless doing the same. He rounded the clamp locking the missile in place and headed for the cab. The soldier was rapidly gaining on him, driven by the fearlessness of youth or the terror of being blamed for failure.

The rungs ended at the base of the rocket's nosecone. With

the warhead not fitted, the truncated tip stopped a few feet short of the transporter's cab. Eddie clambered on to the flat deck beneath it, ducking underneath the missile as if to start back down its other side – then halted.

The pursuing Korean reached the nose—

A brutal uppercut smashed against his jaw. He staggered – and Eddie clamped both hands around the rocket's support arm to pull his feet up and kick the soldier hard in the chest.

The man flew off the transporter's side with a winded scream. He hit the road with a harsh snap of breaking bones – and the jeep ran him over with a deeper, wetter crunch. The impact flung the vehicle off course. It hurtled out over the valley, arcing down to an explosive landing a hundred feet below.

Eddie lowered himself. One soldier down, but where was the other?

A flash of movement in his peripheral vision – and he spun to see the answer in the form of a glinting blade. The second man had climbed over the missile to come along its other side behind him!

Nina finally found secure footing. Panting with exertion and fear, she saw that she was about a third of the way along from the missile's foot. The microlight wing entangled on the clamp obstructed her way forward. A glance back. No sign of Eddie on the side of the last transporter, but nor was there any trace of the jeep following it.

She had no time to wonder what had happened to either. The second jeep was falling back towards her, the transporters moving over to let it by. A soldier in its rear raised his rifle—

Fearful adrenalin forced her into motion. She clambered back towards the missile's tail, expecting shots to come at any moment. But none did. Of course: if the missiles were unfuelled, the Saudis wouldn't pay hard currency for one with bullet holes in the side, and if they *were* fuelled, it might explode.

That would not protect her for long, though. The jeep matched speed with the transporter, the man in the back reaching up to pull her to her death—

Nina kicked at him, knocking him back. Angered, he tried again, but by now she had reached the TEL's rear, passing the erector system's fulcrum. Jutting out behind the missile was its launch stand, a hefty metal framework some eight feet deep that would lower to the ground as the rocket was raised vertically for firing. She climbed up on to it as the soldier made another lunge. He caught her ankle, but a swipe from her boot broke his grip and nearly did the same to his fingers. He let out a shrill cry and retreated.

She negotiated one of the stand's feet to come around the transporter's rear. The gaping bell of the rocket engine loomed menacingly behind the framework. Another soldier in the jeep stood to climb after her—

A bullet clanged off a beam inches from her head.

A private in the cab of the last transporter leaned further out of the passenger-side window. 'I almost got her!' he crowed, adjusting his rifle's aim. 'This time I'll—'

Another shot came – but not from his gun. The driver, a lieutenant, had drawn his sidearm and fired across the broad cab. The bullet hit the soldier in the temple, the other side of his skull exploding outwards. He collapsed, his twitching corpse hanging limply out of the window. His gun rattled against the door on its shoulder strap.

The other members of the transporter's crew reacted with shock. 'You heard Colonel Kang!' the young officer yelled at them. 'If anything happens to the rockets, we're *all* dead!'

'Yes, sir!' gulped a cowed soldier. 'But . . . but what about the spy?'

The lieutenant looked ahead. The men in the jeep had ducked at the rifle shot, but were now raising their heads again. 'They'll catch her. We've got a spy of our own to—'

Something thumped on to the cab roof above them.

Eddie grabbed the soldier's hand as the knife stabbed at him. The two men struggled, the Yorkshireman slowly forcing the blade upwards – then slamming the Korean's wrist against the missile's truncated nosecone. One hit, two, and the man cried out, losing his hold on the weapon. It landed near his feet. Eddie shifted position so he could kick it away, sure he could easily take down his opponent in a contest of raw strength.

The soldier also realised he was physically outmatched. In desperation, he used a large pump mounted on top of one of the vehicle's enormous fuel tanks as a springboard to hurl himself at Eddie. The Englishman fell backwards on to the cab roof, the Korean landing on top of him.

Eddie punched him, but couldn't deliver the blow with full force. The soldier responded with a screaming barrage of flailing fists. The Yorkshireman managed a partial roll to force the smaller man off him, then sent another punch at his face. This one hit home, the Korean shrieking as he lost a couple of front teeth. Eddie shoved him away—

The soldier reacted to something ahead, eyes popping wide. He grabbed a spotlight on the cab's front edge. Eddie followed his gaze – and saw that the transporter was approaching a hairpin bend. Fast.

The TEL lurched as the driver threw it into the corner. Six of its eight axles were steerable, giving it a much tighter turning circle than a conventional articulated truck, but the tyres still tore into the broken road as the mammoth vehicle started to skid. The soldier clung more tightly to his handhold, but Eddie had nothing to grip. He slithered across the roof, his head jarring against the cab's rear edge as he dropped back on to the deck behind it. Coloured stars flared before his eyes.

They cleared just in time to reveal a steep drop looming below—

He threw out his arms, one hand catching the fuel pump as he went over the edge.

The remaining jeep had been forced to brake hard as the second transporter went through the hairpin, dropping behind it to avoid being barged off the road. The soldier in the rear looked back at the third TEL, reacting in shock at the sight of two men on its roof: a soldier of the People's Army and a bald foreigner in a leather jacket. 'Look, behind us!' The other passenger turned, equally startled by the sight. 'We've got to help him!'

'What about the woman?' protested the driver. The redhead was climbing around to the truck's right-hand side.

'He's already killed one of our men!' The soldier pointed at the body hanging out of the third transporter's window. 'He must have taken out the other jeep too – he's more dangerous! If he sabotages the missile . . .'

He didn't need to say more: Kang's threat had been explicit. The driver braked again, preparing to draw alongside the last transporter as it came out of the turn.

Nina hauled herself around the launch stand and sidestepped along it to reach the fulcrum – realising too late that with the truck having turned almost one hundred and eighty degrees around the hairpin, she was once again on the outside of the road with the steeply sloping valley dropping perilously away below her. 'God *damn* it!'

She was about to go back when she saw something different about this side of the vehicle. Partway down the transporter's otherwise featureless flank was a recess, inside which lights were glowing. A control panel?

There were hefty hydraulic jacks at the TEL's rear corners, which she guessed stabilised it while the missile was raised for launch. If she could extend them, the metal feet would act as anchors, dragging the transporter to a halt. That would also force the one behind to stop, as there was not enough room for the hulking vehicles to pass one another.

Gripping the rungs, she climbed along the transporter's side. The valley spread out before her, the SUV and the truck now a long way ahead. The first TEL had also extended its lead over its two siblings.

She quickly reached the recess. It did indeed house a control panel, several red bulbs giving her enough illumination to make out a rank of switches, some gauges and two large twist-grip levers. She hesitated, then started flicking the switches. A motor whined loudly, some of the lights turning green. 'Okay, whatever I'm doing, it's something . . .'

The last bulb changed colour, a hissing thrum joining the sound of the motor – but the powering up of what she assumed were the hydraulic systems had drawn attention. A surprised shout reached her over the noise. She looked forward to see a man glaring out of the cab window at her. He withdrew . . . then the door opened and he climbed out.

Fingers straining, Eddie clung to the fuel pump as the TEL came around the hairpin. Dirt and stones spat up at his legs. The front wheel was directly below him, the long overhanging cab stretching out ahead with a corpse slumped from the window. The skidding vehicle finally straightened out, swinging him back against its side with a bang. He found purchase on the edge of the deck, dragging himself higher.

The soldier was already back on his feet.

Eddie jerked his hand clear as the man's boot stamped down. Another strike caught his thumb as he dodged again. He tried to find a new handhold, but the Korean had seen a fresh target: the dangling man's other hand, gripping the fuel pump. He drew back his leg to strike . . .

Something caught the moonlight. The knife. It too had skittered across the roof, wedging against a filler cap.

Eddie lunged for it. The soldier saw him move, twisting to kick the weapon away—

The Yorkshireman reached it first.

He drove the blade into the soldier's Achilles tendon. The Korean screamed, staggering as his leg buckled. Eddie yanked out the knife and rammed it up into his calf muscle, then pulled him forward. The man toppled over the side with a wail that ended suddenly as he hit the road face-first, breaking his neck.

Breathless, Eddie clamped his free hand around the filler cap, then dragged himself back aboard. He didn't know how many men were still in the cab, but the knife had gone with the soldier, leaving him unarmed again . . .

A metallic clatter reminded him that there was another weapon to hand. The dead soldier was still hanging from the cab window, his Type 58 rifle dangling on its strap.

Eddie swung down on to the door's step. One of the soldiers inside saw him and shouted a warning—

It did no good.

The Englishman grabbed the rifle and pointed it through the window, shooting the nearest man. The gun was set to single-shot, but he simply kept pulling the trigger with almost mechanical timing as he swung it towards each new target. The North Koreans screamed and thrashed in their death throes, blood spattering the windscreen.

The driver collapsed over the steering wheel. The transporter slowed as his foot came off the accelerator, but drifted towards the edge of the road – and the steep drop beyond. Eddie hurriedly threw open the door and scrambled inside, stepping over the bodies sprawled across the wide cabin.

White-painted stones flicked through the headlight beams, the huge truck jolting as the front wheel hit the roadside markers—

He shoved the steering wheel to the left. The TEL veered away from the edge. 'Christ! Too close,' he muttered.

The driver was not wearing a seat belt. Eddie opened the door and pushed the dead man out before taking his place. The second transporter was pulling away, the jeep having fallen back behind it. Its headlights gave him a glimpse of Nina on the other TEL's right-hand side – and a soldier making his way down the vehicle towards her.

Jaw set in determination, he declutched and dropped to a lower gear before revving the engine and re-engaging. The truck lurched forward, picking up speed as he raced to aid his wife.

44

The soldier climbed along the side of the transporter towards Nina, murderous intent clear on his face as he swung around the hydraulic clamp. She hurriedly started back towards the missile's tail, but not before turning the two levers on the control panel. Forcing the truck to stop by lowering the jacks would at least cause enough confusion to give her some slim chance of escape . . .

Confusion struck *her* as her handholds started to move.

The controls weren't for the jacks, she realised with shock. They were for the missile's erector system – which was now rising from its bed!

Mighty hydraulic rams whined, pushing the arms supporting the rocket upwards and lifting the great weapon out of its cradle. 'Oh *crap*!' she gasped.

She looked around at a shrill scream. The soldier's expression was now one of terror: one arm was trapped in the mechanism, dragging him off the footplate as it rose. He squirmed and kicked, trying to free himself, but then a gush of red flowed down the ram's smooth steel. His agonised shrieks became animalistic as his arm was sheared off with a snap of bone. He fell, thudding off the TEL's side and cartwheeling into the black valley below.

Nina cringed, then looked back as the lights of the pursuing jeep grew brighter. The vehicle was catching up again. One of the soldiers shouted into a walkie-talkie; a moment later the transporter drifted towards the inside of the road, making room

533

for the 4x4 to draw alongside. A man in the jeep's rear reached out to pull himself on to the TEL.

A yelled threat in Korean, then he started towards Nina. She hastily reversed direction, starting back towards the cab – only to see a second soldier climb out of it.

Trapped—

Eddie slammed up through the gears as he accelerated in pursuit of the second transporter. He had seen the soldier make the transfer from the jeep behind Nina, and as the road curved, he now saw another man coming at her from the cab. 'Don't you bastards ever give up?' he growled.

The speedometer only went up to seventy kilometres per hour, which with the weight of the missile and its erector crane was highly optimistic, but the needle was still creeping towards the sixty mark. About thirty-five miles per hour, hardly a blistering pace under normal conditions. On this narrow, twisting, precarious route, though, it felt almost supersonic.

He closed on the jeep as it dropped back behind the TEL. The men aboard it had been so focused on Nina that they hadn't realised the third transporter was under new ownership. They were about to find out, though . . .

The 4x4's driver tipped his head up at the mirror as he registered the bright headlights coming up quickly from behind – then looked back in alarm when he saw just *how* quickly. The jeep swung across the road. Eddie spun the wheel to follow it—

The impact barely shook the massive sixteen-wheeled transporter, but the jeep was almost dragged under its sloping steel prow before the driver managed to veer clear down its left side. Eddie swung after the 4x4 as it braked hard. It clipped one of the truck's rear wheels and was thrown against the embankment, spinning to an abrupt stop.

The Yorkshireman checked his mirror. Both occupants were

still alive, and the jeep had only taken superficial damage, quickly reversing and starting after him again. But the second transporter was his most immediate concern: specifically, the two men clambering along its flanks . . .

He did a double-take as he realised the missile was no longer lying flat. The erector arms were lifting it from its bed, the rocket about fifteen degrees from horizontal and steadily rising. 'What the bloody hell have you done?' he asked as he glimpsed Nina scooting along the truck's side. The higher the missile got, the more top-heavy and unstable the TEL would become.

The road widened slightly – just enough for the two transporters to fit side by side. If he overtook the other truck, he could force it to stop. But first he had to help Nina.

He swept the transporter back to the outside of the road, its right wheels dangerously close to the crumbling edge. Down a gear, and he accelerated again, the cab's front corner barely missing the other truck's protruding launch stand as he swept past. The soldier pursuing Nina turned his head in alarm—

There was a muffled bang as Eddie hit him, followed by considerably wetter thumps as the Korean was ground between the two TELs. Blood spouted up on to the side window. What was left of the dead man disappeared under the juggernaut's wheels.

The soldier advancing from the front froze in horror at the carnage. Nina looked back, her concern changing to unexpected hope and delight as she saw her husband waving from inside the cab.

The missile had now risen high enough for a person to fit underneath it. 'Get over!' he shouted, gesturing. She rolled into the curving cradle beneath the huge cylinder.

Eddie accelerated at the second man, who snapped out of his fearful trance and darted on to the back of the truck. He was about to raise his gun when the driver of his own vehicle swerved sharply, trying to ram the chasing TEL off the road. The impact threw the soldier flat.

A second collision jolted both transporters. Eddie was about to shift his foot to the brake, then changed his mind and kept the accelerator down, making a turn of his own to sideswipe the other truck. His cab was just short of halfway along his target, knocking its rear end towards the embankment. The increasingly unsteady TEL lurched. The Korean driver hastily straightened out, deterred from any more attempts at vehicular combat.

Eddie kept up his speed, the two vehicles now side by side with the other ahead by a nose. He glanced back, seeing Nina beneath the missile – and the soldier recovering, snatching his pistol from its holster.

The Englishman ducked and groped for one of the dead men's rifles, but before he could reach it, the side window cracked under bullet impacts. The glass was toughened to withstand a rocket launch – but wasn't bulletproof, he discovered as more rounds shattered the pane beside him—

The gunfire stopped. Like most of the soldiers at the base, the Korean only had one magazine of ammunition. But it was not his only weapon. He scurried forward, shouting to his comrades in the cab, then snatched a hand grenade from his belt. Another man leaned out of the window in alarm, yelling for him to stop, but he had already pulled the pin.

He drew back his arm to lob the grenade through the broken window—

Eddie swung his transporter at its neighbour. The crash knocked the soldier on to his back, but he kept his grip on the explosive, the fuse not yet triggered. The other driver slowed, the Yorkshireman grinding past and slicing off both vehicles' wing mirrors as he drew ahead.

The man in the cab raised his rifle and fired. Eddie dropped lower as bullets lanced over him. His windscreen burst apart.

Wind rushed in through the gaping hole. He squinted and saw the road curving away to the left, rounding a large bowl in the hillside. The lights of Kang's SUV were visible in the distance on its far side, with nothing between them and Eddie's transporter except empty space over the dark forests below.

The Korean driver made another aggressive move, pushing his vehicle against the side of the hijacked TEL and forcing it relentlessly towards the road's edge. If Eddie didn't brake, he would be forced into oblivion over the approaching curve – but slowing would bring him back into the soldier's firing line—

A clunk of metal against metal behind him added a third, equally fatal outcome. The soldier had just thrown his grenade.

Nowhere to go – except *out*.

He flung open the driver's door – and leapt on to the other transporter, catching the bull bars running across its flat front. The unstable TEL rolled like a ship on heavy seas as it entered the turn, the missile straining against its support arms.

The Englishman's former ride continued onwards . . .

Over the edge of the road.

Engine roaring, the massive vehicle hurtled into the void. The grenade exploded, tearing off half the cab's roof – then the missile was thrown free as the truck hit the steep slope, smashing into the trees.

It was indeed fully fuelled.

A monstrous explosion ripped through the woods, engulfing the hillside in flames. A blazing mushroom cloud rolled into the dark sky.

Eddie clung to the transporter's nose, heart racing at his narrow escape – only to see astonished, then angry faces looking back at him through the windscreen.

Hunched in the cradle beneath the rising missile, Nina hadn't seen the other transporter go over the cliff – but she certainly heard, and felt, its destruction. She raised her head as the deafening roar faded behind her.

The soldier had dropped flat to shield himself from his grenade detonation. Now he lifted his head and saw her. His gun was empty, but he still had a knife, which he drew as he rose and advanced.

The missile was now almost forty-five degrees from the horizontal. The microlight's wing rattled and flapped, still caught on the clamp holding the rocket. No hiding places; Nina's only escape route was to climb around the weapon itself. She ducked under the hydraulic arm and sidestepped back along the transporter's flank.

The soldier followed, wielding the knife.

The driver shouted commands to the other man in the cab, who grabbed his rifle and leaned out of the window, trying to curl his gun arm around the transporter's front.

Eddie flattened himself against the bull bars as a bullet cracked past him. The soldier stretched further out. The Yorkshireman hurriedly climbed sideways. There was a gap in the middle of the hefty metal bumper to accommodate a winch. He dropped into the space as another round whipped by. A third shot clanged against the bumper just above him. He tried to squeeze deeper into the recess, a protruding lever jabbing painfully against his chest—

It moved – and the winch whirred, a hefty hook lowering on a heavy-duty steel cable. It hit the road and was immediately snatched backwards to bang noisily against the cab's underside. Eddie considered replicating a famous stunt from *Raiders of the Lost Ark* by grabbing the cable and letting himself be dragged along beneath the transporter, but instantly dismissed the idea as suicide; on the curving road, he would be crushed by the massive wheels.

Instead he shoved the lever back to the stop position before taking hold of the winch assembly itself and dangling from it. His position was precarious in the extreme, but he was as shielded as he could possibly be from the soldier's bullets.

As if to make the point, another round ricocheted off the bumper above him. The North Korean shouted angrily, then withdrew.

Eddie was about to pull himself back up when he heard a bang. The soldier had climbed out on to the cab's ladder-like steps, slamming the door behind him so he could reach the truck's front . . . for a clear shot.

A long dangling line from the microlight's wrecked wing flicked at Nina's face. She ducked away from it, continuing towards the transporter's rear. The rocket rattled and squealed against its restraints above her.

Her wounded arm was slowing her. The Korean soldier closed in, thrusting the knife. She tried to dodge – but the blade slashed the back of her shoulder.

She screamed, almost losing her grip. The soldier smiled, the headlights of the jeep approaching from behind revealing dirty, crooked teeth. He waved the knife at her, taunting, enjoying the moment before he got the rare privilege of killing a foreign spy . . .

The hanging line slapped against the back of his head. Startled by the unexpected touch, he jerked around to see if someone was behind him. Nobody there. He looked back—

Nina seized the line and snapped it like a lasso to loop it around his throat.

The man let out a choked yelp as she pulled it as hard as she could, swinging the wing outwards from the clamp above. It caught the slipstream – and broke free.

The wing acted like a braking parachute. . The soldier was

about to hack the line with his knife when he was abruptly yanked from the transporter by his neck. He landed in front of the jeep, taking the 4x4's solid metal bumper to his face with a gruesome smack.

Nina regained her hold and climbed back on to the cradle. The missile juddered alarmingly above her, rivets straining and tearing—

The TEL lurched sideways. There was a nauseating moment as it teetered on the brink, then wallowed back upright. With the rocket drawing ever closer to the vertical, the transporter was now massively top-heavy . . . and threatening to tip over at any second.

The driver realised the danger and stamped on the brake pedal. Kang had ordered the convoy not to stop out of fear of American saboteurs, but the threat of the transporter capsizing was infinitely more tangible. The speedometer needle plunged.

The sudden deceleration swung Eddie outwards from his cover. One hand lost its grip on the winch. The other held, but he twisted uncontrollably as he dropped back, the jutting lever hitting his ribs.

He cried out, looking up – to see the soldier lean around the cab and take aim.

Nina had been thrown off her feet as the TEL braked, sliding forward and hitting the hydraulic ram. She grabbed it to save herself from falling over the side, only to face a new threat. The jeep started to overtake the transporter as it went around a right-hand bend, the passengers bringing up their rifles. With the missile elevated, they were free to shoot without the risk of hitting it—

More rivets tore free with gunshot snaps, panels buckling as the rocket ground against the clamp – then with a screech of shearing metal the claws broke apart . . .

And the weapon toppled like a felled tree.

Nina screamed—

The missile clashed against the erector arm above her as the TEL turned, rolling over it – on to the jeep.

The 4x4 and the men inside were pounded into the road as the missile landed on top of them. It rolled crazily back across the road behind the transporter, tumbling over the edge into the trees below. The fuel tanks burst open, kerosene and chemical-laced nitric acid splashing together—

Another colossal fireball lit up the night as the missile blew apart. The blast shredded trees into splinters and tore a crater out of the hillside, a stretch of road a hundred feet long sliding into the inferno in the transporter's wake.

The rocket's fall threw the already unstable TEL wildly off balance, slamming the soldier clinging to its front against the cab. He dropped his rifle, the Type 58 bouncing along the road – then the transporter lurched violently back upright. The Korean was flung into the blazing forest. Toppling trees smashed down on top of him.

The driver's foot was still jammed on the brake. The reeling transporter skidded, slewing sideways before juddering to a halt just short of another bend.

The lurch finally cost Eddie his hold on the winch. He fell, landing hard and bowling towards the drop—

He caught a white marker stone, stopping with his legs hanging over the precipice. Aching, winded, he lay still for several seconds as his dizziness subsided.

The crackle of burning trees and the thrum of the transporter's idling engine masked another sound until it was almost upon him. He looked up at a crunch of grit – to see a pair of combat boots just a few feet away.

One of them swung at him—

He jerked up an arm to protect his head. The kick caught his elbow with punishing force, knocking him backwards over the edge. He clawed at the dirty ground, fingers closing around a stone embedded in the earth just before he fell.

The TEL's driver loomed over him, silhouetted by the truck's lights. He had a pistol in one hand, but although he could have simply shot the defenceless Englishman, he had a more sadistic fate in mind.

His foot came down upon Eddie's knuckles.

Eddie gasped at the pain, the driver shifting ever more weight on to his hand. Then suddenly it was gone, but he knew the relief was just the briefest prelude before the man's boot stamped down again—

'Hey! Drop it!'

The shout came from behind the soldier. Nina had jumped from the transporter and retrieved the rifle, aiming it at the Korean.

The man whirled—

She shot him before he could even raise his gun. He fell past Eddie and disappeared down the hillside below.

'Eddie!' Nina ran to him, dropping the gun and pulling him up. 'Oh God, oh my God! I thought I'd lost you.' She held him tightly, tears running down her cheeks with the sudden release of emotion. 'Idiot! Jumping from a plane . . .'

Eddie managed a strained laugh as he hugged her. 'Yeah, okay, it could've gone better. But you weren't exactly Mrs Sensible either.' He looked over her shoulder at the TEL, the empty crane now fully elevated. Beyond it, the night sky was aglow with the light of the burning forest. 'Why did you raise the missile? That's insane!'

'It was an accident! I was trying to lower those jacks to stop the truck.'

'That's only a bit less insane! But it worked, I suppose.'

'And we're both still alive.' She stood, helping him to his feet. 'The explosion took out the road behind us, so nobody can follow.'

Eddie looked across the valley. The SUV, troop truck and last remaining TEL were distant sparks in the blackness as they approached the airbase. 'There's only one way we can go, though – down there.'

'I know.' Nina sighed grimly. 'Great. So we've got another kamikaze mission, then?'

'The first one's always the hardest,' he said with a wry, tired grin. 'The next one's a doddle.' He faced the transporter again. 'It won't be safe to drive like that. How did you lift the crane?'

'There's a control panel at the back.'

'Okay, do the opposite of whatever you did and bring it back down again. I'll get it ready to go.' He collected the rifle, then they went to the two ends of the TEL.

Without the huge weight of the missile upon them, the erector arms lowered considerably faster than they had risen. One had been buckled by the falling rocket, preventing it from returning to its bed. 'That'll have to do,' Eddie called to Nina as it ground against the transporter's side. She shut it down, then ran to join him as he put the truck back into gear and revved the engine. 'You ready?'

She looked down at the airfield. The remnants of Kang's convoy had arrived at the great white cross of the Antonov, ready to load the last missile aboard the giant aircraft. A nod, with a confidence she didn't feel. 'Let's finish this.'

45

Colonel Kang watched with angry impatience as the transporter backed towards the Antonov. The enormous Russian cargo aircraft had opened the clamshell rear doors beneath its tail and lowered a ramp to the runway, but the TEL was not preparing to drive inside. Instead, it was positioning itself beneath the rails running the length of the cavernous hold's ceiling so the missile could be winched up and transferred to a waiting cradle. So huge was the An-124 that it could easily accommodate all three rockets with plenty of room to spare for the ancillary equipment that was also going to their Saudi buyers . . . but this one would be making the trip alone. A second explosion from the mountain had told the Korean that another missile had been destroyed.

The Arabs wouldn't be happy about that, but as Mikkelsson had pointed out, the Hwasong-15s themselves were the least valuable and most easily replaced part of the weapon system. The *most* valuable parts were being loaded aboard right now, Captain Sek and his men taking the trio of warheads and their plutonium cores to the front of the hold. The soldiers would travel with them to Saudi Arabia to ensure that the nuclear materials arrived as agreed – and also to guard them with their lives in case the Russian aircrew had been co-opted by the CIA, or simply decided to hold the bombs ransom. Trust of outsiders was a rare thing in North Korea.

Kang had decided to take the flight himself. Part of his reasoning was to oversee the transfer personally and make sure nothing else went wrong. A second part was his desire to stay away from his superiors in Pyongyang for as long as possible; the obliteration of Facility 17 by foreign spies was a failure that could lead to an instant execution – or, if he had displeased the Supreme Commander sufficiently, a prolonged and agonising one. At the very least, successfully transferring the surviving missile and all three warheads to the Saudis, and returning with their payment, might keep him alive.

The third part of the cargo was being loaded by a forklift. Two wooden crates contained some of Mikkelsson's gold bars. 'Now, you *will* keep them safe, won't you?' asked the Icelander from beside him.

'Of course,' Kang replied. 'As safe as if they were my own.'

Mikkelsson gave him a small smile. 'I am glad we were able to reach an agreement.' He was holding the small Crucible. A close examination of the dense crystal had reassured him that there was nothing that could be used to track its location, while the undoubtedly bugged carrying case had been discarded. 'If you wish, I will arrange for an associate of mine to meet you in Saudi Arabia. He can take care of any financial transactions you may wish to make. For a modest percentage.'

The colonel nodded. 'That would be very helpful, yes. And . . . a Swiss bank account?'

'He can assist you with that too.'

'Good. Good.' Kang glanced across at the small jet that the ashen-faced Sarah was boarding. A pair of soldiers strained to lift a box holding more gold bars aboard. 'Your wife,' he said, more out of a sense of obligation to his benefactor than any particular interest in her well-being. 'Will she be all right? The news about your daughter . . .'

'Sarah will be fine,' Mikkelsson replied. 'In time. As will I.' His jaw muscles tightened with restrained emotion.

'My condolences,' said the Korean dispassionately. He turned back to the Antonov. Several chains had been attached to the missile, the aircraft's internal hoist lifting it from the TEL. He was about to order the Russians to speed up the process when his driver called to him from the nearby SUV. 'What is it?'

'Colonel, an urgent message from the airfield's perimeter guards,' the man replied.

'I will let you take care of it,' said Mikkelsson. 'I assume we have clearance to leave?'

'Yes, yes,' Kang told him with a dismissive wave.

'Then I shall bid you goodbye. Thank you, Colonel. It has been a pleasure doing business with you.' The tall blond man headed to the jet.

Kang took the radio handset. 'What is it?'

'Sir,' said the soldier at the other end of the line, 'a missile transporter is coming down the mountain road.'

'What?' Surely it had been destroyed?

'It's about a kilometre away. What do you want us to do?'

'Does it still have a missile aboard?'

A pause, then: 'No, sir. It's coming very quickly, though.'

An unpleasant realisation struck Kang, echoing his own desire to avoid facing his superiors. If his men were still in control of the transporter, the last thing they would do after allowing their cargo to be destroyed was rush to tell him. 'Under no circumstances are you to let that vehicle through the perimeter!' he snapped. 'Use all means necessary to stop it. Do I make myself clear?'

'Perfectly, sir,' came the reply.

Kang tossed the handset back into the SUV and hurried to the Antonov. 'Get this thing aboard, now! Move faster!'

The loadmaster overseeing the operation was Russian. He might not have understood Korean, but the officer's urgency was clear. 'What is rush?' he asked in halting English.

'We are under attack!' Kang growled in kind. 'We must leave, fast. Tell the pilot to start the engines. We go when the missile is aboard!'

'No, no,' said the loadmaster, shaking his head. 'Missile has to be secured, yes? Cargo strapped down. All safety checks, pre-flight checks, you know? Take twenty minute, thirty minute.'

The colonel drew his sidearm and pushed the muzzle into the other man's stomach. 'We go when the missile is aboard,' he repeated.

The Russian went pale. 'Okay . . .' he said slowly. 'Three minute?'

The transporter thundered down the road, sweeping around the last of the hillside's curves on to the relatively flat ground leading to the airbase. Without the missile's weight, the TEL was considerably more responsive, though it would never break any speed records.

It was still not fast enough for Eddie's liking, either. 'Shit! They've got the fucking thing loaded,' he said. Beyond the perimeter fence he could see the runway, the Antonov at its far end. Even from this distance, it was clear that the missile was no longer on the transporter.

'Look!' said Nina. Flashing lights on the runway turned out to belong to the jet that had brought them to North Korea as it accelerated to take-off speed. Seconds later it was airborne, banking hard to turn north. 'Dammit! There goes our ride.'

'I wasn't really expecting they'd give us a lift home,' said Eddie before returning his focus to the rapidly approaching checkpoint. 'Oh, bollocks.'

'What is it?'

'The unwelcoming committee!' Armed men were dragging concrete blocks in front of the gate, a dazzling searchlight turning towards the TEL.

Nina raised a hand to block the glare. 'I don't suppose this windshield is bulletproof?'

'Nope, found that out the hard way.'

'So what do we do?'

Eddie dropped down through the gears. 'This thing's got sixteen wheels – so it's a four-by-four-by-four!'

He swung the transporter hard to the right, cutting diagonally across a patch of rough open ground towards the fence. Realising their target was going to avoid the roadblock, the soldiers opened fire. Nina and Eddie ducked as bullets clanged against the truck's side. The rear door's window shattered behind the Englishman. He winced, but held his foot on the accelerator. More rounds struck home, but now the fence loomed in the headlights. 'Hold on!'

The transporter crashed through the barrier, mowing down support poles and shredding the chain-link. Coils of razor wire lashed like whips at the cab, the windscreen cracking – then they were clear. Eddie turned the vehicle towards the runway's end. Bullets were still plunking off its flank, but the checkpoint was already falling away behind them.

He sat up, seeing the white-and-blue Antonov in the distance. The other TEL had now moved away from it, ground crew doing the same. 'The bloody thing's getting ready for take-off.'

'How can we stop it?' Nina asked. 'Block the runway?'

'If we stop, we'll get shot, and they'll just drive the truck away. We've got to take out the whole plane.'

'How?' She held up one of the dead crew's Type 58 rifles. 'Shoot it with this? It'd be like a mosquito trying to take down an elephant!'

Eddie stared at the freighter, a memory of a similar situation coming to him. 'Take the wheel,' he said, opening his door.

'What are you doing?'

He waved for her to move into his place. 'Something really stupid.'

'Oh, so business as usual, then?'

He grinned, then clambered out on to the top step to make his way around the front of the cab.

Kang looked on as the missile was lowered, with agonising slowness, into its waiting cradle. Two other spaces sat empty alongside it. The various cases containing the three warheads and their plutonium spheres had been secured at the front of the hold along with numerous crates of equipment and spare parts – and the gold. The two wooden boxes formed a miniature barricade beside the missile's nose. He gave them a greedy look before turning to the loadmaster. 'How long? Hurry!'

'Soon, soon,' the nervous Russian assured him. He called out to another crew member at the winch controls, who responded with a helpless shrug. 'Very soon.'

A soldier hurried into the hold. 'Sir! The transporter just smashed through the fence. It's coming straight at us.'

The colonel ran to a side hatch and looked out. Headlights were visible in the distance. 'Shit!' he growled, hurrying back to the loadmaster. The missile was now in its cradle, the chains going slack. 'We take off now!'

'No, no!' protested the Russian. 'Not safe! Have to fix straps, chain down—'

'Do it on the move.' Kang shouted an order. The other soldiers in the hold instantly responded by snapping their rifles to firing position, all aiming at the loadmaster. 'Tell the pilots to take off *now*, or I kill you.' He switched to Korean to issue another command to Sek. 'Take three men and get up to the cockpit. I want this plane moving in the next sixty seconds.'

The captain saluted, then he and three of his team raced for the ladder to the Antonov's upper deck at the rear of the hold. Kang faced the loadmaster again. 'Well? Do it!'

The Russian licked his dry lips, then shakily drew a walkie-talkie from his belt.

Eddie reached the winch. He let out a few feet of steel cable and supported the hook on one shoulder, then looped the line around its shank. Once it was secure, he started up the winch again, unspooling more cable and collecting it into long coils.

'What are you doing?' Nina shouted over the engine's roar.

'We've got to make sure the warheads never get out of here!' he yelled back.

'How?' One terrifying solution came to her. 'You . . . you want to crash into the plane?'

'We could, but that'd be a bit bad for us too! And we might not even do enough damage; it's a big-arse plane. But if it gets into the air and then comes straight back down again, really hard . . .' He stopped the winch, estimating that he had enough slack in the cable to work with, then glanced over his shoulder. 'Buggeration and fuckery!'

Nina saw the cause of his alarm. 'It's setting off!' The Antonov had left its parking position, heading for the taxiway. It was apparently leaving in a hurry, the aft clamshell doors open and the rear ramp still being raised.

Eddie quickly clambered back to the driver's side of the cab, hanging the heavy steel loops from one of the roof's spot-lights and signalling for Nina to move over. She slid sideways, her husband climbing in to take her place. 'Whatever you're planning, it might be a good time to rethink it,' she said nervously.

'Same plan, just a bit more dangerous. And by a bit, I mean loads. If I can lasso the landing gear before it takes off, it'll drag the transporter with it. It might be a big plane, but this truck's pretty chunky too; having it hanging off the wheels'll seriously fuck up its aerodynamics and hopefully make it crash. I was going to put the cable across the runway and try to catch it as it went past, but now we'll have to chase it.'

'Which means,' Nina said unhappily, 'we'll both have to be *in* the transporter when the plane takes off.'

He gave her a look of grim resignation, putting one of his hands on hers. 'Yeah. I know.'

She stared sadly ahead, seeing not the aircraft but an indelible image from her own mind. 'Goodbye, Macy,' she whispered, a tear trickling down her cheek.

There was nothing he could say in response to that. Instead he angled the TEL to intercept the aircraft, the transporter jolting over the rough expanse of grass. 'Okay, you take over again,' he said. 'I'll climb out and get ready to chuck the cable. Come alongside the plane, and get as close as you can to the wheels.'

They hurriedly made another seat swap, Eddie clambering back on to the step and closing the door behind him. The plane grew ever larger. 'Damn, that thing *is* big,' Nina said.

Eddie couldn't disagree. The An-124's high-mounted wings and broad belly gave it a hulking, overbearing appearance, a towering bully straight from the Cold War. Adding to the impression was its undercarriage; rather than separate sets of landing gear spread out beneath the fuselage, as on an airliner, the Antonov went for brute strength, five massive double-tyred legs in a row on each side of its hull. It even had two sets of nose wheels rather than just one.

All the better, as far as he was concerned. The more wheels, the more chance he had of snagging one. 'Okay!' he shouted as the transporter bounded over a drainage ditch on to the taxiway. 'Catch up with it!'

Nina swung the TEL around – discovering that its twelve-wheel steering system turned it more sharply than she'd expected. Eddie yelped as centrifugal force threw him outwards, the looped cable shimmying around the spotlight. 'Careful!'

'Oh, I'm sorry,' she snapped. 'I should have been learning how to drive a truck rather than raising a child!'

He smiled. 'Love you too.' Steadying himself, he collected the coils of cable and looked up at the Antonov. 'Wow, the last time I chased a massive jet along a runway, I was in a Ferrari . . .'

The TEL came in behind the An-124's starboard wing. Even with the giant freighter only at taxi speed, the jet blast from the two huge engines was fearsome. Searing air, reeking of fuel, scoured Eddie's exposed skin. He waved for Nina to position the truck in line with the fuselage. She did so, the Antonov's stern sliding into view ahead. The rear ramp was almost fully raised, folding to act as a bulkhead at the back of the hold. The two huge clamshell doors forming the tailcone's underside started to close. The aircraft was almost ready for take-off.

The wing loomed above as Nina brought the transporter closer to the row of wheels. Eddie briefly considered using a rifle to strafe and puncture the fuel tanks, but dismissed the idea. Jet fuel was hard to ignite; even a red-hot bullet was unlikely to start a fire, never mind cause an explosion, and the pilots would know within seconds that they had a fuel leak and stop the plane.

If that happened, the warheads would leave North Korea by some other means – and by then he and Nina would be dead. Downing the Antonov was the only way to make their sacrifice count. 'Okay,' he said as he held on to the spotlight and hefted his metallic lasso, 'let's rope us some Russian dogies . . .'

Kang stood in the cockpit with Sek and one of his men, watching over the pilots' shoulders as the runway's lights drew closer. Faced with the threat of having their aircraft impounded and themselves ending up in a North Korean prison – or simply being shot – the Russian aircrew had unwillingly set the Antonov in motion before finishing their pre-flight checks, hurriedly running through as many of the items on their list as possible as the plane trundled towards take-off position.

The colonel's radio crackled. 'Yes?' he said. 'Have you killed the spies?'

'Uh . . . no, sir,' said the worried soldier down the channel. 'We haven't caught up with the missile transporter yet.'

'Why not?'

'It's chasing you!'

Kang and Sek looked at each other in alarm. 'Which side?'

'The right, sir.'

Ignoring the co-pilot's protests, Kang shoved him aside to lean over and peer back through a side window. 'I can't see them,' he said, straightening.

'They might try to crash into us,' said Sek, worried.

Kang addressed the pilot, a man named Petrov, in English. 'We are being chased by a truck! It might ram the plane, or block the runway. We have to go faster and take off.'

The Russian spoke better English than his comrades, the language being a requirement for international pilots. 'No, if they could damage the plane, we have to stop! It is too dangerous to—'

'*Take off!*' roared Kang, drawing his gun for emphasis. The other cockpit crew behind him reacted with shock. 'Go faster! Now!'

Petrov tried to cover his fear and maintain a professional calm, but the weapon pointed at his head – and the rage-crazed expression of the man holding it – made it clear who was now in command of the aircraft. He pushed the throttle levers forward. The engine note rose, the Antonov gaining speed. Kang gave him a contemptuous glare, then withdrew. 'This is what we get for taking a contract from fucking North Korea,' the pilot muttered in his own language to the co-pilot, who swallowed and nodded in agreement.

★ ★ ★

The TEL's cab drew level with the middle set of undercarriage wheels. Eddie had hoped to reach the front to increase his chances of catching one with his lasso but the rising shriek of the engines meant that he had run out of time. 'They're speeding up! Go faster!' he shouted to Nina.

She pushed down the accelerator, but the third set of the Antonov's wheels slipped past, then the fourth. 'It's too slow!' she cried.

'Shit!' The final landing leg rumbled past Eddie. Last chance. He pulled the steel loop wide and tossed it at the huge tyre—

One side fell behind the fat wheel, snagging against the hub as the other was caught by the whirling tread and snatched underneath. The hook slammed into the hydraulics with a bang as the loop snapped tight around the axle.

'Let out the winch!' Eddie yelled, twisting to point at a dash-mounted control box in front of one of the passenger seats; the winch could be operated from both inside the cab and out. 'If there's enough slack, we can slow down and jump off before the plane drags us!'

Nina looked at the box. There were two levers and several switches on it, but all the text was in Korean. She leaned across the cab, straining to reach it. The larger of the two levers was marked with arrows pointing up and down, which she guessed controlled the spool. She stretched out her hand and pushed it forward, to the up position. An electric whine came from outside.

'No, the other one!' Eddie called urgently. 'The winch brake, you need to let it run free—'

Tyres screeched – and a wall of metal filled the windscreen.

The Antonov had turned on to the runway, the massive aircraft rocking on its undercarriage as it changed direction too quickly. Nina gasped and spun the wheel to avoid a collision – and save Eddie from being crushed against the fuselage.

The smell of burning rubber joined the stink of jet fuel. Its port wingtip drooping alarmingly close to the ground, the An-124 continued through its ninety-degree turn, finally coming into line with the runway lights and reeling back upright. Nina struggled to regain control of the transporter as it veered behind the inboard engine. Searing jet exhaust pummelled Eddie. 'Get behind it, behind it!' he shouted, hunching up to protect his face.

She swung the TEL back to the left. The Antonov had now pulled far enough ahead for the vehicle to get beneath its tail. She straightened out, then made another lunge for the winch control—

The four massive engines roared to full thrust.

A superheated hurricane whirled around the transporter. The colossal aircraft accelerated with alarming speed, racing away down the runway – with the cable lashing behind it.

It snapped taut. Eddie lost his footing and swung from the spotlight as the TEL leapt forward. Nina was thrown back in her seat. She stamped at the brake pedal, but to no avail.

The Antonov thundered towards take-off speed, dragging the transporter behind it.

46

The speedometer needle whipped around the dial as far as it would go, and stayed there. Nina gripped the squirming wheel fearfully, trying to hold the truck in a straight line as it snaked down the runway in the Antonov's wake—

The winch! If she let it run freely, it would give the TEL a chance to slow down and let her and Eddie bail out.

Holding the wheel with one hand, she leaned across and clawed at the control box. The winch was still spooling out its cable, the motor shrilling under the strain. Her fingers closed around the second lever, and pushed it.

The winch brake released with a loud clunk. The effect was immediate, the transporter lurching as the acceleration suddenly ceased. Eddie swung back around to the front of the cab, clawing at the roof to find a more secure hold. 'Jump out!' he cried.

'We're going too fast!' The speedometer was still pinned to the top of the dial. She tried the brakes again, but the transporter started to weave, threatening to flip over. All she could do was hold it steady until it slowed enough to risk a leap on to the runway—

The whine of the rapidly spinning winch reel became hollow as the last length of cable unspooled then it slammed to a stop.

The TEL lunged forward again. The sudden burst of speed pounded Eddie against the windscreen. The wind tore at his clothes as the aircraft neared take-off speed.

The transporter started to snake again. Its tyres screamed as they skidded across the concrete. Nina tried desperately to bring it back under control, but the truck was almost at the point of no return, about to overturn . . .

The Antonov's long tailcone dipped towards the runway as its nose rose and it left the ground.

The missile transporter followed it into the sky.

'Oh *God*!' Nina screamed, terror and nausea filling her as the TEL keeled over on to its side. 'Eddie!'

Her husband was pinned against the windshield, the force of the roaring slipstream holding him in place as he clung to the roof with one hand and groped for the bull bars with the other. His palm slapped on glass, flat metal – then clamped around the steel tube. Gasping for breath, he hung spread-eagled against the cab as the runway dropped away.

A squeal of overstressed machinery, audible even over the deafening thunder of the jet's engines – and the unsecured erector arms swung out from the vehicle's back as it rolled over. The wind caught them, yanking them backwards. Hydraulic rams tore apart, bolts shearing and welds cracking—

The arms slammed into their vertical position with such force that the transporter's long chassis snapped in half. The entire launch assembly tore free, taking most of the vehicle's bodywork and the rear eight wheels with it. Tons of metal plunged back down on to the runway, hitting hard enough to smash a crater into the concrete.

The TEL's forward half was still attached to the plane, corkscrewing along in its wake for two full revolutions before levelling out. Nina fell back into the driver's seat, seeing her husband flattened against the window before her. 'Eddie, get in!' she yelled, trying to open the door. The wind instantly slammed it shut again.

Eddie managed to turn his head. He squinted into the gale to see the Antonov banking sharply to starboard, hauling the remains of the transporter after it like a banner.

★ ★ ★

Alarms buzzed in the cockpit, warning lights flashing. 'What is happening?' Kang demanded, trying to cover his fear as the huge aircraft wallowed to one side. He clutched at the back of the pilot's chair to stay upright, Sek and his subordinate backing down the aisle between the other crew stations to find support.

Captain Petrov had higher priorities than answering the Korean, taking several seconds to check readouts and adjust the controls before replying. 'The landing gear is damaged,' he announced, 'and the whole plane is off balance! There's too much extra weight on one side.' He spoke to the co-pilot in Russian, the other man looking back out of his side window. A shocked cry told the others in the cockpit that he had seen something unexpected.

'Well?' snapped Kang after the co-pilot had gabbled a report.

Petrov gave him a disbelieving look. 'We are . . . pulling it behind us.'

'Pulling *what*?'

'The truck, the truck that was chasing us! They must have got a cable around the landing gear.'

'Then close it, cut the cable!'

'*The landing gear is damaged*,' the Russian repeated with impatient contempt. 'It won't close. We have to turn back and land again – it is too dangerous to fly like this.'

'No!' said Kang. 'We do not go back, we must—'

'Are you a pilot? Can you fly a plane? No? Then shut up and let me fly this one!' The pilot turned back angrily to the controls, leaving the colonel fuming impotently.

A voice came through the crew's headsets: the control tower at the airbase. Even without being able to hear the exchange, Kang could tell from its urgency that the situation was about to get worse. Both men in the front seats peered down at the ground, regarding the runway with growing concern as the Antonov made a wide circle over the airfield. 'We . . . we can't land,' Petrov told the Korean. 'The runway is blocked, there is wreckage on it. But we can't reach another airfield if we are pulling the truck; it will make the plane too hard to fly.'

'Then we stop pulling it,' Kang snapped. He glanced at a monitor screen at one of the crew stations, which showed CCTV images of the huge hold below them. The lone missile rocked uneasily in its cradle, only a few of the straps meant to secure it actually in place. But it was the other items of cargo that caught his interest. 'Can the plane fly with the rear ramp down?'

'Yes, it was designed so paratroopers could jump from it. But—'

'Then open it. Now!' He reverted to his native language as he addressed Sek. 'The weapons you were assigned – they're all in the hold, yes?'

'Yes, sir,' Sek replied.

'Good. Then we'll break out a rocket launcher – and blow up the transporter!'

Nina braced herself in the footwell, holding on to the now-useless steering wheel and one of the door handles as the transporter swayed through the sky behind the Antonov. The freighter still had its landing gear extended as it circled the military base. Was it going to land again? If the plane returned to the ground, she and Eddie would be killed. There was no way the broken-backed TEL would touch down neatly on its remaining wheels . . .

Movement on the plane – the clamshell doors cracking apart. Light flooded through the widening gap, spotlights inside illuminating the bare ribbed framework of the fuselage and the giant loading ramp blocking the rear of the hold. What were they doing?

She shouted to Eddie, pointing to alert him of the new development. He twisted painfully to look. 'Shit!' he shouted, the glass muffling his voice. 'The winch – wind it in!'

'Why?'

'The only reason they'd open the back door in flight is to jump out from it – or shoot at us!'

She hurriedly shifted position to push the larger lever forward. She was almost surprised when the winch started, convinced that the punishment it had endured would have destroyed the mechanism. But it began to take up the steel cable again, albeit with a protesting whine.

Eddie looked back at the Antonov. The clamshell doors opened fully. A moment later, the ramp laboriously began to lower. He knew what – or rather who – would be waiting behind it. 'Get a gun!' he called to Nina. 'Soon as that ramp comes down, they'll start shooting – you need to get 'em first!'

'I can't open the door!' she protested as she retrieved a rifle from the footwell, where it had ended up during the truck's wild ride.

'Then shoot out the window!'

Nina reluctantly pointed the Type 58 at the driver's door, turning the fire selector to what she hoped was single-shot mode. 'I'd normally say this is a terrible idea,' she muttered, 'but compared to every other one we've had today, it barely moves the needle . . .'

She cringed – and pulled the trigger.

The noise of the gunshot was excruciating in the cab's confines – but it was nothing against the sudden roar from outside. The bullet itself had only made a coin-sized hole in the glass, but a fraction of a second later the entire pane disintegrated, to be sucked out into the void. The cabin turned into a whirlwind as loose items were snatched up by the vortex.

Eddie stared at her with a *what the hell?* expression. 'I meant shoot out *of* the window – after you wind it down!'

'No, you said— Oh God*damn* it!' Nina shielded her eyes as grit and papers and even the spent bullet cartridge swatted at her face, then squinted past her husband. The Antonov was drawing closer, running lights illuminating its operator's logo on the towering tailfin. Beneath it were the gaping rear doors, the ramp slowly unfolding to reveal the hold beyond.

Kang left Sek in the cockpit to watch the pilots, not trusting the Russians not to lock him and his men out should they be left unattended, while he went with the other soldier and the aircraft's loadmaster to deal with the transporter.

Even though only one missile had been loaded aboard, cradles were in place for all three, so the forward ladder to the hold couldn't be lowered. Instead, the men had to go back down the length of the upper deck, past the little crew cabins and galley and through a small passenger section where the other soldiers anxiously awaited news of what was happening. Their commander didn't deign to inform them, instead continuing onwards until they reached the steep rear ladder. A cold wind gusted up from below.

'Get an RPG, quick,' Kang ordered the soldier. 'Meet me at the ramp.' The young man saluted and scurried down the ladder. The colonel turned to the loadmaster. 'You, come down with me. I want to see what is happening.'

'This very bad idea, you know?' protested the Russian as he descended into the hold. 'Rocket not secure, plane not steady – many bad things can happen! If ramp open, then if plane go up, we all fall out!'

'Then hold on,' Kang growled as he followed him down. By the time he reached the bottom, the soldier had run to the front of the hold and was opening a case containing an RPG-7 rocket launcher. Looking the other way, he saw that the ramp was still only about halfway down. He glared at the loadmaster. 'Make it go faster!'

'I . . . I can't,' the startled man replied.

'Idiot,' Kang snarled. He stalked to the rear of the hold, pausing to maintain his footing as the plane swayed. It had its flaps fully extended for maximum lift at the low speed that was all Petrov dared risk, but even an aircraft as large as the An-124 was susceptible to turbulence, and the pendulous weight of the truck swinging behind it only made the movement more unpredictable. He took hold of one of the ribs running up the hold's wall and peered out through the slowly widening gap.

At first he saw nothing but darkness, but then a flash from one of the Antonov's navigation lights picked out something nearby. He waited a few seconds until it came again. A line in the sky, running back from the plane's starboard underside . . .

He tilted his head, looking around the obstructive ramp – and was startled to see headlights shining back at him. The missile transporter was indeed being hauled behind the An-124, bobbing and weaving like a kite.

Wait – it was getting closer! It took him a moment to realise how: the TELs were fitted with a winch in case they became stuck in muddy ground. But it couldn't be operated remotely, which meant . . .

Astonishment was followed by a sadistic smile as he saw that the man and woman who had destroyed Facility 17 – and almost certainly his career with it – were still in the vehicle. No, not in: *on*! The bald man, Chase, was clinging to the front of the cab, his clothing flapping madly in the wind. Behind him, interior lights picked out the red hair of his wife.

He shouted down the hold to the soldier. 'The spies, they're on the truck! Get over here, quick – we can blow the bastards apart!'

★ ★ ★

The transporter shook and rolled sickeningly as it drew ever closer to the Antonov's tail, caught in its wake turbulence. The ramp was now three quarters lowered, and Nina saw movement behind it, someone wearing a peaked military cap. The figure looked back out through the widening gap, the spotlights inside the doors illuminating his face.

Kang.

Eddie saw him too. 'Shoot him!'

'I can't!' she protested. The Type 58 was almost a yard long, and there wasn't enough room between the seat back and the window frame for her to look down the ungainly weapon's sights at the hold without pushing the barrel out into the hurricane-force wind – which would make it almost impossible to aim.

The ramp kept dropping, the whale-belly hold and the missile inside coming into full view. Another soldier ran past it towards the open doors, carrying a tubular object.

'*RPG!*' Eddie shouted. 'He's got a fucking rocket launcher! Nina, shoot him!'

She had already identified the weapon from unwelcome past experience. But even squeezing as far over as she could, she still couldn't line up the gun on the hold.

The soldier reached Kang. The ramp finally drew level with the floor, then tipped downwards past it. The second Korean gawped at the flying truck, then at a bellowed order from his commander knelt and inserted the warhead's cylindrical rocket motor into the launch tube.

'Nina!' Eddie shouted again, almost pleading. The TEL started to sweep from side to side, pinballing between the fuselage's slipstream and the jet blast from the inboard engine. Each outward swing gave Nina just enough of an angle to aim at the hold. She turned the selector to full-auto, waiting for the North Koreans to slide back through her sights . . .

The soldier stood and raised his own launcher. He flipped up the sights, fixing them on the transporter—

Nina fired first. A spray of bullets scythed through the gaping doorway. Most clanged against the hold's far wall – but a couple found their target.

Kang jerked behind a fuselage rib as two rounds thudded into the soldier's upper body. The man crumpled and fell forwards, sliding down the ramp. He and his weapon slithered off its end and were snatched away by the thunderous wind to vanish into the night.

The rifle's last shot punched through the aluminium hull just behind Kang. The colonel flinched. The loadmaster fled to the ladder, clambering up it for the safety of the upper deck.

Nina dropped the empty gun. 'Okay, now what? We're still not exactly in a great position!'

Eddie looked back at the plane as the straining winch drew them ever closer. With the cable shortening, the transporter's sidelong swings were becoming faster and more forceful, carrying them almost behind the ramp before sweeping back out beneath the engine's churning exhaust plume. 'When we're level with the ramp,' he shouted, 'stop the winch! I'll jump on to it!'

'You'll *what*?'

'Just do it! I can make it!' He shifted towards the corner of the cab.

'Okay, now you're *trying* to get killed!' said Nina, but she still slid back over to reach the winch controls. The transporter swung behind the plane, just a few metres from the foot of the ramp. She briefly glimpsed Kang, then the North Korean disappeared from view as she and Eddie were swept back in the other direction. The next pass brought them almost close enough to touch the ramp's end. Back out towards the engine – and she pulled the lever to brake the winch.

Eddie braced himself, ready to jump.

Kang glanced out from behind the pillar. The woman in the swinging truck had put down her rifle. No more bullets were coming his way.

But he had some of his own to send back at them. He unholstered his pistol and stepped out of cover, raising the gun as he waited for his targets to come back into sight—

The transporter rushed at the ramp. Eddie leapt—

He crossed the terrifying void between the two vehicles in a split second, landing on metal with a bang. He had aimed to grab one of the sets of hydraulic jacks . . .

But missed.

He skidded across the ramp. Its surface was dotted with recessed hooks for attaching chains and cargo straps. He clawed at them as he slid past, catching one with curled fingertips and jerking to a painful stop—

A pounding impact knocked him loose again as the TEL slammed into the plane behind him.

He rolled diagonally down the ramp, snatching at the rearmost jack – and again missed. The black sky opened out hungrily below—

A hefty steel eyelet protruded from the ramp's edge. Eddie thumped hard against it, a fierce pain cutting deep into his chest as a rib cracked – but he grabbed the obstruction to halt his fall just as his legs went over the side. The wind swirling around the Antonov's stern tore at him. He battled to haul his legs back on to the ramp, then looked up.

The transporter was wedged under the An-124's tail, its cab partly crushed between the lower edge of the fuselage and the ramp, and the starboard clamshell door buckled inwards. He couldn't see Nina inside – but he spotted Kang sprawled halfway across the hold where he had been thrown by the collision.

The colonel shook his head dizzily, startled by the sight of the truck half buried in the aircraft's side – then he saw Eddie hanging from the ramp.

His pistol had ended up near the hold's port side. He scrambled up and ran for it.

Eddie realised what he was doing and dragged himself higher, lunging to grab the hydraulic jack. This time he caught it, pulling himself to his feet and swinging around it, using its hinge as a starting block to propel himself up the slope—

Kang snatched up his gun and spun to point it at the Englishman.

47

'What the hell was that?' cried the pilot as the aircraft lurched sideways. 'Something hit us!'

One of the aircrew behind him spotted the cause. 'Look!' he said, pointing at one of the hold's CCTV feeds. The image was of the open rear doors – into which was wedged the truck.

Petrov hurriedly turned back to his controls. 'We've got to shake it loose,' he said. 'If we try to land with that thing stuck there, it'll tear us in half! Everyone hold on!'

He threw the enormous aircraft into a hard bank to starboard.

Kang staggered as the deck tipped beneath him. He fired – but missed, the bullet whipping past Eddie's head. The Antonov's roll continued, its nose dropping as the wings lost lift.

What had foiled the Korean was helping the Yorkshireman. The change in the plane's attitude both angled him away from the ramp's treacherous edge and shallowed the gradient he had to climb. He pounded up it, charging at Kang—

The colonel realised he was losing his footing and hurled himself at the hold's port wall. A dangling strap flapped madly in the wind; he seized it with his free hand and turned to face his foe – just as Eddie dived at him. Both men slammed against the fuselage ribs, grappling for the gun.

Nina fought through a blinding headache and opened her eyes, finding herself sprawled across the seats. Sitting up, she got two shocks: the first discovering the transporter jammed against the ramp; the second the fact that previously clear headroom was now filled with crumpled metal. The cab's ceiling had been crushed by the clamshell door. If she had still been sitting upright, she would have been decapitated.

There was no time to reflect on her lucky escape. The Antonov was banking steeply to the right, and the weight of the transporter's chassis hanging out over nothingness was causing its back end to swing outwards as overstressed steel gave way.

A squeal from the windscreen. Cracks spread down the wide pane as the unyielding fuselage ground down on it—

The window exploded.

A gale blasted into the cab. Instinctual reflex saved her eyesight, but with a hundred-knot slipstream behind it, even laminated safety glass was enough to slash her face. She was thrown backwards, barely able to breathe.

The transporter jolted, twisting out from the tailcone as the An-124's bank steepened . . .

A new alarm shrilled in the cockpit, accompanied by an incongruously calm synthesised female voice. 'Stall warning. Level out. Stall warning. Level out . . .'

'Shit!' gasped Petrov, straining to stay upright in his chair as the artificial horizon banked past forty-five degrees. Increasing power would stop the plane from falling out of the sky, but going any faster with a huge truck jammed into the fuselage ran the risk of losing control. All he could do was obey the robotic instruction and hope the vehicle fell away of its own accord. The Antonov responded sluggishly, nausea rising in its occupants' stomachs.

Sek, clinging to one of the rear seats, looked at the monitor. The transporter was still there, its battered nose slewing around. But his eyes snapped to something on the other side of the ramp

– Colonel Kang, clinging to a strap as he fought with the bald spy.

He knew he had to help his commander, but his lack of either Russian or English meant that getting the aircrew to put him on the plane's loudspeaker system would take too long. Instead he rushed from the cockpit to give orders to the other soldiers in person.

'Lock that fucking door!' Petrov shouted as the plane levelled out. One of the crew slammed the bulletproof hatch and bolted it. 'Don't let any of the little bastards back in!'

The stall warning shut off. He watched the airspeed indicator until it climbed back to its previous mark, then tipped the Antonov into another sharp bank.

Eddie grappled with Kang, one hand clamped around the Korean's gun arm as he drove punches into his stomach with the other. As long as the squat officer was holding the strap, there was little he could do to fight back . . .

The deck rolled beneath him, one sole slipping on the metal. The moment it took to stabilise himself left him open to attack. Kang drove an elbow against his damaged rib.

He cried out in pain, almost falling. Kang jerked his wrist from Eddie's grip and slammed the gun against his head. This time, the Yorkshireman went down. He slithered across the hold as the plane banked more steeply, one flailing hand catching Kang's shin. He grabbed at it, but his fingers only closed around cloth.

It was all he had. He squeezed his fist into a ball, clutching the material like a lifeline.

Kang yelled as Eddie's weight dragged his hand down the strap. He fired at his tormentor, but in his panic the shot went wide. The Antonov's roll steepened, the floor dropping away from the two men.

Fabric slipped through Eddie's fingers. He couldn't hold on—

His free hand found another recessed hook in the deck as he lost his grip on Kang's leg. He swung away, dangling from his new handhold.

With the other man's weight gone, Kang was able to pull himself back up to the wall. His panting fear was quickly supplanted by murderous glee as he saw that his enemy was now at his mercy—

Metal screamed and tore – and the TEL fell away from the ramp.

Nina felt the cab swing around. The transporter was about to go—

She scrambled over the dashboard – and threw herself desperately out through the broken windshield on to the ramp.

Behind her, the roof sheared off as the truck finally broke free. It caught for an instant on the cable – then the winch brake gave way, the steel line unspooling madly as the vehicle tumbled into the empty sky.

Nina landed painfully beside the forward hydraulic jack. She tried to grab the steel column, but missed as the aircraft suddenly rolled upright, throwing her across the ramp.

Kang was flung back against the wall by the Antonov's drunken reel. His shot went high. Eddie scrambled forward, driving himself shoulder-first into the colonel's stomach. Kang folded double, the breath erupting from his lungs.

Eddie hauled him around, about to throw him off the ramp when he saw Nina skidding helplessly down it – and behind her, the transporter falling away—

The cable snapped taut.

Somehow it held, the truck pounding to a stop as if hitting an invisible wall. The aircraft was thrown off balance by a dozen tons of steel abruptly yanking at it like a dropped anchor. It pitched sharply nose-down, rolling back on to its right side. Both Eddie and Kang were catapulted across the hold.

The Korean landed on top of his opponent. Eddie stifled a scream as his ribs took another punishing impact. Kang slid off him, both men clawing for handholds as the floor tipped further forward.

They found them almost simultaneously, but Kang's was more secure. He dragged himself upright as Eddie dangled below him, smiling malevolently as he raised his gun again . . .

A shriek from behind him as Nina flew over the top of the ramp into the hold and rolled down the sloping deck past the two men. Kang glanced at her in surprise—

Eddie swept one leg up to deliver a cartilage-cracking kick to his kneecap.

Kang screeched and tottered backwards – just as the Antonov's pilot pulled back hard on the control yoke, putting it into a steep climb.

The Korean lost his balance and fell on to the ramp. He groped at the metal surface as he slid down it – finding no holds.

He hurtled into open space, screaming in terror—

The last thing he saw was the glare of the transporter's headlights – then he hit the truck's flat front with a gory splat, his innards bursting across it like a bug on a windscreen.

Shrill metallic cracks came from the cable as it started to shear apart, the steel strands snapping one by one . . .

Sek and his men had been hurrying aft through the upper deck when the Antonov began its crazy roller-coaster ride, hurling them all to the floor. After a stomach-churning age, it finally levelled out. 'Get up!' he shouted, struggling to his feet. 'Get down to the hold! We've got to protect the missile, and kill the spies!'

The bruised soldiers doubled their pace towards the plane's rear.

★ ★ ★

'Enjoy your flight!' Eddie yelled after the departed Kang. He crawled to Nina. 'How was yours?'

'It sucked,' she said dizzily, surprised not just at being aboard the huge aircraft, but simply at being alive. 'I didn't even get a bag of peanuts— Oh, you are *kidding* me!' she cried as someone shouted in Korean. They both looked up to see a soldier at the top of the ladder on the hold's starboard side. 'Why can't these assholes just leave us alone?'

'It'd ruin their military Koreas,' said Eddie. The couple ran forward as Sek and his team clattered down the ladder. 'Get on the other side of the missile. They won't dare shoot at it. The whole fucking plane'd blow up!'

The rocket was in a long cradle, empty ones beside it. Stacked beyond the missile at the front of the hold were numerous crates and containers. They would provide cover, but it would not take long for the soldiers to round them. 'There's nowhere to go!' Nina protested.

'There might be guns in those cases,' Eddie said, with little confidence.

They ducked behind the missile and scurried up the hold's port side. Behind them, the soldiers jumped from the ladder. One man brought up his rifle, only for a shrieked order from Sek to stay his trigger finger. By the time some of the others had crossed the hold to get a clear line of sight on their targets, Eddie and Nina had taken cover behind a pair of wooden crates. Like the rest of the boxed cargo, they were held in place by quick-release straps attached to rings set into the deck.

'Uh-oh,' said Nina in alarm, recognising something behind them: the metal case containing one of the plutonium spheres. Two identical containers were secured nearby.

'Those must be the warheads,' Eddie said, seeing three larger crates accompanying them.

572

'Great, so we're five feet from a nuclear bomb.'

'Not the first time.'

'That's hardly something to be proud of!'

'At least this one's not about to explode. Here, give me the—'

He hunched lower as gunfire echoed down the hold. Bullets cracked against the crate shielding them, the wood splintering. Flat metallic clunks came from inside as the rounds hit its contents. One side of the damaged box broke open, spilling gold bars on to the deck with heavy, ringing clunks.

'At least we'll die rich,' said Nina, cringing as another bullet struck the plutonium case – then the shooting stopped.

'Cease fire, *cease fire*!' Sek screamed. 'You'll hit the warheads!'

His men hurriedly broke off the assault. 'What do we do, sir?' asked one.

The captain glared down the hold. 'There are only two of them. You three, advance and take them from the front. The rest of us will go around the other side of the missile and attack from their flank.'

The soldiers who had been assigned to the first group were not happy. 'If we can't shoot at them, sir,' said one, 'what do we do if they shoot at *us*?'

'Don't question my orders, just do it! Go!' He jabbed a finger at the crates, then led the other troops back around the missile to head down its starboard side. The remaining trio exchanged worried looks, then began their advance. When there was no immediate reaction from behind the gold crate, one man took a gamble and charged at it.

Nina heard his rapid approach. 'Here they come!'

Eddie sprang upright and hurled a gold bar at the running man.

It was just as effective a blunt instrument as the one in the cellar of Detsen monastery. The twelve-kilogram brick hit the soldier in the face with a dull smack of flattening bone and gristle. He instantly flopped unconscious to the floor.

One of his comrades darted for the cover of a fuselage rib – then hesitated. Eddie knew what he was thinking: if the Englishman had been reduced to hurling lumps of metal, he was unarmed. And if he believed North Korea's endless propaganda, he would think that all Westerners were cowards who would crumble when faced with the might of his nation's military forces . . .

The man drew a combat knife and ran at them.

Eddie rushed out into the open to intercept him, not wanting to be cornered. The soldier stabbed the knife at him. He twisted to dodge it, his battered ribcage protesting with another burst of pain. The North Korean caught his involuntary grimace and realised he was hurt. He slashed at Eddie's chest to force him back before driving the knife's point at him once more.

This time it found its target, tearing through the flap of Eddie's leather jacket. The Yorkshireman jinked aside just enough to keep it from plunging into his heart, but it still cut into his pectoral muscle. He screamed, lurching backwards as blood seeped from the tear in his clothing. The soldier drew back the knife to make a final, fatal strike—

The TEL's cable snapped.

48

The remains of the truck at last succumbed to gravity and tumbled away. Its release suddenly made the Antonov's load several tons lighter – and the great plane lurched upwards into a steep climb, the pilots caught off guard.

Both Eddie and the soldier fell to the deck, startled cries coming from the other side of the missile as Sek and his men were also knocked down. The Yorkshireman grabbed the nearest missile cradle. The soldier was less fortunate, scrabbling at the floor as he slid backwards towards the open doors. The unconscious man followed, as did the gold bar that had knocked him out – and its scattered companions from the broken crate.

Nina held on to one of the straps securing the bullion container and looked over its top. More men tumbled screaming towards the ramp from the other side of the hold.

The man who had run at Eddie cried out in relief as he found a handhold. He clung to it as his teammates skidded past and dropped from the ramp, howls of raw terror receding into the darkness. Gold bars clattered after them, one almost hitting him. He jerked aside, then looked up to see Nina and Eddie higher up the sloping floor.

North Korean military training was brutal, the punishment for a soldier who lost his weapon severe, and the man had taken the harsh lessons to heart. He was still clutching his rifle in his other hand, and now he swung it towards them—

Nina yanked at the quick-release buckles on the straps securing the gold crate, grabbing one of the floor rings as the heavy wooden box fell away behind her.

It hurtled down the hold straight at the soldier. He fired, but the bullets hit only wood and precious metal—

The crate hit him with a bone-breaking crack and swept him away. It flipped over and its contents flew out, dozens of gleaming golden bricks cascading from the Antonov's rear doors.

Jet engines thundered overhead as the North Korean soldiers who had returned from the muster point closed on their fleeing quarry. The slave workers from Facility 17 had existed on a starvation level, given barely as much food as they needed to perform their back-breaking tasks; now only the adrenalin of fear kept them moving through the dark woods.

But the hunt was almost over, stumbling figures picked out by their pursuers' flashlight beams. 'Stay where you are!' the squad commander yelled. Several prisoners reacted with fearful obedience to his voice, halting and cowering. The braver ones kept going. 'If you surrender now, you will live! If you run, you will die! This is your only warning!'

More of the exhausted fugitives stopped. 'Round them up and kill them,' the commander told his men quietly as they advanced—

One of the soldiers beside him burst apart as something fell from the sky and hit him like a meteorite.

The commander had just enough time to register the gleam of gold in the bottom of the crater that had erupted where the man had been standing – before he and the rest of his troops were obliterated by a hard rain of bullion.

The multi-million-dollar downpour ceased just before it reached the slave workers. They stared in bewilderment at the carnage, still afraid . . . but the fear gradually evaporated to be replaced by jubilation as they realised that not only were they now armed, most of the soldiers' weapons still intact, but they were also very, very rich.

Even in North Korea, gold could buy freedom.

The metal hill from which Nina and Eddie were hanging flattened out as the pilots regained control and pushed the Antonov back to a level attitude. The missile slipped in its cradle, metal grinding on metal.

Eddie stood and looked around. Nina was still gripping a cargo ring where the gold crate had been. A couple of spilled bars had ended up wedged behind the second container next to it. He turned to see how many of the North Koreans had escaped plunging out into the void—

A soldier hurled himself over the rocket at the Yorkshireman.

Eddie fell on to his back. The man straddled his chest and clamped his hands around his throat, snarling in Korean. Eddie tried to force him away, but the pain from his cracked rib was like a red-hot spearhead. The man squeezed harder—

A shadow swept over the pair. The Korean looked up – as Nina clapped his skull between two gold bars. The crack of bone was loud over the ringing thud of the double impact. He slumped on top of Eddie, his clutching hands going limp.

The Englishman gasped, then shoved the unconscious man away. Nina dropped the gold and crouched beside him, seeing the bloody cut across his chest. 'You're bleeding!'

'It's not as bad as it looks,' he wheezed. 'Least I hope it's not, or I'm in trouble! Are there any more of 'em?'

Nina checked the hold's other side. Nobody was in sight. She looked beneath the cradles to see if anyone was crouching behind the missile. The deck was clear. 'Can't see anybody.'

'Okay, help me up.' She brought him to a sitting position. 'Ow! God, that hurt. I've cracked a rib. As if I wasn't in a bad enough way already.'

'We've got to bandage that cut. There must be a first-aid kit somewhere.'

'Probably in the cockpit, and I doubt they'll just let us in if we knock politely.' Another pained groan as he used the cradle to lever himself upright. Nina stood as well. 'We'll have to—'

He saw movement behind her, someone coming around the stacks of cargo at the front of the hold.

Sek.

Eddie shoved Nina away as the captain fired. The bullet tore into his upper thigh. She crashed against the damaged plutonium case, her husband collapsing beside the fallen soldier.

Sek advanced on them. With Eddie down, he turned his gun towards Nina—

She remembered how he had acted in the particle accelerator's control room – and threw open the case's lid to expose the plutonium sphere inside.

He recoiled like a vampire from a crucifix. The ingrained secrecy and compartmentalisation of the activities at Facility 17 and the North Korean military in general meant that all he knew about nuclear materials was that anything marked with the black-and-yellow radiation warning symbol was dangerous, an invisible killer. It took a moment for him to overcome his fear and realise that Nina had not melted or burst into flames—

A moment of which Eddie took full advantage.

The unconscious soldier's sidearm was still in its holster. The Yorkshireman snatched it out and fired three rapid shots into Sek's chest. The Korean fell back against the crates, blood spouting from the closely spaced entry wounds over his heart.

'Oh, Jesus!' Nina cried as she saw Eddie's own bullet hole. She scrambled back to him, pressing her palm over it. He roared in pain. 'I think the bullet's still in there!'

'Leave it, leave it,' he rasped, clenching his jaw. 'Get the gun and go up to the cockpit. We can't let 'em land back at the airbase, or anywhere else in North Korea. If they do, we're dead.'

She took the pistol. 'You're giving up on the kamikaze mission, then?'

'We survived hanging from the back of a fucking jet in a truck, so I'm not going to let some malnourished little cock-end in a stupid hat kill me after all that!' He glanced towards Sek's corpse. 'I'll get his gun and follow you up.'

'Will you be able to climb the ladder with a bullet in your leg?'

'I'll have to if I don't want a bullet in my *head*. Go on.'

'Okay. Oh, and by the way?' She kissed him. 'I love you.'

He smiled. 'Never doubted it for a second.' Nina grinned back, then waited for him to put his own hand over the wound before starting towards the rear ladder.

She had just passed the missile when a voice boomed through the hold. 'Attention! Attention!' said a man with a strong Russian accent. 'The cockpit is locked, and we will not let you enter. We will land at Tonyong airbase as soon as the runway is clear. You cannot escape. Drop your guns and surrender.'

Nina spotted a loudspeaker mounted on a ceiling beam, a closed-circuit camera beside it. Other cameras covered the rest of the cavernous space. 'You think he's bluffing?' she called back to Eddie.

He supported himself against the cradle, wincing as torn muscle pressed against the bullet in his leg. 'This used to be a military plane, so the cockpit door's probably bulletproof. Shit!' He slumped back, defeated. 'Maybe we should just blow up the missile after all, make sure nobody gets it. Or chuck the warheads and the plutonium out of the back. We might get lucky and have 'em land where nobody can reach—'

'The plutonium,' Nina interrupted with inspired urgency. 'The plutonium!' She ran back – not to her husband, but to the open container. The sinister grey sphere squatted within.

'What about it?' Eddie asked, puzzled. 'You going to blow the door open with a nuclear bomb?'

'Not quite.' She went to one of the other metal cases and unlatched it, revealing a second sphere inside. 'But I did some research about nuclear weapons on the flight to China.' She gave him the dark smile of someone who had exhausted all other options but the desperate – or demented. 'You know how much plutonium you need to achieve critical mass? Because I do.'

The freighter's whole crew, including the loadmaster, were now sealed inside the cockpit. 'I can't tell what they're doing,' said one man, watching his CCTV monitor intently. 'Why the hell didn't we get this upgraded to HD?'

'Take over,' Petrov told his co-pilot, leaving his seat to see for himself. The other man continued to guide the An-124 on its long, slow circle of the airbase; the last update from the control tower maintained that the wreckage would be cleared from the runway within minutes, and troops were working flat out to fill the hole in the concrete with earth. Landing would still be risky, but if the North Koreans packed it firmly enough, there was a good chance that the Antonov – built to operate from battle-damaged runways – would make it over the crater with minimal damage.

Minimal *extra* damage, at least; the aircraft had already suffered plenty, one landing wheel all but wrenched off and the rear doors and ramp jammed open. His clients would be paying through the nose for all the repairs . . .

He put financial reparations to the back of his mind as he studied the screen. It showed the front of the hold, looking towards the nose. The bald man appeared injured, bloody patches on his chest and thigh, but he had moved to hunch against the remaining wooden crate. The woman, who seemed somehow familiar, had opened up two other cases.

'Oh, shit,' he whispered. He didn't need high definition to identify the warning trefoils on them. 'She's messing with the nukes!'

The co-pilot, like all the crew a Russian air force veteran, looked around in alarm. 'She can't set one off, can she?'

'I don't think so, but . . .' He watched as the woman lifted out one case's contents and placed it on the deck. It looked like a ball, but from her strained movements it was much heavier than its small size suggested . . . 'Fuck me!' he said, suddenly afraid. 'It must be uranium, or plutonium – it's the only thing that could weigh so much.'

'She won't blow anything up that way,' said the crewman, mystified, as she wrapped the sphere in a cargo strap, then tied it to one of the rings in the floor.

'I still don't like it. We should try to take them out ourselves before landing.'

'The bald guy's still got a gun,' the loadmaster pointed out. The stowaway was in a good position to cover the ladder, and even wounded seemed fully capable of defending himself.

'We can't just sit here and wait for them to do whatever it is they're doing.' Petrov regarded the monitor again as the woman moved to the other open case. Rather than take out its sphere, though, she used a second strap to secure it inside, then carefully tipped the container on its side. She then pushed it across the deck until it was lined up with the sphere on the floor and tied another strap to it. 'Whatever they *are* doing.'

It became clear that an answer would soon arrive as the woman checked her handiwork, then hurried to an intercom system at the side of the hold. She lifted the handset, and a buzzer sounded in the cockpit.

Petrov was still wearing his headset. 'I'll take it,' he said, watching the screen closely as the crewman switched him in. 'This is the captain,' he said in English. 'What do you want?'

'Hi,' the woman replied, her accent American. 'We want a couple of things. First, let us into the cockpit. Second, fly us to South Korea. Sorry for wrecking your plane, by the way.'

'I will not let you into the cockpit, and I will not fly you to South Korea!' Petrov told her firmly. 'We will land at Tonyong in a few minutes. I suggest you jump out the back, it will be quicker and less painful.' The crew, listening in on their own headphones, smiled at his grim joke.

'You know what else is painful?' said the woman. 'Dying of radiation poisoning.'

'You can't set off the bombs. There are safety features.'

'I'm not *going* to set off the bombs. But what I *am* going to do is get down behind that big box full of gold bars,' she pointed at the crate against which her companion was sheltering, 'while I pull these two plutonium spheres together. They're both just below the size at which they'll reach critical mass so if they touch, or even get too close to each other, they'll release a big burst of gamma radiation. You know what that is, I assume?'

The pilot had not worked directly with nuclear weapons during his time in the military, but he had become familiar with their basics. 'Yes, I do,' he said uncomfortably.

'And what it'll do to you?'

'It ain't gonna turn you into the Hulk!' the bald man called out in the background.

'It will kill you too,' said Petrov, starting to sweat.

'Not necessarily. Gold's just as good as lead at blocking radiation. A lot more expensive, obviously, but we've got something like thirty million dollars' worth of it here. We'll be safe behind it, but the gamma rays'll go straight through aluminum like it's tissue paper. Planes are made of aluminum, right? Including the floor?' She pointed at the hold's ceiling above the first sphere directly beneath the cockpit.

'If we die, the plane will crash! You will die too!'

'You won't die right away. It might take hours, days, even weeks. But from everything I've heard about radiation poisoning, you'll wish you'd died instantly. The North Koreans will have killed us by then . . . but if you take us to *South* Korea, we can all stay alive.'

The Antonov's crew exchanged worried looks. 'You would not do this!' said Petrov, trying not to let his concern show in his voice, but not succeeding.

'I would. Because it's the only way we have to get out of this. So are you going to do what I say?'

'No!'

'Your choice.' The figure on the screen hung up the handset, the captain hearing a loud click in his headphones as she disconnected.

'She's bluffing,' he assured his crew, watching her toss the long strap attached to the case over the gold crate and join the man behind it. 'She must be!'

'You know this is the most fucking insane thing you've ever done, right?' said Eddie as Nina crouched beside him.

'I don't even know if it'll work,' she admitted. 'As far as I know it should, but I'm not a nuclear physicist.'

'Shame we haven't got that arsehole Fenrir Mikkelsson here to test it on. And will this gold really block the radiation?'

'Again, I think it *should*, but . . .' She gave him a resigned look. 'Hopefully we won't have to find out.'

She pulled the strap. The case, the plutonium protruding from its open top, slowly scraped along the deck towards the other sphere.

'She's doing it!' cried the loadmaster, staring in horror at the screen. 'She's fucking doing it!'

The co-pilot turned in his seat. 'Will it really kill us?'

'I don't know!' said the pilot. 'She seems to know what she's talking about, but . . . I don't know!'

The sphere in the case inched ever closer to its twin. All eyes were fixed upon it, the Antonov's crew all too aware that it was less than five metres beneath their feet – and that the woman was right about the aluminium floor. 'We can't go to South Korea,' said the co-pilot. 'We're carrying a damn *nuclear missile*! They'll lock us up for breaking the arms embargo!'

'We could dump it out of the rear ramp before we cross the border and say the Koreans never told us what we were transporting,' the loadmaster suggested.

'You think they'd believe that?'

'That doesn't matter right now!' Petrov cut in, close to panic. The spheres were now only a hand-span apart, and still edging nearer. He watched them, paralysed by indecision . . . then hurriedly darted to activate the internal speaker system. 'Okay! Okay! Stop! Don't do it! We'll take you to South Korea!'

Nina and Eddie both looked up at the source of the echoing, panicked voice. 'You think they'll really do it?' he asked, dubious.

'There isn't much we can do if he's lying,' she admitted. 'But he sounds pretty scared, so . . .' She stood and rounded the crate, relievedly pushing the case away from the tied sphere, then returned to the intercom. 'Okay, I've moved the plutonium apart. Now would be a good time to show some good faith, because I can always push them right back.'

'We're changing course now,' said the captain. Seconds passed, the An-124 continuing to circle – then it banked, much less steeply than before, and increased power. The lights of the airbase receded into the distance beyond the rear doors as it levelled out again.

Nina allowed herself a tired smile. 'They're doing it! We're actually going to get out of here!'

Eddie grunted as he stood, keeping one hand over his leg wound. 'This probably isn't the best time to mention that the border between North and South Korea is the most heavily defended in the world, is it?'

49

The Antonov picked its way through the crumpled labyrinth of valleys of North Korea's south-eastern region. The cockpit lights had been all but extinguished to let the pilots adjust their eyesight to the darkness, but despite their tension as they guided the hulking aircraft between the hills and mountains, staying as low as they dared to avoid radar, it was one of the flight crew behind them who was under the most pressure. Using a paper chart, he was trying to plan a route to the border that would both stave off detection for as long as possible – and keep the plane from rounding a peak to find nothing but a wall of rock directly ahead.

With no time to plot a course in advance, he was forced to relay directions to the pilots on the fly. 'In forty seconds turn, uh . . . twenty degrees starboard,' he said, having to approximate the speed-to-distance calculations in his head. 'Next turn after that will be to port.'

Not taking his eyes off the moonlit landscape beyond the windscreen, Petrov spoke to Eddie, who was in the crew seat immediately behind him – both to make sure the pilots were taking them south, and to keep them covered with his gun. 'Please, we have to go higher. The mountains are getting bigger. If we take the wrong route, we will not be able to climb fast enough to get over them.'

'Then don't take the wrong route,' Eddie replied sardonically, trying to mask his nervousness. He could make out enough of the rushing terrain to tell that it would only take a moment of lost concentration to end up embedded in it. Warning lights flashed continuously on the control panels; the pilots had already been forced to switch off the aircraft's verbal alarms because the endless droning of 'Terrain. Pull up. Terrain. Pull up . . .' had driven them to distraction. 'They'll already be looking for us. If they get a radar fix, they'll be on us in no time.'

'Even this low, they may already have one! They have radar everywhere along the border.'

'How far to the DMZ?' Nina asked. She was at the cockpit's rear with the other gun, the rest of the Antonov's crew coralled between her and her husband.

'Dee-em-zed,' Eddie corrected.

'Dee-em-*zee*, and you think *now's* a good time for a transatlantic pronunciation debate?'

The man with the map, who was slowly moving his fingertip over it to mark their current position, glanced at a line below his nail. 'Four, five kilometres.'

'Can you go any faster?' Eddie asked Petrov.

The Russian snorted incredulously. 'You *want* to die?' He saw the valley promised by the navigator and turned as quickly as he dared to follow it. With its landing gear jammed down and the battered rear doors still open, the An-124's aerodynamics – and manoeuvrability – were compromised.

'We made it this far,' said Nina. 'If we keep doing what we're doing, we might—'

Those crew with headphones simultaneously twitched in alarm. Eddie heard a strident voice in Petrov's earpiece. 'Who's that?' he demanded.

'They've found us!' the pilot cried. 'They're ordering us to turn back to Tonyong!'

'It might be a bluff. Keep going.'

'No, they have our position and course!'

A gasp of alarm from the navigator drew everyone's attention.

He spoke urgently – and fearfully – to the pilots. 'This valley splits ahead – and they are both dead ends!' Petrov warned. 'We have to climb.'

'But then they'll be able to shoot at us,' Nina protested.

'Yup,' said Eddie. 'You might want to hold on *really* tight . . .'

The navigator began what sounded to the two Westerners like a countdown as the North Korean kept barking commands over the radio. Petrov kept the Antonov in the valley for as long as he could, then snapped: 'Climbing *now*!'

He pulled back the controls. The An-124 laboured upwards, a tree-covered wall of rock briefly looming beyond the windows before falling out of sight. Eddie glanced at the map. They could only be a couple of kilometres from the DMZ—

The radio voice cut out. Petrov blanched. 'They have gone!'

'What do you mean, gone?' said Nina.

'They have stopped talking! They would only do that if—'

'If they've given up trying to talk us around,' Eddie finished for him. That meant . . .

The co-pilot yelled a Russian obscenity, staring in horror out of his window.

In the distance to the west, an orange pillar of fire and smoke rose from the ground. It headed quickly into the black sky . . . then seemed to slow.

Eddie knew it was an optical illusion. The source of the flames was most likely a telegraph-pole-sized SA-2 surface-to-air missile, like much of North Korea's arsenal an old Soviet weapon, but its age made it barely less deadly. It was still a threat even to fighter aircraft, so the lumbering freighter would be an easy target.

Petrov issued rapid instructions to his crew. Seat belts were hurriedly tightened, those men without chairs racing aft to find secure places in the passenger compartment. 'What's the plan?' Eddie demanded as Nina hurried to join him.

'There is no plan!' Petrov replied, barely controlling his panic. 'This plane is civilian, it has no defences – all we can do is run and hope we do not get blown up!' He turned due south and shoved the throttles further forward.

Eddie looked back through the starboard window. The missile was now a small halo of light around a tiny dark dot, drifting lazily across the sky towards them. 'How far to the DMZ?' The strip of neutral territory bisecting the Korean peninsula was four kilometres wide, and would take just over a minute to traverse at the Antonov's current speed – but the SAM was approaching at more than three times the speed of sound. It would easily reach them before they crossed it.

'We will be there in seconds,' said the Russian. 'Now shut up!'

'All right, keep your hair on! Wish *I* could . . .'

The co-pilot shouted a warning to Petrov, who forced the plane into a hard descending turn. The approaching missile took on terrifying dimensionality as it rolled out of sight beyond the window. Eddie clutched Nina to him—

A bright flash from outside – and the Antonov was thrown sideways as if kicked by an angry god, its hull echoing to the clamour of a thousand burning hailstones. The SA-2 had detonated as it streaked past, its warhead almost two hundred kilograms of high explosive surrounded by a jacket of frangible steel that turned instantly into a cloud of supersonic shrapnel. The explosion was followed a split second later by a deafening bang of disintegrating metal as a chunk of the starboard fuselage tore away, taking a huge bite out of the aircraft's side.

Alarms screamed as the cockpit's occupants regained their senses. Petrov battled with the controls, dragging the enormous plane out of its roll towards earth. A bank of warning lights lit up in a terrifying grid of red. 'We've lost both starboard engines!' he cried, still struggling with the yoke as the co-pilot triggered the crippled engines' fire extinguishers. 'The rudder is damaged, we can't turn well!'

Another horrified warning in Russian from the co-pilot. Another two blazing lines were being etched into the sky—

More fiery flashes from the ground – but these came from *ahead*, lancing from a flattened hilltop a few miles away. 'Oh my God!' Nina yelled. 'They're everywhere!'

'We're over the DMZ!' said the pilot, pushing the Antonov into another desperate evasive turn. 'Those are coming from *South* Korea!'

'Great, now *everyone's* shooting at us!' Eddie held Nina more tightly, watching as another pair of missiles rushed at them —

And shot past.

All heads whipped around in surprise to track them. A second later, two more brilliant flashes lit the sky, followed by thunderous detonations. 'They . . . they shot down the other rockets,' said the co-pilot, stunned.

'Must have been Patriots,' Eddie realised. Both Koreas relied on armaments from their most powerful allies to defend their sides of the border; the difference was that the south had the latest technology from the United States rather than decades-old Soviet weapons. The Antonov had either had the good fortune to cross the DMZ within range of a battery of Patriot interceptors, or – equally likely – South Korea had more of the missiles deployed along the 160-mile dividing line than it let on.

'Okay, so they just saved us,' said Nina. 'Now what?'

The answer came as a new voice crackled through the pilot's headphones. Eddie hurriedly re-donned his own set to listen. The language was English, and the accent American. 'Unknown aircraft, unknown aircraft. You have illegally entered South Korean airspace. Identify yourself, or turn back across the DMZ. You will not be allowed to proceed any further unless you identify yourself. If you do not, we will shoot you down.'

Petrov exchanged worried looks with his crew before answering. 'We are a civilian freight aircraft – I repeat, we have civilians aboard. Do not shoot, do not shoot.'

No reply. Eddie pulled off his headphones and handed them to Nina. 'You should talk to 'em.'

'Why me?' she asked.

'Because you're American, and you're always telling me I can't do the accent!'

She donned the headset. 'Hello, can you hear me? This is Dr Nina Wilde, working for the United Nations. We've uncovered a plot by North Korea to export nuclear weapons, which is why they're trying to kill us! Please respond.'

Still no answer. Petrov glanced back at her with an expression that suggested that desperation had just driven ingenuity. 'Tell them we helped you steal the bombs! We knew nothing about them; the North Koreans told us they were . . . farm equipment! Yes, farm equipment.'

'Uh-huh,' she said, before trying again. 'I repeat, this is Dr Nina Wilde from the United Nations. We have—'

'I say again, unknown aircraft,' the American cut in. 'Identify yourself immediately. We *will* shoot you down if you do not respond.'

'Hello, hello? I'm responding! Can you hear me?' There was no reply. 'Oh crap!' said Nina. 'We can hear them, but they can't hear us!'

One of the crew made a hurried check of his instrument panel. 'Transmitter is out!' he reported. 'Electric systems, many *kaput*!'

The pilot made another attempt to get through, with no success. The voice on the radio returned. 'We have you in sight and are approaching from your eight o'clock. We will attempt visual communication. This is your last chance. If you do not respond, we will kill you.' The threat was delivered with stony calm.

Petrov turned to look back. 'I see two jets!'

Eddie forced himself upright. 'What are you doing?' Nina asked, seeing his obvious pain.

'I'll talk to 'em.'

'How? The radio's broken! And also, why you?'

'I know how to talk to flyboys.' He addressed the crew. 'I need a torch, a flashlight – something I can use for Morse code.'

'The Americans do not use Morse any more,' Petrov protested.

'Then let's hope these guys are old school! Come on, get me a light, quick!'

A pair of F-16 Fighting Falcons, part of the massive US military contingent dedicated to protecting the South Korean border, closed on the lumbering Antonov. One held back, fixing the freighter in its sights, while the second drew alongside to attempt communication with its pilots. Information had been passed on from the ground that the aircraft had been under SAM fire before crossing the DMZ, but that didn't mean it would get a free pass. North Korea was notoriously sneaky, the lead pilot mused, and faking an attack to get its forces into South Korean airspace under the pretence of a defection was exactly the kind of thing they would do . . .

A light flashed from the rearmost window of the Antonov's darkened cockpit. 'They're signalling,' the pilot reported. 'Looks like Morse code.' That made sense: the An-124 was a Russian plane. While the USAF had phased out Morse from standard usage decades ago, other countries still used it.

'Can you tell what they're saying?' asked his wingman.

'Yeah, hold on . . .' The code might no longer have been part of air force training, but many pilots still knew it; he had taught himself in childhood after a diet of movies and TV shows where messages were silently flicked between ships and planes, entranced by the idea of sending secret messages to his friends. His memory was rusty, but he pieced this one together word by word. 'American . . . on board . . . do . . . not . . . shoot . . . you . . . dickhe— *Hey!*'

'Did they just *insult* you?'

'Yeah!' He was affronted – but also oddly intrigued. North Korean insults tended to be much more florid. Maybe there really *was* an American aboard. He let the message continue. 'Working for usint . . . huh? Usintel . . . oh, US intel! Have stolen NK illegal weapons . . . three . . .' He fell silent in shock as he translated the series of flashes into words.

'What?' said his wingman. 'What did they say?'

'He says they, uh . . . they have three nuclear warheads aboard, and do we want them?'

Thirty minutes later, Eddie and Nina were on the ground at Osan airbase south of Seoul – though the landing had been as stressful as the rest of the flight.

Shepherded by more US and South Korean fighters, all primed to blast the Antonov out of the sky if it deviated in the slightest from its assigned course, the battle-scarred aircraft made a hard and terrifying touchdown on its damaged landing gear, the strut to which the TEL had been lassoed collapsing and tearing away. With only two engines providing reverse thrust, it almost overshot the end of the runway, the twin nose wheels stopping just yards from the mud beyond the concrete. It was immediately swarmed by military vehicles, dozens of troops training their weapons upon the plane as its occupants were ordered by loudhailer to disembark and surrender.

Nina supported Eddie, helping him limp down the rear ramp as both raised their hands. 'I was hoping for a reception with, y'know, a lot fewer guns pointed at me,' she said, blinking into the glaring spotlights. 'Or preferably none.'

'Wilde and Chase nuclear delivery service!' Eddie called out as they reached solid ground. 'H-bombs direct to your door. Don't forget to tip!'

The soldiers did not respond well to the joke. 'Get down on the ground with your hands behind your heads!' one bellowed through the speaker. 'Do it now!'

'He's hurt!' Nina protested.

Eddie gritted his teeth as he lowered himself painfully to the runway and lay on his front. 'They really don't care, love.'

The Russians followed them out of the An-124, also lying face-down. A squad of soldiers in armoured hazmat gear ran to surround them. One man hurriedly passed a Geiger counter over the supine prisoners. It crackled, but not enough to cause alarm. 'Where are the bombs?' the leader shouted, voice muffled behind his face mask.

'In there,' said Nina, jerking a thumb towards the hold. 'There's a plutonium sphere tied to the floor; you might want to take care of that first. Long story,' she added, sensing he was about to ask a question that would require a long and convoluted answer. He got the message and quickly led his team inside.

Boots tramped towards her. 'Which of you is Nina Wilde?' another man demanded.

Nina risked raising her head far enough to give the questioner, an air force colonel, a scathing look. 'That would be me, with the breasts.' Eddie had given the F-16's pilot more information via Morse while the Antonov was in flight, including the nature of their mission.

'And Eddie Chase?'

'Me,' said Eddie. 'The one with the bullet in his leg. Which I'd really, *really* like someone to fix, because it fucking hurts!'

'Stretcher!' the colonel called to a medical team waiting beyond the circle of guns, before turning back to the couple. 'The State Department confirmed your story that you were in

North Korea as part of an intelligence-gathering operation. So how the hell did you end up in a Russian cargo plane with a hold full of nuclear weapons?'

'Like I said,' Nina told him wearily, 'it's a long story. Too long.'

Her husband chuckled as the medics carefully lifted him on to a stretcher. 'It'll make a great book, though.'

50

New York City

Oswald Seretse gazed out of the limousine's window as it crossed the Queensboro Bridge into Manhattan, the afternoon sun shining on the rectilinear forest of brick and concrete and glass. 'You have been through a great ordeal, that is for sure,' he said, having listened to Nina and Eddie's account of events in North Korea on the ride from the airport. 'One for which I feel in large part responsible.'

'Mm-hmm,' Nina said stonily, nodding.

He turned back to them. 'Again, you have my most profound and sincere apologies. Had I known that Fenrir was still in the country waiting for you . . . But,' the diplomat went on, 'it at least had a somewhat happy ending.'

Eddie rattled the end of his military-issue crutch against the floor. 'Yeah, I'm smiling like the fucking Joker.'

'I admit, more on an international level than a personal one. The illegal North Korean weapons facility was destroyed, the nuclear warheads it had already produced were captured, and an extremely dangerous escalation of tensions in the Middle East has been averted – to say nothing of the renewed diplomatic pressure that will be placed on North Korea from all sides. You may not appreciate that right now, but I assure you, you have done a tremendous favour for the world. Thank you.'

Nina nodded. 'Has there been any word on Fenrir and the Crucible?'

'Not yet. He seems to have travelled to China, but then we believed that before. The CIA and other agencies are still trying to track him down.'

'Thirty million dollars and a crate of gold bars buys you a lot of anonymity, I guess.'

'So it would seem.' He shook his head. 'I am still in a state of shock about Fenrir, as indeed are many others at the UN. The idea that someone we trusted could have betrayed his principles so completely . . .'

'Some people'll do anything for a shitload of gold,' said Eddie.

Nina knew the comment was not referring entirely to Mikkelsson. 'Yeah. But some of them might realise that other things are more valuable in the end. I hope.'

'Maybe. Right now, though,' he shifted, stretching his injured leg, 'I just want to see *our* most valuable thing.'

'Are you calling our little girl a thing?' The couple grinned at each other.

'I am returning to the United Nations,' said Seretse, smiling again, 'but my driver is at your disposal. He can take you home, or wherever you wish to go.'

'Macy's at her nursery,' Nina told him, checking her watch. 'I already spoke to our niece when we landed; she'll be waiting for us there. They'll be finishing soon.'

'Then I shall delay you as little as possible.' The limo reached the end of the bridge, turning on to 2nd Avenue to make its way southwards.

Seretse said his farewells and exited at the United Nations. Nina gave the driver the nursery's address, and the limo headed back uptown. 'We made it home,' she said, watching familiar surroundings slide past outside. 'I honestly thought we wouldn't, that we'd never get to see Macy again, but . . . we did. We actually made it.' She closed her eyes for a moment, but found the darkness filled with unwelcome visions of everything she had recently endured. 'I'm never going to leave her again.'

'I know how you feel,' said Eddie, his voice filled with weariness. 'But sooner or later, she'll leave *us*. It's what kids do. Holly's out here doing her own thing. One day, Macy'll be the same.'

'One day. But not now. And *definitely* not today.' She leaned against him, holding his hand. 'Oh God, I've missed her so much.'

'Me too, love. Me too.'

The journey to the nursery seemed to take as long as the flight from South Korea. At last they arrived. 'Do you want me to wait for you?' asked the driver.

'Yes please,' said Nina. 'We shouldn't be long.'

He surveyed the street. Parking spaces were, as ever in New York, at a premium, and a section of street alongside scaffolding erected outside the nursery's building had been closed off by road cones. 'I'll circle the block until you come out, if that's okay?'

'No problem,' Eddie told him as they pulled up. 'Don't pick up any hitchhikers, though.'

The driver pulled over and got out to open the door for them. A few passers-by looked on curiously, wondering if celebrities had arrived. 'What, nobody recognises us?' the Yorkshireman mock-complained. 'Tchah! What's the point of having a movie about us if we don't get mobbed by fans every time we're out in public?'

'I'd rather not end up like John Lennon, thanks,' said Nina, helping him out and passing him his crutch. The limo pulled away as they skirted the scaffolding and entered the building.

An unwelcome sight greeted them. 'Oh, great,' Eddie said, seeing a sign on the elevator warning that it was out of service due to the renovation work.

'You want to wait here?' asked Nina.

'No, I'll follow you. It's only one floor up. Just hope the lift in our building's working – I don't want to have to limp up eight flights of stairs!'

'See you up there, Hopalong.' She kissed him, then went to the stairwell and jogged up.

There was nobody in the hallway outside the nursery. Half expecting another reprimand for tardiness, she entered. No one was in reception either. 'Hello?'

Penny Lopez emerged from one of the rooms. 'Oh, hi, Nina. You're back— oh!' She saw the bruises and cuts on the redhead's face. 'My God, are you okay? What happened?'

'I'm fine,' Nina assured her. 'We had a fender-bender.' She saw there were no coats on the hooks. 'Did Macy go with Holly already?'

'Yes, about ten minutes ago. Holly said you were coming, but I assumed she and Macy went to meet you on the street.'

'They weren't outside . . .' Alarm bells started to ring in her mind, worry rising. She went back into the hallway. 'Holly? Macy?'

No reply from either, but Eddie responded from the stairwell. 'What is it?'

Nina looked down over the railing to see him awkwardly ascending. 'Penny said Holly already left with Macy.'

His brow furrowed with concern. 'She knew we were on the way, she wouldn't have left without us.'

'I know. Macy! Holly!'

Her shout echoed from the walls – then a faint cry came from somewhere above. 'Mommy!'

The couple regarded each other with sudden fear. There was absolutely no reason why Holly would have taken their daughter higher into the building.

At least not of her own volition.

'Macy, I'm coming!' Nina shouted as she ran up the stairs.

Eddie struggled up behind her, his crutch thudding off each step. 'Fucking *shit*!' he gasped as he stumbled. 'Find her, don't worry about me!'

Nina pounded up the staircase. Macy's wail had come from one of the higher floors, but she didn't know which one. She reached the third-floor entrance and pulled it open. 'Macy!'

No answer. A wall sign told her this floor was occupied by an accounting firm. The door to its reception area was glass, a woman visible at a desk beyond. She looked up in surprise. Macy and Holly hadn't been here.

She hared up the next flight. The fourth floor was vacant, the lights off. Nina tried the door to the offices. Locked. The next level was undergoing renovation work, piles of drywall panels waiting to replace old plaster and lath. '*Macy!*'

A reply came, another cry of 'Mommy!' from above. Not the next floor, but higher. Nina scaled the stairs even more quickly and rushed into the seventh-floor hallway. This too was being renovated, new glazing units propped vertically on a trolley waiting to be installed. The nearest door was open. She rushed through it—

And froze.

Fenrir Mikkelsson sat on a crate in front of the windows, Sarah standing beside him. He held the frightened and crying Macy on his lap with one hand and a gun in the other. It was not raised, but still pointed in the general direction of Holly, who stood trembling in a corner of the empty, half-decorated room. 'Nina,' said the Icelander with unnerving calm. 'I am so glad to see you again.'

Nina had no time for pleasantries or subtlety. 'Let her go, you bastard! Macy, are you okay?'

The little girl struggled against his unbreakable grip. 'Mommy, I'm scared.'

'I'm sorry, I'm sorry!' said Holly, tears streaming down her cheeks. 'I was bringing Macy downstairs to meet you, he had a gun . . .'

'It's okay, it's not your fault,' Nina assured her. 'What do you want, Fenrir?'

His cold blue eyes flicked towards the door behind her. 'Where is Eddie? I would have thought he would be here to meet his daughter.'

'He's on his way.'

'Then we shall wait for him.' He leaned back slightly, watching her with what seemed almost like admiration. 'I understand that you two achieved what years of diplomacy and military posturing could not by ending part of North Korea's covert nuclear programme.'

'You don't seem too upset about that.' She kept her voice slightly above its normal volume, wanting to give Eddie advance warning of the situation.

'I got what I wanted from the North Koreans.' A glance at a holdall on the floor. From its shape, it contained something spherical, about the size of a basketball: the Crucible. 'Anything that happened subsequently is not my concern.'

'You brought the Crucible with you?'

'Having gone through so much to obtain it, I was not going to leave it behind. I hope you appreciate that I was correct about US hypocrisy, by the way: the Americans kept the warheads for themselves.' He straightened. 'But congratulations on your success. I am sure you returned to this country as heroes.'

'How did *you* get into the country?' she demanded, wanting to keep him talking. As long as he was engaging with her, he would be less likely to hurt Macy. 'You should be on the top of the international most-wanted list.'

'I have my ways. Similar to ones that I know Eddie has used

in the past. All of which are considerably easier when backed by large sums of money.'

'So why are you here? Why not just use that money to hide?'

Mikkelsson's expression barely changed, a slight narrowing of the eyes and a tightening of the lips, but he became almost infinitely more menacing. 'You killed my daughter.'

'*Our* daughter.' Sarah spoke for the first time, her voice barely above a whisper. Nina's attention had until now been on Mikkelsson; she realised his wife was clothed entirely in black. A mother in mourning for her child. There was no anger in her words, only deep sadness.

Mikkelsson did not react to her, his attention fixed upon Nina. 'So I am going to take your daughter from you.'

'Don't you *dare* hurt her,' Nina hissed, filled with sudden rage but powerless to act upon it. If she made a move towards him, he would shoot her before she had gone two steps.

'I am not going to hurt her,' the Icelander replied. 'I am going to *raise* her. As if she were my own. You and Eddie took mine, so I shall take yours.'

Surprise formed on Sarah's numbed, blank face. 'What?'

'Did you really think I would hurt a child?' he said. 'I am not a monster; surely you know that after twenty-six years of marriage. No, I am going to give you a beautiful new daughter.'

'You . . . you think you can *replace* Ana?' she replied, the words quavering with rising emotion. 'Like getting a new phone? It . . . it *doesn't work like that*!' The cry exploded from her, startling Mikkelsson with its intensity. Macy wailed, afraid.

'Sarah, I am doing this for you,' he said. 'For both of us!'

'Our family isn't a machine – you can't just *slot in* a replacement part! You . . . you haven't grieved for Ana, you haven't even cried!'

The accusation seemed to sting him. 'I *am* grieving, Sarah. In my own way.' Nina risked a small step closer, hoping he was distracted but his gaze immediately snapped back, the gun shifting away from Holly and towards her. She froze again.

Sarah did not register the movement. 'You do *everything* in your own way, Fenrir,' she said, eyes brimming with tears. 'You never let me close, and you never know what I'm feeling! You have no idea!'

'Of course I do,' he protested.

'If you did, you wouldn't be talking about making another mother go through what I'm going through now.' Trembling, she looked at Nina. 'You wouldn't let anyone suffer like this! N-not even her.'

The gun rose, now pointing directly at the New Yorker. 'She will not suffer for long, I assure you. She has lived a good life; now she will have a good death.'

Macy shrieked and struggled again, slapping at Mikkelsson's arm. 'Don't hurt my mommy! Don't hurt her!'

He squeezed her more tightly. 'Do not worry, Macy. You will have a new mommy.'

'If you kill me,' said Nina, as fearful for Macy's psyche as her own life, 'you'll traumatise her permanently.'

'She is only three years old,' was his dismissive reply. 'She will not even remember.'

'How would *you* know?' cried Sarah. She stepped out from his side, moving forward and facing him. He had to shift the gun sideways to maintain his aim at Nina. 'What do you know about raising a child? You were never there for Ana, you were always away working! She did everything she could to gain your approval and your love, to get you just to *be* there, but it was never enough. And she tried so hard to be what she thought you wanted her to be that . . . that it got her killed.'

'That is not true,' snapped Mikkelsson, a flash of anger cutting through his icy mask.

'It *is* true!' She stabbed a finger at Nina. 'Her husband was a professional soldier, even better than Rutger. Ana didn't have a chance. But you let her go against him anyway!'

The mention of Eddie made Nina wonder where he was. Even with his wounded leg, surely he should have reached the seventh floor by now? She listened for footsteps or the thud of his crutch from the hallway, but heard nothing. What was he doing?

A small movement of the gun brought her whole attention back to the scene before her. 'Anastasia made her own decisions,' Mikkelsson insisted.

'She would never have made that decision if you hadn't turned her into a killer! She killed Augustine, but she wouldn't have done it without your . . . your permission.'

'I did not tell her to kill anyone!' The ice was starting to melt, heat rising beneath.

'No, but it was what you wanted, and she would do anything to please you! And I won't let you do that to another child.' She took hold of Macy.

'What are you doing?' demanded her husband.

'Giving her back.' She tried to pull the little girl out from Mikkelsson's arm. Nina tensed, desperately afraid that if they struggled the gun would go off, but after another flare of surprised anger he let her go. Sarah lifted her away, holding her for a long moment as she turned towards Nina . . . then put her down. 'Go to your mommy, darling,' she whispered.

Macy needed no prompting, running to her mother, who clutched her protectively. 'Come on, honey,' Nina said. 'We're going. Holly, you too.'

Holly started towards her, but Mikkelsson stood. 'No,' he said. 'You are not leaving.'

'Fenrir, please,' Sarah said. 'Let's just get out of here while we can—'

As if in mocking denial, the warble of a rapidly approaching siren became audible from the street below. Nina knew at once what Eddie had been doing on his ascent: calling the police. But that still didn't explain why he hadn't yet reached her . . .

The answer came from outside as a familiar bald head peered around the side of the windows. Rather than come into the room to face Mikkelsson directly, he had entered one of the adjoining offices and climbed out on to the scaffolding. She suppressed any reaction to the sight. If the Icelander turned, he would see him.

'You can't get away,' she said, trying to keep all attention on her. She held Macy close so she wouldn't see her father and give away his presence. 'Holly, come towards me, slowly. Keep your eyes on me. Everything's going to be okay.' Outside, Eddie carefully sidestepped along the wooden boards, heading for the pane behind the Mikkelssons. He still had his crutch, but now held it under one arm like a lance, ready to use as a weapon.

Nina glanced down. Most of the floor was in shadow, a higher building across the street blocking the sun, but Eddie would have to pass through a line of light angling diagonally across it. 'The cops will be here any second,' she said.

'They will not arrive quickly enough to save you,' Mikkelsson replied. He flicked his gun towards Holly, who stiffened in fear. 'Stop there. I have no quarrel with you.'

'Please don't hurt anyone,' the young woman sobbed, looking around. Nina stopped breathing. If her niece saw Eddie, her surprise would give his presence away—

'Holly, look at me!' she commanded. 'Do what he says, stay still.' To her relief, Holly faced her again. 'Sarah, thank you for giving Macy back to me. Thank you so much. Please, convince him not to do something that'll haunt her for the rest of her life.'

'She's right,' Sarah said to Mikkelsson. 'Fenrir, let's go. Please?' She reached out and placed a hand on top of the gun, gently pushing it downwards. 'If you love me, if you loved Ana like you say you did, you won't do this.'

The Icelander's expression remained unreadable, his unnerving gaze still fixed upon Nina. Then . . .

'No,' he said sharply.

He shoved Sarah away, sending her staggering as he snapped the gun back up – only to glance down at the floor as a shadow flitted across it—

The window behind him exploded.

Eddie swung the crutch like an axe, smashing the glass and hurling himself through the opening. He landed on the crate, rolling off it to tackle the big man and slam him to the floor.

Mikkelsson reflexively fired the gun as he fell. Sarah screamed as the bullet hit her leg. She collapsed. 'Holly, take Macy!' Nina yelled as her niece stared in petrified shock. '*Run!*' Holly snapped into motion and grabbed the little girl, running with her through the door as Nina rushed to help her husband.

Eddie grappled with Mikkelsson. The crutch skittered away from them. The Yorkshireman managed to hook an arm around his opponent's neck and squeezed hard, trying to choke him. Mikkelsson drove an elbow into his side, then twisted to point the gun over his shoulder at Eddie's face. Eddie gripped his wrist and pushed it away as he fired.

The gunshot deafened him, all sounds replaced by a shrill, dizzying ring. Mikkelsson was little better off, but still delivered another blow to the other man's injured ribs. Eddie convulsed in pain. Mikkelsson strained and his raw strength overcame his adversary's grip. He pulled free—

Nina swung the crutch like a baseball bat. Its padded end smacked the gun from his hand. It spun away and hit the broken window's frame, landing on the edge of the boards outside. The siren's howl cut off below as an NYPD patrol car skidded to a stop outside the building.

She tried to send a second strike at Mikkelsson's head, but he kicked her legs out from under her. She fell, her head cracking painfully against the floor. The holdall swam across her blurry vision.

Behind it, Mikkelsson pulled himself up on the crate.

Eddie tried to drag him back down, but the other man lashed out, hitting his bullet wound. The Englishman screamed. Mikkelsson scrambled to the broken window, about to climb through and use the scaffolding to escape—

He saw the gun.

Kicking out the remaining shards of glass, the Icelander ducked on to the scaffold and bent to snatch up the weapon. He turned to kill the couple—

Nina grabbed the holdall containing the Crucible – and threw it at him. 'Don't leave this behind!'

It hit him in the stomach. He stumbled backwards . . . and slipped over the edge.

Mikkelsson snatched at a scaffolding pole as he toppled, but missed. He plunged shrieking towards the ground, the Crucible falling with him—

He landed on the police car. Its roof imploded beneath him, the windows bursting apart and showering the street with glass. People on the sidewalk yelled and ran from the glittering hailstorm.

The holdall hit the kerb beside the car with a bang, the crystalline sphere inside it shattering into thousands of glassy fragments.

The Crucible – the Atlantean artefact that had forged the lost civilisation's supplies of gold, that had driven Talonor's journeys across the world to find another natural nuclear reactor, that had caused an untold number of deaths as men and women were overcome by greed for what it could produce – had been destroyed.

Seven floors above, Nina stared at the empty space beyond the window, then went to assist her husband. 'It's okay, I've got you.'

He put a hand to one ear. 'What?' he replied loudly.

'I said I've got you!'

'All right, no need to shout! Jesus, my ears hurt. What happened, where's—' He regarded the window, then looked back at Nina. 'You got him?'

'Unless he sprouted wings on the way down, yeah.' She helped him up, and they both peered at the street below. 'Oh my God, he's still alive!' A weakly moving figure was splayed across the crushed roof of the police car, embedded in the metal.

'Don't think he'll be making a run for it,' Eddie rumbled. One of the Icelander's legs had acquired an extra joint halfway down the shin. 'What about Macy – where's Macy?' he barked in sudden alarm.

'With Holly.' Nina retrieved his crutch, sparing a moment to glance at Sarah, who was moaning as she clutched her leg. The bullet wound was bloody, but not actually gushing; no major arteries had been torn. 'Keep your hand pressed on it; there'll be an ambulance here soon,' she told her.

Eddie's accumulated injuries barely slowed him as he hobbled determinedly from the room. 'Macy!' he called. 'Holly, where are you? Macy!'

'We're down here!' came a frantic voice from the stairwell. The couple hurriedly descended, finding Holly with their daughter halfway down. Both were crying.

'We're okay, we're okay,' Nina assured them. She took Macy and held her tightly. 'We're here now, we're both here.'

'Mommy!' cried Macy, wrapping her arms around her mother.

'What's Daddy, chopped liver?' said Eddie, managing a pained smile. He joined the huddle, embracing them both. 'Jesus Christ, love, I'm so happy to see you.'

Macy let out a little gasp. 'Daddy! You swore!'

'Get used to it, kid. I'm back.' He gave Nina a look to let her know he was joking, then turned at the sound of someone running up the stairs.

A pair of uniformed NYPD officers arrived. 'You the guy who called Detective Martin?' one asked Eddie.

'Yeah,' replied Eddie, adding to Nina at the mention of his friend on the force: 'Thought it'd be quicker to tell Amy I needed help than go through 911 and have to explain everything.' He looked back at the cops. 'Our little girl's fine, and we're all okay. There's a woman with a gunshot wound on the seventh floor; she's one of the bad guys.'

'There's another bad guy?' the second cop said.

'You might want to go check on your car,' Nina told them. 'And I mean literally *on* your car. He went out the window. He's still alive, though – and currently top of the international most-wanted list, so that should get you some brownie points for catching him.'

The officers exchanged surprised glances, then one took out his radio and reported in as he continued upstairs at a run, the other clattering back down to ground level. Eddie let go of his wife and daughter to hold Holly. 'You all right?'

'I'm fine,' she said, trying not to cry. 'Oh God! I was so scared. When did babysitting become so dangerous?'

'Welcome to our world,' said Nina.

'No offence, but you might want to find someone else in future.'

'We won't be needing anyone. Not any more.' She nuzzled her daughter. 'It's okay, Macy, everything's okay.'

'Are you sure, Mommy?' Macy asked.

She looked at Eddie, who smiled. 'Yeah, I'm sure, honey. Come on. Let's go home.'

Epilogue

One Month Later

Nina strolled through the idyllic calm of Central Park's Shakespeare Garden. It was a beautiful spring morning, the sun climbing in a clear sky and casting a warm light over the carefully maintained flora.

She was in a mood to match the day. Everything had returned to normal – at least, as normal as anything could be in a household containing a three-year-old – and both she and Eddie were well on their way to recovering from the physical wounds of their recent trials.

The mental wounds were another matter, but while her husband preferred to deal with them simply by spending time with Macy, she had her own form of therapy. A third book was already well under way, and she had been approached to produce – or even present – a television documentary series about her archaeological discoveries, an offer that was extremely tempting as it would let her correct the fictionalisations of Hollywood. As for *The Hunt for Atlantis* itself, whatever her personal opinions of the movie, it had been a box-office hit. A sequel had already been green-lit, meaning she was due another payment from Grant Thorn's production company. She and her family would be financially secure for some time.

All without the need for anything from the Midas Legacy.

She rounded a bend in the path to see Olivia on a bench ahead. Her grandmother waved. 'Nina, hello!' she said. 'I'm so happy to see you.'

'Hi,' Nina replied, sitting beside her. 'Are you okay?'

'I'm as fully recovered as anyone my age can hope to be, yes. Thank you. And you?'

'All's good, thanks. Eddie and Macy are both fine. I've taken her to see a specialist a few times, but she doesn't seem to have suffered any trauma. Thank God.'

'Thank God,' Olivia echoed. 'I'm very sorry.'

'For what?'

'For everything that happened. If I'd simply been honest with you from the start . . .'

'What's past is past,' said Nina, not wanting to reopen that line of discussion – or argument. Instead, she leaned back, admiring her surroundings. 'You picked a nice place to meet,' she said meaningfully.

'Yes, I'd hoped you would know it.'

'Of course.' It was the setting for the photograph they both possessed of Olivia and her daughter. 'Was that really the last photo of you and Mom together?'

'It was,' Olivia said, a little sadly. 'She went travelling in Europe with a friend over the summer to help her get through losing her father, then started at university that fall, so I saw much less of her. And then, well . . .'

'She met Dad.'

'And my arrogance, my pride, ruined everything.' She sighed. 'I miss her so much, Nina. I still do, even after all this time. I wish I could go back and change things, or even just see her one more time, but . . . as you said, what's past is past. "The moving finger writes, and having writ, moves on: nor all thy piety nor wit shall move it back to cancel half a line, nor all thy tears wash out a word of it."'

'Omar Khayyam,' said Nina, recognising the words of the Persian poet. 'But considering where we are, maybe Lady Macbeth's "Things without all remedy should be without regard: what's done, is done" might have been more appropriate.'

Olivia nodded. 'Your parents made sure you had a good education.'

'They taught me more than I ever learned in school.'

'I'm glad. I hope you and Eddie do the same for Macy.'

'We will. Although,' a wry smile, 'I'm not sure I want to know what *he'll* teach her.'

'How to survive everything the world will throw at her,' said Olivia, with surprising assurance. 'Though I have no doubt that you'll do your share in that regard as well. She's a wonderful girl, very bright, very determined. With you two to set her on the path, she'll go far.' Another sigh, this one almost mournful. 'I just wish I could be there to see it.'

'It seems like you'll be around for a while yet,' Nina joked.

'That's not what I meant.'

'No?'

She turned to face Nina directly. 'After everything I've done, all the death and destruction that came from my keeping the truth from you – including Macy's life being put in danger – I can't imagine that you would ever want to see me again. And I fully accept that, and that I brought it entirely on myself. Now, I know you want nothing to do with the Legacy or its money. But it exists, so I've arranged for everything I have to be put into trust for Macy after I'm gone. And don't object,' she said, raising a hand on seeing Nina about to do so. 'If she wants to donate every penny to charity, that's up to her. But let her make the decision herself. I'm sure you'll bring her up to make the best one.'

'Thank you,' said Nina in response to the compliment, though she was still far from happy about what she considered the Legacy's dirty money. That disagreement could wait for another day, however, as there was something else she wanted – needed – to say. 'But you're wrong that I don't want to see you again.'

Olivia was genuinely surprised. 'Really?'

'Really. I would like you to be a part of my life. And Macy's. She may never have gotten to meet her grandmother, but her *great*-grandmother's still there for her.'

'I'm . . .' She blinked at Nina, wiping away a small tear. 'I don't know what to say. I'm truly touched. And grateful.'

Nina smiled. 'My pleasure.'

'And mine.' Olivia returned it. 'Laura and Henry raised a most remarkable woman together. And I'm glad that, however long it took, I got to meet her.'

'You say that like it's a one-time deal. So cut it out.' They both laughed. 'Come with me.' Nina stood.

'Where are we going?'

'Eddie's with Macy at the Turtle Pond.' She gestured in the direction of the small lake near the Shakespeare Garden. 'We thought you might like to join us for lunch.'

'I . . . Of course.' Olivia took her proffered hand and stood, a little unsteady on her frostbitten feet. 'I'd be honoured.'

'Good. Because I don't want to make the same mistake that you and Mom did.' She linked an arm with her grandmother's, and they set off down the sunlit path together. 'Whatever else may have happened, you're still part of my family. And my family always sticks together.'

Twenty-four Years Earlier

'What're you doing, honey?' asked Laura Wilde, entering her bedroom to find her daughter stretched across the bed.

Nina took off her Walkman headphones, the tinny sounds of Ace of Base escaping, and rolled over. 'I was looking at these old photos.' A large shoebox full of pictures was beside her.

Laura glanced at the wardrobe where the box normally resided. 'Were you trying on my shoes again?' she said with a smile. 'I've told you before, you're too young for high heels.'

'Ugh, Mom, I'm *fourteen*,' Nina said, rolling her eyes. 'But high heels aren't my thing. They wouldn't be much use on a dig! No, I was looking for the pictures from Morocco – you know, where you found my pendant.' She fingered the scrap of oddly tinted metal that Laura and her husband had found on an unsuccessful attempt to uncover clues to the location of Atlantis six years earlier.

'Yeah, I remember.' She sat on the bed, regarding the pictures spread across it. 'Those aren't from Morocco, though.'

'No, I kinda got sidetracked . . .' Nina giggled. 'These are from before I was born, aren't they?'

'That's right,' said Laura. The print the teen had been examining was of herself and Henry, laughing at the camera – had Jack Philby taken it? – somewhere on the campus at Columbia. 'We were at university in that one; I think we'd just finished our final exams. So apologies for the terrible outfits and haircuts, but it *was* the seventies.'

'I think they're cute,' said Nina, grinning. 'Very retro.' She looked back at the image of her parents. 'You look so happy.'

'We were.' Laura's smile this time was at the memories flooding back. 'You know, from the very first time I spoke to your dad, I knew he was going to be a big part of my life. I couldn't have imagined how much, though.'

'It's so cool that you still love him so much. Loads of the parents of the kids in my class are divorced, or hate each other.'

'Your dad and I'll be together until we die,' Laura assured her.

'That's so romantic. I wonder if I'll ever meet anyone who makes me feel like that?'

'I'm sure you will, honey.' She leaned over to see some of the other photos. 'What else have we got here?'

Her daughter held one up. 'This is you and *your* mom, isn't it?'

Laura felt a pang of guilt that she had over time become practised enough not to show, though it had been a while since she'd covered her feelings in such a way. 'Yeah, it is,' she said, taking the picture from her and gazing at the frozen moment from her past. 'We were at the Shakespeare Garden in Central Park. That's . . . the last photo I have of her.'

'Before she and Grandad died?'

'Mm.' Nina took her non-committal response as an affirmative, but even so Laura was painfully aware that she had just told an untruth by omission. Her mother was still alive and, as far as she knew, well, but they hadn't spoken to each other since just before her wedding. The anger-driven lie she told Henry early in their relationship about Olivia having died in the same car accident as her father had taken on a life of its own out of her fear of revealing the truth; of exposing her betrayal of first her husband's, and now her daughter's, trust . . .

She was so wrapped up in her own regretful thoughts that the next question caught her off guard. 'Do you miss her?'

'I . . . I do, yes,' she admitted. 'I wish there was some way I could see her again without . . . needing a time machine,' she said, catching a questioning look starting to form on Nina's face. 'But I guess that's not going to happen.'

'If you had a time machine, archaeology wouldn't be much fun.'

'If we had a time machine and could go back into the past to see what it was like, we'd be sociologists, not archaeologists,' said Henry Wilde with a chuckle as he entered. 'And I wouldn't wish that on anyone.' He spotted the photo of himself and Laura. 'Oh hey, I remember that!'

Laura got up and kissed him. 'That was a good time, wasn't it?'

'Yeah. And the best thing is, it never stopped.' He returned the kiss.

Nina tutted. 'Get a room.'

'This *is* our room! So, are we going for lunch? There's a new deli a couple of blocks away that I had recommended to me, Aldo's, something like that. I fancy some ridiculous combination of ingredients, give them a proper test.'

Nina slid off the bed. 'Sounds good!'

'Put those away first,' her mother told her, indicating the pictures. The teenager made another impatient sound, but turned to gather them up.

The last one was still in Laura's hand. She contemplated it again. 'You okay?' asked Henry. 'You look sad.'

'Huh? No, I was just . . . you know. Words left unsaid.' Another moment of reverie, then she put the picture in the box and Nina closed the lid on it. Laura smiled at her daughter and husband. 'But things are what they are. And I don't regret any of the choices I've made, because they brought me here.' Her face brightened. 'Come on. Life is good; let's go enjoy it together.'

THRILLINGLY GOOD BOOKS
FROM CRIMINALLY
GOOD WRITERS

CRIME FILES BRINGS YOU THE LATEST RELEASES FROM TOP CRIME AND THRILLER AUTHORS.

GN UP ONLINE FOR OUR MONTHLY NEWSLETTER AND BE THE FIRST TO KNOW ABOUT OUR COMPETITIONS, NEW BOOKS AND MORE.